Ildefonso Falcones is married with four children and lives in Barcelona where he works as a lawyer. *Cathedral of the Sea* is intended as an homage to a people who built one of the most beautiful churches on earth in what was, for that time, a remarkable period of only fifty-four years. First published in Spain where it has become a publishing phenomenon, translation rights have been sold in thirty-six countries. It has won many prizes, including the Euskadi de Plata 2006 for the best novel in Spanish, the Qué Leer 2007 Prize for the best book, and the prestigious Italian Giovanni Boccaccio 2007 award for best foreign author.

ILDEFONSO FALCONES

CATHEDRAL
of the SEA

Translated from the Spanish
by Nick Caistor

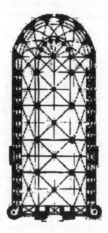

BLACK SWAN

TRANSWORLD PUBLISHERS
61–63 Uxbridge Road, London W5 5SA
A Random House Group Company
www.rbooks.co.uk

CATHEDRAL OF THE SEA
A BLACK SWAN BOOK: 9780552773973

La Catedral del Mar, first published by
Grupo Editorial Random House
Mondadori, SL in 2006

First published in Great Britain
in 2008 by Doubleday
a division of Transworld Publishers
Black Swan edition published 2009

Copyright © Ildefonso Falcones de Sierra 2006
English translation © Nick Caistor 2007

Addresses for Random House Group Ltd companies outside the UK
can be found at: www.randomhouse.co.uk
The Random House Group Ltd Reg. No. 954009

The Random House Group Limited supports The Forest Stewardship Council®
(FSC®), the leading international forest-certification organisation. Our books
carrying the FSC label are printed on FSC®-certified paper. FSC is the only
forest-certification scheme supported by the leading environmental organisations,
including Greenpeace. Our paper procurement policy can be found at
www.randomhouse.co.uk/environment

Typeset in 11/12.5pt Giovanni Book by
Falcon Oast Graphic Art Ltd.
Printed and bound by CPI Group (UK) Ltd, Croydon, CR0 4YY

CATHEDRAL
of the SEA

PART ONE

CHAINED TO THE LAND

1

The year 1320
Bernat Estanyol's farmhouse
Navarcles, in the principality of Catalonia

Bernat realized nobody was looking in his direction, and glanced up at the clear blue sky. The weak late September sun played on the faces of his guests. He had put so much time and effort in preparing the feast that only bad weather could have spoilt it. He smiled up at the autumn sky, and when he looked down again, his smile broadened as he listened to the hum of happy voices in the cobbled courtyard that ran alongside the animal pens at the foot of his farmhouse.

His thirty or so guests were in high spirits: the grape harvest that year had been magnificent. All of them – men, women and children – had worked from dawn to dusk harvesting the grapes, then treading them, without allowing themselves a single day's rest.

It was only when the wine was ready to ferment in its barrels and the grape skins had been stored to distil their liquor during the slack days of winter that the peasant farmers could celebrate their September feast days. And it was then that Bernat Estanyol had chosen to be married.

Bernat surveyed his guests. Many of them had got up

11

at dawn to walk the often great distances separating their properties from the Estanyol farmhouse. They were all enjoying themselves now, talking about the wedding, the harvest, or perhaps both events at once. Some of them, including a group where his Estanyol cousins and the Puig family were sitting, burst out laughing at a ribald comment directed towards him. Bernat felt himself blushing and pretended to take no notice; he did not even want to think about what they might be laughing at. Scattered around the courtyard he could make out the Fontany family, the Vilas, the Joaniquets, and of course the bride's relatives: the Esteve family.

Bernat looked out of the corner of his eye at his father-in-law. Pere Esteve was promenading his immense belly, smiling at some of those invited, saying a few words to others. Then he turned towards Bernat, who found himself forced to wave acknowledgement for the hundredth time that day. He looked for his other in-laws and saw them at different tables among the throng. They had always been slightly wary of him, despite all his attempts to win them over.

He raised his eyes to the sky once more. The harvest and the weather seemed to be on his side. He glanced over at the farmhouse and then again at the wedding party, and pursed his lips. All at once, in spite of the merry hubbub, he felt quite alone. It was barely a year since his father had died; his sister Guiamona, who had gone to live in Barcelona after her marriage, had not bothered to reply to the messages he had sent her, even though he longed to see her again. After his father's death, she was the only immediate family he had left.

That death had made the Estanyol farmhouse the centre of interest for the entire region: matchmakers and parents with unmarried daughters had paid endless visits. Prior to that, no one had paid them much attention, but the demise of the old man – whose rebellious nature had earned him the nickname of 'madcap Estanyol' – had rekindled the hopes of those who were anxious to see their daughter married off to the richest peasant farmer for miles around.

'You're old enough now to get married,' they said to encourage him. 'Exactly how old are you?'

'Twenty-seven, I think,' he replied.

'That's almost an age to have grandchildren,' they scolded him. 'What are you doing all alone in your farm-house? You need a wife.'

Bernat listened to them all patiently. He knew their advice would inevitably be followed by the mention of some candidate or other, a girl stronger than an ox and more beautiful than the most incandescent sunset.

None of this was new to him. Madcap Estanyol, whose wife had died giving birth to Guiamona, had tried to find him a wife, but all the suitable parents had fled the farmhouse cursing the demands he made regarding the dowry any future daughter-in-law was supposed to bring. Little by little, interest in Bernat had waned. The older he grew, the more extreme his father became: his rebelliousness bordered on real lunacy. Bernat had concentrated on looking after his lands and his father; now all of a sudden at twenty-seven he found himself alone and besieged on all sides.

Yet the first visit Bernat received, before the old man had even been properly laid to rest, was of a different nature: it was from the steward of his feudal lord, the lord of Navarcles. How right you were, father! Bernat said to himself when he saw the steward and several soldiers ride up to his farm.

'As soon as I die,' the old man had repeated time and again to him in his brief moments of lucidity, 'they'll be here. You must show them my will.' With that, he pointed to the stone beneath which, carefully wrapped

13

in leather, he had left the document containing the last will and testament of Madcap Estanyol.

'Why is that, Father?' Bernat had asked the first time he heard this.

'As you know,' the old man replied, 'we lease these lands from our lord, but I am a widower, and if I had not drawn up my will, he would have the right to claim half of all our goods and livestock. That is known as the intestate right; there are many others that benefit the lords of Catalonia, and you must make sure you are aware of them all. They will be here, Bernat; they will come to take what is rightfully ours. It's only by showing them my will that you can get rid of them.'

'What if they take it from me?' asked Bernat. 'You know what they are like . . .'

'Even if they did, it is registered in the official account books.'

The steward and his lord's anger soon became common knowledge in the region. It merely served to make the only son's position look all the more attractive, as he had inherited all his father's possessions.

Bernat could clearly recall the visit the man who was now his father-in-law had paid him before the grape harvest. Five shillings, a pallet and a white linen smock: that was the dowry he was offering for his daughter Francesca.

'Why would I want a white linen smock?' Bernat asked, not even pausing as he forked the hay on the ground floor of his farmhouse.

'Look,' was Pere Esteve's only reply.

Leaning on his pitchfork, Bernat looked in the direction Pere Esteve was pointing: the doorway of the stable. He let the pitchfork fall from his hands. Francesca was silhouetted against the light, dressed in the white linen smock . . . Her whole body shone through, just waiting for him!

A shudder ran down Bernat's spine. Pere Esteve smiled.

Bernat accepted his offer. There and then, in the stable, without even going up to the young girl, but never once taking his eyes off her. He realized it was a hasty decision, but so far he had not regretted it: there Francesca was in front of him now, young, beautiful, strong. His breathing quickened. That very night . . . What might she be thinking? Did she feel as he did? Francesca was not joining in with the other women's animated chatter: she sat quietly beside her mother, answering their jokes and laughter with forced smiles. Their gazes met for a moment. She flushed and looked down, but Bernat could tell from the way her breast heaved that she was nervous too. Her white linen smock thrust itself once more into Bernat's fantasies and desire.

'I congratulate you!' he heard a voice say behind him, and felt a hand clapping him on the shoulder. It was his father-in-law. 'Look after her for me,' he added, following Bernat's gaze and pointing to the girl, who clearly did not know where to put herself. 'If the life you have in store for her is as magnificent as this feast . . . This is the most marvellous banquet I have ever seen. Not even the lord of Navarcles could lay on such a treat.'

In order to please his guests, Bernat had prepared forty-seven loaves of wheat bread: the peasants' usual fare of barley, rye or spelt was not good enough for him. Only the whitest bread, as white as his bride's smock, would suffice! He had carried all the loaves to be baked at the Navarcles castle, calculating that, as usual, two loaves would be enough to pay for the privilege. The baker's eyes opened wide when he saw this display of wheaten bread, then narrowed to inscrutable slits. He demanded seven loaves in payment, and Bernat left the castle cursing the laws that prevented peasants like him having their own bread ovens at home, or forges, or bridle and harness workshops . . .

'You're right there,' he told his father-in-law, banishing the unpleasant memory from his mind.

They both stared down the courtyard. Some of his bread might have been stolen, but there was still the wine his guests were drinking – the best, stored away by his father and left to age for several years – or the salt-roasted pig; the vegetable stew seasoned with chickens; and above all the four lambs, split down the middle and roasting slowly on the embers on their spits, oozing fat and giving off an irresistible smell.

All of a sudden the women started bustling about. The stew was ready and the bowls the guests had brought were soon filled. Pere and Bernat sat at the only table laid in the courtyard. The women rushed to serve them, ignoring the four empty seats. The rest stood or sat on wooden benches or the ground and began to eat, still casting glances at the lambs roasting under the watchful eye of some of the cooks. Everyone was drinking wine, conversing, shouting and laughing.

'Yes, a real feast,' Pere Esteve concluded between mouthfuls.

Somebody proposed a toast to the bride and groom. Everybody joined in.

'Francesca!' shouted her father, raising his cup to her as she stood next to the roasting lambs.

Bernat stared hard at her, but again she hid her face.

'She's feeling nervous,' Pere said in excuse, winking at him. 'Francesca, daughter!' he shouted once more. 'Come on, drink with us! Make the most of it now, because soon we'll be leaving – almost all of us, that is.'

The guffaws following this remark only intimidated Francesca still further. She half raised a cup she had been given, but did not drink from it. Then she turned away from the laughter and went on supervising the cooking.

Pere Esteve clinked his cup against Bernat's, spilling some of his wine. The other guests followed suit.

'I'm sure you'll see to it she forgets her bashfulness,' Pere Esteve said out loud, for all to hear.

This led to more guffawing, accompanied by sly comments that Bernat preferred to ignore.

In this merry way, they set to work on large amounts of wine, pork and chicken stew. Just as the women were taking the lambs off the fire, a group of the guests suddenly fell quiet and began to look over to the outskirts of the woods on the edge of Bernat's land, beyond the ploughed fields and the dip in the land that the Estanyols had used to plant the vines that provided them with such excellent wine.

Within a few seconds, the whole wedding party was silent.

Three men on horseback had appeared among the trees. A larger number of men in uniform were walking behind them.

'What can he want here?' Pere Esteve muttered to himself.

Bernat followed the newcomers with his gaze as they drew closer across the fields. The guests began to whisper among themselves.

'I don't understand,' Bernat said eventually, also in a low voice. 'He never comes here: it is not on his way to the castle.'

'I don't like the look of this at all,' said Pere Esteve.

The procession drew slowly closer. As the figures approached, the laughter and remarks the horsemen were making took over from the merriment that had been in evidence in the courtyard; everyone could hear them. Bernat surveyed his guests: some of them could not bear to look, and stood there staring at the ground. He searched for Francesca, who was in the midst of a group of women. The lord of Navarcles's powerful voice rang out. Bernat could feel anger rising inside him.

'Bernat! Bernat!' Pere Esteve hissed, clutching his arm. 'What are you doing here? Run to greet him.'

Bernat leapt up and ran to receive his lord.

'Welcome to this your house,' he panted when he had reached the men on horseback.

Llorenç de Bellera, lord of Navarcles, pulled on his horse's reins and came to a halt in front of Bernat. 'Are you Estanyol, son of the madman?' he asked disdainfully.

'Yes, my lord.'

'We were out hunting, and were surprised to hear your feast on the way back to our castle. What are you celebrating?'

Behind the horses, Bernat caught a glimpse of the soldiers, loaded down with their prey: rabbits, hares, some wild cocks. 'It's your visit that demands an explanation,' he would have liked to reply. 'Or did the castle baker tell you about the white loaves I had baked?'

Even the horses, with their large round eyes focused on him, seemed to be awaiting his response.

'My marriage, your lordship.'

'And whom are you marrying?'

'The daughter of Pere Esteve, my lord.'

Llorenç de Bellera sat silently, looking down at Bernat over his horse's neck. The other mounts snorted impatiently.

'Well?' barked Llorenç de Bellera.

'My bride and I,' said Bernat, trying to hide his discomfort, 'would be very honoured if your lordship and his companions would care to join us.'

'We're thirsty, Estanyol,' was all the lord of Navarcles deigned to reply.

The horses moved on without any need of prodding. Head down, Bernat walked alongside his lord's horse back to the farmhouse. All the guests had gathered at the entrance to the courtyard to receive him: the women stared down at the ground and all the men had removed their caps. A low murmur greeted Llorenç de Bellera when he halted before them.

'That's enough,' he said as he dismounted. 'Carry on with your banquet.'

The guests complied, turning round without a word. Several of the soldiers came up and took care of the horses. Bernat went with his new guests to the table where Pere and he had been seated. Their bowls and cups had disappeared.

The lord of Navarcles and his two companions sat at the table. Bernat withdrew several steps as the newcomers began to talk among themselves. The serving women brought pitchers of wine, loaves of bread, chicken stew, plates of salt pork and freshly roasted lamb. Bernat looked for Francesca, but she was nowhere to be seen. His gaze met that of his father-in-law, who was standing in a group of the guests. Pere Esteve lifted his chin towards the serving women, shook his head almost imperceptibly and turned on his heel.

'Go on with your celebration!' Llorenç de Bellera bawled, waving the leg of lamb he was holding. 'Come on, enjoy yourselves!'

Silently, the guests began to approach the roasted lambs for their share. Unnoticed by the lord and his friends, one group stood their ground: Pere Esteve and a few others. Bernat caught a glimpse of the white linen smock in the midst of them, and hurried over.

'Get away from here, you idiot,' his father-in-law snapped.

Before Bernat could say a word, Francesca's mother thrust a platter of lamb in his hands and whispered: 'Wait on the lord, and don't go anywhere near my daughter.'

The peasants began to devour the lamb, still without

19

saying a word, but from time to time glancing anxiously up at the table where the lord of Navarcles and his two friends were laughing and shouting. The soldiers were resting some way away.

'When we were hunting, we could hear loud laughter from here,' Lord de Bellera complained. 'So loud it drove away all our game. Come on, I want to hear you laugh!'

Nobody obeyed.

'Country bumpkins,' he told his companions, who burst out laughing again.

The three of them sated themselves on lamb and chunks of white bread. The platters of salted pork and chicken stew were pushed to one side of the table. Bernat ate standing up nearby, occasionally glancing anxiously out of the corner of his eye at the gaggle of women surrounding Francesca.

'More wine!' Lord de Bellera demanded, raising his cup. 'Estanyol,' he shouted, seeking him out among the guests. 'Next time you pay me the taxes on my land, I want you to bring this wine, not the vinegar your father has been fooling me with until now.'

Bernat was facing the other way. Francesca's mother thrust a pitcher of wine into his hands.

'Estanyol, where are you?' Llorenç de Bellera pounded the table just as a serving woman was about to serve him more wine. A few drops sprinkled his clothes.

By now, Bernat was close to him, and his friends were laughing at the accident. Pere Esteve lifted his hands to his face.

'Stupid old crone! How dare you spill the wine?' The woman lowered her head in submission, and when the lord made to buffet her with his hand, she fell to the ground. Llorenç de Bellera turned to his friends, cackling at the way the old woman was crawling away from them. Then he became serious once more, and addressed Bernat. 'So there you are, Estanyol. Look what your clumsy old women have done! Are you trying to insult your lord and master? Are you so ignorant you don't realize that your guests should be served by the lady of the house? Where is the bride?' he asked, looking round at everyone in the courtyard. 'Where is the bride?' he repeated, when there was no response.

Pere Esteve took Francesca by the arm and led her to Bernat at the table. She was trembling from head to foot.

'Your lordship,' said Bernat. 'I present you my wife, Francesca.'

'That's better,' said Llorenç, openly staring her up and down. 'Much better. From now on, you are to serve us the wine.'

The lord of Navarcles sat down again and raised his cup. Searching for a pitcher, Francesca ran to serve him. As she poured out the wine, her hand shook. Llorenç de Bellera grasped her wrist and steadied it. When his cup was full, he pushed her to serve his companions. As she did so, her breasts almost brushed his face.

'That is how wine should be served!' the lord of Navarcles bellowed. Standing next to him, Bernat clenched fists and teeth.

Llorenç de Bellera and his friends went on drinking; they kept calling out for Francesca to come and refill their cups. The soldiers laughed with their lord and his friends whenever Francesca had to lean over the table to serve them. She tried to choke back her tears, and Bernat could see a trickle of blood on her hands where she had been digging in her nails. Each time she had to pour out the wine, the guests fell silent and looked away.

'Estanyol,' Llorenç de Bellera finally shouted, clutching Francesca by the wrist. 'In accordance with one of my rights as your lord, I have decided to lie with your wife on her first night of marriage.'

His friends raucously applauded the decision. Bernat leapt towards the table but before he could do anything, the lord's two companions, who had seemed hopelessly drunk, sprang up, hands on the pommels of their swords. Bernat stopped in his tracks. Llorenç stared at him, smiled, then laughed out loud. The girl implored Bernat's help with her eyes.

Bernat stepped forward, but felt one of the swords pressed against his stomach. As the lord dragged her to the outside staircase of the farmhouse, Francesca still looked at him beseechingly. When de Bellera grabbed her round the waist and lifted her over his shoulder, she cried out.

The lord of Navarcles's friends sat down and took up their drinking again. The soldiers stood guard at the foot of the staircase to prevent Bernat making any move.

The sky was still a deep, dark blue.

After some minutes that to Bernat seemed endless, Llorenç de Bellera appeared at the top of the staircase. He was sweaty and was trying to fasten his hunting doublet.

'Estanyol,' he shouted in stentorian tones as he walked past him towards the table, 'now it's your turn. Dona Caterina,' he added, addressing his companions and referring to his new young bride, 'is weary of bastard children of mine turning up all over the place. And I'm weary of her snivelling. So do your duty as a good Christian husband!' he said, turning and addressing Bernat.

Bernat lowered his head, and then walked slowly and reluctantly up the staircase. Everyone was staring at him. He went into the large room on the first floor that served as kitchen and dining room; it had a big hearth on one wall topped by an impressive wrought-iron chimney piece. As he dragged himself over to the ladder that led to the bedroom and granary on the second floor, he heard his footsteps echoing on the wooden boards. Unsure what to do, he stuck his head into the gap at the top of the ladder and peered around him. Now, he could hear nothing.

His chin was level with the boards, and he could see Francesca's clothing scattered all over the floor. The white linen smock, her family's pride and joy, was torn to shreds. He climbed to the top of the ladder.

He found Francesca curled up in a ball. She lay completely naked on the new pallet, which was spattered with blood. She was staring blankly into space, covered in sweat; her body was scratched and bruised. She did not move.

'Estanyol!' Bernat heard Llorenç de Bellera shout from down below. 'Your lord is waiting.'

Bernat could not stop himself retching, then vomiting on to the stored grain until he felt as if he had brought up all his insides. Francesca still did not move. Bernat ran back to the ladder and climbed down. When he reached the bottom of the staircase, pale, revolted, his head spinning, he ran blindly into the imposing shape of the lord of Navarcles.

'It would seem that the husband has not consummated his marriage,' Llorenç de Bellera commented to his companions.

Bernat had to raise his head to face him. 'No . . . your lordship, I could not do it,' he stammered.

Llorenç de Bellera fell silent.

'Well, if you are not up to the task, I'm sure that one of my friends – or my soldiers – will be more ready for it. I told you, I don't want any more bastards.'

'You have no right . . .!'

The wedding guests looking on shuddered as they imagined the consequences of this outburst. With one hand, the lord of Navarcles seized Bernat by the throat. He squeezed, and Bernat was soon gasping for breath.

'How dare you? Are you thinking of using your lord's

legitimate right to lie with the bride to come along later and make claims for your bastard child?' Llorenç buffeted Bernat before letting him go. 'Is that what you're after? I'm the one who decides what the rights of vassalage are. And nobody else! Are you forgetting that I can punish you how and when I choose?'

He landed another blow on Bernat's cheek, sending him crashing to the ground.

'Where's my whip?' he shouted angrily.

The whip! Bernat had been only a child when, together with a crowd of others, he had been forced to accompany his parents to watch the public flogging that the lord of Navarcles had inflicted on a poor wretch, although nobody knew for certain what he had done wrong. The memory of the crack of the leather whip on that man's back resounded in his ears, just as it had on the day, and night after night throughout his childhood. No one who had been there that day had dared make a move; no one did so now. Bernat got to his knees and looked up at his feudal lord, standing there like a great boulder, his hand held out for someone to pass him his whip. Bernat recalled the raw flesh of the other man's back: a bleeding mass so lacerated that not even all the lord's ferocity could tear any more strips from it. Bernat crawled blindly back towards the staircase. He was trembling like a child caught up in a dreadful nightmare. Still no one moved or spoke. Still the sun shone in the clear blue sky.

'I'm so sorry, Francesca,' Bernat whispered after he had struggled back up to the top of the ladder, pushed by one of the soldiers.

He undid his hose and knelt beside her. Glancing down at his limp member, he wondered how on earth he was going to fulfil his lord's command. With one finger, he began to caress Francesca's bare ribs.

She did not react.

'I have . . . we have to do this,' Bernat urged her, gripping her wrist to turn her towards him.

'Don't touch me!' Francesca cried, coming out of her stupor.

'He'll flay me alive!' Bernat protested, staring at her naked body.

'Leave me alone!'

They struggled, until finally Bernat seized both her wrists and forced her upright. Francesca was still fighting him.

'Someone else will come!' he whispered. 'Another man will be the one to force you!'

Her eyes opened wide in an accusing glare.

'He'll have me flayed!' Bernat repeated.

Francesca fought to beat him off, but he flung himself on top of her. Her tears failed to dampen the sudden rush of desire he felt as he rubbed against her naked body. As he penetrated her, she gave a shriek that reached the highest heaven.

Her cries satisfied the soldier who had followed Bernat and was witnessing the whole scene shamelessly, head and shoulders thrust into the room.

Before Bernat had finished, Francesca gradually stopped resisting and her howls turned to sobs. Bernat reached his climax to the sound of his wife's tears.

Llorenç de Bellera also heard the screams from the second-floor window. Once his spy had confirmed that the marriage had been consummated, he called for the horses and he and his sinister troop left the farmhouse. Desolate and terrified, most of the wedding guests did the same.

Calm returned to the courtyard. Bernat was still sprawled across his wife. He had no idea what to do next. He realized he was still gripping her shoulders and lifted his hands away. As he did so, he collapsed again on top of her. He pushed himself up and found himself staring

25

into Francesca's eyes. They seemed to be staring straight through him. Any movement he made would press his body against hers once more, and he could not bear the thought of doing her more harm. He wished he could levitate then and there so that he could separate his body from hers without even touching it.

Eventually, after what seemed an eternity, Bernat pushed himself away and knelt down beside her. He still did not know what to do for the best: to stand up, lie down beside her, get out of the room, or to try to justify himself . . . He could not bear to see Francesca's naked body cruelly exposed on the pallet. He tried to get her to look at him, but her eyes were blank again. He looked down, and the sight of his own naked sex filled him with shame.

'I'm sorr—'

He was interrupted by a sudden movement from Francesca. Now she was staring straight at him. Bernat looked for a glimmer of understanding, but there was none.

'I'm sorry,' he repeated. Francesca was still staring at him without the slightest reaction. 'I'm so sorry. He . . . he was going to flay me alive,' he stammered.

In his mind's eye, Bernat saw the lord of Navarcles standing with his arm outstretched, calling for the whip. He searched Francesca's face: nothing. What he saw in her eyes frightened him still further: they were shouting in silence, as loudly as the screams she had uttered when he had flung himself on her.

Unwittingly, as though trying to make her understand that he knew what she was going through, as if she were a little girl, he stretched out his hand towards her cheek.

'I . . .' he started to say.

His hand never reached her. As it approached, the muscles of her whole body stiffened. Bernat lifted his hand to his own face and burst into tears.

Francesca lay there, staring into space.

After a long while, Bernat stopped crying. He got to his feet, put on his hose and disappeared down the ladder to the floor beneath. As soon as she could no longer hear his footsteps, Francesca got up and went over to the chest that was the only furniture in the room, to find some clothes. When she was dressed, she gently picked up all the things that had been torn from her, including the precious white linen smock. Folding it carefully so that the torn parts did not show, she stowed it in the chest.

2

Francesca wandered about the farmhouse like a lost soul. She carried out all the domestic chores, but never said a word. The sad atmosphere she created soon spread to the farthest corners of the Estanyol family home.

Bernat had several times tried to apologize for what had happened. Once the terror of his wedding day had receded, he had tried to explain what he had felt more clearly: his fear of the lord's cruelty; the consequences for both of them of refusing to obey his orders. Bernat repeated 'I'm sorry' over and over again to Francesca, but she simply stared at him in silence, as though waiting for the moment when, without fail, Bernat's argument led him to the same crux: 'If I hadn't done it, another man would have come . . .' At that point, he always fell silent; he knew there was no excuse, and every time his rape of her rose like an insurmountable barrier between them. The apologies, excuses and silences slowly healed the wound in Bernat, if not in his wife, and his feelings of remorse were tempered by the daily round of work. Eventually, Bernat even resigned himself to Francesca's stubborn refusal to talk.

At daybreak every morning, when he got up to start a hard day's grind, he would stare out of their bedroom window. He had always done this with his father, even in his last illness, the two of them leaning on the thick stone windowsill and peering up at the heavens to see what the day heralded. They would look out over their lands, clearly defined by the different crops growing in each field and extending right across the huge valley beyond the farmhouse. They watched the flight of the birds and listened closely to the noises the animals were making in their pens. These were moments of communion between father and son, and between the two of them and their land: the only occasions when Bernat's father appeared to recover his sanity. Bernat had dreamt of being able to share similar moments with his wife, to tell her all he had learnt from his father, and his father from his own father, and so on back through the generations.

He had dreamt of being able to explain that these fertile lands had in the distant past been free of rent or service, and belonged entirely to the Estanyol family, who had worked them with great care and love. The fruits of their labours were entirely theirs, without their having to pay tithes or taxes or give homage to any arrogant, unjust lord. He had dreamt of being able to share with her, his wife and the mother of the future inheritors of those lands, the same sadness his father had shared with him when he told the story of how it was that, three hundred years later, the sons she would give birth to would become serfs bound to another. Just as his father had told him, he would have liked to have been able to tell her proudly how three hundred years earlier, the Estanyol family, along with many others in the region, had won the right to keep their own weapons as free men, and how they had used those weapons when they had responded to the call from Count Ramon

Borrell and his brother Ermengol d'Urgell and gone to fight the marauding Saracens. He would have loved to tell her how, under the command of Count Ramon, several Estanyols had been part of the victorious army that had crushed the Saracens of the Córdoban Caliphate at the battle of Albesa, beyond Balaguer, on the plains of Urgell. Whenever he had time to do so, his father would recount him that story, tears of pride in his eyes; tears that turned to ones of sadness when he spoke of the death of Ramon Borrell in the year 1017. This was when, he said, the peasant farmers had become serfs again. The count's fifteen-year-old son had succeeded him, and his mother, Ermessenda de Carcassonne, became regent. Now that their external frontiers were secure, the barons of Catalonia – the ones who had fought side by side with the farmers – used the power vacuum to exact fresh demands from the peasants. They killed those who resisted, and took back ownership of the lands, forcing their former owners to farm them as serfs who paid a part of their produce to the local lord. As others had done, the Estanyol family bowed to the pressure; but many families had been savagely put to death for resisting.

'As free men,' his father would tell Bernat, 'we fought alongside the knights against the Moors. But we could not fight the knights themselves, and when the Counts of Barcelona tried to wrest back control of the principality of Catalonia, they found themselves facing a rich and powerful aristocracy. They were forced to bargain – always at our expense. First it was our lands, those of old Catalonia; then it was our freedom, our very lives . . . our honour. It was your grandfather's generation' – Bernat's father would tell him, his voice quavering as he looked out over the fields – 'who lost their freedom. They were forbidden to leave their land. They were made into serfs, people bound to their properties, as were their children, like me, and their grandchildren, like you. Our lives . . . your life, is in the hands of the lord of the castle. He is the one who imparts justice and has the right to abuse us and offend our honour. We are not even able to defend ourselves! If anybody harms you, you have to go to your lord so that he can seek redress; if he is successful, he keeps half of the sum paid you.'

After this his father would invariably recite all the lord's rights. These became etched in Bernat's mind, because he never dared interrupt his father once he had started on the list. The lord could call on a serf's aid at all times. He had the right to a part of the serf's possessions if the latter should die without a will, or when his son inherited; if he had no offspring; if his wife committed adultery; if his farmhouse were destroyed by fire; if he were forced to mortgage it; if he married another lord's vassal; and, of course, if he sought to leave it. The lord had the right to sleep with any bride on her wedding night; he could call on any woman to act as wet-nurse for his children, and on their daughters to serve as maids in the castle. The serfs were obliged to work on the lord's lands without pay; to contribute to the castle's defence; to pay part of what they earned from the sale of their produce; to provide the lord and any companions he brought with lodging in their homes, and food during their stay; to pay to use the woods or grazing land; to pay also to use the forge, the oven and the windmill that the lord owned; and to send him gifts at Christmas and other religious celebrations.

And what of the Church? Whenever Bernat's father asked himself that question, his voice would fill with anger.

'Monks, friars, priests, deacons, canons, abbots, bishops,' he would say, 'every single one of them is just as bad as the feudal lords oppressing us! They have even forbidden us from joining holy orders to prevent us escaping from the land and our enslavement to it!'

'Bernat,' his father would warn him whenever the Church was the target of his wrath, 'never trust anyone who says he is serving God. They will use sweet words on you, and sound so educated you will not understand the half of it. They will try to convince you with arguments that only they know how to spin, until they have seduced your reason and your conscience. They will present themselves as well-meaning people whose only concern is to save you from evil and temptation, but in fact their opinion of us is written in books and, as the soldiers of Christ they say they are, they simply follow what is written there. Their words are excuses, and their reasoning is of the sort you might use with a child.'

'Father,' Bernat remembered he had once asked him, 'what do their books say about us peasants?'

His father had stared out at the fields, up to the line of the horizon dividing them from the heavens: the place he did not care to gaze on, the place in whose name all these monks and clergymen spoke.

'They say we're animals, brutes, people who cannot understand courtly manners. They say we are disgusting, ignoble and an abomination. They say we have no sense of shame, that we are ignorant. They say we are stubborn and cruel, that we deserve no honourable treatment because we are incapable of appreciating it, that we only understand the use of force. They say—'

'Are we really all that, Father?'

'My son, that is what they wish to make of us.'

'But you pray every day, and when my mother died . . .'

'I pray to the Virgin, my son, to the Virgin. Our Lady has nothing to do with friars or priests. We can still believe in her.'

Yes, Bernat Estanyol would have loved to lean on the windowsill in the morning and talk to his young wife; to tell her all his father had told him, and to stare out over the fields with her.

Throughout the rest of September and all October, Bernat hitched up his oxen and ploughed the fields, turning over the thick crust of earth so that the sun, air and manure could bring fresh life to the soil. After that, with Francesca's help, he sowed the grain; she scattered the seed from a basket, while he first ploughed and then flattened the ground with a heavy metal bar once the seed was planted. They worked without talking, in a silence disturbed only by his shouts to the oxen, which echoed round the whole valley. Bernat thought that working together might bring them closer, but it did not: Francesca was still cold and indifferent, picking up her basket and sowing the seed without so much as looking at him.

November arrived, with its yearly tasks: fattening the pig for the kill, gathering wood for the fire and enriching the soil, preparing the vegetable patch and the fields that were to be sown in spring, pruning and grafting the vines. By the time Bernat returned to the farmhouse each day, Francesca had seen to the domestic work, the vegetables, the hens and rabbits. Night after night, she served him his meal without a word, then went off to bed. Every morning, she rose before he did, and by the time he came down, breakfast was waiting for him on the table, and his noon-day meal was in his satchel. As he ate, he could hear her tending the animals in the stable next door.

Christmas came and went, and then in January they finished harvesting the olives. Bernat had only enough trees to provide what was needed at home and what he had to give his lord.

After that, Bernat had to kill the pig. When his father was alive, the neighbours, who rarely visited, were certain never to miss the day the pig was butchered. Bernat remembered those occasions as real celebrations; the pigs were slaughtered and then everyone had plenty to eat and drink, while the women cut up the carcass.

The Esteve family – father, mother and two of the brothers – turned up one morning. Bernat went out into the courtyard to greet them; his wife hung back.

'How are you, daughter?' her mother asked.

Francesca said nothing, but accepted her embrace. Bernat studied the two women: the mother anxiously hugged her daughter, expecting her to put her arms round her too. But Francesca simply stood there stiffly, without responding. Bernat looked anxiously at his father-in-law.

'Francesca,' was all Pere Esteve said, his eyes still looking beyond her shoulder. Her two brothers raised their hands in greeting.

Francesca went down to the pigsty to fetch the pig; the others stayed in the courtyard. No one said a word; the only sound to break the silence was a stifled sob from Francesca's mother. Bernat felt an urge to console her, but when he saw that neither her husband nor her sons made any move, he thought better of it.

Francesca appeared with the animal, which was struggling as if it knew the fate awaiting it. She brought it up to her husband in her usual silent way. Bernat and the two brothers upended it and sat on its belly. The pig's squeals could be heard through the whole Estanyol valley. Pere Esteve slit its throat with a sure hand, and the men sat while the women collected the spouting blood in their bowls, changing them as they filled. Nobody looked at each other.

No one even had a cup of wine while mother and daughter sliced up the meat of the slaughtered animal.

With their work done and the onset of night, the mother again tried to embrace her daughter. Bernat

34

looked on anxiously, to see if this time there was some kind of reaction from Francesca. There was none. Her father and brothers said farewell without raising their eyes from the ground. Her mother came up to Bernat.

'When you think the time for the birth has come,' she said, taking him to one side, 'send for me. I don't think she will.'

The Esteve family set out on the road back to their farm. That night, as Francesca climbed the ladder to bed, Bernat could not help staring at her stomach.

At the end of May, on the first day of harvest, Bernat stood looking across his fields, sickle on shoulder. How was he going to harvest the grain all on his own? For a fortnight now, after she had twice fainted, he had forbidden Francesca to do any hard work. She had listened to him without replying, but obeyed. Why had he done that? Bernat surveyed the vast fields waiting for him. After all, he thought, what if the child were not his? Besides, women were accustomed to giving birth in the fields while they worked, but when he had seen her collapse like that not once, but twice, he could not help but feel concerned.

Bernat grasped the sickle and started to reap the grain with a firm hand. The ears of corn flew through the air. The sun was high in the mid-day sky, but he did not so much as stop to eat. The field seemed endless. He had always harvested it with his father, even when the old man had not been well. Harvesting seemed to revive him. 'Get on with it, son!' his father would encourage him. 'We don't want a storm or hail to flatten it all.' So they reaped row after row. When one of them grew tired, the other took over. They ate in the shade and drank his father's good wine. They chatted and laughed together. Now all Bernat could hear was the whistle of the blade through the air, the swishing noise as it chopped the stems of corn. Scything, scything, and as it sped through the air, it seemed to be asking: Just who is the father of the child-to-be?

Over the following days, Bernat harvested until sunset; sometimes he even carried on working by moonlight. When he returned to the farmhouse, his meal was on the table waiting for him. He washed in the basin and ate without any great appetite. Until one night, when the wooden cradle he had carved that winter, as soon as Francesca's pregnancy became obvious, started to rock. Bernat glanced at it out of the corner of his eye, but went on drinking his soup. Francesca was asleep upstairs. He turned to look directly at the cradle. One spoonful, two, three. It moved again. Bernat stared at it, the soup-spoon hanging in mid-air. He looked all round the room to see if he could see any trace of his mother-in-law, but there was none. Francesca had given birth on her own . . . and then taken herself off to bed.

Bernat dropped the spoon and stood up. Halfway to the cradle, he turned round and sat down again. Doubts about whose child it was assailed him more strongly than ever. 'Every member of the Estanyol family has a birthmark by their right eye,' he remembered his father telling him. He had one, and so did his father. 'Your grandfather was the same,' the old man had assured him, 'and so was your grandfather's father . . .'

Bernat was exhausted: he had worked from dawn to dusk for days on end now. Again he looked over at the cradle.

He stood up a second time and walked over to peer at the baby. It was sleeping peacefully, hands outstretched, covered in a sheet made of torn pieces of a white linen smock. Bernat turned the child over to see its face.

3

Francesca never even looked at her baby. She would bring the boy (whom they had called Arnau) up to one of her breasts, then change to the other. But she did not look at him. Bernat had seen peasant women breast-feeding and all of them, from the well-off to the poorest, either smiled, let their eyelids droop, or caressed their baby's head as they fed it. But not Francesca. She cleaned the boy and gave him suck, but not once during his two months of life had Bernat heard her speak softly to him, play with him, take his tiny hands, nibble or kiss him, or even stroke him. None of this is his fault, Francesca, Bernat thought as he held his son in his arms, before taking him as far away as possible so that he could talk to him and caress him free from her icy glare.

The boy was his! 'We Estanyols all have the birthmark,' he reassured himself whenever he kissed the purple stain close by Arnau's right eyebrow. 'We all have it, father,' he said again, lifting his son high in the air.

But that birthmark soon became something much more than a reassurance to Bernat. Whenever Francesca went to the castle to bake their bread, the women there lifted the blanket covering Arnau so that they could check the mark. Afterwards, they smiled at each other, not caring whether they were seen by the baker or the lord's soldiers. And when Bernat went to work in his lord's fields, the other peasants slapped him on the back and congratulated him, in full view of the steward overseeing their labours.

Llorenç de Bellera had produced many bastard children, but none had ever been able to prove his parentage: his word always prevailed over that of some ignorant peasant woman, even if among friends he would often boast of his virility. Yet it was obvious that Arnau Estanyol was not his: the lord of Navarcles began to notice sly smiles on the faces of the women who came to the castle. From his apartments, he could see them whispering together, and even talking to the soldiers, whenever Estanyol's wife came. The rumour spread beyond the circle of peasants, so that Llorenç de Bellera soon found himself the butt of his friends' jokes.

'Come on, eat, Bellera,' a visiting baron said to him with a smile. 'I've heard you need to build your strength up.'

Everyone at table that day laughed out loud at the insinuation.

'In my lands,' another guest commented, 'I do not allow any peasant to call my manhood into question.'

'Does that mean you ban birthmarks?' responded the first baron, the worse for wear from drink. Again, everyone burst out laughing, while Llorenç de Bellera gave a forced smile.

It happened in the first days of August. Arnau was sleeping in his cradle in the shade of a fig tree at the farmhouse entrance. His mother was going to and fro between the vegetable garden and the animal pens, while his father, keeping one eye all the time on the wooden cot, was busy leading the oxen time and again over the ears of corn to crush the precious grain that would feed them through the year.

They did not hear them arrive. Three horsemen galloped into the yard: Llorenç de Bellera's steward and two others, all three armed and mounted on powerful warhorses. Bernat noticed the horses were not wearing battle armour: they had probably not thought this necessary to intimidate a simple peasant. The steward stayed in the background, while the other two men slowed to a walk, spurring their horses on to where Bernat was standing. Trained for battle, the two horses came straight at him. Bernat backed off, then stumbled and fell to the ground, almost underneath their huge hooves. It was only then that the horsemen reined in their mounts.

'Your lord, Llorenç de Bellera,' shouted the steward, 'is calling for your wife to come and breastfeed Don Jaume, the son of your lady, Dona Caterina.' Bernat tried to scramble to his feet, but one of the riders urged his horse on again. The steward addressed Francesca in the distance. 'Get your son and come with us!' he ordered.

Francesca lifted Arnau from his cradle, and walked, head down, in the direction of the steward's horse. Bernat shouted and again tried to rise to his feet, but before he could do so, he was knocked flat by one of the horses. Each time he attempted to stand up, the same thing happened: the two horsemen took turns to knock him down, laughing as they did so. In the end, Bernat lay on the ground beneath the horses' hooves, panting and dishevelled. The steward rode off, followed by Francesca on foot carrying the child. When they were no more than a dot in the distance, the two soldiers wheeled away and galloped after him.

Once quiet had returned to the farmhouse, Bernat peered at the cloud of dust trailing off towards the horizon, and then looked over at the two oxen, stolidly chewing on the ears of corn they had been trampling.

From that day on, although Bernat continued working with his animals and on the land, his thoughts returned constantly to his son. At night, he wandered around the farmhouse recalling the childish breathing that spoke of life and the future, the creaking of the wooden slats of the cradle whenever Arnau moved, his shrill cry when he was hungry. He tried to discern his son's innocent smell in every corner of the house. Where might he be sleeping now? His cradle, the one Bernat had made with his own hands, was here. When finally Bernat succeeded in falling asleep, the silence would wake him with a start. He curled up on his pallet, listening hour after hour to the sounds of the animals down below that now were all the company he had.

Bernat went regularly to Llorenç de Bellera's castle to have his bread baked. He never saw Francesca: she was shut away to attend to Dona Caterina and her son's unpredictable appetite. The castle, as his father had explained when the two of them had been obliged to come here together, had started out as little more than a watchtower on the summit of a small hill. Llorenç de Bellera's forebears had taken advantage of the power vacuum following Count Ramon Borrell's death to build new fortifications, thanks to the forced labour of the serfs who lived on their ever-expanding territories. Around the keep a hotchpotch of buildings soon grew up, including the bakery, the forge, some new, more spacious stables, kitchens and sleeping quarters.

The castle was more than a league away from the Estanyol farmhouse. On his first visits, Bernat heard no news of his son. Whenever he enquired, he always received the same reply: his wife and boy were in Dona Caterina's private apartments. The only difference was that, while some of those he asked laughed cynically, others lowered their gaze as though ashamed to look the child's father in the eye. Bernat put up with their evasive answers for weeks on end, until one day when he was leaving the bakery with two loaves of bean-flour bread, he ran into one of the scrawny blacksmith apprentices whom he had already questioned several times about his son.

'What do you know about my Arnau?' he asked again.

There was no one else around. The lad tried to avoid him, as if he had not heard, but Bernat seized him by the arm.

'I asked you what you know about my son Arnau.'

'Your wife and son—' the apprentice started with the usual formula, not lifting his eyes from the ground.

'I know where he is,' Bernat interrupted him. 'I'm asking if my Arnau is well and healthy.'

Still not looking at him, the lad started shuffling his feet in the sand. Bernat shook him roughly.

'Is he well?'

When the apprentice still would not look up, Bernat shook him even harder.

'No!' the lad finally admitted. Bernat loosened his grip so that he could look him in the face. 'No,' he said again.

'What's wrong with him?'

'I can't . . . We have orders not to tell you . . .' the apprentice's voice trailed off.

Bernat raised his voice, not caring whether a guard might hear. 'What's wrong with my boy? What's wrong? Tell me!'

'I can't. We cannot . . .'

'Would this change your mind?' asked Bernat, offering him one of the loaves.

The lad's eyes opened wide. Without a word, he snatched the bread from Bernat's hands and bit into it as if he had not eaten in days. Bernat pulled him to one side, away from any prying eyes.

'What's happened to my Arnau?' he asked anxiously.

His mouth stuffed with bread, the apprentice glanced at Bernat, then signalled for him to follow. They crept stealthily along the castle walls until they reached the forge. They crossed it and headed for the back, where the lad opened a door leading into a shed where equipment and tools were kept. He went in and Bernat followed. As soon as he was inside, the boy sat on the floor and started to devour more bread. Bernat peered around the squalid room. It was stiflingly hot, but he could not understand why the apprentice had brought him there: all he could see were piles of tools and old scraps of iron.

Bernat looked enquiringly at the boy. Chewing on the loaf, he pointed to one of the corners of the room and waved Bernat to go and investigate there.

Abandoned and starved, his son lay on a pile of wooden planks inside a torn wicker basket. The strips of white linen bound round him were filthy and in tatters. He was on the verge of death. Bernat could not stop himself uttering a strangled cry that sounded hardly human. He snatched Arnau up and pressed him to his chest. The infant responded only feebly, but he did respond.

'The baron ordered your son be kept here,' Bernat heard the apprentice explain. 'At first, your wife came several times a day, and soothed him by breastfeeding him.' Bernat clutched the child to him, as if trying to breathe life into his tiny lungs. 'One day, the steward came in after her,' the boy went on. 'Your wife fought him off, she shouted as loud as she could . . . I saw him, I was in the forge next door.' He pointed to a crack in the wooden planks of the wall. 'But the steward is a very strong man . . . When he was done with her, the lord and some soldiers came in too. Your wife was lying on the floor; the lord began to laugh at her. All of them did.

42

Since that day, whenever your wife came to feed her child, there would be soldiers waiting at the door. She could not fight them all off. In the past few days, I have hardly seen her here. The soldiers catch her as soon as she leaves Dona Caterina's apartments. She cannot even reach the forge. Sometimes the lord sees what they are doing, but all he does is laugh.'

Without a moment's thought, Bernat lifted his shirt and pushed his son's tiny body inside. He disguised the bulge by holding the other loaf of bread up against his chest. The infant did not even stir. As he made for the door, the apprentice rose to stop him.

'The lord has forbidden it! You cannot—'

'Out of my way, boy!'

The lad stepped in front of Bernat. Once again, Bernat did not hesitate for a second: holding the baby and the loaf of bread in one arm, he snatched an iron bar from the wall and whirled round. Bernat caught the apprentice full on the head. The boy fell to the ground on the threshold of the storeroom before he had time to utter a sound. Bernat did not even look at him; he went out and shut the door behind him.

He had no problem leaving Llorenç de Bellera's castle. No one could have suspected that beneath the loaf of bread he was hiding his son's poor, abused body. It was only after he had emerged through the castle gate that he thought of Francesca and the soldiers. Full of indignation, he mentally reproached her for not trying to contact him, to warn him of the danger their son was in, for not fighting for Arnau . . . Bernat cradled his son's body and thought of his wife being raped by the soldiers while his son was left to die on a pile of rotten planks.

How long would it take them to find the lad he had struck? Was he dead? Had he shut the storeroom door properly? As he strode back to his farm, Bernat's mind was filled with questions. Yes, he dimly remembered shutting the door.

As soon as he had turned the first bend on the twisting path that rose towards the castle, and was out of sight, Bernat uncovered his son. The baby's eyes were dull and lifeless. He weighed even less than the loaf of bread! His arms and legs were so thin! Bernat's stomach churned and a lump came to his throat. Tears began to trickle down his cheeks, but he told himself this was no time to cry. He knew they would set out in search of them, that they would set the dogs on them, but what was the use of running away if the child did not survive? Bernat left the path and hid in some bushes. He knelt down, left the loaf of bread on the ground and lifted Arnau in both hands until he was level with his face. The baby hung there limply, his head lolling to one side. 'Arnau!' whispered Bernat. He shook him gently, over and over again. The baby's eyes seemed finally to be looking straight at him. His own face streaked with tears, Bernat realized that the poor thing did not even have the strength to cry. He cradled him in one arm, then tore off a small piece of bread, wet it with his saliva, and brought it close to his son's mouth. Arnau did not react, but Bernat persisted until he managed to force a tiny piece of bread between his lips. Bernat waited. 'Swallow, son, swallow,' he begged him. His lips trembled when he saw Arnau's throat contract almost imperceptibly. He crumbled some more bread and anxiously repeated the operation. Arnau swallowed seven more fragments.

'We'll get out of this, you'll see,' Bernat told him. 'I promise you.'

He returned to the path. Everything was still calm. That must mean they had not discovered the apprentice's body yet. For a while, Bernat thought of Llorenç de Bellera: cruel, evil, implacable. How much pleasure he would get from hunting down an Estanyol!

'We'll get out of this, Arnau,' he repeated, setting off towards his farmhouse.

Not once did he look back as he ran, and when he reached the farm he did not allow himself even a moment's rest. Leaving Arnau in his cradle, Bernat picked up a sack and stuffed some flour and dried vegetables in it. He put in a wineskin filled with water, and another full of milk, then added salt meat, a bowl, a spoon and some clothing. Last came some coins he had kept hidden, a hunting knife and his crossbow. How proud Father was of this crossbow! he thought, feeling its weight in his hand. He had always told Bernat when he was teaching him how to use it, how he had fought with it alongside Count Ramon Borrell in the days when the Estanyols were free men. Free! Bernat strapped the child to his chest and loaded up all the other items. He would always be a serf, unless . . .

'As of now we are fugitives,' he whispered to his son as he headed off towards the woods. 'Nobody knows these forests as we Estanyols do,' he told him when he had reached cover. 'We have always hunted here.' He pushed through the undergrowth until they came to a stream. He stepped down into the water until it was knee-height, then started walking against the current. Arnau had closed his eyes and was asleep, but Bernat went on talking to him: 'The lord's dogs are not very alert, they've been badly handled. We'll go up to the top, where the woods are denser and no one can hunt us on horseback. That means the lord and his friends have never been up there. They would get their fine clothes torn. As for the soldiers . . . why would they go up there to hunt? They get all they need by stealing from us. We can hide there, Arnau. I swear no one will find us.' He stroked his son's head as he waded upstream.

In mid-afternoon he came to a halt. The woods had become so thick that their branches overhung the stream and blotted out the sky. He sat on a rock and looked down at his legs: the water had made them white and wrinkled. It was only then that he realized how much they ached, but he did not care. He put down the sack and crossbow and untied Arnau. The boy had opened his eyes once more. Bernat diluted some milk in water, added flour, stirred the mixture and then brought the bowl up to the infant's lips. Arnau screwed up his face in disgust. Bernat wiped one of his fingers clean in the stream, dipped it into the mixture, and tried again. After several attempts, Arnau responded, allowing his father to feed him from his finger. Soon afterwards, he closed his eyes and fell fast asleep. All Bernat ate was a chunk of salt meat. He would have liked to rest, but he knew there was still a long way to go.

The Estanyol cave, his father had called it. Night had fallen by the time they reached it, after stopping once more for Arnau to have some food. The cave entrance was a narrow slit in the rocks, which Bernat, his father and grandfather used to close up with branches to protect them from storms or animals on the prowl.

Bernat lit a fire just inside the cave, then took a torch to make sure no wild animal had chosen it for a lair. He settled Arnau on a pallet he made from his sack and some dry twigs, and fed him again. This time, the infant took the food gladly, and then fell into a deep sleep. Before he could eat more than a mouthful of meat, Bernat did the same. They would be safe from Llorenç de Bellera here, he thought as he closed his eyes and matched his breathing to that of his sleeping son.

No sooner had the master blacksmith told him of the discovery of his apprentice's dead body in a pool of blood, than Llorenç de Bellera galloped out of the castle with his men. Arnau's disappearance and the fact that his father had been seen in the castle pointed directly towards Bernat. Now he sat astride his horse in the Estanyol farmhouse yard and smiled when his soldiers informed him that, judging by the disorder inside, it seemed Bernat had fled and taken his son with him.

'You were fortunate when your father died,' he growled, 'but now all this will be mine! Go and find him!' he shouted to his men. Then he turned to his steward and commanded: 'Draw up a list of all the goods, chattels and animals on this property. Make sure it's all there, down to the last grain of corn. Then join the search for Estanyol.'

Several days later, the steward appeared before his lord in the castle keep. 'We've searched all the other farmhouses, the woods and the fields. There is no sign of Estanyol. He must have gone to hide in a town, perhaps in Manresa or—'

With a wave of his hand, Llorenç de Bellera silenced him. 'We will find him. Inform the other barons and our agents in the towns. Tell them one of my serfs has escaped and is to be arrested.' At that moment, Dona Caterina and Francesca appeared. His son Jaume was in Francesca's arms. When Llorenç de Bellera saw her, his face fell: she was of no use to him any more. 'My lady,' he said to his wife, 'I cannot understand how you permit a strumpet like this to give suck to a son of mine.' Dona Caterina gave a start. 'Did you not know that your wetnurse is the whore of all the soldiers in the castle?'

Dona Caterina seized her son from Francesca.

When Francesca learnt that Bernat had fled with Arnau, she wondered what could have become of her son. The Estanyol family lands and properties had all passed into the hands of the lord of Navarcles. She had no one to turn to for help, and all the while the soldiers continued to take advantage of her. A crust of dry bread, a rotten vegetable or two, sometimes a bone to gnaw: that was the price of her body.

None of the peasant farmers who visited the castle even deigned to glance at her. If she tried to approach them, they chased her away. After her mother publicly disowned her outside the castle bakery, she did not dare return to her family home. She was forced to remain close to the castle, one of the army of beggars fighting over the scraps left by the walls. It seemed her fate was to be passed from one man to the next, her only nourishment whatever leftovers the soldier who had chosen her that day cared to give her.

The month of October arrived. Bernat had seen his son smile, but their provisions had almost run out, and winter was approaching fast. It was time for them to leave the cave.

4

The city lay spread at his feet.

'Look, Arnau,' Bernat said to his son, who was sleeping
peacefully strapped to his chest. 'There's Barcelona. We'll
be free there.'

Ever since fleeing with Arnau, Bernat had been unable
to get the city out of his mind. It was the one great hope
all the serfs had. Bernat had heard them talk about it
when they were forced to go and work on their lord's
land, to repair his castle walls or any other of the services
he demanded. When he heard them whispering carefully
so as not to be overheard by the steward or soldiers,
Bernat had been merely curious. He was happy working
on his farm, and would never have abandoned his father
or fled with him. Yet now he had lost his lands, and, as
he watched his son asleep inside the Estanyol cave, what
the others had said came back to haunt him.

'If anyone manages to live in Barcelona for a year and
a day without being arrested by the lord,' he remembered
someone saying, 'they can acquire the status of residents
and become free men.' All the other serfs had fallen
silent. Bernat had looked at them: some had closed their

eyes and clenched their teeth; others were shaking their head in disbelief; still others were smiling up at the sky, dreaming of breaking the chains that tied them to the land.

'So all you have to do is live in the city?' asked one of the youngsters who had been staring skywards. 'Why can people become free men by living in Barcelona?'

The eldest serf confirmed what had been said: 'Yes, you only need to live in Barcelona for a year and a day.'

Eyes shining, the young lad urged him to explain further.

'Barcelona is a very rich city. For many years now, from the days of Jaime the Conqueror to those of Pedro the Great, all our kings have asked it for money to wage war, or for their courts. The citizens of Barcelona granted them the money, but in return won special privileges. One day when he was at war with Sicily, Pedro the Great himself had them all written down in a charter . . .' The old man hesitated. '*Recognoverunt proceres*, I believe it is called. That is where it is laid out how we can become free men. Barcelona needs workmen, people who are free to work.'

The next day, the youth did not appear on the lord of Navarcles's lands. Nor the day after. His father was there, but he did not say a word. Then, three months later, the youth was dragged back in chains, with the threat of the whip at his back; even so, all the other serfs thought they could see a gleam of pride in his eyes.

From the summit of the Serra de Collserola, on the old Roman road between Ampurias and Tarragona, Bernat gazed down at freedom . . . and the sea! He had never even imagined, let alone set eyes on, that vast, seemingly endless expanse. He had heard from traders that Catalonia was the master of lands beyond the waves, but this was the very first time he had been confronted with something he could not see the far end of. 'Beyond that mountain. After you cross that river . . .' He had always been able to point to the spot in the distance that a stranger was asking him about. Now he scanned the horizon, standing silently as he took it all in, gently caressing the unruly curls that had grown on Arnau's head since they had been in hiding.

Then he turned his attention to the land by the shore. He could see five ships close in, near the island of Maians. This was another novelty: until that day, Bernat had only seen drawings of ships. To his right, he saw the mountain of Montjuïc, which also swept down to the sea, and was surrounded by fields and plains; then the city of Barcelona itself. From the low promontory of the Mons Taber in the centre, hundreds of buildings spread out in all directions: low houses built one on top of another, but also magnificent palaces, churches and monasteries . . . Bernat wondered how many people lived there, because, all of a sudden, the buildings came to an end: the city was like a beehive crammed inside walls, with open fields beyond. There were forty thousand people living there, Bernat recalled someone telling him.

'How is anyone going to find us among forty thousand people?' he mused, looking down at Arnau. 'You'll be a free man, my son.'

Bernat was certain they could hide in the city. He would look for his sister. But first he had to get in through a city gate. What if Lord de Bellera had sent out a description of him? That birthmark of his . . . But during the three nights of his walk down from the hills he had been devising a plan. He sat on the ground and picked up a hare he had shot with his crossbow. He slit its throat and let the blood drip on to the small pile of sand he had cupped in his hand. He stirred blood and sand together, and as the mixture dried, spread it around his right eye. Then he put the hare back in his sack.

As soon as he could feel that the mixture had dried, and he could no longer see out of his eye, he set off down the hill towards the Santa Anna gateway, on the northernmost side of the western wall. Lots of people were lined up to get into the city. Arnau was awake by now, and Bernat carried on stroking his head as he slipped in among the crowd, dragging his feet as he did so. A barefoot peasant bent double under an enormous sack of turnips turned towards him. Bernat smiled at him.

'A leper!' shouted the peasant, dropping his sack and jumping out of his way.

To his astonishment, Bernat saw the whole line of people in front of the gate rushing to one side or the other, leaving the track littered with sacks, food, a couple of carts and several mules. Even the blind men clustered around the Santa Anna gateway began to stir.

Arnau started to cry, and Bernat saw some of the soldiers at the gate draw their swords, while others made to close the heavy wooden doors.

'Go to the lazaretto!' someone shouted at him.

'But it's not leprosy!' Bernat protested. 'I simply got a branch in my eye! Look!' He lifted his arms and waved them about. Then, carefully placing Arnau on the ground, he started to take off his clothes. 'Look!' he repeated, showing everybody his strong, healthy body, with no signs of disease or wounds. 'Look! I'm a peasant farmer, but I need a doctor to cure my eye, or otherwise I won't be able to work.'

An official pushed one of the soldiers towards him. He came to a halt a few paces from Bernat and surveyed him.

'Turn round,' he said, gesturing with his finger.

Bernat did as he was told. The soldier looked him up and down, then shook his head to the official. Another man at the gateway pointed with his sword towards the bundle at Bernat's feet.

'What about the boy?'

Bernat bent down to pick Arnau up. He stripped off his clothes with his right side pressed against him, then held him up horizontally, holding him by the side of his head so that no one would spot the birthmark.

Looking back at the gate, the soldier shook his head once more.

'Cover that wound,' he said. 'If you don't, you won't be able to get around the city.'

The line re-formed outside the gate, which swung open. The peasant with the turnips picked up his sack again, avoiding looking at Bernat.

Bernat passed through the gateway with one of Arnau's shirts covering his right eye. The soldiers followed him with their gaze, but then who wouldn't stare at someone with a shirt covering half his face? Leaving Santa Anna church on his left, he followed the rush of people into the city. He turned right into the Plaça de Santa Anna, looking down at the ground the whole time. As the peasants spread out through the streets, gradually Bernat saw fewer and fewer bare feet, or rope and leather sandals, until all at once he found himself staring at a pair of legs covered in flame-red stockings, with tight-fitting shoes, made entirely of some fine material, that ended in such long points that at the tip of each of them was a tiny golden chain which led back to the ankles.

Bernat raised his eyes and found himself staring at a man wearing an elaborate hat. He was dressed in a black robe shot through with gold and silver threads, a belt also decorated with gold, and leather straps sparkling with pearls and other precious stones. Bernat stood there open-mouthed, but the man looked past him as if he did not even exist.

Bernat hesitated, lowered his eyes once more, then gave a sigh of relief. The man had not given him so much as a second look, so he continued on his way down towards the cathedral, which was still under construction. Bit by bit, he plucked up the courage to look around. Nobody seemed to pay him any attention. He stood watching the workmen swarming round the cathedral: some were hewing stone, others were climbing the tall scaffolding that covered the building, still more were hauling on ropes to lift blocks of stone . . . Arnau began to whimper, demanding his attention.

'Tell me,' he said to a passing workman, 'how can I find the potters' quarter?' He knew his sister Guiamona was married to one.

'Carry on down this street,' the man said hastily, 'until you reach the next square, the Plaça de Sant Jaume. There's a fountain in the middle, there you turn right and continue until you come to the new wall, at the Boqueria gate. Don't go out into the Raval district. Instead, walk alongside the wall until you reach the next gateway, Trentaclaus. That's where you'll find the potters.'

Bernat struggled to remember all these different names but just as he was about to ask the man to repeat them, he discovered he had already disappeared.

'Carry on down this street to the Plaça de Sant Jaume,' he whispered to Arnau. 'That much I remember. And once we're in the square, we have to turn right again . . . that's it, isn't it, son?'

Arnau always stopped crying when he heard his father's voice.

'Now what do we do?' Bernat said out loud. They were in a different square, the Plaça de Sant Miquel. 'That man only mentioned one square, but we can't have made a mistake.' Bernat tried to ask a couple of passersby, but none of them stopped. 'Everyone is in such a hurry,' he complained to his son. At that moment, he caught sight of a man standing by the entrance to . . . a castle? 'Ah, there's someone who doesn't seem to be rushing anywhere ... Begging your pardon,' he said, touching the man's black cloak from behind.

Even Arnau, strapped tightly to his father's chest, seemed to give a start when Bernat jumped back as the man turned round.

The old Jewish man shook his head wearily. He knew that Bernat's reaction was the result of the Christian priests' fiery sermons. 'What is it?' he asked.

Bernat could not help staring at the red and yellow badge on the old man's chest. Then he peered inside what he had at first thought was a fortified castle. Everyone going in and out were Jews! And they all wore this distinguishing mark. Was it forbidden to talk to them?

'Did you want something?' the old man repeated.

'How ... how do I find the potters' quarter?'

'Carry on straight down this street,' said the old man, pointing the direction. 'That will take you to the Boqueria gate. Follow the wall down towards the sea, and at the next gate you'll find the district you're looking for.'

In fact, the Church had only forbidden carnal relations with the Jews; that was why it forced them to wear the badge, so that nobody could claim not to have realized whom they were consorting with. The priests always railed against them, and yet this old man ...

'Thank you, friend,' said Bernat with a timid smile.

'Thank you,' the old Jewish man replied. 'But in future, take care that no one sees you talking to one of us ... let alone smiling at us.' His lips twisted in a sad grimace.

At the Boqueria gate, Bernat found himself caught up in a crowd of women who were buying offal and goat's meat. He watched them examining the wares and bargaining with the stallholders. 'This is the meat that gives our lord all his problems,' Bernat muttered to his son, and then laughed at the thought of Llorenç de

Bellera. How often had he heard him threatening the shepherds and the cattlemen who supplied Barcelona with meat! But the lord never dared go any further, because anyone taking livestock to the city had the right to graze them wherever they liked in all Catalonia.

Bernat skirted the market and walked down to the Trentaclaus gate. The streets here were wider, and as he drew close to the gate, he saw dozens of pots, bowls, jars, and bricks drying in the sun in front of the houses.

'I'm looking for Grau Puig's house,' he told one of the soldiers guarding the gate.

The Puig family had been neighbours of the Estanyols. Bernat well remembered Grau, the fourth of eight starving children who could never get enough to eat from their meagre landholding. His mother had a special affection for them, because their mother had helped her give birth to Bernat and his sister. Grau was the brightest and hardest-working of them all; that was why, when Josep Puig received a kinsman's offer for one of them to become a potter's apprentice in Barcelona, it was Grau he chose. Grau was ten years old at the time.

But if Josep Puig found it hard to feed his family, it was going to be impossible for him to find the two bushels of white flour and the ten shillings his relative was demanding in return for taking on Grau for his five years' apprenticeship, not to mention the two additional shillings that Llorenç de Bellera had demanded in order to free a serf from his obligations, and the clothes Grau would need for the first two years of his apprenticeship; the master potter had only agreed to supply what was necessary for the last three.

This was what brought Josep Puig to the Estanyol farmhouse with Grau, who was a few years older than Bernat and his sister. Old man Estanyol listened closely to Puig's proposition: if he endowed his daughter with the list of things he outlined and offered them to Grau at once, he promised his son would marry Guiamona as soon as he reached the age of eighteen and was a qualified craftsman. The old man studied the boy: sometimes, when Grau's family was in dire need, he had come to lend a hand in their fields. The boy had never asked for payment, but Estanyol had always made sure he went home with some vegetables or grain. He trusted him. He accepted the offer.

After five years' hard work as an apprentice, Grau became a qualified craftsman. He was still bound to the master potter, who was sufficiently pleased with him to start paying him a wage. When he reached eighteen, Grau kept his promise and married Guiamona.

'My son,' his father said to Bernat, 'I've decided to give Guiamona a fresh dowry. There are only two of us, and we have the best and most fertile lands in the region. They might need the money.'

'Father,' Bernat interrupted him, 'why do you think it's necessary to give me an explanation?'

'Because your sister has already received her dowry, and you are my heir. The money is yours by right.'

'Do as you see fit.'

Four years later, when he was twenty-two, Grau sat the public examination which took place in front of four officers of the guild. He made his first pieces for them: a water jug, two plates and a bowl. The four men looked on closely, and then unanimously granted him the title of master potter. This allowed him to open his own workshop in Barcelona, and of course to use his own stamp, which was to be put on every piece of pottery made in his workshop, in case there were any complaints about his work. To honour the meaning of the word Grau in Catalan, he chose the outline of a mountain as his stamp.

Grau and Guiamona, who by now was pregnant,

moved into a small, one-storey house in the potters' quarter. By royal decree, this was situated on the western edge of the city, in the land between the new wall built by King Jaime I and the ancient Roman fortifications. They used Guiamona's dowry to buy the property, having saved it for just such an occasion.

It was there, with the pottery workshop and their living quarters sharing the same space as the kiln and the bedrooms, that Grau began his career as a master potter. It was a time when the expansion of Catalan trade was bringing about a revolution among the potters, calling for a specialization that many of them could not accept.

'We're going to make only jugs and storage jars,' declared Grau, 'that's all.' Guiamona glanced at the four masterful pieces he had made for his examination. 'I've seen lots of traders begging for jars to sell their oil, honey or wine in,' he went on. 'And I've seen lots of potters turn them away because their kilns were full of complicated tiles for a new house, bright crockery for a noble, or an apothecary's pots.'

Guiamona ran her fingers over the masterpieces he had created. How smooth they were to the touch! When Grau had triumphantly presented them to her after passing his examination, she had imagined that she would be surrounded with similar beautiful pieces. Even the guild officers had congratulated Grau, because he had shown he was a true master of his craft: the decorations of zigzag lines, palm leaves, rosettes and fleurs-de-lis on the water jug, the two plates and the bowl displayed a wealth of colour on a white tin glaze background: the coppery green so typical of Barcelona that every master potter had to use, but also violet manganese, black iron, cobalt blue and antimony yellow. Each line or design was of a different shade. Guiamona could scarcely wait for the pieces to be fired, in case the clay cracked. As a finishing touch, Grau applied a layer of clear lead glaze which made them entirely waterproof. Guiamona could still feel their smoothness in her fingertips. But now . . . all her husband was going to make were storage jars.

Grau went up to her. 'Don't worry,' he said to calm her fears. 'I'll make more pieces like them just for you.'

Grau's calculation had proved correct. He filled the yard in front of his humble workshop with jugs and storage jars, and soon the traders of the city became aware that in Grau Puig's workshop they could find everything they wanted. No longer would they have to beg for favours from arrogant master craftsmen.

As a result of this, the building that Bernat and little Arnau came to a halt outside was very different from that first tiny workshop. What Bernat could see out of his left eye was a big house on three floors. Open to the street at ground level was the workshop; the master potter and his family lived on the upper two floors. Along one side of the house ran a garden for vegetables and flowers; on the other were sheds leading to the kilns and a terrace where hundreds of jugs and storage jars of all shapes, sizes and colours were displayed. Behind the house, as stipulated in the city regulations, there was empty ground where the clay and other materials could be loaded and stored. It was here too that the potters threw the ashes and other waste from the kilns, which they were forbidden to throw into the city streets.

Bernat could see from outside that there were ten people working non-stop in the workshop. None of them looked like Grau. Bernat noticed two men saying goodbye next to an ox-cart laden with brand-new storage jars. One of them clambered on board the cart and set off. The other man looked well dressed, so before he could disappear back into the workshop, Bernat called to him: 'Wait!'

The other man watched him approach. 'I'm looking for Grau Puig,' said Bernat.

The man stared him up and down. 'If it's work you're after, we don't need anyone. Our master has no time to lose,' he growled, 'and nor have I,' he added, turning his back on the newcomer.

'I'm a relative of Grau's.'

The man stopped in his tracks, then whirled round to face him. 'Hasn't the master paid you enough? Why do you insist on demanding more?' he snarled, pushing Bernat out into the street. Arnau began to cry. 'You've already been told that if you come here again, we'll report you to the authorities. Grau Puig is an important man, you know.'

Although he did not understand any of this, Bernat let the man force him backwards. 'Listen . . .' he protested, 'I . . .'

By now, Arnau was howling in his arms, but then all of a sudden there was an even louder cry from one of the upper-floor windows.

'Bernat! Bernat!'

Bernat and the man turned round together and saw a woman leaning half out of the window, arms whirling like windmills.

'Guiamona!' shouted Bernat, returning her greeting.

The woman pulled her head in. Bernat turned to the man, his eyes narrowed.

'Does Mistress Guiamona know you?' the man asked.

'She's my sister,' Bernat answered curtly. 'And by the way, nobody in this house has ever paid me a penny.'

'I'm sorry,' the man apologized, hoping he was not in trouble. 'I was referring to the master's brothers: first one came, then another, and then still another.'

But Bernat saw his sister coming out of the house, so he cut him short and ran over to embrace her.

'Where's Grau?' he asked his sister once he had cleaned off his eye and handed Arnau over to the Moorish slave who looked after Guiamona's small children. As he watched the boy wolf down the bowl of milk and cereal he was fed, he added: 'I'd like to greet him too.'

Guiamona looked uncomfortable.

'Is something wrong?'

'Grau has changed a lot. He's a rich and important man now.' Guiamona pointed to the many chests lining the walls of the room, the sideboard – a piece of furniture Bernat had never seen in his life before, which was filled with books and crockery – the carpets adorning the floor and the tapestries and curtains hanging from windows and walls. 'He barely attends to the workshop and his potter's trade these days; it's Jaume, his chief assistant, who sees to everything. He's the man you met in the street. Grau is busy as a merchant: ships, wine, oil. Now he is a guild official, which, in accordance with the Laws and Customs of the city, means he is an alderman, a gentleman. Soon he expects to be made a member of the Council of a Hundred.' Guiamona looked around the room. 'He's not the same any more, Bernat.'

'You've changed a lot too,' Bernat said, interrupting her. Guiamona looked down at her matronly body and nodded. 'That man, Jaume,' Bernat continued, 'said something about Grau's relatives. What did he mean?'

Guiamona shook her head, then replied: 'What he meant was that as soon as they heard that Grau was rich all of them – brothers, cousins, nephews – suddenly started turning up at the workshop. They had fled their lands to come and seek Grau's help.' Guiamona could not help noticing her brother's expression. 'So you too . . .?' Bernat nodded. 'But you had the wonderful farm!'

When she heard Bernat's story, she could not hold back her tears. As he told her what had happened to the lad in the forge, she stood up and came to kneel next to his chair.

'Don't mention that to anyone here,' she warned him. Then she laid her head on his lap, and went on listening. 'Don't worry,' she sobbed when Bernat had finished, 'we will help you.'

'Ah, sister,' said Bernat, stroking her head. 'How do you intend to help me when Grau would not even help his own brothers?'

'Because my brother is different!' shouted Guiamona so loudly that Grau took a step backwards.

It was night by the time her husband returned home. Small, skinny Grau, a bundle of nerves, strode up the staircase, cursing. Guiamona was waiting for him. Jaume had told him what had happened: 'Your brother-in-law is sleeping in the hayloft with the apprentices, his boy . . . with your children.'

Grau charged up to his wife. 'How dare you!' he shouted at her when she tried to explain. 'He's a fugitive serf! Do you know what it would mean if they found a fugitive in our house? My ruin, that's what! It would mean my ruin!'

Guiamona let him talk. He whirled round her, flinging his arms theatrically into the air. He was a good head taller than she was.

'You're mad! I've sent my own brothers overseas on ships! I've given my sisters dowries so that they would marry outsiders, and all so that nobody could accuse this family of the slightest thing! And now you . . . Why should I act any differently for your brother?'

'Because he is different!' she shouted, silencing him.

Grau hesitated. 'What? What do you mean?'

'You know very well. I don't think I need to remind you why.'

Grau avoided meeting her gaze. 'This very day,' he muttered, 'I've been meeting one of the five city councillors with a view to being elected to the Council of a Hundred as a guild official. I think I've won three of the five over: I still need to convince the bailiff and the magistrate. Can you imagine what my enemies would say if they found out I had given shelter to a fugitive serf?'

Guiamona reminded him softly: 'We owe him everything.'

'I'm only an artisan, Guiamona. A rich one, but still an artisan. The nobles look down on me, and the merchants despise me, however much they are willing to do business with me. If they found out I had taken in a fugitive . . . do you know what the land-owning nobles would say?'

'We owe him everything,' Guiamona repeated.

'Well then, we'll give him the money and send him on his way.'

'He needs his freedom. A year and a day.'

Grau paced nervously around the room. Then he buried his head in his hands. 'We can't,' he said. 'Guiamona, we can't do it!' he reiterated, peering through his fingers. 'Can you imagine—?'

'Can you imagine! Can you imagine!' she butted in, raising her voice at him. 'Can you imagine what would happen if we threw him out and he was arrested by Llorenç de Bellera's men or one of those enemies of yours? What if they found out that you owe everything to him, a fugitive serf who agreed to give you a dowry that was not yours by right?'

'Are you threatening me?'

'No, Grau, no. But that's how it is. If you won't do it out of gratitude, do it out of self-interest. It's better for you to be able to keep an eye on him. Bernat wants his freedom. He won't leave Barcelona. If you don't take him in, there will be a fugitive and a little boy, both of them with the same birthmark by their right eye as me, wandering the streets of Barcelona. Think how useful they could be to those enemies you're so frightened of.'

Grau stared hard at his wife. He was about to respond, then thought better of it and merely waved his hand. He left the room, and Guiamona could hear him climbing the stairs to the loft.

5

'Your son will stay in the main house; Dona Guiamona will take care of him. As soon as he is old enough, he will become an apprentice in the workshop.'

Bernat paid only scant attention to what Grau's assistant was saying. Jaume had burst into the dormitory at first light. The slaves and apprentices leapt from their pallets as though he were the Devil himself, and rushed pell-mell out of the door. Bernat was satisfied with what he heard: Arnau would be well looked after, and in time would become an apprentice, a free man with a trade.

'Did you hear me?' Jaume asked.

When Bernat did not reply, he cursed: 'Stupid peasants!'

Bernat almost reacted violently, but the smile on the official's face made him think twice.

'Go ahead,' Jaume taunted him. 'Hit me and your sister will be the one who loses. I'll repeat the important things, peasant: you are to work from dawn to dusk, like all the others. In return you will have bed, food and clothing . . . and Dona Guiamona will take care of your son. You are forbidden to enter the main house: on no account may you do so. You are also forbidden to leave the workshop until after the year and a day necessary to win your freedom. Whenever anyone comes into the workshop, you are to hide. You are not to tell a soul of your situation, not even the apprentices in here, although with that birthmark of yours . . .' Jaume shook his head. 'That is the bargain the master has struck with Dona Guiamona. Do you agree?'

'When will I be able to see my son?' asked Bernat.

'That's none of my business.'

Bernat closed his eyes. When they had first set sight on Barcelona, he had promised Arnau he would be a free man. He would not be any lord's vassal.

'What are my tasks?' he said at last.

To carry wood. To carry hundreds, thousands of the heavy branches needed every day for the kilns. To make sure the fires were always lit. To carry clay, and to clean. To clean away the mud, the clay dust and the ashes from the kilns. Over and over again, hauling the ashes and dust to the back of the house. By the time Bernat returned, covered in dust and ashes, the workshop would once again be filthy, so that he had to start all over again. He also had to carry the pottery out into the open with the other workmen, under the watchful gaze of Jaume, who supervised the life of the workshop at all times. Jaume strode around, shouting, cuffing the apprentices and cursing the slaves, on whom he did not hesitate to use the whip if anything was not to his liking.

On one occasion when a big pot slipped out of their hands and rolled on to the ground, Jaume brandished his whip at them. The pot had not even broken, but he lashed the three slaves helping Bernat as hard as he could. He was about to turn on Bernat, until the latter calmly warned him: 'Do that and I'll kill you.'

Jaume hesitated, then flushed and cracked the whip in the direction of the others, who by now were safely out of range. Jaume charged after them. Bernat took a deep breath.

Bernat worked so hard he gave the assistant little opportunity to threaten him. He ate whatever was put before him. He would have liked to tell the stout woman who served them that on his farm the dogs had been better fed than this, but when he saw how the apprentices and slaves threw themselves on the food, he preferred to say nothing. He slept with the rest of them in the loft on a straw pallet, under which he kept his few belongings and what little money he had managed to rescue. The fact that he had stood up to Jaume seemed to have won him the respect of the others, so that he was able to sleep soundly, despite the fleas, the stink of sweat and all the snores.

He put up with everything just for the two evenings a week when Habiba, the Moorish slave girl, brought him Arnau, who was generally fast asleep. Bernat would pick him up, sniffing the smell of clean clothes and fragrance that hung about him. Taking care not to wake his son, he would lift his clothing to look at his legs and arms, his full stomach. Arnau was growing and filling out. Bernat rocked the baby in his arms, pleading with his eyes for Habiba to let him keep the boy a little longer. Sometimes he tried to caress him, but the rough skin of his hands chafed the boy's skin, and Habiba snatched Arnau away from him. As time went by, he came to a tacit agreement with her (she never said a word to him) that he could stroke the boy's pink cheeks with the backs of his fingers. The mere touch of his son's skin made him quiver. When the slave gestured for him to hand the baby back, Bernat would give him one final kiss on the forehead.

As the months went by, Jaume realized that Bernat could do more useful work in the pottery. The two men had come to respect one another.

'There's nothing to be done with the slaves,' Jaume

said one day to Grau Puig, 'they work only because they fear the whip, and don't care what they are doing. But your brother-in-law—'

'Don't call him that!' Grau protested yet again, as this was a frequent liberty his assistant allowed himself.

'The peasant . . .' Jaume corrected himself, pretending to be embarrassed. 'The peasant is different. He takes care over even the most menial job. He cleans the kilns in a way I've never—'

'So what are you suggesting?' Grau butted in, not raising his eyes from the papers he was studying.

'We could give him more responsible work, and besides, he costs us hardly anything.'

This observation finally made Grau look up. 'Don't you believe it,' he said. 'He may not have cost anything to buy, like the slaves do, and he may not have an apprentice's contract, or have a wage like the potters, but he's the most expensive workman I have.'

'I meant . . .'

'I know what you meant.' Grau buried himself in his papers once more. 'Do as you see fit, but let me warn you: that peasant must never forget what his place is in this workshop. If he does, I'll throw him and you out, and you'll never become a master potter. Is that clear?'

Jaume nodded, but from that day on, Bernat helped the potters directly in their work. He was even promoted above the heads of the young apprentices, who were unable to handle the heavy fireproof moulds used to bake the pots in the kilns. From the moulds came big pot-bellied jars with a narrow mouth, a short neck and a small base that could hold up to 280 litres of grain or wine. Previously, Jaume had needed to employ at least two potters to haul the moulds around; with Bernat's help, only one other person was necessary. They would make a jar in the mould, fire it, apply a layer of tin and lead oxides to it, then fire the jar again in a second kiln at a lower temperature so that the tin and the lead would melt together to form a clear waterproof glaze.

Jaume waited anxiously to see whether he had made the right decision. After a few weeks, he was satisfied with the result: production had increased noticeably, and Bernat still took the same trouble over his work. 'More than some of the potters themselves!' Jaume was forced to admit when he went to put the workshop's stamp on the neck of one of the storage jars.

Jaume tried to read the thoughts the peasant concealed behind his placid countenance. There was never any gleam of hatred in his eyes, or any sign of rancour. Jaume wondered what could have happened for him to end up in this situation. He was not the same as the master's other kinsmen who had shown up at the workshop: they had all been bought off. But Bernat . . . the way he fondled his son whenever the Moorish slave girl brought the baby to him! He wanted his freedom, and worked harder than anyone else to make sure he achieved it.

The understanding between the two men produced other results apart from an increase in production. One day when Jaume came over to imprint the master's mark on a jar, Bernat narrowed his eyes and stared pointedly at the base of the piece. *You'll never become a master potter!* Grau's words of warning came immediately to Jaume's mind whenever he considered becoming more friendly with Bernat.

Now, he pretended he was having a coughing fit. He moved away from the jar without stamping it, and looked at the place the peasant had been pointing out to him. He saw a tiny crack which would mean the jar broke in the heat of the kiln. Jaume shouted angrily at the potter . . . and at Bernat.

So the year and the day that Bernat and his son needed to become freemen passed. Grau Puig achieved his longed-for goal of being elected a member of Barcelona's Council of a Hundred. And yet Jaume did not see the peasant react in any way. Anyone else would have demanded his citizenship document and gone off into the streets of the city in search of fun and women, but Bernat did nothing. What was wrong with him?

Bernat could not get the memory of the lad in the forge out of his mind. He did not feel guilty about him: the fool had tried to stop him taking his son. But if he had died . . . Bernat might win freedom from his lord, but even after a year and a day he would not be free of the charge of murder. Guiamona had advised him not to tell his story to anyone, and he had followed her advice. He could not take the risk; Llorenç de Bellera had probably ordered his arrest not only as a fugitive, but as a murderer as well. What would become of Arnau if he were captured? Murder was punishable by death.

His son was growing strong and sturdy. He could not yet talk, but he was crawling everywhere, and gurgled joyfully in a way that made the hair on the back of Bernat's neck stand on end. Despite the fact that Jaume still did not speak to him, his new position in the work-shop (which Grau was too busy with his trading and other commitments to notice) gained him even more respect among the others. With Guiamona's tacit assent, the Moorish girl brought him Arnau more frequently now. His sister was also much busier as a result of her husband's new responsibilities.

There was no way that Bernat was going to risk his son's future by going out into the streets of Barcelona.

PART TWO

CHAINED TO THE NOBILITY

6

Christmas 1329
Barcelona

By now, Arnau was eight years old. He was a quiet, intelligent child with wavy, shoulder-length chestnut locks that framed a face in which shone big, clear, honey-coloured eyes.

Grau Puig's house was decked out for the Christmas celebrations. The youngster who, at the age of ten, thanks to a neighbour's generosity, had been able to leave his father's lands, had finally triumphed in Barcelona. Now he waited alongside his wife to receive his guests.

'They're coming to pay me homage,' he told Guiamona. 'It's unheard of for nobles and merchants to come to a mere artisan's house like this.'

His wife contented herself with listening.

'The King himself has backed me. The King himself! Our King Alfonso!'

That day no work was done in the pottery. Despite the cold, Bernat and Arnau sat on the ground in the yard and watched the constant comings and goings of slaves, craftsmen and apprentices in and out of the house. In all those eight years, Bernat had never set foot again in the Grau mansion, but he did not care. He ruffled Arnau's curls, and thought to himself: I can put my arms around my son, what more could I ask? His boy ate and lived with Guiamona, and even studied with Grau's children. He had learnt to read, write and count at the same time as his cousins. Yet thanks to Guiamona he had never forgotten that Bernat was his father. Grau himself treated the boy with complete indifference.

Bernat insisted time and again that Arnau should be well behaved in the big house. Whenever he came laughing into the workshop, Bernat's own face lit up. The slaves and all the craftsmen – even Jaume – could not help but smile at the boy as he raced out into the yard to wait for his father to complete one of his tasks, then run towards him and hug him tight. Afterwards he would go off and sit down again, watching his father and smiling at anyone who spoke to him. On some nights, after the workshop had closed, Habiba let him out of the house, and father and son had time to talk and laugh together uninterrupted.

Things had changed, even though Jaume still adhered strictly to his master's instructions. Grau paid no attention to the money brought in by the pottery, and had nothing to do with the day-to-day running of it. In spite of this, he could not do without it, because it was the basis of his position as guild official, alderman of Barcelona and member of the Council of a Hundred. However, once he had achieved all this, Grau Puig dedicated himself to politics and high-level finances, as befitted a city alderman.

From the outset of his reign in 1291, Jaime II had tried to impose himself on the old Catalan feudal nobility. To do this, he had turned to the free cities and their citizens, especially Barcelona. Sicily had been part of the Crown's possessions since the days of Pedro the Great. Now, when the Pope granted Jaime II the right to conquer Sardinia, it was the citizens of Barcelona who financed the enterprise.

The annexation of these two Mediterranean islands was in everyone's interests: it guaranteed the supply of grain to Catalonia, as well as sealing Catalan domination of the Western Mediterranean, and with it, control over the sea trade routes. The monarch kept for himself the silver mines and the salt on the island.

Grau Puig had not lived through these events. His opportunity came on the death of Jaime II and the accession of Alfonso III. In that same year, 1327, the Corsicans began to cause trouble in the city of Sassari on Sardinia. At the same time, fearing Catalonia's commercial power, the Genoese declared war, attacking all ships that sailed under the Catalan flag. Neither King nor traders hesitated a moment: the campaign to stifle the revolt in Sardinia and the war against Genoa were to be financed by the burghers of Barcelona. And this was what happened, thanks largely to the efforts of one of the city's aldermen: Grau Puig. He it was who, in addition to contributing generously to the costs of the war, succeeded by his fiery speeches in convincing even the most doubtful to take part. The King himself publicly thanked him for his efforts.

Today, as Grau peered anxiously out of his windows to see if his guests were arriving, Bernat kissed his son on the cheek and sent him back inside.

'It's very cold, Arnau. You should go in.' The boy made as though to protest, but his father insisted. 'You'll eat a fine meal tonight, won't you?'

'Cockerel, nougat and wafers,' his son said enthusiastically.

Bernau gave him an affectionate tap on the behind. 'Run inside. We can talk another day.'

* * *

Arnau arrived just in time to sit down to dinner. He and Grau's two youngest children, Guiamon, who was the same age as him, and Margarida, a year and a half older, were to eat in the kitchen. Josep and Genís, the two older children, were allowed to dine upstairs with their parents.

The arrival of so many guests had made Grau even more nervous than usual.

'I'll see to everything,' he told Guiamona as she was preparing the feast. 'You look after the women.'

'But how are you going to . . .?' she started to protest, but Grau was already giving instructions to Estranya the cook, a plump, impudent mulatto slave, who kept one eye on her mistress while appearing to pay attention to what Grau was saying.

How do you expect her to react? thought Guiamona. You're not talking to your secretary, or in the guild or the Council of a Hundred. So you don't think I'm capable of looking after your guests? Not good enough for you, am I?

Behind her husband's back, Guiamona had tried to restore order among the servants and to make sure that the Christmas feast was a success, but now, as their guests arrived and Grau fussed over everything, including their rich capes, she found she was pushed into the background as her husband had wished, and had to make do with smiling pleasantly at the other women. Grau meanwhile looked like a general in the thick of a battle: he was talking animatedly to his guests, while at the same time showing the slaves what they had to do and whom they were to attend to; the more he shouted and insisted, the more anxious they became. In the end, all of them – except for Estranya, who was in the kitchen preparing the meal – decided that the best thing was to follow Grau wherever he went.

Freed in this way from all supervision – as Estranya and her assistants were all busy labouring over their pots and fires – Margarida, Guiamon and Arnau mixed the chicken with the nougat and stuffed food in each other's mouths, laughing and joking all the while. At one point, Margarida picked up a jug of undiluted wine and swallowed a whole mouthful. She immediately turned bright red and her cheeks flushed, but she succeeded in not spitting any of it out. She encouraged her brother and cousin to do the same. Arnau and Guiamon both drank from the jug, but although they tried to keep their composure like Margarida, they started coughing and spluttering, searching desperately on the table for water, their eyes full of tears. After that, the three of them could not stop laughing: just from looking at each other, at the jug of wine, or Estranya's huge buttocks.

'Get out of here!' the mulatto shouted, tired of their shouts and laughter.

The three of them ran from the kitchen, still laughing and shouting.

'Shh!' another slave warned them at the foot of the main staircase. 'The master does not want any children here.'

'But—' Margarida tried to protest.

'No buts about it,' insisted the slave.

At that moment Habiba came down in search of more wine. The master had shot her a furious look when one of his guests had tried to pour some out and had been rewarded with only a few miserable drops.

'Keep an eye on the children,' Habiba told the slave on the staircase as she passed by. 'More wine!' she shouted at Estranya, going into the kitchen.

Worried that Habiba might bring ordinary wine rather than the special vintage reserved for this occasion, Grau came running after her.

The children had stopped laughing, and instead were keenly watching all this commotion. Grau spotted them with the slave.

'What are you children doing here? And you? Why aren't you doing anything? Go and tell Habiba that the wine is to come from the old jars. Don't forget, otherwise I'll flay you alive. And you children, get off to bed.'

The slave bustled off to the kitchen. Their eyes still glistening from the effects of the wine, the three children smiled at each other. As soon as Grau had rushed back upstairs, they burst out laughing. Bed? Margarida stared at the wide-open front door, pursed her lips and raised her eyebrows.

'Where are the children?' Habiba asked when the slave appeared in the kitchen.

'Wine from the old jars . . .' the slave repeated.

'What about the children?'

'The old ones. The old ones.'

'But what's happened to the children?' Habiba insisted.

'In your bed. The master say go to bed. They with him. From the old jars, yes? He'll flay us alive . . .'

It was Christmas. The streets of Barcelona were empty: no one would be outside until midnight mass and the sacrifice of a cock. The moon shone on the sea so brightly it seemed that the street they were walking down stretched on for ever. The three children stared in wonder at its silver reflection.

'There'll be no one on the beach tonight,' Margarida reasoned.

'Nobody puts to sea at Christmas,' Guiamon agreed.

The two of them turned to Arnau. He shook his head.

'No one will notice,' Margarida insisted. 'We can go and be back very quickly. It's close by.'

'Coward,' hissed Guiamon.

They ran down to Framenors, the Franciscan convent built on the shore at the far western end of the city wall. When they reached it, the children stared across the beach to the Santa Clara convent, which marked Barcelona's eastern limit.

'Look!' Guiamon said excitedly. 'The city fleet!'

'I've never seen the beach like this before,' said Margarida.

Eyes big as saucers, Arnau nodded in agreement.

All the way from Framenors to Santa Clara, the beach was filled with ships of all sizes. There were no buildings to spoil the children's view of this magnificent sight. Once, when Grau had taken them and their tutor down to the strand to watch one of the ships he had an interest in being loaded or unloaded, he had explained that almost a hundred years earlier King Jaime the Conqueror had forbidden any building on the beach in order to leave it free for boats to be grounded. None of the children had thought any more of what Grau had said: wasn't it natural for ships to be beached like that? They had always been there. Grau looked over at the tutor.

'In the ports of our enemies and trading rivals,' the tutor explained, 'none of the boats are left on the beach.'

At that word 'enemy' the four children were suddenly all ears.

'It's true,' Grau went on, finally sure of their interest. 'Our enemy Genoa has a wonderful natural harbour protected from the sea. That means they do not need to beach their ships. Our ally, Venice, has a great lagoon reached by narrow canals: their ships are safe there from any storms. The port of Pisa is connected to the sea by the river Arno; even Marseilles has a natural harbour protected from rough seas.'

'The Phocian Greeks are known to have used the harbour at Marseilles,' the tutor added.

'You say our enemies have better ports than us?' asked Josep, the eldest. 'And yet we defeat them: we're the lords of the Mediterranean!' he exclaimed, repeating the words so often heard from his father. The other children agreed: how was it possible?

Grau turned to their tutor for the explanation.

'Because Barcelona has always had the best sailors. We don't have a harbour, and yet—'

'What do you mean, we don't have a harbour?' protested Genís. 'What's that then?' he said, pointing to the beach.

'That's not a harbour. A harbour needs to be a sheltered place, protected from the open sea, but this . . .' The tutor waved his hands towards the waves lapping on the shore. 'Listen, Barcelona has always been a city of sailors. Many years ago, there was a harbour here, like all the other cities your father mentioned. In Roman times, ships sheltered behind the Mons Taber, which was over there somewhere,' he said, pointing inside the city walls, 'but gradually the land took over from the sea, and the harbour disappeared. Then there was the Comtal harbour, but that has gone too, and so has Jaime the First's, which was also sheltered by another small natural outcrop, the Puig de les Falsies. Do you know where that is now?'

The four children stared at each other, then turned to Grau. Laughingly, he pointed his finger downwards, as if trying to hide his gesture from the tutor.

'Here?' all four of them chimed.

'Yes,' replied the tutor, 'we're standing on it. But that one disappeared too, so Barcelona was left without a harbour, but by then we were a seafaring city, with the best sailors, and we still are . . . even though we have no harbour.'

'Well then,' Margarida objected, 'why is a harbour so important?'

'Your father can explain that better than I,' said the tutor. Grau nodded.

'It's very, very important, Margarida. Do you see that ship?' He pointed to a galley surrounded by small craft.

'If Barcelona had a harbour, we could unload it at a quay without needing all those people to unload the merchandise. Besides, if a sudden storm blew up, the ship would be in great danger because it is so close to shore. It would have to leave Barcelona.'

'Why?' Margarida wanted to know.

'Because it couldn't ride out the storm here: it might sink. Why, it's even made explicit in the *Ordinances of the Barcelona Coast*. There it stipulates that in case of any storm, ships must seek refuge in either the harbour at Salou or at Tarragona.'

'So we don't have a harbour,' said Guiamon sorrowfully, as if he had been robbed of something of the utmost importance.

'No,' said his father, laughing and putting an arm round his shoulder. 'But we're still the best sailors! We're the lords of the Mediterranean! And we do have the beach. Here is where we ground our boats when they are not on a voyage, and it's here that we repair and build them. Can you see the shipyards? There at the far end of the beach, where those arches are.'

'Can we go on to the boats?' Guiamon asked.

'No,' said his father, suddenly serious again. 'Boats are sacred, my boy.'

Arnau never went out with Grau and his children, still less with Guiamona. He was always left at home with Habiba, but later on, his cousins would tell him all they had seen and heard. They had explained everything about the beach and the boats.

And there the boats were that Christmas night. All of them! The small ones: cockboats, skiffs and gondolas. The medium-sized vessels: cogs, dromonds, gallivants, pinks, brigantines, galliots and barques, and even some larger ships: naos, carracks, caravels and galleys, which despite their size were forced by royal decree not to sail between October and April.

'Look at them all!' Guiamon exclaimed.

On the shore at Regomir they could see some fires burning, with watchmen sitting round them. Scattered along the beach from Regomir to Framenors rose the silent boats, lit only by the moon.

'Follow me, sailors!' commanded Margarida, raising her right arm.

Captain Margarida led her men through storms; they fought pirates, boarded ships, won battles. They leapt from one ship to the next, defeating Genoese and Moors, whooping in triumph as they regained Sardinia for King Alfonso.

'Who goes there?'

The three of them stood paralysed with fright in the bottom of a skiff.

'Who goes there?'

Margarida poked her head over the side. Three torches were coming towards them.

'Let's get away from here,' Guiamon whispered, tugging at his sister's dress.

'We can't,' she said. 'They're right in front of us.'

'What about over towards the shipyards?' asked Arnau.

Margarida looked over towards Regomir. Another two lighted torches were heading towards them from that direction.

'It's not safe that way either.'

The boats are sacred! Grau's words echoed in all their minds. Guiamon began to sob, but Margarida silenced him. A cloud covered the moon.

'Into the sea!' ordered the captain.

The three of them jumped overboard into the shallow water. Margarida and Arnau crouched down; Guiamon stretched out at full length. As the torches approached the skiff, the children moved out further into the sea. Margarida looked up at the moon, praying silently that the clouds would keep it hidden.

The search seemed to go on for ever, but none of the men looked out to sea, and if one of them did . . . well, it was Christmas, and they were only three frightened children – frightened, and soaked to the skin by now. It was very cold.

By the time they reached home, Guiamon could hardly stand. His teeth were chattering, his knees trembled and he was shaking uncontrollably. Margarida and Arnau had to lift him under the arms and carry him the last part of the way.

When they arrived, all the guests had already left. Alerted to the children's disappearance, Grau and the slaves were on the point of setting out to look for them.

'It was Arnau,' Margarida said accusingly while Guiamona and the Moorish slave girl plunged the little boy into a bath of hot water. 'He talked us into going down to the beach. I didn't want to . . .' The little girl made sure she accompanied her lies with the tears that always worked so well with her father.

The hot bath, blankets and scalding broth were not enough to revive Guiamon. The fever took hold. Grau sent for the doctor, but his efforts were in vain. The fever grew worse: Guiamon began to cough, and his breathing became shallow and wheezing.

'There's nothing more I can do,' Doctor Sebastià Font said resignedly on the third night he came to visit.

Pale and drawn, Guiamona raised her hands to her head and burst into tears.

'But that's impossible!' shouted Grau. 'There must be some remedy!'

'There may be, but . . .' The doctor was well aware of Grau and his dislikes. But the situation called for desperate measures. 'You will have to call for Jafudà Bonsenyor.'

Grau said nothing.

'Call for him!' Guiamona said between sobs.

A Jew! thought Grau. If you deal with a Jew, you deal with the Devil, he had been taught as a child. And as a child, Grau had joined the other apprentices to run after Jewish women and smash their water jars when they came to fill them at the public fountains. He went on doing so until the King bowed to a petition from the Jewry of Barcelona and prohibited all such attacks. Grau hated Jews. All his life he had harassed or spat at anyone wearing a badge. They were heretics; they were the ones who had killed Jesus Christ . . . how could he allow one of them to cross his threshold?

'Send for him!' shouted Guiamona.

Her anguished cry was so loud that everyone in the neighbourhood heard. Bernat and the apprentices on their pallets shrank back from the sound. Bernat had not been able to see either Arnau or Habiba for three days, but Jaume kept him up to date with what was going on.

'Your son is fine,' he told him when no one was looking.

Jafudà Bonsenyor came as soon as he got the message. He was wearing a plain black hooded djellaba with the badge round his neck. Grau watched him from a distance as he stood in the dining room, hunched over as he listened to Sebastià's explanations. Guiamona stood next to them. Make sure you cure him, Jew! Grau threatened silently when their eyes met. Jafudà Bonsenyor nodded respectfully towards him. Jafudà was a learned man who had devoted his life to studying philosophy and the sacred scriptures. King Jaime II had commissioned him to write the *Book of Sayings of Wise Men and Philosophers*, but he was also a doctor, the most prominent in all the Jewish community. When he saw Guiamon, all he did was shake his head slowly from side to side.

Grau heard his wife's cries. He ran to the stairs.

Guiamona came down from the bedroom on Sebastià's arm. Jafudà appeared behind them.

'Jew!' hissed Grau, spitting as he passed by.

Guiamon died two days later.

No sooner had they all returned to the house after the burial of the boy's body, than Grau signalled to Jaume to come over.

'I want you to go to Arnau at once and make sure he never sets foot inside this house again.'

Guiamona did not say a word.

Grau told him what Margarida had said: that it was Arnau who had led them on. Neither his youngest nor a mere girl could have planned such an escapade. Guiamona listened to his accusations, which blamed her for taking in her brother and nephew. And although deep in her heart she knew it was only a childish prank that had had fatal consequences, the death of her youngest son robbed her of the strength to oppose her husband, while Margarida's blaming of Arnau made it almost impossible for her to bear the sight of him any more. He was her brother's son, and she wished him no harm; but she preferred not to have to see him.

'Tie that Moorish girl to a beam in the workshop,' Grau ordered Jaume before he went off in search of Arnau, 'and make sure everyone gathers round, including the boy.'

Grau had been thinking it through during the funeral service. The slave girl was the one to blame: she should have been looking after them. As he heard Guiamona start crying again, and the priest droned on, he wondered what punishment he should give her. According to the law, he could not kill or maim her, but no one could object if she simply died as a result of the punishment he meted out to her. Grau had never had to deal with such a grievous problem. He ran through all the different tortures he had heard of: covering her body in boiling animal fat (would Estranya have enough in her kitchen?); putting her in chains or shutting her up in a dungeon (that would not be punishment enough); beating her; putting her feet in shackles . . . or flogging her.

'Be careful if you use it,' the captain of one of his ships had told him once as he offered him the gift. 'One lash can take all the skin off a person's back.' Ever since, Grau had kept the whip hidden away. It was a fine Oriental whip made of plaited leather, thick but lightweight and easy to handle. It ended in several thongs, each of them tipped with jagged pieces of metal.

As the priest fell silent and the altar-boys waved the censers round the coffin, Guiamona coughed, but Grau took a deep breath of satisfaction.

The slave girl was waiting, hands tied round a beam, her feet just touching the ground.

'I don't want my son to see this,' Bernat told Jaume.

'This isn't the moment, Bernat,' Jaume warned him. 'Don't go looking for trouble.'

Bernat shook his head again.

'You've worked hard, Bernat; don't cause trouble for your boy.'

In strict mourning clothes, Grau joined the circle of slaves, apprentices and craftsmen surrounding Habiba.

'Take off her clothes,' he ordered Jaume.

When Jaume began tearing off her tunic, Habiba tried to raise her legs to cover herself. But her dark, naked body, gleaming with sweat, was soon exposed to the onlookers' expectant gaze . . . and to the whip that Grau had already laid out on the floor. Bernat grasped Arnau's shoulders tight. The young boy began to cry.

Grau drew his arm back and cracked the whip against Habiba's naked upper half: the leather snaked across her back and the metal thongs wrapped themselves round her, digging into her breasts. A thin trickle of blood started to run down her dark skin. Her breasts were open wounds. Habiba lifted her face to the sky and howled as the pain racked her body. Arnau started to tremble uncontrollably, begging Grau to stop.

But he merely drew back his arm again.

'It was your job to look after my children!'

The whip resounded once more, forcing Bernat to turn his son round and press his face against him. The slave girl howled a second time, while Arnau's shrieks of protest were stifled in his father's body. Grau went on flogging the Moorish girl until not only her back and shoulders but her breasts, buttocks and legs were one bleeding mass.

'Tell your master I am leaving.'

Jaume's mouth thinned into a narrow line. For a second, he was tempted to embrace Bernat, but he could see some of the apprentices staring at them.

Bernat watched the official walk towards the big house. He had tried to talk to his sister, but Guiamona had not responded. For several days, Arnau had not moved from the straw pallet he now shared with his father. He sat there without moving, and when his father came up to see him, he always found him staring at the spot where they had tried to cure Habiba's wounds.

They had cut her down as soon as Grau left the workshop, but did not know where they could safely get hold of her body. Estranya ran in with oil and ointments, but as soon as she saw the bloody mass of flesh, she simply shook her head sadly. Arnau watched all this quietly from the back of the room, tears in his eyes; when Bernat tried to push him outside, he refused to go. Habiba died that same night. The only sign that she had breathed her last was when the low wail, like that of a newborn baby, that she had been making all day, suddenly stopped.

Grau heard of his brother-in-law's decision from Jaume. It was the last thing he needed: the two Estanyols, both of them with the birthmark by their right eye, roaming the streets of Barcelona in search of work, talking about him with everyone who cared to listen . . . and a lot of people would be interested, now that he had reached the summit. He felt his stomach churn and his mouth was dry: Grau Puig, a Barcelona alderman, master of the guild of potters, member of the Council of a Hundred, giving shelter to runaway serfs. The nobles were already against him. The more Barcelona helped King Alfonso, the less the King depended on the feudal lords, and the fewer the rewards they could hope to wring from the monarch. Who had been the chief promoter of this support for the King? He had. And whose interests were harmed when serfs deserted the countryside? The land-owning nobility. Grau shook his head and sighed. He cursed the day he had allowed this peasant to stay under his roof!

'Bring him here,' he told Jaume.

When his brother-in-law appeared, Grau said: 'Jaume tells me that you want to leave us.'

Bernat nodded.

'What do you intend to do?'

'I'll look for work to support my son.'

'You have no trade. Barcelona is full of people like you: peasants who could not earn a living from their lands. They never find work, and end up dying of hunger. Besides,' Grau added, 'you aren't even on the citizens' roll, even though you have lived long enough in the city now.'

'What do you mean by the citizens' roll?' asked Bernat.

'It's the document that proves you have lived a year and a day in Barcelona. It means you are a free citizen, not someone's vassal.'

'Where can I get mine?'

'The city aldermen authorize them.'

'I'll ask for one.'

Grau looked hard at Bernat. He was dirty, dressed in a shabby tunic and wearing a pair of rope sandals. In his mind's eye, he saw him in front of the city aldermen after having already told his story to dozens of clerks: Grau Puig's brother-in-law and nephew, hidden in his workshop for years. The news would spread like wildfire. He himself had used similar gossip against his enemies in the past.

'Sit down,' he said. 'When Jaume told me what you planned to do, I talked to your sister Guiamona' – he lied to conceal his change of attitude – 'and she begged me to take pity on you.'

'I don't need pity,' Bernat objected, thinking of Arnau sitting on the pallet, staring into space. 'I've been working hard for years in return for—'

'That was the offer,' Grau stopped him. 'You accepted it. At that moment it suited you.'

'That may well be,' Bernat admitted. 'But I did not sell myself as a slave, and it doesn't interest me now.'

'Let's leave pity out of it then. I don't think you will find work anywhere in the city, still less if you can't prove you are a free citizen. Without your papers, people will only take advantage of you. Have you any idea how many landless serfs there are here, with children to feed, forced to work for nothing just so that they can live for that precious year and a day in Barcelona? You cannot compete with them, and you will die of hunger before you are listed on the citizens' roll – you . . . or your son, and despite what has happened, we cannot allow little Arnau to suffer the same fate as our Guiamon. One death is enough. Your sister wouldn't be able to bear it.' Bernat remained silent, waiting for his brother-in-law to continue. 'If you are interested,' Grau said, stressing the word, 'you can go on working here, on the same terms . . . and receiving the wage of an ordinary workman, less payment for bed and board for you and your son.'

'And Arnau?'

'What about him?'

'You promised to take him on as an apprentice.'

'And I will – when he is old enough.'

'I want your written promise.'

'You shall have it,' Grau conceded.

'What about the citizens' roll?'

Grau nodded. It would not be hard for him to get Bernat put on it . . . discreetly.

7

'We declare Bernat Estanyol and his son Arnau to be free citizens of Barcelona . . .'

At last! Bernat could not prevent a shudder as he heard these hesitant words from the man reading the documents. He had asked where he could find someone who knew how to read, and had met up with him in the shipyard, offering him a small bowl in return for the favour. With the sounds of ship-building in the background, the smell of tar and the sea breeze caressing his face, Bernat listened as the man read out the second document: Grau agreed to take on Arnau as apprentice when he was ten years old, and promised to teach him the potter's trade. So his son was free, and one day could earn a living that would help him survive in the city.

Smiling broadly, Bernat handed over the bowl and walked back to the workshop. The fact that they had been listed on the citizens' roll meant that Llorenç de Bellera had not denounced them to the authorities, and there was no warrant for his arrest. Could the lad in the forge have survived? he wondered. Even so . . . 'You can keep our lands, Lord de Bellera, we'll keep our freedom,' Bernat muttered defiantly. When they saw Bernat arrive wreathed in smiles, all Grau's slaves and even Jaume interrupted their tasks. There were still traces of Habiba's blood on the ground. Grau had ordered they should not be cleaned up. Bernat's face fell as he tried to avoid them.

'Arnau,' he whispered to his son that night as they lay on the pallet they shared.

'What is it, Father?'

'We are free citizens of Barcelona.'

Arnau did not reply. Bernat felt for his son's head and stroked it. He knew how little this meant to a boy who had been robbed of his happiness. Bernat listened to the slaves' breathing and went on stroking his son's curls, but a sudden doubt assailed him: would the boy agree to work for Grau one day? That night it took Bernat a long time to get to sleep.

At first light each day when the men began their tasks, Arnau would leave Grau's workshop. And every morning, Bernat tried to talk to him and encourage him. You ought to make some friends, he tried to tell him once, but before he could do so, Arnau turned his back on him and walked wearily out into the street. Enjoy your freedom, my son, he wanted to tell him another time, but the boy just stood there looking at him, and when Bernat opened his mouth to speak he noticed a tear rolling down Arnau's cheek. Bernat knelt down. All he could do was hug the boy. Then he watched as he crossed the yard, dragging his feet. As he tried to avoid Habiba's bloodstains, the sound of Grau's whip echoed in Bernat's mind. Bernat promised himself he would never back down when threatened by the whip in the future: once was enough.

Bernat ran after his son, who looked round when he heard him. When he reached Arnau, he began to scrape with his foot at the beaten earth where the traces of the Moorish slave girl's blood still showed. Arnau's face brightened. Bernat scraped even more determinedly.

'What are you doing?' Jaume shouted from the far end of the yard.

Bernat froze. The sound of the whip echoed even more loudly in his mind.

'Father.' Arnau used his rope sandal to push away the small pile of earth Bernat had raised.

'What are you doing, Bernat?' Jaume repeated.

Bernat said nothing. Several seconds went by. Jaume turned and saw all the slaves standing there, staring at him.

'Bring some water, son,' said Bernat, seeing Jaume hesitate.

Arnau hurried off. This was the first time in months his father had seen him run. Jaume nodded.

On their knees, father and son silently scraped at the earth until all traces of injustice were removed.

'Go and play now,' Bernat told him once they had finished.

Arnau looked down. He would have liked to ask his father whom he was meant to play with. Bernat ruffled his hair before pushing him towards the gate. As he did every day, when Arnau was out in the street he walked round the house and climbed a leafy tree that grew above the garden wall. Hidden among the branches, he waited for his cousins and Guiamona to come out.

'Why don't you love me any more?' he muttered to himself. 'It wasn't my fault.'

His cousins looked happy. Over time, Guiamon's death had faded in their memory; it was only on their mother's face that the pain was still visible. Josep and Genís were pretending to fight. Margarida watched them, sitting to one side with her mother, who had her arms round her. Concealed in his tree, Arnau felt a stab of nostalgia as he remembered how that felt.

Morning after morning, Arnau would climb the same tree.

'Don't they love you any more?' he heard someone ask one day.

Arnau was so startled he lost his balance and nearly fell from his perch. He looked all round to discover who had spoken, but could not see a soul.

'Over here,' he heard.

The voice had come from somewhere inside the tree, but he still saw nothing. Eventually he spotted some branches moving, and in among them he could make out the face of a boy who was waving at him. He was sitting astride one of the forks of the tree, peering at him with a serious look on his face.

'What are you doing here, sitting in my tree?' Arnau asked him sharply.

The filthy-looking boy was unimpressed. 'The same as you,' he said. 'Watching.'

'You're not allowed to,' Arnau asserted.

'Why not? I've been doing it a long time now. I used to see you down there before, too.' The boy fell silent. 'Don't they love you any more? Why do you cry so much?'

Arnau realized that a tear was rolling down his cheek, and felt annoyed: he had been caught out. 'Get down from there,' he ordered the other boy, climbing down himself.

The stranger jumped lightly to the ground and stood facing him. Arnau was a head taller than him, but he did not seem afraid.

'You've been spying on me!' Arnau accused him.

'You were spying as well,' the boy retorted.

'Yes, but they're my cousins, so I'm entitled to.'

'Why don't you play with them then, like you used to?'

Arnau could not prevent a sob escaping him, and his voice trembled as he tried to find an answer.

94

'Don't worry,' the other boy said, trying to reassure him. 'I also cry a lot.'

'Why do you cry?' Arnau asked with difficulty.

'I don't know . . . Sometimes I cry when I think of my mother.'

'You have a mother?'

'Yes, but—'

'What are you doing here if you have a mother? Why aren't you playing with her?'

'I can't be with her.'

'Why? Isn't she at your house?'

'No,' the boy said reluctantly. 'Or yes, she is there.'

'So why aren't you with her?'

The grimy boy did not reply.

'Is she ill?' Arnau asked.

The boy shook his head. 'No, she's well enough,' he said.

'What then?' Arnau insisted.

The boy looked at him disconsolately. He bit his lower lip several times, then finally made up his mind. 'Come with me,' he said, tugging at Arnau's sleeve.

The strange little boy ran off at a speed that belied his small size. Arnau followed, trying hard not to let him out of sight. That was easy enough when they were crossing the open yards of the potters' quarter, but became much more difficult when they reached the narrow alleyways of the city, crammed with people and stalls. It was almost impossible for them to make their way through the crowds, or for him to keep the boy in view.

Arnau had no idea where he was, but did not care: he was too busy trying to spot his companion's quick, agile figure as he picked his way among all the people and stallholders, some of whom shouted in protest. He was less adept at avoiding the obstacles, and paid the consequences of the anger his fleet-footed companion's passage aroused. One of the stallholders cuffed him round the ear; another tried to grab him by the shirt. Arnau managed to avoid them both, but by the time he had escaped, the other boy was nowhere to be seen. He found himself all alone, on the edge of a large square full of people.

He recognized the square. He had been there once before, with his father. 'This is Plaça del Blat,' Bernat had told him. 'It's the centre of Barcelona. Do you see that stone in the middle?' Arnau looked in the direction his father was pointing. 'That stone divides the city into quarters: La Mar, Framenors, El Pi and La Salada or Sant Pere.' Now, Arnau reached the end of the silkmakers' street and stood under the gateway of the Veguer castle. There was such a crowd in the square it was impossible for him to make out the figure of the boy. He looked round: on one side of the gateway was the city's main slaughterhouse; on the other stood trestle tables full of bread for sale. Arnau looked again, searching for the boy near the stone benches that lined the square. 'This is the wheat market,' his father had explained. 'On these benches here you can see people who sell it on in the city; on those over there are the peasants who have brought their crops for sale.' But Arnau could see no sign of the boy on either side of the market, only tradesmen haggling over prices, or the country people with their sacks of grain.

While he was still trying to make out where the boy might be, Arnau found himself being pushed into the square by the crush of people making their way in. He attempted to stand to one side near the breadmakers' stalls, but his back brushed against a table and someone cuffed him painfully round the ear.

'Get out of here, you brat!' shouted the baker.

Arnau was quickly submerged again in the rush of people and the noise of the market. He had no idea which way to turn, but was pushed hither and thither by adults much taller than him, some of them bent under sacks of grain, who did not even see him under their feet.

He was starting to feel giddy, when all of a sudden the cheeky, dirt-streaked face of the boy he had been chasing through half of Barcelona popped up in front of him.

'What are you doing standing there?' said the stranger, raising his voice to be heard over the noise of the crowd.

Arnau did not reply, but this time made sure he had a firm grip on the boy's shirt as he was pulled across the square and down Carrer de la Bòria. At the far end they came into the coppersmiths' district. The narrow streets here rang to the sound of hammers beating metal. By now they had stopped running; exhausted, Arnau was still clutching the other boy's shirt sleeve, forcing his rash, impatient guide to slow to a walk.

'This is my house,' the boy said finally, pointing to a small, one-storey building. Outside the door were copper pots of all shapes and sizes. A heavily built man sat there working. He did not even pause to look up at them. 'That was my father,' the little boy said, once they had gone beyond the building.

'Why isn't he—?' Arnau started to ask, turning back to look.

'Wait,' was all the other boy replied.

They went on up the alley and skirted the houses until they were behind them, in a series of small gardens. When they reached the one that belonged to the boy's house, Arnau watched with surprise as the boy climbed the wall and encouraged him to do the same.

'Why . . .?'

'Come on up!' the boy ordered him, straddling the top of the wall.

Then the two of them jumped down into the tiny garden. There, Arnau's companion stood staring at a small hut, which had a small window opening on the side facing the garden. Arnau waited, but the boy did not move.

'What now?' Arnau asked finally.

The boy turned to Arnau.

'What . . .?'

But the little urchin paid him no attention. Arnau watched as he took a wooden crate and put it under the window. Then he climbed on to it, staring inside the dark hole. 'Mother,' he whispered.

A woman's pale arm appeared hesitantly at the window. The elbow rested on the sill, while the hand went straight to the boy's head and started caressing his hair.

'Joanet,' Arnau heard a soft voice say, 'you've come earlier today, the sun is not yet high in the sky.'

Joanet merely nodded his head.

'Has something happened?' the voice insisted.

Joanet did not reply for a few moments. He took a deep breath and then said: 'I've brought a friend.'

'I'm so happy you have friends. What's his name?'

'Arnau.'

How does he know my . . .? Of course! He was spying on me, thought Arnau.

'Is he there with you?'

'Yes, Mother.'

'Hello, Arnau.'

Arnau stared up at the window. Joanet turned towards him.

'Hello . . . madam,' Arnau said, unsure of how to address a voice coming out of a dark window like this.

'How old are you?'

'I'm eight, madam.'

'That means you are two years older than my Joanet, but I hope you get on well and can stay friends. Always remember: there is nothing better in this world than a true friend.'

That was all the voice said. Joanet's mother's hand went on stroking his hair, while the boy sat on the wooden crate, legs dangling.

'Now go and play,' the woman's voice suddenly said, withdrawing her hand. 'Goodbye, Arnau. Look after my boy: you're older than he is.' Arnau tried to say farewell, but the words would not come. 'Goodbye, my son,' the voice added. 'Promise you'll come and see me.'

'Of course I will, Mother.'

'Go now, both of you.'

The two boys walked aimlessly down the noisy streets of the city centre. Arnau waited for Joanet to explain, but when he said nothing, he finally plucked up the courage to ask: 'Why doesn't your mother come out into the garden?'

'She is shut in,' Joanet told him.

'Why?'

'I don't know. She just is.'

'Why don't you climb in the window then?'

'Ponç has forbidden it.'

'Who is Ponç?'

'Ponç is my father.'

'Why has he forbidden it?'

'I don't know.'

'Why do you call him Ponç instead of "Father"?'

'Because he's forbidden that too.'

Arnau came to a halt and tugged at Joanet until the two were face to face.

'I don't know the reason for that either,' the boy said quickly.

They carried on walking. Arnau was trying to make sense of all this, while Joanet was waiting for his new friend's next question.

'What is your mother like?' Arnau finally asked.

'She's always been shut in there,' Joanet said, trying to

force a smile. 'Once, when Ponç was out of the city I tried to climb in, but she would not let me. She said she didn't want me to see her.'

'Why are you smiling?'

Joanet walked on a few paces before replying.

'She always tells me I should smile.'

The rest of that morning, lost in thought, Arnau followed the dirty-looking boy who had never seen his mother's face through the streets of Barcelona.

'His mother strokes his head through a small window in the hut,' Arnau whispered to his father that night as they lay side by side on their pallet. 'He's never seen her. His father won't allow him to, and nor will she.'

Bernat stroked his son's hair exactly as Arnau had told him his new friend's mother had done. The silence between them was broken only by the snores of the slaves and apprentices who shared the same room. Bernat wondered what offence the woman could have committed to deserve such a punishment.

Ponç the coppersmith would have had no hesitation in telling him: 'Adultery!' He had told the same story dozens of times to anyone who cared to listen.

'I caught her fornicating with her lover, a young stripling like her. They took advantage of the hours I was at the forge. Of course, I went to see the magistrate to insist on proper compensation according to the law.' The stocky smith obviously took delight in citing the law which had brought him justice. 'Our princes are wise men, who know the evil of women. Only noblewomen can refute the charge of adultery under oath; all the others, like Joana, have to undergo a challenge and face the judgement of God.'

All those who had witnessed the challenge remembered how Ponç had cut Joana's young lover to ribbons: God had little possibility to judge between the coppersmith, hardened by his work in the forge, and the delicate, lovelorn young man.

The royal sentence was carried out as stipulated in the *Usatges*, the Laws and Customs of Catalonìa: 'If the woman should win the challenge, her husband will keep her honourably, and will meet all the expenses she and her friends might have incurred in this case and challenge, and will make good any harm to her champion. But if she is defeated, she and all her goods will become the possession of her husband.'

Ponç could not read, but he quoted this passage from memory as he showed anyone who cared to see the legal document he had been given:

> We rule that if he wishes Joana to be handed over to him, said Ponç should offer proper surety and swear to keep her in his house in a place twelve feet long, six feet wide and two rods high. That he should give her a straw mattress large enough to sleep on, and a cloak to cover herself with. The place of her confinement is to have a hole in which she may discharge her bodily functions, and a window through which food is to be given her. The said Ponç shall provide each day eighteen ounces of fully baked bread and as much water as she requires. He will not give her or cause her to be given anything which might hasten her death, or to do anything which might lead to the death of said Joana. In respect of all of which, Ponç is to provide a proper guarantee and security, before the aforementioned Joana is handed over to him.

Ponç supplied the magistrate with the required surety, and Joana was handed over to him. He built the brick hut in his garden, making it two and a half yards long by a yard and a half wide. He made sure there was a hole for her to carry out her bodily functions, and left the window through which Joanet, who was born nine months later and was never recognized by Ponç, could have his hair stroked by his mother. In this way, he walled up his young wife for the rest of her days.

'Father,' Arnau whispered to Bernat, 'what was my mother like? Why do you never tell me about her?'

What do you want me to tell you? That she lost her virginity raped by a drunken nobleman? That she was a whore in Lord de Bellera's castle? thought Bernat.

'Your mother . . .' he answered finally, 'was unlucky. She never had good fortune.'

Bernat could hear how Arnau swallowed hard before asking the next question.

'Did she love me?' the boy asked, his voice choking with emotion.

'She didn't get the chance. She died giving birth to you.'

'Habiba loved me.'

'And I love you too.'

'But you're not my mother. Even Joanet has a mother to caress his head.'

'Not all children have . . .' Bernat started to say. The mother of all Christians, he suddenly thought, as the words of the priests surfaced in his memory.

'What were you saying, Father?'

'That you do have a mother. Of course you do.' Bernat could feel his son relax. 'All children who are motherless like you are given another one by God: the Virgin Mary.'

'Where is this Mary?'

'The Virgin Mary,' Bernat corrected him. 'She is in heaven.'

Arnau lay in silence for a few moments before he spoke again.

'What use is it having a mother in heaven? She can't stroke me, play with me, kiss me, or—'

'Yes, she can.' Bernat could clearly recall what his father had explained when he asked these very same questions. 'She sends the birds to caress you. Whenever you see a bird, send your mother a message. You'll see how it flies straight up to heaven to give it to the Virgin Mary. Then the other birds will get to hear of it, and some of them will come to fly round you and sing for you.'

'But I don't understand what birds say.'

'You will learn to.'

'But I'll never be able to see her . . .'

'Yes, of course you can see her. You can see her in some churches, and you can even talk to her.'

'In churches?'

'Yes, my son. She is in heaven and in some churches. You can talk to her through the birds or in those churches. She will answer with birds or at night while you are asleep. She will love and cherish you more than any mother you can see.'

'More than Habiba?'

'Much more.'

'What about tonight?' Arnau asked. 'I haven't talked to her tonight.'

'Don't worry, I did it for you. Now go to sleep, and you'll find out.'

8

The two new friends met every day. They ran down to the beach to see the boats, or roamed the streets of Barcelona. Each time they were playing outside the Puig garden wall and heard the voices of Josep, Genís or Margarida, Joanet could see his friend lifting his eyes to the sky as if in search of something floating above the clouds.

'What are you looking at?' he asked him one day.

'Nothing,' said Arnau.

The laughter grew, and Arnau stared up again at the sky.

'Shall we climb the tree?' asked Joanet, thinking that it was its branches that were attracting his friend's attention.

'No,' said Arnau, trying to spot a bird to which he could give a message for his mother.

'Why don't you want to climb the tree? Then we could see . . .'

What could he say to the Virgin Mary? What did you say to your mother? Joanet said nothing to his, simply listening and agreeing . . . or disagreeing, but of course, he could hear her voice and feel her caresses, Arnau thought.

'Shall we climb up?'

'No,' shouted Arnau, so loudly he wiped the smile from Joanet's lips. 'You already have a mother who loves you. You don't need to spy on anyone else's.'

'But you don't have one,' Joanet replied. 'If we climb . . .'

That they loved her! That was what her children told Guiamona. 'Tell her that, little bird,' Arnau told one that flew up towards the sky. 'Tell her I love her.'

'So, are we going up?' insisted Joanet, one hand already on the lower branches.

'No, I don't need to either . . .'

Joanet let go of the tree and looked inquisitively at his friend.

'I have a mother too.'

'A new one?'

Arnau was unsure.

'I don't know. She's called the Virgin Mary.'

'The Virgin Mary? Who is she?'

'She is in some churches. I know that they' – he went on, pointing to the wall – 'used to go to church, but they never took me with them.'

'I know where she is.'

Arnau's eyes opened wide.

'If you like, I'll take you. To the biggest church in Barcelona.'

As ever, Joanet ran off without waiting for his friend's reply, but by now Arnau knew what to expect, and soon caught him up.

They ran to Carrer de la Boqueria, skirted the Jewish quarter and ran down Carrer del Bisbe until they reached the cathedral.

'Do you think the Virgin Mary is in there?' Arnau asked his friend, pointing to the mass of scaffolding rising round its unfinished walls. He watched as a huge stone was lifted laboriously by several men hauling on a pulley.

'Of course she is,' Joanet said determinedly. 'This is a church, isn't it?'

'No, this isn't a church!' they both heard a voice behind them say. They turned round and found themselves face to face with a rough-looking man who was carrying a hammer and chisel in his hand. 'This is the cathedral,' he corrected them, proud of his position as the master sculptor's assistant. 'Don't ever confuse it with a church.'

Arnau looked daggers at Joanet.

'So where is there a church?' Joanet asked the man as he was about to continue on his way.

'Just over there,' he told the surprised boys, pointing with his chisel back up the street they had just come down. 'In Plaça Sant Jaume.'

They ran back as fast as they could up Carrer del Bisbe to Plaça Sant Jaume. There they saw a small building that looked different from all the others, with a profusion of sculpted images around the doorway, which was raised above street level at the top of a small set of steps. Neither of them thought twice about it: they leapt through the doorway. Inside it was dark and cool, but before their eyes even had time to get used to the darkness, they felt a pair of strong hands on their shoulders and were propelled back down the steps.

'I'm tired of telling you children I'll not have you running around in the church of Sant Jaume.'

Ignoring what the priest had said, Arnau and Joanet stared at each other. The church of Sant Jaume! So this wasn't the church of the Virgin Mary either.

When the priest disappeared, they got back to their feet, only to find themselves surrounded by a group of six boys who were as barefoot, ragged and dirty as Joanet himself.

'He's got a really bad temper,' said one of them, signalling towards the church doors with his chin.

'If you like, we could tell you how to get in without him seeing you,' another one told them. 'But once you're inside, it's up to you. If he catches you . . .'

'No, we don't want to,' Arnau replied. 'Do you know where there is another church?'

'They won't let you into any of them,' a third boy said.

'That's our business,' Joanet retorted.

'Listen to the little runt!' the eldest boy laughed, stepping towards Joanet. He was a good head taller than him, and Arnau was worried for his friend. 'Anything that happens in this square is our business, get it?' he said, pushing him in the chest.

Just as Joanet was about to react and fling himself on the other boy, something on the far side of the square caught the attention of the whole group.

'A Jew!' one of them shouted.

They all ran off after a boy who was wearing the red and yellow badge. As soon as he realized what was about to happen, the little Jewish boy took to his heels. He just managed to reach the entrance to the Jewry before the group caught up with him. They all came to an abrupt halt, unwilling to venture inside. One of them, a boy even smaller than Joanet, had stayed behind. He was wide-eyed with astonishment at the way Joanet had been prepared to stand up to the older boy.

'There's another church down there, beyond Sant Jaume,' he told them. 'If I were you, I'd get away now,' he added, nodding towards the others in the group, who were already heading back to them. 'Pau will be very angry and he'll take it out on you. He's always upset when a Jew gets away from him.'

Joanet bristled, waiting for this boy Pau to reappear.

Arnau tried to pull him away, and finally, when he saw the whole group racing towards them, Joanet allowed himself to be dragged off.

They ran down towards the sea, but when they saw that Pau and his gang – probably more interested in some more Jews in the square – were not pursuing them, they slowed their pace. They had barely gone a street from Plaça de Sant Jaume when they came to another church. They stood at the foot of the steps and looked at each other. Joanet lifted his chin towards the doors.

'We'll wait,' said Arnau.

At that moment an old woman came out of the church and clambered down the steps. Arnau didn't think twice.

'Good lady,' he asked when she reached them, 'what church is this?'

'It's Sant Miquel,' the woman replied without stopping.

Arnau sighed. Sant Miquel.

'Where is there another church?' Joanet asked quickly, when he saw how crestfallen his friend was.

'At the end of this street.'

'Which one is that?' he insisted. For the first time, he seemed to have caught the woman's attention.

'That is the Sant Just i Pastor. Why are you so interested?'

The boys said nothing, but walked away from the old woman, who watched them trudging away disconsolately.

'All the churches belong to men!' Arnau said in disgust. 'We have to find a church for women; that's where the Virgin Mary must be.'

Joanet carried on walking thoughtfully.

'I know somewhere . . .' he said at length. 'It's full of women. It's at the end of the city wall, next to the sea. They call it . . .' Joanet tried to remember. 'They call it Santa Clara.'

'But that's not the Virgin either.'

'But it is a woman. I'm sure your mother will be with her. She wouldn't be with a man who wasn't your father, would she?'

They went down Carrer de la Ciutat to the La Mar gateway, which was part of the old Roman wall near Castell de Regomir. It was from here that a path led to the Santa Clara convent, built in the eastern corner of the new walls close to the shore. They left Regomir Castle behind them, turned left and walked down until they came to Carrer de la Mar, which led from Plaça del Blat to the church of Santa Maria de la Mar before splitting into small parallel alleyways that came out on to the beach. From there, crossing Plaça del Born and Pla d'en Llull, they reached the Santa Clara convent by descending the street of the same name.

In spite of their anxiety to find the church, neither of the two boys could resist stopping to look at the silversmiths' stalls ranged on either side of Carrer de la Mar. Barcelona was a prosperous, rich city, as was obvious from the array of valuable objects on display: silverware, jewel-encrusted jugs and cups made of precious metals, necklaces, bracelets and rings, belts: an endless range of fine objects glinting in the summer sun. Arnau and Joanet tried to examine them more closely, but were chased away by the artisans, who shouted and threatened them with their fists.

Chased by one of the apprentices, they ran off and eventually came to Plaça de Santa Maria. On their right was a small cemetery, the Fossar Major, and on their left was the church.

'Santa Clara is down . . .' Joanet started to say, then suddenly fell silent. What they could see in front of them was truly amazing.

It was a powerful, sturdy church. Sober, stern-looking even, it was windowless and had exceptionally thick walls. The land around the building had been cleared and levelled, and it was surrounded by a huge number of stakes driven into the ground, forming geometrical shapes.

Ten slender columns, sixteen yards high, were placed around the small church's apse. The white stone shone through the scaffolding around them.

The wooden scaffolding that covered the rear of the church rose and rose like an immense set of steps. Even from the distance they were at, Arnau had to raise his eyes to see their top, which was much higher than the columns.

'Let's go,' Joanet urged him when they had seen their fill of the men labouring on the wooden boards. 'This must be another cathedral.'

'No, this isn't a cathedral,' they heard a voice say behind them. Arnau and Joanet looked at each other and smiled. They turned and looked enquiringly at a sturdy man who was toiling under the weight of an enormous block of stone. So what is it then? Joanet seemed to be asking as he smiled at him. 'The cathedral is paid for by the nobles and the city authorities, but this church, which will be more important and beautiful than the cathedral, is paid for and built by the people.'

The man had not even paused: the weight of the stone seemed to push him forward. Yet he had smiled back at them.

The two boys followed him down the side of the church, which was next to another cemetery, the Fossar Menor.

'Would you like us to help you?' asked Arnau.

The man panted, then turned and smiled at them again. 'Thank you, my lad, but you had better not.'

Eventually, he bent down and deposited the stone on the ground. The boys stared at it, and Joanet went over to try to push it, but it did not move. At this, the man burst out laughing. Joanet smiled back at him.

'If it's not a cathedral,' Arnau said, pointing at the tall octagonal columns, 'what is it?'

'This is the new church that the La Ribera district is building in thanks and devotion to Our Lady the Virgin—'

Arnau gave a start. 'The Virgin Mary?' he interrupted the man, eyes opened wide.

'Of course, my lad,' the man replied, ruffling his hair. 'The Virgin Mary, Our Lady of the Sea.'

'And . . . where is the Virgin Mary?' Arnau asked, staring at the church.

'In there, in that small building. But when we finish the new one, she will have the best church that a Virgin has ever had.'

In there! Arnau did not even hear the rest of what the man was saying. His Virgin was in there. All at once, a sound made them all look up: a flock of birds had flown out from the topmost scaffolding.

9

Barcelona's Ribera de la Mar district, where the church in honour of the Virgin Mary was being built, had grown up as an outlying suburb of the Carolingian city, surrounded and protected by the old Roman walls. At the outset it was inhabited by fishermen, stevedores and other humble workmen. It already had a small church, known as Santa Maria de les Arenes, raised on the spot where Saint Eulàlia was said to have been martyred in the year 303. This church got its name from the fact that it was built on Barcelona's sandy shoreline, but the same process of sedimentation that had made the city's ports unusable led to the church becoming separated from the sands of the coast, so that its name gradually lost its meaning. That was when it became known as Santa Maria de la Mar, because although the coast was no longer close by, all the men who made their living from the sea still worshipped there.

The passage of time, which had already robbed the tiny church of its sands, also forced the city to adopt fresh land outside the walls where the emerging middle classes could settle, now that there was no longer enough room for them inside the Roman walls. And of the three boundaries of Barcelona, the middle classes chose the eastern side, where the traffic to and from the port passed by. So it was that Carrer de la Mar became home to the silversmiths; other streets got their names from the moneychangers, the cotton-traders, the butchers and bakers, wine merchants and cheesemakers, the hat- and swordmakers, and the multitude of other artisans who came flocking there. A corn exchange was built, and it was here that foreign traders visiting the city were lodged. Plaça del Born, behind Santa Maria, was also constructed: jousts and tourneys were held there. And it was not merely the rich artisans who were attracted to the new Ribera district; many nobles chose to live there after the Count of Barcelona Ramon Berenguer IV granted the seneschal Guillem Ramon de Montcada the lands that later gave rise to the street bearing his name, which began at Plaça del Born close to Santa Maria de la Mar, and was filled with huge, luxurious palaces.

When the Ribera de la Mar quarter became a rich, prosperous area, the old Romanesque church where the fishermen and others who made their living from the sea went to worship their patron saint seemed too small and poor for the new inhabitants. However, the resources of the Barcelona church authorities and of the nobility were all poured into the rebuilding of the city's cathedral.

United by their devotion to the Virgin, the parishioners of Santa Maria de la Mar, both rich and poor, refused to be discouraged by this lack of official support. Their newly appointed archdeacon, Bernat Llull, asked permission from the ecclesiastical authorities to build what was intended to be the greatest ever monument to the Virgin Mary. Permission was granted.

So from the beginning, Santa Maria de la Mar church was built by and for the common people. This was made explicit by the first stone laid for the new building, which was placed exactly where the main altar was to be raised. Unlike other constructions supported by the authorities, on this stone all that was carved was the coat of arms of the parish. This showed that the construction, and all rights pertaining to it, belonged solely and exclusively to the parishioners who had undertaken the task: the rich, with their money; the poor, with their work. From the moment the first stone had been laid, a group of the faithful and prominent men of the city known as the Twenty-Five met each year with the rector of the parish and an official notary to hand over the keys to the church for that year.

Arnau studied the man who had carried the stone. He was still sweating and out of breath, but he smiled as he looked towards the new building.

'Could I see her?' asked Arnau.

'The Virgin?' the man asked, smiling now at Arnau.

What if children were not allowed into churches on their own? wondered Arnau. What if they had to go with their parents? What had the priest at Sant Jaume told them?

'Of course the Virgin will be delighted to receive a visit from boys like you.'

Arnau laughed nervously, and looked round at Joanet. 'Shall we go?'

'Hey, wait a moment,' the man said. 'I have to get back to work.' He looked over towards the other busy workmen. 'Àngel,' he shouted to a youngster who looked about twelve years old. The boy came running over. 'Take these boys into the church. Tell the priest they would like to see the Virgin.'

With that, he gave Arnau's head a last pat and disappeared back towards the sea. Arnau and Joanet were left with the boy called Àngel. When he looked at them, they both stared down at the ground.

'Do you want to see the Virgin?'

He sounded sincere. Arnau nodded and asked: 'Do you . . . know her?'

'Of course,' laughed Àngel. 'She's the Virgin of the Sea, my Virgin. My father's a boatman,' he added proudly. 'Follow me.'

They went with him to the church entrance. Joanet looked all around him, but Arnau was still troubled, and did not raise his eyes from the ground.

'Do you have a mother?' he asked suddenly.

'Yes, of course,' Àngel said, still striding out in front of them.

Behind his back, Arnau beamed at Joanet. They went through the doors of the church, and Arnau and Joanet paused while their eyes became accustomed to the gloom inside. There was a strong scent of wax and incense. Arnau compared the tall, slender columns being built outside with the squat, heavy ones in the interior. The only light came through a few long, narrow windows cut in the thick walls of the church, casting yellow rectangles on the floor of the nave. Everywhere – on the ceiling, on the walls – there were boats, some of them finely carved, others more rough and ready.

'Come on,' Àngel urged them.

As they walked towards the altar, Joanet pointed to several figures kneeling on the floor that they had not seen at first. As they walked by them, the boys were surprised to hear them murmuring.

'What are they doing?' Joanet whispered in Arnau's ear.

'Praying,' he explained. He knew this because his aunt Guiamona had forced him to pray in front of a cross in his bedroom whenever she came back from church with his cousins.

When they reached the altar, they were confronted by a thin priest. Joanet hid behind Arnau.

'What brings you here, Àngel?' the priest asked him quietly, although his gaze was fixed on the two new-comers. He held out his hand to Àngel, who bent over it.

'These two boys, Father. They want to see the Virgin.'

The priest's eyes gleamed as he spoke directly to Arnau. 'There she is,' he said, pointing to the altar.

Arnau looked in the direction the priest was indicating, until he made out a small, simple stone statue of a woman with a baby on her left shoulder and a wooden boat at her feet. He narrowed his eyes; he liked the serenity of the woman's features. His mother!

'What are your names?' asked the priest.

'Arnau Estanyol,' said the first one.

'Joan, but they call me Joanet,' said the other.

'And your family name?'

Joanet's smile faded. He did not know what his family name was. His mother had told him he could not use Ponç the coppersmith's name, because Ponç would be extremely angry if he found out, but he could not use hers either. This was the first time he had been asked what his name was. Why did the priest want to know? He was still looking at Joanet expectantly.

'The same as his,' he said at length. 'Estanyol.'

Surprised, Arnau turned to him, and saw the look of entreaty in his eyes.

'So you're brothers then.'

'Ye . . . yes,' Joanet stuttered. Arnau backed him up, saying nothing.

'Do you know how to pray?'

'Yes,' Arnau said.

'I don't . . . yet,' Joanet admitted.

'Get your older brother to teach you then,' said the priest. 'You can pray to the Virgin. Àngel, you come with me. I've got a message for your master. There are some stones over there . . .'

The priest's voice died away as the two of them walked off, leaving the two boys by the altar.

'Do we have to get on our knees to pray?' Joanet whispered to Arnau.

Arnau looked back at the shadowy figures that Joanet had pointed out to him. As his friend headed for the red silk prayer cushions in front of the altar, he grabbed him by the arm.

'Those people are kneeling on the floor,' he whispered, pointing towards the others, 'but they are praying as well.'

'What are you going to do?'

'I'm not going to pray. I'm talking to my mother. You don't kneel down when you're talking to your mother, do you?'

Joanet looked at him. No, of course not . . . 'But the priest didn't say we could talk to her. He said we could pray.'

'Don't say a word to him then. If you do, I'll tell him you were lying and that you aren't really my brother.'

Joanet stood next to Arnau and enjoyed studying all the boats decorating the inside of the church. How he would like to have one! He wondered if they could really float. They must do: otherwise, why would anyone have carved them? He could put one of them at the water's edge, and then . . .

Arnau was staring at the stone figure. What could he say to her? Had the birds taken her his message? He had told them that he loved her. He had told them that time and again.

'My father said that even though she was a Moorish slave, Habiba is with you, but said I was not to tell anyone that, because people say Moors cannot go to heaven,' he murmured. 'She was very good to me. She was not to blame for anything. It was Margarida.'

Arnau continued to stare intently at the Virgin.

117

Dozens of candles were lit all around her, making the air quiver.

'Is Habiba with you? If you see her, tell her I love her too. You're not angry that I love her, are you? Even if she is a Moor.'

Through the darkness and the air wavering round the candles, he was sure he saw the lips of the small stone figure curve into a smile.

'Joanet!' he whispered to his friend.

'What?'

Arnau pointed to the Virgin, but now her lips were . . . Perhaps she did not want anyone else to see her smile? Perhaps it was their secret.

'What?' Joanet insisted.

'Nothing, nothing.'

'Have you prayed already?'

They were surprised to find that the priest and Àngel were back.

'Yes,' said Arnau.

'I haven't—' Joanet apologized.

'I know, I know,' the priest interrupted him in a kindly fashion, stroking his head. 'And you, what did you pray?'

'The Ave Maria,' Arnau replied.

'A wonderful prayer. Let's go then,' the priest said, accompanying them to the church door.

'Father,' said Arnau once they were all outside, 'can we come back?'

The priest smiled at them. 'Of course, but I hope that by the time you do, you'll have taught your brother to pray as well.' Joanet looked serious as the priest tapped him on both cheeks. 'Come back whenever you like,' the priest added, 'you will always be welcome.'

Àngel started off towards the pile of large building stones. Arnau and Joanet followed him.

'Where are you going now?' Àngel asked, turning back to them. The two boys looked at each other and shrugged. 'You can't come into our work area. If the overseer—'

'The man with the stone?' Arnau butted in.

'No,' laughed Àngel. 'That was Ramon. He's a *bastaix*.'

Joanet and Arnau both looked at him inquisitively.

'The *bastaixos* are the labourers of the sea; they carry goods from the beach to the merchants' warehouses, or the other way round. They load and unload merchandise after the boatmen have brought it to the beach.'

'So they don't work in Santa Maria?' asked Arnau.

'Yes, they work the hardest.' Àngel laughed at their puzzled expressions. 'They are poor people. They have little money, but they are among those who are most devoted to the Virgin of the Sea. They cannot contribute any funds to the new church, so their guild has promised they will transport the stones free from the royal quarry at Montjuïc to here. They carry them all on their backs,' Àngel said, his face showing no emotion. 'They travel miles under the loads. Afterwards, it takes two of us just to move them.'

Arnau remembered the huge stone that the *bastaix* had left on the ground.

'Of course they work for the Virgin!' Àngel insisted. 'More than anyone else. Now go and play,' he said, before continuing on his way.

10

'Why do they keep building the scaffolding higher and higher?'

Arnau pointed to the rear of Santa Maria church. Àngel looked up and, his mouth full of bread and cheese, muttered an explanation neither of them could understand. Joanet burst out laughing, Arnau joined in, and in the end Àngel himself could not avoid chuckling along with them, until he choked and the laughter turned into a coughing fit.

Arnau and Joanet went to Santa Maria every day. They entered the church and knelt down. Urged on by his mother, Joanet had decided to learn to pray, and repeated the phrases Arnau taught him over and over again. Then, when the two of them split up, he would race to his mother's window and tell her all he had prayed that day. Arnau talked to his mother, except when Father Albert (they had found out that was his name) appeared, in which case he joined Joanet in murmuring his devotions.

Whenever they left the church, they would stand some distance away and survey the carpenters, stonecutters and masons at work on the new building. Afterwards they would sit in the square waiting for Àngel to have a break and join them to eat his bread and cheese. Father Albert treated them affectionately; the men working on Santa Maria always smiled at them; even the *bastaixos*, who came by bent under the weight of their stones, would glance over at the two little boys sitting next to the church.

'Why do they keep building the scaffolding higher?' Arnau asked a second time.

The three of them peered at the rear of the church, where the ten columns stood: eight of them in a semi-circle and two more further back. Beyond them, workmen had started to build the buttresses and walls that would form the new apse. The columns rose higher than the small Romanesque building, but the scaffolding went on up still further into the sky, for no apparent reason. It was not surrounding anything, as though the workmen had gone crazy and were trying to make a stairway to heaven.

'I've no idea,' Àngel admitted.

'None of that scaffolding is supporting anything.'

'No, but it will,' they suddenly heard a man's firm voice say.

The three of them turned round. They had been so busy laughing and coughing they had not noticed that several men had gathered behind them. Some of them were dressed in fine clothes; others wore priests' vestments, enriched with bejewelled gold crosses on their chests, big rings and belts threaded with gold and silver.

Father Albert was watching from the church door. He came hurrying over to greet the newcomers. Àngel leapt up and choked once more on his bread. This was not the first time he had seen the man who had spoken to them, but he had rarely seen him in such splendid company. He was Berenguer de Montagut, the person in charge of the building work on Santa Maria de la Mar.

Arnau and Joanet also stood up. Father Albert joined the group, and bent to kiss the bishops' rings.

'What will they support?'

Joanet's question caught Father Albert just as he was stooping to kiss another ring: Don't speak until you're spoken to, his eyes implored him. One of the provosts made as though to continue on towards the church, but Berenguer de Montagut grasped Joanet by the shoulder and leant down to talk to him.

'Children are often able to see things we miss,' he said out loud to his companions. 'So I would not be surprised if these three have noticed something that has escaped our attention. So you want to know why we're building this scaffolding, do you?'

Glancing towards Father Albert for permission, Joanet nodded.

'Do you see the tops of those columns? Well, from the top of each of them we are going to build six arches. The most important arch of all will be the one that takes the weight of the new church's apse.'

'What is an apse?' asked Arnau.

Berenguer smiled and looked round. Some of the group with him seemed as anxious to hear his explanation as the boys were.

'An apse is something like this.' The master builder joined his hands together in an arch. The children were fascinated by his magic hands, and others in the group crowded forward to see. 'Well, on top of all the rest,' he said, separating one hand and pointing to the tip of the other first finger, 'we put a big stone called the keystone. To do that we first have to raise it to the very highest scaffolding – right up there, can you see?' They all peered up at the sky. 'Once that is in place, we'll build the rib vaults of these arches until they meet the keystone. And that is why we need such tall scaffolding.'

'Why are you doing all that?' Arnau wanted to know. Poor Father Albert flinched, although by now he was growing used to the boys' questions and comments. 'None of this will be visible from inside the church, because it's all above the roof.'

Berenguer and a few of the others laughed. Father Albert sighed.

'Of course it will be visible, my boy, because the roof of the present church will gradually disappear as we build the new structure. It will be as though this tiny church were giving birth to another, bigger one.'

Joanet's obvious disappointment unsettled him. The boy had become accustomed to the small church's sense of intimacy, to its smell, its darkness, the atmosphere there when he prayed.

'Do you love the Virgin of the Sea?' Berenguer asked him.

Joanet glanced at Arnau. They both nodded.

'Well, when we have finished her new church, the Virgin you love so much will have more light than any other virgin in the world. She will no longer be in darkness as she is now. She'll have the most beautiful church you could ever imagine. She won't be shut in by thick, low walls, but will shine among tall, delicate ones, with slender columns and apses that reach up to the heavens: the perfect place for the Virgin.'

They all looked up at the sky.

'Yes,' Berenguer de Montagut went on, 'the Virgin of the Sea's new church will reach right up there.'

He and his companions set off towards Santa Maria, leaving Father Albert and the boys behind.

'Father,' Arnau asked when the others were out of earshot, 'what will happen to the Virgin when they take down the old building, but haven't finished her new church yet?'

'Do you see those buttresses?' the priest replied,

pointing to two of the ones being built as the back part of the ambulatory, behind the main altar. 'In between them they are going to construct the first chapel, dedicated to the Lord Jesus. That's where they will put the Virgin, together with the body of Christ and the sepulchre containing Santa Eulàlia's remains. That way she will come to no harm.'

'Who will look after her?'

'Don't worry,' said the priest with a smile. 'The Virgin will be well looked after. The Jesus chapel belongs to the *bastaixos*' guild; they are the ones who will have the key to its railings, and will make sure she is looked after.'

Arnau and Joanet knew the *bastaixos* well by now. Àngel had reeled off their names when a line of them appeared, bowed beneath their enormous stones: Ramon, the first one they had met; Guillem, as hard as the rocks he carried on his back, tanned by the sun and with a face horribly disfigured by an accident, but gentle and affectionate in his dealings with them; another Ramon, known as 'Little Ramon' because he was smaller and stockier than the other one; Miquel, a scrawny man who did not look strong enough to carry the huge weights, but who succeeded in doing so by straining all the nerves and tendons in his body until it seemed they might explode; Sebastià, the least friendly or talkative of the group, with his son Bastianet. Then there were Pere, Jaume and a seemingly endless list of others, all of them men from La Ribera who had committed themselves to carrying the thousands of stones needed for the new church from the royal quarry at La Roca to Santa Maria de la Mar.

Arnau thought of the *bastaixos* and the way they gazed at the church as they arrived bent double under the weight of a stone; the way they smiled when they were relieved of their load; the mighty strength of their backs. He was sure they would look after the Virgin.

* * *

The operation Berenguer de Montagut had told them about took place within the next week.

'Come at first light tomorrow,' Àngel had told them. 'That's when we'll put the keystone in place.'

The two boys made sure they were there. They ran towards the workmen who had gathered at the foot of the scaffolding. Between labourers, *bastaixos* and priests, there must have been more than a hundred people present. Even Father Albert had taken off his robe and was dressed like all the rest, with a thick piece of red cloth tied round his waist.

Arnau and Joanet joined the throng, saying hello to some and waving at others.

'Boys,' they heard one of the masons say, 'when we start to raise the keystone I want you to stay well away from here.'

The two boys nodded in agreement.

'Where is the stone?' Joanet asked, looking up at the builder.

They ran over to where he pointed, at the foot of the first and lowest scaffold.

'Holy Mother!' they both exclaimed when they saw the huge circular stone on the ground.

Many of the men stared at it as admiringly as they did, but said nothing. They knew how important this day was.

'It weighs more than six tons,' one of them said.

With eyes like saucers, Joanet looked enquiringly at Ramon, the man they had first seen carrying a block of stone.

'No,' he said, reading the boy's mind. 'We didn't carry this one here.'

There was nervous laughter at his comment, but it soon died away. Arnau and Joanet watched the men file past, looking alternately at the stone and at the top of the scaffolding: they had to raise more than six tons some thirty yards in the air, by pulling on cables!

'If anything goes wrong . . .' they heard one of the men say as he crossed himself.

'We'll be caught underneath,' another man replied, twisting his lips.

No one was standing still. Even Father Albert, in his strange attire, kept moving among them, encouraging them, slapping them on the back, talking animatedly. The old church stood there in the midst of all the people and the mass of scaffolding. Curious onlookers from the city began to gather at a safe distance.

Finally, Berenguer de Montagut appeared. He gave nobody time to stop and greet him, but leapt on to the lowest level of scaffolding and began to address all those present. As he did so, some masons tied a huge pulley round the stone.

'As you can see,' he shouted, 'we have rigged up tackle at the top of the scaffolding so that we can raise the keystone. The pulleys up there and the ones round the stone are made up of three separate sets, each of which has another three coming off them. As you know, we cannot use capstans or wheels, because we need to move the stone sideways as well. There are three cables to each pulley system. They go all the way up to the top, and back down again.' He pointed out the path of the cables; a hundred heads followed his gesture. 'I want you to form three groups around me.'

The masons began to divide the men. Arnau and Joanet ran to the rear of the old church and stood with their backs to the wall, watching the preparations. When Berenguer saw that the three groups had formed, he went on: 'Each group will haul on one of the cables. You,' he said, addressing one of the groups, 'are to be Santa Maria. Repeat after me: "Santa Maria!"' The men all shouted: 'Santa Maria!' 'You are Santa Clara.' The second group called out the name of Santa Clara. 'And you over there are Santa Eulàlia. I'll call you by those names. When I shout "Everyone!" I mean all three groups. When you are in position, you have to pull in a straight line, and keep your eyes on the back of the man in front of you. Listen for the instructions from the mason in charge of each group. And remember: always pull in a straight line! Now line up.'

The mason leading each group made sure they were in line. The cables were made ready, and the men picked them up. Before they could start wondering what was going to happen, Berenguer shouted again: 'Everyone! When I give the word, start to pull – gently at first, until you can feel the cables grow taut. Now!'

Arnau and Joanet watched the three lines pull until the cables were taut.

'Everyone! Pull hard!'

The boys held their breath. The men dug their heels into the ground and started to pull. Their arms, backs and faces tensed. Arnau and Joanet stared at the huge block of stone. It had not budged.

'Everyone! Pull harder!'

The order rang out round the church. The men's faces went purple with effort. The wooden scaffolding started to creak. The keystone rose a hand's breadth from the ground. Six tons!

'More!' shouted Berenguer, his gaze fixed on the keystone.

Another few inches. The boys had almost forgotten to breathe.

'Santa Maria! Pull harder! Harder!'

Arnau and Joanet looked towards the Santa Maria line. Father Albert was among them. He had his eyes shut and was pulling with all his might.

'That's right, Santa Maria! That's right. Now everyone: pull!'

The wooden scaffolding creaked again. Arnau and

Joanet glanced at it and then at Berenguer de Montagut. He was staring intently at the stone, which slowly, very slowly, rose into the air.

'Heave! Come on, everyone. Pull harder!'

When the keystone reached the level of the first scaffolding, Berenguer ordered the groups to stop pulling and to keep the stone in the air.

'Santa Maria and Santa Eulàlia, stop pulling,' he ordered. 'Santa Clara, you pull!' The stone moved sideways until it reached the platform Berenguer was standing on. 'Now, everyone! Slacken off the ropes little by little.'

Everyone, including all those hauling on the ropes, held their breath as the stone came to rest on the wooden structure, close to Berenguer's feet.

'Slowly!' he cried out.

The platform buckled under the weight of the stone.

'What if it gives way?' Arnau whispered to Joanet.

If it gave way, Berenguer . . .

It did not give way. But the scaffold had not been built to withstand such a weight for any length of time. The keystone had to be hauled to the top, where Berenguer had calculated that the platforms were more resistant. The workmen changed the cables on to the next set of pulleys, and the men started to haul on them again. The next platform, then the one after that; six tons of stone rose to the spot where the vaulted arches were to come together, high in the heavens above all their heads.

The men were sweating; their muscles had seized up. From time to time, one of them collapsed, and the mason in charge of that line ran to pull him out from under the feet of the man in front. Some strong-looking men from the city were among the crowd, and whenever a man dropped out, they took over.

Berenguer continued to shout orders from high up on the scaffolding. Another man lower down made sure all the groups heard him. When the keystone finally reached the topmost platform, a few smiles appeared on tightly drawn lips, but they all knew that the most crucial moment had arrived. Berenguer de Montagut had calculated the exact position where the keystone had to be placed so that the vaults of the arches would fit perfectly around it. For days he had used ropes and stakes to measure the precise spot in between the ten columns. He had dropped plumb lines from the scaffolding and tied ropes from the stakes on the ground up to the top. He had spent hour after hour scribbling on parchment, then scratching out the figures and writing over them. If the keystone was not placed exactly right, it would not support the stress from the arches, and the whole apse could come crashing down.

In the end, following thousands of calculations, and even more sketches, he traced the outline of where the keystone should go on the top platform of the scaffolding. That was the exact spot, not an inch to one side or the other. When they had hauled the keystone right to the top, the men below almost despaired when Berenguer refused to allow them to rest it on the platform as they had done lower down, but went on shouting orders:

'A little more, Santa Maria. No. Santa Clara, pull, now hold it there. Santa Eulàlia! Santa Clara! Santa Maria . . .! Lower! Higher! Now!' he suddenly shouted. 'Everyone hold it there. A little lower! Little by little. Gently does it!'

All at once, there was no more weight on the cables. The men peered silently up at the sky, where Berenguer de Montagut was kneeling to inspect the positioning of the keystone. He walked round its two yards' diameter, stood up and waved in triumph to everybody down below.

Arnau and Joanet could feel the shout of joy that rose

from the throats of men who had been toiling for hours reverberate against the church wall behind them. Many of them sank thankfully to the ground. A few others hugged each other and danced. The hundreds of spectators who had been watching shouted and applauded. Arnau could feel a knot in his throat, and all the hairs on his body stood on end.

'I wish I were older,' he whispered to his father that night as the two of them lay on the straw pallet surrounded by the coughs and snores of the slaves and apprentices.

Bernat tried to fathom what was behind his son's wish. Arnau had returned home in high spirits and had told him a thousand times how the keystone of the Santa Maria apse had been raised. Even Jaume had listened closely to him.

'Why, son?'

'Because everybody does something. There are lots of boys who help their fathers at Santa Maria, but Joanet and I . . .'

Bernat put his arm round his son's shoulders and drew him towards him. It was true that except when his father had some special errand for him, Arnau spent the whole day at the church. What could he usefully do there?

'You like the *bastaixos*, don't you?'

Bernat had felt his son's enthusiasm whenever he spoke about these men who carried the blocks of stone to the new church. The boys followed them as far as the gates of the city, waited there for them, then walked back with them, all along the beach from Framenors to Santa Maria.

'Yes,' Arnau said.

His father rummaged for something under the pallet. 'Here, take this,' Bernat said, giving him the old waterskin he had taken with them when they first fled his lands.

Arnau felt for it in the darkness. 'Offer them fresh water. You'll see how they thank you for it.'

As always, at dawn the next day Joanet was waiting for him at the gates of Grau's workshop. Arnau showed him the skin, then hung it round his neck, and they both ran off down to the beach. They made for the Àngel fountain, the only one that was on the *bastaixos'* route. The next fountain was down in Santa Maria itself.

When the boys spotted the line of *bastaixos* coming slowly towards them, bent under the weight of their stones, they clambered on to one of the boats on the beach. As the first *bastaix* came level with them, Arnau showed him the waterskin. The man smiled and came to a halt next to the boat so that Arnau could pour the water directly into his mouth. The others waited until the first man had finished, then the next one stepped up. Lightened of their load, on their way back to the royal quarry they paused at the boat to thank the boys for the fresh water.

From that day on, Arnau and Joanet became the water-carriers for all the *bastaixos*. They waited for them close to the Àngel fountain or, whenever the labourers had to unload a ship and could not work for Santa Maria, followed them round the city to pour them water without their having to drop the heavy loads they were carrying.

The two boys still found time to go down to Santa Maria to see the building work, talk to Father Albert or sit and watch how Àngel wolfed down his food. Anyone observing them could see how their eyes shone in a different way whenever they looked at the church. They were doing their bit to help build it! That was what the *bastaixos* and even Father Albert had told them.

The keystone hung high in the sky, and the boys saw how the ribs from each of the ten columns were gradually rising to meet it. The masons built trusses and then placed one block after another on them, curving upwards. Behind the columns, surrounding the first eight of them, the walls of the ambulatory had already been built, with the interior buttresses in place. 'Between these two,' Father Albert told them as he pointed out two of the stone columns, 'we will put the Jesus chapel, the one belonging to the *bastaixos*, where the Virgin will stand.'

He said this because as the walls of the ambulatory were being built, and the new vaults were constructed on the struts from the columns, the old church was gradually being demolished.

'Then above the apse,' Father Albert went on, with Àngel nodding at his side, 'we'll build the roof. Do you know what we will use?' The two boys shook their heads. 'All the faulty pottery jars in the city. First will come the ashlar filling, and then on top of that all the jars, lined up next to each other. Finally there will be the roof covering.'

Arnau had seen all the broken jars piled next to the blocks of stone outside Santa Maria. He had asked his father why they were there, but Bernat hadn't known the answer.

'All I know,' he had said, 'is that we have to pile up all the faulty pieces until someone comes and collects them. I didn't know they were intended for your church.'

In this way, the new church began to take shape behind the apse of the old one, which they carefully dismantled in order to be able to use its stones. The La Ribera district did not want to be left without a church, even while the new, magnificent shrine to the Virgin was rising around them. Masses were said as usual, and yet there was a strange atmosphere in the church. Like everyone else, Arnau went in through the lopsided doorway of the tiny Romanesque construction, but once inside, instead of the welcoming gloom that had protected him while he talked to the Virgin, there was now a flood of light from the windows in the new apse. The old church was like a small box contained in another much larger and more beautiful one, a box destined to disappear as the other one grew, a box whose fourth side was taken up by the new, soaring apse that already boasted a roof.

11

However, there was more to Arnau's life than Santa Maria and giving water to the *bastaixos*. In exchange for bed and board he had, among other duties, to help the Grau family cook whenever she went into the city to buy food.

So every two or three days Arnau left the workshop at dawn and went with Estranya the mulatto slave into the city streets. She walked with splayed legs, her huge body swaying dangerously as she waddled along. As soon as Arnau appeared in the kitchen doorway, she would give him the first things to carry: two baskets of dough they were to take to the ovens in the Carrer dels Ollers Blancs for baking. One basket contained the loaves for Grau and his family: these were made of wheat flour, and became the finest white bread. The other held the loaves for the rest of the household, made from rye, millet or even beans and chickpeas. When baked, this bread was dark, heavy and hard.

Once they had handed over the loaves, Estranya and Arnau would leave the potters' quarter and cross the wall into the centre of Barcelona. In this first part of their journey, Arnau had no problem following the slave, and even found time to laugh at her swaying body and rippling dark flesh.

'What are you laughing at?' the mulatto had asked him more than once.

At that, Arnau would look into her round, flat face and stifle his smile.

'You want to laugh? Laugh at this then,' she said in Plaça del Blat as she gave him a sack of wheat to carry. 'Where's your smile now?' she would say on the way down La Llet as she loaded him with the milk his cousins were to drink. She would repeat the taunt in the narrow Plaça de les Cols, where she bought cabbages, pulses or vegetables, and in Plaça de l'Oli, weighing him down with oil, game or fowl.

After that, struggling under her purchases, Arnau followed the slave all over Barcelona. On the 160 days of abstinence, the mulatto plodded and swayed down to the shore, near Santa Maria. There she fought with the other customers at one of the city's two official fish-mongers (the old and the new) to buy the best dolphins, tunas, sturgeons, or *palomides*, *neros*, *reigs* and *corballs*.

'Now we'll get your fish,' she said. It was her turn to smile as she went round the back of the stalls to buy the leftovers. There were as many people here as at the front, but Estranya did not fight to get the best.

Even so, Arnau preferred these days of abstinence to those when Estranya had to go and buy meat, because whereas to purchase the leftovers of fish she simply had to walk round the stall, when it was meat she brought Arnau to carry all her packages across half the city.

She bought the meat for Grau and his family in one of the butchers situated outside the slaughterhouses. Like everything else sold in the city, this was fresh, first-class meat: no dead animals were allowed inside Barcelona. Everything that was sold was slaughtered on the spot.

That was why, to get the cheap cuts to feed to the servants and slaves in the household, they had to leave the city by Portaferrissa until they reached the market where carcasses were piled alongside meat of unknown origin. Again it was Estranya's turn to smile as she bought and loaded the boy with her new purchases. Then it was back to the baker's to pick up the bread from the oven, and then to Grau's house, Estranya still swaying and waddling her way along, Arnau dragging his feet.

One morning, when Estranya and Arnau were buying meat at the main slaughterhouse by Plaça del Blat, they heard the bells of Sant Jaume church begin to peal. It was not Sunday or a feast day. Estranya came to a halt, legs spread wide. Someone in the square let out a shout. Arnau could not understand what he was saying, but many others soon joined in, and people started running about in all directions. He turned to Estranya, a question on his lips. He dropped his load. The wheat merchants were all scrambling to dismantle their stalls. People were still rushing to and fro, and the bells of Sant Jaume continued to ring out over the square. Arnau thought of running there, but . . . weren't those the bells of Santa Clara he could hear too? He strained to capture the sound, but at that very moment the bells of Sant Pere, Framenors and Sant Just all started up. All the churches in the city were ringing their bells! Arnau stood stock still, open-mouthed and deafened, watching everyone running all round him.

All of a sudden, he saw Joanet's face in front of him. His friend was hopping about nervously. '*Via fora! Via fora!*' he was shouting.

'What's that?' Arnau asked.

'*Via fora!*' Joanet bawled in his ear.

'What does that mean?'

Joanet motioned to him to be quiet, and pointed

towards the ancient Portal Major, beneath the magistrate's palace.

As Arnau watched, one of the magistrate's stewards came out. He was dressed for battle, with a silver breastplate and a broadsword at his side. In his right hand he was carrying the banner of Sant Jordi on a gilded pole: a red cross on a white background. Behind him, another steward, who was also in battledress, held aloft the city banner. The two men ran to the centre of the square and the stone dividing Barcelona into four quarters. When they reached it, waving their banners, the two men cried out as one: '*Via fora! Via fora!*'

All the bells were still ringing, and the cry of *Via fora* was taken up along all the streets around the square. Joanet, who until then had witnessed the spectacle without a word, suddenly began to shout like a madman.

Finally, Estranya reacted. She swatted a hand at Arnau to make him move, but he was still entranced by the sight of the two stewards standing in the centre of the square, with their shining armour and swords, waving their colourful banners, and ducked under her fist.

'Come with me, Arnau,' Estranya ordered him.

'No,' he said, egged on by Joanet.

Estranya grabbed him by the shoulder and shook him. 'Come on. This is no business of ours.'

'What are you saying, slave?' The words came from a woman who, like them, was caught up in the excitement of what was going on, and had heard the argument between Arnau and the mulatto. 'Is the boy a slave?' Estranya shook her head. 'Is he a free citizen?' Arnau nodded. 'How dare you say then that the *via fora* is none of the boy's business?'

Estranya hesitated, her feet slipping under her like a duck on ice.

'Who are you, slave,' another woman said, 'to deny the boy the honour of defending Barcelona's rights?'

Estranya lowered her head. What would her master say if he heard? After all, he was the first to defend the city's honour. The bells were still ringing. Joanet had joined the group of women and was signalling to Arnau to come with him.

'Women don't go with the city *host*,' the first woman reminded Estranya.

'And slaves still less,' another woman added.

'Who do you think will look after our husbands if not boys like them?'

Estranya did not dare raise her eyes from the ground.

'Who do you think will cook for them or run their errands? Who will take off their boots and clean their crossbows?'

'Go where you need to go,' the women told her. 'This is no place for a slave.'

Estranya picked up all the sacks that Arnau had been carrying and started to waddle off. Smiling contentedly, Joanet looked admiringly at the group of women. Arnau had not moved.

'Come on, boys,' the women encouraged them, 'come and look after our menfolk.'

'Make sure you tell my father!' Arnau shouted to Estranya, who had only managed to walk three or four yards.

Joanet saw that Arnau could not take his eyes off the slave, and understood his doubts. 'Didn't you hear the women?' he said. 'It's up to us to look after Barcelona's soldiers. Your father will understand.'

Arnau agreed, hesitantly at first, but then with more conviction. Of course Bernat would understand! Hadn't he himself fought so that they could become free citizens of the city?

When they looked back at the centre of the square, they saw a third man had joined the two stewards: the standard-bearer from the merchants' guild. He did not wear armour, but had a crossbow strapped across his back and carried a sword at his belt. A short while later, the standard of the silversmiths was fluttering alongside the others; slowly the square filled up with banners displaying all kinds of symbols and figures: the furriers' banner, the surgeons and barbers', the ones for the guilds of carpenters, coppersmiths, potters . . .

The freemen of Barcelona began gathering beneath the banners of their trades. As required by law, they all came armed with a crossbow, a quiver with a hundred bolts, and a sword or spear. Within two hours, the *sagramental* of the city of Barcelona was ready to move off in defence of the city's privileges.

By then, Arnau had understood from Joanet what this was all about.

'Barcelona not only defends itself when necessary,' Joanet told him. 'It also goes on the offensive if anyone threatens it.' He spoke excitedly, pointing to the soldiers and their banners, proud of the way the city had responded. 'It's fantastic! You'll see. With any luck, we'll be out of Barcelona for a few days. If anybody mistreats an inhabitant of the city or attacks its rights, they are denounced . . . well, I'm not sure who they are denounced to, whether it's the magistrate or the Council of a Hundred, but if the authorities decide the charge is justified, they call the *host* together beneath the banner of Sant Jordi – can you see it over there in the centre of the square, flying higher than all the others? The bells are rung, and people pour out into the streets shouting "*Via fora!*" so that all the inhabitants know what is going on. The leaders of each guild bring out their banners, and their members gather under them to set off for battle.'

Wide-eyed, Arnau tried to take in everything that was going on around him. He followed Joanet through the different groups congregated in the square.

'What do we have to do? Is it dangerous?' Arnau

asked, impressed by the vast array of arms on display.

'No, usually it's not dangerous,' Joanet replied, smiling. 'Remember that if the magistrate has called the citizens to arms, he has done it not only in the name of the city but of the King as well. That means we never have to fight the royal troops. Of course, it depends on who the aggressor is, but generally when a feudal lord sees the Barcelona *host* approaching, he usually gives in to their demands.'

'So there is no battle?'

'That depends on what the authorities decide, and the feudal lord's attitude. The last time, a castle was destroyed, and then there was a battle, with deaths, attacks, and . . . Look! Your uncle must be over there,' said Joanet, pointing to the potters' banner. 'Let's go and see!'

Beneath the banner, Grau Puig stood in his armour with the three other guild aldermen: he was wearing boots, a leather jacket that protected him down to mid-calf, and a sword. The city's potters crowded round their four leaders. As soon as Grau saw the young boys, he signalled to Jaume, who stepped in front of them, blocking their way.

'Where are you two going?' he asked them.

Arnau looked at Joanet for support.

'We're going to offer to help the master,' said Joanet. 'We could carry his food . . . or whatever else he wants.'

'I'm sorry,' was all Jaume replied.

As he turned away, Arnau asked his friend: 'Now what do we do?'

'It doesn't matter!' said Joanet. 'Don't worry, there are plenty of people here who would be pleased to have our help. Anyway, I'm sure he won't notice if we join in.'

The two boys started to mingle with the crowd, studying the swords, crossbows and lances, and admiring the men dressed in armour. They tried to follow their lively conversation.

'What's happened to the water?' they heard someone shout behind them.

Arnau and Joanet looked round. Their faces lit up when they saw it was Ramon smiling at them. All around him, a group of twenty or more *bastaixos*, armed and powerful-looking, were staring in their direction.

Arnau felt for the waterskin on his back. He must have looked so crestfallen when he could not find it that several of the men laughed and came to offer theirs.

'You always have to be ready when the city calls,' they said jokingly.

The army of citizens left Barcelona behind the banner bearing the red cross of Sant Jordi. They were heading for the village of Creixell, close to Tarragona, where the villagers had seized a flock of sheep that was the property of the city butchers.

'Is that so bad?' Arnau asked Ramon, whom they had decided to accompany.

'Of course it is. Any animals that belong to Barcelona's butchers have the right to travel and graze anywhere in Catalonia. Nobody, not even the King, can stop any flock or herd that is on its way to the city. Our children have to eat the best meat in the land,' said Ramon, ruffling their hair. 'The lord of Creixell has seized a flock and is demanding that the shepherd pay him for grazing and for the right to pass through his lands. Can you imagine what would happen if all the lords and barons between Tarragona and Barcelona did the same? We would never eat.'

If only you knew what sort of meat Estranya gives us . . . thought Arnau. Joanet guessed what was going through his mind and pulled a face. He was the only one that Arnau had told. Arnau had been tempted to warn his father where the scraps of meat floating in the pot had come from, but when he saw not only how eagerly his father devoured them but the way that all the slaves and workmen in Grau's pottery threw themselves on the food, he thought better of it, said nothing and ate along with the rest of them.

'Are there any other reasons for the *sagramental* to be called?' asked Arnau, still with the foul taste in his mouth.

'Of course. Any threat to Barcelona's privileges or against a citizen can mean we are called on. For example, if a citizen is held against his will, then the *sagramental* will go and free him.'

As Arnau and Joanet talked, the army moved up the coast, from Sant Boi to Castelldefels and then Garraf. As the men passed by, everyone stared silently at them, making sure they kept well out of their way. Even the sea seemed to respect the Barcelona *host*, the sound of the waves dying away as the hundreds of armed men marched behind the banner of Sant Jordi. The sun shone on them all day, and as the sea was turning to silver in the evening light, they came to a halt in Sitges. The lord of Fonollar welcomed their leaders into his castle, while the rest of the men made camp outside the town gates.

'Is there going to be a war?' asked Arnau.

All the *bastaixos* stared at him. The only sound was the crackling of their bonfire. Joanet lay fast asleep, his head on Ramon's lap. Some of the men looked at each other, asking themselves the same question: would there be a war?

'No,' said Ramon, 'the lord of Creixell cannot stand against us.'

Arnau looked disappointed.

'He might, though,' one of the guild leaders on the far side of the fire said to encourage him. 'Many years ago, when I was about as young as you are now' – Arnau almost burnt himself on the fire as he leant forward to catch his words – 'the *sagramental* was called out to march on Castellbisbal, where the lord had seized a herd of cattle, just like the lord of Creixell has done now. But at Castellbisbal, he did not back down: he decided to face our army. He probably thought that the citizens of Barcelona – merchants, artisans, or *bastaixos* like us – could not fight. But the men of Barcelona stormed the castle, took the lord and his soldiers prisoner, and razed it to the ground.'

Arnau imagined himself wielding a sword, swarming up a ladder, shouting victoriously on the battlements of Creixell Castle: 'Who dares stand against the Barcelona *sagramental*?' All the men around the fire could see how excited he was: he was staring intently into the flames, his hands clasping a stick he had previously used to poke the fire. 'I, Arnau Estanyol . . .' The sound of their laughter brought him back to Sitges.

'Go and sleep,' Ramon advised him, getting up with Joanet in his arms. Arnau made a face. 'You can dream of battles,' the *bastaix* consoled him.

The night air was cool, but one of the men gave up his blanket for the two boys.

At dawn the next day the army resumed its march on Creixell. They passed through the villages and castles of Geltrú, Vilanova, Cubelles, Segur and Barà. From Barà, they turned inland towards Creixell. About a mile from the sea, the lord of Creixell had built his castle on rocks at the crest of a ridge. It boasted several towers; the houses of the village were clustered round them.

By now it was only a few hours before nightfall. The leaders of the guilds were called together by the councillors and the magistrate. Then the army of Barcelona lined up in battle formation outside Creixell, with banners waving in front of it. Arnau and Joanet roamed behind the lines offering water to any *bastaix* who wanted some. Most of them refused, their eyes fixed on the castle. Nobody spoke, and the children did not dare break the silence. The leaders returned and took their places at the head of each guild. Everyone in the ranks watched as three ambassadors from Barcelona strode towards Creixell; the same number came out of the castle, and the two groups met halfway down the hill.

Like everyone else in the citizens' army, Arnau and Joanet watched the negotiations without a word.

In the end, there was no battle. The lord of Creixell had managed to escape through a secret tunnel that led from the castle to the beach, behind the army. When he saw Barcelona's army drawn up in the valley, the village mayor gave the order to comply with all the city's demands. The villagers released the flock and the shepherd, agreed to pay a large sum of money in compensation, promised to obey and respect Barcelona's privileges in the future, and handed over two men who they said were to blame for the insult. They were taken prisoner at once.

'Creixell has surrendered,' the ambassadors informed the army.

A murmur ran through the ranks. The occasional soldiers sheathed their swords, put down their crossbows and spears and took off their armour. Soon, shouts of triumph, jokes and laughter could be heard on all sides.

'Where's the wine, boys?' Ramon teased them. 'What's the matter?' he asked, seeing them rooted to the spot. 'You would have liked to have seen a battle, wouldn't you?'

The expression on their faces spoke for itself.

'But any one of us could have been wounded, or even killed. Would you have liked that?' Arnau and Joanet quickly shook their heads. 'You should see it in another light: you belong to the biggest and most powerful city in the principality. Everyone is afraid of challenging us.' Arnau and Joanet listened wide-eyed. 'Go and fetch wine, boys. You'll have the chance to drink to our victory too.'

The flag of Sant Jordi returned with honour to Barcelona. Alongside it strode the two boys, proud of their city, its citizens, and of being part of everything. The Creixell prisoners were paraded through the streets in chains. Women and crowds of curious onlookers applauded the army and spat on the captives. Stern-faced and proud, Arnau and Joanet marched with the others all the way to the magistrate's palace, where the prisoners were handed over. Then they went to visit Bernat who, relieved to see his son back safe and sound, soon forgot the scolding he was going to give him, and instead listened contentedly to the account of his new adventures.

12

Several months had gone by since the excitement that had taken him to Creixell, but little had changed in Arnau's life. While he waited for his tenth birthday, when he would become an apprentice in Grau's workshop, he spent his days with Joanet, roaming the streets of the fascinating city, giving the *bastaixos* water and, above all, enjoying watching the new Santa Maria grow. He prayed to the Virgin and told her all his worries, delighting in the smile he thought he could see on her lips.

As Father Albert had told him, when the main altar of the Romanesque church disappeared, the Virgin was taken to the small Jesus chapel in the ambulatory behind the new main altar, between two buttresses and protected by tall, strong iron bars. It was the *bastaixos* who provided for the chapel. They were the ones who looked after it, guarded it, cleaned it and made sure it was always lit by fresh candles. Although it was the most important chapel in the new church, the place where the sacraments were kept, the parish had granted it to these humble workers from the port of Barcelona. Many nobles and rich merchants were happy to pay to build and endow the other thirty-three chapels that would be part of Santa Maria de la Mar, Father Albert told them. But this one, the Jesus chapel, belonged to the *bastaixos*, so the young water-carrier never had any problem getting close to the Virgin.

One morning, Bernat was sorting through the few possessions he kept under their pallet. It was here that he hid the coins he had managed to rescue during their flight from his farmhouse nine years earlier, and the meagre wage his brother-in-law paid him, which would nevertheless help Arnau get on once he had learnt the potter's trade. All of a sudden, Jaume entered the room. Surprised because the assistant never usually came there, Bernat stood up.

'What is it?'

'Your sister has died,' Jaume said hurriedly.

Bernat could feel his legs giving way. He flopped on to the mattress, money bag still in hand.

'Wha . . . What happened?' he stammered.

'The master does not know. Her body was cold this morning.'

Bernat dropped the bag and buried his face in his hands. By the time he lowered them again and looked up, Jaume had disappeared. With a lump in his throat, Bernat recalled the little girl who had worked in the fields alongside him and his father, the girl who never stopped singing as she looked after the animals. Bernat had often seen his father pause in his task and close his eyes, allowing himself to be carried away for a few moments by her happy, carefree voice. And now . . .

Arnau's face showed no reaction when his father told him the news at mealtime.

'Did you hear me, son?' Bernat insisted.

Arnau merely nodded. It was more than a year since he had seen Guiamona, apart from the increasingly rare occasions when he climbed the tree to watch her playing with his cousins. Hidden in the branches, he would shed silent tears as he spied on them while they laughed and ran about, none of them . . . He felt like telling his father that it did not matter, because Guiamona had no love for him, but when he saw how sad his father looked, he said nothing.

'Father.' Arnau went up to him.

Bernat embraced his son.

'Don't cry,' said Arnau, pressing his head against his father's chest. Bernat hugged him, and Arnau responded by wrapping his arms round him.

They were eating quietly with the slaves and apprentices when they heard the first howl. It was a piercing shriek that seemed to rend the air. They all looked towards the big house.

'Professional mourners,' one of the apprentices said. 'My mother is one. It might even be her. She's the best wailer in the city,' he added proudly.

Arnau sought his father's face. Another howl resounded, and Bernat saw his son flinch.

'We'll hear lots more,' he told him. 'I've heard that Grau has hired a lot of wailing women.'

He was right. All that afternoon and night, as people came to visit Grau's house to offer their condolences, women could be heard mourning Guiamona's death. Neither Bernat nor his son could sleep because of the constant keening.

'The whole of Barcelona knows,' Joanet told Arnau the next morning when the two of them managed to meet up in the crush of people that had formed outside Grau's gates. Arnau shrugged. 'They've all come for the funeral,' Joanet added, noticing his friend's indifferent shrug.

'Why?'

'Because Grau is rich, and anyone who accompanies him is to be given mourning clothes,' said Joanet, showing him a long black tunic he was carrying. 'Like this one,' he said with a smile.

By mid-morning, when everyone had donned their black clothes, the funeral procession set off for Nazaret church. It was here that the chapel to Saint Hippolytus, the patron saint of potters, was to be found. The paid mourners walked alongside the coffin, crying, howling and tearing their hair.

The church was full of the rich and famous: aldermen from several guilds, city councillors, and most of the members of the Council of a Hundred. Now that Guiamona was dead, nobody was concerned about the Estanyol family, but Bernat succeeded in pushing his way through people dressed in the simple garments Grau had given out, as well as others wearing silks, byssus and expensive black linen, until he and his son reached his sister's coffin. He was not even allowed to bid her a proper farewell.

Standing at his side while the priests conducted the funeral service, Arnau caught glimpses of his cousins' faces, puffy from crying. Josep and Genís looked calm and composed, but Margarida, although she sat up straight, could not prevent her lower lip constantly trembling. They had lost their mother, just like him. Did they know about the Virgin? Arnau wondered, looking across at his uncle, who sat there stiff as ever. He was sure that Grau Puig would not tell them about her. He had always heard that the rich were different; perhaps they had a different way of finding a new mother.

They certainly did. A rich widower in Barcelona, and one with ambitions . . . even before the period of mourning had finished, Grau began to receive offers of marriage. In the end, the one chosen to be the new mother for Guiamona's children was Isabel. She was young and unattractive, but she was a noble. Grau had weighed up the advantages of all the candidates, but eventually chose the only one from a noble family. Her dowry was a title that brought with it no privileges, lands or riches, but would help him join a class that had always been closed to him. What did he care about the substantial dowries that some merchants offered him in their anxiety to share his wealth? The important noble families in Barcelona were not interested in a widower who, however rich he might be, was nothing more than a potter: only Isabel's father, who was penniless, could see that Grau's character might help him make an alliance that would benefit both parties. And so it proved.

'You will understand that my daughter cannot live in a potter's workshop,' his future father-in-law insisted. Grau nodded. 'And that she cannot marry a simple potter.' Grau tried to protest, but his father-in-law dismissed him with a wave of the hand. 'Grau,' he went on, 'we nobles cannot stoop to working as artisans. You surely understand that? We may not be rich, but we will never be craftsmen.'

We nobles cannot . . . Grau tried to hide his satisfaction at being included as one of them. His father-in-law was right: who among the city nobles had a workshop? My lord baron: from now on that was how he would be known in his commercial dealings, and in the Council of a Hundred . . . My lord baron! How could a Catalan baron have a workshop?

As alderman of the guild, he could smooth the way for Jaume to be made a master potter. They talked the matter over. Grau was in a hurry to wed Isabel, obsessed by the fear that the fickle nobleman might change his mind. The baron-to-be had no time to put his business up for sale. So Jaume would become a master potter, and Grau would sell him the workshop and the house, in instalments. There was only one problem . . .

'I've got four sons,' Jaume told him. 'I'll find it hard enough to pay you for the business . . .' Grau encouraged him to go on. 'I can't take on all the responsibilities you have: the slaves, the craftsmen, the apprentices . . . I wouldn't even be able to feed them! If I want to succeed, I'm going to have to manage with my four sons.'

The date for the wedding had been set. At the urging of Isabel's father, Grau had bought an expensive mansion in Carrer de Montcada, where many of Barcelona's noble families lived.

'Remember,' his father-in-law warned him as they left the new mansion, 'you are not to go into church with a potter's workshop still on your hands.'

They had inspected every nook and cranny of his new house. The baron had nodded condescendingly while Grau was mentally calculating how much it was going to cost him to fill all those rooms. In the mansion behind the gateway on to Carrer de Montcada there was a cobbled yard. At the far end stood the stables, which took up most of the ground floor, together with the kitchens and the slaves' bedrooms. On the right-hand side of the yard was a broad stone staircase, which led up to the first floor of the house proper, with the principal chambers and rooms. Above that there was another floor, with the family bedrooms. The whole mansion was made of stone; the two principal floors had rows of Gothic windows that gave on to the yard.

'Very well,' Grau now said to the man who for years had been his chief assistant, 'you are free of those responsibilities.'

They signed the contract that very day. Grau proudly took it to show his future father-in-law. 'I've sold the workshop,' he announced.

'My lord baron,' the other man said, holding out his hand.

What now? Grau thought when he was alone again. The slaves are no problem; I'll keep those that are of use to me, and those who aren't can be sold. As for the craftsmen and apprentices . . .

151

Grau spoke to the other members of the guild and was able to place them all for modest sums. The only ones left were his brother-in-law and his son. Bernat had no official position within the guild: he was not even a certified craftsman. Nobody would have him in their workshop, even if it was not forbidden. The boy had not even begun his apprenticeship, but there was the question of the contract. Besides, how could he possibly ask anyone to take on members of the Estanyol family? Everybody would find out that those two fugitives were his relatives. They were called Estanyol, just like Guiamona. Everybody would discover that he had sheltered two landless serfs, and now that he was to become a nobleman . . . weren't the nobles the fiercest enemies of all runaway serfs? Wasn't it they who were trying to put pressure on the King to abolish the laws allowing serfs to leave the land? How could he become a noble if the name of the Estanyol family was on every-one's lips? What would his father-in-law say?

'You are to come with me,' Grau told Bernat, who for several days now had been worried by the new turn of events.

As the new owner of the workshop, and consequently free of any commitment to Grau, Jaume had sat Bernat down and talked openly to him. 'Grau won't dare do anything to you. I know, because he told me as much. He doesn't want people to hear of your situation. I've got a good deal here, Bernat. He is in a hurry; he wants every-thing settled before he marries Isabel. You have a signed contract for your son. You should take advantage of that, and put pressure on that rogue. Threaten to take him to the tribunal. You are a good man. I hope you understand that everything that has happened in these past years . . .'

Bernat did understand. And, thanks to the former assistant's support, he had decided to go and confront his brother-in-law.

'What was that you said?' shouted Grau now when Bernat answered him with a brief: 'Where and what for?' 'Where I say, and for whatever I wish,' Grau went on, nervously flinging his arms in the air.

'We are not your slaves, Grau.'

'You don't have much choice.'

Bernat cleared his throat, then followed Jaume's advice. 'I could go to the tribunal.'

Tense, shaken, Grau raised his small, skinny body out of his chair, but Bernat did not back down, however much he would have liked to have run from the room. And the threat of the tribunal worked wonders.

Bernat and his son would look after the horses that Grau had been forced to buy along with the mansion. 'You can't possibly have empty stables,' his father-in-law had commented in passing, as though talking to a slow child. Grau was busy adding up all the costs in his mind. 'My daughter Isabel has always had horses,' the other man added.

But the most important thing for Bernat was the good wage he obtained for himself and for Arnau, who was also going to start working with the horses. They could live outside the mansion in a room of their own, without slaves or apprentices. He and his son would have enough money to get by.

It was Grau himself who urged Bernat to annul Arnau's existing contract as a potter's apprentice, and to sign a new one.

Ever since he had been granted the status of a free man, Bernat had seldom left Grau's workshop. Whenever he had done so, it had been on his own or with Arnau. It did not seem as though there were any outstanding warrants against him: his name was registered on the list of Barcelona citizens. Every time he went out into the street, he reassured himself thinking that they would surely have come for him by now. What he most liked was to walk down to the beach and join the dozens of men who made their living from the sea. He would stand staring out at the horizon, feeling the sea breeze on his face and enjoying the tangy smells from the beach, the boats, the tar . . .

It was almost ten years since he had struck the lad at the forge. He hoped he had not killed him. Arnau and Joanet were scampering around, staring up at him bright-eyed, a smile on their lips.

'Our own house!' shouted Arnau. 'Let's live in La Ribera, please!'

'I'm afraid it will only be one room,' Bernat tried to explain, but his son went on smiling as though they were moving to the city's grandest palace.

'It's not a bad area,' Jaume said when Bernat told him his son's suggestion. 'You can find a good room there.'

That was where the three of them were heading now. The boys were running around as usual; Bernat was carrying their few belongings.

On the way down to Santa Maria church, the two boys never stopped greeting people they met.

'This is my father!' Arnau shouted to a *bastaix* weighed down under a sack of grain, pointing to Bernat who was some twenty yards behind them.

The *bastaix* smiled but continued walking, bent double under his load. Arnau turned and started to run back towards his father, but then realized Joanet was not following him.

'Come on,' he said, waving to him.

Joanet shook his head.

'What's wrong?'

The little boy lowered his head. 'He is your father,' he muttered. 'What will become of me now?'

He was right. Everyone they knew thought they were brothers. Arnau had not considered that.

154

'Come on, run with me,' he said, tugging at Joanet's sleeve.

Bernat watched them approach: Arnau was pulling at Joanet, who seemed reluctant. 'Congratulations – you have fine sons,' said the *bastaix* as he walked past. Bernat smiled. The two boys had been playing together for more than a year now. What about little Joanet's mother? Bernat imagined him sitting on the crate, having his head stroked by an arm that had no face. A lump rose in his throat.

'Father—' Arnau began to say when they reached him. Joanet hid behind his friend.

'Boys,' Bernat interrupted his son, 'I think that—'

'Father, how would you like to be Joanet's father too?' Arnau said hurriedly.

Bernat saw the smaller boy peep out from behind Arnau's back.

'Come here, Joanet,' said Bernat. 'Would you like to be my son?' he asked as the boy approached.

Joanet's face lit up.

'Does that mean yes?'

The boy clung to his leg. Arnau beamed at him.

'Now go and play,' said Bernat, his voice choking with emotion.

The boys took Bernat to meet Father Albert.

'I'm sure he can help us,' said Arnau. Joanet nodded.

'This is our father!' the smaller boy said, rushing in front of Arnau and repeating the words he had been telling everyone on their way to the church, even those they knew only by sight.

Father Albert asked the boys to leave them for a while. He offered Bernat a cup of sweet wine while he listened to his story.

'I know where you can stay,' he told him. 'They are good people. Now tell me, Bernat: you've found a good job for Arnau. He'll earn a wage and will learn a trade. There is always a need for grooms. But what about your other son? What are your plans for Joanet?'

Bernat looked uncomfortable, and told the priest the truth.

Father Albert took them to the house of Pere and his wife. They were an old, childless couple who lived in a small, two-storey house close to the beach. The kitchen was on the ground floor, and there were three rooms above it, one of which they could rent.

The whole way there, and while he was introducing them to Pere and his wife, then watching Bernat offer them payment, Father Albert held Joanet firmly by the shoulder. How could he have been so blind? Why had he not realized how much the little boy suffered? To think of all the occasions he had seen him sitting there, gazing into space with a lost look on his face!

Father Albert pulled the boy towards him. Joanet glanced up and smiled.

The room was simple but clean. The only furniture was two mattresses on the floor; the only company the sound of the waves on the beach. Arnau strained to hear the noise of the men working on Santa Maria, which was nearby, behind them. They ate the stew that Pere's wife prepared most days. Arnau looked down at the food, then looked up and smiled at his father. Estranya's concoctions were a thing of the past now! The three of them ate heartily, watched by the old woman, who seemed ready to refill their bowls whenever they wished.

'Time for bed,' said Bernat, when he had eaten his fill. 'We have to work tomorrow.'

Joanet hesitated. He stared at Bernat and, when everybody had got up from the table, headed for the door.

'This is no time to be going out, son,' said Bernat, in front of the old couple.

13

'They are my mother's brother and his son,' Margarida explained to her stepmother when she expressed surprise that Grau had taken on two more people for only seven horses.

Grau had told Isabel he wanted nothing to do with the horses. In fact, he did not even go down to inspect the magnificent stables on the ground floor of the mansion. His new wife took care of everything: she chose the animals and brought her chief stableman, Jesús, with her. He in turn advised her to employ an experienced groom, whose name was Tomàs.

But four men to look after seven horses was excessive even for the way of life the baroness was used to, and she said as much on her first visit to the stables after the two Estanyols had arrived.

Now she encouraged Margarida to tell her more.

'They were peasants, serfs on a lord's lands.'

Isabel said nothing in reply, but a suspicion was planted in her mind.

Margarida went on: 'It was the son, Arnau, who was responsible for my little brother Guiamon's death. I hate

157

them both! I've no idea why my father has kept them on.'

'We'll soon find out,' muttered the baroness, her eyes fixed on Bernat's back as he brushed down one of the horses.

When she brought the matter up that evening, Grau was dismissive.

'I thought it was a good idea,' was all he said, although he did confirm that they were fugitives.

'If my father got to hear of it . . .'

'But he won't, will he, Isabel?' said Grau, looking at her intently. She was already dressed for dinner, one of the new customs she had introduced into the life of Grau and his family. She was only just twenty, and like Grau was extremely thin. She was not particularly attractive, and lacked the voluptuous curves that he had once found alluring in Guiamona, but she was noble – and her character must be noble too, Grau thought. 'I'm sure you wouldn't want your father to discover that you are living with two fugitives.'

The baroness looked at him, eyes ablaze, then swept out of the room.

In spite of the baroness and her stepchildren's dislike of him, Bernat soon showed his worth with the horses. He knew how to deal with them, feed them, to clean their hooves and frogs, and to look after them when they were sick. He moved easily among the animals: the only part of his work where he lacked experience was in turning them out spotlessly.

'They want them to shine,' he told Arnau one day as they walked back home. 'They don't want to see a speck of dust. We have to scrape and scrape to get all the grit out of their hair, then brush them until they really glisten.'

'What about their manes and tails?'

'We have to cut them, plait them and put ribbons in them.'

'Why do they want horses with so many ribbons?'

Arnau was forbidden to go near the horses. He looked at them admiringly in the stables, and could see how they responded to his father's care. What he most enjoyed was when only he and Bernat were there and he was allowed to stroke them. As a treat, when there was no one around, Bernat allowed him to sit on the back of one or other of them inside the stable. Usually though, his tasks meant he was never allowed to leave the harness room. He would clean the harnesses over and over again, greasing the leather then rubbing it with a cloth until the grease was completely absorbed and the surface of the saddles and reins gleamed. He cleaned the bits and stirrups, then combed the blankets and other pieces of tackle until he had got rid of every last horse hair. Often he had to finish the job by using his hands as a pair of pincers to pull out the fine, needle-like hairs that stuck so closely to the cloth they seemed to be part of it. If there was any time left after he had done all this, he would polish and polish the new carriage that Grau had bought.

As the months went by, even Jesús had to admit Bernat's worth. Whenever he went into one of the stables, not only did the horses not become alarmed, but more often than not they moved towards him. He touched and stroked them, whispering to reassure them. When Tomàs came in, on the other hand, the steeds flattened their ears and retreated to the furthest wall when he shouted at them. What was the matter with him? Until now he had been perfectly competent, thought Jesús each time he heard a fresh outburst.

Every morning when father and son set off for work, Joanet stayed to help Mariona, Pere's wife. He would clean and tidy the house, then accompany her to market. After that, while she busied herself with her cooking, he would head off to the beach to find Pere. The old man had spent his life fishing, and apart from receiving occasional aid from their guild, he also earned a few coins by helping the younger fishermen repair the nets. Joanet went with him, listening to all his explanations and running off to get whatever he might need.

Apart from all this, whenever he could he escaped and went to visit his mother.

'This morning,' he explained to her one day, 'when Bernat went to pay Pere, he gave him back some of the money. He told him that the little one . . . that's me, Mother, that's what they call me . . . Well, he said that seeing the little one helped so much at home and on the beach, there was no need for him to pay for me.'

The imprisoned woman listened, hand on her son's hair. How everything had changed! Ever since he had been living with the Estanyols her little one no longer sat there sobbing, waiting for her silent caresses and words of affection. A blind affection. Now he spoke, told her about his life. Why, he even laughed!

'Bernat hugged me,' Joanet said proudly, 'and Arnau congratulated me.'

The hand closed on the boy's head.

Joanet went on talking, in a rush to tell her everything. About Arnau, Bernat, Mariona, Pere, the beach, the fishermen, the nets they repaired. But his mother was no longer listening: she was only happy that her son finally knew what it was like to be hugged, to be happy.

'Run, my boy,' his mother interrupted him, trying to conceal the tremor in her voice. 'They'll be waiting for you.'

From inside the walls of her prison, she heard how her little one jumped down from the crate and ran off. She imagined him climbing the wall she wished she had never seen.

What was left for her? She had survived for years on bread and water within these four walls, every last inch of which her fingers had explored hundreds of times. She had fought against solitude and madness by staring up at the sky through the tiny window the King, in his great mercy, had allowed her. She had fought off fever and other illnesses, and had done all this for her son, to be able to stroke his head, to give him encouragement, to make him feel that, in spite of everything, he was not alone in the world.

Now he was not alone. Bernat hugged him! It felt as though she knew him. She had even dreamt of him during the endless hours of her imprisonment. 'Take care of him, Bernat,' she had whispered to the thin air. And now Joanet was happy. He laughed, ran everywhere, and . . .

Joana sank to the ground and stayed there. That day she did not touch any of the bread or water left for her; her body did not need it.

Joanet came back the next day, and the day after, on and on. She could hear how he laughed and talked of the world so full of hope. All that came out of the window were faint words: *yes, no, look, run, run and live.*

'Run and enjoy the life that because of me you have never enjoyed until now,' she whispered as he climbed back over the wall.

The pieces of bread formed a pile on the floor of Joana's prison.

'Do you know what has happened, Mother?' said Joanet, pulling the crate against the wall to sit on: his feet still did not touch the ground. 'No, how could you?' He sat curled up and pressed his back against the wall exactly where he knew his mother's hand could reach down and touch his head. 'I'll tell you. Well, yesterday one of Grau's horses . . .'

But no arm appeared through the window.

'Mother, listen. It's funny, I tell you. It's about one of the horses . . .'

He turned and looked up at the window.

'Mother?'

He waited.

'Mother?'

He strained to hear above the sounds of the copper-smiths hammering in the streets all around: nothing.

'Mother!' he shouted.

He knelt up on the crate. What could he do? She had always forbidden him to approach the window.

'Mother!' he shouted again, standing up on the crate.

She had always insisted he should not try to look in and see her. Yet there was no answer! Joanet peered inside: it was too dark for him to see anything.

He climbed up and lifted his leg through the window. He was too big – he would have to slide in sideways.

'Mother?' he said again.

He grabbed the top of the window, lifted both legs on to the sill, then squeezed in on his side. He jumped to the floor.

'Mother?' he said as his eyes grew used to the gloom.

Gradually he could make out a point of light that gave off an unbearable stench, and then on the other side of the room, to his left, he saw a body curled up on a straw pallet against the wall.

Joanet waited without moving. The noise of hammers on metal had faded into the distance.

'I wanted to tell you a funny story,' he said, stumbling towards the shape on the floor. Tears started to course down his cheeks. 'It would have made you laugh,' he stammered, coming up to her.

Joanet sat for a long while next to his mother's body. As though she had guessed her son might come into her cell, Joana had buried her face in her arms, as if trying to avoid him seeing her like this even after her death.

'Can I touch you?'

The little one stroked his mother's hair. It was filthy, dishevelled, dry as dust.

'You had to die for us to be together.'

Joanet burst into tears.

Bernat knew what to do as soon as he returned home and was met by Pere and his wife, interrupting each other as they tried to tell him that Joanet had not come back. They had never asked him where he disappeared to. They always thought he went to Santa Maria, but nobody had seen him there that afternoon. Mariona raised her hand to her mouth: 'What if something has happened to him?'

'We'll find him,' Bernat said, trying to reassure her.

Joanet was still sitting beside his mother's body. First he stroked her hair; then he curled it between his fingers, getting some of the knots out. After that, he got up and stared up at the window.

Night fell.

'Joanet?'

Joanet looked back up at the window.

'Joanet?' he heard once more from beyond the wall.

'Arnau?'

'What's happened?'

He answered: 'She's dead.'

'Why don't you . . .?'

'I can't. I don't have a crate inside here. The window is too high up.'

'There's a very bad smell,' concluded Arnau. Bernat beat on the door of Ponç the coppersmith's house once more. What could the little one have been doing, shut up in there all day? He called out again, in a loud voice. Why did nobody answer? At that moment, the door opened, and a gigantic figure almost filled the entire doorway. Arnau took a step back.

'What do you want?' the man growled. He was bare-foot, and was wearing only a threadbare shirt that came down to his knees.

'My name is Bernat Estanyol, and this is my son,' he said, grasping Arnau by the shoulder and pushing him forward. 'He's a friend of your son Joa—'

'I don't have a son,' Ponç protested, making as though to shut the door in their faces.

'But you do have a wife,' said Bernat, pushing the door open despite Ponç's efforts. 'Well,' he explained to the coppersmith, 'you did have one. She has died.'

Ponç showed no reaction. 'So what?' he said, with an almost imperceptible shrug of his shoulders.

'Joanet is inside the hut with her.' Bernat tried to make his voice sound as threatening as he could. 'He can't get out.'

'That's where that bastard should have spent his entire life.'

Squeezing Arnau's shoulder tight, Bernat looked steadily at the other man. Arnau was frightened again, but when Ponç looked down at him, he stood defiantly straight.

'What are you going to do?' Bernat insisted.

'Nothing,' the coppersmith replied. 'Tomorrow, when they knock the hut down, the boy will get out.'

'You can't leave a child all night in—'

'I can do what I like in my own house.'

'I'll go and tell the magistrate,' Bernat said, knowing it was an empty threat.

Ponç's eyes narrowed. Without another word, he disappeared inside, leaving the door open. Bernat and Arnau waited. He finally came back carrying a rope, which he handed directly to Arnau.

'Get him out of there,' he ordered the boy, 'and tell him that now his mother is dead I don't ever want to see him here again.'

'How . . .?' Bernat began to ask.

'The same way he has been getting in there all these years,' Ponç said. 'By climbing over the wall. You are not going through my house.'

'What about his mother?' Bernat asked before he could shut the door again.

'The King handed me the mother with orders that I should not kill her. Now that she is dead, I'll give her back to the King,' Ponç quickly replied. 'I paid a lot of money as surety and, by God, I have no intention of forfeiting it for a whore like her.'

Only Father Albert, who already knew Joanet's story, and old Pere and his wife, whom Bernat had no choice but to tell, ever found out about the boy's terrible misfortune. All three of them paid him special attention, but he still refused to talk. Whereas before he had constantly been on the move, now he walked slowly and deliberately, as if he were carrying an unbearable weight on his shoulders.

'Time is a great healer,' Bernat said to Arnau one morning. 'We have to wait and offer him our love and help.'

Yet Joanet remained silent, except when, each night, he was overcome by tears. Bernat and Arnau lay quietly on their mattress, until it seemed the poor boy ran out of energy and was overcome by a fitful sleep.

'Joanet,' Bernat heard his son call out to him one night. 'Joanet!'

There was no answer.

'If you like, I can ask the Virgin Mary to be your mother too.'

Well said, son! thought Bernat. He had not wanted to suggest it, because the Virgin was Arnau's secret. It was up to him to decide if he wanted to share it.

Now he had done so, but Joanet had made no reply. The room remained completely silent.

'Joanet?' Arnau insisted.

'That was what my mother called me.' These were the first words he had spoken in days. Bernat lay on his mattress without moving. 'She's no longer here. Now my name is Joan.'

'As you like. Did you hear what I said to you about the Virgin, Joanet . . . Joan?'

'But your mother doesn't speak to you – mine did.'

'Tell him about the birds,' Bernat whispered.

'Well, I can see the Virgin, and you could never see your mother.'

Joan was silent again.

'How do you know she listens?' he asked finally. 'She is only a stone figure, and stone figures don't listen.'

Bernat held his breath.

'If it's true they don't listen,' Arnau responded, 'why does everyone talk to them? Even Father Albert. You've seen him. Do you think Father Albert is making a mistake?'

'She isn't Father Albert's mother,' the other boy insisted. 'He's already told me he has one. How will I know if the Virgin wants to be my mother if she doesn't speak to me?'

'She'll tell you at night when you sleep, and through the birds.'

'The birds?'

'Well,' said Arnau hesitantly. The truth was he had never really understood what the birds were meant to do, but he had never dared tell his father so. 'That's more complicated. My . . . our father will explain it to you.'

Bernat felt a lump in his throat. Silence filled the room again, until Joanet spoke once more.

'Arnau, could we go right now and ask the Virgin?'

'Now?'

Yes, now, my son, now. He needs it, thought Bernat.

'Please.'

'You know it's forbidden to go into the church at night. Father Albert—'

'We won't make any noise. Nobody will find out. Please!'

Arnau gave in. The two boys stole out of the house and ran the short distance to Santa Maria de la Mar.

Bernat curled up on the mattress. What could possibly happen to them? Everyone in the church loved them.

Moonlight played over the outlines of the scaffolding, the half-built walls, the buttresses, arches and apses . . . Santa Maria lay silent, with only the occasional flames from bonfires showing there were watchmen in the vicinity. Arnau and Joan sneaked round the church to the Carrer del Born entrance, but it was closed, and the side by the Les Moreres cemetery, where much of the building material was kept, was the most closely guarded. But on the side where the new work was being carried out there was only one fire. It was not hard to get in: the walls and buttresses led down from the apse to the Born doorway, where a wooden board marked the site of the new steps into the church. The two boys walked over the chalk lines drawn by Master Montagut, showing the exact position for the new door and steps, and entered Santa Maria. They headed silently towards the Jesus chapel in the ambulatory. There, behind strong and wonderfully wrought iron railings, they found the Virgin, lit as ever by the candles that the *bastaixos* made sure never went out.

They crossed themselves. 'That's what you should always do when you come into church,' Father Albert had told them. They grasped the iron bars of the chapel.

He wants you to be his mother, Arnau said silently to the Virgin. *His mother has died, and I don't mind sharing you.*

Clinging to the bars, Joan stared in turn at the Virgin and at Arnau.

'What?' he asked.

'Be quiet!'

Father says he must have suffered a lot. His mother was im-
prisoned, you see. She could only reach her arm out through a
window, and he couldn't see her. Not until she had died, but
even then he says he didn't really look at her because she had
forbidden him to.

The smoke rising from the pure beeswax candles in
the rack below the statue clouded Arnau's sight once
more, and the lips of the Virgin smiled at him.

'She will be your mother,' he declared to Joan.

'How do you know, if you say she replies through—'

'I know, and that's all there is to it,' Arnau cut in.

'What if I asked her?'

'No,' said Arnau, interrupting him again.

Joan stared at the stone figure: how he wanted to be
able to talk to her the way Arnau did! Why did she listen
to his brother and not to him? How could Arnau
know . . .? Joan was promising himself that one day he
would be worthy of her talking to him when they heard
a noise.

'Shhh!' Arnau whispered, looking towards the empty
Les Moreres doorway.

'Who goes there?' A lantern appeared in the doorway.

Arnau started to run towards the Born entrance, where
they had got into the church, but Joan stood rooted
to the spot, staring at the light that was now coming
along the ambulatory.

'Let's go!' said Arnau, tugging at him.

When they looked outside they saw more lanterns
heading towards them. Arnau looked back; there were
more lights inside the church too.

There was no way out. The watchmen were talking and
shouting to each other. What could the boys do? The
wooden floor! He pushed Joan down. The planks did
not quite reach the wall. He pushed Joan down again,
until the two of them were in the church foundations.

The lights reached the platform above them. The foot-steps on the wooden boards echoed in Arnau's ears, and the voices hid the sound of his wildly beating heart.

They waited while the watchmen searched the build-ing. It took them a lifetime! Arnau peered upwards, trying to work out what was going on. Each time he saw light filtering through the boards, he crouched down to hide still further in.

In the end the watchmen completed their search. Two of them stood on the wooden boards and for a few moments shone their lanterns all round. How could they possibly not hear the beating of his or Joan's heart? The men moved away. Arnau turned his head to look at the spot where his brother had been crouching. One of the watchmen placed a lamp by the wooden planks; the other one was already walking away. Joan was not there! Where could he have got to? Arnau went over to where the church foundations joined the wooden floor. There was a hole, a small underground passage into the foundations of the church.

When Arnau had pushed him down into the found-ations, Joan had crawled under the wooden floor. He found nothing in his way, so went on crawling along the passageway, which angled slowly down towards the main altar. Arnau had encouraged him onwards, whispering 'Be quiet' several times. The noise of his body scraping against the sides of the tunnel prevented him hearing anything more, but he was sure Arnau was right behind him: he could hear him clambering under the floor. It was only once the tunnel broadened out, allow-ing him to turn round and get to his knees, that Joan realized he was all alone. Where was he? It was com-pletely dark.

'Arnau?' he called out.

His voice echoed round him. It was . . . it was like a cave. Beneath the church!

He called out again and again. Quietly at first, then much louder, but he was frightened by the sound of his own shouts. He could try to get back, but where was the mouth of the tunnel? Joan stretched out his arms, but could feel nothing: he had crawled too far.

'Arnau!' he shouted again.

Nothing. He began to cry. What might he find in the cave? Monsters? What if this was hell? He was underneath a church; didn't they say that hell was down there somewhere? What if the Devil appeared?

Arnau meanwhile was crawling down the passage. That was the only place Joan could have gone. He would never have climbed back out from under the floor. Arnau struggled on for a few yards, then called out once more. No one would hear outside the tunnel. No reply. He crawled on.

'Joanet!' he shouted, then corrected himself. 'Joan!'

'Here,' he heard the reply.

'Where is here?'

'At the end of the tunnel.'

'Are you all right?'

Joan stopped shaking. 'Yes.'

'Come back then.'

'I can't. This is like a cave, and I can't find the way back.'

'Feel the walls until you— No!' Arnau changed his mind. 'Don't do that, Joan, do you hear me? There might be other tunnels. If only I could reach you . . . can you see anything, Joan?'

'No,' the other boy replied.

Arnau could crawl on until he found him, but what if he got lost too? Why was there a cave down there? Ah, now he had an idea! He needed light. If they had a lamp, they could find their way back.

'Wait where you are! Do you hear me, Joan? Stay still, all right? Can you hear me?'

'Yes, I can. What are you going to do?'

'I'm going to get a lamp and come back. Stay where you are and don't move, promise?'

'Yes . . .' said Joan reluctantly.

'Think that you are underneath your mother, the Virgin.' Arnau did not hear any reply. 'Did you hear me, Joan?'

Of course he heard him. He had said: 'Your mother'. Arnau could hear her, even if he could not. But he had not let him talk to her. What if Arnau did not want to share his mother, and had deliberately shut him up down there, in hell?

'Joan?' Arnau insisted.

'What is it?'

'Wait for me, and don't move.'

With difficulty, Arnau managed to crawl back until he was under the boards by the Born doorway. He quickly snatched the lamp that the watchman had left there, then disappeared into the tunnel again.

Joan could see the light approaching. When the walls opened out, Arnau took his hand away from the lantern to give more light. His brother was kneeling a couple of yards from the mouth of the passageway.

'Don't be afraid,' Arnau said, trying to calm him.

He raised the lamp, and the flame rose higher. Where were they . . .? It was a cemetery! They were in a cemetery. A tiny cave which for some reason had survived beneath Santa Maria like an air bubble. The roof was so low they could not stand up. Arnau looked over at several huge amphorae. They looked just like the jars he was used to seeing in Grau's workshop, but more rounded. Some of them were broken, showing the skeletons inside, but others were still intact: big clay vessels cut in half, stacked together and sealed at the top.

Joan was still shaking: he was staring straight at a skeleton.

'It's all right,' Arnau insisted, going over to him.

Joan drew away from him.

'What is—?' Arnau started to ask.

'Let's get out of here,' said Joan, interrupting him.

Without waiting for a reply, he plunged into the tunnel. Arnau followed, and when they reached the boards at the entrance, blew out the lamp. There was no one in sight. He put the lantern back where he had found it and they returned to Pere's house.

'Don't say a word of this to anyone,' he warned Joan on the way. 'Agreed?'

Joan didn't reply.

14

Ever since Arnau had told him that the Virgin was his
mother too, Joan had run to the church whenever he had
a free moment. He would cling to the grille of the Jesus
chapel, push his head in between the railings, and stare
at the stone figure with the child on her shoulder and
boat at her feet.

'One of these days you won't be able to get your head
out,' Father Albert said to him once.

Joan pulled back and smiled at him. The priest ruffled
his hair and knelt down beside him.

'Do you love her?' he asked, pointing inside the
chapel.

Joan hesitated.

'She's my mother now,' he replied, more as a wish than
a certainty.

Father Albert was choked with emotion. How much
he could tell the little boy about Our Lady! He tried to
speak, but the words would not come. He put his arm
round Joan's shoulders until he could safely speak again.

'Do you pray to her?' he asked when he had recovered.

'No. I just talk to her.' Father Albert looked

inquisitively at him. 'Well, I tell her what's been happening to me.'

The priest looked at the Virgin. 'Carry on, my son, carry on,' he said, leaving him at the chapel.

It was not hard. Father Albert considered three or four possible candidates, and finally settled on a rich silversmith. During his last annual confession, the craftsman had seemed very contrite about several adulterous affairs he had been involved in.

'If you really are his mother,' Father Albert muttered, raising his eyes to the heavens, 'you won't hold this little subterfuge against me, will you?'

The silversmith could not say no.

'It's only a small donation to the cathedral school,' the priest told him. 'It will help a child, and God . . . God will thank you for it.'

Now all that was left was to speak to Bernat. Father Albert went to find him.

'I've managed to get a place for Joanet at the cathedral school,' he told him as they walked along the beach near Pere's house.

Bernat turned to look at him. 'I don't have the money for that,' he apologized.

'It won't cost you anything.'

'But I thought that schools . . .'

'Yes, but those are the public ones in the city. For the cathedral school, it's enough . . .' What was the point explaining the details? 'Well, I've seen to that.' The two men continued walking. 'He will learn to read and write, first from hornbooks and then from psalms and prayers.' Why did Bernat not say anything? 'Then when he is thirteen, he can start secondary school. There he will study Latin and the seven liberal arts: grammar, rhetoric, dialectics, arithmetic, geometry, music and astronomy—'

'Father,' Bernat interrupted him, 'Joanet helps out in

the house, and because of that Pere does not charge me for his food. But if the boy goes to school . . .'

'He'll be fed at school.' Bernat looked at him again, and shook his head slowly, as though thinking it over. 'Besides,' the priest went on, 'I've already spoken to Pere, and he's agreed you should pay the same as now.'

'You've done a lot for the boy.'

'Yes, do you mind?' Bernat shook his head, smiling. 'Just imagine if one day Joanet went to university, to the main centre in Lleida, or even to somewhere abroad, like Bologna or Paris . . .'

Bernat burst out laughing. 'If I refused, you'd be really disappointed, wouldn't you?' Father Albert nodded. 'He's not my son, Father,' Bernat added. 'If he were, I wouldn't allow one boy to work for the other, but it's not going to cost me anything, so why not? He deserves it. And perhaps one day he will go to all those places you mentioned.'

'I'd prefer to be with the horses, like you,' Joanet told Arnau as they walked along the same part of the beach where Father Albert and Bernat had decided his future.

'But it's very hard work, Joanet . . . Joan. All I do is clean and polish, and just when I've got everything gleaming, a horse gets taken out and I have to start all over again. That's when Tomàs doesn't come in shouting and throwing a bridle or harness at me for me to see to. On the first day he cuffed me round the ear as well, but my father came in, and . . . oh, you should have seen him! He had a pitchfork, and pinned Tomàs against the wall with it. The tines were pressing into his chest, so he started stammering and begging for forgiveness.'

'That's why I'd like to be with you.'

'Oh, no!' Arnau replied. 'It's true that he hasn't laid a hand on me since then, but he always finds something wrong with what I do. He rubs dirt into things on purpose – I've seen him!'

'Why don't you tell Jesús?'

'Father tells me not to. He says Jesús wouldn't believe me, that Tomàs is his friend, and so he would always take his side. He says the baroness hates us and would use any argument against us. So you see, there you are learning lots of new things at school, while I have to put up with someone deliberately making things dirty and shouting at me.' They both fell silent for a while, kicking sand and staring out to sea. 'Make the most of it, Joan,' Arnau said all of a sudden, repeating the words he had heard Bernat say.

Joan was soon making the most of his classes. He took to them from the day when the priest who taught them congratulated him in front of the whole class. Joan felt an agreeable tingling sensation as the other boys stared at him. If only his mother were still alive! He would immediately run and sit on the crate in the garden and tell her exactly what the priest had said: 'the best', he had called him, and all the others, all of them, had looked at him! He had never been the best at anything before!

That evening, Joan walked home wreathed in a happy cloud. Pere and Mariona listened to him with contented smiles, asking him to repeat clearly phrases the boy thought he had already said, but had only gabbled incomprehensibly in his excitement. When Arnau and Bernat arrived, the three in the house looked towards the door. Joan made as if to rush over to them, but stopped when he caught sight of his brother's face: it was obvious he had been crying. Bernat had a hand on his shoulder, and was holding him close.

'What . . .?' asked Mariona, going up to Arnau to give him a hug.

Bernat held her off with a gesture. 'We have to put up with it,' he said to no one in particular.

Joan tried to catch his brother's gaze, but he was looking at Mariona.

They put up with it. The groom Tomàs did not dare cross Bernat, but he took it out on Arnau.

'He's looking for a fight, son,' Bernat said to calm Arnau when he grew angry again. 'We mustn't fall into the trap.'

'But we can't carry on like this all our lives,' Arnau complained another day.

'We won't. I've heard Jesús warn him several times already. He's not a good worker, and Jesús knows it. The horses in his care are wild: they kick and bite. It won't be long before he's in trouble, my son, it won't be long.'

Bernat was right. The consequences of Tomàs's attitude were soon felt. The baroness was determined that Grau's children should learn to ride. It was acceptable for Grau not to do so, but the two boys had to learn. So several times a week after lessons, Jesús drove Isabel and Margarida in the carriage, and the boys, the tutor and Tomàs the groom walked alongside, the latter leading a horse on a halter. They went out of the city to a small field outside the walls, where each of them in turn had riding lessons from Jesús.

Jesús held a long rope attached to the horse's bit in his right hand, and led the animal round in circles, while in the other he had a whip to control its movements. The young riders climbed on to their mount one after another and circled round the head stableman, listening to his instructions and advice.

That day, from beside the carriage where he was supervising the team, Tomàs stared fixedly at the horse's mouth: all that was needed was a stronger pull than normal, just one. And there was always a moment when the horse took fright.

Genís Puig was astride the mount. Tomàs looked at the boy's face. Panic. He was terrified of horses, and sat stiff as a board. There was always a moment when the horse took fright.

Jesús cracked the whip, urging the horse into a gallop. The horse reared its head and pulled on the rope.

When the leading rein came away from the halter and the horse ran free, Tomàs could not stop himself smiling. He quickly stifled it. It had been easy for him to sneak into the harness room and cut the rope until it hung by a thread.

Isabel and Margarida gave strangled cries. Jesús dropped the leading rein and tried to stop the horse. It was no use.

When he saw the rope fall away, Genís started to shriek, and clung to the horse's neck. This meant that his feet and legs dug into his mount's flanks, which spurred it into a full gallop. It headed straight for the city gate, with the boy still hanging on desperately. When the horse leapt over a small mound, he was thrown off into the air, landed hard, then rolled on the ground until he came to rest in a clump of bushes.

Bernat was in the stables. The first he heard was the thunder of horses' hooves on the cobblestones, and then the baroness shouting. Instead of walking in quietly as they usually did, the horses clattered across the yard. Bernat went out to look, and came across Tomàs leading in the horse. It was in a lather, panting heavily through its nostrils.

'What . . .?' Bernat started to ask.

'The baroness wants to see your son,' Tomàs shouted, hitting the animal's side.

The baroness's shrieks could still be heard outside the stables. Bernat looked pityingly at the horse, which was pawing the ground.

'The mistress wants to see you,' Tomàs shouted again as Arnau came out of the harness room.

Arnau looked at his father, who merely shrugged.

They went out into the yard. The baroness was livid, waving the whip she always took when she went riding, and shouting at Jesús, the tutor and all the slaves who had come out to see what was going on. Margarida and Josep were still hanging behind. Genís stood next to her, dirty, bleeding and with torn clothes. As soon as Arnau and Bernat appeared, the baroness strode towards the boy and slashed his face with her whip. Arnau lifted his hand to his mouth and cheek. Bernat darted forward, but Jesús stepped in between them.

'Look at this,' the head stableman roared, showing him the severed rope. 'This is your son's work!'

Bernat took the rope and the halter and examined them. Hands still to his face, Arnau looked at them as well. He had checked them the previous day. He peered up at his father just as he in turn was glancing towards the stable door, where Tomàs was observing the scene.

'It was fine,' Arnau shouted, picking up the rope and halter and shaking them in Jesús's face. He glanced at the stable door again. 'It was fine,' he repeated, as the first tears welled in his eyes.

'Look at him cry,' a voice suddenly said. Margarida was pointing at Arnau. 'He's the one to blame for your accident, and now he's crying,' she added to her brother Genís. 'You didn't cry when you fell off the horse because of him,' she lied.

Josep and Genís were slow to react, but then they too joined in making fun of Arnau.

'That's right, cry, little girl,' one of them said.

'Yes, go on, cry,' repeated the other.

Arnau saw them pointing at him and laughing. He could not stop crying! The tears ran down his cheeks and his chest heaved as he sobbed. He stretched out his arms to show everyone, including the slaves, what had happened to the rope and the halter.

'Instead of crying, you should say you're sorry for your

carelessness,' the baroness chided him, smiling broadly at her stepchildren.

Say he was sorry? Arnau looked at his father, a puzzled look on his face. Bernat was staring at the baroness. Margarida was still pointing at him and sniggering with her brothers.

'No,' he objected. 'It was fine,' he added, throwing the rope and halter on to the ground.

The baroness began to wave her arms in the air, but stopped when she saw Bernat take a step towards her. Jesús caught Bernat by the elbow.

'She is a noblewoman,' he whispered in his ear.

Arnau looked at them all, then ran out.

'No!' shouted Isabel when Grau said he would get rid of father and son after he learnt what had happened. 'I want the father to stay here, working for your sons. I want him to be aware at all times we are waiting for his son to apologize. I want that boy to apologize publicly in front of your children. And that won't happen if you get rid of them. Tell the father that his son cannot come back to work until he has said he is sorry . . .' Isabel was shrieking and waving her arms. 'Tell him he will only receive half his wage until that happens, and that if he looks for other work we'll make everyone in Barcelona aware of what happened here, so that he won't be able to make a living. I want an apology!'

We'll make all of Barcelona aware . . . Grau could feel the hair on his body prickle. All those years trying to keep his brother-in-law hidden, and now . . . now his wife wanted the whole of Barcelona to hear of him!

'Be discreet, I beg you.' He could think of nothing else to say.

Isabel looked at him, her eyes bloodshot with rage. 'I want them humiliated!'

Grau was about to say something, but thought better

of it, and pursed his lips. 'Discretion, Isabel, that's what we need,' was all he said.

Grau gave in to his wife's demands. After all, Guiamona was no longer alive; there were no more birthmarks in the family, and they were all known as Puig rather than Estanyol. When Grau left the stables Bernat listened with narrowed eyes as the stableman told him of the new conditions.

'Father, there was nothing wrong with that halter,' Arnau complained that night when the three of them were back in the small room they shared. 'I swear it!' he said, when Bernat said nothing.

'But you can't prove it,' Joan butted in. He had already heard what had happened.

You don't need to swear it, thought Bernat, but how can I explain to you . . .? He remembered how horrified he had been at his son's reaction in Grau's stables: 'I'm not to blame, so there's nothing I need to apologize for.'

'Father,' Arnau repeated, 'I swear to you . . .'

'But—'

Bernat told Joan to be quiet. 'I believe you, son. But now, to bed with you.'

'But—' This time it was Arnau who protested.

'To bed!'

Arnau and Joan blew out their candles, but Bernat had to wait long into the night until he heard the rhythmic breathing that told him they were fast asleep. How could he possibly tell his son the family was demanding a public apology?

'Arnau . . .' His voice shook when he saw his son stop dressing and glance over at him. 'Grau . . . Grau wants you to apologize; unless you do . . .' Arnau looked at him inquisitively. 'Unless you do, he will not allow you back in the stables.'

He had not even finished speaking when he saw his boy's eyes take on a seriousness he had never seen before. Bernat looked towards Joan, who had also stopped dressing and stood there open-mouthed. Bernat tried to speak again, but the words would not come.

'Well then?' asked Joan, breaking the silence.

'Do you think I should apologize?'

'Arnau, I gave up everything I had for you to be free. Although they had belonged to the Estanyol family for centuries, I left our lands so that nobody could do to you what they had done to me, to my father and my father's father . . . and now we're back in the same situation, at the mercy of people who call themselves noble. But there's a big difference: we can say no. My son, learn to use the freedom it's cost us so much to win. You and only you can decide.'

'But what would you advise, Father?'

Bernat was silent for a moment.

'If I were you I wouldn't give in.'

Joan tried to have his say. 'They are no more than Catalan barons! Only the Lord can grant true forgiveness.'

'How will we live?' asked Arnau.

'Don't worry about that, son. I have some money saved that we can use. And we'll find somewhere else to work. Grau Puig is not the only man with horses.'

Bernat did not let a single day go by. That same evening, once his work was finished, he started to look for another job for him and Arnau. He found a nobleman's house with stables where the stableman was happy to see him. There were many in Barcelona who were jealous of the care Grau's horses received, and when Bernat explained that he was the person responsible, the man was keen to take both of them on. But the next day, when Bernat returned to the stables to confirm something he had already celebrated with his sons, they did not even receive him. 'They were not offering enough money,' he lied that night over supper. Bernat tried in several other households that kept horses, but just when it seemed they were happy to take them on, by the next day the situation had changed completely.

'You won't find any work,' a stable hand finally told him when he saw the desperation in Bernat's face as he stared down at the cobbles of the umpteenth stable that refused him. 'The baroness will not permit it,' the man explained. 'After you came to see us, my master received a message from the baroness begging him not to give you employment. I'm sorry.'

'Bastard,' he whispered in his ear in a low but steady voice, drawing out the vowels. Tomàs the groom jumped and tried to get away, but Bernat grabbed him by the neck from behind and squeezed until he was almost bent double. Only then did he relax the pressure. If all the nobles are getting messages, Bernat had thought, it's because someone is following me. 'Let me go out through another door,' he had begged the stableman. Tomàs, who was keeping watch on a street corner opposite the stables, did not see him leave. Bernat came up behind him. 'You tampered with the halter so it would give way, didn't you? And now what do you want?' He pressed down on the groom's neck once more.

'What . . . what does it matter?' Tomàs said, gasping for breath.

'What do you mean?' said Bernat, tightening his grip. The groom thrashed his arms in the air, but could not break free. A few moments later, Bernat could feel Tomàs's body go limp. He let go of his neck and turned him round. 'What did you mean by that?' he asked again.

Tomàs took several deep gulps of air before answering. As soon as the colour returned to his cheeks, he smiled a mocking smile. 'Kill me if you like,' he said, still panting for breath, 'but you know very well that if it hadn't been the halter, it would have been something else. The baroness hates you, and always will. You are nothing more than a runaway serf, and your son is the son of a runaway. You will never find work in Barcelona: those are the baroness's orders, and if it's not me, it will be someone else who spies on you.'

Bernat spat in his face. Not only did Tomàs not move, but his smile broadened.

'You have no option, Bernat Estanyol. Your son will have to beg for forgiveness.'

'I'll do it,' Arnau said wearily that night, fists clenched as he fought back tears after listening to his father's account. 'We can't fight the nobles, and we have to work. The swine! They're all swines!'

Bernat looked at his son. *We'll be free there*, he remembered promising him a few months after his birth, when they had first set eyes on Barcelona. Was this what he had struggled so hard for?

'No, my son. Wait. We'll find another—'

'They're the ones who give the orders, Father. The nobles are in charge. In the countryside, in our lands, here in the city.'

Joan looked on in silence. 'You must obey and submit yourselves to your princes,' his teachers had taught him. 'Man will find freedom in the Kingdom of God, not in this one.'

'They can't control the whole of Barcelona. The nobles may be the ones who have horses, but we can learn some other trade. We'll find something.'

Bernat saw a gleam of hope appear in his son's eyes. They widened as if he were trying to absorb strength from his father's words. 'I promised you freedom, Arnau. I must give it you, and I will. Don't give up so quickly, little one.'

Over the next few days, Bernat roamed the streets in search of freedom. At first, once he had finished his work in Grau's stables, Tomàs followed him, without even bothering to keep hidden. Soon, though, he stopped spying on him: the baroness understood she had no influence over artisans, small traders or builders.

'It'll be hard for him to find anything,' Grau tried to re-assure his wife when she came to complain about the peasant's attitude.

'Why do you say that?' she asked him.

'Because he won't find work. Barcelona is suffering the consequences of a lack of planning.' The baroness urged him to continue; Grau was never wrong in his judgements. 'The last few years' harvests have been disastrous,' he explained. 'There are too many people in the country-side, so what little they do harvest never reaches the cities. They eat it all themselves.'

'But Catalonia is big,' said the baroness.

'Make no mistake, my dear. Catalonia may be big, but for many years now the peasants have not grown cereals, which is what is needed. Nowadays they produce linen, grapes, olives or dried fruit, but not cereals. The change has made their lords rich, and we merchants have done very well out of it too, but the situation is becoming impossible. Until now we've been able to eat grain from Sicily and Sardinia, but the war with Genoa has put a stop to that. Bernat will not find work, but all of us, we nobles included, are going to face problems. And all because of a few useless noblemen . . .'

'How can you talk like that?' the baroness cut in, feeling herself under attack.

'Look at it this way, my love.' Grau was serious in his attempt to explain. 'We earn our livelihood from trade, and we've done very well out of it. We invest part of what we earn in our own businesses. We don't use the same ships as we had ten years ago, and that's why we go on making money. But the noble landowners have not invested a thing in their lands or their working methods: they are still using the same implements and techniques as the Romans did. The Romans! They should let their fields lie fallow every two or three years; that way they could produce two or three times as much as they do. But those noble landlords you are so keen to defend never think of the future; all they want is easy money. They are the ones who will be the ruin of Catalonia.'

'Things can't be as bad as all that,' the baroness insisted.

'Have you any idea how much a sack of wheat costs?' When his wife made no reply, Grau shook his head and went on: 'Close to a hundred shillings. Do you know what the normal price is?' This time, he did not wait for an answer. 'Ten shillings unground, sixteen ground. So a sack has increased tenfold in price!'

'What will we eat then?' his wife asked, unable to conceal her preoccupation.

'You don't understand. We'll still be able to buy wheat . . . if there is any, because there could come a moment when it runs out – if we haven't got there already. The problem is that whereas wheat has gone up ten times in price, ordinary people are still receiving the same wages—'

'So we will have wheat,' his wife butted in.

'Yes, but—'

'And Bernat will not be able to find work.'

'I don't think so, but . . .'

'Well, that's all that matters to me,' the baroness said. With that, she turned her back on him, weary of listening to all his explanations.

'. . . something terrible is brewing,' Grau said, but his wife could no longer hear.

A bad year. Bernat was tired of hearing that excuse time and again. Wherever he tried to find work, the bad year was to blame. 'I've had to lay off half my apprentices: how can I offer you work?' one artisan told him. 'This is a bad year, I can't even feed my children,' said another. 'Haven't you heard?' a third man told him. This is a bad year; I've had to spend half my savings just to feed my family. Normally a twentieth would have been enough.' How could I not have heard? Bernat thought, but went on searching until winter and the cold weather came on. By then there were some places where he did not even dare ask. The children went hungry; their parents did not eat so they could give them something; and smallpox, typhus and diphtheria began to make their deadly appearance.

Arnau looked into Bernat's money bag when his father was at work. At first he checked it each week, but soon looked every day, often more than once. He could clearly see that their reserves were rapidly being eaten up.

'What is the price of freedom?' he asked Joan one day as they were both praying to the Virgin.

'Saint Gregory says that at the beginning all men were born equal and were therefore free.' Joan spoke in a quiet, steady voice as though repeating a lesson. 'But it was those men who had been born free who for their own good chose to submit to a lord who would take care of them. They lost part of their freedom, but gained a lord who would take care of them.'

Arnau listened to him, staring intently at the Virgin's statue. *Why don't you smile for me? Saint Gregory . . . Whenever did Saint Gregory have an empty purse like my father's?*

'Joan.'

'What is it?'

'What do you think I should do?'

'It's your decision.'

'But what do you think?'

'I've already told you. It was the free men who decided they wanted a lord to take care of them.'

That same day, without telling his father, Arnau presented himself at Grau Puig's mansion. In order not to be seen from the stables, he slipped in through the kitchen. There he found Estranya, as huge as ever, as if hunger had made no mark on her. She was busy with a pot over the fire.

'Tell your masters I've come to see them,' he told her when the cook noticed him.

A blank smile spread across the slave's face. She went to tell Grau's steward, who informed his master. Arnau was kept waiting for hours, standing in the kitchen. Everyone in Grau's service filed past to take a look at him. Most of them smiled, although a few looked sad at his capitulation. Arnau met all their gazes, responding defiantly to those who mocked him, but he was unable to wipe the smiles from their faces.

The only person who did not appear was Bernat, although Tomàs the groom had made sure he knew his son had come to apologize. 'I'm sorry, Arnau, so sorry,' Bernat muttered over and over to himself as he brushed down one of the horses.

After many hours, with aching legs – Arnau had tried to sit down, but Estranya had prevented him from doing so – he was led into the main room of Grau's house. He did not even notice how richly it was appointed: his eyes immediately went to the five members of the family waiting for him at the far end of the room. The baron and his wife were seated; his three cousins stood beside them. The men wore brightly coloured silk stockings with jerkins and gold belts; the women's robes were adorned with pearls and precious stones.

The steward led Arnau to the centre of the room, a few feet from the family. Then he returned to the doorway, where Grau had told him to wait.

'What brings you here?' Grau asked, stiff and distant as ever.

'I've come to ask your forgiveness.'

'Well, do so then,' Grau ordered him.

Arnau was about to speak, but the baroness interrupted him.

'Is that how you propose to ask for forgiveness? Standing up?'

Arnau hesitated for a moment, but finally sank down on one knee. Margarida's silly giggle echoed round the room.

'I beg forgiveness from you all,' Arnau intoned, his eyes fixed on the baroness.

She looked straight through him.

I'm only doing this for my father. Arnau stared back at her defiantly. *Trollop.*

'Our feet!' the baroness shrieked. 'Kiss our feet!' Arnau tried to stand again, but she stopped him. 'On your knees!' she crowed.

Arnau obeyed, and shuffled over to them. *Only for my father. Only for my father. Only for my father . . .* The baroness put forward her silk slippers, and Arnau kissed them, first the left one, then the right. Without looking up, he moved on to Grau. When he saw the boy kneeling at his feet, Grau hesitated, but then he noticed his wife staring furiously at him, he raised his feet in turn up to the boy's mouth. Arnau's boy cousins did the same as their father. When Arnau tried to kiss Margarida's silk slipper, she jerked it away and started giggling once more. Arnau tried again, and she did the same. Finally, he waited for her to lift the slipper to his mouth . . . first one . . . then the other.

15

Bernat counted the money Grau had paid him. He growled as he dropped it into his purse. It ought to be enough, but . . . those cursed Genoese! When would they end their siege against the principality? Barcelona was going hungry.

Bernat tied the bag to his belt and went to find Arnau. The boy was undernourished. Bernat looked at him anxiously. A hard winter. At least they had got through the winter. How many others could say the same? Bernat drew his mouth into a tight line, stroked his son's hair, then let his hand fall on his shoulder. How many in Barcelona had died from the cold, hunger or disease? How many fathers could still rest their hands on their sons' shoulders? At least you're alive, he thought.

That day a grain ship, one of the few that had succeeded in evading the Genoese blockade, arrived in the port of Barcelona. The cereals were bought by the city itself at exorbitant prices, to be resold to the inhabitants for more accessible sums. That Friday there was wheat in Plaça del Blat, and people had started congregating there since first light. They were already fighting to see how the official measurers were going to divide the stocks.

For a few months now, despite the best efforts of the city councillors to silence him, a Carmelite friar had been preaching against the rich and powerful. He blamed them for the food shortages and accused them of keeping wheat hidden away. The friar's diatribes had struck a chord among the faithful. The rumours about the hidden wheat spread throughout the city. That was why this particular Friday people were crowding noisily into Plaça del Blat, arguing and pushing their way forward to the tables where city officials were weighing the grain.

The authorities had calculated how much wheat there was for each inhabitant, and put the cloth merchant Pere Juyol, the official inspector for Plaça del Blat, in charge of supervising its sale.

'Mestre doesn't have a family,' came the cry a few minutes later as a ragged-looking man with an even more ragged child stepped up to the table. 'They all died over the winter.'

The weighers took back the grain from Mestre, but this was just the start: one man had sent his son to another table; another had already had his share; a third had no family; that is not his son, he's only brought him to get more . . .

The square became a hive buzzing with rumours. People abandoned the queues, started to argue and were soon swapping insults. Someone shouted that the authorities should put the wheat they were hiding on public sale; the crowd backed him. The officials found they could no longer control the swarm of people pushing and shoving round the tables. The King's stewards began to confront the hungry mob, and it was only a quick decision by Pere Juyol that saved the situation. He ordered the grain be taken to the magistrate's palace at the eastern side of the square, and suspended all sales that morning.

Frustrated in their attempts to buy the precious grain, Bernat and Arnau went back to work at Grau's mansion. In the yard outside the stables they told the head stableman and anyone else who cared to listen what had happened in Plaça del Blat. Neither of them was slow to accuse the authorities, or to complain how hungry they were.

The noise brought the baroness to one of the windows overlooking the yard. She was delighted at the sufferings of the runaway serf and his shameless son. As she looked down on them, a smile spread across her face: she recalled the instructions Grau had given her before he left on a journey. Hadn't he told her his prisoners must eat?

The baroness picked up the bag of money reserved for buying food for those prisoners who were in gaol for debts they owed Grau. She called the steward and ordered him to entrust the task to Bernat Estanyol. His son Arnau was to go with him in case of trouble.

'Don't forget to tell them that this money is to buy food for my husband's prisoners,' she said.

The steward carried out his mistress's orders. He too enjoyed the look of disbelief on their faces, which grew greater still when Bernat felt the weight of coins in his hand.

'This is for the prisoners?' Arnau asked his father as they set off to carry out the order.

'Yes.'

'Why for the prisoners?'

'They're in gaol because they owe Grau money, but he is obliged to pay for their food.'

'What if he didn't?'

They went on walking down towards the beach.

'Then they would be set free. That's the last thing Grau

192

wants. He pays the royal taxes, he pays for the prison governor, and he pays for his prisoners' food. That's the law.'

'But . . .'

'Just leave it, my lad.'

They walked on in silence back to their house.

That evening, Arnau and Bernat went to the gaol to fulfil their strange task. They had heard from Joan, who had to cross the square on his way back from the cathedral school, that feelings were still running high. Even in Carrer de la Mar, which ran from Santa Maria up to the square, they could hear the crowd shouting. People were thronging round the magistrate's palace, where the grain that had been withdrawn from sale that morning was being stored. It was also here that Grau's prisoners were kept.

The crowd wanted wheat, and the city authorities did not have enough people to distribute it in an orderly way. The five councillors met the magistrate to try to find a solution.

'Everyone should take a solemn oath,' said one of them. 'If they don't swear, they won't get any grain. Every person who buys must swear that they need the amount they are asking for to feed their family, and nothing more.'

'Do you think that will work?' another councillor said doubtfully.

'The oath is sacred!' the first one retorted. 'Don't people swear oaths for contracts, to claim their innocence, or to fulfil their duties? Don't they go to Saint Felix's altar to swear on the holy sacraments?'

They announced their decision from a balcony in the magistrate's palace. Word spread to those who had not heard the proclamation, and the devout Christians clamoured to swear their oath . . . yet again, as they had done so often in their lives.

The wheat was brought out into the square again. The crowd's hunger was plain to see. Some people took the oath, but soon arguments, shouting and scuffles broke out again. The crowd grew angry and started to demand the wheat that the Carmelite friar had told them the authorities were hiding.

Arnau and Bernat were still at the end of Carrer de la Mar, at the opposite side of the square to the magistrate's palace, where the wheat was being sold. All round them, the crowd was shouting and protesting.

'Father,' asked Arnau, 'will there be any wheat left for us?'

'I believe so,' said Bernat, trying not to look at his son. How could there be any left for them? There was not enough wheat for a quarter of the citizens demanding it.

'Father,' Arnau insisted, 'why are the prisoners guaranteed food when we're not?'

Bernat pretended he had not heard his son's question above all the uproar, but could not help glancing down at him. He was starving: his legs and arms were like sticks, and his eyes, which had once been so carefree and joyous, now stood out from his gaunt face.

'Father, did you hear me?'

Yes, thought Bernat, but what can I tell you? That we poor are united by hunger? That only the rich can eat? That only the rich can allow themselves the luxury of keeping their debtors? That we poor mean nothing to them? That the children of the poor are worth less than even one of the prisoners being held in the magistrate's palace? Bernat said nothing.

'There's wheat in the palace!' he shouted, adding his voice to the clamour of the crowd. 'There's wheat in the palace!' he yelled even louder when those around him fell silent and turned to stare at him. Soon many of them had noticed this man who was insisting that there was grain in the magistrate's palace. 'If there wasn't, how could they feed the prisoners?' he cried, holding up Grau's money bag. 'The nobles and the rich pay for the prisoners' food! Where do the prison governors get the wheat for their prisoners? Do they have to buy it like us?'

The crowd gave way to let Bernat through. He was beside himself. Arnau rushed after him, trying to catch his attention.

'What are you doing, Father?'

'Do the governors have to take an oath like we do?'

'What's wrong with you, Father?'

'Where do the governors get the wheat for the prisoners from? Why isn't there enough for our children, when the prisoners get plenty?'

Bernat's words inflamed the crowd still further. This time the officials were unable to withdraw the supplies as the mob engulfed them. Pere Juyol and the city magistrate were about to be lynched, and were only saved by some soldiers who ran to their defence and then escorted them back inside the palace.

Few managed to satisfy their needs. The wheat was spilt across the square, and trodden on and wasted by the mob. Those who tried to scoop it up risked being trampled on as well.

Somebody shouted that the city councillors were to blame. The crowd rushed off to drag them out of their houses.

Bernat joined in this collective madness, bawling as loud as anyone and allowing himself to be carried away on the tide of enraged citizens.

'Father, Father!'

Bernat looked down at his son. 'What are you doing here?' he asked, still striding along and yelling at the top of his voice.

'I . . . What has happened to you, Father?'

'Get away from here. This is no place for children.'

'Where should I . . .?'

'Here, take this.' Bernat handed him two money bags: his own and the one for the prisoners.

'What am I to do with these?' asked Arnau.

'Go home, son, go home.'

Arnau saw his father disappear in the midst of the crowd. The last thing he saw of him was the glint of hatred in his eyes.

'Where are you going, Father?' he shouted after him.

'In search of freedom,' said a woman who was standing nearby, also watching the mob swarming through the streets of the city.

'But we're already free,' ventured Arnau.

'There is no freedom where there is hunger, my lad,' the woman declared.

In tears, Arnau fought his way through the rushing crowd.

The disturbances lasted two entire days. The homes of the councillors and many other noble residences were sacked. The enraged crowd went round the city, at first in search of food . . . and then in search of vengeance.

For two whole days the city of Barcelona was submerged in chaos. The authorities were powerless to stop it, until an envoy from King Alfonso arrived with sufficient soldiers to put an end to the violence. A hundred men were arrested, and many others fined. Of the hundred, ten were hanged after the briefest of trials. Among those called to testify, there were few who did not point to Bernat Estanyol, with the birthmark over his right eye, as one of the instigators of the citizens' revolt in Plaça del Blat.

16

Arnau ran the length of Carrer de la Mar to Pere's house without glancing at Santa Maria even once. His father's eyes were engraved on his mind; his shouts echoed in his ears. He had never seen him like that before. What's happened to you, Father? Is it true as that woman said that we are not free? He rushed into Pere's house without paying heed to anyone or anything, and shut himself in his room. Joan found him there, sobbing.

'The city has gone mad,' he said, opening the door. 'What's wrong?'

Arnau did not answer. His brother looked round the room.

'Where's Father?'

Arnau choked back his tears, and pointed back up into the city.

'Is he with them?'

'Yes,' Arnau managed to stutter.

Joan recalled the rioting he had been forced to avoid on his way back from the bishop's palace. The soldiers had sealed off the Jewry and were standing guard outside the gates to keep out the mob, who had turned their attention to looting the houses of rich Christians. How could Bernat be with them? Images of groups of enraged people battering down doors and emerging with armfuls of possessions filled Joan's mind. There was no way that Bernat could be one of them.

'It can't be,' he said out loud. Arnau looked up at him from the pallet. 'Father is not like the others . . . How can it be possible?'

'I don't know. There were lots of people. They were all shouting . . .'

'But . . . Father? Father couldn't do things like that. Perhaps he was just . . . trying to find someone?'

Arnau stared at Joan. *How can I tell you it was he who was shouting the loudest, who was leading the others on? How can I tell you when I don't believe it myself?* 'I don't know, Joan. There were a lot of people.'

'They are stealing, Arnau! They're attacking the city aldermen!'

Arnau's look silenced him.

That night the two boys waited in vain for their father to return. The next day, Joan got ready for school.

'You shouldn't go,' Arnau advised him.

Now it was Joan's turn to silence him with a look.

'King Alfonso's soldiers have put an end to the revolt,' was Joan's only comment when he came back that evening.

But Bernat did not return to sleep that night either.

The next morning, Joan said goodbye to Arnau once more. 'You ought to get out of the house,' he said.

'What if Father comes home?' said Arnau, his voice choking with emotion.

The two brothers hugged each other. *Where are you, Father?*

It was Pere who went out in search of news. It was

easier to find out what had happened than it was to make his way back home.

'I'm sorry, my lad,' he told Arnau. 'Your father has been arrested.'

'Where is he?'

'In the magistrate's palace, but—'

Before he could finish, Arnau had run out of the door. Pere looked at his wife and shook his head. The old woman buried her face in her hands.

'They held summary trials,' Pere explained. 'Lots of witnesses recognized Bernat because of his birthmark, and swore he was one of the leaders of the rising. Why did he do it? He seemed—'

'Because he has two children to feed,' his wife interrupted him, tears in her eyes.

'Because he had . . .' Pere said wearily. 'He has already been hanged along with nine others in Plaça del Blat.'

Mariona raised her hands to her face again, but then suddenly dropped them. 'Arnau . . .' she exclaimed, heading for the door. Her husband's words brought her to a halt.

'Let him go. From today he's no longer a boy.'

Mariona nodded. Pere went over and held her in his arms.

By order of the King, the executions were carried out immediately. There was not even time to build a scaffold, and so the prisoners were hanged from carts.

Arnau stopped running as soon as he got to Plaça del Blat. He was panting, out of breath. The square was full of silent people standing with their backs to him, staring at . . . Above their heads, next to the palace, hung ten lifeless bodies.

'No . . .! Father!'

His anguished cry echoed round the square. Hundreds of heads turned towards him. Arnau walked slowly through the crowd, which pulled back to let him through. He searched the ten deadfaces . . .

'At least let me go and tell the priest,' Pere's wife pleaded.
'I've already told him. He must be there by now.'

When he identified his father, Arnau vomited. The people around him jumped back. The boy took another look at the swollen purplish-black face, tilted to one side, with its contorted features and eyes that would now fight for all eternity to burst from their sockets. His tongue lolled lifelessly from the corner of his mouth. The second and third times he looked, all Arnau brought up was bile.

He felt a hand on his shoulder.

'We should go, my boy,' said Father Albert.

The priest tried to pull him in the direction of Santa Maria, but Arnau would not move. He looked over again at his father, and shut his eyes. He would never be hungry again. Arnau trembled like a leaf. Father Albert tried again to pull him away from the macabre scene.

'Leave me, Father, please.'

With the priest and the others in the square looking on, Arnau ran unsteadily over to the improvised gallows. He was clutching his stomach and was still shaking all over. When he reached his father, he turned towards one of the soldiers standing guard beside the bodies. 'Can I take him down?' he asked.

Faced with the boy's insistent gaze from below his father's body, the soldier hesitated. What would his own children have done if he had been hanged?

'No,' he had to tell him. If only he could have been somewhere else! He would have preferred to be fighting a band of Moors, or to be with his children. What kind of death was this? The hanged man had simply been fighting for his children, for this boy begging him with his eyes, like everyone else in the square. Where was the city magistrate? 'The magistrate has ordered that they be left hanging in the square for three days.'

'I'll wait.'

'After that they are to be placed above the city gates, like everyone executed in Barcelona, so that anyone passing by will heed the laws.'

With that, the soldier turned his back on Arnau and continued his patrol round the hanged bodies.

'Hunger,' he heard behind him. 'He was only hungry.'

When his futile patrol brought him back alongside Bernat's body, the boy was sitting on the ground beneath him, head in hands, crying. The soldier hardly dared look at him.

'Come with me, Arnau,' said the priest, who had joined him again.

Arnau shook his head. Father Albert was about to say something, but a sudden shout silenced him. The families of the other victims were arriving in the square. Mothers, wives, children and brothers flocked round the hanged men. They were silent except for the occasional howl of grief. The soldier went on his way again, trying to remember the war-cries of the heathen foe. Joan, who had to pass through the square on his way home, saw the terrible spectacle and fainted immediately, before he had even noticed Arnau, who still sat in the same spot, rocking himself back and forth. Joan's schoolmates picked him up and took him into the bishop's palace. Arnau did not see his brother either.

The hours went by. Arnau was oblivious to the comings and goings of townspeople visiting the square out of a sense of pity, or morbid curiosity. Only the sound of the soldier's boots pacing up and down seemed to bring him out of himself.

Arnau, I gave up everything I had for you to be free. Although they had belonged to the Estanyol family for centuries, I left our lands so that nobody could do to you what

*they had done to me, to my father and my father's father . . .
and now we're back in the same situation, at the mercy of people
who call themselves noble. But there's a big difference: we can
say no. My son, learn to use the freedom it's cost us so much to
win. You and only you can decide . . . If I were you I wouldn't
give in.* When had his father said that? Not long ago.

Is it true we can refuse, Father? The soldier's boots
passed in front of his eyes once more. *Where there is
hunger there is no freedom. You aren't hungry any more,
Father. What about our freedom?*

'Take a good look at them, children.'

That voice . . .

'They are criminals. Take a good look.' For the first
time, Arnau lifted his head and looked at the people who
had come to see the hanged men. The baroness and her
three stepchildren were peering at Bernat Estanyol's
contorted features. Arnau stared first at Margarida's feet,
then at her face. His cousins had gone pale, but the
baroness was smiling, and looking directly at him. Arnau
got shakily to his feet. 'They didn't deserve to be citizens
of Barcelona,' he heard Isabel say. He dug his fingers into
the palms of his hands; he flushed and felt his bottom
lip start to tremble. The baroness was still smiling. 'What
else could one expect from a runaway serf?'

Arnau was about to throw himself at the baroness. But
the soldier moved to intercept him.

'Is something wrong, my lad?' The soldier followed
Arnau's gaze. 'I wouldn't do it, if I were you,' he
warned. Arnau tried to get round him, but the soldier
grabbed his elbow. Isabel was no longer smiling, but
stood there stiffly arrogant, challenging him to attack
her. 'I wouldn't do it, if I were you. That would be the
end of you,' Arnau heard the man say. He looked up at
him. 'Your father is dead,' the soldier insisted. 'You aren't.
Sit down again.' The soldier could feel Arnau stop straining against him. 'Sit down,' he repeated.

Arnau gave way, and the soldier stood beside him.

'Take a good look at them, children,' said the baroness again, the smile back on her face. 'We'll come here again tomorrow. The hanged men will be here until they rot, just like all runaway criminals should be left to rot.'

Arnau could feel his lower lip tremble uncontrollably. He stared at the Puig family until the baroness decided to turn her back on him.

Some day . . . some day I'll see you dead . . . I'll see you all dead, he promised himself. Arnau's hatred pursued the baroness and her stepchildren across Plaça del Blat. She had said she would be back the next day. Arnau looked up at his father's body.

I swear to God they will never rejoice again at the sight of you, but what can I do? He saw the soldier's boots pass in front of his face once more. *Father, I won't allow your body to rot here on the end of a rope.*

Arnau spent several hours trying to think how he could remove his father's corpse, but all his plans came up against the boots marching past him. He could not even get Bernat down without being seen: at night they were bound to have torches lit . . . torches lit . . . torches lit? At that precise moment he saw Joan come into the square. White as a sheet, with bloodshot eyes swollen from tears, his brother wearily came across to him. Arnau stood up and Joan flung himself into his arms.

'Arnau . . . I . . .' he stuttered.

'Listen to me,' Arnau said, still clinging to him. 'Keep on crying.' I couldn't stop if I wanted to, thought Joan, surprised at the tone of his brother's voice. 'Tonight at ten o'clock I want you to hide on the corner of Carrer de la Mar and the square. Make sure nobody sees you. Bring . . . bring a blanket. The biggest one you can find at Pere's house. Now, go home.'

'But—'

'Go home, Joan. I don't want the soldiers to get a good look at you.'

Arnau had to push his brother away from him. Joan stared first at his brother's face, then up at their father's body. He started shaking with sobs.

'Go home, Joan.'

That night, when the only people left in the square were the relatives grouped underneath the swinging corpses, there was a change of guard. The new soldiers stopped patrolling round the bodies, and instead sat by a fire they had lit at one end of the line of carts. Everything was quiet in the cool of the night. Arnau stood up and walked past the soldiers, trying to conceal his features.

'I'm going to get a blanket,' he told them.

One of them glanced across at him.

He crossed Plaça del Blat to the corner of Carrer de la Mar. He stood there a few moments, wondering what had happened to Joan. It was ten o'clock: where had he got to? Arnau called out softly. Silence.

'Joan?' he whispered.

A shadow emerged from a doorway opposite.

'Arnau?' he heard in the darkness.

'Of course it's me.' Joan's sigh of relief was clearly audible. 'Who did you think it was? Why didn't you answer me at first?'

'It's very dark,' was Joan's only reply.

'Have you brought the blanket?' The shadowy figure lifted a bundle. 'Good. I've already told them I was going to fetch one. I want you to wrap it round you, and go and take my place. Walk on tiptoe so you look taller.'

'What are you planning to do?'

'I'm going to burn him,' Arnau said when Joan was beside him. 'I want you to take my place. I want the soldiers to think you're me. All you have to do is sit underneath . . . sit where I was, and do nothing. Just keep your face concealed, and don't move. Whatever you see, whatever happens, don't move. Is that clear?' He did not wait for Joan to answer. 'When it's all over, you will be me. You'll be Arnau Estanyol, your father's only son. Do you understand that? If the soldiers ask . . .'

'Arnau.'

'What is it?'

'I can't do it.'

'Wh . . . what?'

'I can't do it. They'll find me out. When I see our father—'

'Do you prefer to see him rot? Do you prefer to see him hanging at the city gate for the crows and worms to devour his body?'

Arnau waited, giving his brother time to imagine the scene for himself.

'Do you want the baroness to go on mocking him even after his death?'

'Isn't this a sin?' Joan suddenly asked.

Arnau tried to catch his brother's features in the darkness, but could only see a shadow. 'His only crime was to be hungry! I don't know if this is a sin, but I will not let our father's body rot, dangling from a rope. I'm going to do it. If you want to help, wrap yourself in that blanket and sit still. If you don't . . .'

At that, Arnau headed off down Carrer de la Mar, while Joan walked across Plaça del Blat. He wrapped the blanket round himself and stared up at Bernat: one ghost among ten dangling from the carts, dimly lit by the glow from the bonfire the soldiers had made. Joan did not want to see his face. He did not want to have to look at his purple, lolling tongue, but despite himself he found he could not take his eyes off Bernat. The soldiers watched as he approached.

Arnau ran to Pere's house. He found his waterskin and poured the contents out. Then he filled it with the oil

205

from the lamps. Sitting by the hearth in their kitchen, Pere and his wife looked on.

'I don't exist,' he told them in a faint voice. He took Mariona's hand as she gazed affectionately at him. 'Joan is to be me. My father only had one son . . . Take care of him if anything happens.'

'But Arnau—' Pere started to say.

'Shhh!' hissed Arnau.

'What are you going to do?' the old man insisted.

'What I have to,' said Arnau, getting up.

I don't exist. I am Arnau Estanyol. The soldiers were still watching him. Burning a body must be a sin, thought Joan. Bernat was staring at him! Joan came to a halt a few paces from the hanged man. No, it was just Arnau who had put that idea in his head.

'You there, is something wrong?' said one of the soldiers, making to stand up.

'No, nothing,' Joan replied. He walked forward again, towards the dead eyes that seemed to follow him everywhere.

Arnau picked up the lamp and waterskin and ran out of the house. He found some mud and smeared it on his face. How often his father had talked to him about this city that now had brought about his death. He went round Plaça del Blat by La Llet and La Corretgeria squares, until he was at the end of Carrer de la Tapineria, right next to the line of carts with the hanged men. Joan was sitting beneath their father's body, trying to stop shaking so as not to give himself away.

Arnau hid the lantern in the street, slung the waterskin across his back and started to crawl towards the far side of the carts drawn up against the palace wall. Bernat was in the fourth one. The soldiers were still talking round their fire at the opposite end of the line. Arnau crawled behind the carts. As he reached the second one, a woman saw him; her eyes were puffy from crying. Arnau paused, but the woman looked away and went on weeping. He climbed up on the cart where his father was hanging. Joan heard him and turned round.

'Don't look!' His brother lowered his gaze. 'And try not to shake so much!'

Arnau stretched up towards his father's body, but a sudden noise made him crouch down again. He waited a few moments, and stood up once more: again he heard a noise, but this time he remained upright. The soldiers were still talking to each other. Arnau raised the waterskin and began to pour oil over his father's body. His head was too high for him, so he stretched up as far as he could and squeezed the skin hard so that the oil shot out. A greasy patch of oil began to soak Bernat's hair. When the wineskin was empty, Arnau headed back to Carrer de la Tapineria.

He would only have one chance. Arnau hid the lamp behind his back to conceal its weak flame. *I have to get it right the first time.* He looked over at the soldiers. Now it was his turn to tremble. He took a deep breath and stepped into the square. Bernat and Joan were ten paces from him. He lifted the lamp, casting light over himself. As he entered the square the lamplight seemed to him as bright as a radiant dawn. The soldiers looked in his direction. Arnau was about to start running when he realized that none of them was stirring. *Why would they? How are they supposed to know I'm going to burn my father? Burn my father!* The lantern shook in his hand. With the soldiers looking on, he reached Joan. Nobody moved. Arnau came to a halt beneath Bernat's dangling body and looked up at him one last time. Oil glistened on his face, hiding the terror and pain so evident there before.

Arnau threw the lamp at the body. Bernat started to burn. The soldiers leapt up, glancing at the flames as they ran after the fleeing Arnau. The lamp fell on to the floor of the cart, where a pool of oil also caught fire.

'Hey, you!' he heard the soldiers shouting.

Arnau was about to run out of the square when he spied Joan still sitting in front of the cart. He was completely covered by the blanket, and seemed paralysed with fear. Immersed in their grief, other mourners looked on in silence.

'Stop! Stop in the King's name!'

'Move, Joan!' Arnau looked back at the soldiers, who were almost upon him. 'Move, or you'll be burnt!'

He could not leave Joan where he was. The burning oil was snaking across the ground towards his brother's trembling figure. Arnau was about to pull him away, when the woman who had seen him earlier stepped in between them.

'Run. Run for it,' she urged him.

Arnau ducked under the first soldier's hand and sprinted off. He ran down Carrer de la Bòria to the Nou gate, the soldiers' shouts echoing in his ears. The longer they chase me, the longer it will take them to get back to Father and put the fire out, he thought as he darted along. The soldiers, none of them young and all of them laden with weapons, would never catch a lad like him, running with the speed of fire.

'In the King's name, halt!' he heard behind him.

Something whistled past his right ear. Arnau heard the spear clatter to the ground in front of him. He sped across Plaça de la Llana as more spears fell around him. He went past the Bernat Marcús chapel and reached Carrer dels Carders. The soldiers' cries were fading in the distance. He could not carry on running to the Nou gateway, because there were bound to be more soldiers guarding it. If he headed down towards the sea, he would reach Santa Maria; if instead he went up towards the mountains he could reach as far as Sant Pere de les Puelles, but then he would come up against the city walls again.

He chose to aim for the sea. He skirted the Sant Agustí convent, then lost himself in the maze of streets of the Mercadal district. He climbed walls, ran through gardens, wherever looked darkest. As soon as he was convinced there was no sound behind him apart from the echo of his own footsteps, he slowed to a walk. He followed the Rec Comtal down to Pla d'en Llull, beside the Santa Clara convent. From there it was an easy matter to reach Plaça del Born, then the street of the same name, and finally Santa Maria, his refuge. But just as he was about to squeeze in through the boards of the doorway, something caught his attention: there was a guttering lantern on the floor of the church. He peered into the shadows beyond its feeble light, and soon saw the figure of the watchman stretched out on the ground, blood trickling from the corner of his mouth.

Arnau's heart started to pound. What was going on? The watchman was meant to look after Santa Maria. Why would anyone . . .? The Virgin! The Jesus chapel! The *bastaixos'* collection box!

Arnau did not think twice. His father had been executed; he could not allow anyone to bring dishonour to his mother. He crept into Santa Maria through the boarded-up doorway and headed for the ambulatory. The Jesus chapel was on his left between two buttresses. He walked round the church and hid behind one of the columns near the main altar. He could hear sounds coming from the Jesus chapel, but as yet could not see anything. He slid to the next column. From there he could see into the chapel, which as usual was lit by dozens of candles.

A man was climbing out over the chapel railings. Arnau looked at the Virgin: everything seemed to be all right. What was going on? He scanned the interior of the chapel: the collection box had been forced open. As the thief continued to climb over the iron grille, Arnau could almost hear the clink of coins the *bastaixos* dropped into the box in aid of their orphans and widows.

'Thief!' he shouted, lunging at the iron railings and striking the man on the chest. Taken by surprise, the thief fell to the floor. He had no time to think. The man leapt to his feet and delivered a tremendous blow to Arnau's face. He crashed to the floor of Santa Maria.

17

'He must have fallen trying to escape after he had robbed the *bastaixos'* collection box,' said one of the King's guards standing next to Arnau, who was still unconscious. Father Albert shook his head. How could Arnau have done such a terrible thing? The *bastaixos'* collection box, in the Jesus chapel, underneath the statue of his Virgin! The soldiers had come to tell him a couple of hours before dawn.

That cannot be true, he told himself.

'Yes, Father,' the captain insisted. 'The boy was carrying this purse,' he added, showing him the bag with the money Grau had given to pay for his prisoners. 'What's a young lad like him doing with so much money?'

'And look at his face,' another soldier said. 'Why would he smear his face with mud if he wasn't planning to steal something?'

Staring at the purse the officer was holding up, Father Albert shook his head again. What could Arnau have been doing there at this time of night? Where had he got the money?

'What are you doing?' he asked the soldiers, who were busy lifting Arnau from the floor.

'Taking him to prison.'

'No you aren't,' he heard himself say.

Perhaps . . . perhaps there was an explanation for all this. It was impossible that Arnau had tried to steal from the *bastaixos'* collection box. Not Arnau.

'He's a thief, Father.'

'That's for a court to decide.'

'And that's what will happen,' said the captain as his men supported Arnau under the arms. 'But he can wait for the judgement in gaol.'

'If he goes to any gaol, it will be the bishop's,' said the priest. 'The crime was committed on holy ground, therefore it is under ecclesiastical jurisdiction, not that of the city magistrate.'

The captain looked at his soldiers and Arnau. Shrugging his shoulders, he ordered them to release him, which they did by simply letting him go and allowing him to fall to the ground again. A cynical smile spread across his face when he saw how the youngster's face struck the paving stones.

Father Albert glared at them. 'Bring him round,' he ordered, taking out the keys to the chapel. He opened the grille and stepped inside. 'I want to hear what he has to say.'

He went over to the collection box. He saw that the three clasps had been broken. It was empty. There was nothing else missing in the chapel, and nothing had been destroyed. What happened, Our Lady? he asked the Virgin silently. How could you allow Arnau to do something like this? He heard the soldiers splashing water on the boy's face, and reappeared outside the chapel just as several *bastaixos* who had heard about the robbery came rushing into the church.

The freezing water roused Arnau. He looked up and saw he was surrounded by soldiers. In his mind, he heard the spear whistling past his head in Carrer de la

Bòria once again. He was running in front of them: how had they managed to catch him? Had he stumbled? The soldiers' faces bent towards him. His father! His body was burning! He had to escape! Arnau struggled to his feet and tried to push one of them off, but they easily succeeded in pinioning him.

Dejected, Father Albert saw how Arnau was trying to wriggle free from the soldiers.

'Do you need to hear any more, Father?' the officer growled. 'Isn't this confession enough?' he insisted, pointing at Arnau.

Father Albert raised his hands to his face and sighed. He walked slowly over to where the soldiers were holding Arnau.

'Why did you do it?' he asked when he came up to them. 'You know that box belongs to your friends the *bastaixos*. They use the money to help the widows and orphans of their guild, or to pay for the burial of any member who dies. It's also for works of charity, and to decorate the Virgin, your mother, with candles that are always alight. So why did you do it, Arnau?'

Seeing the priest reassured Arnau: but what was he doing there? The *bastaixos*' collection box! The thief! He remembered being punched, but then what? Wide-eyed, he looked around him. Beyond the soldiers, countless faces that he knew were waiting for his answer. He recognized Ramon and Little Ramon, Pere, Jaume, Joan – who was trying to see more by standing on tiptoe – Sebastià and his son Bastianet, and many more he had given water to and with whom he had shared unforgettable moments when the Barcelona *host* had marched on Creixell. So that was it! He was being accused of the robbery!

'I didn't . . .' he muttered.

The King's captain held up Grau's purse. Arnau felt on his belt for where it should have been. He had not wanted to leave it under his mattress in case the baroness reported them to the authorities and accused Joan, and now . . . Damn Grau! Damn the purse!

'Is this what you're looking for?' the captain said.

'It wasn't me, Father,' Arnau defended himself.

The captain guffawed, and the soldiers joined in the laughter.

'Ramon, it wasn't me. I swear it,' Arnau insisted, staring directly at the *bastaix*.

'What were you doing here so late at night then? Where did you get that money? Why did you try to run away? Why is your face covered in mud?'

Arnau felt his face: it was caked with mud.

The purse! The King's officer was continually waving it in front of his eyes. More and more *bastaixos* kept arriving, and remarking on what had happened. Arnau watched the purse swinging. That damned purse! He spoke imploringly to Father Albert: 'There was a man,' he said. 'I tried to stop him but couldn't. He was very big and strong.'

The captain's incredulous laugh echoed once more round the ambulatory.

'Arnau,' the priest said, 'just answer the captain's questions.'

'No . . . I can't,' Arnau admitted, producing more hilarity among the soldiers, and consternation among the *bastaixos*.

Father Albert said nothing. He stared at Arnau. How often had he heard those words? 'I can't,' someone would say to him, a terrified look on their face. 'If it got out . . .' Of course, the priest always thought on those occasions, if it got out that I had stolen, or committed adultery, or blasphemed, then I would be arrested. And so he had to insist, swearing that he would never tell, until they opened their conscience to God and to forgiveness.

'Would you tell me in private?' he asked.

Arnau nodded.

The priest pointed to the Jesus chapel. 'The rest of you wait here,' he told them.

'It was our box that was robbed,' came a voice from behind the group of soldiers. 'A *bastaix* should be present too.'

Father Albert agreed, and glanced down at Arnau. 'Ramon?' he suggested.

The boy nodded again. The three of them walked inside the chapel. Arnau immediately told them everything. He told them about Tomàs the groom, his father, Grau's purse, the baroness's orders, the riots, the execution, the fire . . . He told them about being chased, about stumbling upon the man stealing from the box, his fruitless attempt to stop him. He told them of his fear that the soldiers would find out he had Grau's purse, or that he would be arrested for setting fire to his father's body.

His explanations went on and on. Arnau could not give a proper description of the man who had hit him: it was too dark, he said in answer to their questions. All he remembered was that he was big and strong. Finally, the priest and the *bastaix* exchanged glances: they believed him, but how could they prove to all the people congregated outside the chapel that it had not been him? The priest looked at the Virgin, then at the forced collection box, and left the chapel.

'I think the boy is telling the truth,' he told the small crowd gathered in the ambulatory. 'I don't think he stole from the box; in fact, I think he tried to prevent the robbery.'

Ramon, who had come out of the chapel behind him, agreed.

'Well then,' said the officer, 'why can't he answer my questions?'

'I know the reasons,' Father Albert replied and Ramon nodded agreement again. 'And they are convincing ones. If anyone doesn't believe me, let them say so now.' Nobody spoke. 'Now, where are the three aldermen of the guild?' Three *bastaixos* stepped forward. 'Each of you has a key to open the box, don't you?' The three men agreed. 'Do you swear that it has only ever been opened by all three of you together, in the presence of ten guild members, as your statutes specify?' The men swore that it had. 'Do you also swear therefore that the final total in the account book should tally with what was in the box?' The three aldermen swore that too. 'And you, captain, do you solemnly swear that this was the purse the boy had on him?' The captain swore. 'And that it contains as much as when you found it?'

'You are insulting an officer of King Alfonso!'

'Do you solemnly swear it or not?'

Some of the *bastaixos* pressed round him, demanding an answer.

'I swear.'

'Good,' said Father Albert. 'Now I'll go and fetch the account book for the box. If this boy is the thief, what is in the purse should match or be more than the last entry in the book. If there is less, then we ought to believe him.'

A murmur of agreement spread through the assembled *bastaixos*. Most of them looked at Arnau: all of them at one time or another had been given fresh water from his waterskin.

Father Albert gave the chapel keys to Ramon for him to lock the grille. Then he went to the priest's house to find the account book, which according to the guild's statutes had to be kept by a third person outside the association. As far as he could recall, the amount of money in the box was much greater than the sum Grau had set aside to pay for his prisoners' food. That should be irrefutable proof of Arnau's innocence, he thought with a smile.

While Father Albert went to fetch the book, Ramon set about locking the chapel grille. As he was doing so, he saw something glint inside. He went over and, without moving it, examined the shiny object. He said nothing to anyone. He locked the grille, then rejoined the group of *bastaixos* waiting for the priest by the boy and the soldiers.

Ramon whispered something to three of them, and they immediately left the church without anyone else noticing.

'According to the account book,' Father Albert said as he showed it to the three guild aldermen, 'there were seventy-four pence and five shillings in the collection box. Now count what there is in the purse,' he said to the captain.

Even before opening it, the soldier shook his head. There was nothing like that sum inside.

'Thirteen pence!' he declared. 'But' – he was shouting now – 'the boy's accomplice could have run off with the rest.'

'Why would that accomplice leave thirteen pence with Arnau then?' said one of the *bastaixos*.

A murmur of assent ran through the crowd.

The captain stared at all the *bastaixos*. He almost made the mistake of saying something hasty that he might regret, but thought better of it. Some of the stone-carriers had already gone up to Arnau, clapping him on the back and ruffling his hair.

'If it wasn't the boy, who was it?' he asked.

'I think I know who it was,' came the voice of Ramon from the far side of the main altar.

Behind him, two of the *bastaixos* he had spoken to earlier were dragging in a third, stocky man.

'It would be him,' someone in the crowd agreed.

'That was the man!' shouted Arnau as soon as he saw him.

The Mallorcan had always caused trouble in the guild, until one day they discovered he had a concubine and expelled him. No *bastaix* was allowed to have a relationship with anyone other than his wife. Nor could his wife: if she did, he was also dismissed from the guild.

'What is that boy saying?' the Mallorcan protested as he was pushed into the ambulatory.

'He accuses you of having stolen the money from the *bastaixos*' collection box,' Father Albert told him.

'He's lying!'

The priest sought out Ramon, who nodded his head slightly.

'I also accuse you!' Ramon shouted, pointing at him.

'He's lying too!'

'You'll get the chance to prove it in the cauldron at the Santes Creus monastery.'

A crime had been committed in a church. The *Constitutions of Peace and Truce* established that innocence had to be proved by the ordeal of boiling water.

The Mallorcan went pale. The aldermen and the soldiers looked enquiringly at the priest, but he indicated that they should not say anything. In reality, the ordeal by boiling water was no longer used, but the priests often still employed the threat of plunging a suspect's limbs into a cauldron of boiling water to obtain a confession.

Father Albert narrowed his eyes and studied the Mallorcan. 'If the boy and I are lying, I'm sure you will withstand the boiling water on your arms and legs without having to confess to any crime.'

'I'm innocent,' the Mallorcan protested.

'As I've told you, you'll have the chance to prove it,' said the priest.

'And if you're innocent,' Ramon butted in, 'explain to us what your dagger was doing inside the chapel.'

The Mallorcan turned on him. 'It's a trap!' he said quickly. 'Somebody must have put it there to make me look guilty! The boy! It must have been him!'

Father Albert opened the chapel grille again, and came out carrying the dagger. 'Is this yours?' he asked, thrusting it in his face.

'No . . . no.'

The guild aldermen and several *bastaixos* came over to the priest and asked to examine the knife.

'It is yours,' one of the aldermen said, weighing it in his hand.

Six years earlier, as a consequence of all the fights that had broken out in the port, King Alfonso had banned the stone-carriers and other free workmen from carrying hunting knives or other similar weapons. The only knives they could carry were blunt ones. The Mallorcan had refused to obey the order and had often shown off his magnificent dagger to the others. It was only when he was threatened with expulsion from the guild that he had agreed to go to a blacksmith's to have the point filed smooth.

'Liar!' one of the *bastaixos* cried.

'Thief!' shouted another.

'Someone must have stolen it to incriminate me!' the Mallorcan protested, trying to break free from the two men holding him.

It was then that the third *bastaix* who had gone with Ramon to find the Mallorcan came back. He had been to search the man's house.

'Here it is,' he called out, waving a purse. He handed it to the priest, who passed it on to the captain.

'Seventy-four pence and five shillings,' the captain announced after counting the coins.

As he had been doing so, the *bastaixos* had encircled

the Mallorcan. None of them could ever hope to have so much money! When the count was finished, they flung themselves on the thief. Insults, kicks, punches, all rained down on him. The soldiers did not intervene. The captain looked across at Father Albert and shrugged.

'This is the house of God!' shouted the priest, pushing the stone-carriers away. 'We're in the house of God!' he repeated until he was next to the Mallorcan, who was rolled up into a ball on the floor of the church. 'This man is a thief, and a coward too, but he deserves a fair trial. You cannot take the law into your own hands. Take him to the bishop's palace,' he ordered the captain.

Someone took advantage of him talking to the captain to aim one last kick at the Mallorcan. When the soldiers dragged him to his feet, others spat on him. The soldiers led him out.

After the soldiers had left Santa Maria with their prisoner, the *bastaixos* came up to Arnau, smiling and apologizing. Then they gradually drifted away. Eventually, the only people left outside the Jesus chapel were Father Albert, Arnau, the three guild aldermen, and the ten witnesses called for whenever the guild's collection box was involved.

The priest put the money back in the box. He noted what had happened that night in the account book. Day had dawned, and someone had gone to ask a locksmith to come and repair the three clasps. All of them had to wait until the box could be locked again.

Father Albert rested his hand on Arnau's shoulder. It was only then that he remembered how he had seen him sitting beneath Bernat's body dangling from a rope. He tried not to think about the fire. He was only a boy! He looked up at the Virgin. He would have been left to rot at the city gate, he explained silently. What does it matter? He's only a boy, and now he has nothing: no father, no job to help feed himself . . .

'I think,' he said all of a sudden, 'that you should make Arnau Estanyol a member of your guild.'

Ramon smiled. He too, once things had calmed down, had been thinking about all Arnau had confessed to them. The others, including Arnau, gave the priest puzzled looks.

'But he's only a boy,' one of the guild aldermen said.

'He's not strong enough. How will he be able to carry sacks or stones on his back?' asked another.

'He's very young,' insisted a third.

Arnau gazed at them all, eyes open wide.

'Everything you say is true,' the priest admitted, 'but neither his size, his strength nor his youth prevented him from defending money that was rightfully yours. But for him, your collection box would be empty.'

The *bastaixos* studied Arnau a while longer.

'I think we could try him out,' Ramon said finally, 'and if he is not up to it . . .'

Someone in the group agreed.

'All right,' one of the aldermen said eventually, looking across at his two companions. Neither of them demurred. 'We'll take him on trial. If he shows his worth over the next three months, we'll accept him fully into the guild. He will be paid in proportion to the work he does. Here,' he said, handing him the Mallorcan's dagger, which he was still holding, 'this can be your *bastaix* knife. Father, write that in the book too, so that the boy has no problems of any kind.'

Arnau could feel the priest's hand gripping his shoulder. He did not know what to say, but smiled his thanks to the stone-carriers. He was a *bastaix*! If only his father could see him!

18

'Who was it? Do you know him, lad?'

The noise of the soldiers running and shouting as they chased Arnau still filled the square, but all Joan could hear was the burning crackle of Bernat's body above him.

The captain of the guard had stayed near the scaffold. He shook Joan and asked again: 'Do you know who it was?'

Joan was transfixed by the sight of the man who had been a father to him burning like a torch.

The captain shook Joan until he turned towards him. He was still staring blindly ahead of him, and his teeth were chattering.

'Who was it? Why did he burn your father?'

Joan did not even hear the question. His whole body started to shake.

'He can't speak,' said the woman who had urged Arnau to run off. It was she who had pulled Joan away from the flames, and had recognized Arnau as the boy who had been sitting guard over the hanged man all that afternoon. If I only dared do the same, she thought, my husband's body wouldn't be left to rot on the walls, to be pecked at by the birds. Yes, that lad had done something all the relatives there wished they had done, and the captain . . . he had only come on duty that night, so could not have recognized Arnau: he thought the man's son must be this one. The woman put her arms round Joan and hugged him tight.

'I need to know who set fire to him,' the captain insisted.

'What does it matter?' the woman murmured, feeling Joan trembling uncontrollably in her embrace. 'This boy is half-dead from fear and hunger.'

The captain rolled his eyes, then slowly nodded. Hunger! He himself had lost an infant child: the boy had grown thinner and thinner until a simple fever had been enough to carry him off. His wife used to hold him just as this woman was doing now. He used to stare at the two of them: his wife in tears, the little boy pressing up against her, desperate for warmth . . .

'Take him home,' the captain told her.

'Hunger,' he muttered, turning to look at Bernat's burning corpse. 'Those cursed Genoese!'

Dawn had broken over the city.

'Joan!' shouted Arnau as soon as he opened the door.

Pere and Mariona, sitting close to the hearth, motioned to him to be quiet.

'He's asleep,' said Mariona.

The woman in the square had brought him home and told them what had happened. The two old folk cosseted him until he fell asleep, then went to sit by the fireside.

'What will become of them?' Mariona asked her husband. 'Without Bernat, the boy will never survive in the stables.'

And we won't be able to feed them, thought Pere. They could not afford to let them keep the room without paying, or to feed them every day. It was then he noticed how Arnau's eyes were shining. His father had just been executed! His body had been burnt, so why was he looking so excited?

'I'm a *bastaix*!' Arnau announced, heading for the few cold scraps left in the pot from the previous evening.

The two old folk looked at each other, and then at the boy, who was eating directly from the ladle, his back to them. He was starving! The lack of grain had affected him, as it had all Barcelona. How was such a puny boy going to carry those heavy loads?

Mariona looked back at her husband, shaking her head.

'God will find a way,' Pere said.

'What did you say?' asked Arnau, turning to face them, his mouth full of food.

'Nothing, my lad, nothing.'

'I have to go,' said Arnau, picking up a piece of stale bread and biting off a chunk. His desire to tell them all that had happened in the square was outweighed by his longing to join his new companions. He said: 'When Joan wakes up, tell him where I've gone.'

In April the ships put out to sea again, after being hauled up on the beach since October. The days grew longer, and the big trading vessels began to enter and leave the city. No one involved – the merchants, owners or pilots – wanted to spend longer than was strictly necessary in the dangerous port of Barcelona.

Before he joined the group of *bastaixos* waiting on the shore, Arnau stared out to sea. It had always been there, but when he had been with his father they had turned their backs on it after a few steps. Today he looked at it with different eyes: it was going to be his livelihood. The port was filled with countless small craft, two big ships which had just arrived, and a fleet of six enormous men-o'-war, with 260 small boats and twenty-six rows of oarsmen each.

Arnau had heard of this fleet; it was Barcelona itself which had paid for it to help King Alfonso in his war against Genoa, and the city's fourth councillor, Galcerà Marquet, was in command. Only victory over Genoa could open the trade routes again and guarantee the Catalan capital's prosperity: that was why the city had shown the King such generosity.

'You won't let us down, will you, lad?' someone said as he stood on the shore. Arnau turned and saw it was one of the guild aldermen. 'Come on,' the man said, hurrying on to where the other guild members had congregated.

Arnau followed him. When they reached the group, all the *bastaixos* smiled at him.

'This isn't like giving people water,' one of them said. The others laughed.

'Here,' said Ramon. 'It's the smallest we could find in the guild.'

Arnau took the headpiece carefully.

'Don't worry, it won't snap!' laughed one of the *bastaixos* when he saw how gently Arnau was holding it.

Of course not! thought Arnau, smiling back at him. How could it? He put the pad on the support, and made sure the leather thongs fitted round his forehead.

Ramon checked that the support was in the right place. 'Good,' he said, patting him on the back. 'All you need is the callus.'

'What callus?' Arnau started to ask, but just at that moment the arrival of the guild aldermen diverted everyone's attention.

'They can't agree,' one of the aldermen explained. All the *bastaixos*, including Arnau, looked a little further down the beach, where a group of finely dressed men were arguing. 'Galcerà Marquet wants his war galleys to be loaded first, but the merchants want their two ships unloaded beforehand. So we have to wait.'

The men muttered among themselves; many of them sat down on the sand. Arnau sat next to Ramon, the leather strap still on his forehead.

'It won't break, Arnau,' the *bastaix* said, pointing to it, 'but don't get any sand in it: that would hurt when you lift the load.'

The boy took off the headpiece and put it away carefully, making sure no sand got in it.

'What's the problem?' he asked Ramon. 'We can unload or load first one lot, then the other.'

'Nobody wants to be in Barcelona longer than necessary. If a storm blew up, all the boats would be in peril, defenceless.'

Arnau surveyed the port, from Puig de les Falsies round to Santa Clara, then turned his gaze on the group of men who were still arguing. 'The city councillor is in charge, isn't he?'

Ramon laughed and ruffled his hair. 'In Barcelona it's the merchants who are in charge. They are the ones who have paid for the royal men-o'-war.'

In the end, the dispute was settled with a compromise: the *bastaixos* would first go and collect the supplies for the royal galleys from the city, while the small boats unloaded the merchant ships. The *bastaixos* ought to be back before the others had reached the shore with the ships' goods, which would be left under cover in a suitable place rather than immediately distributed to their owners' storehouses. The boatmen would take the supplies out to the warships while the *bastaixos* went back for more, then go on from them to the merchant ships to pick up the goods there. This would be repeated until the process was complete, with the warships loaded and the others empty. After that, the goods would be distributed to their corresponding storehouses, and if there was any time left, the merchant ships would be loaded again.

Once the agreement had been struck, all the men set to work. Different groups of *bastaixos* headed into Barcelona and the city warehouses where the supplies for the crews and oarsmen of the galleys were kept. The boatmen headed out to the recently arrived merchant ships and began to unload their cargoes, which could not be taken on shore directly because of the lack of a harbour.

Each boat, catboat, cog or barge had a crew of three or four men: the boatman and, depending on the guild, slaves or free men who were paid a wage. The boatmen from the Sant Pere guild, the oldest and richest in the city, used two slaves per boat, as stipulated in their ordinances. Those in the more recent and less wealthy guild of Santa Maria had only paid hands. Whoever was in the crew, the operation to load and unload the cargoes was slow and cautious, even when the sea was calm, because the boatmen were held responsible by the ship-owners for any loss or damage to their goods. They could even be sent to gaol if they could not pay the compensation demanded.

When the sea grew rough in the port of Barcelona, things became even more complicated, not only for the boatmen but for everyone involved in the sea trade. Firstly because the boatmen could refuse to go out and unload the cargo (which they were not allowed to do in fine weather) unless a special price was agreed with the owner. But it was the owners, captains and even the crews of the ships who were most affected by storms. There were severe penalties if they left their ship before the cargo had been completely taken off; and the owner or his clerk, who were the only ones allowed off the ship, had to return at the first sign of any tempest.

So while the boatmen began to unload the first merchant ship, the *bastaixos*, divided into groups by their leaders, began to transfer the supplies for the galleys from different storehouses in the city. Arnau was put with Ramon, to whom the alderman gave a meaningful look as he did so.

They walked down the shoreline to the doors of the Forment, the city's grain warehouse. It had been heavily guarded by soldiers since the popular uprising. When they reached it, Arnau attempted to hide behind Ramon, but the soldiers soon saw there was a young lad among all the robust men.

'What's this fellow going to carry?' one of them asked, pointing to him and laughing.

When he saw all the soldiers staring at him, Arnau felt his stomach churn, and tried harder to conceal himself behind Ramon, but the *bastaix* grasped him by his shoulder, put the leather headpiece on his forehead, and answered the soldier in a similarly jocular tone: 'It's time he started work!' he shouted. 'He's thirteen and has to help his family.'

The soldiers nodded and stepped aside. Arnau walked between them head down. As he entered the warehouse, the smell of grain hit him. The beams of sunlight filtering through the windows picked out the particles of fine dust that soon made Arnau and many other *bastaixos* cough.

'Before the war against Genoa,' Ramon told him, stretching out his hand in a sweeping gesture as though trying to encompass the entire storehouse, 'all this was filled with wheat, but now . . .'

Arnau spotted the big earthenware jars that Grau had manufactured lined up next to each other.

'Get started!' shouted their leader.

Holding a parchment in his hand, the manager of the warehouse started pointing to the jars. How on earth are we going to carry such full jars? Arnau wondered. It was impossible for one man to carry all that weight. But the *bastaixos* formed pairs, and after tipping the jars slightly to put ropes round them, they threaded a long pole through the ropes, lifted it together and set off for the beach. Clouds of dust started to swirl around. Arnau coughed still more. When it was his turn, he heard Ramon shout: 'Give the boy one of the small ones, one with salt in it.'

The warehouse manager looked at Arnau and shook his head. 'Salt is expensive,' he said, addressing Ramon. 'If he drops the jar . . .'

'Give him one with salt!'

The grain jars measured about three feet in height, but the one Arnau had to carry was about half that size. Even so, when Ramon helped him lift it on to his back, he could feel his knees buckle.

Ramon squeezed his shoulders. 'It's time to show your worth,' he whispered.

Bent over, Arnau took a step forward. He grasped the handles of the jar firmly, and pushed his head until he could feel the leather thong biting into his forehead.

Ramon watched as he set off unsteadily, putting one foot in front of the other slowly and carefully. The warehouse man shook his head again. The soldiers said nothing as the boy passed by them.

'This is for you, Father!' Arnau muttered between clenched teeth when he felt the heat of the sun on his face. The weight was going to split him in two! 'I'm not a child any longer, Father: can you see me?'

Ramon and another *bastaix* walked behind him, carrying a large grain jar on a pole. They watched as Arnau almost fell over his own feet. Ramon shut his eyes.

Are you still hanging there? Arnau was thinking, the image of Bernat's body imprinted on his mind. Nobody can make fun of you any more! Not even that witch and her stepchildren! He steadied himself under the load and set off again.

He reached the shore. Ramon was smiling behind

him. Nobody said a word. The boatmen came and relieved him of the salt jar before he reached the sea. It took Arnau several moments before he could straighten up again. 'Did you see me, Father?' he muttered, peering at the sky.

When he had unloaded his grain jar, Ramon patted Arnau on the back.

'Another one?' the boy asked in all seriousness.

Two more. When Arnau had deposited the third salt jar on the beach, Josep, one of the guild officials, came up to him. 'That's enough for today, my lad,' he told him.

'I can do more,' replied Arnau, trying not to show how much his back was hurting.

'No, you can't. Besides, I can't have you going round Barcelona bleeding like a wounded animal,' he said in a fatherly way, pointing to thin trickles of blood running down Arnau's sides. Arnau put a hand to his back, then glanced at it. 'We're not slaves; we're free men, working for ourselves, and that's how people should see us. Don't worry,' the alderman said, seeing how disappointed Arnau looked, 'the same has happened to all of us at one time or another, and we all had someone who told us to stop working. The blisters you have on your neck and back have to harden, to form a callus. That will only take a few days, and you can be assured that from then on, I won't let you rest any more than the others.'

Josep handed him a small bottle. 'Make sure you clean the wound properly, then have some of this ointment rubbed on. It will help dry out the wound.'

As he listened to the man, Arnau relaxed. He would not have to carry anything more that day, but the pain and tiredness from the sleepless night he had just experienced left him feeling faint. He muttered a few words of goodbye and dragged himself home. Joan was waiting for him at the door. How long had he been there?

'Did you know I'm a *bastaix* now?' Arnau said when he reached the doorway.

Joan nodded. He knew. He had watched his brother on his last two journeys, clenching teeth and fists as he saw each unsteady step, praying he would not fall, shedding tears at the sight of his blotched purple face. Now Joan wiped away the last of his tears and held out his arms. Arnau fell into his embrace.

'You have to put this ointment on my back,' Arnau managed to say as Joan helped him upstairs.

That was all he did say. A few seconds later, collapsed flat out on the pallet with his arms outstretched, he fell into a deep, restorative sleep. Trying not to wake him, Joan cleaned his wound with hot water that Mariona brought up to him. The ointment had a strong, sharp smell. He spread it on, and it seemed to take effect immediately, because Arnau stirred but did not wake up.

That night it was Joan who could not sleep. He sat on the floor next to his brother, listening to him breathe. He allowed his own eyelids to droop whenever the sound was regular and quiet, but started awake whenever Arnau moved uncomfortably. What's going to become of us now? he wondered from time to time. He had talked to Pere and his wife; the money Arnau earned as a *bastaix* would not be enough to keep them both. What would happen to him?

'Get to school!' Arnau ordered the next morning, when he saw Joan busy helping Mariona with her household chores. He had thought about it the previous day: everything should stay the same, just as his father had left it.

Mariona was leaning over her fire. She turned to her husband, who spoke before Joan could even answer.

'Obey your elder brother,' he told him.

Mariona's face creased in a smile. Her husband, though, looked serious: how were the four of them going

231

to live? Mariona went on smiling, until Pere shook his head as if trying to clear it of all the doubts they had talked over endlessly the previous evening.

Joan ran out of the house. As soon as he had gone, Arnau tried to stretch. He could not move a single muscle. They had all seized up, and he felt stiff from head to toe. Bit by bit, however, his young body came back to life, and after eating a frugal breakfast he went out into the sunshine. He smiled when he saw the beach, the sea and the six galleys still at anchor in the port.

Ramon and Josep made him show them his back.

'One trip,' the guild alderman told Ramon before rejoining the group. 'Then he can go to the chapel.'

Arnau turned to look at Ramon as he struggled to replace his shirt.

'You heard him,' Ramon said.

'But . . .'

'Do as you're told, Arnau. Josep knows what he is doing.'

He did. As soon as Arnau lifted the first jar on to his back, his wound started bleeding again.

'But if it has started bleeding already,' he said when Ramon unloaded his jar of grain on the beach behind him, 'what's the problem if I make a few more journeys?'

'The callus, Arnau, the hard skin. The idea is not to destroy your back, but to let the hard skin form. Now go and wash, put more ointment on, and get down to our chapel in Santa Maria.' As Arnau made to protest, Ramon insisted: 'It's our chapel – it's your chapel, Arnau. We have to look after it.'

'My boy,' said the *bastaix* who had carried the jar with Ramon, 'that chapel means a lot to us. We're nothing more than port workers, but La Ribera has offered us something that no nobleman or wealthy guild has: the Jesus chapel and the keys to the church of Santa Maria de la Mar. Do you understand what that means?' Arnau nodded thoughtfully. 'There can be no greater honour for any of us. You'll have plenty of time to load and unload; don't worry about that.'

Mariona tended his back, and then Arnau headed for Santa Maria. He went to find Father Albert to get the keys to the chapel, but the priest first took him to the cemetery outside Les Moreres gate.

'This morning I buried your father,' he told him, pointing to the cemetery. Puzzled, Arnau looked at him. 'I didn't want to tell you in case any soldiers appeared. The magistrate decided he did not want people to see your father's burnt body either in Plaça del Blat or above the city gates. He was frightened others might do the same. It wasn't hard to convince him to let me bury the body.'

They both stood silently outside the cemetery for a while.

'Would you like me to leave you on your own?' the priest eventually asked.

'I have to clean the *bastaixos*' chapel,' said Arnau, wiping away his tears.

For several days after that, Arnau made only one trip carrying a load, then went back to the chapel. The galleys had already weighed anchor, and the goods from the merchant ships were the usual items of trade: fabrics, coral, spices, copper, wax . . . Then one day, Arnau's back did not bleed. Josep inspected it again, and Arnau spent the whole day carrying heavy bundles of cloth, smiling at every *bastaix* he met on the way.

He was also paid his first wage. Barely a few pence more than he had earned working for Grau! He gave it all to Pere, together with a few coins he still had from Bernat's purse. It's not enough, the boy thought as he counted out the coins. Father used to pay Pere a lot more. He peered inside the purse again. That would not last very long, he realized. His hand still inside the purse, he looked at the old man. Pere grimaced.

'When I can carry more,' said Arnau, 'I'll earn more.'

'You know as well as I do that will take time, Arnau. And before that, your father's purse will be empty. You know this house isn't mine . . . No, it isn't,' he added, when the boy looked up at him in surprise. 'Most of the houses in the city belong to the Church: to the bishop or a religious order. We only have them in emphyteusis, a long lease for which we pay rent every year. You know how little I can work, so I rely on the money from the room to be able to pay it. If you can't cover it . . . What am I to do?'

'So what's the point of being free if citizens are chained to their houses just as peasants are to their lands?' asked Arnau, shaking his head.

'We're not chained to them,' Pere said patiently.

'But I've heard that all these houses are passed down from father to son; they even get sold! How is that possible if they don't belong to you and you are not tied to them?'

'That's easy to understand, Arnau. The Church is very rich in lands and properties, but according to its laws it cannot sell ecclesiastical possessions.' Arnau tried to intervene, but Pere raised a hand to stop him. 'The problem is that the bishops, abbots and other important positions in the Church are appointed by the King. He always chooses his friends, and the Pope never says no. All those friends of the King hope to receive a good income from what they own, and since they cannot sell any properties, they have invented this system called emphyteusis to get round the ban.'

'So that makes you tenants,' said Arnau, trying to understand.

'No. Tenants can be thrown out at any time. The emphyteuta can never be thrown out . . . as long as he pays his rent to the Church.'

'Could you sell the house?'

'Yes. That's known as subemphyteusis. The bishop would get a part of the proceeds, known as the laudemium, and the new subemphyteuta can carry on just as I do. There is only one caveat.' Arnau looked at him enquiringly. 'The house cannot be passed on to anyone of a higher social position. It could never be sold to a nobleman . . . although I doubt whether any noble would be interested in this place, don't you?' he said with a smile. When Arnau did not join in, Pere became serious once more. He said nothing for a while, then added: 'The thing is, I have to pay the annual rent and between what I earn and what you pay me . . .'

What are we going to do now? Arnau thought. With the miserable wage he earned, he and his brother could not even pay enough for food, and yet it was not fair to cause Pere problems: he had always treated them well.

'Don't worry,' he said hesitantly, 'we'll leave and then you—'

'Mariona and I have been thinking,' Pere interrupted him. 'If you and Joan didn't mind, you could sleep down here by the fire.' Arnau's eyes opened wide. 'That way . . . that way we could rent the room to a family and be able to pay the rent. You would only have to find two pallets for yourselves. What do you think?'

Arnau's face lit up. His lips began to tremble.

'Does that mean yes?' Pere prompted him.

Arnau steadied his mouth and nodded enthusiastically.

'Now it's time we helped the Virgin!' one of the guild aldermen shouted.

Arnau felt the hairs prickle on his arms and legs.

That day there were no ships to load or unload. The sea in the port was dotted with small fishing boats. The *bastaixos* had gathered on the beach as usual. The sun was climbing in the sky, heralding a fine spring day.

This was the first time since Arnau had become a *bastaix* at the start of the seagoing season that they had been able to spend a day working for Santa Maria.

'We'll help the Virgin!' the group of *bastaixos* shouted.

Arnau surveyed his companions: their drowsy faces were suddenly all smiles. Some of them swung their arms back and forth to loosen their back muscles. Arnau recalled when he used to give them water, and saw them going by, gritting their teeth, bent double under the weight of the enormous stones. Would he be up to it? Fear tightened his muscles, and he began to exercise like the others.

'This is your first time, isn't it?' said Ramon, congratulating him. Arnau said nothing, and allowed his arms to drop to his sides. 'Don't worry, my lad,' Ramon added, resting his hand on Arnau's shoulder and encouraging him to catch up with the others, who were already leaving the beach. 'Remember that when you are carrying stones for the Virgin, she carries part of the weight.'

Arnau looked at him.

'It's true,' the *bastaix* insisted with a smile. 'You'll discover that today.'

They started from Santa Clara, at the eastern end of the city, and had to cross the entire city, then out of the walls and up to the royal quarry at La Roca, in Montjuïc. Arnau walked without talking: from time to time he could sense that some of the others were watching him. They left La Ribera behind, then the exchange and the Forment storehouse. As they passed by the Àngel fountain, Arnau could see the women waiting to fill their pitchers; many of them had let him and Joan in when they came running up with the waterskin. People waved as they went by. Some children ran and jumped around the group of men, whispering and pointing at Arnau with respect. The *bastaixos* left behind the gates of the shipyard and reached the Framenors convent at the western end of the city. It was here that the city walls petered out: beyond them were the unfinished royal dockyards, and further on still, open countryside and vegetable plots: Sant Nicolau, Sant Bertran and Sant Pau del Camp. This was where the track up to the quarry began.

Before they could reach it, however, the *bastaixos* had to cross Cagalell. The stench from the city's waste hit them long before they could see it.

'They're draining it,' one of the men said when the smell overwhelmed them.

Most of the others agreed.

'It wouldn't smell so bad if they weren't,' another *bastaix* explained.

Cagalell was a pond that formed at the mouth of the gully by the walls. It was here that all the waste and sewage from the city accumulated. The ground was so rough it could not run off properly across the beach, so the water lay stagnant until a city workman dug a channel through and pushed the waste out into the sea. That was when Cagalell smelt its worst.

They skirted round it until they came to a narrow part they could jump across, then walked on through the fields until they reached the slopes of Montjuïc.

'How do we get back across Cagalell?' asked Arnau, pointing to the foul-smelling stream.

'I've never yet met anybody who could jump with a block of stone on their back,' laughed Ramon.

As they climbed up to the royal quarry, Arnau peered back down at the city. It looked far, far below. How was he going to walk all that way with a huge stone on his back? He could feel his legs giving way just at the thought of it, but he ran to catch up with the rest of the group, who were still talking and laughing as they climbed ahead of him.

They went round a bend, and there the royal quarry lay in front of them. Arnau could not help gasping in astonishment. It was like Plaça del Blat or any other of the city markets, except that there were no women! On a flat expanse of ground, the King's officers were dealing with everyone who had come seeking stone. Carts and mule trains were lined up on one side, where the walls of the mountain had not yet been excavated. The rest looked as though it had been sliced through; it was a mass of glistening rock. Countless stonemasons were levering off enormous blocks of stone – a hugely dangerous task – and down on the flat ground others cut them into smaller stones.

The *bastaixos* were greeted with great affection by all those waiting for stones. While their leaders talked to the quarry officials, the others embraced or shook hands with the people waiting. They laughed and joked together, and skins of wine or water were raised.

Arnau could not help watching the stonecutters at work. He was equally fascinated by the way the labourers loaded the carts and mules, always supervised by a clerk noting everything down. Just as in the markets, people were talking or waiting their turn impatiently.

'You weren't expecting anything like this, were you?'

Arnau turned and saw Ramon handing back a wine-skin. He shook his head. 'Who is all this stone for?'

'Oh!' said Ramon, then began to reel off the list: 'For the cathedral, for Santa Maria del Pi, Santa Anna, for the Pedralbes monastery, for the royal dockyards, for Santa Clara, for the city walls. Everything is being built or changed; and then there are the new houses for the rich and the noblemen. Nobody wants wood or bricks. They all want stone.'

'And the King gives them all this stone?'

Ramon burst out laughing. 'The only stone he gives free is for Santa Maria de la Mar . . . and possibly for

Pedralbes monastery too, because that is being built at the Queen's behest. He charges a lot for all the rest.'

'Even the stone for the royal dockyards?' asked Arnau. 'They are for the King, aren't they?'

Ramon smiled again. 'They may be royal, but the King isn't the one paying for them.'

'The city?'

'No.'

'The merchants?'

'Not them either.'

'Well then?' asked Arnau, turning to face him.

'The royal dockyards are being paid for by—'

'The sinners!' The man who had offered him his wine-skin took the words out of Ramon's mouth. He was a mule-driver from the cathedral.

Ramon and he laughed out loud at Arnau's bewildered look.

'The sinners?'

'Yes,' explained Ramon, 'the new shipyards are being built thanks to money from sinful merchants. Look, it's very simple: ever since the crusades . . . you know what the crusades were, don't you?' Arnau nodded: of course he knew what they were. 'Well, ever since the Holy City was lost for ever, the Church has banned all trade with the sultan of Egypt. But as it happens, it's there that our traders can find their best goods, so none of them is willing to give up trading with the sultan. Which means that whenever they want to do so, they go to the customs office and pay a fine for the sin they are about to commit. They are also absolved beforehand, and therefore they don't fall into sin. King Alfonso ordered that all the money collected in this way should go to financing Barcelona's new dockyards.'

Arnau was about to say something, but Ramon raised his hand to cut him short. The guild aldermen were calling them. He signalled to Arnau to follow him.

'Are we going before them?' asked Arnau, pointing to the muleteers who they were leaving behind.

'Of course,' said Ramon, still striding ahead. 'We don't need to be checked as thoroughly as they do: our stone is free, and easy to count: one *bastaix*, one stone.'

'One *bastaix*, one stone,' Arnau repeated to himself when the first *bastaix* and the first stone came past him on their way down the mountain. He and Ramon had reached the spot where the stonecutters were cutting the huge blocks. He looked at his companion's taut, tense face. Arnau smiled, but his fellow *bastaix* did not respond: the time for jokes and pleasantries was over. Nobody was laughing or talking now; everyone was staring at the heap of stones on the ground. They all had the leather thongs fixed tightly round their foreheads: Arnau slipped his over his head. The *bastaixos* were coming past him now, one by one. They were silent, and did not wait for the next one. The group around the stones was growing smaller all the time. As Arnau stared at the stones, he could feel his stomach wrench. A *bastaix* bent over, and two labourers lifted a block of stone on to his back. Arnau could see him flinch under the weight. His knees were knocking! The man stood still for a few moments, straightened up, then walked past Arnau on his way down to Santa Maria. My God, he was three times as strong as Arnau, and yet his legs had almost given way! How was he going to . . .?

'Arnau,' called out the guild aldermen.

There were still a few *bastaixos* waiting. Ramon pushed him forward. 'You can do it,' he said.

The three aldermen were talking to one of the stone-cutters. He kept shaking his head. The four of them were surveying the pile of stones, pointing here and there, and then shaking their heads again. Standing by the pile, Arnau tried to swallow, but his throat was too dry. He was shaking: he had to stop! He moved his hands, then extended his arms backwards and forwards. He could not allow them to see him trembling!

Josep, one of the aldermen, pointed to a stone. The stonecutter shrugged, glanced at Arnau, shook his head once more, and then waved to the masons to pick it up. 'They're all the same,' he had told the *bastaixos* over and over.

Seeing the two masons approaching with the stone, Arnau went up to them. He bent over, and tensed all the muscles in his body. Everyone fell silent. The masons slowly let go of the block and helped him grasp it with his hands. As the weight pressed down on him, he bent still further over, and his legs started to buckle. He clenched his teeth and shut his eyes. 'You can do it!' he thought he heard. In fact, nobody had said a word, but everyone had said it to themselves when they saw the boy's legs wobble. *You can do it!* Arnau straightened under the load. Many of the others gave a sigh of relief. But could he walk? Arnau stood there, his eyes still closed. Could he walk?

He put one foot forward. The weight of the block of stone forced him to push out the other foot, then the first one again . . . and the other one a second time. If he stopped . . . if he stopped, the stone would crush him.

Ramon took a deep breath and covered his face in his hands.

'You can do it, lad!' one of the waiting muleteers shouted.

'Go on, braveheart.'

'You can do it!'

'For Santa Maria!'

The shouting echoed off the walls of the quarry and accompanied Arnau as he set off on his own down the path to the city.

But he was not alone. All the *bastaixos* who set off after him soon caught up and made sure that they fell in with him for a few minutes, encouraging him and helping him on his way. As soon as another one reached them, the first would continue at his own pace.

Arnau could hardly hear what they said. He could scarcely even think. All his attention was on the foot that had to come from behind, and once he saw it moving forward and touching the ground under him, he concentrated on the other one; one foot after the other, overcoming the pain.

As he crossed the gardens of Sant Bertran, his feet seemed to take an eternity to appear. By now, all the other *bastaixos* had overtaken him. He remembered how when Joan and he used to give them water they would rest the block on the gunwale of a boat while they drank. Now he looked for something similar, and soon came across an olive tree. He rested the stone on one of its lower branches; he knew that if he put it on the ground, he would never be able to raise it again. His legs were stiff as boards.

'If you stop,' Ramon had advised him, 'make sure your legs don't go completely stiff. If they do, you won't be able to carry on.'

So Arnau, freed from at least part of the weight, continued to move his legs. He took deep breaths. Once, twice, many times. The Virgin will take part of the weight, Ramon had told him. My God! If that was true, how much did his stone really weigh? He did not dare move his back. It hurt terribly. He rested for a good while. Would he be able to set off again? Arnau looked all around him. He was completely alone. Not even the mule-drivers took this path, because they had to go down to the Trentaclaus gate.

Could he do it? He stared up into the sky. He listened to the silence, then with one pull managed to lift the block of stone again. His feet began to move. First one, then the other, one, then the other . . .

At Cagalell he stopped again, this time resting the stone on the ledge of a huge rock. The first *bastaixos* reappeared, on their way back to the quarry. Nobody spoke, merely exchanged glances. Arnau gritted his teeth once more and lifted the stone again. Some of the *bastaixos* nodded their approval, but none of them halted. 'It's his challenge,' one of them commented later, when Arnau was out of earshot, and he turned to look at his painful progress. 'He has to do it on his own,' another man agreed.

After he had passed the western wall and left Framenors behind, Arnau came across the first inhabitants of Barcelona. All his attention was still on his feet. He was in the city! Sailors, fishermen, women and children, men from the boatyards and ships' carpenters all stared in silence at the boy bent double under the stone, his face sweaty and mottled from the effort. They looked at the feet of this youthful *bastaix*, and he could see nothing else. Everyone was silently willing him on: one foot, then the other, one after the other . . .

Some of them fell in behind him, still without saying a word. After more than two hours' effort, Arnau finally arrived at Santa Maria accompanied by a small, silent crowd. Work on the church came to a halt. The workmen stood at the edge of the scaffolding. Carpenters and stonemasons downed their tools. Father Albert, Pere and Mariona were there, waiting for him. Àngel, the boatman's son who by now was a craftsman, came up to him.

'Keep going!' he shouted. 'You're there! You've made it! Come on, you can do it!'

Shouts of encouragement came from the highest scaffolding. The crowd that had followed Arnau through the city cheered and applauded. All Santa Maria joined in, even Father Albert. Yet Arnau still stared down at his feet: one, then the other, one, then the other . . . all the way to the area where the stones were stored. As he reached it, apprentices and craftsmen rushed to receive the block the boy had carried.

Only then did Arnau look up. He was still bent double, and his body was shaking all over. But he smiled. People crowded all round to congratulate him. Arnau found it hard to tell who they all were: the only one he recognized was Father Albert. He was staring in the direction of Les Moreres cemetery. Arnau followed his gaze.

'For you, Father,' he whispered.

When the crowd had dispersed and Arnau was preparing to head back towards the quarry as his companions had done – some of them by now had made as many as three journeys – the priest called out to him. Josep, the guild alderman, had given him instructions.

'I've got a job for you,' he said. Arnau came to a halt and looked at him, puzzled. 'You have to clean the Jesus chapel, to sort out the candles and tidy everything.'

'But . . .' Arnau protested, pointing to the blocks of stone.

'There are no buts about it.'

19

It had been a hard day. Midsummer had only just past, and nightfall came late. The *bastaixos* had to work from dawn to dusk loading and unloading the ships that came into the port, and were always under pressure from merchants and captains, who wanted to stay the shortest time possible in the port of Barcelona.

Arnau entered Pere's house dragging his feet and carrying his leather strap in his hand. Eight faces turned towards him. Pere and Mariona were seated at table with another man and woman. Joan, a boy and two girls were sitting on the floor by the wall. All of them were eating from bowls.

'Arnau,' Pere said to him, 'these are our new tenants. Gastó Segura, an artisan tanner.' The man merely nodded his head slightly, still eating. 'His wife, Eulàlia.' She did smile at him. 'And their three children: Simó, Aledis and Alesta.'

Arnau was exhausted. He waved his hand sketchily in the direction of Joan and the tanner's three children, and went to take the bowl Mariona was offering him. Yet something made him take a second look at the three young newcomers. What was it . . .? Their eyes! The two girls were openly staring at him. Their eyes were . . . they were huge, a rich chestnut brown, sparkling with life. They both smiled at him.

'Eat, lad!'

Their smiles vanished. Alesta and Aledis quickly dropped their gaze to their bowls again, while Arnau turned to the tanner, who had stopped eating and was lifting his chin towards Mariona, who was offering Arnau his bowl from the fire.

Mariona gave him her place at the table, and Arnau started to eat. Opposite him, Gastó Segura was chewing his food with his mouth wide open. Every time Arnau looked up, the tanner was staring at him.

After a while, Simó got up and handed his empty bowl and those of his sisters to Mariona.

'To bed with you,' Gastó said, breaking the silence.

The tanner's eyes narrowed as he concentrated his gaze on Arnau once more; the young *bastaix* felt so uncomfortable he stared down at his bowl and only heard the sound of the girls getting up and bidding everyone a timid goodnight. When their steps had faded on the stairs, he looked up again. Gastó's interest in him seemed to have waned.

'What are they like?' he asked Joan that night, the first they spent on their straw pallets each side of the hearth.

'Who?' asked Joan.

'The tanner's daughters.'

'What do you mean? They're normal enough,' said Joan, gesticulating to show his incomprehension in a way that his brother could not see in the darkness. 'They're normal girls. At least I suppose so.' He hesitated. 'In fact, I don't really know. I haven't been allowed to speak to them; their brother didn't even let me shake their hands. When I went to do so, he stepped between us so I couldn't reach them.'

But Arnau was not even listening. How could eyes like theirs be normal? And they had both smiled at him.

At first light next morning, Pere and Mariona came down to find that Arnau and Joan had already put away their mattresses. A short time later, the tanner and his son appeared. None of the women were with them: Gastó had forbidden them to appear until the two lads had gone. Arnau left Pere's house with their huge brown eyes still imprinted on his mind.

'Today you're at the chapel,' one of the guild aldermen told him when he reached the shore. The previous evening he had noticed Arnau was staggering under his last load.

Arnau nodded. He was no longer upset whenever he was sent to the chapel. Nobody cast any doubt on the fact that he was a *bastaix* now; the guild aldermen had confirmed it and even though he could still not carry as much as Ramon or most of the others, he had shown he was as willing as any of them to work hard. They all appreciated him. Besides, those brown eyes . . . they would probably distract him from his work. And he felt tired: he had not slept well next to the hearth. He went into Santa Maria through the main door of the old church, which was still standing. Gastó Segura had not even let them glance at his daughters. Why shouldn't he look at two perfectly normal girls? And that morning he had probably forbidden them— He tripped over a rope and almost fell. He stumbled on a few yards, getting caught up in more ropes, until he felt a pair of strong hands grip his shoulders. He had twisted his ankle, and cried out in pain.

'Hey!' he heard the man who had grabbed him say. 'You should be more careful. Look what you've done!'

His ankle was hurting, but he looked down at the floor. He had pulled out the ropes and stakes that

Berenguer de Montagut used . . . but . . . surely this couldn't be him? He turned slowly round to see who had helped him. It couldn't be the master builder! He flushed when he saw he was face to face with none other than Berenguer de Montagut. Then he looked round and saw that all the craftsmen had halted in their work and were staring at them.

'I . . .' he stammered. 'If you like . . .' He pointed to the mess of ropes entangled round his feet. '. . . If you like I could help you . . . I . . . I'm sorry, master.'

All at once, Berenguer de Montagut's face relaxed. He was still holding Arnau by the arm. 'You're the *bastaix*,' he said with a smile. Arnau nodded. 'I've seen you here often.'

His smile grew broader. The workmen seemed relieved. Arnau looked down again at the ropes round his feet.

'I'm sorry,' he repeated.

'Don't worry.' The master builder waved to the others to sort out the mess. 'Come and sit with me. Does it hurt?'

'I don't want to be any trouble,' said Arnau, grimacing with pain as he bent down to free himself of the ropes.

'Wait.' Berenguer de Montagut got him to straighten up, and knelt down himself to untangle the ropes. Arnau hardly dared look at him, but glanced instead at the workmen. They were watching in astonishment. The master builder on his knees before a simple *bastaix*!

'We have to take care of these men,' he shouted to everyone once he had freed Arnau's feet. 'Without them, we would have no stones for the church. Come and sit down by me. Does it hurt?'

Arnau shook his head, but he was limping, trying not to cling on to the master. Berenguer de Montagut took him firmly by the arm and led him towards some pillars that were lying flat on the ground, waiting to be hoisted into position. The two of them sat on one. 'I'm going to tell you a secret,' he said as soon as they were settled. Arnau turned towards him. Berenguer de Montagut was going to tell him a secret! What more could possibly happen to him that morning?

'The other day I tried to lift the block of stone you brought here. I could hardly manage it.' Berenguer shook his head. 'I couldn't imagine taking even a few steps with it. This church belongs to you,' he said, surveying the building work. Arnau felt a shiver run through him. 'Some day, when our grandchildren, or their children, or the children of their children are alive, and people look at this, they won't mention Berenguer de Montagut: it will be you they talk of, my boy.'

Arnau could scarcely speak. The master! What did he mean? How could a *bastaix* be more important than the great Berenguer de Montagut, the man who had built Santa Maria and Manresa Cathedral? Surely he was the important one.

'Does it hurt?' insisted the master builder.

'No . . . a little. It's only a slight twist.'

'I hope so.' Berenguer de Montagut patted him on the back. 'We need your stones. There's still a lot to do.'

Arnau followed his gaze as he surveyed the work going on.

'Do you like it?' Berenguer de Montagut asked him suddenly.

Did he like it? It was a question Arnau had never asked himself. He had watched the church growing: its walls, apses, its magnificent, slender columns, its buttresses, but . . . did he like it?

'They say it will be the best church to the Virgin in the whole of Christianity,' he said finally.

Berenguer turned to him and smiled. How could he explain to a youth, a *bastaix*, what the church would be like, when not even bishops or noblemen could envisage his creation?

'What's your name?'

'Arnau.'

'Well, Arnau, I don't know if it will be the best' – Arnau forgot his aching foot and turned to face him – 'but what I can assure you is that it will be unique, and to be unique does not mean to be better or worse, but simply that: unique.'

Berenguer de Montagut stared intently at the construction work. He went on: 'Have you heard of France or Lombardy, or Genoa, Pisa, Florence?' Arnau nodded – of course he had heard of his country's enemies. 'Well, all those places are building churches as well: magnificent cathedrals, grandiose and lavishly decorated. The princes of those realms want their churches to be the biggest and most beautiful in the world.'

'But isn't that what we want too?'

'Yes and no.' Arnau shook his head, confused. Berenguer de Montagut turned to him and smiled. 'Let's see if you can understand. We want this to be the finest church ever, but we want to achieve that by different means than the others. We want the home of the patron saint of the sea to be a home for all Catalans, to be like the homes in which the faithful themselves live. We want it to be conceived and built in the same spirit that has made us what we are, making use of what is uniquely ours: the sea, the sunlight. Do you understand?'

Arnau thought for a few moments, then shook his head again.

'At least you're sincere,' laughed the master builder. 'Those princes create things for their personal glory. We do it for ourselves. I've noticed that sometimes, instead of carrying a load on your own, two of you use a pole and carry it between you.'

'Yes, when it's too big and heavy to carry on our backs.'

'What would happen if we made that pole twice as long?'

'It would snap.'

'Well, that's exactly what happens with those princes' churches . . . No, I don't mean they break,' he added, seeing the boy's surprised look. 'What I mean is that they want them to be so big, tall and long that they have to make them as narrow as possible. Big, long and narrow: do you see?' This time, Arnau nodded. 'But our church will be the opposite. It won't be as long or as tall, but it will be very broad, so that every Catalan will be able to find room to be with their Virgin. Once it's finished, you'll be able to appreciate it: there will be a shared space for all the faithful, without distinction. And the only decoration will be the light: the light of the Mediterranean. We don't need anything more than that: space and the light that will pour in from down there.' Berenguer de Montagut pointed to the apse, and drew his hand down towards the floor. 'This church will be for the common people, not for the greater glory of any prince.'

'Master . . .' The ropes and stakes had been sorted out, and one of the craftsmen had appeared next to them.

'Do you understand now?'

It would be for the common people! 'Yes, master.'

'Remember, your blocks of stone are like gold to this church,' Montagut said, clambering to his feet. 'Does it still hurt?'

Arnau had completely forgotten about his ankle. He shook his head.

Since he did not have to work with the *bastaixos* that day, Arnau returned home early. He had cleaned the chapel quickly, replaced the spent candles with new ones, said a rapid prayer and bid the Virgin farewell. Father Albert saw him running from the church, and Mariona saw him running into the house.

'What's wrong?' the old woman asked. 'What are you doing here so early?'

Arnau glanced quickly round the kitchen: there the three of them were – mother and two daughters, sewing at the table. The three of them gazed at him.

'Arnau!' Mariona repeated. 'Is something wrong?'

He realized he was blushing. 'No . . .' He had not even thought of an excuse! How could he have been so stupid? And they were staring at him: all three of them, peering at him standing in the doorway, panting. 'No,' he said, 'it's just that I finished early today.'

Mariona smiled and glanced at the girls. Their mother Eulàlia could not help smiling either.

'Well, if you've finished early,' said Mariona, disturbing his thoughts, 'you can go and fetch me some water.'

She had looked at him again, thought Arnau as he carried the bucket to the Àngel fountain. Did that mean something? He swung the bucket: of course it did.

He did not have much opportunity to find out. If it was not Eulàlia who got in his way, he came up against Gastó's few remaining blackened teeth; and if neither of them was in the house, Simó mounted guard over his two sisters. For days, Arnau had to be content with casting glances at them out of the corner of his eye. Occasionally he could get a good look at their faces: they had delicate features, with strong chins and prominent cheekbones. Their noses looked Roman, and both had shining white teeth and those amazing brown eyes. On other occasions, when the sun shone in through the windows, Arnau felt he could almost touch the blue sheen on the silky locks of their jet-black hair. Once or twice, when he felt really safe, he allowed his gaze to travel downwards from the elder sister Aledis's face to her chest, where he could just make out her breasts that could be glimpsed even through the coarse cloth of her smock. The sight made his body quiver. And when he was sure no one was watching him, he even dared to look lower still, at the curves of her body and legs.

Gastó Segura had lost everything during the months of hunger. This had made him even more bitter than he already was by nature. His son Simó worked with him as an apprentice, but his greatest concern was his two daughters, whom he could not provide with dowries in order to secure good husbands. Yet their beauty was in their favour, and Gastó was sure they would make good matches. If they did, that would be two fewer mouths to feed.

For that reason, he was desperate for them to remain untouched, so that no one in Barcelona could have the slightest doubt about their good character. This was the only way, he told Eulàlia and Simó, that Aledis and Alesta could make good marriages. Father, mother and elder brother had all taken this task upon themselves, but whereas Gastó and Eulàlia thought there would be no problem fulfilling it, Simó was more worried about them living for any length of time in the same house as Arnau and Joan.

Joan had become the outstanding pupil at the cathedral school. He had mastered Latin in no time at all, and his teachers were delighted at this thoughtful, sensitive pupil who in addition was deeply devout. He was so gifted that nearly all of them foresaw a great future ahead of him in the Church. Joan gradually won Gastó's and Eulàlia's respect, and the two of them would often sit with Pere and Mariona and listen in rapt attention to the way the young lad explained the holy scriptures. As a rule it was only the priests who could read those books written in Latin and yet now, in this humble house by the sea, the four of them could enjoy the sacred teachings, the ancient parables and other messages from the Lord which they had previously only heard from the pulpit.

If Joan had won the respect of all those around him, Arnau could say the same; even Simó regarded him with great admiration: a *bastaix*! Almost everyone in La Ribera knew of the efforts Arnau made to carry stone for the Virgin. 'They say that the great Berenguer de Montagut got on his knees to help him,' another apprentice had told Simó, hands spread wide in astonishment. Simó imagined the great master, respected by noblemen and bishops, kneeling at Arnau's feet. When the master spoke, everyone, including his father, kept silent, and when he shouted . . . when he shouted, everyone trembled. Simó watched Arnau when he came home at night. He was always the last to arrive. He looked tired and sweaty, carrying the leather headpiece in his hand, and yet . . . he was smiling! When had Simó ever come home from work smiling? On several occasions, he had crossed Arnau's path as he was carrying stones down to Santa Maria: his legs, arms and chest seemed made of iron. Simó stared at the block of stone and then at Arnau's straining face: how could he possibly have seen him smile?

All this explained why, despite being older than the Estanyols, when Simó had to look after his sisters and Arnau or Joan appeared, he kept in the background and the two girls could enjoy the freedom they were denied when their parents were there.

'Let's go for a walk on the beach!' Alesta suggested one day.

Simó wanted to refuse. Walking along the beach? What would his father say if he saw them?'

'All right,' said Arnau.

'It will do us good,' Joan agreed.

Simó said nothing. So the five of them went out into the sunshine: Aledis with Arnau, Alesta alongside Joan, and Simó bringing up the rear. Both the girls let the sea breeze play with their hair, and mould their loose smocks against their bodies, outlining their breasts, stomach and thighs.

They walked along in silence, looking out to sea or kicking at the sand, until they came across a group of *bastaixos* relaxing on the beach. Arnau waved at them.

'Would you like me to introduce you to them?' he asked Aledis.

She glanced over at the group of men. They were all staring at her. What could they be looking at? The breeze pressed her smock up against her breasts and nipples. Dear God! It seemed as though they were trying to burst out of the material. Aledis blushed and shook her head, although Arnau was already going over to the men. She turned on her heel, and Arnau was left standing there.

'Run and catch her, Arnau,' he heard one of his colleagues shout.

'Don't let her get away,' another one said.

'She's a pretty one!' a third man added.

Arnau ran until he had caught up with Aledis.

'What's wrong?'

She did not answer. She turned her face away and held her arms folded across her chest, but did not insist they return home. So they walked on along the beach, with only the sound of waves for company.

20

That same night, as they were eating by the hearth, Aledis rewarded Arnau with an extra second's attention, a second when she kept those enormous brown eyes of hers fixed on him.

It was a second when Arnau once more heard the waves on the shore, and felt his feet sinking into the sand. He glanced round to see if anyone else had noticed, but Gastó was still talking to Pere, and nobody else seemed to have seen a thing. No one seemed to hear the waves.

When he dared look at her again, Aledis had lowered her gaze and was pushing her food around the bowl.

'Eat, child!' Gastó the tanner ordered, seeing her toying with the food rather than putting it in her mouth. 'Food isn't for playing with.'

Gastó's words brought Arnau back down to earth. For the rest of the meal, not only did Aledis avoid looking at him again, but she made a deliberate show of ignoring him.

It was several days before she offered him a silent gift like the one she had given him that night after their walk along the beach. Until then, on the few occasions they met, Arnau had been longing to see her eyes on him, but Aledis always managed to avoid him, or kept her face turned away.

'Goodbye, Aledis,' he said to her absent-mindedly one morning as he left for the beach.

It so happened that they were alone at the time. Arnau was about to shut the door behind him, but something he could not describe made him turn and look at the girl instead. There she stood, erect and beautiful by the hearth, an invitation in her great brown eyes.

Finally! Finally. Arnau blushed and looked away. Flustered, he made to shut the door, but as he was doing so, he stopped a second time: Aledis was still standing there, calling out to him with those eyes of hers. And she smiled. Aledis had smiled at him!

His hand slipped off the door latch. He stumbled and almost fell. He did not dare look at her again, but rushed off towards the beach, leaving the door wide open.

'He gets embarrassed,' Aledis whispered to her sister that same evening, when the two of them were lying on their own on the pallet they shared before their parents and brother came upstairs.

'Why should he be?' Alesta asked. 'He's a *bastaix*. He works in the port and carries blocks of stone for the Virgin. You're only a young girl. He's a man,' she added, with more than a hint of admiration.

'You're the silly young girl!' her sister snapped.

'Oh, and you're a grown woman, are you?' Alesta replied, turning her back on her sister as she spoke the same words their mother used whenever either of them asked for something they were not old enough to have.

'That's enough,' Aledis said, to calm her.

A grown woman. I am, aren't I? Aledis thought of her mother and her friends, of her father. Perhaps . . .

257

perhaps her sister was right. Why would somebody like Arnau, a *bastaix* who had shown the whole of Barcelona his devotion to the Virgin of the Sea, become embarrassed when a young girl like her looked at him?

'He gets embarrassed. I'm sure of it,' Aledis insisted the following night.

'Silly goose! Why would he?'

'I don't know,' Aledis replied, 'but he does. He gets embarrassed when he looks at me. And when I look at him. He gets flustered, he turns red, he runs away . . .'

'You're crazy!'

'Maybe so, but . . .' Aledis was sure she was right. Although the previous night her sister had made her doubt it, she would not succeed again. She had proven it. She had watched Arnau, and waited for the right moment, when nobody could catch them by surprise. She went up to him, so close she breathed in his body smell. 'Hello, Arnau.' Nothing more than that, a simple greeting accompanied by a gentle smile, so close to him they were almost touching. Arnau blushed again, looked away, and tried to retreat. When Aledis saw him pull away from her, she smiled again, this time out of pride at discovering a power she did not know she had. 'You'll see tomorrow,' she told her sister.

The fact that her sister was there as a witness led her to take her coquettishness still further: she was sure she would succeed. That morning, as Arnau was about to leave the house, Aledis stood between him and the door, leaning against it. She had planned the move over and over again in her mind while her sister slept.

'Why don't you want to talk to me?' she said softly to Arnau, staring him straight in the eye.

She was amazed at her own audacity. She had said the sentence so many times to herself she was uncertain whether she would be able to get it out without stumbling over the words. If Arnau answered, she would be lost, but to her delight this did not happen. Aware of the presence of Alesta, Arnau turned instinctively towards Aledis, his cheeks reddening as they always did. He could not leave; nor did he dare look at Alesta.

'I, yes . . . I—'

'You, you, you,' Aledis interrupted him, growing bolder. 'You run away from me. We used to talk and laugh together, but now, whenever I try to approach you . . .'

Aledis stood as straight as she could in front of him. Her young breasts poked through her smock. Despite the rough cloth, her nipples stood out like crossbow bolts. Arnau saw them, and not all the stones in the royal quarry could have made him take his eyes off what Aledis was offering him. His whole body quivered.

'Girls!'

Eulàlia's voice as she came down the stairs brought them all back to reality. Aledis opened the door and went out before her mother could reach the ground floor. Arnau turned to Alesta, who was still standing watching everything open-mouthed, then rushed out of the door as well. Aledis had already vanished.

That night in bed the two girls were whispering to each other again, trying to find answers to the questions raised by this new experience that they could not share with anyone. What Aledis was sure of, although she did not know how to explain it to her sister, was the power her body had over Arnau. This feeling delighted her, filling her entirely. She wondered if all men would react in the same way, but was unable to see herself with anyone other than Arnau: she would never have behaved like this with Joan or any of the tanning apprentices who were friends of her brother Simó. Just imagining it made her . . . And yet, when it came to Arnau, something inside her broke free . . .

*   *   *

'What's wrong with the lad?' Josep the guild alderman asked Ramon.

'I don't know,' Ramon answered in all sincerity.

The two men looked across at the boats, where Arnau was vigorously demanding they give him one of the heaviest loads. When he succeeded, Josep, Ramon and the others saw him stagger off under its weight, with clenched jaw and strained face.

'He won't be able to keep this pace up,' Josep asserted.

'He's young,' Ramon said, trying to defend him.

'He won't be able to withstand it.'

They had all noticed. Arnau demanded the heaviest loads and stones as if his life depended on it. He almost ran back to get the next job, again calling for them to load him down with more weight than was good for him. At the end of the day, he limped back exhausted to Pere's house.

'What's the matter, lad?' Ramon asked him the next day, as they were both carrying heavy bundles to the city storehouses.

Arnau said nothing. Ramon was unsure whether his silence was because he did not want to talk, or because for some reason he could not do so. His face was strained again because of the weight on his back.

'If you have a problem, perhaps I—'

'No, no . . .' Arnau managed to stutter. How could he tell Ramon his body was burning with desire for Aledis? How could he tell him he could only find peace and quiet by loading heavier and heavier weights on his back until his mind was fixed only on reaching his destination, and forgot her eyes, her smile, her breasts, her entire body? How could he tell him that whenever Aledis played her little games with him, he lost all control of his thoughts and imagined her naked beside him, caressing his body? It was then that he would recall the priest's warnings about forbidden relationships: 'They're a sin! A sin!' he would warn the faithful loudly. How could he tell Ramon he wanted to return home so exhausted that he would crumple on to the pallet and fall asleep at once, despite the fact that she was so close by? 'No, no,' he repeated. 'But thanks, Ramon.'

'He'll collapse,' Josep insisted at the end of that day.

This time Ramon did not dare contradict him.

'Don't you think you're going too far?' Alesta asked her sister one night.

'Why?'

'If Father found out . . .'

'What is he supposed to find out?'

'That you love Arnau.'

'I don't love Arnau! It's just that . . . I feel good, Alesta. I like him. When he looks at me . . .'

'You love him,' her younger sister insisted.

'No! How can I explain it? When I see him looking at me, when he blushes, it's as though a little caterpillar were crawling through me.'

'You love him.'

'No. Go to sleep! What would you know about it?'

'You love him! You love him! You love him!'

Aledis decided to say nothing: but did she love him? She only knew she liked being looked at and desired. She was pleased that Arnau could not take his eyes off her body. She was content that he was so obviously upset when she ceased flirting with him: was that loving someone? Aledis tried to find an answer, but before long she lapsed into a state of pleased contentment, and then fell asleep.

One morning, Ramon left the beach when he saw Joan coming out of Pere's house. 'What's wrong with your brother?' he asked straight out.

Joan thought it over. 'I think he's in love with Aledis, Gastó the tanner's daughter.'

Ramon burst out laughing. 'Well, that love is driving him mad,' he warned Joan. 'If he carries on like this, he'll collapse. No one can work as hard as he is doing. He can't take all that exertion. He wouldn't be the first *bastaix* to drop . . . but your brother is very young to be crippled. Do something, Joan.'

That same night, Joan tried to talk to his brother. 'What's bothering you, Arnau?' he asked, lying on his pallet.

Arnau said nothing.

'You ought to tell me. I'm your brother and I want . . . I'd like to help. You've always shared my worries; let me do the same for you.'

Joan waited while his brother struggled to find the words.

'It's . . . it's because of Aledis,' Arnau admitted finally. Joan did not want to interrupt. 'I don't know what's happened to me with her, Joan. Ever since we went for that walk on the beach, something's changed between us. She looks at me as though she'd like to . . . I don't know what. And I . . .'

'And you what?' Joan prompted him when he fell silent.

I'm not going to tell him about anything except for the way she looks at me, Arnau decided, as the image of Aledis's breasts flashed through his mind.

'Nothing.'

'So, what's the problem?'

'I have bad thoughts. I imagine I can see her naked. Well, that I'd like to see her naked. I'd like . . .'

Joan had recently been asking his tutors to tell him more about women, without realizing his interest came from his concern about his brother, and his fears that he could be led astray. His teachers had been only too glad to explain at length all the theories on the character and perverse nature of women.

'You're not to blame for that,' Joan told Arnau.

'Why not?'

'Because wickedness is one of the four natural illnesses mankind is born with as a result of original sin,' he told him, whispering across the hearth where they slept, 'and women's wickedness is greater than any other in the world.' Joan repeated word for word what he had heard his masters tell him.

'What are the other three illnesses?'

'Avarice, ignorance and apathy, or the inability to do good.'

'But what has wickedness got to do with Aledis?'

'Women are wicked by nature, and take pleasure in tempting men on to the paths of evil.'

'Why?'

'Because women are like moving air, like vapour. They shift constantly, like the breeze.' Joan could remember the priest who had made that comparison standing there, his arms outstretched, his hands waving around his head. 'Secondly, because women, by nature – because they were made that way – have so little common sense, and therefore have no way of keeping their natural wickedness in check.'

Joan had read all this, and a lot more besides, but was unable to put the ideas into words. The wise men further stated that women were also by nature cold and phlegmatic, and it is well known that when something cold finally catches fire, it burns fiercely. According to authority, women were without doubt the antithesis of men, and were therefore incoherent and absurd. One had only to look at the difference in their bodies: women's bodies were broad at the base and narrow at the top, whereas a well-formed man's body should be the opposite, narrow from the chest down, but broad in the chest and back, with a short, vigorous neck and a large head. When a woman is born, the first letter she pronounces is an 'e', which is a letter to complain with; men by contrast first say the letter 'a', the first letter of the alphabet, opposed to 'e'.

'It's not possible. Aledis is not like that,' Arnau objected.

'Don't be fooled. Apart from the Virgin, who conceived Jesus without sin, all other women are the same. Even your guild's ordinances say so! Don't they prohibit adulterous relations? Don't they insist that any man who has a friendship or lives with an immodest woman be expelled?'

Arnau had no reply to that argument. He had no opinion about the theses of wise men and philosophers, and however much Joan insisted, he was not really interested; but he could not go against the rules of his guild. He knew what they were, and the guild aldermen had warned that if he broke them he would be expelled. And the guild could not be wrong!

Arnau was extremely confused. 'So what's to be done? If all women are evil—'

'First you must marry,' Joan butted in, 'and once you are married, follow the teachings of the Church.'

To get married . . . the thought had never crossed Arnau's mind, but if that were the only solution . . .

'What does one have to do once one is married?' he asked, his voice trembling at the thought of being with Aledis for ever.

Joan returned to the arguments he had learnt from his masters: 'A good husband should strive to control his wife's natural wickedness by applying the following principles: firstly, the woman should be governed by the man, and should submit to him. "*Sub potestate viri eris,*" we are told in Genesis. Secondly, as Ecclesiastes says: "*Mulier si primatum haber . . .*"' Joan hesitated. '"*Mulier si primatum habeat contraria est viro suo,"* which means that if it is the woman who rules at home, she will stand against her husband. Another principle is to be found in Proverbs: *"Qui delicate a pueritia nutrit servum suum, postea illum sentiet contumacem."* That means that whoever is gentle with people meant to serve them – among whom are included women – will find rebellion where there should be humility, submission and obedience. If, despite all this, wickedness is still apparent in a man's wife, he should punish her by putting her to shame and through fear. He should correct her from the start, when she is still young, rather than wait for her to grow old.'

Arnau listened in silence to his brother's words.

'Joan,' Arnau said once he had finished. 'Do you think I could marry Aledis?'

'Of course! But you ought to wait a while until you have made your way in the guild and can support her. In any case, it would be wise to speak to her father before he promises her to anyone else, because if he does that, you are lost.'

The image of Gastó Segura and his few blackened teeth seemed to Arnau like an unsurmountable obstacle. Joan guessed what his brother was afraid of.

'You have to do it,' he insisted.

'Would you help me?'

'Of course.'

Silence returned to the two straw pallets ranged either side of the hearth.

'Joan,' said Arnau after a few moments.

'What is it?'

'Thank you.'

'It's nothing.'

The two brothers tried hard to sleep, but found it impossible. Arnau was too excited at the idea of marrying his beloved Aledis. Joan was lost in memories of his mother. Could Ponç the coppersmith have been right?

Wickedness is natural in women. A woman should be ruled by man. A man should punish his wife. Could the coppersmith have been acting justly? How could he respect his mother's memory and give his brother this kind of advice? Joan remembered his mother's hand poking out of the tiny window of her prison, caressing his head. He remembered how he had hated – and still did – the coppersmith Ponç . . . *but what if he had been right?*

Over the next few days, neither of them had the courage to speak to the bad-tempered Gastó, whose situation as tenant in Pere's house constantly reminded him of his misfortune at losing his own home. He became increasingly sour whenever he was in the house, which was the one time the two brothers had the opportunity to raise the question with him. His endless growls, protests and insults continually made them postpone the idea.

Arnau was still bewitched by the atmosphere Aledis generated. He watched her, followed her with his eyes and in his imagination. There was no moment in the day when he did not think of her, except when Gastó made his appearance: the presence of her father made his heart shrink.

This was because however much the priests and his own guild might forbid him from doing so, he could not take his eyes off Aledis when she, knowing she was alone with her plaything, seemed to take every opportunity to allow her loose, faded smock to press against her body. Arnau was ensnared by the vision: those nipples, breasts – Aledis's entire body was calling out to him. You will be my wife. One of these days you will be my wife, he thought, his mind ablaze. He imagined her naked, his mind wandering along forbidden, unknown paths: the only naked female body he had ever seen had been that of the tortured Habiba.

On other occasions, Aledis bent over in front of Arnau. She did not kneel down, but bent from the waist, deliberately showing off her rear and the curves of her hips. She also took advantage of every opportunity she had to raise her smock above her knees and show her thighs. Or she would put her hands on the small of her back, pretending to feel a non-existent pain, and bend backwards so that he could see how flat and smooth her stomach was. Afterwards she would smile or, making as if she had suddenly discovered Arnau's presence, would seem embarrassed. When she went out, Arnau was left to struggle to wipe the images from his mind.

Whenever something like this happened, Arnau became even more determined to find the right moment to talk to Gastó.

'What the devil are you two doing just standing there?' Gastó spluttered once, when the two lads came up to him with the ingenuous idea of asking for his daughter's hand in marriage. Joan's tentative smile vanished as soon as the tanner stepped between them, pushing them away from him.

'You ask,' Arnau said to him on another occasion.

Gastó was alone at the table downstairs. Joan sat opposite him, cleared his throat and was just about to speak when the tanner suddenly looked up from the hide he was busy examining.

'I'll flay him alive! I'll tear his balls off!' the tanner exploded, spitting saliva out between the gaps in his blackened teeth. 'Simóoo!' Joan shrugged in despair towards the figure of Arnau, who was hiding in the corner of the room.

Simó came running. 'How could you have stitched this so badly?' Gastó said, pushing the piece of leather under his nose.

Joan got up from his chair and left them to it.

But he and Arnau did not give up.

'Gastó!' Joan shouted after him one evening when the tanner had left the house after supper, apparently in a good mood, and the two boys had followed him down to the beach.

'What do you want?' he said, still striding on.

At least he's letting us speak, the two boys thought.

'I wanted . . . to talk to you about Aledis . . .'

Hearing his daughter's name, Gastó came to a sudden halt. He turned and brought his face so close to Joan's that his rotten breath made the boy reel.

'What's she done?' Gastó respected Joan; he took him to be a serious young man. Hearing him mention Aledis, combined with his naturally suspicious nature, made him think the lad was about to accuse her of something. The tanner could not allow the slightest stain on his precious jewel's reputation.

'Nothing,' said Joan.

'What do you mean, nothing?' Gastó pressed him, his face still only inches away from Joan. 'Why did you mention Aledis then? Tell me the truth, what has she done?'

'Nothing, she's done nothing, I swear.'

'Nothing? And you, what about you?' he barked, turning to Arnau. Joan was relieved. 'What have you got to say for yourself? What do you know about Aledis?'

'Me? . . . Nothing . . .' Arnau's hesitation only served to increase the tanner's obsessive suspicions.

'Tell me!'

'There's nothing . . . no . . .'

'Eulàlia!' Gastó did not wait to hear any more. He bawled for his wife, and set off back to Pere's house to find her.

That night the two boys were overcome with guilt when they heard Eulàlia cry out in pain as Gastó tried to beat an impossible confession out of her.

They tried to broach the subject twice more, but got nowhere. After several weeks, disheartened, they decided to speak to Father Albert. He smiled and promised to talk to Gastó on their behalf.

'I'm sorry, Arnau,' Father Albert told him a week later. He had called the two boys to meet him on the beach. 'Gastó Segura does not agree to you marrying his daughter.'

'Why?' Joan wanted to know. 'Arnau is a good person.'

'Do you want my daughter to marry a slave from La Ribera?' the tanner had told the priest. 'A slave who doesn't earn enough to pay for a room?'

Father Albert tried to convince him: 'There are no slaves working in La Ribera. That was in olden times. You know it's forbidden for slaves to work—'

'It's work for slaves.'

'That's in the past too,' the priest insisted. 'Besides,' he added, 'I've found a good dowry for your daughter.' Gastó Segura, who thought the conversation had already finished, suddenly turned back to hear what the priest had to say. 'It will allow them to buy a house—'

Gastó interrupted him once more: 'My daughter doesn't need any rich man's charity! Keep your wiles for others!'

When he heard Father Albert's words, Arnau stared out to sea. Moonlight was shimmering across the water from horizon to shore, dying in the foam of the waves breaking on the beach.

Father Albert let the lapping of the waves calm them. What if Arnau asked the reasons behind the tanner's refusal? What could he tell him?'

'Why?' stammered Arnau, still staring out at the horizon.

'Gastó Segura is . . . a very strange man.' Father Albert could not break the boy's heart still further. 'He wants a nobleman to marry his daughter! How can a mere tanner aspire to something like that?'

A nobleman. Had the lad believed him? Nobody should feel belittled by the nobility. Even the waves lapping patiently, endlessly, on the shore seemed to be waiting for Arnau's reply.

A sob echoed along the beach.

Father Albert put his arm round Arnau's shoulder. He could feel his body shaking. He put his other arm round Joan, and the three of them stood gazing out to sea.

'You will find a good wife,' said the priest after a while.

Not like her, thought Arnau.

PART THREE

CHAINED TO PASSION

21

Four years had passed since Gastó Seguro refused to give
his daughter's hand in marriage to Arnau the *bastaix*. A
few months later, Aledis was married off to an old master
tanner, a widower for whom his young bride's charms
more than made up for her lack of dowry. Until the
moment she was given away, Aledis's mother never let
her out of her sight.

Arnau himself was now a tall, strong and good-
looking young man of eighteen. During those four years
he had lived from and for the guild of the *bastaixos*, the
church of Santa Maria and his brother Joan. He carried
more than his share of goods and stone blocks; he gave
money to the guild; he attended religious services
devoutly. But he had not married, and the guild aldermen were worried that a lusty young man like him might
fall into temptation, which would mean they would
have to expel him from the brotherhood.

Yet Arnau would not hear of marrying. When the
priest told him Gastó wanted nothing to do with him,
Arnau stood staring at the sea, thinking of the women
who had been part of his life: he had not even known

who his mother was; Guiamona had shown him affection, but then turned against him; Habiba had vanished in a welter of blood and pain – at night Arnau still often dreamt of Grau's whip lashing her naked body; Estranya had treated him like a slave; Margarida had laughed at him at his moment of greatest humiliation; and Aledis: what could he say about her? It was thanks to her that he had discovered the man inside him, but she had soon abandoned him.

'I have to take care of my brother,' he told the aldermen whenever they brought the matter up. 'You know he has dedicated his life to the Church, to serve God,' he would say while they thought of how to persuade him. 'What better aim could there be in life?'

At this the aldermen invariably fell silent.

This was how Arnau lived throughout those four years: calmly, wrapped up in his work, Santa Maria and, above all, Joan.

That second Sunday in July 1339 was a historic day for Barcelona. In January 1336, King Alfonso the Kind had died in the city, and after Easter that same year, his son Pedro was crowned in Zaragoza. He became Pedro III of Catalonia, Pedro IV of Aragon, and Pedro II of Valencia.

Between 1336 and 1339, the new monarch did not once visit Barcelona, the capital of Catalonia. Both the nobility and the merchants were concerned at this failure to pay homage to the kingdom's most important city. They were all well aware of the new King's dislike of the Catalan nobility: Pedro III was the son of Alfonso's first wife, Teresa de Entenza, Countess of Urgell and Viscountess of Ager. Teresa had died before her husband became king, and Alfonso remarried, this time to Eleonor of Castile, an ambitious and cruel woman by whom he had two sons.

Despite his conquest of Sardinia, King Alfonso was a weak, easily led man: Queen Eleonor quickly won large tracts of land and honours for her sons. Her next goal was to pursue her stepchildren, the children of Teresa de Entenza who were the heirs to the throne. Throughout the eight years of Alfonso the Kind's reign, Eleonor never missed an opportunity to attack the Infante Pedro, who was still a young boy, as well as his brother Jaime, Count of Urgell. Only two Catalan nobles, Pedro's godfather Ot de Montcada, and Vidal de Vilanova, the Knight Commander of Montalbán, supported the cause of Teresa's children. It was they who warned King Alfonso and the two brothers to escape before they were poisoned. Pedro and Jaime followed their advice, and hid in the mountains of Jaca in Aragon before finally securing the protection of the nobles of Aragon and seeking refuge in the city of Zaragoza, where they were protected by Archbishop Pedro de Luna.

This was the reason why Pedro's coronation broke with a tradition that had been upheld ever since the kingdom of Aragon had been united with the principality of Catalonia. While he ascended the throne of Aragon in Zaragoza, the right to rule Catalonia, which belonged to him as the Count of Barcelona, had always been granted in Catalan territory. Until Pedro III, new monarchs first took the oath in Barcelona, and were later crowned in Zaragoza. Whereas the King took the crown of Aragon simply because he was the new monarch, as Count of Barcelona he had to swear allegiance to the laws and customs of Catalonia, a ceremony that was regarded as essential before he could be crowned king.

As Count of Barcelona, Prince of Catalonia, the monarch was seen by the Catalan nobility simply as *primus inter pares*. This was evident from the oath that they swore him: 'We, who are as good as you, swear to your majesty, who is no better than us, that we will accept you as our king and sovereign liege, for as long as you respect all our freedoms and laws; if not, not.' As a result, when Pedro III was to be crowned, the Catalan nobles went to Zaragoza to demand that he come first to Barcelona to swear the oath there as all his predecessors had done. When the King refused, the Catalans walked out of the coronation. However, the King knew he must receive their oaths of loyalty, and so, despite renewed protests by the nobility and authorities in Barcelona, he chose to do so in the city of Leida. In June 1336, after swearing to respect the Catalan customs and laws, he duly received their expressions of loyalty.

So it was that on the second Sunday of July 1339, King Pedro paid his first visit to Barcelona, the city he had humiliated. Three reasons brought him there: the oath that his brother-in-law Jaime III, King of Mallorca, Count of Roussillon and Cerdagne and Lord of Montpellier, had to swear as a vassal of the Crown of Aragon; the general council of bishops of the province of Tarragona (to which Barcelona belonged); and the transfer of the remains of Saint Eulàlia the martyr from the church of Santa Maria to the cathedral.

The first two events took place out of sight of ordinary people. Jaime III expressly asked that his oath of allegiance be given not in front of the populace, but in the palace chapel before a small group of chosen nobles.

The third event, however, became a public spectacle. Nobles, churchmen and all the inhabitants of the city came out on to the streets. The most privileged among them accompanied the royal party as they first heard mass in the cathedral, then walked in procession down to Santa Maria, before finally returning to the cathedral with the martyr's remains.

All along the route, the streets were lined with people anxious to proclaim their King. Santa Maria's apse was already roofed over; work had begun on the second vault, but a part of the original Romanesque church still survived.

Saint Eulàlia was martyred during Roman rule, in the year 303. Her remains were kept first in the Roman cemetery and then in the church of Santa Maria de les Arenes, which was built on the pagan burial ground once Emperor Constantine had issued his edict authorizing Christian worship. When the Arabs invaded Spain, the men in charge of the tiny church decided to hide the martyr's remains. In 801, when the French King Louis the Pious liberated the city, Frodoí, the then Bishop of Barcelona, decided to search for the saint's relics. Once found, they were laid to rest in a small coffer in Santa Maria.

In spite of being draped in scaffolding and surrounded by stones and building material, Santa Maria looked splendid for the royal visit. The archdeacon, Bernat Rosell, together with members of the commission of works, noblemen, beneficiaries and other church dignitaries, all of them dressed in their finest robes, were there to greet the King. The bright colours of their garments were spectacular: the July morning sun poured in through the unfinished roof and windows of the church, glinting on the gold and metal adorning the vestments of those privileged enough to wait for the King inside.

The sun also glinted on the blunt tip of Arnau's dagger: the humble *bastaixos* had taken up a place of honour alongside all the important dignitaries. Some of them, Arnau included, stood outside the Jesus chapel, the one they looked after. Other *bastaixos* stood guard at the front doorway to the church, which was still part of the old Romanesque building.

The *bastaixos*, former slaves or *macips de ribera*, enjoyed many privileges in Santa Maria de la Mar. As well as being responsible for the church's main chapel and being the guardians of the main entrance, the masses for their celebrations were said at the high altar, the chief alderman of the guild kept the key of the Jesus chapel, and during Corpus Christi they were the ones who carried the statue of the Virgin, and also the lesser ones of Saints Tecla, Catherine and Macià. In addition, whenever a *bastaix* was close to death, the holy eucharist was carried to him, at whatever time of day or night, through the main doorway under its canopy.

That July morning, Arnau and his companions were allowed through the lines of soldiers protecting the royal party. He knew he was the envy of all the citizens thronging the streets in the hope of seeing the King. A mere labourer in the port, here he was striding into Santa Maria alongside noblemen and merchants, as if he were one of them. As he walked through the church on the way to his chapel, he found himself opposite Grau Puig, Isabel and his three cousins, all of them decked out in silk, as haughty and condescending as ever.

'Arnau,' he heard someone call just as he was continuing on past Margarida. Was it not enough for them to have ruined his father's life? Could they possibly be so cruel as to want to humiliate him still further in front of his colleagues, here in the church? 'Arnau,' he heard someone call again.

He looked up and saw Berenguer de Montagut standing in front of him, only a yard from the Puig family.

'Your excellency,' said the master builder, addressing the archdeacon. 'May I present Arnau . . .'

'Estanyol,' Arnau stammered.

'He is the *bastaix* I have often told you about. When he was only a boy, he was already carrying stones for the Virgin.'

The prelate nodded, and held out his ringed finger, which Arnau leant forward to kiss. Berenguer de Montagut patted him on the back. Arnau saw Grau and his family bowing to the prelate and the master builder, but neither paid them any attention, moving on to greet other nobles. Arnau straightened and strode away from the Puig family towards the Jesus chapel, where he joined his guild companions to stand guard.

Shouts from the crowd outside announced the arrival of the King and his retinue. King Pedro III; King Jaime of Mallorca; Queen María, Pedro's wife, the Infantes Pedro, Ramón Berenguer and Jaime – the first two the King's uncles, the last his brother; the Queen of Mallorca, also a sister of the King's; Cardinal Rodés, the papal envoy; the Archbishop of Tarragona; other bishops and prelates; nobles and knights: they all headed in procession down Carrer de la Mar to Santa Maria. Never before had Barcelona seen such a display of personalities, such wealth and pomp.

Pedro III, the Ceremonious, wanted to impress the people of Barcelona whom he had neglected for more than three years. He succeeded. The two Kings, the cardinal and the archbishop were carried on litters by bishops and nobles. At the provisional high altar, they received the chest with the martyr's remains. The entire congregation looked on closely and Arnau could scarcely contain his nervousness. The King himself carried the coffer with the holy relics from Santa Maria to the cathedral. He went inside, and handed over the remains for burial in the specially constructed chapel beneath the high altar.

22

After the interment of Saint Eulàlia's remains, the King held a banquet in his palace. Together with Pedro at the royal table sat the cardinal, the Kings of Mallorca and Aragon and the Queen Mother, the Infantes of the royal house and several prelates: twenty-five people in total. More noblemen occupied the other tables, as well as a large number of knights – the first time they had been included in a royal celebration. But not only the King and his court celebrated the occasion: the whole of Barcelona was given over to merriment for eight days.

Early each morning, Arnau and Joan attended mass and took part in the solemn processions that wound their way through the city to the tolling of the church bells. Then, like everyone else, they wandered the streets of Barcelona, enjoying the jousts and tournaments in Plaça del Born, where nobles and knights demonstrated their martial skills, either on foot wielding their big broadswords, or on horseback, charging each other with lances at the ready. The two young men were also fascinated by the mock sea battles staged in the streets. 'Out of the water they look much bigger,' Arnau commented to Joan, pointing out the men-o'-war and galleys mounted on wheels that were hauled round the city while their crews pretended to board and do battle with each other. Joan looked disapprovingly at Arnau whenever he made a small wager on cards or dice, but smiled and joined in the games of bowls, the *bòlit* and *escampella*, at which the young seminarian showed remarkable skill in knocking down the pins in the first and hitting the coins in the second.

But what Joan most enjoyed was to hear the songs about the heroic deeds of Catalans in history from the mouths of the many troubadours who had flocked to the city. 'This is the chronicle of King Jaime the First,' he told Arnau when they heard the tale of the conquest of Valencia. 'That is the story of Bernat Desclot,' he explained on another occasion when the troubadour had finished his account of the battles of Pedro the Great during his conquest of Sicily, or the French crusade against Catalonia.

'Today we have to go to Pla d'en Llull,' said Joan when another day's procession was over.

'Why is that?'

'A troubadour from Valencia who knows Ramon Muntaner's chronicle is going to perform there.' Arnau looked at him quizzically. 'Ramon Muntaner is a famous chronicler from Valencia. He was a leader of the Almogavars when they conquered the duchies of Athens and Neopatras. He wrote the history of the wars seven years ago, and I'm sure it will be interesting. At least it will be true.'

The Pla d'en Llull, an open area situated between Santa Maria and the Santa Clara convent, was filled to overflowing. People were sitting on the ground, talking among themselves but not taking their eyes off the spot where the Valencian troubadour was to appear: so great was his reputation that even noblemen had come to listen, accompanied by slaves carrying seats for their families. 'They're not here,' Joan told Arnau when he saw him looking anxiously among the nobles. Arnau had told him about his meeting with the Grau family in Santa Maria. The two found a good place to sit alongside a group of *bastaixos* who had been waiting for some time for the spectacle to begin. Arnau sat on the ground, but not before he had scanned all the noble families who stood out higher than all the rest.

'You should learn to forgive,' Joan whispered. Arnau said nothing, but gave him a hard look. 'A good Christian—'

'Joan,' Arnau interrupted him, 'never. I'll never forget what that harpy did to my father.'

At that moment the troubadour appeared, and the crowd broke into applause. Martí de Xàtiva was a tall, thin man with easy, fluent gestures. He raised his hands to call for silence.

'I am about to tell you the story of how and why six thousand Catalans conquered the Orient, how they defeated the Turks, the Byzantines, the Alans and all the other warlike peoples who tried to stand against them.'

Again, applause rang out all round the square. Arnau and Joan joined in.

'I will also recount how the Emperor of Byzantium murdered our admiral Roger de Flor and many other Catalans, after inviting them to a feast . . .' Someone shouted: 'Traitor!' and the rest of the public growled more insults. 'I will end by telling you how the Catalans took revenge for the death of their leader, devastating the Orient and sowing death and destruction in their wake. This is the story of the company of Catalan Almogavars who in the year of 1305 set sail under the command of Admiral Roger de Flor . . .'

The Valencian troubadour knew how to capture his audience's attention. He gesticulated and acted out his words, accompanied by two assistants. He also invited members of the public to take part.

'Now I turn again to our Caesar,' he said, as he began the story of the death of Roger de Flor. 'Accompanied by three hundred horsemen and a thousand footsoldiers, our admiral went to Adrianople where *xor* Miqueli, the emperor's son, had invited him to a feast in his honour.' At this point, the troubadour pointed to one of the most elegantly dressed nobles in the crowd and asked him to come up on to the stage to play the role of Roger de Flor. 'If you involve your audience,' the troubadour's master had explained, 'especially if they are nobles, they will give you more money.'

On the platform, the figure of Roger de Flor was received with adulation by the two assistants, acting out the first six days of his stay in Adrianople. On the seventh, *xor* Miqueli summoned Girgan, the leader of the Alans, and Melic, chief of the Turcopoles, and their eight thousand cavalrymen.

The troubadour strode restlessly round the stage. The crowd started to shout again: some of them got to their feet, and it took all the efforts of the two assistants to prevent them intervening to defend Roger de Flor. The troubadour himself stabbed the admiral, and the nobleman playing the part fell to the ground. The crowd bayed for revenge for the treachery. Joan looked across at Arnau, who sat there staring at the fallen nobleman. The eight thousand Alans and Turcopoles assassinated all the thirteen hundred Catalans who had followed Roger de Flor – the assistants made stabbing gestures at each other time and again.

'Only three men survived,' the troubadour continued, raising his voice. 'Ramon de Arquer, a knight from Castelló d'Empúries, Ramon de Tous . . .'

He went on to tell how the Catalans wreaked their revenge, laying waste to Thrace, Chalcidice, Macedonia and Thessaly. The crowd cheered whenever the singer mentioned any of these names. 'May the vengeance of the Catalans be upon you!' they cried over and over again. They all knew of the feats of the Almogavars when they reached the duchy of Athens. There they killed twenty thousand men and won another victory, after making Roger des Laur their captain. All this the troubadour sang, and then went on to relate how they gave the woman who had been married to the lord of La Sola as wife to their new leader. At this point, the troubadour sought out another nobleman, invited him up on stage, and then picked a woman from the audience and brought her up to accompany the new chief of the Almogavars.

'In this way,' sang the troubadour, joining the hands of the nobleman and the woman, 'the Almogavars shared out the city of Thebes and all the castles and lands of the duchy, and married off all the women to the men of the Almogavar company, according to their merits.'

As he was singing the final verses of Muntaner's chronicle, the two assistants chose men and women from the audience and formed them into two lines. Many were happy to be chosen: they saw themselves in the duchy of Athens, as Catalans who had avenged the death of Roger de Flor. The group of *bastaixos* caught the assistants' attention. The only unmarried man among them was Arnau, and so his companions hauled him to his feet and offered him as someone to join in the revelry. To the delight of his colleagues, he was immediately selected. Arnau went up on to the stage.

As soon as Arnau joined the line of Almogavars, a woman stood up from among the crowd and stared at him with her huge brown eyes. The assistants saw her: she was hard to miss, being so young and beautiful, and so insistent that she be allowed on the stage. When the two men came to lead her away, a surly old man grabbed her by the arm and tried to force her to sit down again. The crowd laughed as she tried to free herself from him. The assistants looked towards the troubadour, but he urged them to carry on: don't worry about humiliating someone, he had been told, if that means you get the rest on your side – and the rest of the audience was laughing openly at the old fellow, who by now was on his feet struggling with the young woman.

'She's my wife,' he tried to explain to one of the assistants, pushing him off.

'The vanquished have no wives,' the troubadour cried out from the stage. 'All the women of the duchy of Athens now belong to the Catalans.'

At this, the old man hesitated for just long enough to allow the troubadour's assistants to snatch the young woman from him and place her in the line of women. The crowd cheered.

The troubadour carried on with his chronicle, pairing off the Athenian women with the Almogavars to loud applause. Arnau and Aledis stared at each other. How long has it been, Arnau? those huge brown eyes of hers were asking him. Four years? Arnau glanced back at the group of *bastaixos*, all of whom were smiling and encouraging him. He could not meet Joan's gaze. Look at me, Arnau. Aledis had not opened her mouth, but Arnau could hear her calling him. Arnau's eyes sank deep into hers. The Valencian troubadour took her hand and led her across to Arnau. He lifted Arnau's hand and joined the two together.

Another shout of joy rang out. All the couples were in pairs facing the public, headed by Arnau and Aledis. Aledis could feel her whole body tremble as she gently squeezed Arnau's hand. He was looking out of the corner of his eye at the old tanner who was standing in the audience glaring at them.

'And so the Almogavars were married,' sang the

troubadour, pointing to the couples. 'They settled in the duchy of Athens and there, in the distant Orient, they still live, to the glory of Catalonia.'

The Pla d'en Llull burst into noisy applause. Aledis squeezed Arnau's hand again to catch his attention. They stared at each other. Take me, Arnau, those brown eyes of hers were begging him. All of a sudden, she was no longer beside him: her husband had grabbed her by the hair and was dragging her off in the direction of Santa Maria, to hoots of derision from everyone in the crowd.

'A few coins for the performance,' the troubadour said, stepping in front of him.

As reply, the tanner spat and carried on dragging Aledis away.

'Whore! Why did you do it?'

The old man still had strong arms, but Aledis felt nothing when he slapped her.

'I . . . I don't know. It was all the people, the way they were shouting; all at once I felt I was really in the Orient . . .'

'In the Orient? Harlot!'

The tanner picked up a leather strap, and Aledis forgot Arnau and how she had been unable to resist the temptation to join him.

'Please, Pau, please. I've no idea why I did it. Forgive me. I beg you, forgive me.' Aledis sank to her knees in front of her husband and lowered her head. The leather strap wavered in his hand.

'You are to stay inside the house until I give you permission to leave it,' he said, finally relenting.

Aledis said nothing more. She stayed on her knees until she heard the door to the street close behind him.

Four years earlier, her father had given her away in marriage. Since she had no dowry, this was the best Gastó could arrange for his daughter: an old master tanner who was a childless widower. 'One day you will inherit from him,' had been her father's only comment. He did not add that when the old man died it would be he, Gastó Segura, who would take his place at the head of the business. In his view, daughters did not need to know such trivial details.

On their wedding day, the old man had not waited for the end of the celebration to haul his young bride off to the bedroom. Aledis allowed herself to be undressed by his unsteady hands, and her breasts to be kissed by his drooling mouth. As he touched her, Aledis shuddered at the contact with his calloused, rough fingers. Pau quickly led her to the bed then fell on top of her, still in his clothes. He was slobbering, quivering, panting. He smothered her in kisses and bit her breasts. He thrust his hand between her legs. Then, still dressed, he started to pant more and more loudly, moved jerkily and finally sighed, rolled off and fell fast asleep.

It was the next morning that Aledis lost her virginity beneath a frail, weak body that pressed on her with clumsy desire. She wondered if she would ever feel anything other than disgust.

Each time she had to go down to the workshop for some reason or other, Aledis stared intently at her husband's apprentices. Why did none of them look at her? She could see them: her eyes followed the way their muscles tensed, and rejoiced at the drops of sweat that formed on their brows and then ran across their faces, down their necks and on to their strong, powerful chests. Aledis's desire moved to the rhythm of their arms as they tanned the hides, back and forth, back and forth . . . but her husband's orders had been very clear: 'Ten lashes of the whip for any of you who looks at my wife once; twenty for the second time; the third, no food.' So night after night Aledis asked herself what had happened to the pleasure she had heard so much about, the pleasure her young body demanded, the pleasure the decrepit husband she had been forced to marry could never offer.

Some nights the old man clawed at her with his rasping hands. On others, he forced her to stimulate him, or chivvied her to let him penetrate her as quickly as possible before his urge faded. Afterwards, he always fell sound asleep. On one such night, being careful not to wake him, Aledis got up silently. Her husband did not even move as she left the bed.

She went down to the workshop. The work benches stood out in the darkness. She walked between them, caressing the smooth surfaces with the fingers of one hand. What's the matter? Don't you desire me? Aledis was thinking dreamily of the apprentices as she stepped between the tables, stroking her breasts and thighs, when a dim glow in the corner of a wall caught her eye. A knot had fallen out of one of the planks separating the workshop from the area where the apprentices slept. Aledis went over and peeped through the hole. She immediately took a step back. Her whole body was trembling. She pressed her eye to the hole once more. They were all naked! For a moment she was afraid her breathing might give her away. One of the apprentices was touching himself as he lay on his mattress!

'Who are you thinking about?' asked the lad who lay closest to the wall where Aledis was hiding. 'The master's wife?'

The other apprentice made no reply, but kept on rubbing his penis, back and forth, back and forth . . . Aledis began to perspire. Without realizing what she was doing, she slid a hand between her legs and, staring at the boy who was thinking of her, quickly learnt how to give herself pleasure. She came even before the young lad did, and slumped to the ground beside the wall.

The next morning, Aledis walked by the apprentices' bench exuding desire. Without thinking, she came to a halt in front of the apprentice she had seen the night before. Eventually, he could stand it no longer, and surreptitiously glanced up. She knew it was true that he had been thinking of her, and smiled to herself.

That afternoon, Aledis was called back down to the workshop. The tanner was waiting for her behind the apprentice.

'My love,' he said when she came up to him, 'you know I don't like anyone disturbing my apprentices.'

Aledis saw the lad's back. It was crisscrossed by ten thin bloody lines. She said nothing. She did not return to the workshop that night, or the next one, or the one after that, but by mid-July she was there time and again, caressing her body with Arnau's hands. He was on his own! His eyes had told her so. He had to be hers!

23

Barcelona was still in the midst of celebrations.

It was a humble dwelling, like all those the *bastaixos* lived in, even if this one belonged to Bartolomé, one of the guild aldermen. Like most of their houses, it was situated in one of the narrow side streets that led down from Santa Maria, Plaça del Born or Pla d'en Llull to the beach. The big kitchen was situated on the ground floor, with walls made of adobe bricks. Above it was another floor, with wooden walls, that had been added later.

Arnau could feel his mouth watering at the meal Bartolomé's wife had prepared: fresh white wheat bread; beef with vegetables fried with strips of bacon right in front of them in a big pan on the fire, and seasoned with pepper, cinnamon and saffron! There was also wine with honey, cheese and sweetmeats.

'What are we celebrating?' asked Arnau. He was seated at table with Joan opposite him, Bartolomé on his left, and Father Albert to his right.

'You'll find out soon enough,' said the priest.

Arnau turned to Joan, but he said nothing.

'You'll soon see,' Bartolomé repeated. 'For now, just eat.'

Arnau shrugged and gladly accepted the bowl of meat and half-loaf of bread that Bartolomé's eldest daughter handed him.

'This is my daughter Maria,' said Bartolomé.

Arnau nodded, without lifting his gaze from his bowl. When the four men had been served, and the priest had blessed the meal, they made a start on the food. Bartolomé's wife, their daughter and four other young children did the same sitting on the floor, although they had only the usual stew.

Arnau savoured the meat and vegetables. What strange flavours he could taste! Pepper, cinnamon and saffron: they were what noblemen and rich merchants ate. 'When we boatmen unload sacks of spices,' one of them had told him on the beach one day, 'we pray that they don't fall into the sea or get spoilt somehow. If they did, there would be no way we could pay to replace them: it would be prison for sure.' Arnau tore off a chunk of bread and put it in his mouth, then picked up the glass of wine with honey . . . Why were they all staring at him like that? Although they tried to hide it, he was convinced the other three were studying him. Joan seemed to be looking steadfastly down at his food. Arnau concentrated on his own food once more: he took one, two, three spoonfuls, and then suddenly looked up: he could see Joan and Father Albert making signs at each other.

'All right, what's going on?' Arnau insisted, putting his spoon down on the table.

Bartolomé grimaced. 'What can we do?' he seemed to be asking the others.

'Your brother has decided to take the habit and join the Franciscan order,' Father Albert said at last.

'So that's what it was!' Arnau picked up his cup of wine, turned to Joan and raised it, a smile on his lips. 'Congratulations!'

But Joan did not raise his cup. Nor did Bartolomé or

the priest. Arnau sat with his cup of wine in mid-air. What was going on? Apart from the four smaller children who were still blithely eating their food, all the others were gazing intently at him.

Arnau put his cup down. 'Well?' he asked his brother.

'I can't do it.'

Arnau twisted his mouth.

'I can't leave you on your own. I will only enter the order when I see that you are with . . . a good woman, the future mother of your children.' As he spoke, Joan glanced over at Bartolomé's daughter, who hid her face.

Arnau sighed.

'You ought to get married and have a family,' Father Albert insisted.

'You can't stay on your own,' Joan repeated.

'I would consider it a great honour if you were to accept my daughter Maria as your wife,' Bartolomé quickly added. The young girl clung to her mother. 'You're a good, hardworking man. You're healthy, and a devout Christian. I am offering you a good woman, and would give you a large enough dowry for you to buy your own house. Besides, as you know, the guild pays married men more.'

Arnau could not bring himself to look Bartolomé in the eye.

'We have looked around a lot, and we think Maria is the right person for you,' added the priest.

Arnau stared at him.

'Every good Christian has a duty to marry and bring children into this world,' insisted Joan.

Arnau turned to look at his brother, but even before Joan had finished, a voice on Arnau's left claimed his attention.

'I don't think it's a very difficult decision, my boy,' Bartolomé advised him.

'I won't join the Franciscans if you don't marry,' Joan repeated.

'You would make us all very happy if you became a married man,' added the priest.

'The guild would not look kindly on the fact that you refused to marry and as a result your brother could not continue in the Church.'

Nobody said another word. Arnau pursed his lips. The guild! There was no way out.

'Well, brother?' asked Joan.

Arnau turned to face him, and for the first time saw someone he did not recognize: someone who was asking him a question in deadly earnest. How could the change in his brother have escaped him? He still had an image of him as a smiling young boy running everywhere to show him the city, a boy with legs dangling over the side of a crate while his mother stroked his hair. How little the two of them had talked during the past four years! He had always been at work, loading and unloading the ships, arriving home at nightfall too tired to speak, content to have done his duty.

'Would you really not take the habit because of me?'

All at once it was just the two of them.

'Yes.'

Just him and Joan.

'We've worked very hard for that.'

'Yes.'

Arnau rested his chin on his hand and thought for a few moments. The guild. Bartolomé was one of the aldermen: what would his colleagues say? He could not let Joan down after all the efforts they had made. Besides, if Joan left, what would become of him? He looked at Maria.

Bartolomé waved for her to come over. The girl shyly left her mother's side.

Arnau saw a simple young woman, with wavy hair and a generous smile.

'She is fifteen,' he heard Bartolomé say when Maria was next to the table. Feeling the pressure of all their gazes, the girl crossed her hands in front of her and looked down at the floor. 'Maria!' her father called out.

She raised her eyes and blushed as she sought out Arnau's face. She was still squeezing her hands together tightly.

This time it was Arnau who looked away. When he saw how Arnau was avoiding his daughter, Bartolomé became concerned. The girl gave a deep sigh. Could she be crying? Arnau had not meant to offend her.

'Very well,' he said.

Joan raised his cup, closely followed by Bartolomé and the priest. Arnau reached for his own wine.

'You're making me very happy,' said Joan.

'To the happy couple!' cried Bartolomé.

A hundred and sixty days a year! By order of the Church, Christians were meant to avoid eating meat 160 days each year, and each and every one of them saw Aledis, along with all the other housewives of Barcelona, go down to the beach near Santa Maria to buy fish at one of the two stalls in the city.

Where are you? As soon as she saw a ship, Aledis peered along the shoreline to where the boatmen were loading or unloading the goods. Where are you, Arnau? She had seen him once, his muscles so taut it seemed as though they would burst through the skin of his body. My God! Aledis shuddered, and began to count the hours until nightfall, when her husband would fall asleep and she could go down to the workshop to be with Arnau, his image still fresh in her memory. Thanks to the many days of abstinence, Aledis came to understand the *bastaixos'* routine: when there were no ships to unload, they carried blocks of stone to Santa Maria, and after their first trip they no longer stayed in line, but worked as each man saw fit.

That morning Arnau was on his way back for another stone. On his own. He was carrying his leather headpiece in one hand, and was bare-chested. Aledis saw him walk past the fish stall. The sun was glinting off the sweat covering his whole body, and he was smiling at everyone he met. Aledis stepped out of the queue. Arnau! She longed to be able to call out to him, but knew she could not. The women waiting in line were already staring at her, and the old woman who was behind her pointed to the gap she had left. Aledis waved for her to take her place. How could she escape the attention of all these gossips? She pretended to retch. One of the women came to help her, but Aledis pushed her away; the others smiled. Aledis retched again, then ran off, while the other pregnant women gestured knowingly.

Arnau was striding along the beach on his way to the royal quarry at Monjuïc. How could she catch him? Aledis ran along Carrer de la Mar to Plaça del Blat. From there she turned left beneath the old gateway in the Roman wall, next to the magistrate's palace, and then ran all the way down Carrer de la Boqueria until she reached the gate. Everyone stared at her: what if someone recognized her? What did she care! Arnau was on his own. Aledis left the city by La Boqueria and flew down the track leading to Montjuïc. He must be somewhere near . . .

'Arnau!' This time she did shout out loud.

Halfway up the path to the quarry, Arnau halted, and turned to see the woman who was running towards him. 'Aledis! What are you doing here?'

Aledis fought for breath. What could she tell him?

'Is something wrong, Aledis?'

What could she say?

She bent double, clutching her stomach, again pretended to be retching. Why not? Arnau came up to her and took her by the arms. Just to feel his touch made her tremble.

'What's the matter?'

Those hands of his! They gripped her forearm fiercely. Aledis looked up: she was pressed close to Arnau's chest, still glistening with sweat. She breathed in his smell.

'What's the matter?' Arnau repeated, trying to get her to straighten up. Aledis seized her chance and flung her arms round him.

'My God!' she whispered. She buried her face in his shoulder and began to kiss him and lick his sweat.

'What are you doing?'

Arnau tried to push her away, but Aledis clung even more tightly to him.

Arnau was startled to hear voices beyond a bend in the path. The other *bastaixos*! How could he explain . . .? It might be Bartolomé himself. If they found him there, with Aledis clinging to him, kissing him like that . . . they would throw him out of the guild! Arnau lifted Aledis round the waist and plunged off the path behind some bushes. He covered her mouth with his hand.

The voices came near and then continued on their way, but Arnau was no longer paying them any heed. He was seated on the ground, with Aledis on top of him: one of his hands was still round her waist, the other was on her mouth. She was staring at him. Those brown eyes of hers! Suddenly Arnau realized he was holding her close. One hand was across her stomach, and her breasts . . . her breasts were heaving next to his chest. How many nights had he dreamt of holding her like this? How often had he dreamt of her body? Aledis did not struggle in his grasp; she simply stared at him with those huge brown eyes.

He took his hand from her mouth.

'I need you,' he heard her lips whisper.

Then her lips came close to his, and kissed them. They were soft, sweet, filled with desire.

The taste of her! Arnau shuddered.

Aledis was trembling too.

Her taste, her body . . . her desire.

Neither of them said anything more.

That night, Aledis did not go down to spy on the apprentices.

24

It was almost two months since Maria and Arnau had been married in Santa Maria de la Mar. The ceremony had been led by Father Albert, and all the members of the guild of *bastaixos* had been present, as well as Pere and Mariona, and Joan, who already had the tonsure and the white habit of the Franciscan order. With the promise of a wage increase after his marriage, Arnau and his wife chose a house down by the beach. Maria's family and many others, who all wanted to contribute, helped them furnish it: Arnau did not have to do a thing. House, furniture, crockery, linen: all appeared thanks to the efforts of Maria and her mother, who insisted he do nothing. On their wedding night, Maria gave herself to him willingly, although with little passion. When Arnau woke at dawn the next morning, his breakfast was waiting for him: eggs, milk, salt meat, bread. The same scene was repeated at mid-day, and that evening, and the next day, and the one after that: Maria always had Arnau's food on the table. She also took his shoes off, washed him and helped treat any cuts or wounds he might have. She was always willing in bed. Day after day, Arnau encountered everything a man could want: food, cleanliness, obedience, care and attention, and the body of a young, attractive woman. Yes, Arnau. No, Arnau. Maria never argued with him. If he wanted a candle, Maria dropped whatever she was doing to fetch him one. If he complained, she smothered him in kisses. Whenever he breathed, Maria ran to bring him air.

The rain was pouring down. The sky suddenly darkened, and flashes of lightning pierced the dark clouds, illuminating the stormy sea. Soaked to the skin, Arnau and Bartolomé were standing on the beach. All the ships had left the dangerous open port of Barcelona to seek refuge in Salou. The royal quarry was shut. There would be no work for the *bastaixos* that day.

'How are things with you, my boy?' Bartolomé asked his son-in-law.

'Good, very good . . . except . . .'

'Is there a problem?'

'It's just that . . . I'm not used to being treated as well as Maria treats me.'

'That was what we brought her up to do,' said Bartolomé proudly.

'But it's too . . .'

'I said you would not regret marrying her.' Bartolomé looked at Arnau. 'You'll get used to it. Enjoy the love of a good woman.'

They were still discussing the matter when they came to Carrer de les Dames, a small side street that gave on to the beach. They saw a group of about twenty poor-looking women, young and old, pretty and ugly, healthy and sick, walking up and down in the rain.

'Do you see them?' asked Bartolomé, pointing in their direction. 'Do you know what they are waiting for?' Arnau shook his head. 'On stormy days like today, when the captains of fishing-boats who are not married have done all they can to stay afloat, when they have commended their souls to all the saints and virgins in the Church and still cannot ride out the storm, they have only one choice. Their crews know it and demand they keep the tradition. In his moment of despair, a captain must swear to God in front of his crew that if they reach port safely he will marry the first woman he sets eyes on when he steps on dry land. Do you understand, Arnau?' Arnau looked more closely at the group of women pacing nervously up and down the street, staring out to sea. 'That's what women are born for: to get married, to serve their man. That was how we brought Maria up, and that's how we gave her to you.'

The days went by, with Maria utterly devoted to Arnau, while he could think only of Aledis.

'Those stones will ruin your back,' said Maria as she massaged him and applied ointment to the wound Arnau had near his shoulder-blade.

Arnau said nothing.

'Tonight I'll check your headpiece. It can't fit properly if the stones cut into you like that.'

Arnau still said nothing. He had returned home after dark. Maria had helped him off with his footwear, served him a cup of wine and forced him to sit down while she massaged his back, in the same way as she had seen her mother do to her father all through her childhood. As always, Arnau let her get on with it. If he said nothing, it was because the wound had nothing to do with the stones for the Virgin, or with his headpiece. His wife was caring for a wound that shamed him, a wound made by the nails of another woman, a woman Arnau could not renounce.

'Those stones will destroy all your backs,' Maria repeated.

Arnau drank down the wine in one gulp, feeling Maria's hands gently rubbing his shoulders.

* * *

Ever since her husband had brought her down to the workshop to see the punishment he had meted out to the apprentice who had dared look at her, Aledis did no more than spy on the young men at night. She discovered that they often slipped out into the garden, where they met women who climbed over the wall to be with them. The apprentices had the leather, the tools and the knowledge to make themselves thin sheaths, which they greased and put on their penises before they penetrated any of the women. The guarantee that they would not become pregnant, added to the youthful vigour of their partners and the darkness of the night, meant that many local women succumbed to the temptation of an anonymous nocturnal adventure. Aledis had no difficulty getting into the apprentices' sleeping area and stealing some of these ingenious sheaths; the lack of any risk in her relations with Arnau only served to inflame her passion still further.

Aledis told him that with these sheaths they would not have children. Could it be the grease from them that stuck to his penis? Was it a punishment for going against divine law? Maria was still not pregnant. She was a strong, healthy young woman. What other reason apart from Arnau's sins could there be for her not being with child? Why else would the Lord not reward her with the offspring she so desired? Bartolomé needed a grandson. Father Albert and Joan both wanted to see Arnau a father. The entire guild of *bastaixos* was waiting for the moment when the young couple would announce the good news: the men joked about it with Arnau; their wives visited Maria to offer their advice and to extol the virtues of family life.

Arnau also wanted a son.

'I don't want you to put that on me,' he said to Aledis one day when she pounced on him on the way up to the quarry.

Aledis would not listen. 'I've no intention of losing you,' she said. 'Before that happens, I would leave the old man and come and find you. Then everyone would know what's been going on between us. It would mean your downfall: they would expel you from the guild, and probably from the city as well. Then you would only have me; I would be the only one willing to follow you. My life makes no sense without you: otherwise I'm condemned to live my days alongside an old, obsessed man who can't satisfy me in any way.'

'You would see me ruined? Why would you do that?'

'Because I know that deep down you love me,' Aledis said firmly. 'In fact, I would only be helping you take a step you're too frightened to take on your own.'

Hidden among the bushes on the slopes of Montjuïc hill, Aledis slid the sheath on to her lover's penis. Arnau let her do it. Was what she had said true? Was it true that deep down he wanted to live with her, to abandon his wife and all he had in order to run away with her? If only his body did not clamour so to be with her . . . What charms did she have that so completely undermined his willpower? Arnau thought of telling her the story of Joan's mother, and of the possibility that if their relationship became known, her husband could have her walled up for the rest of her days. Instead, he climbed on top of her . . . yet again. Aledis panted as he thrust into her, but all he could hear were his own fears: Maria, his work, the guild, Joan, disgrace, Maria, his Virgin, Maria, his Virgin . . .

25

Seated on the royal throne, King Pedro raised his hand. To his right stood the Infantes Don Pedro and Don Jaime; on his left were the Count of Terranova and Father Ot de Montcada. The King waited for the rest of the council to fall silent. They were in the great chamber of the royal palace at Valencia, where they had received Pere Ramon de Codoler, steward and messenger from King Jaime of Mallorca. According to Ramon de Codoler, the King of Mallorca, Count of Roussillon and Cerdagne and lord of Montpellier, had resolved, because of the constant affronts the French had committed against him, to declare war on the King of France. As a loyal vassal of King Pedro's, King Jaime called on Pedro to present himself at the head of the Catalan armies at Perpignan on 21 April of the following year, 1341, to support and defend him in that war.

King Pedro and his council had been studying the request all morning. If they did not respond to the King of Mallorca's call, he would renounce his vassalage and be free of all obligations. But if they did respond – everyone was agreed on this – they would be falling into a trap; as soon as the Catalan forces entered Perpignan, Jaime would take sides with the King of France against them.

When there was silence in the hall, the King spoke: 'You have all been considering this matter, and trying to find a way to refuse the request the King of Mallorca has made. I think I have found the answer: we shall go to Barcelona and call our parliament. Then we shall require the King of Mallorca to come to Barcelona to attend the sessions on the twenty-ninth of March, as is his duty. What can happen? Either he comes, or he does not. If he comes, he will have fulfilled his obligations, and we will do the same . . .' At this, some of the royal counsellors stirred uneasily: if the King of Mallorca came to Barcelona, then there would be war against France – at the same time as Catalonia was fighting Genoa! One of them even raised his voice to protest, but Pedro lifted his hand again to calm him, and smiled before going on to say: '. . . by asking the advice of our vassals, who will be the ones to take the final decision.' Some of the councillors smiled with the King; others nodded their agreement. The Catalan parliament held authority over decisions such as whether or not to start a war. It would therefore not be the King who was refusing to come to the aid of the King of Mallorca, but the Catalan parliament. 'If he does not appear,' Pedro went on, 'he will have broken the terms of his vassalage. In that case, we will have no obligation to help him, or to get mixed up in his war against the King of France.'

Barcelona, 1341

Nobles, churchmen and representatives from the free cities of the principality of Catalonia – the three branches who made up the parliament – had congregated in Barcelona. They filled the city streets with their colourful attire: silks from Almeria, Barbary, Alexandria and Damascus; wool from England or Brussels; lace from Flanders, Mechlin and Orlanda; or the fabulous black linen from Byssus; all of their garments shot through with threads of gold or silver in the most exquisite designs.

Yet Jaime of Mallorca had not arrived. For several days now, boatmen, *bastaixos* and all the other port workers had been on standby in case the King of Mallorca appeared. The port of Barcelona was not prepared for the arrival of such great figures: they could hardly be carried from the lowly craft that went out to meet the big ships in the same way the merchants were, in order not to get their clothes wet. Instead, whenever someone important came to Barcelona, the boatmen lined up their craft from the shore to well into the sea, and built a temporary bridge over them to allow kings and princes to disembark with the required dignity.

The *bastaixos*, including Arnau, had already brought all the necessary planks of wood down to the beach. Like many of the inhabitants of Barcelona and members of the parliament who had congregated on the shore, they scanned the horizon for a glimpse of the lord of Mallorca's galleys. Everyone was talking about what was going on: the King of Mallorca's request for aid and King Pedro's ruse were common knowledge.

'It seems to me,' Arnau said one morning to Father Albert as he was tidying up the candles in the Holy Eucharist chapel, 'that if the entire city is aware of what King Pedro is proposing, then King Jaime must know as well: so why would he come?'

'He will not come,' replied the priest, without pausing in his tasks in the chapel.

'What will happen then?' Arnau looked at the priest, who stopped and shrugged nervously.

'I am afraid Catalonia will embark on a war against Mallorca.'

'Another war?'

'Yes. Everybody knows how much King Pedro wishes to reunite the ancient Catalan kingdoms that Jaime the First divided among his heirs. Ever since then, the Kings of Mallorca have constantly betrayed the Catalans. It was scarcely fifty years ago that Pedro the Great had to defeat the armies of France and Mallorca at the Col de Panissars. After that victory, he went on to conquer Mallorca, Roussillon and the Cerdagne, only to be ordered to return them to Jaime the Second by the Pope.' The priest turned to face Arnau. 'There is going to be war, Arnau. I don't know when or with what excuse, but there is going to be war.'

Jaime of Mallorca did not appear before the Barcelona parliament. The King granted him a further three days, but at the end of that time there was still no sight of his galleys in the port of Barcelona.

'There you have the excuse,' Father Albert told Arnau when they met again in the chapel. 'I still do not know when, but now there is the excuse.'

When the sessions of parliament had concluded, King Pedro began the legal process to try his vassal for disobedience. He added the accusation that Catalan money was being minted in the territories of Roussillon and the Cerdagne, whereas the royal currency could by right only be struck in Barcelona.

Jaime of Mallorca still did not comply, but the trial, headed by the magistrate of Barcelona, Arnau d'Erill, and assisted by Felip de Montroig and the royal vice-chancellor Arnau Çamorera, took place in his absence. Soon, however, the King of Mallorca grew concerned when his envoys informed him of what the outcome could be: the requisition of all his kingdoms and territories. He then turned to the King of France, to whom he paid homage, and to the Pope, for them to intercede on his behalf with his brother-in-law King Pedro.

The Holy Pontiff took his side, and asked King Pedro for a safe conduct for Jaime and his followers to come to Barcelona to present his apologies and to defend himself against the accusations. The King could not go against the Pope's wishes, and so granted Jaime the safe conduct, although he also made sure he sent word to Valencia for them to dispatch four galleys under the command of Mateu Mercer to keep watch on the King of Mallorca's fleet.

When the sails of the King of Mallorca's galleys appeared on the horizon, all Barcelona rushed down to the port. The squadron under Mateu Mercer was waiting for them, just as heavily armed. The Barcelona magistrate Arnau d'Erill ordered the port workers to start building the pontoon bridge: the boatmen lined up their vessels, and the *bastaixos* began laying the planks over them.

As soon as the King of Mallorca's ships had dropped anchor, the remaining boatmen sailed out to the royal galley.

'What's going on?' asked one of the *bastaixos* when he saw the royal standard still flying from the ship, and only one nobleman disembarking from it.

Arnau and his companions were already soaked. They all looked across the beach at the magistrate, who in turn was staring at the small boat now approaching the shore.

Just one person made use of the bridge they had constructed: Viscount Èvol, a nobleman from Roussillon. He was richly attired and armed and, instead of stepping down on to the beach, he remained standing at the end of the wooden planks.

The magistrate went to meet him. From the sandy shore, he listened to what Lord Èvol had to say. The others could see Èvol pointing towards Framenors, and then back at the King of Mallorca's galleys. When the two men had finished talking, the viscount returned to the royal galley, while the magistrate headed up into the city. Soon afterwards he returned, with instructions from King Pedro.

'King Jaime of Mallorca and his wife Constanza, Queen of Mallorca and sister of our beloved King Pedro,' he shouted for everyone on the beach to hear, 'intend to stay in Framenors convent. A fixed wooden bridge, with a roof and enclosed sides, is to be built from where his ships are anchored to the royal apartments.'

At this, a murmur of protest spread along the shore, but the magistrate stifled it with a stern gesture. Most of the workmen turned to look at the convent of Framenors, perched on the edge of the sea.

'This is madness,' Arnau heard one of his companions mutter.

'If a storm blows up,' another one said, 'the bridge will never withstand it.'

A bridge with a roof and enclosed sides! Why on earth would the King of Mallorca demand something like that?

Arnau turned back towards the magistrate, and saw Berenguer de Montagut arriving on the beach. Arnau d'Erill pointed to the Framenors convent, then with his right hand drew an imaginary line out into the sea.

All the *bastaixos*, boatmen, ships' carpenters, caulkers, oarsmen, smiths and ropemakers stood silently as the magistrate finished his explanation and the master builder considered the problem.

The King gave orders to suspend all work on Santa Maria and the cathedral: all the labourers were trans-ferred to building the new bridge. Berenguer de Montagut oversaw the dismantling of part of the scaffolding round the church, and that same morning the *bastaixos* started carrying material over to Framenors.

'This is nonsense,' Arnau complained to Ramon as the two of them were carrying a heavy tree trunk. 'We break our backs carrying stones down to Santa Maria, and now here we are undoing our work on the church, and all at the whim—'

'Be quiet!' Ramon urged him. 'We're following the King's orders; he must know what he is doing.'

The King of Mallorca's galleys – still closely watched by the ones from Valencia – were rowed across to Framenors, where they anchored at a considerable distance from the shore. Workmen and carpenters began to put up scaffolding round the façade of the convent, then extended it down towards the shore. The *bastaixos* and anyone without a precise task to fulfil went back and forth carrying tree trunks and planks for the bridge itself.

Work ended at nightfall. Arnau came home exhausted.

'Our King has never demanded anything so crazy; he is happy to come ashore using the traditional bridge we build over the small craft. Why should we allow a traitor to do as he wishes?'

His protests and grumbling gradually ceased as he felt Maria's hands gently massaging his shoulders.

'Your wounds are getting better,' said his young wife. 'Some people use ointment with geranium and raspberry, but in our family we've always preferred hearts-ease. My grandmother treated my grandfather with it, my mother does the same for my father . . .'

Arnau closed his eyes. Heartsease? He had not seen Aledis for days. That was the only reason his back was getting better!

'Why are you tensing your muscles?' Maria reproached him, interrupting his thoughts. 'Relax: you need to relax so that . . .'

He still paid her little attention. Why should he? Relax so that she could treat the wounds another woman had made? If only she would get angry with him . . .

But instead of shouting at him, that night Maria gave herself to him again: she sought him out, and gently embraced him. Aledis had no idea what it meant to be gentle. They fornicated like animals! Arnau let Maria wrap her arms round him, keeping his eyes tight shut. How could he look at her? The young girl caressed his body . . . and his soul. She brought him pleasure, so intense it became a torment.

At dawn the next day, Arnau got up to set off for Framenors. Maria was already downstairs, by the kitchen fire, preparing his breakfast.

Throughout the three days that it took to build the bridge down from the convent, no member of the King of Mallorca's court left their galleys; nor did anyone from the Valencian fleet. When the construction from the convent reached the water's edge, the *bastaixos* formed into groups to transport the material for the rest of the bridge. Arnau worked ceaselessly: if he stopped, he knew he would only feel Maria's hands caressing him, and that would bring back memories of how a few days earlier Aledis had bitten and scratched the same body.

Now their task was to lower piles into the water from small boats between the shore and the galleys. Berenguer de Montagut again took personal charge of the operation. He stood in the prow of a catboat, peering down over the side to make sure the wooden piles were set firmly in the sea bottom before any weight was put on them.

On the third day, a new wooden bridge more than fifty yards long appeared on the horizon of the port of Barcelona. The royal galley came alongside it, and a short while later, Arnau and all the others who had built the bridge heard the King and his court walking along the wooden boards; many of them looked up.

When they were safely installed in Framenors, Jaime

sent a messenger to King Pedro to tell him that the rigours of the sea crossing had affected both him and Queen Constanza, and that in consequence his sister begged him to come and visit her in the convent. As King Pedro was preparing to do so, the Infante Don Pedro appeared before him, accompanied by a young Franciscan friar.

'What do you have to tell me, friar?' said the King, visibly annoyed at this delay to the visit to his sister.

Joan bent over to disguise the fact that he was almost a head taller than the monarch. 'The King is very short,' he had been told, 'and he never receives his subjects standing up.' The two men were on their feet now, however, and the King's gaze was piercing.

Joan was lost for words.

'Tell him,' the Infante urged him.

Joan broke into a sweat; he could feel the rough cloth of his habit sticking to his body. What if it were not true? The thought occurred to him for the first time. He had heard it from an old friar who had disembarked with the King of Mallorca, and had not hesitated a moment. He had come running to the royal palace, struggled with the guard because he had refused to give the message to anyone but the King himself, had relented when he saw the Infante Don Pedro, but now . . . what if it were not true? What if it were just another of the King of Mallorca's ruses?

'Well, come on, out with it!' the King shouted.

'Your majesty, you should not go and visit your sister Queen Constanza. It's a trap laid by King Jaime of Mallorca. Using the excuse that his wife is so ill and weak, he has instructed the usher at the door to her apartment not to let anyone but you and the Infantes Don Pedro and Don Jaime in. Nobody else is to have access to the Queen's chamber; but inside twelve armed men will be waiting to seize you and take you down the covered bridge, and on to the King's galley. Then you will be taken to the island of Mallorca and the castle of Alaró. The plan is to keep you prisoner until you set King Jaime free from his vassalage and grant him fresh lands in Catalonia.'

He had done it!

The King narrowed his eyes, and asked: 'And how does a young friar like you come to know all this?'

'I heard it from Brother Berenguer, a relative of yours.'

'Brother Berenguer?'

Don Pedro nodded; then the King apparently suddenly remembered who this friar was.

'Brother Berenguer was told this in confession by a repentant traitor,' Joan went on. 'He was asked to give you the message, but he is so old and infirm that he entrusted it to me.'

'That was why he wanted the bridge covered on all sides,' the Infante Don Jaime said. 'That way, nobody would see we had been taken prisoner.'

'It would have been easy,' Don Pedro agreed.

'You are well aware that if my sister the Queen is ill,' said the King to his sons, 'I have to go and see her if she is in my dominions.' Joan listened, not daring to look at any of them. The King fell silent for a while. 'I will postpone tonight's visit, but I need – do you hear me, friar?' Joan gave a start. 'I need this repentant sinner to permit us to make this act of treachery public. For as long as it is a secret of the confessional, I will be obliged to go and see the Queen. Now, be off with you!'

Joan ran back to Framenors and told Brother Berenguer of the King's demand. King Pedro did not visit his sister that night and, in what he took as a sign that divine providence was protecting him, he suddenly developed a swelling on his face near his eye. This had to be bled, which meant that he spent several days in bed, during which time Brother Berenguer succeeded in obtaining permission for King Pedro to make the plot public.

This time Joan did not doubt for a moment the truth of what he was told.

'Brother Berenguer's penitent is your own sister,' he told the King as soon as he was brought before him. 'Queen Constanza, who begs that you bring her to your palace, by force if necessary. Once here, free from her husband's pressure and placed under your protection, she will reveal all the details of the treachery.'

Accompanied by a squad of soldiers, the Infante Don Jaime presented himself at Framenors to carry out Queen Constanza's wishes. The friars allowed him in, and the Infante and his soldiers went directly to see the King. All his protests were in vain: Constanza left for the royal palace soon afterwards.

The King of Mallorca had little more success when he appeared before his brother-in-law.

'Since I gave my word to the Pope,' King Pedro told him, 'I will respect your safe conduct. Your wife will remain here under my protection. Now leave my kingdom.'

As soon as Jaime of Mallorca and his four galleys had departed, King Pedro ordered Arnau d'Erill to make haste with the trial against his brother-in-law. A few days later, the magistrate ruled that all the lands of the unfaithful vassal, who had been tried in his absence, were to pass into the hands of King Pedro. Now the King had the legitimate excuse he had been seeking to be able to declare war on the King of Mallorca.

Overjoyed at the possibility of reuniting the kingdoms that his forebear Jaime the Conqueror had divided, King Pedro sent for the young friar who had revealed the plot to him.

'You have served us well and faithfully,' the King told him. This time, he was seated on his throne. 'I shall grant you a favour.'

Joan had already been told by the royal messengers that this was what the King intended to do. He had thought hard about it. He had joined the Franciscan order at his teachers' suggestion, but as soon as he had entered the Framenors convent, he had been sorely disappointed: where were the books? Where was the knowledge? Where could he work and study? When he finally spoke to the prior, the old man patiently reminded him of the three principles of the order, as established by Saint Francis of Assisi: 'Complete simplicity, complete poverty, and complete humility. That is how we Franciscans must live.'

But Joan wanted to investigate, to study; to read and learn. Hadn't his masters taught him that this too was the way of the Lord? Whenever he met a Dominican monk, he was filled with envy. The Dominican order was mainly devoted to the study of philosophy and theology, and had created several universities. What Joan most wanted was to join their order and to be able to continue his studies in the prestigious university at Bologna.

'So be it,' the King decreed after hearing Joan's argument. All the hairs on the young friar's body stood on end. 'We trust that one day you will return to our kingdoms endowed with the moral authority that comes from knowledge and wisdom, and that you will apply that authority for the benefit of your King and his people.'

26

Almost two years had gone by since the Barcelona magistrate had ruled against King Jaime III of Mallorca. All the bells in the city were ringing incessantly; inside Santa Maria, still without walls, Arnau listened to them with a shrinking heart. The King had declared war on Mallorca, and the city had filled with nobles and soldiers. On guard outside the Jesus chapel, Arnau could see them among the ordinary people who had flocked to the church and the square outside. Every church in the city was holding a mass for the Catalan army.

Arnau felt weary. The King had assembled his fleet in the port of Barcelona, and for several days now, the *bastaixos* had been working non-stop. One hundred and seventeen ships! No one had ever seen such an array: twenty-two huge galleys all fitted out for war; seven pot-bellied transports for carrying horses, and eight big troop ships with two or three decks for housing soldiers. The rest of the fleet was made up of medium-sized or small boats. The sea was covered in masts as the ships manoeuvred in and out of the port.

It must have been in one of those galleys that Joan, in

his black habit, had sailed off to Bologna a year earlier. Arnau accompanied him to the shore. Joan jumped into the boat and sat with his back to the sea, smiling at him. Arnau watched him settle, and as soon as the oarsmen began to row, he felt his stomach wrench and had to fight back his tears. He was on his own.

He felt the same even now. He looked around him. The church bells were still ringing from every bell-tower in the city. Nobles, clergymen, soldiers, merchants, artisans and the ordinary inhabitants of Barcelona were thronging Santa Maria. His fellow guild members stood on guard beside him, and yet how lonely he felt! All his hopes, all his life's dreams had vanished just like the old church that had given way to the new one. There was nothing left of it. No trace at all of the Romanesque church: all he could see was the huge wide central nave of the new Santa Maria, bounded by the soaring octagonal columns which supported the roof vaults. Beyond the columns, the exterior walls of the church were rising, hoisting themselves skyward, stone by patient stone.

Arnau looked up. The keystone of the second vault in the central nave was already in position, and now work was going on to place the ones in the side aisles. The birth of Our Lord: that had been the subject chosen to be sculpted on the boss. The presbytery roof was almost completely finished. The next vault, the first over the immense central nave, was still incomplete. It looked like a huge spider-web: the ribs of the four arches were still open to the skies, while the keystone hung in the centre like a great spider ready to leap out on the finest threads to devour its prey. Arnau could not help staring up at the slender columns. He knew how it felt to be trapped in a spider's web! Aledis was pursuing him more and more insistently every day. 'I'll tell your guild aldermen,' she threatened whenever Arnau hesitated, and so he sinned with her, again and again. Arnau turned to observe his fellow *bastaixos*. If they only knew . . . There was Bartolomé, an alderman, and Ramon, his friend and protector. What would they say? And now he did not even have Joan with him.

Santa Maria itself seemed to have turned its back on him. Now that it was partly roofed over, and with the buttresses in place to hold up the side aisles of the second vault, the city noblemen and rich merchants had begun work in the side chapels, determined to leave their mark in the shape of coats of arms, images, sarcophagi and every kind of decoration sculpted in stone.

Whenever Arnau came to the church these days in search of help from his Virgin, there was always some merchant or nobleman busy among the building work. It was as though his church had been stolen from him. The newcomers had appeared all of a sudden, and they often paused proudly at the eleven chapels around the ambulatory that, of the thirty-four planned, had already been built. By now the birds of the coat of arms of the Busquets family could be seen in the All Saints' chapel; the hand and lion rampant of the Junyent family in the Saint James' chapel; Boronat de Pera's three pears carved in the keystone of the Saint Paul chapel; the horseshoe and stripes of Pau Ferran in the marble of the same chapel; the arms of the Duforts and the Dussays and the font of the Font family in the Saint Margaret chapel. They had even forced their way into the Jesus chapel! There, in his chapel, the chapel of the *bastaixos*, work had begun on the sarcophagus for Bernat Llull, the Archdeacon of the Sea who had begun the building work on the new church, next to the coats of arms of the Ferrers.

Arnau passed by nobles and merchants with his gaze lowered. All he did was carry stone and kneel before his Virgin to ask her to free him from the spider pursuing him.

When the religious services were over, the entire city made its way down to the port. King Pedro III was there, decked out for war and surrounded by his barons. While the Infante Don Jaime, Count of Urgell, was to stay in Catalonia to defend the frontier of the Empordà, Besalú and Camprodon which were adjacent to the lands on the mainland ruled by the King of Mallorca, the other nobles were all sailing off with the King to conquer the island. They included the Infante Don Pedro, the seneschal of Catalonia; Pere de Montcada, admiral of the fleet; Pedro de Eixèrica and Blasco de Alagó; Gonzalo Díez de Arenós and Felipe de Castro; Father Joan de Arborea; Alfonso de Llòria; Galvany de Anglesola; Arcadic de Mur; Arnau d'Erill; Father Gonzalvo García; Joan Ximénez de Urrea; as well as many other noblemen and knights, all of them equipped for battle with their soldiers and those of their vassals.

Maria, who had met Arnau outside the church, pointed to them, shouting for him to look where she was pointing.

'The King! The King, Arnau. Look at him! Look at the way he bears himself! What about his sword? Can you see it? And that nobleman over there? Who is he, Arnau? Do you know? Look at all those shields, their armour, the pennants fluttering . . .'

Maria dragged Arnau all the way along the beach to Framenors. There, some distance from the nobles and soldiers, stood a large group of filthy, poorly dressed men. They had no shields or armour, and wore only long, stiff tunics, greaves and leather caps. They were busily climbing on board small boats that would take them out to the warships. Their only weapons were flat swords and spears!

'Is that the Company?' Maria asked her husband.

'Yes. The Almogavars.'

The two of them watched in the same respectful

silence as all the others on the beach, staring at these mercenaries who had been taken on by King Pedro. The conquerors of Byzantium! Even the children and women who, like Maria, had been impressed by the nobles' swords and armour, surveyed the Almogavars with pride. They fought on foot and wore no protection, relying entirely on their skill and dexterity. Who could possibly laugh at the way they were dressed or the weapons they carried?

Arnau was told this was what the Sicilians had done: they had laughed at them on the field of battle. How could such a ragged group hope to fight nobles on horseback? And yet the Almogavars defeated them and conquered the island. The French had done the same: the story was told throughout Catalonia to anyone who would listen. Arnau had heard it on several occasions.

'They say,' he murmured to Maria now, 'that some French knights captured one of the Almogavars and led him before Prince Charles of Salerno, who insulted him, calling him a poor wretch and laughing at the Catalan Company.' Arnau and his wife were still watching the Almogavars climb on board the boats. 'So then the Almogavar, in front of the Prince and all his knights, challenged their best captain to single combat. He said he would fight on foot, armed only with his spear. The Frenchman could be on horseback, in full armour.' Arnau fell silent, but Maria turned and urged him to go on. 'The French laughed at the Catalan, but accepted the challenge. They all made their way to an open field near the French camp. There, the Almogavar first killed the Frenchman's horse, then took advantage of how unwieldy he was when fighting on foot to overcome him easily. As he was preparing to cut the knight's throat, Charles of Salerno promised the Almogavar his freedom.'

'It's true,' someone added behind their backs, 'they fight like real devils.'

Arnau could feel Maria clinging to him, gripping his arm as hard as she could while she stared at the mercenaries. *What are you looking for, woman? Protection? If you only knew! I'm not even capable of facing my own weaknesses. Do you think any of them could hurt you more than I am doing? They fight like devils.* Arnau stared at them: men who were happy to go off to fight, leaving their families behind. Why . . . why could he not do the same?

It took hours for all the men to board the ships. Maria went home, while Arnau wandered among the others gathered on the beach. He met several of his companions on the way.

'What's all the hurry?' he asked Ramon, pointing to the small craft that were continuously coming to take on more and more soldiers.

'You'll soon see,' Ramon answered.

At that very moment he heard the first whinny of a horse, soon followed by hundreds more. The army's horses had been drawn up outside the city walls; now it was their turn to embark. Several of the seven transports were already full of horses, brought from Valencia with the noblemen from that city, or from the ports of Salou, Tarragona or from the north of Barcelona.

'Let's get away from here,' Ramon warned Arnau. 'This is going to turn into a real battlefield.'

Just as they were leaving the beach, the grooms led the first steeds down to the water. They were huge warhorses, which kicked, snorted and threatened to bite, while their handlers struggled to control them.

'They know they're off to war,' Ramon told Arnau as they sought cover behind the boats drawn up on the beach.

'They know?'

'Of course. Whenever they're put on ships, it's to go to war. Look.'

Arnau peered out to sea. Four of the flat-bottomed transports drew up as close to the beach as they could, and opened their stern doors: they splashed into the water, revealing the gaping hulls inside. 'And those that don't know,' Ramon went on, 'are made nervous by the ones that do.'

Soon the beach was filled with horses. There were hundreds of them, all big, strong, powerful beasts, warhorses trained for combat. The grooms and squires dodged in and out, trying to avoid the rearing, biting animals. Arnau saw several of them fly through the air or flinch as they were on the receiving end of a flashing hoof. Everything was bedlam.

'What are they waiting for?' asked Arnau.

Ramon pointed to the ships once more. Some of the grooms were wading out to them, leading their horses.

'They are the most experienced ones. Once they are on board, they will attract the others.'

And so it proved. As soon as the first horse reached the ships' ramps, the grooms headed back to the shore. The horses immediately started whinnying loudly.

That was the signal.

The rest of the herd plunged into the water, splashing so much that for a few moments they disappeared entirely from view. Behind them and on either side, a handful of the most expert horsemen followed, cracking their whips and driving them towards the ships. Most of their grooms had lost the reins by now, and the horses swam or floundered on their own, careering into each other. For a while, there was total chaos: shouts from all sides, the lash of whips, animals neighing and struggling to climb up on to the ramps, roars of encouragement from the beach. Then gradually, calm returned to the shore. The ramps were raised, and the horse transports were ready to set sail.

The order to depart came from Admiral Pere de

Montcada's ship. All 117 vessels began to pull out of the harbour. Arnau and Ramon walked home along the beach.

'Off they go,' said Ramon. 'To conquer Mallorca.'

Arnau nodded without a word. Yes, off they went. On their own, leaving behind their problems and their heartbreak. Cheered off as heroes, their minds set on one thing: war. What he wouldn't have given to be among their number!

On 21 June of that same year, Pedro III attended mass in the cathedral of Mallorca, *in sede majestatis*, wearing the traditional robes, attributes and crown of the King of Mallorca. Jaime III had fled to his territories in Roussillon.

The news reached Barcelona and spread through the mainland: King Pedro had taken the first step towards fulfilling his oath to reunite the kingdoms split on the death of Jaime I. Now all that was left was for him to conquer the territory of the Cerdagne and the Catalan lands on the far side of the Pyrenees: Roussillon.

Throughout the long month that the Mallorca campaign had lasted, Arnau could not get the image of the royal fleet leaving the port of Barcelona out of his mind. When the ships were already some way from the shore, everyone on the beach dispersed and returned home. What reason did he have to follow them? To receive care and affection he did not deserve? He sat in the sand until long after the last sail had disappeared beyond the horizon. 'Lucky them, to be able to leave their problems behind,' he said to himself over and over again. Throughout that month, whenever Aledis lay in wait for him on the track up to Montjuïc, or when after-wards he had to face Maria's loving attention, Arnau could hear the shouts and laughter of the Almogavar company, and see the fleet slipping into the distance.

Sooner or later, he would be found out. A short while earlier, while Aledis was still panting on top of him, someone had shouted from the track. Had they heard the two lovers? They lay for a while holding their breath, then Aledis laughed and fell on him again. The day he was found out . . . it would mean disgrace, expulsion from the guild. What would he do then? How would he manage to live?

When on 29 June 1343 the whole city of Barcelona came down to meet the royal fleet assembled in the mouth of the river Llobregat, Arnau had made his decision. The King had to fulfil his promise to conquer Roussillon and the Cerdagne, and he, Arnau Estanyol, would be part of his army. He had to get away from Aledis! Perhaps if he did that, she would forget him, and when he got back . . . He shuddered: after all, this was war; men would die. But perhaps when he returned he could take up his tranquil life with Maria once more, and Aledis would no longer pursue him.

King Pedro III ordered his ships to enter the port of Barcelona in strict order of hierarchy: first the royal galley, then that of Infante Don Pedro, then Pere de Montcada's, followed by the one Lord de Eixèrica commanded, and so on.

While the rest of the fleet waited, the royal galley made its way into port and sailed round it, so that everyone who had gathered on the shore could see it and cheer.

Arnau heard how everyone roared their approval as the ship passed in front of them. The *bastaixos* and boatmen were standing close to the water, ready to build the pontoon for the king. Also waiting next to the *bastaixos* were Francesc Grony, Bernat Santcliment and Galcerà Carbó, all of them Barcelona aldermen, and other guild aldermen. The boatmen began to manoeuvre their craft into place, but the aldermen told them to wait.

What was going on? Arnau looked at the other *bastaixos*. How was the King to disembark if not across their bridge?

'He should not land,' he heard Francesc Grony tell Lord Santcliment. 'The army should go straight on to Roussillon, before King Jaime can reorganize, or make a pact with the French.'

All those around him were of similar mind. Arnau stared out at the royal galley, still triumphantly sailing around the port. If the King did not land, if the fleet continued on to Roussillon without calling in at Barcelona . . . his legs almost gave way under him. The King had to disembark!

Even Count de Terranova, the King's counsellor who had been left in charge of the city, seemed to agree with the others. Arnau glared at him.

The three city aldermen, Count de Terranova and several other leading citizens got into a catboat and were taken to the royal galley. Arnau could hear his own guild companions were also in favour of it: 'He mustn't give the King of Mallorca time to rearm,' they argued.

The discussions went on for several hours. Nobody moved from the beach, awaiting the King's decision.

In the end, the boatmen did not build their bridge, but not because the fleet had left to conquer Roussillon and the Cerdagne. Instead, King Pedro decided he could not continue the campaign in the present circumstances: he did not have sufficient money; a large number of his cavalry had lost their steeds during the sea crossing and needed to disembark; and, above all, he needed fresh arms and provisions to pursue the war. He rejected the city authorities' suggestion that he give them some days to organize festivities to celebrate the conquest of Mallorca, declaring that there was to be no celebration until he had reunited his kingdoms. So finally, when on 29 June 1343 Pedro III did disembark in the port of

Barcelona, it was like any other seaman: leaping into the water from a small boat.

How could Arnau tell Maria he was thinking of joining the army? He did not have to worry about Aledis: what would she gain by making their adultery public? If he went off to war, why would she seek to harm both him and herself? Arnau remembered Joan and his mother: that was the fate awaiting her if their adultery became known of, and Aledis was well aware of it. But Maria? How could he possibly tell her?

Arnau tried. He tried to say goodbye to her when she was massaging his back. 'I'm off to the wars,' he thought he could say. Just that: 'I'm off to the wars.' She would cry: what had she done to deserve it? He tried to tell her when she was serving him his food, but her sweet eyes looking at him prevented him saying a word. 'What's wrong?' she said. He even tried it after they had made love, but Maria simply went on caressing him.

Meanwhile, Barcelona had become a hive of activity. The common people wanted the King to leave to conquer the Cerdagne and Roussillon, but the King seemed to be in no hurry. The nobles were demanding he pay them for the soldiers they had contributed, and for the loss of their horses and weapons, but the royal coffers were empty, so that the King had to allow many of them to return to their own lands. Ramon de Anglesola, Joan de Arborea, Alfonso de Llòria, Gonzalo Díez de Arenós and many others departed in this way.

So King Pedro was forced to call on the Catalan *host*: it would be his people who fought for him. The bells rang out all through the principality, and on the King's orders, the priests in their weekly homilies called on all free men to enlist. The nobility had deserted the Catalan army! Father Albert spoke passionately, whirling his arms in the air. How was the King going to defend Catalonia? What if, when he saw the nobles abandoning King

Pedro, the King of Mallorca joined with the French to attack them? It had already happened once! Father Albert cried out above the congregation's heads in Santa Maria: who among them had not heard of the French crusade against Catalonia? On that occasion, the invaders had been defeated. But now? What would happen if King Jaime were allowed to rearm?

Arnau stared at the stone Virgin with the child at her shoulder. If only he and Maria had had a child. If that had happened, he was sure none of this would have taken place. Aledis would not have been that cruel. If only he had been given a son . . .

'I've made a promise to the Virgin,' Arnau whispered to Maria while the priest was still haranguing the congregation, recruiting soldiers from the high altar. 'I'm going to join the royal army so that she will give us the blessing of a child.'

Maria turned towards him before looking at the Virgin, took his hand and held it tight.

'You can't do this!' Aledis shouted at him when Arnau announced his decision. Arnau raised his hands to get her to speak more quietly, but she paid him no heed: 'You can't leave me! I'll tell everyone—'

'What good would that do, Aledis?' he interrupted her. 'I'll be with the army. All you will do is ruin your own life.'

They stared at each other, crouching in the bushes as they always did. Aledis's bottom lip started to tremble. How pretty she was! Arnau lifted a hand towards her cheek to wipe away her tears, but thought better of it.

'Goodbye, Aledis.'

'You can't leave me,' she sobbed.

Arnau turned back to her. She had fallen forward on her knees, her head between her hands. When he said nothing, she peered up at him.

'Why are you doing this to me?' she moaned.

Arnau saw the tears roll down her face; her whole body was racked with sobs. Arnau bit his lip and looked up at the top of the hill, where he went to fetch his blocks of stone. Why hurt her any more than necessary? He spread his arms wide.

'I have to do it.'

She crawled over and reached out to clutch his legs.

'I have to do it, Aledis!' he repeated, jumping backwards. Then he ran off down Montjuïc hill.

27

She could tell by the vivid colours of their clothes that they were prostitutes. Aledis was uncertain whether she should approach them, but the smell from their stewpot was irresistible. She was hungry – no, she was starving. The girls, who looked as young as she was, were moving and talking animatedly around their fire. When they saw her close to the camp, they invited her to join them: but they were prostitutes. Aledis looked down at herself: ragged, evil-smelling, filthy. The whores called out to her again; she was dazzled by the way their silk robes caught the sun. Nobody else had offered her anything to eat. Hadn't she tried at every tent, hut or fireside she had come across? Had anyone else taken pity on her? No, they had treated her like a common beggar. She had begged for help: a crust of bread, a piece of meat, a vegetable even. They had spat on her outstretched hand and laughed. These women might be whores, but they had asked her to share their meal with them.

The King had ordered his armies to assemble in the town of Figueres, in the north of the principality. All those nobles who had not abandoned him headed there, together with the *hosts* of Catalonia, including the citizens of Barcelona. Among these was Arnau Estanyol. He felt free and hopeful, and carried his father's cross-bow and his blunt *bastaix*'s dagger.

But if King Pedro succeeded in bringing together an army of twelve hundred men on horseback and four thousand footsoldiers in Figueres, he also managed to attract another army: the relatives of soldiers – mostly of the Almogavars, who lived like gypsies and took their families with them wherever they went; tradesmen sell-ing all kinds of goods, and hoping to be able to buy whatever booty the soldiers obtained; slave-traders, clergymen, card sharps, thieves, prostitutes, beggars and all kinds of hangers-on whose only aim was to try to cream off the army's spoils. Together they formed an astonishing rearguard that moved at the same pace as the army, but obeyed its own rules – often crueller ones than those to be found in the conflicts they lived off like parasites.

Aledis was simply one more among this motley crowd. The farewell from Arnau was still ringing in her ears. She could still feel the way that her husband's rough, clumsy hands had forced their way between her legs. The old man's panting mingled with Arnau's words in her memory. He had pushed at her, but she had not moved. He had grasped her more firmly, hoping for that fake generosity with which she usually rewarded his efforts. But this time, Aledis closed her legs. Why did you leave me, Arnau? was all she could think as Pau fell on her, pushing his penis into her with his hands. She gave way, and opened her legs. She felt so bitter she had to stifle a desire to retch. The old tanner started to squirm like a snake on top of her. She was sick beside the bed, but he did not even notice. He was still thrusting away feebly, supporting his flaccid manhood with his fingers, and nibbling at her breasts, where the nipples lay flat, unaroused. As soon as he had finished, he rolled off and fell fast asleep. The next morning, Aledis made a small bundle of her scant possessions, took a few coins she had managed to steal from her husband, and went out into the street as usual.

That morning, however, she headed for the monastery at Sant Pere de los Puelles, then left Barcelona and started along the old Roman road that led to Figueres. She walked through the city gates head down, avoiding looking at the soldiers and restraining the urge to break into a run. Once she was beyond the city walls, she looked up at the bright blue sky and set off towards her new future, smiling broadly at all the travellers coming in the opposite direction towards Barcelona. Arnau had also left his wife, she was sure of it. He must have joined the army to get away from Maria! He could not love that woman. When the two of them made love, she could tell! When he was on top of her, she could feel his passion! He could not fool her. It was she, Aledis, whom he loved. And when he saw her . . . Aledis had a vision of him running towards her, arms outstretched. Then they would escape! Yes, they would run away and be together . . . for ever!

For the first few hours of her journey, she fell in with a group of peasants returning to their farms after selling their produce. She explained she was going in search of her husband because she was pregnant, and wanted him to know before he went into battle. From them she learnt that Figueres was a good five or six days' walk away, following the same road through Girona. She also had the chance to hear the advice of a couple of toothless old women who seemed so frail that they must break under the weight of the empty baskets they were carrying on their backs, but who nevertheless kept going, barefoot, showing unbelievable strength for such ancient, frail creatures.

'It's not good for a woman to be travelling these roads alone,' one of them told her, shaking her head.

'No, it isn't,' agreed the other.

A few seconds went by, while they both paused for breath.

'Especially if you are young and beautiful,' the second one added.

'That's true, that's true,' the first one concurred.

'What can happen to me?' Aledis asked naively. 'The road is full of good people such as yourselves.'

Again she had to wait, while the old women struggled to catch up with their group.

'On this stretch, there are plenty of people. There are lots of villagers who make their living in Barcelona as we do. But a bit further on,' one old woman added, still staring at the ground, 'when the villages are fewer and there is no large city nearby, the paths become lonely and dangerous.'

This time her companion did not add an immediate comment. Instead she walked on another few steps, then turned to Aledis: 'If you are alone, make sure you're not seen. Hide as soon as you hear a noise. Keep away from other people.'

'Even if they are knights?' laughed Aledis.

'Especially if they are!' one of the old women cried.

'As soon as you hear a horse's hooves, hide and pray!' added the other.

This time they both shouted the warning together, without even needing to pause for breath. They were so insistent that they came to a halt, and allowed the other peasants to get some way ahead. Aledis's look of disbelief must have been so obvious that, as they set off again, the two old women repeated their warning.

'Listen, my girl,' said one of them, while the other crone nodded agreement even before she knew what her companion was going to say, 'if I were you, I'd go back to the city and wait for your man there. The roads in the countryside are very dangerous, especially now they are full of soldiers and knights off to fight. That means there is no authority, nobody is in charge, nobody is worried about being caught and punished by the King, because he is so busy with other matters.'

Aledis walked thoughtfully alongside the two old women. Hide from knights on horseback? Why on earth should she do that? All the knights who had ever been to her husband's workshop had always been courteous and shown her respect. Nor had she ever heard from the many traders who supplied the tanner with his materials of any stories of robberies or problems on the roads of Catalonia. Instead, they had regaled the old man and her with terrifying stories of what could happen during sea voyages, which took them into the lands of the Moors or even further, to the territory of the sultan of Egypt. Her husband had told her that for more than two hundred years, Catalan roads were protected by law and by the King's authority, and that anyone who dared commit a crime anywhere along them would be punished far more severely than for a similar offence committed elsewhere. 'Trade depends on peace on the highway!' he would declare, adding: 'How could we sell our products all over Catalonia if the King could not guarantee peace?' He would go on to tell her, as though she were a child, how two hundred years earlier it had been the Church which had first started to take measures to defend the roads. First came the *Constitutions of Peace and Truce*, drawn up at church synods. If anyone broke them, they faced instant excommunication. The bishops established that the inhabitants of their sees were not to attack their enemies from the ninth hour of Saturdays to the first hour on Monday, nor during any religious festival. This truce also benefited all members of the clergy and churches, and everyone who was headed towards a church or coming away from one. He went on to explain that these constitutions had gradually been broadened to protect a greater number of people and goods, until they included merchants and farm animals, as well as those used for transport, and then farming implements and houses, the inhabitants of villages, women, crops, olive groves, wine . . . and finally, King Alfonso I extended this official peace to all public highways and paths in his kingdom, ruling that anyone who broke these provisions was committing a crime of *lèse-majesté*.

Aledis looked at the old women, who had carried on walking in silence, bowed down under their burdens, dragging their bare feet through the dust. Who would dare commit a crime of *lèse-majesté*? What Christian would want to run the risk of being excommunicated for attacking someone on a Catalan road? She was still turning all this over in her mind when the group of peasants headed off towards the village of Sant Andreu.

'Goodbye, my girl,' the old women said. 'Take heed of what we've told you. If you decide to carry on, be careful. Don't go into any town or city. You could be seen and followed. Only stop at farmhouses, and then only when you see women and children in them.'

Aledis watched the group move off, with the two old women struggling to keep up with the others. A few minutes later, she was all alone. Until now she had been in the company of the peasants, talking with them and allowing her thoughts to fly free as she imagined herself with Arnau again, excited by the adventure she had experienced after her sudden decision to leave everything and follow him. Now, as the voices and sounds of her companions faded into the distance, Aledis felt suddenly lonely. She had a long way ahead of her: she put a hand to her forehead to try to make out where she should go, protecting her eyes from the sun, which was already high in the bright blue sky. Not a single cloud spoilt the magnificent dome joining the horizon to the vast, rich lands of Catalonia.

Perhaps it was not only a feeling of loneliness that Aledis felt when the peasants departed, or the strangeness of finding herself in this unknown landscape. The fact was that Aledis had never seen the earth and sky laid out thus, with nothing to prevent her looking all round and seeing everything stretched out in front of her . . . whenever she liked! She stared and stared. She stared towards the horizon, beyond which she had been told lay the town of Figueres. Her legs trembled at the thought. She turned and looked back the way she had come. Nothing. She had left Barcelona behind, and could see nothing she recognized. Aledis looked in vain for the rooftops that until now had always come between her and this unknown marvel: the sky. She searched desperately for the smells of the city, the aroma of her husband's leather workshop, the noise of people, the sounds of a living city. She was on her own. All at once, the words of warning the two old women had offered her came flooding into her mind. She tried to catch some last glimpse of Barcelona. Five or six days! Where was she to sleep? How would she eat? She raised her bundle. What if their warning was true? What should she do? What could she do against a mounted knight or an outlaw? The sun was high in the sky. Aledis turned again towards where they had told her she could reach Figueres . . . and Arnau.

She tried to be careful. She was constantly on the alert, listening for any sound that might disturb the road's peace and quiet. As she drew near Montcada, where the castle stood proud on its hill, defending access to the plain of Barcelona, the road filled once more with peasants and traders. It was almost mid-day, and Aledis joined them as though she were part of one of the groups heading for the town, but when they came to its gates she remembered the old women's advice, and instead skirted it and continued on her way on the far side.

Aledis was pleased to find that the further she walked, the more the fears that had assailed her when she found herself alone gradually subsided. To the north of Montcada, she met up with more peasants and traders. Most of them were on foot too, although some rode on carts or on mules and donkeys. They all greeted her cheerfully, and this generosity of spirit also cheered Aledis. As she had done earlier, she joined a group, this time of merchants headed for Ripollet. They helped her ford the river Besós, but as soon as they had crossed it, they veered off left towards Ripollet itself. On her own again, Aledis avoided Val Romanas, but then found herself facing the real river Besós: a river which at that time of year was high enough to make it impossible for her to cross on foot.

Aledis looked down at the rushing water and at the boatman waiting unconcernedly on the riverbank. When he smiled a condescending smile at her, he revealed two rows of horribly blackened teeth. If she wanted to continue on her way, Aledis knew she had no choice but to use the services of this grinning fool. She tried to draw the top of her dress tighter over her bosom, but having to carry her bundle made it difficult. She slowed down. She had always been told how gracefully she moved: until now, she had been pleased at the idea. But now . . . the man was a big black bear! A filthy mess. What if she dropped her bundle? No: he would notice. After all, she had no reason to fear him. His shirt was stiff with dirt. What about his feet? My God! His toes were almost invisible under the grime. Slowly. Slowly. What a dreadful man! she could not help thinking.

'I'd like to cross the river,' she said in her bravest voice.

The boatman gazed up from her breasts to her big brown eyes. 'Ha,' was all he said, before brazenly staring at her bosom once more.

'Didn't you hear me?'

'Ha,' he repeated, without looking up.

The only sound came from the water rushing by. Aledis could feel the boatman's eyes on her. She breathed more rapidly, which only served to make her breasts stand out even more. The man's bloodshot gaze seemed to penetrate to the furthest corners of her body.

Aledis was all alone, lost in the Catalan countryside, on the banks of a river she had never heard of and which she thought she had already crossed with the traders heading for Ripollet. Alone with a big, strong brute of a fellow who was staring at her with bloodshot eyes in the most disgusting way. Aledis looked all round her. There was not a soul in sight. A few yards to her left, at some distance from the riverbank, stood a rough cabin built of tree trunks thrown together. It looked as vile and filthy as its owner. In among a pile of rubbish near the entrance a fire was heating a cooking pot hanging from an iron tripod. Aledis could scarcely bear to think what might be inside the pot: the smell it gave off was enough to make her feel nauseous.

'I have to catch up with the King's army,' she began to say hesitantly.

'Ha,' was all she got from him again.

'My husband is a captain,' she lied, speaking more firmly now, 'and I have to tell him I'm pregnant before he goes into combat.'

'Ha,' said the boatman, showing his blackened teeth once more.

A trickle of saliva appeared in one corner of his mouth. He wiped it away with his sleeve.

'Don't you have anything else to say?'

'Yes,' he replied. His eyes narrowed. 'The King's captains usually die quickly.'

Aledis did not see it coming. The boatman hit her swiftly and powerfully across the side of the face. Aledis spun round and fell at the filthy feet of her aggressor.

The man bent down, grabbed her by the hair and started dragging her towards his hut. Aledis dug her fingernails into the flesh of his hand, but he kept on dragging her along. She tried to get to her feet, but stumbled and fell again. She struggled, and threw herself against his legs, trying to stop him. The boatman evaded her clutching hands and kicked her in the pit of the stomach.

Inside the hut, as she tried to get her breath back, Aledis felt earth and mud scraping against her as the ferryman discharged his lust.

While he waited for the *hosts* and other armies to assemble, and for their supplies to arrive, King Pedro established his headquarters at an inn in Figueres. This was a town that sent representatives to the Catalan parliament, close to the border with Roussillon. Infante Don Pedro and his knights gathered in Pereleda, while Infante Don Jaime and the other noblemen – Lord de Eixèrica, Count Luna, Blasco de Alagó, Joan Ximénez de Urrea, Felipe de Castro and Joan Ferrández de Luna, among others – made camp outside the town walls of Figueres.

Arnau Estanyol was among the royal army. At the age of twenty-two, he had never experienced anything like it. The royal camp, with more than two thousand men still excited by their victory in Mallorca, and keen for more fighting, violence and booty, had nothing to do but await the order to march on Roussillon. It was the opposite of the quiet routine he knew from the *bastaixos* in Barcelona. Except for the periods when they were receiving training or practising with their weapons, life in the camp revolved around gambling, listening to the tales of war that the veterans used to terrify the newcomers with, petty thefts and quarrels.

Arnau spent his time strolling round the camp with three other youths who were from Barcelona and were as unused to the ways of war as he. They stared in admiration at horses and suits of armour, which the squires kept spotless at all times and displayed outside their tents in a kind of competition to show whose arms and equipment could shine the most. But if these steeds and armour impressed them, they could not help but be sickened by the amount of filth, the dreadful smells and clouds of insects attracted by the mounds of waste created by the thousands of men and animals. The royal officials had ordered that several long, deep trenches be dug to make latrines, as far as possible from the camp and close to a running stream which would carry away the soldiers' waste. But the stream was almost dry, and the refuse piled up every day and rotted, giving off a sickly, unbearable stench.

One morning when Arnau and his new companions were walking among the tents, they saw a knight on horseback returning from training. The horse was anxious to get back to its stable for a well-earned feed and to have the heavy armour removed from its breast and flanks. It snorted, raising its legs and kicking out, while the rider tried to control it and reach his tent without doing any damage to the soldiers or gear strewn about the lanes that had been created between the rows of tents. Held in check by a fierce iron bit, the huge, powerful animal chose instead to perform a spectacular dance, spraying anyone and anything it met with the white foaming sweat lathering its sides.

Arnau and his companions tried to get as far as possible out of the way, but unfortunately just at that moment the horse lunged sideways and knocked over Jaume, the smallest of the group. He was not hurt, and the rider did not even notice, continuing on his way back to his tent. But Jaume had fallen on to another group of soldiers, who were busy gaming with dice. One of them had already lost all he could hope to gain from whatever future campaigns King Pedro undertook, and was looking for a fight. He stood up, more than ready to vent the anger he felt towards his gaming colleagues on poor Jaume. He was a strongly built man with long, dirty hair and beard. The desperate, frustrated look on his face which came from losing steadily hour upon hour would have deterred even the bravest of foes.

The soldier lifted Jaume clear off the ground until he was level with his face. The poor lad did not even have time to realize what had happened to him. In the space of a few seconds, he had been knocked down by a horse, fallen into a dice game and now he was being attacked by a great roaring brute who shook him and then all of a sudden punched him so hard in the face that blood started to trickle from his mouth.

Arnau saw Jaume dangling from the man's grasp. 'Let go of him, you swine!' he shouted, surprising even himself.

The others rapidly moved away from Arnau and the soldier. Jaume, so astounded at Arnau's words that he had stopped struggling, found himself on his backside on the ground as the veteran dropped him and turned to face the person who had been foolish enough to insult him. All at once, Arnau found himself at the centre of a circle of onlookers curious to see what would happen between him and this enraged soldier. If only he had not insulted him . . . Why had he called him a swine?

'It wasn't his fault . . .' Arnau stammered, pointing to Jaume, who still had little idea of what was going on.

The soldier said nothing, but charged straight at Arnau like a rutting bull. His head struck Arnau in the midriff and sent him flying several yards, right through the ring of spectators. Arnau's chest felt as if it had exploded. The foul-smelling air he had got used to breathing seemed

339

suddenly to have disappeared. He gasped for breath, and tried to get to his feet, but a kick in the face sent him sprawling again. His head throbbed violently as he struggled again to breathe in, but before he could do so, another kick, this time to his kidneys, flattened him once more. After that, the blows rained down on him, and all Arnau could do was roll into a ball on the ground.

When the madman finally paused, Arnau felt as if his body had been smashed to pieces, and yet despite all the pain, he also thought he could hear a voice. Still curled in a ball, he tried to make out what it was saying.

He heard it quite clearly, speaking directly to him.

First once, then over and over again. He opened his eyes and saw the circle of people around him, all of them laughing and pointing at him. It was his father's words that were echoing in his abused ears: *I gave up everything I had for you to be free.* In his befuddled mind images and flashes of memory blurred and blended: he saw his father hanging from the end of a rope in Plaça del Blat . . . Arnau got to his feet, his face a bloody mess. He remembered the first stone he had carried to the Virgin of the Sea . . . The veteran had turned his back on him. Arnau recalled the effort it had taken to lift the stone on to his back, the pain and suffering, and then his pride when he unloaded it outside the church . . .

'Swine!'

The bearded veteran whirled round. 'Stupid peasant!' he roared, before launching himself again full length at Arnau.

No stone could have weighed as much as that swine did. No stone . . . Arnau stood up to the man's charge, grappled with him, and the two men fell on to the sandy ground. Arnau managed to get to his feet before him, but instead of punching him, grabbed him by his hair and his leather belt, lifted him above his head like a rag doll, and threw him right above the heads of the watching circle.

The bearded veteran fell in a heap on top of them.

But the soldier was not daunted by this show of Arnau's strength. He was used to fighting, and in a few seconds was again in front of Arnau, who was standing with feet spread wide in order to meet his charge. This time, however, instead of flinging himself on his opponent, the soldier tried to punch him, but once more Arnau was too quick for him: he parried the blow by grasping the man's forearm, then spun round quickly and sent him crashing to the ground, several yards away. This did not hurt the soldier, and so again and again he returned to the charge.

Finally, just when the soldier was expecting him to throw him off once more, Arnau instead punched him straight in the face, putting all his pent-up rage into the blow. The soldier fell at his feet, out cold. Arnau wanted to clutch his own hand to try to stop the stinging pain he could feel in his knuckles, but instead stood staring defiantly at the small crowd that had gathered, fist raised as though he might strike again. Don't get up, he said silently to the fallen man. For God's sake, don't get up.

The veteran tried drunkenly to stagger to his feet. *Don't do it!* Arnau put his foot in the other man's face and pushed him to the ground. *Don't get up, you whoreson.* The soldier lay still, until he was dragged away by his friends.

'You there!' The voice was one of command. Arnau turned and saw himself confronted by the knight who had caused the fight in the first place. He was still in full armour. 'Come over here.'

Arnau went over to him, secretly nursing his bruised hand.

'My name is Eiximèn d'Esparça, shield-bearer to His Majesty King Pedro the Third. I want you to serve under me. Go and see my attendants.'

28

The three young women fell silent and looked at each other as Aledis threw herself on the stew like a starving animal. She kneeled down and scooped up the meat and vegetables directly from the cooking pot, without even pausing for breath, although she did keep an eye on them over the food. The youngest of the three, who had blond curls that cascaded down over a sky-blue robe, twisted her lips at the other two: which of them had not been in the same situation? she seemed to be saying. Her companions exchanged knowing glances with her, and all three moved away from Aledis.

As she did so, the girl with the golden curls turned to look inside the large tent where, protected from the July sun that beat down on the camp, four other women, slightly older than the first three, were also staring intently at Aledis. So too did their mistress, who sat in the middle of them on a stool. She had nodded when Aledis appeared, and agreed she should be given food. Since then, she had not taken her eyes off her: she was dressed in grimy rags, but she was beautiful ... and young. What could she be doing here? She was not a vagabond: she did not seem to want to beg. Nor was she a prostitute: she had instinctively recoiled when she saw whom she was with. She was filthy, wearing a torn smock and with a mass of dishevelled, greasy hair. But her teeth were gleaming white. She had obviously never known hunger, or the kinds of disease that left teeth blackened. What was she doing there? She must be running away from something, but what?

The mistress gestured towards one of the women inside the tent with her. 'I want her cleaned and tidied up,' she whispered as the other woman leant over her.

The woman looked at Aledis, smiled and nodded.

Aledis could not resist. 'You need a bath,' said another of the prostitutes, who had come out of the tent. A bath! How many days had it been since she had even washed? They got ready a tub of fresh water for her inside the tent. Aledis sat in it, her knees drawn up, while the three prostitutes who had watched her eat began to wash her. Why not let them fuss over her? She could not appear before Arnau looking the way she did. The army was camped close by, and he must be with them. She had done it! So why not let them look after her? She also allowed them to dress her. They looked for the least garish robe, but even so . . . 'Streetwalkers must wear brightly coloured clothes,' her mother had once told her as a child, when she had mistaken a prostitute for a noble lady and stepped aside to let her by. 'So how do we tell the two apart?' Aledis had asked. 'The King obliges them to dress that way, but he prohibits them from wearing any cape or cloak, even in wintertime. That's how you can tell the prostitutes: they always have bare shoulders.'

Aledis looked down at herself now. Women of her social rank, the wives of artisans, were not allowed to wear bright colours, but how lovely this cloth was! But how could she go and find Arnau dressed like this? The soldiers would take her for . . . She raised an arm to see how the sides of the robe looked.

'Do you like it?'

Aledis turned and saw the mistress standing in the entrance to the tent. At a sign from her, Antònia, the young girl with blond curls who had helped her dress, vanished outside.

'Yes . . . no . . .' Aledis looked at herself once more. The robe was bright green. Perhaps these women had something she could wrap round her shoulders? If she covered them, then nobody would think she was a prostitute.

The mistress looked her up and down. She had been right: the girl had a voluptuous body that would delight any of the army captains. And those eyes! The two women stared at each other. They were huge. Chestnut brown. And yet there was a sad look in them.

'What brought you here, my girl?'

'My husband. He's in the King's army, and left before he could learn he's going to be a father. I want to tell him now, before he goes into combat.'

She said this as quickly as she could, just as she had done to the traders who had rescued her at the river Besós when the ferryman, after he had raped her, was trying to get rid of her by drowning her in the river. They had taken him by surprise, and he had run away as fast as his legs could take him. Aledis had not been able to fight him off, and after she had let him have his way with her he had dragged her by the hair down to the river. The outside world no longer existed. The sun had ceased to shine, and all she could hear was the boatman's panting, which echoed inside her and mingled with her memories and sense of helplessness. When the traders arrived and saw how badly she had been treated, they took pity on her.

'You have to tell the magistrate about this,' they said.

But what could she tell the King's official? What if her husband were looking for her? What if she were found out? There would be a trial, and she could not . . .

'No. I have to reach the royal camp before the armies leave for Roussillon,' she said, after explaining that she was pregnant and that her husband was unaware of it. 'I'll tell him, and he will decide what we should do.'

The traders went with her as far as Girona. Aledis left them at Sant Feliu church, outside the city walls. The oldest among them shook his head sadly when he saw her so lonely and bedraggled by the church walls. Aledis remembered the old women's warning, 'Don't go into any town or city,' and so she avoided Girona, where some six thousand people lived. From outside the city, she could see the outline of the Santa Maria cathedral, still under construction; with next to it the bishop's palace and, alongside that, the tall, imposing Gironella Tower, the city's main defensive point. She gazed at all these fine buildings for a few moments, then continued on her way to Figueres.

The mistress, who was watching as Aledis remembered her journey, saw that the young girl was trembling.

The presence of the royal army in Figueres attracted hundreds of people. Aledis joined them, already in the grip of hunger. She could no longer recall what they looked like, but she was given bread and water, and somebody offered her some vegetables. They came to a halt for the night north of the river Fluviá, at the foot of Pontons Castle, which guarded the river approach to the town of Bàscara, halfway between Girona and Figueres. It was there that two of the travellers took payment for the food they had offered her: both of them raped her brutally in the night. Aledis was past caring. She sought in her memory for the image of Arnau's face, and took refuge there. The next day, she followed the group like an animal, walking several paces behind them. But this time they did not give her any food, or even talk to her. At long last, they reached the royal camp.

And now . . . what was this woman staring at? She did nothing but stare . . . at Aledis's stomach! Aledis could see that the robe fitted snugly over her flat, smooth stomach and she squirmed beneath the other woman's gaze.

The mistress pursed her lips in satisfaction, but Aledis did not see the gesture. How often had she witnessed silent confessions of this sort? Girls who made up stories, but at the slightest pressure were unable to sustain their lies: they always grew nervous and looked down at the ground, just as this one did. How many pregnancies had she seen? Dozens? Hundreds? Never had a girl with such a flat, smooth stomach like that really been pregnant. Had she missed a month? Possibly, but that was not enough to lead her to undertake such an arduous journey to see her husband before he went off to fight.

'There is no way you can go to the army camp dressed like that.' Aledis looked up when she heard the other woman speak. She glanced down at the robe again. 'We are forbidden to go there. If you wish, I could find your husband for you.'

'You? You would help me? Why would you do that?'

'Haven't I already helped you? I've given you food, had you washed and dressed. Nobody else has done as much in this hellish camp, have they?' Aledis nodded, and shuddered as she recalled the way she had been treated. 'Why does it seem so odd to you then?' the woman added. Aledis hesitated. 'We may be whores, but that doesn't mean we don't have feelings. If someone had given me a helping hand some years ago . . .' The woman gazed into space, and her words floated up into the roof of the tent. 'Well, that doesn't matter now. If you

346

wish, I can help you. I know many people in the army camp, and it wouldn't be difficult to locate your husband.'

Aledis thought it over. Why not?

The other woman was thinking of her new recruit. It would be easy enough to have the husband disappear . . . all it would take was a scuffle in the camp . . . many of the soldiers owed her favours. And then what would the girl do? Whom could she turn to? She was on her own . . . she would be hers. And the pregnancy, if it was real, was no problem either; she had dealt with many others in the past, for the price of a few coins.

'I thank you,' said Aledis.

That was it. She was hers.

'What's your husband's name? Where does he come from?'

'He's part of the Barcelona *host*. His name is Arnau, Arnau Estanyol.'

At this, Aledis saw the other woman tremble. 'Is there something wrong?' she asked.

The woman fumbled for the stool and sat down. Perspiration beaded her brow. 'No,' she said. 'It must be this ghastly hot weather. Pass me that fan, will you?'

It was impossible! she told herself, while Aledis carried out her request. The blood was beating at her temples. Arnau Estanyol! Impossible.

'Describe your husband to me,' she said, fanning herself as she sat.

'Oh, it ought to be very easy to find him. He's a *bastaix* from the port of Barcelona. He's young, strong, tall and good-looking. He has a birthmark right next to his right eye.'

The mistress went on fanning herself in silence. She was gazing far beyond Aledis, to a village called Navarcles, to a wedding feast, a straw mattress, a castle . . . to Llorenç de Bellera, her disgrace, hunger, pain . . .

How many years had gone by since then? Twenty? Yes, at least that many. And now . . .

Aledis interrupted her thoughts: 'Do you know him?'

'No . . . no.'

Had she ever known him? In fact, she remembered little about him. She had been so young!

'Will you help me find him?' Aledis asked, bringing her back to the present once more.

'Yes, I will,' said the other woman, indicating that Aledis should leave the tent.

Once she had gone, Francesca buried her face in her hands. Arnau! She had managed to forget him, and now, twenty years later . . . If this girl were telling the truth, the child she was bearing in her belly would be . . . her grandchild! And she had been planning to kill it! Twenty years! What could he be like? Aledis had said he was tall, strong, handsome. Francesca had no image of him, even as a newborn baby. She had succeeded in making sure he had the forge to warm him, but soon it had become impossible for her to go and visit him. *Those wretches! I was only a girl, but they queued up to rape me!* A tear coursed down her cheek. How long had it been since she had cried. She had not done so twenty years earlier. The boy will be better off with Bernat, she had thought. When she learnt what had happened, Dona Caterina had slapped her and sent her off to be the soldiers' plaything. When they had finished with her, she had lived off the scraps thrown over the castle wall. She wandered among the heaps of rubbish and waste, fighting with other beggars for whatever mouldy, worm-ridden remains they could find. That was how she had met another young girl. She was skinny, but still pretty. Nobody seemed to be looking after her. Perhaps if . . . Francesca offered her some scraps she had saved for herself. The girl smiled, and her eyes lit up; she had probably known no other life than this. Francesca washed her in a stream, scrubbing her skin with sand until she cried out with pain and cold. Then all she had to do was present her to one of the captains at Lord de Bellera's castle. That was how it had all started. *I grew hard, my son, so hard that my heart turned to stone inside me. What did your father tell you about me? That I left you to die?*

That same night, when the King's captains and those soldiers who had been fortunate at dice or cards came to her tent, Francesca asked if any of them knew Arnau.

'The *bastaix*, you mean?' said one of them. 'Of course I do, everyone knows who he is.' Francesca's head tilted to one side as she listened. 'They say he defeated a veteran everybody was afraid of,' the man explained, 'and then Eiximèn d'Esparça, the King's shield-bearer, took him on as part of his personal guard. He has a birthmark by his right eye. He's being trained to fight with a dagger. He's fought on several more occasions, and always won. He's well worth betting on.' The officer smiled. 'Why are you so interested in him?' he said, his smile broadening still further.

Why not feed his lascivious imagination? thought Francesca. Explaining anything different would be complicated. So she winked at the captain.

'You're too old for a man like him,' the soldier laughed.

Francesca did not give way. 'Bring him to me and you won't regret it.'

'Where? Here?'

What if Aledis had been lying? But Francesca's first impressions had never let her down.

'No, not here.'

Aledis walked a few steps away from the tent. It was a beautiful warm and starry night, with a big yellow moon lighting the darkest corners. She looked up at the sky, and then at the men who went into the tent and emerged soon afterwards on the arm of one or other of the girls. They would head for some small huts in the distance, and then a short while later reappear, sometimes laughing, sometimes in silence. The same scene was repeated again and again. Each time, the prostitutes headed for the tub where Aledis had bathed, and washed their private parts in the water, staring at her brazenly as they did so. It reminded Aledis of the woman her mother had once told her she should not step aside for.

'Why don't they arrest her?' Aledis had asked her mother on that occasion.

Eulàlia had looked down at her daughter, calculating whether she was of an age to receive a proper explanation. 'She can't be arrested,' she told her. 'The King and the Church allow them to ply their trade.'

Aledis looked up at her in disbelief.

'Yes, daughter, that's right. The Church says that fallen women should not be punished by earthly laws, because divine law will do so.' How was she to explain to a child that the real reason for the Church being so lenient was to prevent adultery or unnatural relationships? Eulàlia observed her daughter again. No, she was not old enough to understand about unnatural relationships.

Antònia, the girl with the golden curls, smiled at her from beside the tub. Aledis pursed her lips in response, but went no further.

What else had her mother told her? she wondered, trying to take her mind off what she was seeing. That prostitutes could not live in any village, town or city where honest citizens lived, under threat of being thrown out of their own homes if their neighbours so demanded. That they were obliged to listen to religious sermons aimed at rehabilitating them. That they could only visit public baths on Mondays and Fridays, the days reserved for Jews and Saracens. And that they could use their money for works of charity, but never for any holy oblation.

Standing next to the tub, Antònia was holding her skirt up with one hand while she washed herself with the other. And she was still smiling! Every time she bent to scoop up water, she looked at Aledis and smiled. Aledis did her best to respond, and tried not to let her gaze wander downwards towards her groin, clearly visible in the moonlight.

Why was the girl smiling at her? She was no more than a girl, but already she was condemned. A few years earlier, just after her father had refused to allow her to be betrothed to Arnau, her mother had taken her and her sister Alesta to the Sant Pere convent in Barcelona. 'Let them see it,' had been the tanner's terse command. The convent atrium was full of doors that had been torn off their hinges and left leaning against the convent arches or thrown on the ground. King Pedro had given the abbess of Sant Pere's the sole authority to order all the prostitutes out of her parish, and then to tear the doors off their dwellings and bring them all to be displayed at the convent. The abbess had been more than happy to oblige!

'Have all these people been forced out of their homes?' Aledis had asked, flapping her hand at the sight and remembering what had happened to her own family before they had rented a room with Pere and Mariona: their front door had also been torn off because they had been unable to pay their taxes.

'No, daughter,' her mother had replied. 'This is what happens to women who abandon chastity.'

Aledis could vividly remember that moment, and the way her mother had narrowed her eyes and peered at her.

Aledis shook her head to rid it of that painful memory. She found herself staring once more at Antònia and her exposed pubis, where the hairs were as blond and curly as the hair on her head. What would the abbess of Sant Pere do with someone like Antònia?

Francesca came out of her tent, looking for Antònia. 'Come here, girl!' she shouted at her. Aledis watched as Antònia skipped away from the tub, pulling up her hose, and ran into the tent. Then her gaze met that of Francesca, before the older woman turned back into the tent. Why was she looking at her like that?

Eiximèn d'Esparça, King Pedro III's shield-bearer, was an important person. In fact, his position was more impressive than his physique, because the moment he dismounted from his huge warhorse and took off his armour, he was merely a short, skinny-looking fellow. A weak man, thought Arnau, hoping the nobleman could not read his mind.

Eiximèn d'Esparça commanded a company of Almogavars that he paid for out of his own purse. Whenever he surveyed them, he began to worry. Where did those mercenaries' loyalty really lie? To whoever paid them, that was all. That was why he liked to surround himself with a praetorian guard, and explained why he had been so impressed by Arnau.

'What weapons are you skilled in?' d'Esparça's captain had asked Arnau. The *bastaix* showed him his father's crossbow. 'Yes, I thought as much. All you Catalans are good with crossbows, it's your duty. Any other weapons?'

Arnau shook his head.

'What about that knife?' The officer pointed to the weapon Arnau was wearing tucked into his belt, but when he took it out, the officer burst out laughing. 'That blunt thing wouldn't even be able to tear a virgin's hymen. I'll show you how to use a real dagger.'

He reached inside a big chest and handed him a hunting knife that was much longer and broader than the *bastaix* dagger. Arnau drew his finger along its sharp blade. From that moment on, day after day, he joined Eiximèn's guard to train in hand-to-hand combat with this new knife. He was also given a coloured uniform, with a coat of mail, a helm – which he polished until it shone – and strong leather shoes that were tied up round his ankles. The tough training alternated with real hand-to-hand combats, without weapons, that were organized by the nobles in the camp. Arnau soon became the champion of the shield-bearer's guard, and not a day went by without him fighting once or twice in front of a noisy crowd which wagered on the winner.

It took only a few of these fights for Arnau to become famous among all the troops. Whenever he walked around the camp, in the few free moments left to him, he could sense he was being watched and talked about. How strange it felt to have people fall silent when you went by!

Eiximèn d'Esparça's captain smiled when the soldier told him who was looking for Arnau.

'Do you think I could pay a visit to one of her girls too?' he asked.

'I'm sure you could. The old woman is crazy for your man. You can't imagine how her eyes shine at the mention of him.'

The two of them laughed out loud.

'Where do I have to take him?'

Francesca chose a small tavern on the outskirts of Figueres for their meeting.

'Don't ask questions, and do as you're told,' the captain warned Arnau. 'There's somebody who wants to see you.'

The two soldiers led him to the tavern. When they got there, they showed him up to the wretched little room where Francesca was waiting for him. As soon as Arnau was inside, they shut the door and barred it from the outside. Arnau turned and tried to open it: when he failed, he began banging on it with his fists.

'What's going on?' he cried. 'What is this?'

All he got by way of response was the two men's cackles.

Arnau listened to them for a few moments. What was happening? Then he suddenly realized he was not alone. He turned round again: Francesca was watching him. She was leaning against the window, her figure dimly lit by a candle on one of the walls. In spite of the gloom, he could see her bright green robe. A prostitute! How many stories about women had he heard in the warmth of the camp fires; how many soldiers had boasted of spending all their pay on a girl who was always so much better, more beautiful and more voluptuous than the one talked about before. Arnau said nothing, and looked down at the floor of the room. He was in the army because he was running away from two women! Perhaps . . . perhaps this trick was because he never said anything, because he never showed any interest in women . . . he had often been scoffed at for it round the camp fire.

'What kind of joke is this?' he asked Francesca. 'What do you want from me?'

The candlelight was so dim she still could not make him out properly, but that voice . . . his voice was already that of a man, and she could see that he was big and tall, as the girl had said. She could feel her legs trembling, and felt weak at the knees. Her son!

Francesca had to clear her throat several times before she could speak.

'Don't worry. I don't intend to do anything that could bring you dishonour. Besides,' she went on, 'we are on our own. What could a weak old woman like me do to a strong young man like you?'

'So why are those two outside laughing?' asked Arnau, still standing close to the door.

'Let them laugh if they like. Men have twisted minds:

they like to think the worst. Perhaps if I had told them the truth, if I had told them why I was so anxious to see you, they wouldn't have been as keen as they were to bring you when they imagined it was for a baser reason.'

'What were they to think of a prostitute and a man shut in a room in a tavern? What else can one expect from a whore?'

Arnau spoke harshly, woundingly. It took Francesca some time to recover.

'We are people too,' she said, raising her voice. 'Saint Augustine wrote that it was for God to judge fallen women.'

'So you brought me here to talk about God?'

'No.' Francesca went over to him; she had to see his face. 'I brought you here to talk about your wife.'

Arnau staggered as though he had been hit. She could see he truly was handsome.

'What's wrong? How do you—'

'She is pregnant.'

'Maria?'

'Aledis,' said Francesca without thinking. Had he said Maria?

'Aledis?'

Francesca could see he was dazed. What did that mean?

'What are you two doing talking all the time?' they heard the soldiers shout outside, and they banged on the door, laughing. 'What's wrong? Is he too much of a man for you?'

Arnau and Francesca looked at each other. She signalled for him to move away from the door, and Arnau followed her. They began to talk in a whisper.

'Did you say Maria?' asked Francesca when they were on the far side of the room by the window.

'Yes. My wife's name is Maria.'

'Who is Aledis then? She told me that . . .'

Arnau shook his head. Was that a sad gleam in his eyes? wondered Francesca. Arnau seemed to have crumpled before her: his arms hung loosely by his sides, and his head seemed too heavy for his neck. But he said nothing. Francesca felt a stab of pain deep inside. What is going on, my son?

'Who is Aledis?' she insisted.

Arnau simply shook his heavy head. He had abandoned everything; Maria, his work, the Virgin . . . and now, *she* was here! And pregnant! Everybody would find out. How could he ever return to Barcelona, to his work, or his home?

Francesca looked out of the window. The night was dark. What was the pain gripping her so tightly? She had seen men crawling through the dirt, women with nowhere to turn; she had been a witness to death and misery, to sickness and torment, but never until this moment had she felt anything like this.

'I don't think she is telling the truth,' she said, struggling to speak as she continued to gaze out of the window. She sensed Arnau stirring behind her.

'What do you mean?'

'I don't think she is pregnant, I think she is lying.'

'What does that matter?' Arnau heard himself say.

Aledis was in the camp, and that was more than enough. She was following him, and she would pursue him everywhere. Nothing that he had done was of any use.

'I could help you.'

'Why would you want to?'

Francesca turned to face him. They were almost side by side: she could reach out and touch him. She could smell his body. Because you are my son! she could tell him. Now was the moment if ever – but what had Bernat told him about her? What good would it do for him to learn his mother was a common whore? Francesca stretched out a trembling hand. Arnau did not move. What good would it do? She held back. More than twenty years had gone by, and she was nothing more than a prostitute.

'Because she lied to me,' she answered. 'I gave her food and clothing, I took her in. I don't like being lied to. You look like a good person, and I think she is lying to you too.'

Arnau looked her straight in the eye. What did it matter? Aledis was free of her husband and was far from Barcelona. Aledis would tell everything, and besides, this woman . . . what was it in her that somehow made him feel at peace?

He leant towards her and began to explain.

29

King Pedro III had already been in Figueres for seven days when on 28 July 1343 he ordered the army to strike camp and begin the march on Roussillon.

'You'll have to wait,' Francesca told Aledis while the girls were taking down their tent to follow the soldiers. 'When the King orders them to set off, none of them can leave the ranks. Perhaps when we make camp again . . .'

Aledis looked at her enquiringly.

'I've already sent him a message,' said Francesca in an offhand way. 'Are you coming with us?'

Aledis nodded.

'Well, help out then,' Francesca told her sharply.

Twelve hundred men on horseback and more than four thousand footsoldiers, all of them armed and with provisions for eight days, set off towards La Jonquera, a town little more than half a day's march from Figueres. Behind them came a huge train of carts, mules and all sorts of camp followers. When they reached La Jonquera, King Pedro ordered them to set up camp once more: a new papal messenger, an Augustinian friar this time, had brought another letter from Jaime III. When King Pedro had conquered Mallorca, King Jaime had turned to the Pope for aid; on that occasion, monks, bishops and even cardinals had tried unsuccessfully to mediate.

Now, as before, King Pedro refused to listen to the new papal envoy. His army spent the night at La Jonquera. Was this the moment? Francesca wondered as she watched Aledis helping the others prepare the food. No, it was not, she decided. The further they were from Barcelona and Aledis's former life, the more opportunity she would have. 'We have to wait,' she told Aledis when she enquired anxiously about Arnau.

The next morning, King Pedro ordered everyone on the march again.

'To Panissars! In battle formation! Four columns ready for combat!'

The order ran through the ranks. Arnau heard it as he was ready to move off with the rest of Eiximèn d'Esparça's personal guard. To Panissars! Some of the men shouted the word, others merely whispered it, but all spoke of it with pride and respect. The pass at Panissars! The way through the Pyrenees between Catalan territory and Roussillon. That night, only half a league from La Jonquera, stories of the feats of arms from the legendary battle of Panissars could be heard round every camp fire.

Panissars was where the Catalans – the fathers or grandfathers of the current army – had defeated the French. The Catalans standing alone! Many years earlier, Pedro the Great of Catalonia had been excommunicated by the Pope for conquering Sicily without his consent. The French, led by Philippe the Bold, had declared war on the heretic in the name of Christianity, and with the help of some traitors had crossed the Pyrenees by the pass at La Maçana.

Pedro the Great had been forced to withdraw. The

nobles and knights of Aragon had abandoned him and returned to their own lands.

'Only we Catalans were left!' said someone in the night, silencing even the crackling fire.

'And Roger de Llúria!' shouted another man.

His armies depleted, King Pedro had to allow the French to invade Catalonia while he awaited reinforcements from Sicily, under the command of Admiral Roger de Llúria. He ordered Viscount Ramon Folch de Cardona, the defender of Girona, to withstand the French siege until Roger de Llúria could reach Catalonia. Viscount Cardona mounted an epic defence of the city until at length King Pedro authorized him to surrender.

Roger de Llúria arrived and defeated the French navy. On land, the French army was swept by an epidemic.

'When they took Girona, they desecrated the shrine of Sant Narcís,' one of the soldiers at a camp fire explained.

According to local legend, millions of flies had come buzzing out of the sepulchre when the French defiled it. It was these insects which spread the epidemic through the French camp. Defeated at sea, weakened by sickness on land, King Philippe the Bold called a truce in order to allow him to retreat without a massacre.

Pedro the Great granted him the truce, but only in his name and that of his nobles and knights.

Now, Arnau could hear the cries of the Almogavar company as they entered the pass at Panissars. Shielding his eyes, he looked up at the steep mountainsides off which the mercenaries' blood-curdling shouts echoed. It had been here, alongside Roger de Llúria and watched from on high by Pedro the Great and his nobles, that the Almogavars had slaughtered the retreating French army, killing thousands of men. The next day Philippe the Bold died in Perpignan, and the crusade against Catalonia was over.

The Almogavars kept up their shouting all the way through the pass, challenging an enemy which failed to appear. Perhaps they too remembered what their fathers and grandfathers had told them had happened on this very spot fifty years earlier.

Those ragged men, who when they were not fighting as mercenaries lived in the forests and mountains and spent their time plundering and laying waste to the lands ruled by the Moors, ignoring whatever treaty the Christian kings might have made, took orders from no one. Arnau had seen it during the march from Figueres to La Jonquera, and it was obvious again now: of the four columns into which the King had divided the army, three advanced in formation beneath their banners, but the Almogavars swarmed in an unruly mass, shouting, threatening, laughing at their enemy, daring them to come and show themselves.

'Don't they have any leaders?' asked Arnau when he saw how the Almogavars ignored Eiximèn d'Esparça's call for a halt and instead continued their disorderly advance through the pass.

'It doesn't look like it, does it?' said a veteran who had come to a halt beside him, as all the royal shield-bearer's personal guard had done.

'No, it doesn't.'

'Well, they do have their leaders, and they are careful not to disobey them. They're not commanders like ours, though.' The veteran pointed to Eiximèn d'Esparça, then caught an imaginary fly in his fingers and waved it in front of Arnau's eyes. The *bastaix* and several other soldiers laughed at his gesture. 'They have real leaders,' the veteran said, growing serious all of a sudden. 'In their company, it doesn't matter whose son you are, if you have a name, or are some count or other's favourite. The most important of their leaders are the *adalils*.' Arnau looked at the Almogavars who were still swarming past them. 'No, don't bother,' the soldier said, 'you won't be able to pick them out. They all dress the same, but all the Almogavars know who they are. You need four things to become an *adalil*: skill at leading troops; to give your all and to inspire your men to do the same; to have the qualities of a born leader; and, above all, to be loyal.'

'That's what they say our commander has,' Arnau interrupted him, pointing to the royal shield-bearer.

'Yes, but nobody has ever challenged his position. To get to be an Almogavar *adalil* you need to have twelve other *adalils* swear on pain of death that you possess all these qualities. There would be no nobles left in the world if they had to do the same in front of their peers – especially when it came to loyalty.'

The soldiers listening to him all nodded their agreement. Arnau looked at the Almogavars once more. How could they bring down a charging warhorse with nothing more than a spear?

'Below the *adalils*,' the veteran went on, 'come the *almogatens*. They have to be expert in battle, to give everything for their cause, to be mobile and loyal. They are chosen in the same way: twelve *almogatens* have to swear that the candidate possesses all the required qualities.'

'On pain of death?'

'On pain of death,' the veteran confirmed.

What Arnau could not have imagined was that these mercenaries' independent spirit was so great that they would disobey even the King's orders. Pedro III had ordered that once all his army had successfully crossed the Panissars pass, they should head directly for Perpignan, the capital of Roussillon. Despite this, as soon as they had emerged from the pass, the Almogavars split off from the main army and headed for Bellaguarda Castle, which guarded its northern entrance.

Arnau and the royal shield-bearer's man stood and watched as the mercenaries rushed up the slope to the castle. They were still whooping and shouting as they had done all the way through the pass. Eiximèn d'Esparça turned towards the King, who was also observing the attack.

But Pedro III did nothing. How could he stop them? He turned back and continued on his way to Perpignan. This was Eiximèn d'Esparça's signal. The King had sanctioned the assault on Bellaguarda, but he was the one paying the Almogavars, and if there was any booty to be shared out, he wanted to be there. And so, while the main force followed the King in battle formation, Eiximèn d'Esparça and his men set off after the Almogavars.

The Catalans laid siege to the castle. That afternoon and through all the next night, the mercenaries took turns to chop down trees to make their siege weapons: assault ladders and a big battering ram mounted on wheels that was swung using ropes suspended from another, higher tree trunk, and was covered with hides to protect the men underneath.

Arnau stood guard below the walls of Bellaguarda. How were they going to storm the castle? They would be advancing unprotected, uphill, while the defenders could fire down on them from behind their battlements. He could see them up there, peeping out and observing the besiegers. On one occasion he even thought someone was staring straight at him. The defenders seemed calm, though his own legs shook at the idea of them watching him.

'They seem very sure of themselves,' he remarked to one of the veterans standing guard beside him.

'Don't be fooled,' the man said. 'Inside the castle they're having a far worse time than us. Besides, they've seen the Almogavars.'

The Almogavars. There they were again. Arnau turned to look at them. They were working tirelessly, and now seemed to be perfectly well organized. None of them was laughing or arguing; they were all getting on with the task in hand.

'How can they possibly frighten the people inside the castle so much?' asked Arnau.

The veteran laughed. 'You've never seen them fight, have you?' Arnau shook his head. 'Just wait and see.'

Arnau waited, dozing on the hard ground through a long night during which the mercenaries kept on building their machines by torchlight.

As day dawned and the sun rose over the horizon, Eiximèn d'Esparça ordered his troops to deploy round the castle. The shadows of the night had barely dispersed in the first timid light of day. Arnau looked round to see where the Almogavars were. This time they had obeyed the order, and were drawn up beneath the walls of Bellaguarda. Arnau peered up at the lofty castle. All the lights inside had been extinguished, but he knew they were waiting inside the walls. He shivered. What was he doing there? The morning air was chill, but his hands were sweaty on the crossbow. There was complete silence. He could die. The day before, he had often seen the defenders staring straight at him, a mere *bastaix*: the faces of those men, which then had been blurred in the distance, now appeared clearly before him. They were there, waiting for him! He shivered again. His knees were knocking, and he had to make a great effort to stop his teeth chattering. He clasped his crossbow firmly to his chest so that nobody could see how his hands were shaking. The captain had told him that when the order to advance was given, he should run towards the castle, seek cover behind some boulders and fire his crossbow up at the defenders. The problem would be to reach those boulders. Could he do it? Arnau found himself staring at them. He had to run there, hide behind them, fire his bow, duck down again, fire a second time—

A command rent the air.

The order to attack! The boulders! Arnau got ready to sprint towards them, but felt the captain's gloved hand holding him back.

'Not yet,' said the officer.

'But . . .'

'Not yet,' the captain repeated. 'Look.' He pointed towards the Almogavars.

From among their ranks, another cry went up: 'Awake, iron!'

Arnau could not take his eyes off them. Suddenly, all of them took up the cry: 'Awake, iron!'

At this, all the Almogavars beat their spears and knives together until the sound drowned out their voices.

'Awake, iron!'

Their steel weapons did start to awaken, sending out showers of sparks as the blades clashed against each other or on rocks. The thunderous noise deafened Arnau. Little by little, hundreds and then thousands of sparks flashed in the gloom, and the mercenaries were soon surrounded by a halo of bright light.

Arnau found himself waving his crossbow in the air and shouting with them: 'Awake, iron!' He was no longer sweating or trembling. 'Awake, iron!'

He glanced up at the castle walls: it seemed as if the Almogavars' battle cry would bring them tumbling down. The ground was shaking, and the bright glow from the sparks grew and grew. All of a sudden, there was the sound of a trumpet, and the shouting changed into a mighty roar:

'Sant Jordi! Sant Jordi!'

'Now you can go,' shouted the captain, pushing Arnau forwards in the wake of about two hundred men who were charging ferociously up the castle mound.

Arnau ran to seek cover behind the boulders alongside the captain and a company of crossbowmen. He concentrated on one of the scaling ladders the Almogavars had placed against the wall, trying to aim at the figures who were fighting off the mercenaries from the top of the battlements. The Almogavars were still shrieking like madmen. Arnau's aim was true: he twice saw his bolts strike defenders below their chain-mail protection, and the bodies fall back.

As one group of attackers managed to scale the castle walls, Arnau felt the captain's hand on his shoulder, telling him to stop firing. There was no need to use the battering ram: as soon as the Almogavars had appeared on the battlements, the castle gates opened and several knights galloped out to avoid being taken hostage. Two of them fell to the Catalan crossbow fire; the others succeeded in escaping. Deserted by their leaders, some of the castle defenders started to surrender. Eiximèn d'Esparça and his cavalry forced their way into the castle and laid about them, killing anyone who resisted. The footsoldiers poured in after them.

After he had rushed inside the castle, Arnau came to a halt, crossbow over his shoulder, dagger in hand. It was not needed. The castle yard was strewn with the dead, and those still alive were on their knees, unarmed, begging for mercy from the knights who strode around, broadswords at the ready. The Almogavars were already plundering the castle's riches: some had entered the castle keep; others were stripping the bodies with a greed that Arnau could not bear to watch. One of them came up and offered him a handful of crossbow bolts. Some of them had missed their aim, but others were stained with blood, and a few still had lumps of flesh caught on them. Arnau hesitated. The Almogavar, an older man who was as tough and wiry as the bolts he was holding out, was surprised at Arnau's reaction. Then he smiled a toothless smile and offered them to another soldier.

'What are you doing?' the soldier asked Arnau. 'Do

you think Eiximèn is going to replace your bolts for you? Clean these off,' he said, throwing them at Arnau's feet.

In a few hours it was all over. The surviving men were shepherded together and manacled. That same night they would be sold as slaves in the camp that followed the Catalan army. Eiximèn d'Esparça's men set off again to rejoin the main army. They took their wounded with them, leaving behind seventeen Catalan dead and a blazing fortress that would no longer be of any use to King Jaime III and his allies.

30

Eiximèn d'Esparça and his men caught up with the royal army near the town of Elne the Proud, barely two leagues from Perpignan. The King decided to make camp there for the night. He received the visit of yet another bishop who once again tried unsuccessfully to mediate on behalf of Jaime of Mallorca.

Although King Pedro had not objected to Eiximèn d'Esparça and his Almogavars taking Bellaguarda Castle, he did try to prevent another group of knights over-running the tower of Nidolères on the way to Elne. He arrived too late: by the time he got there, the knights had already taken it, killed all its inhabitants, and set fire to everything.

Nobody, however, dared go near Elne or threaten the people living there. The entire royal army gathered round their camp fires and stared at the lights of the town. In open defiance of the Catalan army, its gates were left wide open.

'Why—' Arnau started to ask, seated at one of the fires.

'Why is it called Elne the Proud?' one of the veterans interrupted him.

'Yes, and why are we showing it so much respect? Why don't they even bother to shut the gates?'

The soldier stared at the city for a long while before answering.

'Elne the Proud weighs on our consciences . . . as Catalans,' he explained. 'They know we won't dare touch them.' With that, he fell silent. Arnau had learnt to respect the experienced soldiers' ways. He knew that if he hurried him, the man would look down on him and refuse to say anything more. All the veterans liked to take their time telling their stories and reminiscences, whether they were true or false, had actually happened or not. And they liked to build up the suspense. In his own good time, the soldier continued his explanation: 'In the war against the French, when Elne was our possession, Pedro the Great promised to defend it. He sent a detachment of Catalan knights to do so. But they betrayed the town, fleeing at night and leaving it at the enemy's mercy.' The veteran spat into the fire. 'The French profaned the churches, killed the children by beating their heads against the walls, raped the women and executed all the men . . . all except one. That's why the massacre at Elne is on our consciences. No Catalan would dare touch the town.'

Arnau looked again at the open gates of Elne the Proud. Then, as he gazed at the camp fires of the Catalan forces, he could see that men round each of them were also staring down at Elne in silence.

'Whose life did they spare?' he asked, breaking his own rules about not being impatient.

The veteran studied him through the flames. 'A man called Bastard de Rosselló.' This time, Arnau waited for him to go on. 'Years later, that same man guided the French troops through the La Maçana pass to invade Catalonia.'

* * *

The army slept in the shadow of the town of Elne.

A short way from them the hundreds of camp followers also slept. Francesca gazed at Aledis. Was this the right place? Elne's history had been told in this camp too, and an unusual silence reigned. Francesca had found herself looking time and again at the town's open gates. Yes, they were in inhospitable territory; no Catalan would ever be well received in Elne or the surrounding area. Aledis was a long way from home. All that was needed was for her to feel she was completely alone.

'Your Arnau is dead,' Francesca told her straightaway after she had sent for her.

Aledis crumpled before her eyes: Francesca could see her visibly shrink inside her green robe. Aledis raised her hands to her face, and the strange silence was broken by the sound of her sobbing.

'How . . . how did it happen?' she asked after a while.

'You lied to me,' was all Francesca said coldly.

Shaking and with eyes brimming with tears, Aledis gazed at the older woman, and then looked down.

'You lied to me,' Francesca repeated. Aledis said nothing. 'You want to know how it happened? Your husband – the real one, the tanner – killed him.'

Pau? That was impossible. Aledis looked up. It was impossible that an old man like him . . .

'He turned up at the royal camp and accused Arnau of abducting you,' Francesca went on, disturbing Aledis's thoughts. She wanted to observe her reactions, especially as Arnau had told her she was afraid of her husband. 'He denied it, and your husband challenged him.' Aledis tried to interrupt – how could Pau challenge anyone? 'He paid a captain to fight on his behalf,' Francesca insisted, forcing Aledis to remain quiet. 'Didn't you know? When someone is too old to fight, he can pay somebody else to do it for him. Your Arnau died defending your honour.'

Aledis grew desperate. Francesca could see her whole

body quake. Her legs gradually gave way, and she sank to her knees on the ground in front of the older woman. Francesca was ruthless.

'I've heard that your husband is looking for you.'

Aledis covered her face in her hands again.

'You'll have to leave us. Antònia will give you your old clothes back.'

That was what she had been after: the look of fear and panic on Aledis's face!

A host of questions flooded Aledis's mind. What could she do? Where could she go? Barcelona was at the far end of the earth and besides, what did she have left there? Arnau was dead! The journey from Barcelona to Figueres flashed through her mind, and she felt all the horror, humiliation and shame in her every bone. And now Pau was looking for her!

'No . . .' Aledis stammered out, 'I couldn't do that!'

'I don't need other people's problems,' Francesca told her.

'Protect me!' Aledis begged her. 'I've nowhere to go. I have no one to turn to.' She was sobbing out loud, still on her knees in front of Francesca. She did not dare look up.

'I can't. You're pregnant.'

'That was a lie too,' wailed the girl. She crawled over to Francesca's legs. Francesca did not move.

'What would you do in return?'

'Whatever you wish!' Aledis cried. Francesca hid her smile. That was the promise she had been waiting for. How often had she wrung a similar one out of girls like Aledis? 'Whatever you wish,' Aledis said again. 'Protect me, hide me from my husband, and I'll do whatever you wish.'

'You know what we are,' the other woman insisted.

What did that matter? Arnau was dead. She had nothing. She had no one left . . . apart from a husband who would stone her if he found her.

'Please, I beg you, hide me. I'll do whatever you want!'

* * *

Francesca ordered Aledis not to go with any of the soldiers; Arnau was well known in the royal army.

'You're to work in secret,' she told her the next day, as they prepared to move on. 'I wouldn't want your husband . . .' Aledis agreed before she had even finished. 'You mustn't let yourself be seen until the war is over.' Aledis nodded again.

That same night, Francesca sent Arnau a message: 'It's all arranged. She won't bother you any more.'

The next day, instead of heading for Perpignan where King Jaime of Mallorca was installed, Pedro III decided to lead his army towards the coast and the town of Canet. Here, Ramon, the local viscount, was honour bound to hand over his castle because of the vassalage he had sworn after the conquest of Mallorca, when the Catalan King had allowed him to go free after he had taken Bellver Castle.

So it turned out. Viscount Canet handed over his castle to King Pedro, and the army was able to rest and eat well, thanks to the generosity of the local peasantry, who were counting on the fact that the royal army would soon move on to Perpignan. At the same time, King Pedro linked up with his navy.

While he was at Canet, he received yet another mediator. This time it was no less a figure than a cardinal, the second to intercede on Jaime of Mallorca's behalf. King Pedro dismissed this emissary as well, and set about studying the best way to lay siege to the city of Perpignan. While the King waited for more supplies from the sea, the six days that the army was camped at Canet saw them attacking the castles and fortresses that lay between the coast and Perpignan.

In the name of the King, the Manresa *host* took the castle of Santa Maria de la Mar. Other companies assaulted the castle at Castellarnau Sobirà, and Eiximèn d'Esparça, with his Almogavars and other knights, besieged and finally took Castell-Rosselló.

Castell-Rosselló was not a simple frontier post like Bellaguarda. It was one of the forward defences of the Roussillon capital. Outside its walls the same war-cries of the Almogavars were heard, and the same crash of their spears and daggers. This time they were reinforced by the blood-curdling shouts of several hundred more soldiers, all of them anxious for combat. The fortress proved much harder to over-run than Bellaguarda: the fight for the walls was bitter, and several battering rams had to be swung into action to force a way through.

The crossbowmen were the last to rush in through the gaps in the defences. This was nothing like the victory at Bellaguarda. Soldiers and civilians, including women and children, were ready to defend the castle with their lives. Arnau was soon involved in vicious hand-to-hand fighting.

He dropped his crossbow and drew his knife. All around him, hundreds of men were locked in combat. The whistle of a sword blade jolted him back to his own situation. He jumped aside instinctively, and the sword skimmed past him. With his free hand, Arnau grabbed the wrist holding the weapon and lunged with his dagger. He did this mechanically, as he had been taught during the endless lessons Eiximèn d'Esparça's captain had given him. He had been shown how to fight; he had been shown how to kill, and yet nobody had shown him how to thrust a knife into another man's abdomen. His adversary's chain mail deflected the blade, and although still held by the arm, the man succeeded in whirling his sword and wounding Arnau in the shoulder.

It was only a second, but it was long enough for Arnau to realize he had to dispatch the man as quickly as possible. He gripped his dagger even more firmly and jabbed it under the chain mail into his enemy's stomach. The defender was still brandishing his sword, but with less strength now. Arnau thrust the dagger upwards. He could feel the warmth of the man's insides on his hand. He lifted the soldier off the ground; the sword fell from his grasp. Arnau found himself staring at the soldier face to face. The man's lips were moving, only a few inches from his own mouth. Was he trying to tell him something? Over the din of battle, Arnau could hear his death rattle. What was he thinking? Could he see death coming? As if his bulging eyes had sent him a warning, Arnau removed his blade and wheeled round just as another defender was about to leap on him.

He did not hesitate. Arnau's dagger sliced through the air, then through his new adversary's throat. Arnau stopped thinking. It was he who looked for more death. He fought; he shouted at the top of his lungs. He thrust and sank his blade into the flesh of his enemies not once but many times, without paying any attention to their faces or their pain.

He killed.

When it was all over and the defendants of Castell-Rosselló had surrendered, Arnau looked down at himself. He was spattered with blood, and his whole body was trembling from his exertions.

He looked around him; bodies lay in heaps: stark evidence of the battle. He had not had the time to see any of his adversaries as people. He had not shared their pain or taken pity on their souls. Now, though, the faces he had not seen through their veil of blood came back to haunt him, claiming the respect due to the vanquished. Arnau would often remember the blurred features of all those he had killed.

* * *

In mid-August, the royal army made camp once more between Canet Castle and the coast. Arnau had stormed Castell-Rosselló on 4 August. Two days later, King Pedro ordered his troops to strike camp, and since the city of Perpignan refused to pay homage to him, the Catalan armies laid waste to the surrounding area: Basoles, Vernet, Solés, Sant Esteve . . . They uprooted vines, olive groves and all other trees in their way. The only ones they did not touch were fig trees: was this merely a whim on the part of King Pedro? They burnt mills and crops, destroyed farmland and villages, but never once laid siege to the capital, Perpignan, where King Jaime had sought refuge.

15 August 1343
Solemn campaign mass

Drawn up on the beach, the entire royal army paid homage to the Virgin of the Sea. Pedro III had yielded to the pressure from the Holy Father and agreed to call a truce with Jaime of Mallorca. The news ran through the ranks like wildfire. Like most of the others, Arnau could not concentrate on what the priest was saying in the mass: they all stood sad and contrite. This time, the Virgin was no consolation to Arnau. He had killed. He had chopped down trees. He had destroyed vines and crops before the terrified gaze of peasants and their children. He had help raze entire villages: the homes of honest people. King Jaime had secured his truce; King Pedro had given way. Arnau remembered the priests haranguing them in Santa Maria de la Mar: 'Catalonia needs you! King Pedro needs you! Go to war!' What war? There had only been killing. Skirmishes in the country-side, when the ones to suffer had been ordinary people and loyal soldiers . . . and children, who would go hungry the next winter when the supplies of grain ran out. What war? The one that bishops and cardinals had fought, acting as go-betweens for sly, scheming kings? The priest went on with his homily, but Arnau was not listening. Why had he been made to kill? What use were all those dead?

The mass ended. The soldiers split into small groups.

'What about the booty we were promised?'

'Perpignan is rich, very rich,' Arnau heard someone say.

'How is the King going to pay his soldiers now, when he did not have enough before?'

Arnau strolled among the different groups. What did he care about booty? What was important to him was the way the children had looked at him, like the one who, clutching his sister's hand, had watched fearfully as Arnau and other soldiers had trampled their vegetables and scattered the grain that was meant to feed them that winter. Why? his innocent eyes seemed to implore. What harm have we done you? The children had probably been left in charge of the vegetable patch: they stood rooted to the spot, tears rolling down their cheeks, until the great Catalan army had finished destroying their meagre possessions. As they left, Arnau did not have the heart to cast them a backward glance.

The army was going home. The columns of soldiers filtered along the roads of Catalonia, still followed by all the hangers-on, prostitutes and traders who had also seen their dreams of riches dashed.

Barcelona drew nearer. The different *hosts* dispersed to return to the towns they had come from. Others were to cross the city. Arnau noticed that, like his companions, he had a new spring in his step. Some of the soldiers were smiling openly: they were going home.

Maria's face flashed into his mind. 'All arranged,' he had been told, 'Aledis will not trouble you any more.' That was all he wanted; that was what had driven him to war.

Maria's face smiled at him.

31

The end of March 1348
Barcelona

Day was dawning. Arnau and the other *bastaixos* were
waiting at the water's edge to unload a Mallorcan galley
that had arrived during the night. The guild aldermen
were organizing their men. The sea was calm, with the
waves gently lapping the shore, calling the inhabitants of
Barcelona to start their day. The sun's rays were
beginning to pick out colours on the rippling waters, and
while the *bastaixos* waited for the boatmen to arrive
with the ship's cargo, they allowed themselves to be
carried away by the magic of the moment, gazing at the
distant horizon or mentally following the dancing
waves.

'That's odd,' said one of them, 'they're not unloading
the ship.'

They all stared out at the galley. The boatmen had
drawn alongside, but some of them were already heading back to the shore with empty vessels. Others were
shouting to the sailors on board, some of whom dived
into the sea and clambered aboard their craft. But no one
was unloading any of the merchandise from the galley.

'The plague!' The first boatmen's cries could be heard

on the beach long before they landed. 'The plague has reached Mallorca!'

Arnau shuddered. How could such a beautiful sea be bringing such dreadful news? If it had been a grey, stormy day . . . but everything about this morning had seemed bathed in magic. For months there had been talk of the plague in Barcelona: it was ravaging the Orient and now was spreading west: whole communities had been wiped out.

'Perhaps it won't reach Barcelona,' some said. 'To do that, it would have to cross all the Mediterranean.'

'The sea will protect us,' said others.

For several months, everyone had wanted to believe that the plague would not reach Barcelona.

Mallorca, thought Arnau. The plague had reached Mallorca: it had crossed league upon league of the Mediterranean.

'The plague!' the boatmen repeated when they reached the shore.

The *bastaixos* crowded round them to hear the news. The galley captain was in one of the boats.

'Take me to the magistrate and the city councillors,' he said, leaping ashore. 'Quick about it!'

The aldermen did as he asked; the other *bastaixos* pressed round to hear what the newcomers had to say. 'Hundreds are dying,' they were told. 'It's terrible. No one can do anything. Children, women, men, rich and poor, nobles and common people . . . even animals are victims. The bodies are piling up in the streets and rotting. The authorities are at their wits' end. People die within two days, howling with pain.' Some of the *bastaixos* ran off towards the city, shouting and waving their arms in the air. Arnau stayed to listen, horrified by what he heard. They said that those who caught the plague developed huge purulent ganglions on their necks, armpits or groins, which grew until they burst.

The news spread quickly through the city. Many people ran down to the beach to hear it from the new arrivals, then swiftly ran back to their homes.

The whole of Barcelona became a hive of rumours: 'When the ganglions burst, a host of devils come pouring out. The plague sufferers go mad and start biting others; that's how the illness is spread. The eyes and genitals burst. If anyone looks at the ganglions, they catch it too. The victims have to be burnt before they die, otherwise the disease attacks someone else. I've seen the plague!' Anyone who made this last claim immediately became the centre of attention: a crowd would gather round to hear their story; after that, imagination magnified the horror as the details were repeated from mouth to mouth. The only precaution the city authorities could think of was to recommend strict measures of hygiene. In consequence, the inhabitants crowded into the public baths . . . and the churches. Masses, prayers, processions: nothing sufficed to ward off the evil creeping ever nearer the city. After a fearful month's wait, the plague reached Barcelona.

The first case was a caulker who worked in the royal shipyard. When the doctors came to see him, all they could do was confirm what they had read in books and medical treatises.

'They're the size of small tangerines,' said one, pointing to the large swellings on the man's neck.

'They're black, hard and hot to the touch,' added a second doctor.

'Cold cloths for his fever.'

'We have to bleed him. If we do, the bleeding around the ganglions will disappear.'

'We have to lance the ganglions,' a third one opined.

The other doctors looked at the sick man and then at their colleague.

'According to our books, lancing is of no use.'

'After all,' said another one, 'he's only a caulker. Let's look at his armpits and groin.'

There were big, hard ganglions there too. Shrieking with pain, the plague victim was bled, and what little life he had left seeped out through the cuts the medical experts made in his suffering body.

That very same day, more cases were discovered. The next day, more still, and even more the day after that. The inhabitants of the city shut themselves in their houses, where some of them died amid terrible suffering. Others were left out on the streets for fear of contagion, and met slow, agonizing deaths. The authorities ordered a whitewash cross to be daubed on the door of every house where an outbreak had occurred. They continued to insist on hygiene, and for people to avoid all contact with the plague sufferers. They had the bodies burnt in huge funeral pyres. Many of the inhabitants scrubbed at their skin until it came away in clumps, and wherever they could, stayed away from the victims. But nobody thought of getting rid of the millions of fleas in the city, and to the astonishment of doctors and authorities, the disease continued to spread.

Several weeks went by, and like many others Arnau and Maria went every day to Santa Maria, offering prayers that received no response from the heavens. All around them, close friends such as Father Albert were dying. The plague also took the old couple Pere and Mariona, who were not able to resist the disease for long. The bishop organized a pilgrimage that would go round the entire city perimeter; it was to leave the cathedral, head down Carrer de la Mar to Santa Maria. There the Virgin of the Sea would be waiting on her dais, and she would become part of the procession.

The Virgin was in Plaça de Santa Maria, with the *bastaixos* who were to carry her on their shoulders. The men looked sadly at each other, silently wondering about all those who were no longer among them. Nobody said a word. They all clenched their teeth and stared at the ground. Arnau remembered earlier processions, when there had been so many of them they had to fight to get near the dais. The aldermen had to organize them so that everybody could have a turn carrying the statue, whereas now . . . now there were not enough *bastaixos* even to be relieved. How many had died? How long would this go on? The sound of people murmuring their prayers came down Carrer de la Mar. Arnau looked at the head of the procession: everyone was shuffling along despondently. Where were all the nobles who were usually so proud to walk alongside the bishop? Four of the city's five councillors had died; three-quarters of the Council of a Hundred had met the same fate. The others had fled the city. The *bastaixos* lifted their Virgin in silence, balanced the dais on their shoulders, let the bishop go past, and then joined the procession and the prayers. The pilgrims went from Santa Maria down to the Santa Clara convent via Plaça del Born. At Santa Clara, despite the incense the priests had lit, the smell of burnt flesh was all too obvious; many of those present burst into tears. At Sant Daniel gate they turned left and headed towards the Nou gateway and the Sant Pere de les Puelles monastery; as they advanced they had to avoid several dead bodies and tried not to look at the dying who lay on every street corner and in front of doors daubed with a white cross that would never again open for them. Holy Mother, thought Arnau, carrying the statue on his shoulder, what have we done to deserve this? From Sant Pere the pilgrims carried on down to the Santa Anna gateway, where they turned left again in the direction of the sea, until they reached the Forn dels Arcs district, and headed back towards the cathedral.

Despite this public display of faith, many people were

beginning to doubt whether the Church or the city authorities were doing anything useful: they prayed and prayed, but the plague continued to cause havoc everywhere.

'They say it's the end of the world,' Arnau complained one day when he returned home. 'All Barcelona has gone mad. They call themselves the flagellants.' Maria had her back to him. Arnau sat down, waiting for his wife to take his footwear off as usual. He went on: 'There are hundreds of them out in the streets, naked from the waist up. They shout that the day of judgement is at hand, confess all their sins openly to anyone who cares to listen, and lash their backs with whips. Some of them are cut to ribbons, but they go on . . .' Arnau stroked Maria's forehead as she knelt before him. She was burning up. 'What . . .?'

He lifted her chin in his hand. No, it could not be! Not her! Maria looked at him, glassy-eyed. She was sweating, and her whole face was swollen. Arnau tried to lift her head further in order to see her neck, but she winced with pain.

'Not you!' he wailed.

On her knees, Maria gripped his sandals and stared up at him. Tears began to course down her cheeks.

'My God, not you!' Arnau knelt beside her.

'Get away, Arnau,' Maria stuttered. 'Don't stay close to me.'

Arnau tried to put his arms round her, but as he did so, she whimpered with pain once more.

'Come here,' he said, helping her up as gently as he could. Sobbing, Maria continued to insist that he leave her. 'How could I? You're all that I have . . . everything! What would I do without you? Some people recover from it, Maria. You will, you'll see. You'll get better.' Trying to comfort her, he led her to the bedroom and laid her on the bed. There he could get a clear view of her neck: the beautiful outline was tinged with black. 'A doctor! We need a doctor!' he shouted, flinging open the window and running out on to the balcony.

Nobody seemed to hear him. Yet that night, when the ganglions started to swell on Maria's neck, someone came to paint a white cross on their door.

All Arnau could do was press cold cloths on his wife's brow. She was shivering uncontrollably in bed. Every time she moved, the pain was such that she could not help moaning: her muffled groans made the hairs on Arnau's arms stand on end. She was staring blankly up at the ceiling, but Arnau could see the lumps on her neck growing and turning ever darker. 'I love you, Maria. How often would I have liked to tell you so.' He took her hand and knelt by the bed. He spent the whole night on his knees, clutching her hand and shivering and sweating along with her, imploring the skies for help each time Maria writhed in pain.

He used the best sheet they had as a shroud to wrap her in, then waited for the cart for the dead to pass by. He was not going to leave her out in the street. He wanted to hand her body over himself. And that is what he did. When he heard the weary clop of horses' hooves outside his house, he picked Maria up and went out into the street.

'Farewell,' he said, kissing her on her forehead.

The two officials, who were wearing gloves and had thick scarves to protect their faces, were taken aback when they saw Arnau unwrap the shroud and kiss his wife. Nobody wanted to go near the plague victims, not even their loved ones, who usually left them out in the street or at most called the officials in to take them from their death beds. When Arnau handed them Maria's body they were so astonished that they laid her gently on top of the dozen or so bodies already in their cart.

With tears in his eyes, Arnau watched as the cart disappeared down the streets of Barcelona. He would be next: he went back into his house and sat to wait for the death that would reunite him with Maria. For three days, Arnau awaited the plague, constantly feeling his neck for a swelling that refused to appear. There were no ganglions, and so Arnau finally had to accept that, for the moment, the Lord was not calling him to his side to be with Maria.

Arnau walked along the beach, tramping through the waves that lapped the shore of his cursed city. He wandered through the streets of Barcelona, oblivious to the misery, the dying and the cries from house windows. Something took him once more to Santa Maria. Building work had been suspended, and the scaffolding was empty. Blocks of stone lay all around, waiting for the masons, yet ordinary people still flocked to the church. Arnau went in. The faithful were clustered around the unfinished high altar, standing or kneeling to pray. Although the church still did not have walls around the main apses, the atmosphere was filled with the perfume of incense that was burnt to conceal the smell of death that penetrated everywhere. As Arnau was heading for the Virgin's statue, he heard a priest talking to the congregation.

'You should know,' he told them, 'that our Supreme Pontiff, Pope Clement the Sixth, has published a bull in which he absolves the Jews of all blame for causing the plague. The disease is a trial sent by God to test his Christian people.' There were murmurs of disapproval from the flock. 'Pray,' the priest said, 'and commend yourselves to the Lord . . .'

As they left the church, many of the worshippers were arguing about what the priest had said.

Arnau paid no attention to the homily, but walked on to the Jesus chapel. The Jews? What could they possibly have to do with the plague? As ever, his little Virgin was waiting for him in the same place. As usual, the *bastaixos'* candles kept her company. Who could have lit them? This time, though, because of the thick clouds of incense, Arnau could not see his holy mother's face; he did not see her smile. He tried to pray but found it impossible. *Why did you allow her to die?* The tears rolled down his cheeks again as he remembered Maria and all her suffering, her body racked with pain, the dreadful ganglions that had devoured her. If it had been a punishment, he should have been the one to suffer: he was the one who had sinned by being unfaithful with Aledis.

Standing there in front of his Virgin, he swore a solemn oath that never again would he allow himself to be carried away by lust. He owed that to Maria. Whatever happened. Never.

'Is something wrong, my son?' he heard someone ask. Arnau turned and found himself face to face with the priest who a few minutes earlier had been addressing the congregation. 'Oh, it's you, Arnau,' the man said, recognizing him as one of the *bastaixos* who frequented Santa Maria. 'Is something wrong?'

'Maria.'

The priest nodded sadly. 'Let us pray for her,' he said.

'No, Father,' said Arnau. 'Not yet.'

'It's only in God that you will find comfort, Arnau.'

Comfort? He had no hope of finding that anywhere. Arnau peered again towards his Virgin, but the incense still obscured his view.

'Let us pray,' insisted the priest.

'What were you saying about the Jews?' Arnau asked, still trying to avoid having to pray.

'Throughout Europe they are saying that the Jews are to blame for the plague.' Arnau looked at him enquiringly. 'They say that in Geneva, at Chinon Castle, some

Jews have confessed that the plague was spread by one of their number from Savoy who poisoned wells with a potion prepared by rabbis.'

'Is that true?' Arnau asked him.

'No. The Pope has absolved them, but the people want someone to blame. Shall we pray now?'

'You do it for me, Father.'

Arnau left Santa Maria. In the square outside he found himself surrounded by a group of about twenty flagellants. 'Repent!' they shouted at him, all the while whipping their own backs. 'It's the end of the world!' others spat in his face. Arnau could see blood running down their raw backs and legs, past the hair shirts wound round their waists. He surveyed their faces, their wild, staring eyes. He ran away from them down Carrer de Montcada until he could no longer hear their cries . . . but something here caught his attention too. The doors! Very few of the huge doorways to the palaces on Carrer de Montcada displayed the white crosses that seemed to be everywhere in the rest of the city. Arnau found himself opposite the Puig family palace. There was no cross there either: all the windows were closed, and he could see no sign of life inside the building. Arnau willed the plague to find them wherever they had taken refuge, and for them to suffer as much as Maria had done. Then he hurried away even more quickly than he had from the flagellants.

When he reached the corner of Carrer de Montcada and Carders, he again ran into a noisy crowd, this time armed with sticks, swords and crossbows. They're all crazy, Arnau told himself, stepping back to let them by. The homilies preached in every church of the city had been of little use. Clement VI's bull had not succeeded in calming people desperate to unleash their anger on someone. 'To the Jewry!' he could hear them shouting. 'Heretics! Murderers! Repent!' The flagellants were part of the crowd, still lashing their backs and spattering all those around them with blood.

Arnau fell in behind the mob, among a group who were following them silently. Several plague victims were with them. It seemed as though the whole of Barcelona had converged on the Jewry, surrounding the partly walled neighbourhood on all four sides. Some took up position to the north, next to the bishop's palace. Others were on the western side, by the old Roman walls; still others filled Carrer del Bisbe, which bordered the Jewry to the east; the rest, including Arnau's group, were to the south, in Carrer de la Boqueria and outside Castell Nou, where the entrance to the Jewry stood. The noise was deafening. They wanted revenge, even though for the moment they were content to stay outside the gates, shaking their sticks and crossbows.

Arnau found room for himself on the crowded steps of Sant Jaume church, the same one he and Joanet had been thrown out of all those years ago when they were searching for the Virgin he could call his mother. Sant Jaume rose close to the southern wall of the Jewry, and from its steps Arnau could see what was happening over the heads of the mob. The garrison of royal soldiers, headed by the city magistrate, was preparing to defend the Jewish quarter. Before launching any attack, a group of citizens went to talk with the magistrate beside the half-open gates of the Jewry and persuade him to withdraw his troops. The flagellants kept up their shouting and dancing around them, while the crowd continued to hurl threats against the Jews, whom they could not even see.

'They won't withdraw,' Arnau heard a woman next to him say.

'The Jews are royal property, they depend entirely on the King,' another man agreed. 'If the Jews die, the King will lose all the taxes he's imposed on them . . .'

'And all the loans he's had from those usurers.'

'Not just that,' said a third man. 'If the Jewry is attacked, the King will lose even the furniture the Jews offer him and his court whenever they come to Barcelona.'

'The nobles will have to sleep on the floor,' someone shouted, to general laughter.

Arnau himself could not help smiling.

'The magistrate will defend the King's interests,' the woman asserted.

She was proved right. The magistrate did not back down, and as soon as the two sides had finished talking, he shut himself inside the Jewry. That was the signal the mob had been waiting for. Before the gate was even shut, those closest to the walls rushed at it, while the others flung sticks, arrows and stones over the walls. The assault had begun.

Arnau watched as the hate-filled crowd threw themselves at the gates and walls of the Jewry. No one was leading them; the only thing resembling orders were the cries of the flagellants who were still whipping themselves beneath the walls, and urging the others to scale them and kill the heretics. When they did succeed in climbing over, many of them fell to the royal soldiers' swords, but the Jewry was under siege from all four sides now, and many more over-ran the defenders and began to attack any Jews they could find.

Arnau stayed on the steps of Sant Jaume for two hours. The war-cries reminded him of his days as a soldier: Bellaguarda and Castell-Rosselló. The faces of those who fell mingled with those of the men he himself had killed; the smell of blood took him back to Roussillon, to the lies that had led him to that absurd war, to Aledis and Maria . . . overcome with memories, he left his vantage point.

Leaving behind the massacre, Arnau walked down

towards the sea, still thinking of Maria and what had forced him to seek a way out in fighting. All at once, his thoughts were interrupted. He was level with Castell de Regomir, a tower in the old Roman wall, when shouting close by forced him back to reality.

'Heretics!'

'Murderers!'

Arnau found himself confronted by a group of about twenty people filling the street. They were brandishing sticks and knives and shrieking at some others who must be pressed up against a house wall. Why could they not simply mourn their dead? Arnau did not want to stop, and pushed his way through the enraged attackers. As he was forcing a path for himself, he glanced briefly at the spot they had surrounded: in a house doorway a bloody-faced Moorish slave was using his body to try to protect three children dressed in black with the yellow badge on their chests. Arnau suddenly found himself in between the Moor and his attackers. Silence fell, and the children's terrified faces peeped out from behind their protector. Arnau glanced at them: how he regretted never having given Maria any children! A stone flew through the air towards them. It grazed Arnau, and when the Moor stepped into its path, hit him in the stomach. He doubled up with pain. A child's tiny face peered directly at Arnau. His wife had loved children: she had not cared whether they were Christians, Moors or Jews. She would gaze at them on the beach, in the streets of the city . . . her eyes would follow them tenderly, and then she would look back at him . . .

'Move away! Get out of our way, will you?' Arnau heard a voice shout behind his back.

Arnau looked again at the pair of terrified eyes in front of him. 'What do you want with these children?' he growled.

Several men armed with knives confronted him. 'They're Jews,' they said as one.

'And just for that you're going to kill them? Aren't their parents enough for you?'

'They've poisoned the wells,' one of the men said. 'They killed Jesus. They kill Christian children for their heretical rites. Yes, they tear their hearts out . . . they steal the sacred host.'

Arnau was not listening. He could still smell the blood of the Jewry . . . of Castell-Rosselló. He seized the man closest to him by the arm, punched him in the face and took his knife. Then he confronted the others: 'Nobody is to harm any children!'

The attackers watched Arnau wielding the knife, drawing circles with it in the air. They saw the look of determination in his eyes.

'Nobody is going to harm any children,' he repeated. 'Go and fight in the Jewry, against the soldiers, against grown men.'

'They will kill you,' warned the Moor, who now was behind him.

'Heretic!' the attackers cried.

'Jew!'

Arnau had been taught to attack first, to catch his enemy unawares, not to let him gain confidence, to frighten him. Shouting 'Sant Jordi!' Arnau launched himself at the nearest men. He plunged his dagger into the first one's stomach, then whirled round, forcing the others to back off. His dagger sliced the chests of several more. From the ground, one of the wounded men stabbed him in the calf. Arnau looked down, seized him by the hair, pulled his head back and slashed his throat. Blood came spurting out. Three men were lying on the ground; the others began to draw back. 'Withdraw when you are outnumbered' was another piece of advice Arnau remembered. He made as if to charge again, and the assailants fell over each other trying to get away. Without looking behind him, Arnau gestured to the Moor to gather the children to him, and when he could feel them around his legs, he backed away down towards the beach, still glaring at the armed group.

'They're waiting for you in the Jewry,' he shouted at them, still shepherding the children away.

When they reached the old gate of Castell de Regomir, they broke into a run. Without giving any explanation, he prevented them heading back to the Jewry.

Where could he hide the children? Arnau led them down to Santa Maria. He came to a halt outside the main entrance. From where they stood, they could see inside the unfinished church.

'You're not planning to take the children into a Christian church, are you?' the slave asked, panting for breath.

'No,' replied Arnau. 'But very close to it.'

'Why didn't you let us return home?' asked the young girl, who was obviously the eldest of the three and had recovered from their escape more quickly than the others.

Arnau felt his calf. The blood was pouring out.

'Because your homes are being attacked,' he told them. 'They blame you for the plague. They say you poisoned the wells.' None of them said anything. 'I'm sorry,' he added.

The Moorish slave was the first to react: 'We can't stay here,' he said, forcing Arnau to look up from his wound. 'Do as you think best, but hide the children.'

'What about you?' asked Arnau.

'I have to find out what has happened to their families. How will I meet you again?'

'You won't,' said Arnau, realizing he would not have the chance to show him how to get to the Roman cemetery. 'I'll come and find you. Go down to the beach at midnight, by the new fish stall.' The slave nodded. As they were about to separate, Arnau added: 'If in three nights you haven't appeared, I'll presume you are dead.'

The Moor nodded again, and gazed at Arnau with his big black eyes. 'Thank you,' he said, before running off towards the Jewry.

The smallest child tried to follow him, but Arnau held him back by the shoulders.

That first night, the Moor did not appear at the meeting point. Arnau waited more than an hour for him after midnight, listening to the distant sounds of disturbances in the Jewry and staring at the red glow that filled the sky. While he was waiting, he had time to think about everything that had happened on this insane day. He had three Jewish children hidden under the high altar of Santa Maria, beneath his own Virgin. The entrance to the underground cemetery that he and Joanet had discovered long ago was still the same as the last time they had been there. The stairs to Plaça del Born had not yet been completed, so it was easy to get in under the wooden platform at the entrance, although they had to wait crouching outside for almost an hour until the guards who were patrolling around the church had left.

The children followed him along the dark tunnel without a word of protest until Arnau told them where they were and warned them not to touch anything if they did not want an unpleasant surprise. At that, the three of them burst into tears, and Arnau had no idea how to respond. Maria would have known how to calm them.

'They're only dead people,' he shouted. 'And they didn't die of the plague. What do you prefer: to be here, alive among the dead, or outside so that you can be killed?' The sobbing stopped. 'I'm going out again now to fetch a lamp, water and some food. All right? Is that all right?' he repeated when they said nothing.

'All right,' he heard the girl reply.

'Let's see. I've risked my life for you, and I'm going to risk it again if anybody discovers I am hiding three Jewish children under Santa Maria church. I'm not prepared to do so if when I get back here you've all run off. What do you say? Will you wait for me here, or do you want to go out into the streets again?'

'We'll wait,' the girl said resolutely.

Arnau returned to an empty house. He washed and tried to tend his wound. He bound it up, filled his old wineskin with water, took a lantern and oil to fill it with, a loaf of dry bread and salt meat, and then limped back to Santa Maria.

The children had not moved from the end of the tunnel where he had left them. Arnau lit the lantern and found himself facing three fearful young fawns too frightened to respond to his attempt to reassure them with a smile. The girl had her arms round the other two. All three were dark-skinned, with long, clean hair. They looked healthy and attractive, with gleaming white teeth, especially the girl.

'Are they your brothers?' Arnau asked her.

'We're brother and sister,' she said eventually, pointing to the smaller of the other two. 'He is a neighbour.'

'Well, I think that after all that's happened and what's still to come, we had better introduce ourselves. My name is Arnau.'

The girl did the honours: she was called Raquel, her brother was Jucef, and their neighbour's name was Saul. Arnau asked them more questions by the light of the lantern, while every so often the children cast anxious glances towards the cemetery behind them. They were thirteen, six and eleven years old. They had been born in Barcelona and lived with their parents in the Jewry. They had been going back there when the mob had attacked them. The slave, whom they had always called Sahat, belonged to Raquel and Jucef's parents. If he had said he would go to the beach, he would do so; he had never failed them.

'Well,' said Arnau after listening to them, 'I think it might be useful to have a look at where we are. It's been a long time, more or less since I was your age, since I've been here: although I don't think anybody has moved.' He was the only one to laugh. He held the lantern up and crawled to the centre of the necropolis. The children remained rooted to the spot, terrified at the sight of the open tombs and skeletons. 'This is the best I could think of,' he apologized when he saw their look of terror. 'I'm sure nobody will find you here while we wait for things to calm down outside—'

'What will happen if they kill our parents?' Raquel interrupted him.

'Don't think of that. I'm sure nothing will happen to them. Look, come over here. There's a space with no tombs that's big enough for all of us. Come on!' He gestured energetically for them to approach him.

In the end he succeeded, and the four of them gathered in a small space where they could sit on the floor without having to touch any tombs. The Roman cemetery was exactly the same as the first time Arnau had seen it, with its strange pyramidal tiles and big amphorae with skeletons inside. Arnau placed the lantern on one of them, and offered the children the water, bread and salt meat. They all drank avidly, but would only eat the bread.

'It's not kosher,' explained Raquel, pointing to the meat.

'Kosher?'

Raquel explained what kosher meant, and the rituals that had to be performed before members of the Jewish community were allowed to eat meat. They went on talking until the two boys had fallen fast asleep on the girl's lap. Then, whispering so as not to wake them, Raquel asked Arnau: 'Don't you believe what they say?'

'What about?'

'That we poisoned wells.'

Arnau did not reply for some time.

'Have any Jews died of the plague?' he asked.

'Lots.'

'In that case, no,' Arnau asserted. 'I don't believe it.'

When Raquel also fell asleep, Arnau crawled back out of the tunnel and headed for the beach.

The attack on the Jewry lasted two days. All that time, the outnumbered royal forces, together with members of the Jewish community, tried their best to defend the district from the constant assault of an enraged, zealous mob who in the name of Christianity dedicated themselves to pillaging and murder. In the end, the King sent enough soldiers to quell the riot, and matters slowly returned to normal.

On the third night Sahat, who had fought alongside his masters, was able to get away and meet Arnau on the beach opposite the fish stall, as agreed.

'Sahat!' came a voice in the darkness.

'What are you doing here?' asked the slave when Raquel threw herself on him.

'The Christian is very ill.'

'Is it—?'

'No,' the girl interrupted him, 'it isn't the plague. He doesn't have any swellings. It's his leg. The wound has become infected and he has a high fever. He can't walk.'

'What about the other two?' asked the slave.

'They're fine. And . . .?'

'They're waiting for you.'

Raquel took the slave to the platform by the Plaça del Born doorway at Santa Maria.

'Here?' asked the Moor in a puzzled way when the girl slipped in underneath the wooden planks.

'Quiet,' she said. 'Follow me.'

They made their way along the tunnel to the Roman cemetery. They all had to help get Arnau out; Sahat crawled backwards pulling him by the hands while the children pushed him by the feet. Arnau had lost consciousness. The five of them, with Arnau draped over Sahat's shoulders and the children dressed in Christian clothes the slave had brought them, headed for the Jewry, making sure they stayed as much as possible in the darkest corners. When they arrived at the Jewry gates, which were guarded by a large contingent of the King's men, Sahat explained to the captain who the children really were and why they were not wearing their yellow badges. Arnau, he said, was a Christian, but had a fever and needed to see a doctor, as the captain could see for himself. The captain took a quick look at the wound, but soon moved away in case it was a plague victim. But what in fact opened the gates to the Jewry was the generous purse of money that the slave slipped into the captain's hands while he was talking to him.

32

'Nobody is going to harm those children. Father, where are you? Why, Father? There's grain in the palace. I love you, Maria . . .'

Whenever Arnau was delirious, Sahat made the children leave the room. He called for Raquel and Jucef's father Hasdai to come and help keep Arnau still when he started fighting the soldiers of Roussillon and threatened to reopen the wound on his leg. Master and slave kept watch at the foot of the bed, while another female servant put cold compresses on his forehead. This had already been going on for a week, during which time Arnau received the best care from Jewish doctors as well as constant attention from the Crescas family and their slaves – most of all Sahat, who watched over him day and night.

'The wound is not that serious,' said the doctors, 'but the infection has spread to the whole body.'

'Will he live?' asked Hasdai.

'He's a strong man,' was all the doctors would say as they left.

'There's grain in the palace!' Arnau shouted again a

few minutes later. He was sweating and writhing on his bed.

'If it hadn't been for him,' said Sahat, 'we'd all be dead.'

'I know,' said Hasdai, who was standing next to him.

'Why did he do it? He's a Christian.'

'He's a good person.'

At night, when Arnau was resting and the house was quiet, Sahat would turn to the east to kneel and pray for the Christian. During the day, he patiently made him drink as much water as possible, and take the potions the doctors had prepared. Raquel and Jucef often came into the room, and if Arnau was not delirious, Sahat let them stay.

'He's a warrior,' Jucef said on one occasion, his eyes wide open in amazement.

'I'm sure he has been,' agreed Sahat.

'He said he was a *bastaix*,' Raquel objected.

'In the cemetery, he told us he was a warrior. Perhaps he's a warrior *bastaix*.'

'He only said it to keep you quiet.'

'I would wager he is a *bastaix*,' said Hasdai. 'From what he says now, at least.'

'He's a *warrior*,' the young boy insisted.

'I don't know, Jucef.' The slave ruffled his black locks. 'Why don't we wait until he's better and can tell us himself?'

'Will he get better?'

'Of course. When have you heard of a warrior dying from a leg wound?'

After the children left, Sahat would go up to Arnau and touch his burning brow. 'It's not only the children who are alive thanks to you, Christian. Why did you do it? What drove you to risk your life for a slave and three Jewish children? Live! You must live! I want to be able to talk to you, to thank you. Besides, Hasdai is very rich; I'm sure he will want to reward you.'

A few days later, Arnau began to recover. One morning, Sahat found that his fever was noticeably reduced.

'Allah, whose name be praised, has heard my prayers.'

Hasdai smiled when he was able to confirm the improvement.

'He will live,' he went so far as to tell his children.

'Will he tell me about his battles?'

'Son, I'm not sure . . .'

But Jucef started to imitate Arnau, whirling the dagger about to take on an imaginary group of attackers. Just as he was about to slash the wounded man's throat, his sister grasped him by the arm.

'Jucef!' she said to him sternly.

They turned to look at Arnau, and saw him staring at them from the bed. Jucef was terrified.

'How do you feel?' Hasdai asked him.

Arnau tried to answer, but his mouth was too dry. Sahat gave him a glass of water.

'Good,' he managed to say after a few sips. 'What about the children?'

Pushed forward by their father, Jucef and Raquel came to his bedside. Arnau tried to smile.

'Hello,' he said.

'Hello,' they replied.

'What about Saul?'

'He's well,' Hasdai reassured him. 'But now you must rest. Come on, children.'

'When you're better, will you tell me all about your battles?' Jucef asked before his father and sister dragged him out of the room.

Arnau nodded, and smiled again.

Over the next week, the fever completely disappeared, and the wound began to heal. Arnau and Sahat talked whenever the *bastaix* felt strong enough.

'Thank you,' were his first words to the Moorish slave.

'You've already thanked me, remember? Why . . . why did you rescue us?'

'The boy's eyes . . . my wife would never have allowed me to . . .'

'Maria?' asked Sahat, remembering how Arnau had said the name during his delirium.

'Yes,' said Arnau.

'Would you like us to tell her you are here?' Arnau's mouth tightened and he shook his head. 'Is there anyone you'd like us to tell?' But when he saw Arnau's sorrowful expression, the slave did not persist.

'How did the siege of the Jewry end?' Arnau asked him on another occasion.

'Two hundred men and women murdered. Many houses looted or burned.'

'That's terrible!'

'It's not as bad as it might have been,' Sabat insisted. Arnau cast him a surprised glance. 'We were lucky in the Barcelona Jewry. From the Orient to Castile, Jews have been slaughtered without mercy. More than three hundred communities have been completely destroyed. In Germany Emperor Charles the Fourth promised a personal pardon to any criminal who killed a Jew or helped destroy a Jewry. Can you imagine what would have happened in Barcelona if instead of protecting us, your King had granted a pardon to everyone who killed a Jew?' Arnau closed his eyes and shook his head. 'In Mainz, they burnt six thousand Jews at the stake. In Strasbourg, they burnt two thousand in a huge funeral pyre in the Jewish cemetery, including women and children. Two thousand at once . . .'

The children were only allowed in Arnau's room when Hasdai was visiting him and could see they did not disturb him. One day, when Arnau was able to get out of bed and beginning to take his first steps, Hasdai appeared on his own. Tall and thin, with long black hair, a piercing gaze and hook nose, the Jewish man sat opposite him.

'You ought to know . . .' he said gravely, 'well, I suppose you do know,' he added, correcting himself, 'that your priests forbid Christians and Jews to live together.'

'Don't worry, Hasdai; as soon as I can walk—'

'No,' the Jew interrupted him, 'I'm not saying you have to leave my house. You saved my children from certain death, putting your own life at risk. All I own is yours, and I will be eternally grateful to you. You can stay here as long as you wish. My family and I would be very honoured if you would do so. All I wanted to do was warn you, especially if you do decide to stay, to be very discreet about it. Nobody will hear about it from us – and by that I mean all our community; you can be sure of that. It's your decision, but I repeat that we would be very honoured and happy if you did decide to do so. What do you say?'

'Who else could tell your son of the battles I've seen?'

Hasdai smiled and held out his hand. Arnau took it.

'Castell-Rosselló was a mighty fortress . . .' Little Jucef sat opposite Arnau in the garden behind the Crescas house, legs crossed and eyes wide open. He loved to hear the *bastaix*'s stories: alert when he was listening to details of the sieges; anxious during the fighting; smiling once victory had been won.

'The defenders fought valiantly,' Arnau told him, 'but we soldiers of King Pedro were too strong for them . . .'

When he had finished, Jucef was desperate to hear another tale. Arnau told him both true and invented ones. I only attacked two castles, he had almost confessed, the rest of the time we plundered the land and tore up the crops . . . except for the fig trees.

'Do you like figs, Jucef?' he asked him once, remembering the twisted branches rising out of a devastated landscape.

'That's enough, Jucef,' his father told him, coming into the garden and hearing his son insist on being told yet another story. 'Go to bed now.' Jucef obediently left his father and Arnau. 'Why did you ask the boy if he liked figs?'

'It's a long story.'

Without a word, Hasdai sat opposite him on a seat. Tell me, his eyes said.

'We destroyed everything,' Arnau said, after briefly describing what had happened, 'except for the fig trees. It's absurd, isn't it? We laid waste to the land, but in the midst of all that destruction, a solitary fig tree still stood, as though it were looking at us and asking what we were doing.'

Arnau was lost in the maze of his memories, and Hasdai could not bring himself to interrupt him.

'It was a meaningless war,' concluded the *bastaix*.

'But the following year,' said Hasdai, 'the King regained Roussillon. Jaime of Mallorca knelt bareheaded before him and surrendered his armies. Perhaps that first war you were involved in helped to—'

'To kill peasants, children and poor people of hunger,' Arnau cut in. 'It may have meant that Jaime's army had no provisions, but many innocent people had to die for that. We're nothing more than playthings in the hands of our nobles. They settle their affairs without caring how much death or misery they bring to other people.'

Hasdai sighed. 'Don't I know it? We're royal property, we belong to him . . .'

'I went to war to fight, and in the end all I did was burn poor people's houses.'

The two men sat for a while lost in thought.

'Well,' said Arnau at length, 'now you know the story of the fig trees.'

Hasdai got up and patted Arnau on the shoulder. Then he suggested they go inside. 'It's grown cooler,' he said, glancing up at the sky.

When Jucef left them on their own, Arnau also talked to Raquel in the small back garden. Instead of telling her about the war, Arnau liked to describe his life as a *bastaix*, and about Santa Maria.

'We don't believe Jesus Christ was the Messiah. He still hasn't come: the Jewish people are still waiting for him,' Raquel explained on one occasion.

'They say you killed him.'

'That's not true!' she replied, indignantly. 'It's we who have always been killed and driven out, wherever we tried to settle!'

'They say', insisted Arnau, 'that at Easter you sacrifice a Christian child. You eat his heart and limbs as part of your rituals.'

Raquel shook her head vigorously. 'That's nonsense! You yourself have seen we don't eat any meat that isn't kosher, and that our religion doesn't allow us to drink any blood: what would we do with a child's heart, let alone his arms or legs? You know my father and Saul's; can you imagine them eating a child?'

Arnau thought about Hasdai's face and his wise words; he recalled his patience and the way his eyes shone whenever he looked at his children. How could such a man ever eat the heart of a child?

'What about the host?' he asked Raquel. 'They also say you steal them to torture them and make Christ suffer again.'

Raquel waved her hands in denial. 'We Jews don't believe in transubs . . .' She snapped her fingers in frustration. She always stumbled over that word whenever she talked about it with her father! 'Transubstantiation,' she said quickly.

'In what?'

'In transubs . . . stantiation. To you it means that your Jesus Christ is present in the host, that it really is his body. We don't believe that. To Jews, your host is nothing more than a piece of bread. So it would be stupid of us to torture a bit of bread, wouldn't it?'

'So nothing you are accused of is true?'

'Nothing.'

Arnau wanted to believe Raquel, especially when she stared at him wide-eyed, begging him to reject the prejudices the Christians held about her community and its beliefs.

'But you are usurers. That's something you can't deny.'

Raquel was about to respond, when they both heard her father's voice.

'No, we are not usurers,' said Hasdai, interrupting them and sitting down next to his daughter. 'At least not in the way it is usually meant.' Arnau waited for him to go on. 'Look, until a little more than a century ago, in the year 1230, Christians also lent money and charged interest. Both Jews and Christians did so, until a decree from your Pope Gregory the Ninth forbade Christians to make money in this way. Since then, only Jews and a few other groups such as the Lombards have been able to do so. But for twelve hundred years, you Christians lent money with interest. It's only been a little more than a hundred years that you haven't been permitted to *officially*,' said Hasdai, stressing the word, 'and yet you condemn us as usurers.'

'Officially?'

'Yes, officially. There are many Christians who lend money using us as intermediaries. But anyway, I wanted to explain to you why we do it. Throughout history, wherever we Jews have been, we've depended on the king. We've been expelled from many countries; first from our own lands, then from Egypt. Later on, in 1183, from France, and some time afterwards, in 1290, from England. Jewish communities were forced to emigrate from one country to another. They had to leave all their possessions behind, and to beg permission to settle from the rulers of the countries where they arrived. In response, the kings, as happened here in Catalonia, take over the Jewish community and demand heavy contributions for their wars and other expenses. If we did not make any profits from our money, we wouldn't be able to fulfil your kings' exorbitant demands, and we would end up being thrown out yet again.'

'But it's not only kings you lend money to,' Arnau insisted.

'No, that's true. And do you know why?' Arnau shook his head. 'Because the kings never repay our loans. On the contrary, they are always asking for more and more money for their wars and other extravagances. We have to make money somehow to lend them, or to make a generous contribution when it turns out not to be a loan.'

'You can't refuse?'

'They would expel us . . . or worse, they wouldn't defend us from Christians attacking us as they did in this city. We would all die.' This time, Arnau nodded, bringing a smile of satisfaction to Raquel's face when she saw that her father was convincing him. Arnau himself had been a witness to the enraged Barcelona mob howling their anger against the Jews. 'Anyway, remember that we don't lend money to any Christians who aren't either merchants or have permits to buy and sell. Almost a century ago, your King Jaime the Conqueror brought in a law which said that any commission or deposit made by a Jew to someone who was not a merchant was to be considered false, invented by the Jews, which means we cannot make a claim against anyone who isn't a merchant. We can't place commissions or deposits with anyone but merchants – otherwise we would never see our money again.'

'What's the difference?'

'It's completely different, Arnau. You Christians are proud that you follow the dictates of your religion by not lending money for interest, and it's true that you don't do it; not openly, at least. Yet you do lend money, but call it something else. Before the Church forbade loans with interest between Christians, business went on much as it does now between Jews and merchants: there were Christians with a lot of money who lent it to other Christians, the merchants – and they repaid the capital with interest.'

'What happened when it was forbidden to lend with interest?'

'It's simple. As ever, you Christians found a way round the Church's prohibition. It was obvious that no Christian was going to lend money to another one without making money, as the Church intended. If that were the case, he might as well keep his money and not run any risk. That was when you Christians invented the idea of the commission. Have you heard about that?'

'Yes,' Arnau admitted. 'In the port they talk a lot about commissions when a boat loaded with goods arrives, but the truth is, I've never really understood what it means.'

'It's not hard. A commission is nothing more than a loan with interest . . . but in another guise. Someone, usually a moneychanger, lends money to a merchant for him to buy or sell goods. Once the operation is complete, the merchant has to give back the same amount to the moneychanger, plus a part of the profits he has made. It's exactly the same as a loan with interest, but called by another name. The Christian who lends the money is making a profit, which is what the Church wants to prohibit – that profit comes from money and not from work. You Christians carry on doing exactly as you did a hundred years ago, before gaining interest from money was forbidden. Only now you call it something different. And when we Jews lend money for a deal we are usurers, whereas if a Christian makes money through a commission, that's fine.'

'Is there really no difference?'

'Just one. In commissions, the person who lends the money runs the same risk over the deal: in other words, if the merchant does not come back or loses his goods – if for example his ship is attacked by pirates – then the person making the loan loses too. The same isn't true of a loan as such, because in that case the merchant would still be obliged to return the money plus interest. In reality, though, it's exactly the same, because a merchant who has lost his goods cannot pay us anyway, and we Jews have to fit in with customary practice: merchants want commissions without risk, and we have to accept them because if we didn't, we would not make enough money to pay what your kings demand. Do you understand now?'

'We Christians do not give loans with interest, but offer commissions, which comes down to the same thing,' Arnau said in clarification.

'Exactly. What your Church is trying to prevent is not interest in itself, but making a profit by using money, not by working for it. And they only prohibit loans to those who are not kings, the nobility, or knights: a Christian can lend any of them what is known as a soft loan, because the Church considers this must be for war, and that makes the interest gained right and proper.'

'But only Christian moneychangers do that,' Arnau argued. 'You can't judge all Christians by what a few—'

'Make no mistake, Arnau,' Hasdai warned him, smiling and raising a finger. 'Those moneychangers get money from Christians, and use it to set up commissions. If they make money from them, they have to repay those Christians who gave them the money in the first place. The moneychangers are the public face of this business, but the money comes from Christians – from all those who put money into their exchanges. Arnau, there is something that never alters throughout history: whoever has money wants more; a person like that has never given it away, and never will. If your bishops don't do so, why should their flocks? Call it a loan, a commission, or whatever you like, but people never give anything for nothing. And yet we Jews are the usurers.'

As they talked, night fell: a calm, starry Mediterranean night. For a while longer, the three of them sat and enjoyed the peace and tranquillity of the small back garden behind the Crescas family home. Eventually they were called in for supper, and for the first time since he had been living there, Arnau considered this Jewish family as being the same as him: people with different beliefs, but good people, as good and charitable as the most saintly of Christians. That evening he sat at Hasdai's table and enjoyed to the full all the flavours of Jewish cooking served by the women of the house.

33

Time was passing, and the situation was becoming uncomfortable for all of them. The news reaching the Jewish quarter about the plague was encouraging: cases were becoming rarer and rarer. Arnau needed to get back to his own house. The night before he left, he and Hasdai met in the garden. They tried to talk about unimportant things in a friendly way, but there was an air of sadness to the meeting, and they both avoided looking at each other.

'Sahat is yours,' Hasdai unexpectedly announced, handing over the documents that sealed the matter.

'What do I need a slave for? I won't even be able to feed myself until our ships are put to sea again, so how could I feed a slave? The guild does not allow slaves to work. No, I don't need Sahat.'

'But you will need him,' Hasdai replied with a smile. 'He belongs to you. Ever since Raquel and Jucef were born, Sahat has looked after them as though they were his own children, and I can assure you he loves them as if they were. Neither he nor I can ever repay you for what you did for them. We think that the best way to settle our debt is by making life easier for you. To do that, you will need Sahat's help, and he is ready to give it.'

'Make life easier for me?'

'We both hope to help make you rich.'

Arnau smiled back at the man who was still his host. 'I'm nothing more than a *bastaix*. Wealth is for nobles and merchants.'

'You can have wealth too. I'll provide the means for you to do so. If you act wisely and follow Sahat's advice, I have no doubt you will become rich.' Arnau looked at him to learn more. 'As you know,' Hasdai continued, 'the plague is slackening. There are fewer and fewer cases, but it has had terrible consequences. No one knows exactly how many people have died in Barcelona, but we do know that four of the five city councillors have perished. That could have disastrous consequences. As regards our affairs, a good number of those who died were money-changers who worked in the city. I know, because I used to deal with them and they are no longer there. I think that if you were interested, you could become a money-changer.'

'I know nothing about business or changing money,' Arnau protested. 'Besides, every professional in a trade has to pass an examination. I know nothing about any of that kind of thing.'

'Moneychangers don't have to pass any test,' Hasdai replied. 'I know the King has been asked to establish some rules, but he has not yet done so. Anyone can be a moneychanger, as long as your counting house has sufficient backing. Sahat has enough knowledge for both of you. He knows all there is to know about the business. He has been part of my own dealings for many years now. I bought him in the first place because he was already an expert. If you allow him to, he can teach you and you will soon prosper. He may be a slave, but he is someone you can trust; besides which, he feels an extra loyalty towards you because of what you did for my children. They're the only people he has ever loved, because they are his family.' Hasdai looked enquiringly at Arnau through narrowed eyes. 'Well?'

'I'm not sure . . .' Arnau said doubtfully.

'You'll be backed not only by me, but by all the other Jews who are aware of what you did. We are a grateful people, Arnau. Sahat knows all my agents throughout the Mediterranean, Europe and in the Orient – even in the distant lands of the sultan of Egypt. You will start with a great deal of support for your business, and you can count on all of us to help you. It's a good offer, Arnau. You won't have any problems.'

Unsure if he was doing the right thing, Arnau accepted. This was enough to set all the machinery Hasdai had already prepared into motion. First rule: nobody, absolutely nobody was to know that Arnau was being helped by the Jews of Barcelona; that could only be used against him. Hasdai gave him a document which purported to show that all his funds came from a Christian widow living in Perpignan: this was the formal cover he needed.

'Should anyone ask,' Hasdai told him, 'don't say anything, but if they insist, tell them you have inherited it. You will need a lot of money to begin with,' he went on. 'First of all you will need to underwrite your counting house with the Barcelona magistrates. That is a thousand silver marks. Then you will have to buy a house or the lease on a house in the moneychangers' district, that is, either in Carrer dels Canvis Vells or Canvis Nous, and equip it as befits your station. Finally, you will need more money to be able to start trading.'

Moneychanging? Why not? What was left of his old life? All the people he loved had died from the plague. Hasdai seemed convinced that with Sahat's aid he could succeed. He had not the slightest idea of what a money-changer's life might be like: Hasdai assured him he would be rich, but what was it like to be rich? All of a sudden he remembered Grau, the only rich man he had ever known. He felt his stomach wrench. No, he would never be like Grau.

He underwrote his counting house with the thousand silver marks Hasdai gave him. He swore to the magistrates he would denounce any counterfeit money he came across – wondering to himself how on earth he would recognize it if by chance Sahat were not with him – and would slice it in two with the special shears all moneychangers kept for that purpose. The magistrate signed the enormous ledgers where he was to write down all his transactions, and, at a time when Barcelona was still in chaos following the effects of the bubonic plague, he was given official approval to operate as a money-changer. The days and times when he was to keep his business open were also established.

The second rule that Hasdai proposed concerned Sahat.

'No one should ever suspect he is my gift. Sahat is well known among the moneychangers, and if anyone finds out, you could have problems. As a Christian you are allowed to do business with Jews, but you should avoid anyone thinking you are a friend of Jews. There's another problem regarding Sahat: very few in the profession would understand why I have sold him to you. I have had hundreds of offers for him, each one more generous than the last, but I've always turned them down, because of both his abilities and his love for my children. Nobody would understand why he is with you. We thought in fact that Sahat could convert to Christianity.'

'Why would he do that?'

'We Jews are forbidden to have Christian slaves. If any

of our slaves convert, we have either to free them, or sell them to another Christian.'

'Will the other moneychangers believe it?'

'An outbreak of the plague is enough to undermine any religious belief.'

'Is Sahat willing to do it?'

'He is.'

They had spoken about the matter not as master and slave, but as the two close friends they had become over the years.

'Would you be capable of it?' Hasdai asked him.

'Yes,' answered Sahat. 'Allah, all praise and glory to him, will understand. You know the practice of our faith is forbidden in Christian lands. We fulfil our obligations in secret, in the privacy of our own hearts. That is how it will continue to be, however much holy water they sprinkle over me.'

'Arnau is a devout Christian,' Hasdai went on. 'If he ever found out . . .'

'He never will. We slaves more than anyone know the art of dissembling. No, not while I've been with you, but I have been a slave all my life. Our lives often depend on it.'

The third rule remained a secret between Hasdai and Sahat.

'Sahat, I have no need to tell you,' his former master said with trembling voice, 'how grateful I am to you for this decision of yours. My children and I will be eternally grateful to you.'

'It is I who should thank you.'

'I suppose you know where you should concentrate your efforts.'

'I believe so.'

'Stay away from spices, from fabrics, oils or wax,' Hasdai warned him, while Sahat nodded, already expecting this kind of advice. 'Until the situation has settled,

414

Catalonia will be unable to import these kinds of things. Slaves, Sahat, slaves. After the plague, Catalonia needs people to work. Until now, it's not something we have done much of. You will find them in Byzantium, Palestine, Rhodes and Cyprus. And in the markets of Sicily as well, of course. There are lots of Turks and Tartars on sale there. But I think it's better if you buy them in their own countries. We have agents in each of them who can help you. Your new master should amass a considerable fortune in no time at all.'

'What if he refuses to deal in slaves? He doesn't look the kind of person—'

'He is a good person,' Hasdai interrupted him to confirm his suspicions. 'He's scrupulous, of humble origin, and he's very generous. He might well refuse to have anything to do with the slave trade. Therefore, don't bring them to Barcelona. Don't let Arnau see them. Take them directly to Perpignan, Tarragona or Salou, or simply sell them in Mallorca – one of the biggest slave markets in all the Mediterranean is there. Let others bring them to Barcelona or wherever else they want to take them. Castile also needs a lot of slaves. Anyway, by the time Arnau has worked out how these things function, he will have made a lot of money. If I were you – and I'll say the same thing to him myself – I would tell him to become familiar with all the different currencies, how money is changed, the various markets, the routes and the main sorts of goods that are exported or imported. While he is doing that, you can be getting on with your own affairs. Just remember that we are no more intelligent than anyone else, and that anybody who has money will be importing slaves. There's a chance to make a lot of money, but it won't last. Make the most of it while you can.'

'Will you help?'

'In any way I can. I'll give you letters for all my

agents – you know them already. They will supply you with whatever credit you may require.'

'What about the account books? The slaves will have to appear there, and Arnau could find out.'

Hasdai smiled knowingly at his former slave. 'I'm sure you'll be able to sort out a small detail like that.'

34

'This one!' Arnau pointed to a small, two-storeyed house that was shut up and had a white cross daubed on the door. Sahat, who had been baptized a Christian with the name of Guillem, nodded at him. 'Is that all right?' asked Arnau.

Guillem nodded again, this time with a smile.

Arnau looked at the house and shook his head. All he had done was point to it, and Guillem had immediately consented. This was the first time in his life that his wishes had been so easily granted. Would it always be the same from now on? He shook his head again.

'Is something wrong, master?'

Arnau glared at him. How often had he told Guillem not to call him that? But the Moor did not agree. According to him, they had to keep up appearances. Now he stared back steadily at Arnau. 'Don't you like it, master?' he added.

'Yes . . . of course I like it. Is it suitable?'

'It couldn't be better. Look,' said Guillem, pointing to its position, 'it's right on the corner of the two streets where the moneychangers live: Canvis Nous and Canvis Vells. What could be better?'

Arnau followed Guillem's finger. Canvis Vells ran down to the sea, to the left of where they were standing. Canvis Nous was immediately opposite them. But that was not why Arnau had chosen it: he had not even realized these were the moneychangers' streets, although he had walked up and down them hundreds of times. No, the important thing was that the house was on the corner of the square of Santa Maria, just by what would be the church's main doorway.

'A good omen,' he muttered.

'What was that, master?'

Arnau turned angrily towards Guillem. He could not bear being called that.

'What appearances do we have to keep between the two of us?' he growled. 'Nobody can hear or see us.'

'Keep in mind that since you've become a money-changer, a lot of people are listening and watching you without your realizing it. You have to get used to the idea.'

That same morning, while Arnau wandered along the beach among the boats looking out to sea, Guillem investigated who the owners of the house were. As he had thought, it was the Church. The emphyteutas had died: who better than a moneychanger to take their place?

That afternoon, they visited the house. The upper floor contained three small rooms. They furnished two, one for each of them. The ground floor was made up of a kitchen, with a door to what must once have been a small vegetable patch, and, on the other side of a partition, an airy room in which over the next few days Guillem installed a wardrobe, several lanterns and a long hardwood table, with two chairs behind it and four in front.

'Something's missing,' said Guillem, and left the room.

Arnau was left sitting alone at what was to be his moneychanging table. The long wooden surface shone where he had polished it time and again. He ran his fingers over the backs of the two chairs.

'Choose where you'd like to sit,' Guillem had told him.

Arnau chose the right-hand chair, the one that would be to the left of any future clients. Guillem changed the seats around: to the right he placed an elegant chair with arms, covered in red silk; his own was of less expensive cloth.

Arnau surveyed the empty room. It was so strange! Only a few months earlier, he had spent his days unloading boats, and now . . . He had never before sat in such a wonderful chair! His ledgers were piled up at one end of the table; unused parchment, Guillem had assured him when they purchased them. They also bought quills, inkwells, a balance, several money chests, and a large pair of shears for cutting fake coins.

Guillem took from his purse more money than Arnau had ever seen in his life.

'Who is paying all that?' he asked.

'You are.'

Arnau raised his eyebrows and stared at the purse hanging from Guillem's belt.

'Would you like it?' asked the Moor.

'No,' replied Arnau.

In addition to all the things they purchased, Guillem had brought one item of his own: a fine abacus with a wooden frame and ivory counters that Hasdai had given him. As he sat, Arnau picked it up and moved the counters from one side to another. What had Guillem told him? The Moor had flicked the counters one way and another, calculating rapidly. Arnau had asked him to show him more slowly, and Guillem had obediently tried to explain how an abacus worked, but Arnau could not remember even the essentials.

He put the abacus down and decided to tidy the table. The ledgers should go opposite his chair – no, better put them in front of Guillem. He would be the one making the entries. The money chests could go on his side; the shears could go a bit further away. The quills and the inkwells next to the account books, alongside the abacus. Who else was going to use them?

He was still busy sorting all this out when Guillem reappeared.

'What do you think of it?' Arnau asked him, smiling and showing him all he had done with the table.

'Very good,' said Guillem, smiling back at him, 'but that way we will never get any clients, least of all any willing to place their money with us.' Arnau's face fell. 'Don't worry, there's only one thing missing. That's what I went to buy.'

Saying this, Guillem handed him a cloth. Arnau carefully unrolled it: it was made of the most expensive scarlet silk, with golden threads round the edges.

'This is what you need on your table,' said the Moorish slave. 'It is the public sign that you have fulfilled all the official requirements and that your counting house has been underwritten with the city magistrate for a thousand silver marks. There are severe penalties for anyone who keeps a cloth of this kind without proper authorization. Unless you are able to display one, nobody will deposit any money with you.'

From then on, Arnau and Guillem devoted themselves to the new business. As Hasdai Crescas had advised, the former *bastaix* first spent some time learning the basics of the profession.

'The first thing a moneychanger must be good at,' said

Guillem as they both sat behind the table, keeping an eye open to see if anyone were venturing inside, 'is exchanging different kinds of money.'

With that he stood up, walked round the table, and dropped a bag of money in front of Arnau.

'Look closely,' he said, taking a coin out of the purse. 'Do you recognize it?' Arnau nodded. 'It's a Catalan silver croat. They are minted in Barcelona, only a short distance from here.'

'I've only ever had a few in my purse,' said Arnau, 'but I've carried a lot more on my back. It seems the King only trusts the *bastaixos* to transport them.'

Guillem smiled and agreed. He dipped his hand into the purse again.

'And this,' he said, taking out another coin and placing it alongside the first one, 'is a gold florin from Aragon.'

'I've never had any of them,' said Arnau, picking it up and admiring it.

'Don't worry, you'll have lots.' Arnau stared at him, but the Moor merely nodded slightly. 'This is an old Barcelona coin, the tern.' Guillem put this third coin on the table, and before Arnau could say anything more, continued pulling out different coins. 'Traders use many different kinds of currencies, and you have to be able to recognize them all. There are ones the Muslims use: bezants, mazmudinas and gold bezants.' Guillem lined up one of each of them in front of Arnau. 'Then there are French tournois, the Castilian gold doblas, the gold florins struck in Florence and those minted in Genoa, ducats from Venice, coins from Marseilles and other Catalan coins; reales from Valencia and Mallorca, the gros from Montpellier, coins from the eastern Pyrenees and the ones minted in Jaca that are usually found in Lleida.'

'Holy Mother of God!' Arnau exclaimed when the Moor had finished the list.

'You need to be able to recognize them all,' Guillem insisted.

Arnau looked up and down the line of coins several times. He sighed.

'Are there any more?' he asked, peering up at Guillem.

'Yes, lots. But these are the most common ones.'

'How are they changed?'

This time it was the Moor's turn to sigh. 'That's more complicated.' Arnau encouraged him to go on. 'Well, to do that we use the standard currencies: pounds and marks for large sums, shillings and pence for smaller ones.' Arnau nodded at this: he had always talked in shillings and pence, whatever the coins he had been using, although they were usually the same. 'If you are given a coin, you need to calculate its value according to these standard currencies, then do the same for the currency you have to change it to.'

Arnau struggled to keep up with his explanations. 'How do I know what the values are?'

'They are fixed periodically on the Barcelona exchange, at the Consulate of the Sea. You need to go there regularly to check the official rate of exchange.'

'Does it vary then?' Arnau shook his head in despair. He did not know any of these different currencies, had no idea how to exchange one for another, and on top of that, their values changed!

'Constantly,' the Moor told him. 'And you have to know the variations. That's how a moneychanger makes his money. One of the most important parts of his business is to buy and sell currency.'

'To buy money?'

'Yes, buying or selling money. Buying silver with gold, or the other way round, juggling with all the various sorts of currency there are, and doing it here in Barcelona if the rate of exchange is good, or elsewhere if it is better there.'

Arnau threw up his hands helplessly.

'It's quite easy, in fact,' Guillem insisted. 'Look: in Catalonia it's the King who determines the parity between the gold florin and the silver croat. He has set it at thirteen to one: a gold florin is worth thirteen silver croats. But in Florence, Venice or Alexandria, they don't care what the King says, and to them, the gold in a florin is not worth thirteen times the silver there is in a croat. Here, the King sets the rate for political reasons; there, they weigh the gold and silver and set their own exchange rate. In other words, if you save silver croats and sell them abroad, you will get more gold than you would here in Catalonia for the same coins. Then if you bring the gold back here, you will still get thirteen croats for each gold florin.'

'Why doesn't everyone do that then?' Arnau objected.

'Everyone who can does. But someone who has only ten or a hundred croats does not bother. The people who do are the ones who have many other people prepared to deposit their ten or hundred croats with them.' The two men looked at each other. 'And that is us,' the Moor concluded, spreading his palms.

Some time later, when Arnau was already becoming skilled in recognizing the different currencies and understanding how to exchange them, Guillem started to explain the trade routes and the goods bought and sold along them.

'Nowadays,' he said, 'the main one is the route from Crete to Cyprus, from there to Beirut, and from there to Damascus or Alexandria . . . although the Pope has forbidden trade with Alexandria.'

'So how is it done?' asked Arnau, playing with the abacus in front of him.

'With money, of course. You buy a pardon.'

Arnau remembered the explanation he had heard in the royal quarries about how the royal dockyards were being paid for.

'And do we only trade around the Mediterranean?'

'No. We trade with everyone. With Castile, with France and Flanders, although you are right, it is mostly around the Mediterranean. The difference is the kind of goods we trade: we buy cloth in France, England and Flanders, especially expensive materials: wool from Toulouse, Bruges, Malines, Diest or Vilages, although we sell them Catalan linen too. We also buy copper and tin goods. In the Orient, in Syria and Egypt, we buy spices—'

'Pepper,' said Arnau.

'Yes, pepper. When people talk about the spice trade to you, they also mean wax, sugar and even elephant tusks. If they talk of fine spices, then they are referring to what you commonly imagine them to be: cinnamon, cloves, pepper, nutmeg and so on . . .'

'Did you say wax? Do we import wax, then? How can it be that we import wax when the other day you told me we export honey?'

'That's how it is,' the Moor interrupted. 'We export honey but import wax. We have too much honey, but the churches use a lot of wax.' Arnau recalled the *bastaixos'* first duty in Santa Maria: to ensure there were always candles lit beneath the statue of the Virgin of the Sea. 'Wax comes from Dacia via Byzantium. The other main goods we trade in are foodstuffs,' Guillem went on. 'Many years ago, Catalonia exported wheat, but now we have to import all kinds of cereals: wheat, rice, millet and barley. We export olive oil, wine, dried fruits, saffron, bacon and honey. We also sell salt meat—'

At that moment, a client came in. Arnau and Guillem fell silent. The man sat opposite them and, after an exchange of greetings, deposited a sizeable sum of money with them. Guillem was pleased: he did not know the client, which was a good sign, as it meant they were beginning not to have to depend on Hasdai's clients. Arnau dealt with him in a professional way, counting out the coins and verifying their authenticity – although for good measure he passed them one by one to Guillem. Then he wrote down the sum deposited in his ledger. Guillem watched him write. Arnau had improved: his efforts were bearing fruit. The Puig family's tutor had taught him the alphabet, but he had not written anything for years.

While waiting for the seagoing season to begin, Arnau and Guillem spent nearly all their time preparing commission contracts. They bought goods for export, joined with other traders to charter ships or contracted them and discussed what cargoes to fill them with on the return journeys.

'What profits do the merchants we are contracting make?' Arnau wanted to know.

'That depends on the commission. On normal ones, they take a quarter of the profits. If the transaction is in gold or silver money, it does not amount to that much. We state the exchange rate we want, and the merchants make their profits from whatever they can get above that.'

'How do they manage in such distant lands?' Arnau asked, trying to imagine what these places were like. 'They are foreign countries, where people speak other tongues . . . everything must be different.'

'Yes, but don't forget that in all those cities Catalonia has consulates,' Guillem replied. 'They're like the Consulate of the Sea here in Barcelona. There is a consul appointed by the city of Barcelona in every port. He tries to see that everything in commerce is carried out fairly, and mediates in any disputes which might arise between Catalan traders and local merchants or authorities. All the consulates have their own warehouse. They are walled premises where Catalan merchants can stay and where their goods can be stored until they are sold or loaded on board ship. Every warehouse is like a part of Catalonia on foreign soil. The person with authority over them is the consul, not the authorities of the country they are in.'

'Why is that?'

'Every country is interested in trade. They can levy taxes and fill their coffers from it. Trade is a different world, Arnau. We may be at war with the Saracens, but, for example, since last century Catalonia has had consulates in Tunis or Bugia and, make no mistake, no Arab leader would ever attack one.'

Arnau Estanyol's moneychanging business was thriving. The plague had decimated Barcelona's moneychangers; the presence of Guillem was a guarantee for investors; and, as the plague receded, more and more people wanted to put the money they had hidden at home to good use. And yet Guillem could not sleep. 'Sell them in Mallorca,' Hasdai had recommended, referring to slaves, so that Arnau would not find out. Guillem had followed the advice: would that he hadn't! he told himself, tossing and turning on his bed. He had used one of the last ships to leave Barcelona, at the start of October. Byzantium, Palestine, Rhodes and Cyprus: those were the destinations of the four merchants who set sail in the name of Arnau Estanyol, supplied with bills of exchange that Guillem had handed to Arnau for signature. The former *bastaix* had scarcely even glanced at them. Now the merchants were to buy slaves and transport them to Mallorca. Guillem shifted once more in bed.

The political situation was conspiring against him. Despite the Holy Pontiff's efforts to mediate, King Pedro had conquered the Cerdagne and Roussillon a year after his first attempt, when the truce he had agreed to had run out. On 15 July 1344, after most of his villages and towns had capitulated, King Jaime III knelt bareheaded before his brother-in-law. He begged for mercy and handed over his lands to the Count of Barcelona. King

Pedro left him as lord of Montpellier and Viscount of Omelades and Carlades, but recovered the Catalan territory his ancestors had once possessed: Mallorca, Roussillon and the Cerdagne.

However, after surrendering in this way, Jaime of Mallorca gathered a small army of sixty knights and three hundred footsoldiers and made for the Cerdagne to fight his brother-in-law again. King Pedro did not even deign to go and do battle against him, but instead sent his lieutenants. Weary, unhappy and defeated yet again, King Jaime sought refuge from Pope Clement VI, who still supported him. While he was under the Church's safe protection, he thought up the last of his schemes: he sold Henri VI of France the title of lord of Montpellier for twelve thousand golden crowns, then used that, together with loans from the Church, to equip a fleet conceded him by Queen Joanna of Naples. In 1349, he and his fleet disembarked in Mallorca.

Guillem had planned for the slaves to arrive with the first ships of the year 1349. A great deal of money was at stake. If anything went wrong, Arnau's name – however strongly he was backed by Hasdai Crescas – would suffer among the agents he would need to work with in the future. He was the one who had signed the bills of exchange, and, even though they were guaranteed by Hasdai, they would have to be paid. Relations with agents in far-off countries depended on trust, absolute trust. How could a moneychanger succeed if his first operation was a failure?

'Even he told me to avoid having anything to do with Mallorca,' Guillem confessed one day to Hasdai, the only person he could admit his fears to, as they walked in the Jewish man's garden.

They did not look each other in the eye, and yet they both knew they were thinking the same. Four slave ships! If they failed, it could even be the ruin of Hasdai.

427

'If King Jaime will not keep the word he gave the day he surrendered,' said Guillem, finally looking at Hasdai, 'what will become of Catalan trade and goods?'

Hasdai said nothing: what was there to say?

'Perhaps your merchants will choose another port,' he said at length.

'Barcelona?' mused Guillem, shaking his head.

'Nobody could have foreseen this,' said the Jew, trying to reassure him. Arnau had saved his children from certain death. What was this in comparison?

In May 1349 King Pedro sent the Catalan fleet to Mallorca, right in the middle of the seagoing season, right in the middle of the trading season.

'What good fortune we did not send any ships to Mallorca,' Arnau commented one day.

Guillem had to sit down.

'What would happen if we had sent any?' asked Arnau.

'What do you mean?'

'We take money from people and invest it in commissions. If we had sent ships to Mallorca and King Jaime had requisitioned them, we would lose both the money and the goods on board; we wouldn't be able to return the deposits. The commissions are at our own risk. What happens in cases like that?'

'*Abatut,*' the Moor replied tersely.

'*Abatut?*'

'If a moneychanger cannot repay the deposits, the magistrate gives him six months to settle the debts. If by the end of that time he has been unable to pay them off, he is declared *abatut*, or bankrupt. He is imprisoned on bread and water, and all his possessions are sold to pay his debtors . . .'

'I don't have any possessions.'

'If those possessions are insufficient,' Guillem continued reciting from memory, 'he is beheaded

428

outside his counting house as a warning to all the others.'

Arnau said nothing.

Guillem did not dare look at him. How was Arnau to blame for any of this?

'Don't worry,' he told him, 'it will never happen.'

35

The war continued in Mallorca, but Arnau was happy. Whenever there was no work to do, he stood at the door of his counting house and looked out. Now that the plague had ceased, Santa Maria was coming back to life. The tiny Romanesque church he and Joanet had known no longer existed; work on the new church was steadily advancing towards the main doorway. He could spend hours watching the masons placing the blocks of stone; he had a vivid memory of all those he had carried. Santa Maria meant everything to Arnau: his mother, his acceptance into the guild . . . and, of course, a place of refuge for the Jewish children. Occasionally a letter from his brother made him even happier. Joan's letters were always short, and only told him about his health and the fact that he was studying hard.

As he looked out, a *bastaix* appeared carrying a stone. Few of the guild members had survived the plague. His own father-in-law Bartolomé, Ramon and many others had died. Arnau had wept for them on the beach with his former companions.

'Sebastià,' he muttered when he recognized the man.

'What did you say?' he heard Guillem ask behind him.

Arnau did not turn round. 'Sebastià,' he repeated. 'That man carrying the stone over there is called Sebastià.'

As he passed by, the *bastaix* called a greeting, without turning his head or pausing. His lips were drawn in a tight line from the effort.

'For many years, that could have been me,' Arnau went on, his voice choked with emotion. Guillem made no comment. 'I was only thirteen when I took my first stone to the Virgin.' At that moment, another *bastaix* walked past the door. Arnau greeted him. 'I thought I was going to snap in two, that my spine was going to break, but you can't imagine the satisfaction I felt when I finally got there . . . my God!'

'There must be something good about your Virgin for people to sacrifice themselves for her like that,' he heard the Moor say.

At that they both fell silent, watching the line of *bastaixos* passing by on their way to the church.

The *bastaixos* were the first to turn to Arnau.

'We need money,' Sebastià, who by now was one of the guild aldermen, told him straight out one day. 'Our coffers are empty, our needs are great, and at the moment there is little work, and what there is of it is badly paid. After the plague, our members are finding it hard to survive, so I cannot force them to contribute to our funds until they have recovered from the disaster.'

Arnau looked across at Guillem. He sat next to him behind the table with its glittering scarlet silk cloth without showing the slightest emotion.

'Is the situation really that bad?' asked Arnau.

'Worse than you could imagine. Food has become so expensive we *bastaixos* cannot even provide for our families. On top of that, there are the widows and orphans of those who died. We have to help them. We need money, Arnau. We'll pay you back every last penny you lend us.'

'I know.'

Arnau looked across again at Guillem to seek his approval. What did he know about lending money? Until now he had only taken in money, never lent it out.

Guillem covered his face in his hands. He sighed.

'If it's not possible . . .' Sebastià started to say.

'It is possible,' said Guillem. The war had been going on for two months now, and there was no news of his slaves. What did a few pence matter? Hasdai would be the one facing ruin. Arnau could allow himself to make the loan. 'If your word is enough for my master—'

'It is,' Arnau said emphatically.

Arnau counted out the money the guild of *bastaixos* was asking him for and solemnly handed it over to Sebastià. Guillem saw them shake hands across the table, both of them standing there trying clumsily to hide their emotions as their handshake went on and on.

During the third month of the war, just as Guillem was losing all hope, the four merchant ships arrived together in Barcelona. When the first of them had called in at Sicily and heard about the war in Mallorca, the captain had chosen to wait for more Catalan ships to arrive, including Guillem's three other galleys. Together, they all decided to avoid Mallorca, and instead sold their cargoes in Perpignan, the second city of Catalonia. On their return to Barcelona, they met the Moor, as agreed, not in Arnau's counting house but in the city warehouse in Carrer dels Carders. There, once they had deducted their quarter of the profits, they gave him bills of exchange for the rest, plus everything that was due to Arnau. A fortune! Catalonia needed people to work, and the slaves had been sold at exorbitant prices.

When the merchants had left the warehouse and no

one could see him, Guillem kissed the bills of exchange once, twice, a thousand times. He set off back to Arnau's counting house, but when he reached Plaça del Blat he changed his mind and went into the Jewry instead. After giving Hasdai the good news, he headed for Santa Maria, beaming at the sky and everyone he met.

When he entered the counting house, he saw that Arnau was with Sebastià and a priest.

'Guillem,' said Arnau, 'this is Father Juli Andreu. He has replaced Father Albert.'

Guillem nodded awkwardly to the priest. More loans, he thought.

'It's not what you might imagine,' Arnau told him. Guillem felt the bills of exchange in his pocket and smiled. What did he care? Arnau was a rich man. He smiled again, but Arnau misinterpreted his smile. 'It's even worse,' he said seriously. What could be worse than lending to the Church? the Moor almost asked, but thought better of it, and greeted the guild alderman instead. 'We have a problem,' Arnau concluded.

The three men sat gazing at the Moor for a few moments. 'Only if Guillem accepts,' Arnau had insisted, ignoring the reference the priest had made to him being only a slave.

'Have I ever told you about Ramon?' Guillem shook his head. 'He was a very important person in my life. He helped . . . he helped me a lot.' Guillem was still standing next to them, as befitted a slave. 'He and his wife died of the plague, and the guild cannot continue to look after his daughter. We've been talking . . . they've asked me . . .'

'Why do you want my opinion, master?'

When he heard this, Father Juli Andreu turned and looked triumphantly at Arnau.

'The Pia Almoina and the Casa de la Caritat can't cope any more,' Arnau went on. 'They can't even hand out bread, wine and stew to beggars every day as they used to. The plague has hit them badly too.'

'What is it that you want, master?'

'They are suggesting I adopt her.'

Guillem felt for the bills of exchange once more. You could adopt twenty children if you wished, he thought. 'If that is your desire,' was all he said.

'I don't know anything about children,' Arnau objected.

'All you have to do is give them affection and a home,' said Sebastià. 'You have the home . . . and it seems to me you have more than enough affection.'

'Will you help me?' Arnau asked Guillem, ignoring Sebastià.

'I'll obey you in whatever way you wish.'

'I don't want obedience. I want . . . I'm asking for your help.'

'Your words do me honour. I will willingly help you,' Guillem promised. 'In whatever you need.'

The girl was eight years old, and was called Mar, like Arnau's Virgin. In little more than three months, she recovered from the shock of losing her parents to the plague. From then on, it was not the clinking of coins or the scratching of pens on vellum that could be heard in the house: it was laughter and the sound of running feet. At their places behind the table, Arnau and Guillem would scold her whenever she managed to escape from the slave Guillem had bought to look after her and ran into the counting house, but as soon as she had gone, both men always smiled at each other.

Arnau had been angry when Donaha the slave first appeared.

'I don't want any more slaves!' he shouted, cutting across Guillem's arguments.

At that the thin, filthy girl dressed only in rags had burst into tears.

'Where would she be better off than here?' Guillem asked Arnau. 'If you're really so against it, set her free, but she will only sell herself to someone else. She has to eat – and we need a woman to look after the child.'

The girl clung to Arnau's knees. He tried to struggle free.

'Do you know how much she must have suffered?' Guillem said, his eyes narrowing. 'If you reject her . . .'

In spite of himself, Arnau agreed to take her on.

As well as employing the girl, Guillem found the answer to the problem of the fortune they had gained from the sale of the other slaves. After he had paid Hasdai as the sellers' agent in Barcelona, he gave all the remaining profits to a Jew whom Hasdai trusted who happened to be in Barcelona at the time.

Abraham Levi arrived one morning at the counting house. He was a tall, gaunt man with a scrawny white beard, wearing a black coat and the yellow badge. He greeted Guillem, who presented him to Arnau. Then he sat opposite Arnau and gave him a bill of exchange for the total of the profits.

'I want to deposit this amount with you, Messire Arnau,' he said.

Arnau's eyes opened wide when he saw how much was involved, and quickly passed the document to Guillem for him to read.

'But . . .' he started to say, while Guillem feigned surprise at what he was reading, 'this is a lot of money. Why do you want to deposit it with me, and not someone of your own . . .'

'Faith?' said the Jew. 'I've always trusted Sahat. I don't think his change of name' – he glanced at the Moor – 'will have affected his judgement. I'm going on a journey, a very long one, and I want you and Sahat to put my money to work.'

'For depositing a sum this large, we will immediately

owe you a quarter, isn't that right, Guillem?' The Moor nodded. 'But how can we pay you your profit if you're about to leave on such a long journey? How can we keep in touch with you?'

Why all this fuss? Guillem wondered. He had not given the Jew precise instructions, but Levi was more than capable of coping.

'Reinvest it all,' he told Arnau. 'Don't worry about me. I don't have any children or family, and I won't need the money where I'm going. Some day, perhaps far off in the future, I will claim it back, or send someone to claim it. Until then, you are not to worry. I'll be the one who gets in touch with you. Is that a problem?'

'Of course not,' replied Arnau. Guillem breathed a sigh of relief. 'If that is what you want, so be it.'

They completed the transaction and Abraham Levi stood up.

'I have to say goodbye to some friends in the Jewry,' he said as he bid the two of them farewell.

'I'll go with you,' said Guillem, making sure Arnau had no objection.

From the counting house the two men went to a scribe, in whose presence Abraham Levi signed away his rights to the money he had just deposited with Arnau Estanyol, and ceded him any profits which might accrue from this capital. Guillem returned to the counting house with the document hidden in his clothing. It was only a matter of time, he thought as he walked through the city. Formally, the money belonged to the Jew: that was what Arnau's account books showed. But nobody could ever claim it from him, as Abraham Levi had signed away all his rights to it. And the three-quarters of the profits made on this capital that corresponded directly to Arnau would be more than enough for him to multiply his fortune.

That night while Arnau slept, Guillem crept down to

the counting house. He had found a loose stone in the wall. He wrapped Abraham Levi's document in a cloth and hid it behind the stone, which he replaced as best he could. One day he would ask one of the workmen at Santa Maria to seal it properly. That was where Arnau's fortune could lie until he found a way to tell him where it had come from. It was all a matter of time.

A matter of a long time, Guillem had to admit to himself one day when he and Arnau were walking back along the beach after attending to some business at the Consulate of the Sea. Slaves were still arriving at Barcelona; human goods that the boatmen transported to the shore crowded into their small craft. Men and boys who could work, but also women and children whose wailing led both men to stop and look at what was going on.

'Listen to me, Guillem. No matter how bad a situation we may find ourselves in,' said Arnau, 'we will never finance any trade in slaves. I would prefer to be beheaded by the city magistrate before I did that.'

They watched as the galley was rowed further out to sea.

'Why is he leaving?' Arnau asked without thinking. 'Why doesn't he take on another cargo for the return journey?'

Guillem turned towards him, shaking his head gently.

'He'll be back,' he assured Arnau. 'He's only going out to open sea . . . to carry on unloading,' he ended, with trembling voice.

Arnau watched the galley heading out to sea. For a few moments, he said nothing.

'How many of them die?' he asked at length.

'Too many,' said the Moor, remembering one such ship.

'Never, Guillem! Remember that: never!'

36

1 January 1354
Plaça de Santa Maria de la Mar
Barcelona

Of course it would have to be outside Santa Maria, thought Arnau. He was standing at one of his windows watching as the whole of Barcelona crowded into the square, the adjoining streets, on to the scaffolding and even inside the church, all of them staring at the dais the King had ordered erected in the square. King Pedro III had not chosen Plaça del Blat, the cathedral, the exchange building or the magnificent shipyards he himself was building. He had chosen Santa Maria, the people's church, the church being constructed thanks to the united efforts and sacrifices of all the citizens of Barcelona.

'There's nowhere in all Catalonia that better represents the spirit of the people of Barcelona,' Arnau had commented to Guillem that morning as they surveyed the work going on to erect the platform. 'The King knows it, and that's why he chose here.'

Arnau shivered. His whole life had revolved around that church!

'It will cost us money,' the Moor complained.

Arnau turned towards him to protest, but the Moor

would not take his eyes off the platform, so Arnau chose not to say anything more.

Five years had gone by since they had opened the counting house for business. Arnau was thirty-two years old, happy . . . and rich, very rich. He lived austerely, but his ledgers showed he had amassed a considerable fortune.

'Let's have breakfast,' he said finally, putting his hand on Guillem's shoulder.

Downstairs in the kitchen Donaha was waiting for them with Mar, who was helping her set the table. When the two men appeared, Donaha carried on working, but Mar ran towards them.

'Everyone's talking about the King's visit!' she cried. 'Do you think we could get near him? Will his knights be with him?'

Guillem sat down at the table and sighed. 'He's come to ask us for more money,' he explained to her.

'Guillem!' Arnau rebuked him when he saw the girl's puzzled expression.

'But it's true,' said the Moor in self-defence.

'No, Mar, it's not,' said Arnau, winning the reward of a smile. 'The King has come to ask for our help in conquering Sardinia.'

'Help meaning money?' asked Mar, winking at Guillem.

Arnau looked at her, and then at Guillem: they were both smiling at him mischievously. How the girl had grown! She was almost a woman now: beautiful, intelligent, and with a charm that could entrance anyone.

'Money?' the girl repeated, interrupting his thoughts.

'All wars cost money!' Arnau was forced to admit.

'Aha!' said Guillem, spreading his palms.

Donaha began to fill their bowls.

'Why don't you tell her', Arnau went on when Donaha

had finished, 'that in fact it doesn't cost us money, it makes us more?'

Mar stared wonderingly at the Moor.

Guillem hesitated. 'We have had three years of special taxes,' he said, refusing to accept that Arnau was right. 'Three years of war that we people of Barcelona have financed.'

Mar smiled once more, and looked towards Arnau.

'That's true,' Arnau conceded. 'Exactly three years ago we Catalans signed a treaty with Venice and Byzantium to declare war on Genoa. Our aim was to conquer Corsica and Sardinia, which according to the Treaty of Agnani ought to be feudal possessions of Catalonia and yet are still controlled by the Genoese. Sixty-eight armed galleys!' Arnau raised his voice. 'Sixty-eight armed galleys – twenty-three from Catalonia, the rest of them from Venice or Greece – joined battle with sixty-five Genoese men-o'-war.'

'What happened?' asked Mar, when Arnau unexpectedly fell silent.

'Neither side won a victory. Our admiral, Ponç de Santa Pau, died in the battle. Only ten of our twenty-three galleys came back. What happened then, Guillem?'

The Moor shook his head.

'Go on, Guillem, tell her,' Arnau insisted.

Guillem sighed. 'The Byzantines betrayed us,' he intoned. 'They made peace with Genoa and in return gave them the exclusive monopoly on trade with their city.'

'What else happened?' insisted Arnau.

'We lost one of the most important trade routes in the Mediterranean.'

'Did we lose money?'

'Yes.'

Mar continued to switch her gaze between the two men. Over by the fire, Donaha was following their argument.

'A lot of money?'

'Yes.'

'More than we have given the King since?'

'Yes.'

'Only if the Mediterranean is ours can we trade in peace,' Arnau concluded triumphantly.

'What about the people from Byzantium?' Mar wanted to know.

'The following year, King Pedro equipped a fleet of fifty galleys commanded by Bernat de Cabrera, and defeated the Genoese off Sardinia. Our admiral captured thirty-three enemy galleys and sank another five. Eight thousand Genoese died, and a further three thousand two hundred were taken prisoner. But only forty Catalans lost their lives! After that the Byzantines changed their minds,' he added, gazing into Mar's eyes, which were sparkling with curiosity, 'and opened up their ports to trade with us once more.'

'Three years of special taxes we are still paying,' Guillem noted.

'But if the King now rules over Sardinia and we can trade with Byzantium, why has he come here now?' asked Mar.

'The Sardinian nobles, led by a certain judge in the city of Arborea, have risen up against King Pedro. He has to go and quash the uprising.'

'The King should be satisfied with having his trade routes open and receiving his taxes,' Guillem protested. 'Sardinia is a rough, inhospitable land. We will never succeed in taming it.'

The King spared no pomp in appearing before his people. Up on his dais, his short stature went unnoticed. He was dressed in his finest robes, the vivid scarlet of his doublet glinting in the winter sunlight as brightly as the precious stones adorning it. He had made sure he was wearing his golden crown, and the small dagger of office hung at his belt. His retinue of nobles and courtiers were not to be outdone, and wore equally magnificent costumes.

The King spoke to his people, whipping them up into a frenzy. When before had they ever heard a King addressing ordinary citizens in this way, explaining what his plans were? He spoke about Catalonia, its lands and its interests. When he went on to talk of the betrayal of Arborea in Sardinia, the crowd raised their fists in the air and clamoured for vengeance. He continued to stir them up, until finally he asked them for the help he needed: by then, they would have handed over their children to him if he had requested it.

Everyone in Barcelona had to pay their contribution: Arnau was taxed heavily as an authorized moneychanger. Soon afterwards, King Pedro set off for Sardinia in command of a fleet of a hundred ships.

After the King's army had left Barcelona, the city returned to normal. Arnau went back to his counting house, to Mar, Santa Maria, and to helping all those who came asking for a loan.

Guillem had had to get used to a very different way of doing business from the one he had known with the other moneychangers and merchants he had worked with, including Hasdai Crescas. At first he was opposed to it, and made no secret of his position whenever Arnau opened his purse to lend money to one of the many workmen who seemed to need it.

'Don't they pay? Don't they return all our money?' Arnau asked him.

'But they don't pay any interest,' Guillem objected. 'That money could be making a profit.'

'How often have you told me we should buy a palace, that we should be living in more luxury than we do? How much would that cost, Guillem? You know it's infinitely more than all the sums I've lent to these people.'

Guillem was forced to keep quiet. Above all, because it was true. Arnau lived modestly in his house on the corner of Canvis Nous and Canvis Vells. The only thing he spent money on was Mar's education. The girl went to a merchant friend's house to learn from the tutors there, and also at Santa Maria. It had not been long before the commission of works at the church had come to ask Arnau for funds as well.

'I already have a chapel,' Arnau told them when they suggested he might like to dedicate one of the side chapels. 'Yes,' he said when they looked at him in surprise, 'my chapel is the Jesus chapel, the one the *bastaixos* look after. That will always be mine. But anyway . . .' he said, opening his money chest, 'how much do you need?'

How much do you need? How much could you make do with? Will this be enough? These were questions Guillem had to get used to hearing. As people started greeting him on the street, smiling at him and thanking him whenever he was on the beach or in the La Ribera district, he came to accept Arnau's approach. Perhaps he's right, he began to think. Arnau was constantly giving to others, but had he not done the same with him and the three Jewish children who were about to be stoned – complete strangers to him? If Arnau had been different, he, Raquel and Jucef would in all likelihood have been killed. Why should he change now, simply because he was rich? So Guillem, just like Arnau, began to smile at everyone he met and to thank strangers who made way for him in the street.

Yet some decisions Arnau had taken over the years seemed to have nothing to do with that attitude. It was logical enough that he should refuse to take part in the slave trade, but, Guillem wondered, why did he sometimes turn down opportunities that had nothing to do with slaves?

At the beginning, Arnau simply announced his

decision: 'I'm not convinced.' 'I don't like it.' 'I don't understand it.'

On one such occasion, the Moor's patience was eventually exhausted.

'It's a good opportunity, Arnau,' he said as the traders left their counting house. 'What's wrong? Sometimes you reject things that would bring us a good profit. I don't understand. I know I have no right to—'

'Yes you have,' Arnau butted in, without turning towards him. 'I'm sorry, it's just that . . .' Guillem waited for him to make up his mind. 'Look, I will never have anything to do with a deal that involves Grau Puig. I never want to see my name associated with his.' Arnau stared straight in front of him, at somewhere in the distance.

'Will you tell me why one day?'

Why not? mused Arnau. He turned to him and began to explain all that had happened between him and the Puig family.

Guillem knew Grau Puig, because he had worked with Hasdai Crescas. The Moor wondered why, when Arnau was so adamant about having nothing to do with him, the baron seemed willing to do business with Arnau? Could it be, after all that Arnau had told him, that he did not feel the same way?

'Why?' he asked Hasdai Crescas one day, after he had briefly told him Arnau's story, confident it would not leave those four walls.

'Because there are many people who will not have any dealings with Grau Puig. I haven't done so for some time now. And there are many more like me. He's a man obsessed with being somewhere he was not born to be. While he was an artisan, you could trust him, but now . . . now he is aiming for something else. He did not really know what he was doing when he married a noblewoman.' Hasdai shook his head. 'To be a noble you have to have been born one, you have to have imbibed it with your mother's milk. I'm not saying that's a good thing, or trying to defend it, but that's the way the nobility survives and succeeds in overcoming the difficulties of their position. Besides, if a Catalan baron is ruined, who would dare challenge him? They are proud, arrogant even, born to give orders and to feel they are superior to everyone else, even when they are ruined. But Grau Puig has only managed to be a noble through his money. He spent a fortune on his daughter Margarida's dowry, and that has almost bankrupted him. All Barcelona is aware of it! People laugh at him behind his back, and his wife knows it! What is a simple artisan doing living in a palace on Carrer de Montcada? The more people laugh at him, the more he has to prove himself by spending more. What would Grau Puig be without money?'

'You mean to say that . . .?'

'I don't mean to say anything, but I won't have any dealings with him. In that sense, if for a different reason, your master is quite right.'

From then on, Guillem paid particular attention to any conversation where Grau Puig's name came up. At the exchange, the Consulate of the Sea, in business deals, when goods were being bought or sold, or during general conversations about the trade situation, the baron's name featured far too often.

'His son, Genís Puig . . .' he said to Arnau one day after coming back from the exchange as they stood gazing at the sea, which seemed calmer and gentler than ever. When he heard the name, Arnau turned sharply to his companion. 'Genís Puig has had to ask for a loan on easy terms in order to follow the King to Mallorca.' Were Arnau's eyes shining? Guillem looked at him steadily. He had not said anything, but wasn't that a gleam in his eye? 'Do you want to know more?'

Arnau still said nothing, but eventually nodded. His eyes had narrowed, and his lips were drawn in a tight line. He nodded again as he heard the details from Guillem.

'Do I have your authority to take all the decisions I consider necessary?' asked the Moor.

'I don't give you the authority, I beg you to do it, Guillem.'

Discreetly, Guillem began to use his knowledge and all the contacts he had acquired over years of doing business in Barcelona. The fact that the son, Don Genís, had been forced to take up one of the special loans reserved for the nobility meant that his father could no longer meet the costs of going to war. Those soft loans, thought Guillem, still meant a high rate of interest had to be paid: they were the only ones where Christians could lend money with interest. Why would a father accept that his son paid interest unless he himself did not have the capital? And what about Isabel? That harpy who had destroyed Arnau's father and Arnau himself, who had forced Arnau to crawl on his knees to kiss her feet, how could she accept something like that?

Over the next few months, Guillem cast his nets wide. He talked to friends, to anyone who owed him favours, and sent messages to all his agents: what kind of situation was Grau Puig, the Catalan baron and merchant, really in? What did they know about him, his business affairs, his finances . . . his solvency?

As the seagoing season was coming to an end, and ships were heading back to the port of Barcelona, Guillem started to receive replies to his enquiries. Invaluable information! One night, after they had closed the counting house, Guillem remained seated at the table.

'I have things to do,' he told Arnau.

'What things?'

'I'll tell you tomorrow.'

The next morning as the two men sat at the counting table before breakfast, the Moor said to Arnau: 'Grau Puig is in desperate straits.' Was that another gleam in Arnau's eye? 'All the moneychangers and merchants I've talked to are agreed: his fortune has been swallowed up.'

'Perhaps it's only malicious gossip,' Arnau said, interrupting him.

'Wait, look at this.' Guillem handed him his agents' letters. 'Here's the proof. Grau Puig is in the hands of the Lombards.'

Arnau thought about what that meant: the Lombards were moneychangers and merchants, agents of the big banking concerns in Florence or Pisa. They were a tight-knit group who always looked after their own interests; their members dealt with each other or with their head-quarters. They had a monopoly on the trade in luxury cloths: woollen fleeces, silks, brocades, Florence taffeta, Pisan veils, and many other goods. The Lombards helped no one, and only allowed others to have a part of their trade so as not to be expelled from Catalonia. It was never a good idea to be in their hands. Arnau glanced at the letters, then dropped them on the table.

'What are you suggesting?'

'What do you want?'

'You know what I want: his ruin!'

'They say that Grau Puig is an old man now, and it is his wife and children who run his business affairs. Just imagine! His finances are precarious: if any venture failed, everything would come crashing down, and he would not be able to pay his debts. He would lose everything.'

'Buy up their debts.' Arnau spoke coldly, without moving a muscle. 'Do it discreetly. I want to be their chief creditor, but I don't want anyone to know. Make sure one of his ventures does fail . . . No, not one,' he said, correcting himself, 'all of them!' He thumped the table so hard even the heavy ledgers shook. 'As many as you can,' he added more calmly. 'I don't want them to escape me.'

20 September 1355
The port of Barcelona

At the head of his fleet, King Pedro III returned victorious to Barcelona after conquering Sardinia. The whole of the city rushed down to the beach to receive him. As everyone cheered, the King disembarked on a special wooden bridge built in front of Framenors convent. His retinue of nobles and soldiers also came ashore to a Barcelona willing and ready to celebrate his victory over the Sardinians.

Arnau and Guillem shut the counting house and went down to the beach along with all the others. Later Mar joined them to help celebrate in honour of the King: they sang and danced, listened to troubadours, ate sweetmeats and then, as the sun was setting and the September night air began to grow cool, they returned home.

'Donaha!' shouted Mar as soon as Arnau opened the front door.

Bubbling with excitement from the celebrations, the girl ran into the house, still shouting for Donaha. But when she reached the kitchen doorway, she suddenly came to a halt. Arnau and Guillem looked at each other. What was going on? Had something happened to Donaha?

They ran to Mar's side.

'What is—?' Arnau started to ask.

'Arnau, I don't think all this yelling is the proper way to receive someone you haven't seen in such a long time,' said a male voice that sounded familiar to him.

Arnau had been pushing Mar out of the way, but stood rooted to the spot when he heard these words.

'Joan!' he cried after a few moments' pause.

Mar watched as he went into the kitchen, arms opened wide, to greet the figure in black who had so frightened her. Guillem put his arm round her.

'It's his brother,' he whispered in her ear.

Donaha was crouched in a corner of the kitchen, trying to hide.

'My God!' exclaimed Arnau, clasping Joan round the waist. 'My God!' he went on repeating, as he lifted him clean into the air not once but several times.

Smiling broadly, Joan managed to struggle free from his grasp. 'You'll snap me in two!'

But Arnau was not listening to him. 'Why didn't you tell me?' he asked, this time seizing him by the shoulders. 'Let me look at you! You've changed!'

'It's been thirteen years,' Joan tried to say, but Arnau would not listen.

'How long have you been in Barcelona?'

'I came—'

'Why didn't you tell me?' With each question, Arnau shook his brother's shoulders. 'Are you here to stay this time? Tell me you are!'

Guillem and Mar could not help smiling. The friar saw them: 'That's enough,' he said, pushing Arnau away. 'Enough. You'll squeeze me to death.'

Arnau stood back to survey him. Only the bright, lively eyes reminded him of the Joan who had left Barcelona. Now he was almost bald, thin, and hollow-cheeked . . . and the black habit hanging from his shoulders only made him look worse. Joan was two years younger than him, but he looked much older.

'Haven't you been eating? If the money I sent wasn't enough—'

'No,' Joan butted in, 'it was more than enough. Your money served to nourish . . . my spirit. Books are very expensive, Arnau.'

'You should have asked for more.'

Joan waved away the suggestion, then sat down at the table opposite Guillem and Mar.

'Aren't you going to present me to your god-daughter? I see she's grown a lot since your last letter.'

Arnau signalled to Mar and she came round the table to stand in front of Joan. Abashed by the stern look in the friar's eyes, she kept her own on the floor. When he had finished his examination of her, Arnau presented Guillem.

'This is Guillem,' he said. 'I've talked a lot about him in my letters.'

'Yes.' Joan made no effort to shake him by the hand, and Guillem was forced to withdraw his own outstretched arm. 'Do you fulfil your Christian obligations?' he asked coldly.

'Yes . . .'

'Yes, Brother Joan,' Joan corrected him.

'Brother Joan,' Guillem repeated.

'And over there is Donaha,' Arnau said quickly.

Joan nodded without so much as glancing in her direction.

'Good,' he said, turning to Mar and indicating with his eyes that she could sit down. 'You're Ramon's daughter, aren't you? Your father was a good man, a hard-working Christian who feared his Lord, like all *bastaixos*.' He looked at Arnau. 'I've prayed a lot for him since Arnau told me of his death. How old are you, my child?'

Arnau ordered Donaha to serve their supper, then sat at the table. He realized that Guillem was still standing some way away, as though he did not dare sit down with the newcomer. 'Come and sit, Guillem,' he said. 'This is your home too.'

Joan said nothing.

Nobody spoke during supper. Mar was unusually quiet, as if the presence of the friar had robbed her of all spontaneity. For his part, Joan ate frugally.

'Tell me, Joan,' Arnau said when they had finished eating, 'what are you doing here? When did you come back?'

'I took advantage of the King's return. I boarded a ship to Sardinia when I learnt of his victory there, and came from the island to Barcelona.'

'Have you seen the King?'

'He hasn't received me yet.'

Mar asked permission to leave the table. Guillem did the same. They both said goodnight to Brother Joan. After that, the two brothers talked until dawn; with the aid of a bottle of sweet wine, they made up for thirteen years apart.

37

To the relief of everyone in Arnau's family, Joan decided to move to Santa Caterina convent.

'That is the proper place for me,' he told his brother, 'but I'll come and visit you every day.'

Arnau, who had noticed how uncomfortable his goddaughter and Guillem had been during supper the previous evening, did not insist more than was strictly necessary.

'Do you know what he said to me?' he whispered to Guillem when they were getting up from their meal at mid-day. The Moor bent closer. 'He asked what we have done to see that Mar is married.'

Without straightening up, Guillem looked across at the girl, who was helping Donaha clear the table. Find a husband for her? Why, she was only . . . a woman! Guillem turned to Arnau. Neither of them had ever looked at her as they did now.

'What has become of our little girl?' Arnau whispered.

The two men gazed at her again: she was lively, beautiful, serene and self-assured.

As she picked up the food bowls, Mar looked back at them.

Her body was already that of a woman: it was curved and shapely, and her breasts were beginning to show underneath her smock. She was fourteen.

Mar glanced at them again, and saw them staring open-mouthed at her. This time instead of smiling she looked embarrassed, if only momentarily.

'What are you two staring at?' she bridled. 'Don't you have anything better to do?' she added, standing in front of them defiantly.

They both nodded as one. There was no doubt about it: she had turned into a woman without them even noticing it.

When they were safely in the counting house, Arnau said: 'She'll have a princess's dowry. Money, clothes, a house . . . no, a palace!' At this, he turned towards his companion. 'What has happened about the Puig family?'

'That means she'll leave us,' said Guillem, as if he had not heard Arnau's question.

The two men sat for a while in silence.

'She'll give us grandchildren,' Arnau said eventually.

'Don't fool yourself. She'll give her husband children. Besides, if we slaves cannot have children, we have even less right to grandchildren.'

'How often have I offered to free you?'

'What would I do with freedom? I'm fine as I am. But Mar . . . a married woman! I don't know why, but I'm already beginning to hate her husband, whoever he may be.'

'Me too,' Arnau admitted.

They turned towards each other, and both of them burst out laughing.

'But you didn't answer my question,' said Arnau once they had recovered their composure. 'What's happened with the Puig family? I want that palace for Mar.'

'I sent instructions to Filippo Tescio in Pisa. If anyone can achieve what you are after, he's the one.'

'What did you tell him?'

'That he was to pay pirates if necessary, but that the Puigs' commissions were not to reach Barcelona, and those that had left the port should not arrive at their destinations. That he should steal the goods or set fire to them if need be, but that none of them should arrive.'

'Did he reply?'

'Filippo? No, he would never do that. He won't put anything in writing or entrust the affair to anyone else. If it got out . . . We have to wait for the end of the seagoing season. That will be in less than a month. If the Puig family's commissions have not returned by then, they won't be able to pay their debts. They'll be ruined.'

'Have you bought up their credit notes?'

'You are Grau Puig's main creditor.'

'They must be suffering by now,' Arnau muttered to himself.

'Haven't you seen them?' Arnau turned sharply to him. 'They're down at the beach all the time. Before it was the baroness and one of her stepchildren; now that Genís is back from Sardinia, he has joined them. They spend hours scanning the horizon in search of a mast . . . and when a ship appears and comes into port but isn't one of theirs, the baroness curses the waves. I thought you knew . . .'

'No, I didn't know.' Arnau said nothing for a few moments. 'Tell me when one of our ships is due in port.'

'Several ships are coming in together,' Guillem told him one morning as they were walking back from the Consulate of the Sea.

'Are the Puig family there?'

'Of course. The baroness is so close to the water the waves are licking her shoes . . .' Guillem fell silent. 'I'm sorry, I didn't mean to . . .'

Arnau smiled. 'Don't worry,' he said, reassuring him.

Then he went up to his bedroom, where he slowly put on his finest clothes, the ones Guillem had finally convinced him he should buy.

'A man in your position cannot appear badly dressed at the exchange or the consulate,' he had argued. 'That is what the King decrees, and so do your saints; Saint Vincent, for example . . .'

Arnau made him be quiet, but listened to his advice. Now he donned a white sleeveless shirt made of the finest Malines cloth, which was trimmed with fur, a red silk damascene doublet that came down to his knees, black hose and black silk shoes. He fastened the doublet round his waist with a wide belt that had gold threads and was studded with pearls. Arnau completed his attire with a marvellous black cloak that Guillem had discovered in one of their ships' expeditions beyond Dacia. It was lined with ermine and embroidered with gold and precious stones.

When he stepped into the counting house, Guillem nodded his approval. Mar was about to say something, but changed her mind. She watched as Arnau went out of the door: she ran to it and from the street outside saw him walk down to the beach, his cloak rippling in the sea breeze, and the precious stones sparkling all round him.

'Where's Arnau going?' she asked Guillem, coming back into the counting house and sitting opposite him in one of the clients' chairs.

'To collect a debt.'

'It must be a very important one.'

'It is, Mar,' said Guillem, pursing his lips, 'but this is only the first instalment.'

Mar began to play with the ivory abacus. How often, hidden in the kitchen, had she watched as Arnau worked on it? His face was always serious, and he concentrated hard while he moved the counters and noted down figures in his books. Mar shivered the length of her spine.

'Is something wrong?' asked Guillem.

'No . . . no.'

Why not tell him? Guillem would understand, she said to herself. Except for Donaha, who could not help but smile whenever she saw Mar hiding in the kitchen to spy on Arnau, nobody else was aware of it. All the girls who met in the merchant Escales' house talked about the same thing. Some of them were already betrothed, and liked nothing better than to praise the virtues of their husbands-to-be. Mar listened to them, but always avoided their questions to her. How could she mention Arnau? What if he found out? Arnau was thirty-four; she was only fourteen. But one of the girls was betrothed to someone even older than Arnau! She would have loved to be able to tell someone. Her friends could chatter about money, appearance, attractiveness, manliness or generosity, but she knew that Arnau was better than any of them! Did not the *bastaixos* Mar occasionally met on the beach tell her that Arnau had been one of King Pedro's bravest soldiers? Mar had discovered his old weapons in the bottom of a chest. When she was all alone she would pick them up and caress them, imagining Arnau surrounded by enemies and fighting them off valiantly as the *bastaixos* had told her he did.

Guillem studied the young girl. Mar sat there, the tip of her finger on one of the abacus counters, staring into space. Money? Bags and bags of it. Everyone in Barcelona knew that. And as for his kindness . . .

'Are you sure nothing's wrong?' Guillem asked again, startling her out of her daydream.

Mar blushed. Donaha always claimed that anybody could read her thoughts, that the name of Arnau was on her lips, her eyes, her whole face. What if Guillem knew this too?

'No . . .' she repeated, 'nothing.'

Guillem replaced the abacus counters and Mar smiled

at him . . . with a sad expression? What could be going through her mind? Perhaps Brother Joan was right; she was already of marriageable age, and here she was, shut up in a house with two men . . .

Mar took her finger off the abacus. 'Guillem.'

'Tell me.'

She fell silent.

'Oh, it's nothing,' she said finally, getting up from her chair.

Guillem watched her as she left the room; it was hard to admit it, but the friar was probably right.

He went up to them. He had walked to the shore while the ships, three galleys and a carrack, had entered the port. The carrack belonged to him. Isabel was dressed in black, and held on to her hat with one hand. Her stepsons Josep and Genís were standing beside her, with their backs to him. All three were peering desperately at the ships. They won't bring you any relief, thought Arnau.

As he strode by in his best clothes, *bastaixos*, boatmen and merchants all fell silent.

Look at me, you harpy! Arnau waited, a few steps from the water's edge. *Look at me! The last time you did . . .* The baroness turned slowly towards him; her sons did the same. Arnau took a deep breath. *The last time you did, my father was hanging above my head.*

The *bastaixos* and boatmen were muttering to each other.

'Is there something you need, Arnau?' asked one of the aldermen.

Arnau shook his head, not taking his eyes off Isabel's face for a moment. The others moved away, and Arnau found himself next to the baroness and his cousins.

He breathed deeply once more. Defiantly, his gaze locked with Isabel's for a few more seconds, then he glanced at his cousins and finally looked out to sea, smiling.

The baroness's lips tightened. She too turned towards the sea, following Arnau's gaze. When she looked towards him again, he was already striding away, the sunlight glinting off the precious stones on his cloak.

Joan was still intent on seeing Mar married. He proposed several candidates: it was not difficult to find them. As soon as they heard the size of Mar's dowry, nobles and merchants came running, but . . . how was the girl herself to be told? Joan offered to do it, but when Arnau told Guillem as much, the Moor was resolutely against the idea.

'You have to do it,' he said. 'Not a monk she hardly knows.'

Ever since Guillem had insisted thus, Arnau found he could not take his eyes off the girl. Did he know her? They had lived in the same house for years now, but it had been Guillem who always looked after her. All he had done had been to enjoy her being there, to hear her laughter and cheery banter. He had never talked to her about anything serious. Now, whenever he considered approaching her and asking her to go for a walk with him, on the beach, or – why not? – to Santa Maria, whenever he thought of telling her they had to discuss a serious matter, he realized he knew little about her . . . and hesitated. Where was the little girl he used to carry on his shoulders?

'I don't want to marry any of them,' she told them. Arnau and Guillem looked at each other. Eventually, Arnau had persuaded the Moor they should bring the subject up together.

'You have to help me,' Arnau had pleaded with him.

Mar's eyes lit up when the two men mentioned marriage to her. They were sitting behind their accounting table, with her in front of them on the other side, as if this were another commercial transaction. But she shook her head at the mention of each of the five candidates that Brother Joan had suggested.

'But, Mar,' Guillem insisted, 'you have to choose someone. Any girl would be proud to marry one of the names we have mentioned.'

Mar shook her head again. 'I don't like them.'

'Well, you have to do something,' said Guillem, looking to Arnau for support.

Arnau studied the young girl. She was on the verge of tears. Her head was lowered, but he could tell from her trembling bottom lip and troubled breathing that tears were not far away. Why would a girl react in that way when they had just proposed such good matches for her? The silence lasted an eternity. Eventually, Mar raised her eyes slightly and peered at Arnau. Why make her suffer?

'We'll go on looking until we find someone she does like,' he said to Guillem. 'Do you agree, Mar?'

She nodded, got up from the chair and left the room. The two men sat staring at each other.

Arnau sighed. 'And I thought the difficult part was going to be telling her!'

Guillem said nothing. He was still gazing at the kitchen doorway through which Mar had disappeared. What was going on? What was his little girl trying to hide? When she had heard the word 'marriage' she smiled, and her eyes had lit up, but then afterwards . . .

'Just wait until you see how Joan reacts when he hears,' Arnau grumbled.

Guillem turned to him, but did not reply for a moment. What did it matter what the friar thought?

'You're right. We'd best go on looking.'

Arnau turned towards Joan. 'Please,' he said, 'this isn't the moment.'

They had gone into Santa Maria to calm down. The news was not good, but here, with his Virgin, the constant sounds of the stonemasons and the smiles of all the workmen, Arnau felt at ease. Joan, though, had found him and would not let him be: it was Mar here, Mar there, Mar everywhere. After all, what business was it of his?

'What reasons can she have against marriage?' Joan insisted.

'This isn't the moment, Joan,' Arnau said again.

'Why not?'

'Because we are facing another war.' The friar looked startled. 'Didn't you know? King Pedro the Cruel of Castile has just declared war on us.'

'Why?'

Arnau shook his head. 'Because he's been wanting to do so for some time now,' he growled, raising his arms. 'The excuse was that our admiral, Francesc de Perellós, captured two Genoese boats carrying olive oil off the coast of Sanlúcar. The Castilian King demanded they be released, and when our admiral paid no attention, he declared war on us. That man is dangerous,' muttered Arnau. 'I understand that he has earned his nickname: he is spiteful and vengeful. Do you realize what this means, Joan? We are at war with Genoa and Castile at the same time. Does it seem like a good moment to be bothering ourselves with getting the girl married?'

Joan hesitated. They were standing beneath the keystone for the nave's third arch, surrounded by scaffolding erected for the construction of the ribs.

'Do you remember?' asked Arnau, pointing up at the keystone. Joan looked up and nodded. They had been children when the first stone had been put in place! Arnau waited a moment and then added: 'Catalonia is not going to be able to finance this. We're still paying for the campaign against Sardinia, and now we have to fight on another front.'

'I thought you merchants were in favour of conquest.'

'We wouldn't open any new trade routes in Castile. No, it's a difficult situation, Joan. Guillem was right.' At the mention of the Moor's name, Joan looked askance. 'We have only just conquered Sardinia and the Corsicans have risen against us: they did so as soon as the King left the island. We are at war with two powers, and the King's coffers are empty; even the city councillors seem to have gone mad!'

They began to walk towards the high altar.

'What do you mean?'

'I mean that there is no money available in Barcelona. The King is pressing ahead with his building schemes: the royal dockyards and the new city wall—'

'But both of them are needed,' said Joan, interrupting him.

'The dockyards, possibly, but after the plague there is no need for the wall.'

'Well then?'

'Well, the King is still exhausting his reserves. He has obliged all the surrounding villages to contribute to the new wall, because he says one day they will take refuge inside it. He has also created a new tax for it: the fortieth part of all inheritances is to be set aside for its construction. As for the dockyards – all the fines that the consulates collect are poured into building them. And now here we are with another war.'

'Barcelona is rich.'

'Not any longer, Joan, that's the problem. The more money the city gave him, the more privileges the King has granted it. As a consequence, the councillors have taken on so much they cannot finance everything. They've increased the taxes on meat and wine. Did you know that part of the city's budget went to keeping those prices down?' Joan shook his head. 'It used to be half of the city's budget. Instead of that, now they've brought in new taxes. The city's debts will bring ruin to us all, Joan, you mark my words.'

The two men stood lost in thought in front of the high altar. When they finally left the church, Joan returned to the attack.

'What about Mar?'

'She will do whatever she wants, Joan.'

'But—'

'No buts about it. That is my decision.'

'Knock,' Arnau said to him.

Guillem pounded on the heavy door with the door-knocker. The sound echoed along the deserted street. Nobody came to open.

'Knock again.'

Guillem knocked again, not once but seven, eight times. At the ninth, the peephole opened.

'What's the matter?' the eyes on the other side of the door asked. 'What's all this fuss? Who are you?'

Clinging to Arnau's arm, Mar could feel him grow tense.

'Open up!' Arnau commanded.

'In whose name?'

'Arnau Estanyol,' Guillem said solemnly, 'owner of this building and of everything there is in it, including your-self if you are a slave.'

Arnau Estanyol, owner of this building . . . Guillem's words resounded in Arnau's ears. How long had it been? Twenty years? Twenty-two? Behind the spyhole, the eyes hesitated.

'Open up!' Guillem insisted.

Arnau looked up at the heavens. He was thinking of his father.

'What . . .?' the girl began to ask.

'Nothing, nothing,' Arnau said with a smile, just as one

462

of the doors that allowed people on foot into the palace opened in the huge double gate.

Guillem stood back to let Arnau past.

'Both gates, Guillem. I want them to open both gates wide.'

Guillem went inside, and Arnau and Mar could hear him giving orders.

Can you see me, Father? Do you remember? This was where they gave you that bag of money that led to your downfall. What else could you have done? Arnau recalled the rising in Plaça del Blat; people shouting, his father one of them, all of them pleading to be given grain! Arnau could feel a lump rise in his throat.

The gates opened and Arnau went in.

Several slaves were standing in the courtyard. On the right was the staircase up to the principal rooms. Arnau did not look up at them, but Mar had no hesitation, and could see shadows moving behind the windows. The stables were in front of them: the grooms were lined up outside. My God! Arnau's whole body shook. He leant on Mar, and she glanced at him.

'Here you are,' said Guillem to Arnau, handing him a rolled-up parchment.

Arnau did not take it. He knew what was in it. Since Guillem had shown it to him the previous day he had learnt its contents by heart. It was an inventory of all Grau Puig's possessions that the magistrate had awarded him in payment of his debts: the palace, the slaves – Arnau looked in vain for the name of Estranya on the list – together with several properties outside Barcelona, among which was a small house in Navarcles in which he decided to allow the Puig family to live. Some jewels, two pairs of horses with all their harnesses, a carriage, suits and other clothing, pots, pans and crockery, carpets and furniture: everything in the palace was detailed on this rolled-up parchment that

Arnau had read time and again the previous evening.

He glanced once more at the door to the stables, then surveyed all the cobbled courtyard . . . until his eyes alighted on the foot of the staircase.

'Shall we go up?' asked Guillem.

'Yes. Take me to your mas— to Grau Puig,' Arnau corrected himself.

The slave led them upstairs. Mar and Guillem looked all around them; Arnau stared straight ahead. The slave led them to the main chamber.

'Announce me,' Arnau said to Guillem before the doors were opened.

'Arnau Estanyol!' his friend cried out, flinging them open.

Arnau did not remember what this main chamber was like. As a young boy he had not even looked when he had crossed it . . . on his knees. Nor did he pay much attention this time. Isabel was seated in a chair next to one of the windows. Josep and Genís were standing on either side of her. The former, like his sister Margarida, was married now. Genís was still unmarried. Arnau looked for Josep's family, but could not see them. In another chair sat Grau Puig, a drooling old man.

Isabel confronted him, eyes blazing.

Arnau stood in the middle of the room, next to a hard-wood dining table that was twice as long as the one in his counting house. Mar and Guillem were both behind him. The family slaves had clustered in the doorway.

Arnau spoke in a voice loud enough for everyone in the room to hear. 'Guillem, those shoes are mine,' he said, pointing to Isabel's feet. 'Get her to take them off.'

'Yes, master.'

Mar was taken aback, and turned towards the Moor. Master? She knew Guillem was a slave, but had never before heard him speak to Arnau in this way.

Guillem signalled to two of the slaves standing in the

doorway, and the three of them walked over to Isabel. The baroness still sat there haughtily, challenging Arnau with her gaze.

One of the slaves knelt down, but before he could touch her, Isabel took off her own shoes and let them fall to the floor. She stared straight at Arnau.

'I want you to gather up all the shoes in the house and burn them out in the yard,' said Arnau.

'Yes, master,' said Guillem once more.

The baroness was still glaring at him defiantly.

'Those chairs,' said Arnau, pointing to the ones she and Grau Puig were sitting in. 'Take them out of here.'

'Yes, master.'

Grau's children lifted him out of his chair. The baroness stood up before the slaves could take the chair from under her and stack it with the others in a corner of the chamber.

But she was still defying him.

'That robe is mine too.'

Did he see her tremble?

'You don't mean to say . . .?' spluttered Genís Puig, still carrying his father.

'That robe is mine,' Arnau insisted, staring straight at Isabel.

Was she trembling?

'Mother,' said Josep, 'go and change.'

Yes, she was trembling.

'Guillem,' shouted Arnau.

'Mother, please.'

Guillem went up to the baroness.

She was trembling!

'Mother!'

'What do you want me to put on?' howled Isabel to her stepson. Then she turned again to face Arnau. Her whole body shook. Do you really want me to take my robe off? her eyes asked him.

Arnau frowned sternly and slowly, very slowly, Isabel lowered her gaze to the floor. She was sobbing with rage.

Arnau waved to Guillem to leave her. For a few moments, the only sound in the main chamber of the palace was of her sobbing.

'By tonight,' Arnau said at length to Guillem, 'I want this building empty. Tell them they may go back to Navarcles, which they should never have left.' Josep and Genís stared at him; Isabel was still weeping. 'I'm not interested in those lands. Give them some of the slaves' clothes, but no footwear. Burn it all. Sell everything else and close this house up.'

Arnau turned round and saw Mar, her face flushed. He had forgotten all about her. He took her by the arm and they walked out of the room.

'You can close the gates now,' he told the old man who had let them into the palace.

The two of them walked in silence to his counting house, but before they went in, Arnau came to a halt. 'Shall we go for a walk on the beach?'

Mar nodded.

'Has your debt been repaid now?' she asked him when they could see the sea in front of them.

They walked on a few steps.

'It never will be, Mar,' she heard him murmur. 'Never.'

38

Arnau was working in the counting house. The seagoing season was at its height. Business was thriving, and Arnau had become one of the richest men in all Barcelona. Even so, he still lived in the small house on the corner of Canvis Vells and Canvis Nous, together with Guillem, Mar and Donaha. Arnau would not heed Guillem's advice and move to the Puig family palace, which had been shut for four years. Mar was proving to be quite as stubborn as Arnau, and had still not agreed to be married.

'Why do you want to push me away from you?' she said to him one day, her eyes bathed in tears.

'I . . .' Arnau stammered, 'I don't want to push you away from me!'

She went on weeping, and leant against his shoulder.

'Don't worry,' Arnau reassured her, stroking her head. 'I'll never force you to do anything you don't want to.'

So Mar went on living with them.

But on the morning of 9 June, a church bell suddenly began to ring. Arnau stopped what he was doing. A moment later, another bell began to sound, and soon afterwards many more joined in.

'*Via fora,*' Arnau said to himself.

He went out into the street. At Santa Maria, the workmen were quickly swarming down the scaffolding; masons and labourers emerged from the main doorway. In the streets all around, people were running and shouting, '*Via fora!*'

Arnau met Guillem, who was walking quickly towards the house, a worried look on his face. 'War!' he shouted.

'They're calling out the *host,*' said Arnau.

'No . . . no.' Guillem stopped to get his breath back. 'It's not the city *host*. It's Barcelona and all the towns and villages for two leagues around.'

That meant the *hosts* from Sant Boi and Badalona. From Sant Andreu and Sarrià; from Provençana, Sant Feliu, Sant Genís, Cornellà, Sant Just Desvern, Sant Joan Despí, Sants, Santa Coloma, Esplugues, Vallvidrera, Sant Martí, Sant Adrià, Sant Gervasi, Sant Joan d'Horta . . . the ringing of bells could be heard all round the city.

'The King has invoked the *usatge princeps namque,*' explained Guillem. 'It's not the city going to war, it's the King! We're at war! We're being attacked. King Pedro of Castile has launched an attack—'

'He's attacking Barcelona?'

'Yes. Barcelona.'

The two men ran into their house.

Shortly afterwards, they came out again. Arnau was carrying the weapons he had used when he served under Eiximèn d'Esparça. They ran down Carrer de la Mar towards Plaça del Blat, but soon realized that the crowd shouting '*Via fora*' was headed in the opposite direction.

'What's going on?' Arnau asked one of the men, grabbing him by the arm as he sped past.

'To the beach!' the man shouted, struggling free of him. 'Down to the beach!'

'An attack from the sea?' Arnau and Guillem asked themselves, then joined the hundreds of others running down to the shore.

By the time they arrived, it seemed as though the whole of Barcelona was there, gazing out at the horizon and waving their crossbows in the air. The bells were still ringing in their ears. The shouts of '*Via fora*' gradually subsided, and everyone stood quietly on the sand.

Guillem raised a hand to his eyes to protect them from the fierce June sun, and began to count the ships he could see: one, two, three, four . . .

The sea was dead calm.

'They'll destroy us,' Arnau heard someone say behind him.

'They'll lay waste to Barcelona.'

'What can we do against an army?'

Twenty-seven, twenty-eight . . . Guillem was still counting.

'They'll destroy us,' Arnau said to himself. How often had he discussed this with other merchants and traders? Barcelona was defenceless from the sea. From Santa Clara to Framenors, it was open to the Mediterranean. There were no defences at all! If a fleet sailed into its port . . .

'Thirty-nine, forty. Forty ships!' exclaimed Guillem.

Thirty galleys and ten men-o'-war. Pedro the Cruel's fleet. Forty ships filled with battle-hardened men, up against ordinary citizens suddenly forced to become soldiers. If the ships landed, there would be fighting on the beach and the streets of the city. Arnau shuddered as he thought of all the women and children . . . of Mar. Barcelona would be defeated. Then the city would be pillaged, the women raped. Mar! As he thought of what might happen to her, he leant on Guillem for support. She was young and beautiful. He imagined her being overpowered by Castilian soldiers, screaming, crying for help . . . Where would he be then?

More and more people crowded on to the beach. The King himself appeared, and began to give his men orders.

'The King!' the shout went up.

What could he do? Arnau thought desperately.

The King had been in Barcelona for three months, organizing a fleet to sail and defend Mallorca, which Pedro the Cruel had threatened to attack. But there were only ten of the King's galleys in port – the rest of the fleet had yet to arrive. And it was in the port that they would do battle!

Arnau shook his head as he surveyed the sails coming closer and closer to the coast. The King of Castile had fooled them. Ever since the war had started three years earlier, there had been a succession of battles and truces. First, Pedro the Cruel had attacked the kingdom of Valencia, and then that of Aragon, where he took the city of Tarazona and directly threatened Zaragoza. At that point, the Church had become involved, and Tarazona was handed over to Cardinal Pedro de la Jugie. It was for him to decide to which of the two Kings the city was to belong. A year-long truce was also signed, although this did not include the frontier regions of the kingdoms of Murcia and Valencia.

During this truce, Pedro the Ceremonious succeeded in persuading his half-brother Ferrán, who had been allied to Castile, to change sides and attack Murcia. He did so, and reached as far as Cartagena in the south.

Now King Pedro was on the beach, taking command. He ordered the ten galleys to be made ready, and that the citizens of Barcelona and surrounding towns, who were beginning to arrive at the shore, should embark together with the small number of soldiers he had with him. Every vessel, big or small, merchant or fishing, was to head out to repel the Castilian fleet.

'This is madness,' complained Guillem when he saw

everyone scrambling on board the boats. 'Any one of those galleys can ram our vessels and split them in two. Huge numbers of people will be killed.'

It would still take some time before the Castilian fleet reached the harbour.

'They will show no mercy,' Arnau heard someone say. 'They'll massacre us.'

Pedro the Cruel was not someone to show mercy. Everyone was aware of his fearsome reputation: he had executed his bastard brothers, Federico in Seville and Juan in Bilbao. A year later, after holding her prisoner all that time, he had beheaded his aunt Eleonor. What mercy could they expect from someone who did not shrink from killing his own family? The Catalan King had not put Jaime of Mallorca to death despite his constant betrayals and all the wars they had fought.

'It would make more sense to try to defend ourselves on land,' Guillem shouted in Arnau's ear. 'We'll never do it at sea. As soon as the Castilians get beyond the *tasques*, they will over-run us.'

Arnau agreed. Why was the King so determined to defend the city at sea? Guillem was surely right, once the enemy had got beyond the *tasques* . . .

'The *tasques*!' Arnau shouted. 'What boat do we have in the harbour?'

'What do you mean?'

'The *tasques*, Guillem! Don't you understand? What ship do we have?'

'That whaler over there,' said Guillem, pointing to a huge, pot-bellied boat.

'Come on. We've no time to lose.'

Arnau started running towards the sea, in among the crowd of other people doing the same. He looked behind to encourage Guillem to follow him.

The shoreline was buzzing with soldiers and citizens of Barcelona, wading into the sea up to their waists.

Some of them were trying to clamber on board the small fishing-boats that were already heading out to sea; others were waiting for boatmen to come and pick them up and take them to one or other of the bigger men-o'-war or merchant vessels anchored further out.

Arnau saw a boat approaching the shore. 'Come on!' he shouted to Guillem and plunged into the water, trying to make sure he reached the boat before all the others around them. By the time they got there, it was already full, but the boatman recognized Arnau and made room for him and Guillem.

'Take me out to the whaling ship over there,' Arnau shouted when the man was about to set sail.

'First to the galleys. That's the King's order—'

'Take me to my ship!' Arnau insisted. The boatman looked at him doubtfully, and the others in the boat started to protest. 'Silence!' shouted Arnau. 'You all know me. I have to reach my ship. Barcelona . . . your family depends on it. All your families might depend on it.'

The boatman gazed out at the big, lumbering ship. It was only a little out of his way. Why would Arnau Estanyol not be telling the truth?

'Head for the whaler!' he ordered his two oarsmen.

As soon as Arnau and Guillem had grasped the rope ladders thrown to them by the ship's captain, the boatman headed off for the nearest galley.

'Get all your men rowing!' Arnau ordered the captain before his feet had even touched deck.

The captain gave the order to the oarsmen, who immediately took their places on the rowing benches.

'Where are we headed?' he asked.

'To the *tasques*,' Arnau told him.

Guillem nodded. 'May Allah, whose name be praised, grant you success.'

But if Guillem understood what Arnau was trying to do, the same could not be said of the King's army and the citizens of Barcelona. When they saw his ship begin to move off with no soldiers or weapons on board, one of them shouted: 'He wants to save his ship!'

'Jew!' another man cried.

'Traitor!'

Many others joined in the insults. Soon, the entire beach was filled with angry cries against Arnau. What was Arnau Estanyol up to? *bastaixos* and boatmen wondered as they watched the heavy ship slowly gather speed when a hundred pairs of oars dipped rhythmically into the water.

Arnau and Guillem stood at the ship's prow, staring at the Castilian fleet that was drawing dangerously close. As they passed the rest of the Catalan fleet, they had to protect themselves from a hail of arrows, but as soon as they were out of range they went to the prow once more.

'This has to work,' Arnau told Guillem. 'Barcelona must not fall into the hands of that traitor.'

The *tasques* were a chain of sandbanks parallel to the coast. They were Barcelona's only natural defence, although they also represented a danger for any boat wishing to enter the city harbour. There was only one channel that was deep enough to allow large ships in; anywhere else could mean they ran aground on the sands.

Arnau and Guillem drew ever nearer to the *tasques*, no longer having to hear the obscene insults of thousands of voices on the beach. Their shouting had even managed to drown out the noise of the bells.

'It will work,' Arnau repeated, this time under his breath. Then he told the captain to have the oarsmen stop rowing. As the hundred pairs of oars were raised out of the water and the ship started to glide towards the *tasques*, the shouts from the beach gradually died away until there was complete silence. The Castilian fleet was drawing closer. Above the sound of the distant

473

bells, Arnau could hear the ship's keel scraping over sand.

'It has to work!' he muttered.

Guillem seized him by the arm and squeezed it tightly. It was the first time he had ever reacted like this.

The whaler glided slowly on and on. Arnau glanced at the captain. Are we in the channel? he asked merely by raising his eyebrows. The captain nodded: ever since Arnau had told him to stop rowing, he had realized what he was trying to do.

The whole of Barcelona realized.

'Now!' shouted Arnau. 'Turn the ship!'

The captain gave the order. The oarsmen on the larboard side plunged their oars into the water, and the whaler began to swing round until prow and stern were stuck firmly in the two sides of the deep channel.

The ship listed to one side.

Guillem squeezed Arnau's arm even harder. The two men looked at each other and Arnau drew the Moor close to embrace him, while the beach and the King's galleys exploded with cries of congratulation.

The entrance to the port of Barcelona had been sealed.

In full battle armour on the beach, the King watched as Arnau deliberately ran his ship aground. The nobles and knights grouped around him said nothing as he stared out to sea.

'To the galleys!' he ordered.

With Arnau's whaling ship blocking the harbour, Pedro the Cruel deployed his fleet in the open sea. King Pedro III did the same on the port side of the sandbanks, and so before nightfall the two fleets – one a proper armada, made up of forty armed and prepared warships, the other a picturesque motley of craft, with ten galleys, dozens of small merchant ships and fishing-boats crammed with ordinary citizens – were drawn up facing each other in a line that ran from Santa Clara to Framenors. No one could either enter or leave the port of Barcelona.

There was no battle that day. Five of Pedro III's galleys took up position close to Arnau's ship, and that night, by the light of a glorious moon, a company of royal soldiers came aboard.

'It seems as though we're at the centre of the battle,' Guillem commented to Arnau as the two men sat on deck, close to the side in order to shelter from any Castilian crossbowmen.

'We've become the city wall, and all battles start at the walls.'

At that moment, one of the King's captains came up. 'Arnau Estanyol?' he asked. Arnau raised a hand. 'The King authorizes you to leave the ship.'

'What about my crew?'

'The galley slaves?' Even in the darkness, Arnau and Guillem could see the look of surprise on the officer's face. What did the King care about a hundred convicts? 'We might need them here,' he said, to avoid the question.

'In that case,' said Arnau, 'I'm staying. This is my ship, and these are my crew.'

At that the officer shrugged and went on deploying his men.

'Do you want to leave?' Arnau asked Guillem.

'Aren't I part of your crew?'

'No, as you know very well.' The two men fell silent, watching shadows passing by them as the soldiers ran to take up their positions in response to their officers' half-whispered commands. 'You know you haven't been a slave for many years now,' added Arnau. 'All you have to do is ask for your letter of emancipation and it's yours.'

Some of the soldiers came to take up position next to them.

'You should go down to the hold with the others,' one of the soldiers muttered as he pushed in beside them.

'In this ship we go where we please,' Arnau replied.

The soldier bent over the two men. 'I'm sorry,' he said. 'We are all grateful for what you've done.' Then he went off to search for another place by the gunwale.

'When will you want to be free?' Arnau asked Guillem again.

'I don't think I would know how to be free.'

At this, the two men fell silent. Once all the King's soldiers had boarded the ship and taken up their positions, the night went slowly by. Arnau and Guillem slept fitfully while the others coughed or snored around them.

At dawn, Pedro the Cruel ordered the attack. His fleet approached the sandbanks, and his men began to fire their crossbows and to shoot stones from catapults and bricolas. From the other side of the banks, the Catalan fleet did the same. There was fighting all the way down the coast, but especially around Arnau's whaler. Pedro III could not allow the Castilians to board it, and stationed several galleys close by.

Many men died from the crossbow bolts fired from both armies. Arnau remembered the whistle of the arrows as he had fired them from his crossbow, crouching behind the boulders outside Bellaguarda Castle.

The sound of raucous laughter brought him back to reality. Who on earth could be laughing in the midst of battle? Barcelona was in danger, and men were dying. What was there to laugh about? Arnau and Guillem stared at each other. Yes, it was laughter. Laughter that was growing louder and louder. The two men sought a sheltered spot from where they could survey what was going on. They soon realized that it was the men aboard ships in the second or third line of the Catalan fleet, who were out of range of the Castilians, and were making fun of their enemy, laughing and shouting insults at them.

The Castilians continued firing their catapults at the Catalans, but their aim was so poor that time and again the stones fell harmlessly into the water. Some of them raised plumes of spray in the sea around Arnau's ship. He and Guillem looked at each other again, and smiled. The men on the other ships were still taunting the Castilians, and from the beach more hoots of derision could be heard.

Throughout the day, the Catalans ridiculed the Castilian artillerymen, who constantly failed in their attempts to strike home.

'I wouldn't like to be in Pedro the Cruel's galley,' Guillem said to Arnau.

'No,' Arnau replied, laughing, 'I can't bear to think what he'll do to those bunglers.'

That night was very different from the previous one. Arnau and Guillem tended the many wounded men on the ship. They staunched their wounds and then helped lower them into the smaller boats to be taken back to land. A fresh detachment of soldiers boarded the ship, and it was only towards the end of the night that the two men could rest a while and prepare themselves for the next day.

At first light, the mocking shouts of the Catalans started again. The insults and laughter were taken up by the crowds still lining the shore.

Arnau had run out of crossbow bolts, so he took cover beside Guillem and the two of them surveyed the battle.

'Look,' his friend said, 'they are coming much closer than they did yesterday.'

It was true. The Castilian King had decided to put a stop to all the insults as soon as possible, and was heading straight for Arnau's ship.

'Tell them to stop laughing,' said Guillem, staring at the oncoming armada.

King Pedro III saw the danger. Determined to defend Arnau's whaler, he brought his galleys as close to the sandbanks as he dared. This time, the battle was so near that Arnau and Guillem could almost touch the royal galley, and could clearly see the King and his knights on board.

The two opposing galleys drew up side by side with the sandbanks in between them. The Castilians fired catapults they had mounted on the prow. Arnau and Guillem turned to look at the Catalan King's vessel. It had not been touched. The King and his men were still on deck, and the ship did not seem to have suffered any damage.

'Is that a bombard?' asked Arnau as he saw Pedro III striding towards a cannon on his own galley.

'Yes,' said Guillem. He had seen them loading it on board when the King had been preparing his fleet for the defence of Mallorca against a Castilian attack.

'A bombard on a ship?'

'Yes,' Guillem said again.

'This must be the first time that's happened,' commented Arnau, still watching closely as the King gave orders to his gunners. 'I've never seen . . .'

'Nor have I—'

Their conversation was interrupted by the roar from the cannon as it shot a huge stone. They quickly turned to survey the Castilian ship.

'Bravo!' they shouted when they saw the cannonball smash the galley's mast. A great cheer went up from the whole Catalan fleet.

The King ordered his men to reload the bombard. Taken by surprise and hampered by the fallen mast, the Castilians were unable to return fire. The next Catalan stone was a direct hit on the fo'castle.

The Castilians began to manoeuvre away from the sandbanks.

Thanks to the constant mockery and to the ingenious bombard on the royal galley, the Castilian sovereign was forced to rethink. A few hours later, he ordered his fleet to lift the siege of Barcelona and head for Ibiza.

Standing on deck with several of the King's officers, Arnau and Guillem watched the Castilian ships recede into the distance. The bells of Barcelona began to ring out once more.

'Now we'll have to get the ship off the sandbanks,' said Arnau.

'We'll take care of that,' he heard someone say behind him. He turned and came face to face with an officer who had just climbed aboard. 'His majesty is waiting for you on the royal galley.'

King Pedro III had heard all about Arnau Estanyol during the two nights of battle. 'He's rich,' the city councillors had told him, 'immensely rich, your majesty.' The King nodded unenthusiastically at everything they told him about Arnau: his years as a *bastaix*, his service as a soldier under Eiximèn d'Esparça, his devotion to Santa Maria. It was only when he heard that Arnau was a widower that his eyes opened wide. Rich and a widower, thought the King, perhaps we can get rid of that . . .

'Arnau Estanyol,' one of his camerlingos announced. 'Citizen of Barcelona.'

The King sat on a throne on deck, flanked by a large group of nobles, knights and leading figures of the city who had flocked on board the galley following the Castilian retreat. Guillem stood at the ship's gunwale, some way away from the group surrounding Arnau and the monarch.

Arnau made to kneel before Pedro, but the King told him to rise.

'We are very pleased with your action,' said the King.

'Your intelligence and daring were vital in helping us win this victory.'

The King fell silent. Arnau did not know quite what to do. Was he meant to speak? Everybody was looking at him.

'In recognition of your valiant action,' the monarch continued, 'we wish to grant you a favour.'

Was he meant to speak now? What favour could the King possibly grant him? He already had all he could wish for . . .

'We offer you the hand of our ward Eleonor in marriage. As her dowry, she will be baroness of Granollers, Sant Vicenç dels Horts and Caldes de Montbui.'

Everyone on board the galley murmured their approval; some applauded. Marriage! Had he said marriage? Arnau turned to find Guillem, but could not see him. All the nobles and knights were smiling at him. Had the King said marriage?

'Are you not pleased, lord baron?' the King asked, seeing Arnau turn his head aside.

Arnau looked back at him. Lord baron? Marriage? What did he want all that for? When he said nothing, the nobles and knights fell silent too. The King's eyes pierced him. Had he said Eleonor? His ward? He could not . . . he must not offend the King!

'No . . . I mean yes, your majesty,' he stammered. 'I thank you for your generosity.'

'So be it then.'

At that, Pedro III stood up and his courtiers closed around him. As they passed by Arnau, some of them slapped him on the back, congratulating him with phrases he could not catch. He was soon left standing all on his own. He turned towards Guillem, who was still over by the ship's side.

Arnau spread his palms in bewilderment, but the

Moor gestured towards the King and his retinue, and so he quickly dropped his arms to his side.

Back on shore Arnau was greeted with as much enthusiasm as the King himself. It seemed as though the entire city wanted to congratulate him: hands stretched out to him, others patted him on the back. Everybody wanted to get near the city's saviour, but Arnau could not hear or recognize any of them. Just when everything was going well and he was happy, the King had decided to arrange a marriage for him. The crowd swarmed round and followed him all the way from the beach to his counting house. Even after he had disappeared inside, they stood in the street calling out his name and shouting their joy.

As soon as Arnau stepped into the house, Mar flung herself in his arms. Guillem was already there; he had sat in a chair without saying a word. Joan, who had also arrived, was looking on with his usual taciturn expression.

Mar was taken aback when Arnau, perhaps more vigorously than necessary, freed himself from her embrace. Joan came up to congratulate him, but Arnau brushed him off too. He sank into a chair next to Guillem. The others all stared at him, not daring to say a word.

'What's wrong?' Joan asked at length.

'I'm to be married!' said Arnau, raising his hands above his head. 'The King has decided to make me a baron and to marry me to his ward. That's the favour he's granting me for having saved his capital! He's marrying me off!'

Joan thought about what he had heard, then smiled and responded: 'Why are you complaining?'

Arnau glanced at him out of the corner of his eye. Next to him, Mar's whole body had begun to shake. Donaha, who was standing in the kitchen doorway, was the only one to notice. She came bustling over and helped her stay on her feet.

'What is so bad about the idea?' Joan insisted. Arnau did not even bother to look at him. As she heard the friar speak, Mar began to retch. 'What is wrong with you marrying? And with the King's ward, no less. You will become a Catalan baron.'

Afraid she was going to be sick, Mar went with Donaha to the kitchen.

'What's the matter with Mar?' asked Arnau.

The friar took a few moments to answer.

'I'll tell you what's the matter,' he said finally. 'She should be getting married too! Both of you should be married. It's a good thing that King Pedro has more sense than you.'

'Leave me, will you, Joan?' said Arnau wearily.

The friar lifted his arms in the air and left the room.

'Go and see what's wrong with Mar,' Arnau asked Guillem.

'I don't know what's wrong,' he told Arnau a few minutes later, 'but Donaha told me not to worry. It's a woman's thing.'

Arnau turned to him. 'Don't talk to me about women,' he moaned.

'We can't go against the King's wishes, Arnau. Perhaps . . . given a bit of time, we can find a solution.'

But they were not given any time. King Pedro III fixed 23 June as the date when he would set off in pursuit of the King of Castile. He ordered his fleet to assemble in the port of Barcelona that day, and let it be known that before leaving he wanted the matter of the marriage of his ward Eleonor to the rich merchant Arnau settled. A court official came one morning to Arnau's counting house to tell him as much.

'That means I only have nine days left!' Arnau

complained to Guillem as soon as the official had left. 'Less perhaps!'

What could this Eleonor be like? Just thinking about her kept him awake. Old? Beautiful? Friendly, pleasant, or arrogant and cynical like all the other nobles he had known in his life? How could he marry a woman he had never even met? He confided the task of finding out about her to Joan.

'You have to do it for me. Find out what she is like. I can't stop worrying about what's in store for me.'

'It's said,' Joan told him the same day that the official had appeared in the counting house, 'that she is the bastard daughter of one of the Catalan infantes, one of the King's uncles, although nobody dares say for certain exactly which one. Her mother died giving birth to her, that's why she was taken into court—'

'But what is she like, Joan?' Arnau interrupted him.

'She is twenty-three years old and attractive.'

'What about her character?'

'She's a noblewoman,' was all Joan would say.

Why tell Arnau what he had heard about Eleonor? She's definitely attractive, they had told him, but she always looks as though she is angry with the whole world. She is spoilt, fickle, haughty and ambitious. The King married her to a nobleman, but he died soon afterwards, and as she had no children she returned to court. Was the King granting Arnau a favour? A royal reward? The people Joan spoke to had laughed at the idea. The King could not tolerate Eleonor any more, so who better to marry her off to than one of the richest men in Barcelona, a moneychanger who could well be a source of loans? Whatever happened, King Pedro came out winning: he was getting rid of Eleonor and at the same time gaining access to Arnau and his wealth. No, there was no reason to tell him all this.

'What do you mean when you say she is a noble-woman?'

'Exactly that,' said Joan, trying to avoid Arnau's eyes. 'She's noble, she's a woman, and therefore she has a well-defined character, as all of them do.'

Eleonor had also been making enquiries on her own side. The more she heard, the angrier she became: her husband-to-be had been a *bastaix*, member of a guild that derived from the slaves employed in the port, the freed slaves. What was the King doing, marrying her to a *bastaix*? Everyone told her he was rich, very rich: but what did she care about his money? She lived at court and wanted for nothing. Then when she discovered Arnau was the son of a runaway serf who had himself been born a serf, she decided she must see the King. How could he expect her, the daughter of an infante, to marry someone of that ilk?

Pedro III would not see her. He ordered that the wedding should take place on 21 June, two days before he left for Mallorca.

He was to be married the next day. In the royal chapel at Santa Àgata.

'It's a small chapel,' Joan explained. 'It was built at the start of the century by Jaime the Second at the behest of his wife, Blanche of Anjou. It's dedicated to the relics of Christ's passion in the same way as the Sainte-Chapelle in Paris, where the Queen was born.'

It was to be an intimate affair: Joan was the only person accompanying Arnau. Mar had refused to attend. Ever since Arnau had announced his marriage, she had shied away from him. Whenever they were in a room together, she said nothing, and all her previous smiles had stopped.

That was why this final evening Arnau approached her and asked her to go for a walk with him.

'Where?' asked Mar.

Where?

'I don't know . . . what about Santa Maria? Your father adored the church. Did you know it was there that I met him?'

Mar agreed, so they left the counting house and walked down to the still unfinished façade of Santa Maria. The masons had begun work on the two octagonal towers that were to flank it, and the sculptors had already set to with hammer and chisel on the tympanum, door posts, mullions and archivolts. Arnau went into the church with Mar. The ribbed vaults of the central nave's third arch were already stretching up towards the keystone, like a spider's web protected by the wooden scaffolding as they grew.

Arnau was only too aware of Mar standing beside him. She was almost as tall as he was, and her hair flowed down to her shoulders. She smelt of freshness, of herbs. Most of the workmen stared admiringly at her; he could see it in their eyes, even if they turned away as soon as they realized Arnau was looking at them. Her fragrance wafted across to him in waves as she walked down the nave.

'Why don't you want to come to my wedding?' he asked her point-blank.

Mar said nothing. She looked desperately around the church.

'They haven't even allowed me to be married in my Santa Maria,' muttered Arnau.

The girl still made no response.

'Mar . . .' Arnau waited for her to turn towards him. 'I would have liked you to be with me on my wedding day. You know I don't want to do it, that it's against my will, but the King . . . I won't insist any more, all right?' Mar nodded. 'If I don't insist, can things be the same between us as they were before?'

Mar stared at the ground. There was so much she would have loved to tell him . . . But she could not refuse him what he asked; she could not refuse him anything.

'Thank you,' said Arnau. 'If you had failed me . . . I don't know what would happen to me if those I most care about failed me!'

Mar shivered. That was not the sort of affection she was looking for. She wanted love. Why had she agreed to come with him like this? She gazed up at the apse of the church.

'You know, Joan and I saw them raising that keystone,' Arnau told her when he saw the direction she was looking in. 'We were only boys then.'

At that moment, the master glassmakers were hard at work on the clerestory, the set of windows under the apse roof. They had already finished the upper tier, where the Gothic arch was rounded off with a small rose window. After the clerestory, they would work on the set of big arched windows underneath. They placed small pieces of coloured glass, held by strips of lead, into the window space. The sunlight streamed in through the glass.

'At that time,' Arnau went on, 'I was lucky enough to talk to the great Berenguer de Montagut. I remember him saying that we Catalans need no more decoration than space and light. He pointed to the apse where you're looking now, then drew his hand down towards the high altar as though the light were pouring down. I told him I understood what he was talking about, but in fact I could not imagine what he meant.' Mar looked at him. 'I was only young,' he said to justify himself, 'and he was the master builder, the great Berenguer de Montagut. Now I do understand.' He went closer to Mar and raised a hand up towards the rose window high in the apse. Mar tried to hide the shiver that ran through her when he touched her. 'Do you see how the light comes into the church?' Then he drew his hand down towards the altar, just as Berenguer had done all those years ago, although now he could point to shafts of coloured light flooding in. Fascinated, Mar followed Arnau's hand. 'Take a good look. The stained glass facing the sun is in bright colours: reds, yellows and greens, to take advantage of the strong Mediterranean light. The others are white or blue. All through the day as the sun moves round, the colour in the church interior changes, and the stones reflect all the different hues. How right Berenguer was! It's like having a new church every day, every hour, as if a new one were constantly being born, because although the stone is dead, the sun is alive and different each day; the reflections change with it.'

The two of them stood enthralled by the warm, coloured light.

After a while, Arnau took Mar by the shoulders and turned her towards him. 'Don't leave me, Mar, I beg you.'

Next day at dawn, in the dark, over-ornate chapel of Santa Àgata, Mar tried to hide her tears as she witnessed the ceremony.

Arnau and Eleonor stood stiff and unmoving in front of the bishop. Eleonor looked straight ahead of her all the time. At the beginning of the ceremony, Arnau turned to her once or twice, but she did not deign to turn her head in his direction. From then on, he merely glanced at her occasionally out of the corner of his eye.

39

As soon as the wedding ceremony was over, the new
Baron and Baroness of Granollers, Sant Vicenç and
Caldes de Montbui left for Montbui Castle. Joan told
Arnau of the questions that Eleonor's steward had asked.
Where did Arnau think she was going to sleep? In rooms
above a vulgar counting house? What about her
servants? And her slaves? Arnau made him be quiet, but
agreed to leave Barcelona that same day, provided Joan
went with them.

'For what reason?' the friar asked.

'Because I think I am going to need your good offices.'

Eleonor and her steward left on horseback. She rode
side-saddle, while a groom walked alongside holding the
reins. Her scribe and two maidens rode mules, and a
dozen or so slaves dragged along as many mules loaded
down with all her possessions.

Arnau hired a cart.

When the baroness saw the ramshackle vehicle arrive,
drawn by two mules and carrying the scant possessions that
Arnau, Joan and Mar were bringing with them – Guillem
and Donaha had stayed in Barcelona – her eyes blazed

fiercely enough to light a torch. This was the first time she had really looked at Arnau and her new family; they had been married, they had gone through the ceremony before the bishop and with the King and his wife in attendance, but she had never even deigned to glance at them.

They left Barcelona with an escort provided by the King. Arnau and Mar sat up on the cart, while Joan walked alongside. The baroness urged her horse on so that they would arrive at the castle as quickly as possible. It came into view before sunset.

Perched on the top of a hill, it was a small fortress where until their arrival the local thane had lived. Many peasants and serfs were curious to see their new lords, so that by the time they were close to the castle, more than a hundred people had thronged around them, wondering who this man could be, so richly dressed but travelling in a broken-down cart.

'Why are we stopping now?' asked Mar when the baroness gave the order for everyone to come to a halt.

Arnau shrugged.

'Because they have to hand over the castle to us,' Joan explained.

'Don't we have to go in for them to do that?' asked Arnau.

'No. The Customs and Practices of Catalonia prescribe something different: the thane, his family and their retinue have to leave the castle before they hand it over.' As he was saying this, the heavy gates of the fortress swung slowly open, and the thane appeared, followed by the members of his family and all his servants. When he reached the baroness, he gave her something. 'You're the one who should receive those keys,' Joan told Arnau.

'What do I want with a castle?'

As the thane and his party passed by the cart, he could not hide a sly smile. Mar flushed. Even the servants stared openly at them.

'You shouldn't allow it,' Joan said again. 'You are their lord now. They owe you respect and loyalty—'

'Listen, Joan,' said Arnau, interrupting him, 'let's get one thing clear: I don't want any castle, I am not and have no wish to be anyone's lord and master, and I have not the slightest intention of staying here any longer than is strictly necessary to sort out whatever needs sorting out. As soon as that's done, I am going back to Barcelona. If the lady baroness wishes to live here in her castle, so be it. It's all hers.'

This outburst brought the first smile of the day to Mar's face.

'You can't leave,' Joan insisted.

Mar's face fell. Arnau turned to confront the friar.

'What do you mean, I can't? I can do as I choose. Am I not the baron? Don't the barons leave home for months on end to follow the King?'

'Yes, but they're going to war.'

'Thanks to my money, Joan, thanks to my money. It seems to me more important that somebody like me accompanies the King than any of those nobles who are always asking for easy loans. Well,' he added, looking towards the castle, 'what are we waiting for now? It's empty, and I'm tired.'

'By law, there still has to be—' Joan began.

'You and your laws,' Arnau snapped at him. 'Why are you Dominicans so concerned about legal matters? What is there still—?'

'Arnau and Eleonor, Baron and Baroness of Granollers, Sant Vicenç and Caldes de Montbui!' The cry echoed out over the valley that lay beneath the castle hill. Everyone looked up to the tallest tower in the fortress. Eleonor's steward, his hands cupped to amplify the sound, was shouting at the top of his voice: 'Arnau and Eleonor, Baron and Baroness of Granollers, Sant Vicenç and Caldes de Montbui! Arnau and Eleonor . . .!'

'That was still to come: the official announcement that the castle has changed hands,' Joan concluded.

The baroness moved forwards.

'At least he mentioned my name.'

The steward was still shouting with all his might.

'Without that, your possession of the castle would not be legal,' the friar concluded.

Arnau was about to say something, but thought better of it and merely shook his head wearily.

Inside the castle yard, behind the walls and around the keep, the usual conglomeration of buildings had been put up haphazardly over the years. There was a long hall with a vast dining room, kitchens and pantries, with other rooms on the upper floor. Scattered around outside the hall were a handful of wooden buildings for the servants and the small garrison of soldiers to live in.

The captain of the guard, a small, broad-beamed man who looked unkempt and filthy, came out to greet Eleonor and her party officially. They all went into the large dining chamber.

'Show me where the thane lived,' Eleonor shouted.

The captain pointed to a stone staircase whose only adornment was a stone balustrade. The baroness started up the steps, followed by her steward, the scribe, and her maidens. She completely ignored Arnau.

The three Estanyols stood in the middle of the hall, watching as the slaves carried in all Eleonor's possessions.

'Perhaps you should—' Joan started to say.

'Don't interfere, Joan,' Arnau said curtly.

For some moments, they surveyed the great hall: the high ceiling, huge hearth, armchairs, the candelabra and the table with room for a dozen guests. Then Eleonor's steward appeared on the stairs. He came down towards them but stopped three steps before the bottom.

'The lady baroness' – he spoke in fluted tones, without addressing anyone in particular – 'says she is very tired tonight and does not want to be disturbed.'

The steward was about to turn on his heel when Arnau halted him.

'Hey, you!' he shouted. The steward turned back towards him. 'Tell your lady mistress not to worry, no one is going to disturb her . . . ever,' he hissed. Mar's eyes opened wide, and she raised her hands to her mouth. The steward turned to make his way up the stairs once more, but Arnau again called out to him: 'Hey! Which are our rooms?' The steward shrugged. 'Where's the captain of the guard?'

'He's attending my lady.'

'Well, go upstairs and find her, and get the captain to come down. And be quick about it, because if you aren't I'll see to it you are castrated, and the next time you announce the handover of a castle you'll be singing it falsetto.'

The steward gripped the balustrade tightly, confused at this violent threat. Could this be the same man who had sat quietly the whole day as his cart bumped and jolted along? Arnau's eyes narrowed. He strode over to the staircase, pulling out the *bastaix* dagger he had insisted on wearing to his wedding. The steward did not have time to see that it was in fact completely blunt: before Arnau had taken three steps, he fled upstairs.

Arnau turned back to the others: Mar was laughing, but Joan scowled disapprovingly. Behind them, several of Eleonor's slaves had seen what had happened and were smiling to themselves as well.

'You over there!' Arnau shouted when he saw them. 'Stop laughing and unload the cart. Then take the things up to our rooms.'

By now they had been living in the castle for more than a month. Arnau had tried to sort out the affairs of his new possessions, but whenever he began to pore over the account books, he ended by closing them with a sigh. Torn pages, figures scratched out and written over, contradictory or even false dates. They were incomprehensible, completely undecipherable.

It had taken only a week in Montbui Castle for Arnau to long to get back to Barcelona and leave his lands in the hands of a capable administrator. But while he was making up his mind what to do, he decided he should get to know his property a little better. To do this, he did not turn to the noblemen who were his vassals and who, whenever they came to the castle, completely ignored him but bowed their knee to Eleonor. Instead, he sought out the ordinary people, the peasants, the serfs chained to his vassals.

Taking Mar with him, he toured his lands. He was curious to know if what he had heard in Barcelona was true. The traders there often based their decisions on the news they received from the countryside. Arnau knew, for example, that the 1348 epidemic had depopulated the countryside, and that as recently as the previous year, 1358, a plague of locusts had made the situation even worse by devouring all the crops. The lack of resources was beginning to show even in the city, forcing the traders there to change their way of doing business.

'My God!' muttered Arnau behind the back of the first peasant, who had run into his farmhouse to present his family to the new baron.

Mar too found it impossible to take her eyes off the ruin of a house and its outbuildings, all of them as filthy and uncared for as the man who had come out to greet them, and who now reappeared with a woman and two small children.

The four of them lined up in front of the newcomers and tried awkwardly to bow to them. Their eyes were filled with fear. Their clothes were rags, and the children . . . the children could hardly stand up straight. Their legs were spindle-thin.

'Is this all your family?' asked Arnau.

The peasant was about to nod when the sound of a feeble wail came from inside the house. Arnau frowned, and the man shook his head slowly. The look of fear in his eyes changed to one of sadness.

'My wife has no milk, your honour.'

Arnau looked at her. How could anyone with a body like that have milk! First she would need to have breasts . . .

'Is there no one near who could . . .?'

The peasant anticipated the question.

'Everyone is in the same situation, your honour. The children are dying.'

Arnau saw Mar raise a hand to her mouth.

'Show me your farm: your granary, the stables, your house and fields.'

'We can't pay any more, your honour!' The woman had fallen to her knees and was crawling over to where Arnau and Mar stood.

Arnau went to her and took her by her skinny arms. She shrank beneath his touch.

'What . . .'

The children began to cry.

'Don't hit her, please, your honour, I beg you,' pleaded the peasant, coming up to Arnau. 'It's true, we can't pay any more. Punish me if you must.'

Arnau let go of the woman and withdrew to where Mar was standing, watching in horror what was happening.

'I'm not going to hit her,' Arnau told the man, 'or you, or anyone else in your family. Nor am I going to ask you for more money. I just want to see your farm. Tell your wife to stand up, please.'

First their eyes had shown fear, then sadness; now the

man and woman's sunken eyes stared at him in bewilderment. Are we meant to play at being gods? thought Arnau. What had been done to this family for them to act this way? They were allowing one of the children to die, and yet thought that someone had come to ask them to pay even more.

The granary was empty. So was the stable. The fields were untended, and the ploughing gear had fallen into disrepair. As for the house . . . if the child did not die of hunger it would die of disease. Arnau did not dare touch it, it seemed . . . it seemed as though the infant might snap in two just by moving it.

He took his purse from his belt and pulled out a few coins. He was about to give them to the man, but thought again and got out several more.

'I want this child to live,' he said, leaving the coins on the remains of what must once have been a table. 'I want you, your wife and your two other children to eat. This money is for you, and you alone. Nobody has the right to take it from you. If there are any problems, come to the castle to see me.'

None of the family moved: they were all staring at the coins. They did not even look up when Arnau said farewell and left the house.

Arnau returned to his castle in silence, deep in thought. Mar shared his silence with him.

'They're all the same, Joan,' Arnau told him one evening when the two men were walking in the cool air outside the castle. 'Some of them have been lucky enough to take over uninhabited farmhouses whose owners have died or simply fled the land: who could blame them? They use the land for woods and pasture: that gives them some chance to survive even though they can't produce crops. But the rest . . . the rest are in a terrible state. The fields are barren, and so they are dying of hunger.'

'That's not all,' Joan added. 'I have heard that the nobles, your vassals, are forcing the remaining peasants to sign *capbreus*.'

'*Capbreus*?'

'They're documents which accept all the feudal rights that had been allowed to lapse during the years of plenty. There are so few men left that the nobles are making more and more demands so that they can get as much out of them as before, when there were far more serfs.'

Arnau had not been sleeping well for some time now. He had nightmares with all the haggard faces he had seen. Now he found he could not get back to sleep. He had visited all his lands and been generous. How could he allow things to stay as they were? All those peasant families depended on him: they were directly responsible to their lords, but they in turn owed their allegiance to him. If he, as their feudal baron, demanded the nobles pay their rents and duties, they would in turn force the wretched peasants to meet the new demands that the thane had through his negligence allowed to be reintroduced.

They were slaves. Chained to the land. Slaves on his lands. Arnau turned to and fro on his bed. His slaves! An army of starving men, women and children whom nobody considered important . . . except to extort more and more out of until they died. Arnau recalled the nobles who had come to pay homage to Eleonor: they were all healthy, strong, dressed in fine clothes; fortunate people! How could they turn their backs so completely on the reality their serfs were forced to live? And what could he do about it?

He was generous. He gave money where he could see it was needed: to him it was a pittance, but it brought delight to the children he saw, and a warm smile to the face of Mar, who never left his side. But he could not carry on doing it for ever. If he went on handing out money, the nobles would soon find a way to get their hands on it. They would still refuse to pay him, but would exploit the poorest peasants still further. What could he do?

Each day Arnau rose feeling increasingly pessimistic. Eleonor, however, was in a very different frame of mind.

'She has summoned the nobles, peasants and other inhabitants on Assumption Day,' said Joan, who as a Dominican friar was the only one among them who had any contact with the baroness.

'What for?'

'So that they can pay her . . . pay you both homage,' he said. Arnau waved for him to continue. 'According to the law' – Joan spread his palms, as though to say 'it was you who asked', and went on – 'according to the law, any noble may at any time demand of his vassals that they renew their vows of fealty and homage to them. It's logical that, as they have not done so before, Eleonor wishes them to do so now.'

'Do you mean to say they will come?'

'Nobles and knights are not obliged to attend a commendation ceremony of this kind. They can instead come and swear fealty in private, provided they do so within a year, a month and a day of being called upon to do so. However, Eleonor has been talking to them, and it appears they will come. After all, she is the King's ward. Nobody wants to offend her.'

'What about the husband of the King's ward?'

Joan made no reply. Yet there was something in his look . . . Arnau knew he was keeping something back.

'Do you have anything more to say to me, Joan?'

The friar shook his head.

Eleonor ordered a platform be built on the plain below the castle. She dreamt of nothing but Assumption Day.

How often had she seen not merely noblemen but whole towns swear fealty to her guardian, the King? Now they would do the same for her. She was the queen, the sovereign in her own lands. What did she care that Arnau would be next to her? Everyone knew that it was to her, the King's ward, that they were swearing allegiance.

She grew so nervous that as the day drew closer, she even allowed herself to smile at Arnau. He was some distance from her, and it was only the ghost of a smile, but it was a smile nonetheless.

Arnau hesitated, then forced his own lips into a curling grimace.

Why did I smile at him? Eleonor cursed herself, and clenched her fists. *Stupid woman! How could you humiliate yourself like that before a vulgar moneychanger, a runaway serf?* They had been at Montbui for more than six weeks now, yet Arnau had not once come near her. Wasn't he a man? When no one was looking, she would glance at his strong, powerful body, and at night all alone in her room she even dreamt of him mounting and fiercely taking possession of her. How long had it been since she felt like this? But he humiliated her with his disdain. How dare he? Eleonor bit her bottom lip savagely. His time will come, she told herself.

On the feast day of the Assumption, Eleonor rose at dawn. From the window of her lonely bedroom she could see the plain and the high dais she had ordered built. The peasants were beginning to gather round it; many of them had gone without sleep in order not to be late for their lord's summons. Not a single nobleman was yet to be seen.

40

The sun heralded a hot, glorious day. The clear cloudless
sky, similar to the one that almost forty years earlier had
greeted the wedding celebration of a serf called Bernat
Estanyol, arched like a bright blue dòme over the heads
of the thousands of vassals. The hour was fast approaching, and Eleonor, dressed in her finest robes, paced
nervously up and down the great hall of Montbui Castle.
What had happened to the nobles and knights? Dressed
as usual in his black habit, Joan was resting in an armchair, while Arnau and Mar, as though detached from the
scene, shot each other amused looks whenever they
heard Eleonor sighing anxiously.

At last the nobles arrived. As impatient as his mistress,
a servant came rushing into the room to tell Eleonor they
were coming. The baroness went to look out of a
window; when she turned again towards the others, her
face was beaming with delight. The nobles and knights
who lived on her lands had obviously made great efforts.
Their fine clothes, swords and jewels stood out
among the crowd of peasants dressed in their grey, sad
tunics. The grooms led their horses behind the platform,

from where their neighing and stamping broke the silence with which the poor peasants had greeted the arrival of their lords. The servants set up elaborate seats, covered in bright silks, beneath the dais. This was where noblemen and knights were to swear fealty to their new masters. The peasants instinctively moved away from the final line of seats in order to leave a space between them and the privileged.

Eleonor looked out of the window again. She smiled as she saw the wealth and power her new vassals were displaying so openly. Followed by her retinue, she made her way to the dais, and sat before them all like a true queen.

Eleonor's scribe, who today was acting as master of ceremonies, began by reading King Pedro III's decree which gave as dowry to the royal ward Eleonor the baronies of Granollers, Sant Vicenç and Caldes de Montbui, with all the vassals, lands and rents that it contained . . . As the scribe was reading this, Eleonor drank in his words: she felt herself observed and envied – hated even, why not? – by all those who until now had been vassals of the King. They would still owe him their loyalty, of course, but from now on there would be someone else between them and their sovereign: her. Arnau by contrast was not even listening to the scribe's speech: he merely smiled back at all the peasants he had visited and helped when they greeted him.

In the midst of the crowd of people were two women dressed in vivid colours, as befitted their condition as common prostitutes. One was already old; the other was mature but still beautiful, and unabashedly displayed her charms.

'Nobles and knights,' shouted the scribe, this time succeeding in capturing Arnau's attention, 'do you swear fealty to Arnau and Eleonor, Baron and Baroness of Granollers, Sant Vicenç and Caldes de Montbui?'

'No!'

The refusal seemed to rend the sky. The dispossessed thane of Montbui Castle had risen to his feet to reject the oath in a thunderous voice. A low murmur spread among the peasants grouped behind the nobles. Joan shook his head as though he had expected something of this sort; Mar looked uneasy, as if she did not know what she was doing up on the platform in front of all these people; Arnau was at a loss; and Eleonor's face had turned as pale as wax.

The scribe turned to the platform, expecting instructions from his mistress. When none were forthcoming, he took the initiative.

'You refuse?'

'We refuse,' boomed the thane, sure of himself. 'Not even the King can oblige us to pay homage to someone who is of lower rank than ourselves. That is the law!' Joan nodded sadly. He had not wanted to tell Arnau as much. The nobles had tricked Eleonor. 'Arnau Estanyol is a citizen of Barcelona,' the thane went on, 'the son of a runaway serf. We will not pay homage to the runaway son of a landed serf, even if the King has granted him the baronies you spoke of!'

The younger of the two women in the crowd stood on tiptoe to get a better view of the dais. Seeing all the nobles seated in front of it had aroused her curiosity, but now, when she heard the name of Arnau, citizen of Barcelona and a peasant's son, her legs began to give way beneath her.

With the crowd still murmuring in the background, the scribe once again turned towards Eleonor. So did Arnau, but she made no sign to either of them. She sat transfixed. After the initial shock, her astonishment had turned to anger. Her face had gone from white to bright red; she was shaking with rage and her hands were grasping the arms of her chair so tightly it seemed as though she wanted to claw into the wood.

'Why did you tell me he had died, Francesca?' asked the younger of the two prostitutes.

'He's my son, Aledis.'

'Arnau is your son?'

Francesca nodded, at the same time gesturing to Aledis to keep her voice down. The last thing in the world she wanted was for anyone to find out that Arnau was the son of a common prostitute. Fortunately, the people around them were too absorbed in the dispute among the nobles in front of them.

The argument was unresolved. When he saw that no one else would take the lead, Joan decided to intervene.

'You may be right in what you affirm,' he cried from behind the outraged baroness, 'and may refuse to pay homage, but that does not absolve you from fulfilling your duties and pledging your obedience to them. That's the law! Are you willing to do so?'

The thane of Montbui knew the friar was right. He looked around the other nobles to judge their opinion. Arnau gestured for Joan to come closer.

'What does this mean?' he whispered to him.

'It means they save face. Their honour is intact if they do not swear fealty and homage to . . .'

'To a person of lower rank,' Arnau helped him out. 'You know that has never troubled me.'

'They refuse to swear homage to you or to be your vassals, but the law obliges them to fulfil their duties to you and pledge their obedience, recognizing that they hold their lands and honours in your name.'

'Is that something similar to the *capbreus* they make the peasants accept?'

'Something similar.'

'We will pledge our obedience,' said the thane.

Arnau paid him no attention. He did not even look at him. He was thinking: perhaps this was the solution to

502

the peasants' misery. Joan was still leaning over him. Eleonor was there in body but not in spirit: her eyes were staring out beyond the spectacle in front of her, at her lost illusions.

'Does that mean,' Arnau asked Joan, 'that although they will not legally recognize me as their feudal lord, I can still give them orders which they must obey?'

'Yes. They are concerned above all about their honour.'

'Good,' said Arnau, standing up unobtrusively and gesturing to the scribe to come over. 'Do you see the gap between the nobles and the others?' he asked when he was beside him. 'I want you to stand there and repeat word for word in the loudest voice you can everything I am about to say. I want everyone to hear what I am saying!' As the scribe made his way to the open ground behind the nobles, Arnau smiled wryly at the thane, who was waiting for some response to his pledge of obedience. 'I, Arnau, Baron of Granollers, Sant Vicenç and Caldes de Montbui . . .'

Arnau waited for the scribe to repeat his words:

'I, Arnau,' the scribe duly called out, 'Baron of Granollers, Sant Vicenç and Caldes de Montbui . . .'

'. . . declare null and void on my lands all those privileges known as malpractices . . .'

'. . . declare null and void . . .'

'You cannot do that!' shouted one of the nobles over the scribe's words.

When he heard this, Arnau glanced at Joan to confirm that he did indeed have the power to do what he was suggesting.

'Yes I can,' he said shortly, after Joan had backed him up.

'We will petition the King!' shouted another noble.

Arnau shrugged.

Joan came up to him on the dais. 'Have you thought what will happen to all those poor people if you give them hope and then the King rules against you?'

'Joan,' said Arnau, with a self-confidence that was new to him, 'I may know nothing about honour, nobility or the rules of knighthood, but I do know what is written in my account books regarding all the loans I have made to his majesty. Which, by the way,' he added with a smile, 'have been considerably increased for the Mallorca campaign since my marriage to his ward. That I do know. I can assure you that the King will not question my decisions.'

Arnau looked at the scribe and gestured to him to continue.

'. . . declare null and void on my lands all those privileges known as malpractices . . .' shouted the scribe.

'I annul the right of *intestia*, by which a lord has the right to inherit part of the possessions of his vassals.' Arnau went on speaking clearly and slowly, so that the scribe could repeat his words. The peasants listened quietly, caught between astonishment and hope. 'Also that of *cugutia*, by which lords may take half or all of the possessions of an adulterous woman. That of *exorquia*, which gives them part of the inheritance of married peasants who die without issue. That of *ius maletractandi*, which allows nobles to mistreat peasants at their will, and to seize their goods.' Arnau's words were met with a silence so complete that the scribe decided the crowd could hear their feudal lord's proclamation without any help from him. Francesca gripped Aledis's arm. 'I annul the right of *arsia*, which obliges peasants to compensate their lord for any fire on his land. Also the right of *firma de espoli forzada* which gives the lord the right to sleep with a bride on her wedding night . . .'

The son could not see it, but in the crowd that was starting to react joyously as they realized Arnau meant what he was saying, an old woman – his mother – let go of Aledis's arm and raised her hands to her face. Aledis instantly understood. Tears welled in her eyes, and she turned to embrace the older woman. At the foot of the dais, nobles and knights were noisily debating the best way to present the problem to King Pedro.

'I declare null and void all other duties that peasants have been obliged to fulfil, apart from the right and proper levies on their lands. I declare you free to bake your own bread, to shoe your animals and repair your equipment in your own forges. I declare you women and mothers free to refuse to give suck to the children of your lords without payment.' At this, lost in her memories, the old woman could not stop the tears flowing. 'And also to refuse to serve unpaid in their households. I further free you from having to offer gifts to your lords at Christmas and to work on their lands for no reward.'

Arnau fell silent for a few moments, his eyes fixed not on the squabbling nobles but on the throng of peasants beyond them. They were waiting to hear something more. One thing more! They all knew it, and were waiting impatiently for Arnau to speak again. One more thing!

'I declare that you are free!'

The thane leapt up and shook his fist at Arnau. All around him, the nobles stood and shouted their fury.

'Free!' sobbed the old woman as the peasants cheered wildly.

'From this day on, a day when nobles have refused to pay homage to the King's ward, the peasants who work on the lands that are part of the baronies of Granollers, Sant Vicenç and Caldes de Montbui are to be treated exactly the same as those in New Catalonia, the baronies of Entença, Conca del Barberà, the counties of Tarragona and Prades, La Segarra and La Garriga, the marquisate of Aytona, the territories of Tortosa and Urgell . . . the same as in all the nineteen regions of the Catalonia conquered thanks to the efforts and the blood of your fathers. You are free! You are peasants but never again in these lands will you be serfs, and nor will your children or your children's children!'

'Nor will your mothers,' Francesca murmured to herself. 'Nor will your mothers,' she repeated, before dissolving into sobs once again, and clutching Aledis, who was close to tears herself.

Arnau had to leave the dais in order not to be overwhelmed by the peasants rushing to congratulate him. Joan helped Eleonor away: she was unable to walk on her own. Behind them, Mar was trying to control the emotions she felt were about to explode inside her.

When Arnau set off back towards the castle, the plain began to empty of people. After agreeing on how they would present their complaint to the King, the nobles galloped off, paying no heed to anyone on foot, who were forced to leap off the tracks into the fields to avoid being knocked down by the furious horsemen. Nevertheless, as they headed back to their farms, there were smiles on all the peasants' faces.

Soon the only ones left near the dais were the two women.

'Why did you lie to me?' asked Aledis.

This time the old woman turned to face her. 'Because you did not deserve him . . . and he was not meant to live with you. You were never meant to be his wife.' Francesca said this without hesitation. She said it coldly, despite the emotion still choking her.

'Do you really think I don't deserve him?' asked Aledis.

Francesca wiped away her tears, and soon was once again the energetic, determined woman who had run her business for so many years.

'Haven't you seen what he has become? Didn't you hear what he just said? Do you think his life would have been the same if he had been with you?'

'What you said about my husband and the duel . . .'

'All a lie.'

'That I was being pursued?'

'That too.' Aledis frowned and glared at Francesca. The old woman was not intimidated. 'You lied to me too, remember?'

'I had my reasons.'

'So did I.'

'You wanted me for your business . . . I see that now.'

'That was one of the reasons, I admit. But do you have anything to complain about? How many naive girls have you fooled in the same way since then?'

'I wouldn't have had to if you—'

'Remember, the choice was yours.' Aledis looked doubtful. 'Some of us never had a choice.'

'It was very hard, Francesca. To reach Figueres, dragging myself there with all that I went through, and with what result?'

'You live well, better than many of those nobles here today. You lack for nothing.'

'My honour.'

Francesca straightened as far as her bent body would permit. She turned to confront Aledis. 'Listen, Aledis, I know nothing about honour or honours. You sold me yours. Mine was stolen when I was still a girl. Nobody gave me any choice. Today I cried in a way I have never allowed myself to do before, and that is enough. We are what we are, and it serves no purpose for either of us to think about how we became it. Let others fight for their honour. You saw what they are like. Who among them knows what honour really is?'

'Perhaps now that those privileges have been abolished . . .'

'Don't fool yourself; the peasants will continue to be poor, wretched souls with nowhere to lay their heads. We have had to struggle hard to gain what little we have, so forget about honour: that is not for ordinary people.'

Aledis looked around her at the peasants streaming away. They might no longer have to submit to their lords' abusive privileges, but they were still the same men and women deprived of hope, the same starving, barefoot children dressed in rags. She nodded and folded her arms round Francesca.

41

'You're not thinking of leaving me here, are you?'

Eleonor flew down the staircase. Arnau was in the great hall, seated at the table signing the documents that annulled the malpractices and privileges on his lands. 'As soon as I've signed them, I'm leaving,' he had told Joan. The friar was standing with Mar behind Arnau, watching him sign.

Arnau finished what he was doing, and then looked up to confront Eleonor. This must have been the first time they had spoken since their marriage. Arnau did not stand up. 'Why do you want me to stay with you?'

'You don't expect me to stay in a place where I've suffered so much humiliation, do you?'

'I'll put it another way then: why would you want to come with me?'

'You're my husband!' screeched Eleonor. She had gone over it time and again: she could not stay at Montbui, but she could not return to court either. Arnau grimaced. 'If you go and leave me here, I'll protest to the King.'

This time, her words gave Arnau pause for thought. 'We'll petition the King!' the nobles had threatened him. He thought he could deal with the threat from the nobles, but . . . he looked at the documents he had signed. If the King's ward Eleonor added her voice to theirs . . .

'Sign these,' he said, passing her the parchments.

'Why should I? If you abolish all the privileges, we'll not receive any revenues.'

'Sign and you will live in a palace on Carrer de Montcada in Barcelona. You won't need the revenues: you'll have all the money you could wish for.'

Eleonor walked across to the table, picked up the quill and leant over the documents.

'What guarantees do I have that you will keep your word?' she asked suddenly, glancing at Arnau.

'The fact that the bigger the palace is, the less I'll see of you. That's one guarantee. The fact that the better life you have, the less you'll bother me. That's another: is that enough? I've no intention of offering any more.'

Eleonor looked up at the two figures standing behind Arnau. Was that a smile on the girl's face?

'Are they going to live with us?' she asked, pointing at them with the quill.

'Yes.'

'The girl too?'

Mar and Eleonor glared at each other.

'Wasn't I clear enough for you, Eleonor? Are you going to sign or not?'

She signed.

Arnau did not wait for Eleonor to pack all her things. To avoid the August heat he set off that evening in the same hired cart he had arrived in.

None of them looked behind as the cart emerged from the castle gates.

'Why do we have to go and live with her?' Mar asked Arnau during the journey back to Barcelona.

'I cannot afford to offend the King, Mar. One never knows how a monarch may react.'

Mar sat silently for a few moments, deep in thought.

'Is that why you offered her all you did?'

'No . . . well, yes in part, but the main reason was the peasants. I don't want her to make any complaint. The King has supposedly given us the revenues from these lands to live on, even if in fact they are tiny or non-existent. If she goes to the King and says that through my fault those revenues have vanished, he could possibly overturn my decisions.'

'The King? Why would the King . . .?'

'You need to know that only a few years ago the King published a decree against the serfs, a decree that even went against privileges he and his predecessors had given the cities. The Church and nobility had demanded he take measures against any serfs who escaped and left their lands untended . . . and the King did so.'

'I didn't think he would do anything like that.'

'He's just another noble, Mar, even if he is first among them.'

They spent the night in a farmhouse outside the village of Montcada. Arnau paid the peasants generously. They rose at dawn and were in Barcelona before the heat of the day.

'The situation is dramatic, Guillem,' Arnau told him once everyone had finished their greetings and the two men were on their own. 'The Catalan countryside is in a far worse state than we thought. We only hear about it when there is news, but when you see how bad the fields and properties are, you realize we are in real trouble.'

'I've been taking that into account for some time now,' Guillem said, to Arnau's surprise. 'It's a real crisis, but I could see it coming. We've talked about it, if you remember. Our currency is constantly losing value in foreign markets, but the King is not doing anything about it here in Catalonia, and the exchange rate is unsustainable. The city is falling deeper and deeper into debt in order to finance everything it has created in Barcelona. Nobody is making any profit from trade, and so people are looking for more secure places to invest.'

'What about our business?'

'I've moved it outside the country. To Pisa, Florence, even Genoa. Those are places where we can trade with logical exchange rates.' The two men fell silent. 'Castelló has been declared *abatut*,' Guillem said eventually. 'Disaster is looming.'

Arnau remembered the fat, sweating moneychanger who had always been very friendly to him.

'What happened?'

'He wasn't sufficiently cautious. His clients began to reclaim their deposits, and he couldn't meet their demands.'

'Will he be able to?'

'I don't think so.'

On 29 August, the King disembarked after his victorious campaign in Mallorca. As soon as the Catalan fleet arrived at the islands, Pedro the Cruel had fled Ibiza after taking and plundering it.

A month later, Eleonor arrived. All the Estanyol family, including Guillem, despite his initial protests, moved to the palace on Carrer de Montcada.

Two months later, the King granted an audience to the thane of Montbui. The previous day, Pedro III had sent envoys to ask for a fresh loan from Arnau. When it was granted, he gave short shrift to the thane, and upheld all Arnau's proclamations.

Two months later, when the six months the law allowed for an *abatut* to settle his debts had elapsed, the moneychanger Castelló was beheaded outside his counting house in Plaça dels Canvis. All the city's moneychangers were forced to witness the execution from the front row of spectators. Arnau saw Castelló's head severed from his body at the executioner's first sure blow. He would have liked to close his eyes as many others did, but found it impossible. He had to see it. It was a reminder to exercise caution, and he would never forget it, he told himself as his colleague's blood ran down the scaffold.

42

He could see her smile. Arnau could still see his Virgin smile, and life was smiling at him too. He was forty now, and despite the crisis his business ventures were prospering, bringing him handsome profits, part of which he donated to the poor or to Santa Maria. With time, Guillem was forced to admit he was right: the common people repaid their loans, coin by coin. His church, the temple to the sea, was still growing: work was now going on to build the third central vault and the octagonal towers on either side of the west front. Santa Maria was filled with artisans: marble-cutters and sculptors, painters, glassmakers, carpenters and the smiths working on the iron railings. There was even an organist, whose work Arnau followed with interest. What would music sound like in this marvellous church, he wondered? After the deaths of the archdeacon Bernat Llull and two canons who had followed him, the post was now filled by Pere Salvete de Montirac. Arnau had a good relationship with him. Others who had died by now were the master builder Berenguer de Montagut and his successor Ramon Despuig. Work on the church was now directed by Guillem Metge.

It was not only with the provosts of Santa Maria that Arnau had close relations. His economic situation and his newly acquired social rank brought him into contact with the city councillors, aldermen and members of the Council of a Hundred. His opinion was much sought after in the exchange, and his advice was followed by traders and merchants alike.

'You ought to accept the position,' Guillem told him.

Arnau thought about it. He had just been offered one of the two posts of Consul of the Sea of Barcelona. The consuls were the highest authorities for all aspects of trade in the city. They acted as judges in mercantile matters, and had their own jurisdiction, independent of all other institutions in Barcelona. This gave them the authority to mediate in any problem related to the port or port workers, as well as to ensure that the laws and customs of commerce were respected.

'I don't know whether I could—'

'Nobody could do it better, Arnau, believe me,' Guillem interrupted him. 'You can do it. Of course you can.'

Arnau agreed to take over as consul when the two currently in office had finished their term.

The church of Santa Maria, his business concerns, his future duties as Consul of the Sea: all this created a wall around Arnau behind which he felt comfortable, so that when he went back to his new home, the palace in Carrer de Montcada, he did not realize what was going on inside its imposing gateway.

Although he had fulfilled the promises made to Eleonor, he also made sure that the guarantees he had given her were respected, so that his dealings with her were reduced to an absolute minimum. Mar meanwhile was a wonderful twenty-year-old who still refused to be married. Why should I when I have Arnau? What would he do without me? Who would take his shoes off? Who would look after him when he gets back from work? Who would talk to him and listen to his problems? Eleonor? Joan, who's more and more devoted to his studies? The slaves? Or Guillem, whom he spends most of the day with anyway? she reasoned to herself.

Every day, Mar waited impatiently for Arnau to return home. Her breathing quickened whenever she heard him knocking at the door in the gate, and the smile returned to her lips as she ran to greet him at the top of the staircase that led up to the principal rooms of the palace. When Arnau was out during the day, her life was both boring and a torture.

'Not partridge!' she heard the shout from the kitchens. 'Today we are going to eat veal.'

Mar turned to confront the baroness, who was standing in the kitchen doorway. Arnau liked partridge. She had gone with Donaha to buy them. She chose them herself, hung them from a rack in the kitchen and checked on them each day. When she decided they had hung long enough, she went down early in the morning to pluck them.

'But . . .' Mar tried to object.

'Veal,' Eleonor insisted, glaring at her.

Mar turned to look at Donaha, but the slave merely gave a slight shrug of her shoulders.

'I decide what is eaten in this house,' the baroness went on, addressing all the slaves in the kitchen. 'I say what happens here!'

With that, she turned on her heel and left.

Eleonor waited to see what would happen following this explosion. Would the girl turn to Arnau, or keep their argument secret? Mar also thought it over. Should she tell Arnau? What would she gain by that? If Arnau took her side, he would argue with Eleonor, who after all was mistress of the house. And if he didn't support her? Her stomach churned. Arnau had once said that he could not afford to offend the King. What if Eleonor complained to the sovereign over this? What would Arnau say then?

By the end of the day, when Arnau had still not said a word to her, Eleonor smiled scornfully at Mar. From then on, she stepped up her attack on the girl. She forbade her to go with the slaves to the markets, or to go into the kitchens. She put slaves on the door of whichever room she was in. 'The lady baroness does not wish to be disturbed,' they would tell Mar if she tried to enter. Day after day, Eleonor found new ways of making her life difficult.

The King. They had to avoid offending the King. Those words were engraved in Mar's memory; she repeated them to herself time and again. Eleonor was still his ward; she could go and see him whenever she wished. Mar was not going to be the one who gave Eleonor that excuse!

She could not have been more wrong. Eleonor took little satisfaction from these domestic disputes. All her tiny victories were as nothing when Arnau came home and Mar flung herself in his arms. The two of them laughed, talked together . . . their bodies touched. Sitting in an armchair, Arnau would tell her everything that had happened during the day: the discussions at the exchange, his business deals, his ships, while Mar knelt at his feet, entranced by his stories. Wasn't that the place of his legitimate spouse? At night after dinner he would sit in one of the window openings with Mar in his arms, staring up at the starry sky. Behind them, Eleonor would dig the nails into her hands until they began to bleed; the pain would eventually make her get up and withdraw to her own apartments.

All alone, she considered her situation. Arnau had not touched her since their marriage. She stroked her body, ran her hands over her breasts . . . they were still firm! Then her hips, and between her legs . . . as pleasure began to surge through her, she was jolted back to reality: that girl . . . that girl had taken her rightful place!

'What will happen when my husband dies?'

She asked the man straight out, as soon as she had taken a seat at his book-laden table. She could not help coughing; the chamber was full of books, paper, and dust.

Reginald d'Area studied his visitor unhurriedly. Eleonor had been told he was the best lawyer in Barcelona, an expert interpreter of the *Usatges*, the Laws and Customs of Catalonia.

'I understand you have no children with your husband? Is that right?' Eleonor frowned. 'I need to know,' he said placidly. Everything about him, from his plump frame and friendly expression to his white flowing hair and beard, inspired confidence.

'No, I haven't had any.'

'I imagine your enquiry concerns the inheritance?'

Eleonor stirred uneasily in her chair. 'Yes,' she said at length.

'Your dowry will be returned to you. As far as your husband's own inheritance is concerned, he can dispose of it as he wishes in his will.'

'Do I get nothing as of right?'

'You may have use of his goods and properties for a year, the year of strict mourning.'

'Is that all?'

Reginald d'Area was taken aback by her violent retort. Who did she think she was?

'You can thank your guardian King Pedro for that,' he said dryly.

'What do you mean?'

'Until your guardian came to the throne there was a law in Catalonia laid down by King Jaime the First by which the widow could enjoy the whole of her

518

husband's inheritance for life, if she did not misuse it. But the merchants of Barcelona and Perpignan are very jealous of their wealth, even when their wives are involved. It was they who won the concession from King Pedro that widows should have access to the inheritance for only a year. And your guardian has made this provision into a law throughout the entire principality . . .'

Eleonor was not listening, and got up even before the lawyer had finished speaking. She started coughing again and surveyed his chamber. Why did he need so many books? Reginald stood up as well.

'If you need anything else . . .'

Still with her back to him, Eleonor merely raised her hand.

One thing was clear: she needed a child from her husband to secure her future. Arnau had kept his word, and Eleonor had been able to enjoy a very different kind of life: one of luxury, which she had seen while she lived at court, but had been unable to enjoy for herself because of all the royal treasurers' petty regulations. Now she could spend as much as she wanted; she had all she could wish for. But if Arnau were to die . . . And the only thing that stood in her way, the only thing keeping him from her, was that voluptuous young witch. If that witch were not there . . . if she disappeared . . . Arnau would be hers! Surely she would be capable of seducing a runaway serf?

A few days later, Eleonor summoned the friar to her apartments. He was the only one among the Estanyol family with whom she had any dealings.

'I don't believe it!' said Joan.

'But it's true, Brother Joan,' said Eleonor, face buried in her hands. 'He has not even touched me since we were married.'

Joan knew that Arnau had no love for Eleonor and that they slept in different chambers. That was unimportant: nobody married for love, and most nobles slept apart. But if Arnau had never lain with Eleonor, they were not properly married.

'Have you spoken to him about it?' he asked.

Eleonor lowered her hands from her face, making sure that Joan got a good view of her reddened eyes. 'I do not dare. I wouldn't know what to say. Besides, I think . . .' Eleonor let her suspicions float on the air.

'What do you think?'

'I think Arnau is much closer to Mar than to his own wife.'

'You know Arnau adores her.'

'I am not talking about that kind of love, Brother Joan,' she insisted, lowering her voice. Joan sat upright in his chair. 'Yes. I know you find it hard to believe, but I'm sure that girl, as you call her, wants my husband for herself. It's like having the Devil in my house, Brother Joan!' Eleonor brought a tremble to her voice. 'My weapons, Brother Joan, are those of a simple woman who merely wishes to comply with the precepts of the Church regarding married women, but every time I try to, I find that my husband's so blinded by her charms that he is prevented from even seeing me. I have no idea what to do!'

Was that why Mar refused to get married? Could it be true? Joan reflected on it: the two were always together, and he had seen her fling herself into his arms. And the way they looked at each other, the way they laughed and smiled! How stupid he had been! He was sure the Moor knew it, and that was why he always defended her.

'I don't know what to say,' he said evasively.

'I have a plan . . . but I need your help and above all, your advice.'

43

As he listened to Eleonor's plan, a shudder ran through Joan's body.

'I have to think about it,' he told her when she insisted how dramatic her situation was.

That evening he shut himself up in his room. He excused himself from dinner. He avoided Mar and Arnau. He avoided Eleonor's inquisitive looks. Instead, he consulted his volumes of theology, which were neatly arranged in a cupboard. He was confident he could find the answer to his dilemma there. During all the years he had spent apart from his brother, he had always thought of him. He loved Arnau; he and his father were the only ones Joan had had to turn to in his childhood. Yet there were as many hidden folds to his affection as there were in his black habit. Lurking somewhere among them was an admiration that came close to envy. Arnau, with that frank smile of his, those easy gestures: a little boy who claimed he could talk to the Virgin. Brother Joan clenched his fists when he remembered how often he himself had tried to hear that voice. Now he knew it was almost impossible, and that only a chosen few were blessed with that honour. He studied and disciplined himself in the hope that he might be one of them. He fasted until his health was threatened, but all in vain.

Brother Joan buried himself in the doctrines of Bishop Hincmar of Reims, those of Saint Leo the Great, of Master Gratian, the epistles of Saint Paul, and many others.

It was only through the carnal communion of the married couple, the *coniunctio sexuum*, that matrimony among human beings reflected the union of Christ with the Church, which was the main objective of the sacrament. Without that *carnalis copula*, matrimony did not exist, according to the first of these authors.

Only when a marriage has been consummated through carnal relations is it regarded as valid by the Church, ruled Saint Leo the Great.

Gratian, his master at the university of Bologna, went further in this doctrine, linking the symbolism of marriage, the consent freely given by the bride and groom at the altar, and sexual relations between man and woman: the *una caro*. Even Saint Paul, in his famous epistle to the Ephesians, had written: 'So ought men to love their wives as their own bodies. He that loveth his wife loveth himself. For no man ever yet hated his own flesh; but nourisheth and cherisheth it, even as the Lord the church . . . For this cause shall a man leave his father and mother, and shall be joined unto his wife, and they two shall be one flesh. This is a great mystery: but I speak concerning Christ and the church.'

Joan pored over the teachings and doctrines of the doctors of the Church until far into the night. What was he searching for? He opened one of the treatises a second time. For how long was he going to ignore the truth? Eleonor was right: without copulation, without the union of the flesh, there could be no true matrimony.

Why have you not lain with her? You are living in sin. The Church does not recognize your marriage. By the light of a candle he reread Gratian, following the words with his finger. He was looking for something that did not exist. *The royal ward! The King himself gave her to you, and yet you have not copulated with her. What would the King say if he found out? Not even all your money . . . It's an insult to him. He gave you Eleonor in marriage. He himself led her to the altar, and you have spurned the offer he gave you. What about the Bishop? What would he say?* He went back to Gratian. And all because of a stubborn young girl who was refusing to fulfil her destiny as a woman.

Joan spent hours with his books, but his mind continually strayed to thoughts of Eleonor's plan and possible alternatives. He ought to tell Arnau straight out. He imagined himself sitting face to face with Arnau, or possibly standing, yes, both of them standing . . . 'You must lie with Eleonor. At the moment, you are living in sin,' he would tell him. What if this made him angry? After all, he was a Catalan baron, and Consul of the Sea. Who was he, Joan, to tell Arnau what to do? He returned to his books. Why on earth had they ever adopted that girl? She was the cause of all their problems. If Eleonor was right, his brother might feel closer to Mar than to her. Mar was the guilty one. She had rejected all offers of marriage in order to keep tempting Arnau with her charms. What man could resist her? She is the Devil! The Devil made flesh, temptation, sin. Why should he risk losing his brother's love when she was the Devil? Yes, she was the evil one. She was the guilty one. Only Christ was strong enough to resist temptation. Arnau was not God, he was a man. Why should men suffer if the Devil was the guilty one?

Joan plunged into his books again, until finally he found what he was looking for:

See how this evil inclination is so ingrained within us, that human nature of itself and through its original corruption, without need of any other motive or instigation, turns towards this vileness, and were it not for the grace of our Lord in repressing this natural inclination, the whole world would fall into this loathsome temptation. So it is that we read that a young and pure boy, brought up by saintly hermits in the desert far from contact with any female, was sent to the city where his mother and father dwelt. And as soon as he entered the place where they were living, he asked those who had brought him what all the new sights he had seen might be: and as he had seen beautiful, finely adorned women, he asked what they might be, and the saintly hermits told him that these things were devils who brought turmoil everywhere they went, and while they were in his father and mother's house, the hermits who had brought him there asked him as follows: 'Of all the beautiful, new things you have seen and had never seen before, which did you most admire?' And the boy replied: 'Of all the beautiful things I have seen, what I most liked are those devils which bring turmoil to the world.' And when the saintly fathers replied: 'Oh, wretched creature! Have you not often heard and read of the evil that are devils and their works, and that their dwelling place is Hell: how then can they have so much pleased you on your first sight of them?' They say the boy answered them: 'Even though the devils are so evil, and do so much harm, and although they may dwell in Hell, I would not care about all that evil or to be in Hell if I could be and live with devils of that sort. Now I know that the devils of Hell are not as evil as is said. Now I know it would be good to be in Hell, since those devils are there and I would like to be with them. Would that I could join them, God willing.'

It was dawn by the time that Brother Joan had finished reading and closed his books. He was not going to take the risk. He was not going to be the saintly hermit who confronted the little boy who preferred the Devil. He was not going to be the one who called his brother a wretched creature. It was there in his books, the ones Arnau himself had paid for. There was no other possible way. He knelt on the footstool in his room beneath an image of the crucified Christ, and prayed.

That night, before he finally succeeded in finding sleep, he thought he could detect a strange smell, the smell of death seeping into his room and threatening to choke him.

On Saint Mark's day, the members of the Council of a Hundred, together with the city aldermen, elected Arnau Estanyol, Baron of Granollers, Sant Vicenç and Caldes de Montbui, as Consul of the Sea of Barcelona. Then, as laid down in the *Llibre de Consolat de Mar*, to popular acclaim Arnau and the other newly chosen consul led a procession of councillors and prominent citizens down to the exchange, where the Consulate of the Sea was housed. The exchange was also being rebuilt, on the shore close to Santa Maria church and Arnau's counting house.

The *missatges*, as the soldiers belonging to the consulate were known, were drawn up to greet them as the party entered the palace, and the councillors of Barcelona handed possession of the building over to the newly elected consuls. As soon as the others had left the exchange, Arnau immediately set to work: a merchant was claiming the value of a shipment of pepper which had fallen into the sea while a young boatman was unloading it. The pepper was brought to the court-room for Arnau to verify that it had been damaged as claimed.

Arnau listened to the different versions from the merchant, the boatman and the witnesses both sides had brought. He knew the merchant personally, as he did the boatman. The latter had recently asked him for a loan. He was newly married. On that occasion, Arnau had congratulated him and wished him well.

'I rule that the boatman must pay the price of the pepper,' he said, his voice trembling. 'This is as laid down in . . .' Arnau consulted the heavy tome the clerk passed him, 'article sixty-two of our Customs of the Sea.' The young boatman had just asked him for a loan. He was newly married, in Santa Maria as befitted all men of the sea. Was his wife pregnant already? Arnau recalled the gleam of excitement in the young bride's eyes the day he had congratulated them. He cleared his throat: 'Do you have . . .' – he coughed again – 'Do you have the money to pay?'

Arnau could not look at him. He had just given him a loan. Could it have been for his house? For linen? For furnishings, or perhaps for the boat itself? The young man's negative reply rang in his ears.

'I therefore sentence you to . . .' The lump rising in his throat almost prevented him going on. 'I sentence you to prison until you pay off the entire amount of your debt.'

How could he pay it if he were not able to work? Was his wife pregnant? Arnau forgot to rap the bench with his gavel. The *missatges* stared at him. He remembered, and hit the wooden bench in front of him. The young boatman was led away to the consulate's cells. Arnau lowered his head.

'It's something you have to do,' the clerk said when all the others had left the courtroom.

Seated to the right of the clerk in the centre of the immense judge's bench, Arnau sat and said nothing.

'Look,' the clerk insisted, showing him another thick book that contained the consulate's rules and regulations. 'Here's what it says concerning prison sentences: "This is how the consul shall demonstrate his power, from greater to less." You are the Consul of the Sea and have to demonstrate your power. Our prosperity, the prosperity of this city, depends on it.'

He did not have to send anyone else to prison that day, but on many others found himself forced to do so. The Consul of the Sea's jurisdiction included everything that had to do with commerce: prices, the crews' wages, the security of ships and goods . . . and anything else related to the sea. Arnau quickly established himself as an authority independent of the city bailiff and magistrate; he passed sentence, embargoed ships, seized debtors' goods, sent others to gaol, backed up by the army of *missatges*.

While Arnau was busy at the consulate, obliged to send young boatmen and others to prison, Eleonor summoned Felip de Ponts. He was a knight she had known since her first marriage. He had been to see her on several occasions to ask her to intercede on his behalf with Arnau, whom he owed a considerable amount of money he could not repay.

'I've tried everything I could, Don Felip,' Eleonor lied when he appeared before her, 'but it is impossible. He is going to call in your debt soon.'

When he heard this, Felip de Ponts, a tall, strong-looking man with a bushy blond beard and small eyes, turned pale. If his debts were reclaimed, he would lose what little land he possessed . . . and even his warhorse. A knight without land to provide him with income and without a horse to go to war on was no knight at all.

Felip de Ponts bent on one knee. 'I beg you, my lady,' he pleaded. 'I'm sure that if you so desired, your husband would postpone his decision. If he recovers his debt, my life will not be worth living. Do it for me! For old times' sake!'

Eleonor stood in front of the kneeling knight for some time, giving the impression she was thinking the matter over.

'Stand up,' she ordered him. 'There might be a possibility . . .'

'I beg you!' Felip de Ponts said, before rising.

'It is very hazardous.'

'That does not matter! I'm not afraid of anything. I've fought with the King in all—'

'It would involve abducting a young girl,' Eleonor blurted out.

'I don't . . . I don't understand,' the knight stuttered after a few moments.

'You understood perfectly,' Eleonor replied. 'It involves abducting a young girl and then . . . deflowering her.'

'That is punishable by death!'

'Not always.'

This was what Eleonor had heard. She had never dared ask, especially with this plan of hers in mind, but she turned to Joan to confirm it.

'We need to find someone who will abduct her,' she told him, 'and then rape her.' Joan buried his face in his hands. 'As I understand it,' she went on, 'the *Usatges* of Catalonia state that if the girl or her parents agree to the marriage, then the rapist will not face punishment.' Joan's hand was still in front of his face. 'Is that true, Brother Joan?' she insisted, when he made no reply.

'Yes, but . . .'

'Is it true or not?'

'It is true,' Joan concurred. 'Rape is punishable by life-long exile if no violence is involved, and with death if there is. But if the two agree to marry, or the rapist pro-poses a husband of similar social rank whom the girl accepts, then there is no punishment.'

A smile stole across Eleonor's face, which she quickly

tried to stifle when Joan again tried to get her to change her mind. She adopted the position of the wronged wife.

'I don't know, but I can tell you there is nothing I would not try in order to win my husband back. Let's find someone who will abduct her,' she insisted, 'then rape her, and then we will consent to him marrying the girl.' Joan shook his head. 'What's the difference?' Eleonor stressed. 'We could force Mar to marry, even against her will, if Arnau were not so blind . . . so bewitched by that girl. You yourself have said you wanted to see her marry, but Arnau will not hear of it. All we would be doing is resisting that woman's pernicious influence on my husband. We would be the ones who chose Mar's future husband, just as if she were being married in an ordinary way. The only difference is we do not need Arnau's agreement. We cannot count on that, because he has lost his reason over that girl. Do you know any other father who would allow his daughter to grow old without marrying? However much money they may have, or however noble they are. Do you know anyone? Even the King gave me away against . . . without asking my opinion.'

Joan gradually yielded to Eleonor's arguments. She used the friar's weakness to insist over and over again on her precarious situation, the sin that was being committed in her own home. Joan promised to think it over . . . and did so. Eventually, he agreed they should approach Felip de Ponts: with conditions, but he did agree.

'Not always,' Eleonor said again.

Knights were expected to know what was in the *Usatges*.

'Are you sure the girl would agree to the marriage? Why hasn't she married already then?'

'Her guardians will give their permission.'

'Why don't they simply arrange a marriage for her?'

'That is none of our business,' Eleonor cut in. That, she thought, will be for me to sort out . . . me and the friar.

'You are asking me to abduct and rape a girl, and yet you tell me the reason behind it is none of my business. You have chosen the wrong man, my lady. I may be a debtor, but I am a knight . . .'

'She is my ward.' Felip de Ponts looked surprised. 'Yes. I'm talking about my ward, Mar Estanyol.'

Felip de Ponts well remembered the girl Arnau had adopted. He had seen her several times in the counting house, and had even shared a pleasant conversation with her one day when he had gone to visit Eleonor.

'You want me to abduct and rape your own ward?'

'I think I have been sufficiently clear, Don Felip. I can assure you that there will be no punishment.'

'What reason—?'

'The reasons are my affair! Well, what do you say?'

'What will I gain by it?'

'Her dowry will be generous enough to cancel all your debts. Believe me, my husband will be exceedingly generous towards his daughter. Besides, you would win my favour, and you know how close I am to the King.'

'What about the baron?'

'I will deal with him.'

'I don't understand—'

'There's nothing more to understand: ruin, disrepute, dishonour . . . or my support.' At this, Felip de Ponts sat down. 'Ruin or riches, Don Felip. If you reject my offer, tomorrow will see the baron calling in your debt and disposing of your lands, your weapons and your animals. You can rest assured of that.'

44

Ten days of anguished uncertainty went by until Arnau received the first news of Mar. Ten days during which he suspended all activity beyond that of trying to find out what had become of the girl, who had disappeared without trace. He met the city magistrate and councillors to press them to do all they could to discover what had happened. He offered huge rewards for any information about Mar's fate or whereabouts. He prayed more than he had ever prayed before, until finally Eleonor, who said she had heard something from a passing merchant who had been looking for him, confirmed his worst suspicions. The girl had been kidnapped by a knight by the name of Felip de Ponts who was one of his debtors. The knight was keeping her by force in a fortified farmhouse close to Mataró, which was less than a day on foot north of Barcelona.

Arnau sent the consulate's *missatges* to the farmhouse. He himself returned to Santa Maria to pray to his Virgin of the Sea once more.

Nobody dared interrupt him; out of respect, the workmen took greater care with whatever they were doing.

On his knees beneath the small stone figure which had always meant so much to him, Arnau tried to ward off the scenes of horror and panic that had assaulted him over the past ten days and now came flashing into his mind once again, interspersed with images of Felip de Ponts's face.

Felip de Ponts had seized Mar inside her own house. He bound and gagged her, and beat her until she was so exhausted she could no longer resist. He bundled her into a sack and sat with it up on the back of a cart loaded with harnesses driven by one of his servants. Then, making as though he had come to buy or repair bridles and saddles, he was able to pass through the city gates without arousing the slightest suspicion. Back in his own farmhouse, he took her into the fortified tower lying alongside it, and there raped her time and again, his violence and passion only increasing as he realized how beautiful his captive was and how obstinately she tried to defend her body even after she had lost her virginity. Felip de Ponts had promised Joan he would rob her of her virtue without even undressing her, without showing her his own body and using only the minimum force. He kept his promise the first time, which was meant to be the only occasion he came near her, but soon desire overcame his knight's sense of honour.

Nothing that Arnau imagined, with tears in his eyes and quaking heart, could compare to what Mar really suffered.

When the *missatges* entered Santa Maria, all work on the church stopped. Their captain's words echoed as loudly as they did in the consulate courtroom: 'Most honourable consul, it is true. Your daughter has been seized and is being held by the knight Felip de Ponts.'

'Have you spoken to him?'

'No, your honour. He has barricaded himself in his tower and refused to accept our authority. He claims that this has nothing to do with commerce or the sea.'

'Do you know how the girl is?'

The captain lowered his gaze.

Arnau clawed at the footstool. 'He is challenging my authority? If it's authority he wants,' he growled between clenched teeth, 'I'll see he gets it.'

The news of Mar's abduction spread rapidly. At dawn the next morning all the bells of Barcelona began to ring. The cry of 'Via fora' came from the throats of all the citizens in the streets: a woman from Barcelona had to be rescued.

As so often in the past, Plaça del Blat became the meeting point for the *sometent*, the army of Barcelona. Soon all the guilds of the city were present in the square. Not one was missing; they all lined up beneath their pennants, fully armed. Instead of wearing his fine merchant's clothes, Arnau donned the tunic he had worn when he had fought under Eximèn d'Esparça and later against Pedro the Cruel. He still had his father's precious crossbow, which he had never wanted to replace and which he now stroked as he had never done before. He tucked into his belt the dagger he had used so skilfully years before to kill his enemies.

When he appeared in the square, more than three thousand men cheered him. The standard-bearers raised their pennants. Swords, spears and crossbows were waved above the heads of the crowd, as they shouted a deafening 'Via fora!' Arnau did not react, but Joan and Eleonor turned pale. Arnau searched beyond the sea of weapons and pennants: the moneychangers did not belong to any guild.

'Was this part of your plans?' the Dominican asked Eleonor above the hubbub.

Eleonor was staring fearfully at the massed guilds. The whole of Barcelona had come out to support Arnau.

They were waving their weapons in the air and howling. All for that wretched young girl!

At last Arnau saw the pennant he was looking for. The crowd opened in front of him to allow him to join the *bastaixos'* guild.

'Was this part of your plans?' the friar asked again. Both of them watched Arnau striding away into the crowd. Eleonor made no reply. 'They'll eat your knight alive. They'll destroy his lands, raze his farmhouse, and then . . .'

'Then what?' grunted Eleonor, still staring straight ahead of her.

Then I'll lose my brother. Perhaps we're still in time to do something. This is going to end badly . . . thought Joan.

'Speak to him,' he insisted.

'Are you mad, friar?'

'What if he won't accept the marriage? What if Felip de Ponts tells him everything? Talk to him before the *host* sets off. For the love of God, do it, Eleonor!'

'For the love of God?' As she spat out the words, she turned to face him. 'You speak to your God. Do it, friar.'

They followed Arnau towards the *bastaixos'* pennant. They met Guillem, who as a slave was not allowed to bear arms.

When he saw her arriving, Arnau frowned.

'She's a ward of mine as well,' she said.

The city councillors gave the order. The army of the people of Barcelona began to march out of the square. The pennants of Sant Jordi and the city were at the head, followed by that of the *bastaixos* and then all the other guilds. Three thousand men against a single knight. Eleonor and Joan fell in beside them.

Outside the city, the *host* was joined by more than a hundred peasants from Arnau's lands. They were happy to come to the defence of someone who had treated them so generously. Arnau noticed that no other nobles or knights were among them.

Grim-faced, Arnau walked alongside the pennant with the *bastaixos'* column. Joan tried to pray, but the words that usually came so readily to him now stubbornly refused to appear in his mind. Neither he nor Eleonor had ever imagined that Arnau would call out the *host*. Joan was still deafened by the noise of the three thousand men clamouring for justice and vengeance for a citizen of Barcelona. Many of them had kissed their daughters before they left; more than one, already strapped into their armour, had cupped their wife's chin in their hand and told them: 'Barcelona defends its own . . . especially its women.'

They will lay waste to poor Felip de Ponts's lands as if it were their own daughter who had been abducted, thought Joan. They will try him and execute him, but first they will give him the chance to talk . . . Joan looked at Arnau, who was still marching along in silence.

By evening, the *host* had reached Felip de Ponts's lands. It came to a halt at the foot of a small hill atop which the knight's fortress was perched. It was nothing more than a peasant farmhouse; its only defences consisted of a small tower rising on one side. Joan studied the farmhouse, then surveyed the army awaiting its orders from the city councillors. He looked at Eleonor, who avoided his gaze. Three thousand men to take one simple farmhouse!

Joan shook himself and ran to where Arnau and Guillem were standing, next to the councillors and other prominent citizens of Barcelona, beneath the Sant Jordi pennant. As he drew near, he could hear them discussing what to do next. His stomach clenched when he realized most of them were in favour of attacking the farmhouse without warning or offering Ponts the chance to surrender.

The councillors began to give orders to the guild aldermen. Joan looked at Eleonor, but she was staring straight ahead at the farmhouse. Joan went up to Arnau: he wanted to speak to him, but found it impossible. Guillem was standing proudly beside him; he glanced at the friar with a look of scorn. The guild aldermen passed on the orders to their columns. Sounds of preparation for battle could be heard. Torches were lit; the sound of swords being drawn and crossbows tightened rose through the evening air. Joan turned to look at the farmhouse, and then again at the *host*. The men began to march on the building. There would be no concessions: Barcelona would show no mercy. Arnau drew his dagger and set off with all the rest, leaving the friar behind as he advanced on the house. Joan glanced despairingly towards Eleonor; still she showed no reaction.

'No . . .!' shouted Joan as his brother strode away from him.

His cry was swallowed up in a murmur that spread through the ranks of the entire *host*. A man on horseback had emerged from the farmhouse. It was Felip de Ponts, slowly riding his horse down towards them.

'Seize him!' shouted one of the councillors.

'No!' shouted Joan again. Everyone turned in his direction. Arnau looked enquiringly at him. 'A man who surrenders should not be seized and made captive.'

'What's this, friar?' one of the councillors asked. 'Do you think you can give orders to the Barcelona *host*?'

Joan looked imploringly at Arnau. 'A man who surrenders should not be taken captive,' he repeated.

'Let him give himself up,' Arnau conceded.

Felip de Ponts looked first for his accomplices, then turned to face the men gathered beneath the pennant of Sant Jordi, among them Arnau and the city councillors.

'Citizens of Barcelona,' he shouted, loud enough for the whole army to hear, 'I know the reason why you are here today. I know you are seeking justice for one of your citizens. Here I stand. I confess to being the perpetrator of the crimes I am accused of, but before you take me prisoner and lay waste my buildings, I beg you for the chance to speak.'

'Do so,' one of the councillors authorized him.

'It is true that, against her will, I have abducted and lain with Mar Estanyol . . .' At this, a murmur ran through the ranks of the *host*, forcing him to break off for a moment. Arnau's hands gripped his crossbow. 'I did so at the risk of losing my life, aware that this is the punishment for such an offence. I did it, and if I were born a second time I would do it again because such is the love I have for this girl, such the despair I felt at see-ing her waste her youth without a husband beside her to help her enjoy the fruits God blessed her with, that my emotions overcame my reason, and I behaved more like an animal crazed with passion than one of King Pedro's knights.' Joan could sense the entire army listening intently, and willed the knight to say the right thing. 'For being an animal, I hand myself over to you; but as the knight I long to become once more, I solemnly swear to marry Mar Estanyol and to love her for the rest of my life. Judge me! I am not prepared, as our laws provide, to give her up to another husband of the same social rank. I would kill myself rather than see her with anyone else.'

Felip de Ponts finished his speech and waited, proud and erect on his steed, defying an army of three thousand men. The *host* was silent, trying to take in all that they had heard.

'Praised be the Lord!' shouted Joan.

Arnau stared at him in astonishment. Everyone, including Eleonor, turned to look at the friar.

'What do you mean by that?' Arnau asked him.

'Arnau,' Joan insisted, taking hold of his arm and speaking loud enough for all those around them to hear, 'this is nothing more than the result of our own negligence.' Arnau looked startled. 'For years we have gone along with Mar's whims, neglecting our duties towards a beautiful young woman who should already have brought children into the world, as the laws of God decree – and who are we to go against our Lord's intentions?' Arnau started to say something, but Joan raised his hand to cut him short. 'I feel guilty about this. For years I have felt guilty about being too complaisant with a headstrong girl whose life was without meaning according to the precepts of the holy Catholic Church. This knight,' he went on, pointing to Felip de Ponts, 'is nothing more than the hand of God, someone sent by Our Lord to carry out a task we have proved ourselves unequal to. Yes, for years I have felt guilty seeing how God-given beauty and health was being wasted by a girl fortunate enough to be adopted by somebody as good and kind as you. I have no wish also to feel guilt for the death of a knight who, risking his own life, has merely accomplished what we ourselves were incapable of doing. Give your consent to the marriage. I, if my opinion is of any worth, would accept the knight's proposal.'

Arnau said nothing for some time. The whole army was waiting to hear what he had to say. Joan took advantage of the delay to glance round at Eleonor, and thought he could see a triumphant smile on her lips.

'Do you mean to say that all this is my fault?' Arnau asked Joan.

'Mine, Arnau, mine. It's I who should have instructed you concerning the laws of the Church, and what God's designs for mankind are, but I never did . . . and am sorry for it.'

Guillem's eyes were blazing.

'What are the girl's wishes?' Arnau asked Felip de Ponts.

'I am a knight of King Pedro,' the other man replied, 'and his laws, the exact same ones which have brought you here today, take no account of the wishes of a woman of marrying age.' A mutter of approval ran through the ranks of the *host*. 'I, Felip de Ponts, a Catalan knight, am offering my hand in marriage. If you, Arnau Estanyol, Baron of Catalonia and Consul of the Sea, do not consent to the marriage, then take me prisoner and judge me. But if you do consent, then the girl's wishes are of little importance.'

'This is not about her wishes, Arnau,' Joan insisted, lowering his voice. 'It's about your duty. Fulfil it. Nobody asks their daughters' or their wards' opinion. The decision as to what is best for them is taken on their behalf. This man has lain with Mar. What she wishes does not really matter now. Either she marries him or her life will be hell. You are the one to decide, Arnau: another senseless death, or the divine solution to our lack of care.'

Arnau turned to his companions. He saw Guillem still staring at the knight, bristling with hatred. He saw Eleonor, the wife the King had forced on him. They met each other's gaze. Arnau gestured to her for her opinion. Eleonor nodded. Arnau turned back to Joan.

'It's the law,' Joan insisted.

Arnau looked at the knight, then at the army. They had all lowered their weapons. None of the three thousand men seemed to dismiss Felip de Ponts's arguments: none of them wanted war. They were all waiting for Arnau's decision. Such was the law of Catalonia, the law regarding women. What was to be gained by fighting, killing the knight and freeing Mar? What would her life be like now that she had been abducted and raped? Would she spend it in a convent?

'I give my consent.'

There was a moment's silence. Then, as Arnau's

decision spread through them, a murmur rose from the ranks of soldiers. Someone shouted his approval. Another man agreed. Several more joined in, until the entire *host* acclaimed it.

Joan and Eleonor glanced at each other.

A hundred yards away, locked in the tower of Felip de Ponts's farmhouse, the woman whose future had just been decided was watching the army massed at the foot of the hill outside. Why did they not charge up it? Why did they not attack? What could they be discussing with that wretch? What were they shouting?

'Arnau? What are your men shouting?'

45

It was the shouts from the *host* that convinced Guillem
that what he had heard was true: *I consent*. He clenched
his teeth. Somebody clapped him on the back and
joined in the shouting. *I consent*. Guillem stared at Arnau
and then at the knight. His face seemed relaxed. What
could a mere slave like him do? He looked again at Felip
de Ponts: now he was smiling. 'I have lain with Mar
Estanyol . . .' That was what he had said. 'I have lain with
Mar Estanyol!' How could Arnau . . .?

Someone thrust a wineskin at him. Guillem pushed it
away.

'Don't you drink, Christian?' Guillem heard someone
ask.

He caught Arnau's eye. The city councillors were
congratulating Felip de Ponts, who was still on his
steed. All around him, soldiers were drinking and
laughing.

'Don't you drink, Christian?' Guillem heard again
behind him.

Guillem pushed the man off and looked in Arnau's
direction once more. The councillors were congratulating

him as well. Despite being surrounded, Arnau met Guillem's gaze.

Then the crowd, with Joan among them, forced Arnau to head up the hill to the farmhouse. Arnau was still looking back at Guillem.

The entire *host* was celebrating the agreement reached. Some soldiers had lit camp fires and sat around them singing.

'Drink to our consul and the happiness of his daughter,' said another man, again offering him a wineskin.

Arnau had disappeared on the track up to the house.

Guillem pushed the wineskin away again.

'Are you refusing to drink to . . .?'

Guillem stared the man in the eye, then turned his back on him and set off in the direction of Barcelona. Gradually the noise of the *host* faded in the distance. Guillem found himself alone on the road back to the city. He walked along, dragging his feet . . . dragging with him his feelings, and what little pride as a man he could still feel as a mere slave. All this he dragged along with him back to Barcelona.

Arnau refused the cheese that the trembling old woman who looked after Felip de Ponts's farmhouse offered him. Aldermen and councillors had all crowded into the large room above the stables, where the big stone hearth stood. Arnau looked in vain for Guillem among the crowd of people. Everyone was talking and laughing, calling out to the old woman for her to serve them cheese and wine. Joan and Eleonor stayed close to the hearth; whenever Arnau looked in their direction, they glanced away.

A sudden whisper in the crowd made him switch his attention to the far end of the room.

Mar had come in on Felip de Ponts's arm. Arnau saw her pull herself free and come running over to him. She was smiling. She threw her arms open, but instead of embracing him, suddenly stopped and let them fall by her sides.

Arnau thought he could see a bruise on her cheek.

'What is going on, Arnau?'

Arnau turned to Joan for help, but his brother was still looking down at the floor. Everyone in the room was waiting for him to speak.

'The knight Felip de Ponts has invoked the *usatge: Si quis virginem . . .*' he muttered at length.

Mar did not move. A tear started to roll down her cheek. Arnau lifted his hand to brush it away, then thought better of it, and the teardrop slid down Mar's neck.

'Your father,' Felip de Ponts began to say from behind them, before Arnau could silence him, 'the Consul of the Sea, has consented to your marriage before the entire *host* of Barcelona.' He rushed through the words before Arnau could stop him . . . or change his mind.

'Is this true?' asked Mar.

The only thing that's true is that I would like to hold you . . . kiss you . . . have you with me always. Is that what a father should feel? Arnau thought.

'Yes, Mar.'

No more tears appeared in Mar's eyes. When Felip de Ponts came up and took her arm again, she did not object. Somebody behind Arnau gave a cheer, and all the others joined in. Arnau and Mar were still staring at each other. When a shout of congratulation to the bride and groom rang out, Arnau felt he was drowning. Now it was his cheeks that were streaming with tears. Perhaps his brother was right, perhaps Joan had understood what he himself had been unable to see. He had sworn to the Virgin that he would never again be unfaithful to a wife, even if that wife were not of his choosing, out of love for another woman.

'Father?' Mar beseeched him, reaching out her hand to dry his tears.

Arnau's whole body shook when he felt her fingers on his face. He turned on his heel and fled.

At that moment, out on the lonely, dark road back to the city of Barcelona, a slave raised his eyes to the heavens and heard the ghastly cry of pain issuing from the throat of the girl he had loved and looked after as his own child. He was born a slave, and had lived all his life as one. He had learnt to love in silence and to stifle his emotions. A slave was not an ordinary man, which was why in his solitude – the only place where no one could restrict his freedom – he had learnt to see much further than all those whose souls were clouded by life. He had seen the love they had for each other, and had prayed to his twin gods that the two he loved most in the world would seize the chance and free themselves from the chains that bound them far tighter than those a slave had to endure.

Then Guillem did something that as a slave he never permitted himself. He allowed his tears to flow.

Guillem never entered Barcelona. He reached the city while it was still dark, and stood outside the closed Sant Daniel gate. His little girl had been snatched from him. Perhaps he had not been aware of it, but Arnau had sold her just as if she had been a slave. What would Guillem do in Barcelona? How could he sit where once Mar had sat? How could he walk down streets where he had walked with her, talking, laughing, sharing the secrets of her innermost feelings? What would he do in Barcelona apart from remember her day and night? What future could he have alongside the man who had put an end to both their dreams?

Guillem turned away from the city and continued along the coast. After two days' travel he reached the port of Salou, the second most important in Catalonia. He stared out at the horizon. The sea breeze brought him memories of his childhood in Genoa, of a mother and brothers and sisters he had been cruelly separated from when he was sold to a merchant who began to teach him his trade. Then during a sea voyage, master and slave had been captured by the Catalans, who were constantly at war with Genoa. Guillem passed from master to master until Hasdai Crescas saw in him qualities far beyond those of a simple workman. Guillem gazed out to sea again, at the ships, the people on board . . . why not Genoa?

'When does the next ship leave for Lombardy, for Pisa?'

The young man rummaged in the papers strewn all over the table in the store. He did not know Guillem, and had at first treated him with a great show of disdain, as he would have any dirty, foul-smelling slave, but as soon as the Moor told him who he was, he remembered what his father had often said to him: 'Guillem is the right-hand man of Arnau Estanyol, the Consul of the Sea, and someone who provides us with our livelihood.'

'I need writing materials and a quiet place to write,' Guillem said.

'I accept your offer of freedom,' he wrote. 'I am leaving for Genoa via Pisa. I will travel there in your name, still a slave, and await my letter of emancipation.' What else should he write: that he could not live without Mar? Would his master and friend Arnau be able to? Why remind him of that? 'I am going in search of my roots, of my family,' he wrote. 'Together with Hasdai, you have been my best friend. Take care of him. I shall be forever grateful to you. May Allah and Santa Maria keep watch over you. I will pray for you.'

As soon as the galley Guillem had embarked on was making its way out of Salou harbour, the young man who had attended him left for Barcelona.

* * *

Very slowly, Arnau signed the letter setting Guillem free. Each stroke of the pen reminded him of something from the past: the plague, the confrontation, the counting house, day after day of work, talk, friendship, shared happiness . . . As he reached the end, his hand shook, and when he had finished, the feather quill bent double. Both he and Guillem knew the real reason why he had been driven away from Barcelona.

Arnau returned to the exchange. He ordered that his letter be sent to his agent in Pisa, together with a bill of payment for a small fortune.

'Should we not wait for Arnau?' Joan asked Eleonor when he came into the dining room and saw her already seated at table, ready to eat.

'Are you hungry?' Joan nodded. 'Well, if you want supper you had better have some now.'

The friar sat beside Eleonor at one end of Arnau's long dining table. Two servants offered them white wheat bread, wine, soup and roast goose with pepper and onions.

'Didn't you say you were hungry?' asked Eleonor when she saw that Joan was merely pushing the food around his plate.

Joan looked across at his sister-in-law and said nothing. They did not exchange another word that evening.

Several hours after he had trudged upstairs to his room, Joan heard noises in the palace. Several servants had gone out into the yard to receive Arnau. They would offer him food and he would refuse, just as he had done on the three previous occasions that Joan had decided to wait up for him: Arnau had sat in one of the chambers, and waved away their offers with a weary gesture.

* * *

Joan could hear the servants coming back. Then he heard Arnau's footsteps outside his door, as he slowly made for his bedroom. What could he say to him if he went out and greeted him? He had tried to talk to him on the three occasions he had waited up for him, but Arnau had been completely withdrawn and had answered his brother's questions in monosyllables: 'Do you feel well?' 'Yes.' 'Did you have a lot of work at the exchange?' 'No.' 'Are things going well?' No answer. 'What about Santa Maria?' 'Fine.' In the darkness of his room, Joan buried his face in his hands. Arnau's footsteps had faded away. What could he talk to him about? About her? How could he hear from Arnau's lips the fact that he loved her?

Joan had seen Mar wipe away the tears running down Arnau's cheeks. 'Father?' he had heard her say. He had seen Arnau tremble. He had turned and seen Eleonor smile. He had needed to see Arnau suffer to understand . . . but how could he confess the truth to him now? How could he tell him he had been the one . . .? The sight of those tears came back into his mind. Did he love her so much? Would he be able to forget her? Nobody was there to comfort Joan when yet again he got down on his knees and prayed until dawn.

'I should like to leave Barcelona.'

The Dominican prior studied the friar: he looked haggard, with sunken eyes circled with dark lines. His black habit was filthy.

'Do you think, Brother Joan, that you are capable of taking on the role of inquisitor?'

'Yes,' Joan assured him. The prior looked him up and down. 'If I can only leave Barcelona, I will feel better.'

'So be it. Next week you are to leave for the north.'

His destination was a region of small farming villages dedicated to growing crops or raising livestock. They were hidden in valleys and mountains, and their inhabitants were terrified of the arrival of an inquisitor. The Inquisition was nothing new to them: since more than a century earlier, when Ramon de Penyafort was charged by Pope Innocent IV with bringing the institution to the kingdom of Aragon and the principality of Narbonne, these villages had suffered visits from the black friars. Most of the doctrines that the Catholic Church considered heretical came through Catalonia from France: first the Cathars and the Waldensians, then the Beghards and finally the Templars when they were chased out by the French King. The border regions were the first to come under these heretical influences, and many of their nobles were condemned and executed: Viscount Arnau and his wife Ermessenda, Ramon the lord of Cadí, Guillem de Niort, the deputy of Count Nuño Sanç in the Cerdagne and Coflent. These were the lands Brother Joan was called upon to work in.

'Your excellency,' he was greeted by a party of the leading citizens of one of these villages. They all bowed before him.

'Do not call me "excellency",' insisted Joan, urging them to straighten up. 'Simply say "Brother Joan".'

In his brief experience, this scene had already been repeated time and again. The news of his arrival, accompanied by a scribe and half a dozen soldiers from the Holy Office, always preceded him.

Now he found himself in the main square of the village. He surveyed the four men, who still stood in front of him with bowed heads. They had taken off their caps, and shifted uneasily. Although there was no one else in the square, Joan knew that many pairs of hidden eyes were watching him. Did they have so much to conceal?

After being received in this way, Joan knew they would offer him the best lodgings in the village. There he would find a table that was too well stocked for the means of people like these.

'I only want a piece of cheese, some bread and water. Take away all the rest and make sure my men are seen to,' he repeated once again after installing himself at table.

The kind of house he was put up in was becoming familiar as well. It was a humble, simple dwelling, but stone-built, unlike most of the other buildings, which were nothing more than mud or wooden hovels. The table and a few chairs were the only furniture in the room, the centre of which was the hearth.

'Your excellency must be tired.'

Joan stared at the cheese on his plate. To get here, he and his men had walked for several hours up rocky tracks in the chill of early morning, their feet muddy and wet from dew. Under the table, he rubbed his aching calf and crossed his right foot over his left to rub that too.

'Don't call me "excellency",' he repeated yet again, 'and I am not tired. God does not tolerate tiredness when it is a question of defending his name. We will start as soon as I have had something to eat. Gather the people in the square.'

Before he had left Barcelona, Joan had asked in Santa Caterina convent to consult the treatise that Pope Gregory IX had written in 1231 describing the procedures to be adopted by itinerant inquisitors.

'Sinners! Repent!' First came the sermon to the people. The sixty or so inhabitants of the village who had gathered in the square lowered their heads when they heard the friar's opening words. The black friar's stern expression paralysed them. 'The fires of hell await you!' The first time he had spoken, he had not been sure whether he would be able to find a way to address them, but the words had flowed, one after the other, and as he became aware of the power he had over these terrified peasants, the more easily they came. 'Not one of you will escape! God will not allow black sheep in his flock.' They had to speak out: heresy had to be brought to light. That was his task: to seek out the sins committed in secret, the ones only neighbours, friends or spouses knew about . . .

'God knows this. He knows you. His all-seeing eye is upon you. Anyone who sees sin and does not denounce it will burn in the eternal fires, because it is even worse to tolerate sin than to commit it; he who sins may be forgiven, but he who hides sin . . .' Having said this, he would study them closely: an uneasy shuffling here, a furtive glance there. They would be the first. 'He who hides sin . . .' Joan fell silent again, saying nothing until he could see them quaking at his threatening words. '. . . will never be forgiven.'

Fear. Fire, pain, sin, punishment . . . the black friar shouted and persisted in his diatribe until he controlled their minds: his grip over them began with this first sermon.

'You have a period of grace of three days,' he said finally. 'Anyone who comes voluntarily to confess their guilt will be dealt with mercifully. After those three days . . . the punishment will be exemplary.' He turned to the captain. 'Investigate that blonde woman over there, that barefoot man and the one with the black belt. And that girl with the baby . . .' Joan pointed them all out discreetly. 'If they do not come forward themselves, you are to bring them to me, together with another three chosen at random.'

Throughout the three days of grace, Joan remained seated, unmoving, behind the table in his lodging. With him were the scribe and the soldiers, who shifted from foot to foot as the hours slowly went by.

Only four people appeared to relieve their boredom: two men who had not fulfilled their obligation to attend mass, a woman who had disobeyed her husband on several occasions, and a child who poked his head, wide-eyed, round the door. Someone was pushing him from behind, but the boy refused to enter the room properly, and stood in the doorway, half in and half out.

'Come in, boy,' Joan urged him.

At this, the boy drew back, but once again a hand pushed him inside the room, then shut the door behind him.

'How old are you?' asked Joan.

The boy stared at the soldiers, at the scribe who had already begun to write, and at the black friar. 'Nine,' he said hesitantly.

'What is your name?'

'Alfons.'

'Come closer, Alfons. What do you want to tell us?'

'That . . . that two months ago I picked some beans from our neighbour's garden.'

'You picked?' asked Joan.

Alfons lowered his gaze. 'I stole,' he said in a faint voice.

Joan got up from his pallet and trimmed the lantern. The village had been silent for hours, and he had spent all that time trying to get to sleep. Whenever he shut his eyes and felt drowsy, a teardrop falling down Arnau's cheek would jerk him back awake. He needed light. He tried many times to sleep, but always found himself sitting up on the pallet, sometimes fearful, at others bathed in sweat, always engulfed by memories that haunted him.

He needed light. He checked there was still oil in the lamp. Arnau's sad face peered at him out of the shadows.

He fell back on the pallet. It was cold. It was always cold. For a while he lay and watched the flickering flame and the shadows dancing in its light. The only window in the room had no glass, and the wind was whistling through it. *We are all dancing a dance . . . mine is . . .*

He curled up under the blankets and forced himself to close his eyes once more.

Where was the light of day? One more morning, and their three days of grace would be up.

Joan fell into an uneasy sleep, but half an hour later he woke up again, in a sweat. The lantern was still burning, the shadows still dancing. The village was completely quiet. Why did day not dawn?

He wrapped himself in the blankets and went over to the window.

Another village. Another night waiting for day to dawn.

Waiting for the next day . . .

That morning a line of villagers stood outside the house, guarded by the soldiers.

She said her name was Peregrina. Joan pretended not to be paying much attention to the blonde woman who was fourth in line. He had got nothing out of the first three. Peregrina stood in front of the table where Joan and the scribe were sitting. The fire crackled in the hearth. Nobody else was inside the house: the soldiers were posted outside the front door. Suddenly Joan looked up. The woman began to tremble.

'You know something, don't you, Peregrina? God sees everything,' Joan told her. Peregrina nodded, but did not raise her eyes from the beaten earth floor. 'Look at me. I need you to look at me. Do you want to burn in everlasting flames? Look at me. Do you have children?'

Slowly, the woman looked up. 'Yes, but—' she stammered.

'But they are not the sinful ones, is that it?' Joan interrupted her. 'Who is then, Peregrina?' The woman hesitated. 'Who is it, Peregrina?'

'Blasphemy,' she said.

'Who is committing blasphemy, Peregrina?'

The scribe was poised to write.

'She is . . .' Joan waited without saying anything. There

was no going back now. 'I've heard her blaspheme when she is angry . . .' Peregrina's gaze darted back to the floor. 'My husband's sister, Marta. She says terrible things when she is angry.'

The scratch of the scribe's quill on the parchment drove out all other noises.

'Is there anything more, Peregrina?'

This time the woman raised her eyes and looked at him calmly. 'No, nothing more.'

'Are you sure?'

'I swear it. You have to believe me.'

Joan had only been mistaken about the man with the black belt. The barefoot man had denounced two shepherds who did not follow the rules of abstinence: he swore he had seen them eat meat during Lent. The girl with the baby, a young widow, also denounced her neighbour. He was a married man who was continually making advances to her . . . and had even stroked her breast.

'What about you? Did you allow him to do that?' Joan asked her. 'Did you enjoy it?'

The girl burst into tears.

'Did it give you pleasure?' Joan insisted.

'We were hungry,' she sobbed, holding up her baby.

The scribe wrote down her name. Joan stared at her. What did he give you? he thought. A crust of dry bread? Is that all your honour is worth?

'Confess!' he shouted, pointing a finger at her.

Two more people denounced their neighbours, claiming they were heretics.

'Some nights I hear strange noises and see lights in their house,' one of them said. 'They are Devil-worshippers.'

What could your neighbour have done for you to denounce him like this? wondered Joan. You know he will never find out who betrayed him. What do you stand to gain if I condemn him? A strip of land perhaps?'

'What is your neighbour's name?'

'Anton the baker.'

The scribe copied out the name.

By the time Joan had finished the interrogations, night was falling. He called the captain in and the scribe read out the names of all those who were to present themselves to the Inquisition at first light the next day.

Then again it was the silence of the night, the cold, the flickering flame . . . and his memories. Joan got up once more.

A blasphemous woman, a lecherous man and a Devil-worshipper. 'At dawn I shall have you,' he muttered. Could it be true about the Devil-worshipper? He had heard many similar accusations, but only one had borne fruit. Could it be true this time? How was he going to prove it?

He felt weary, and returned to the pallet to close his eyes. A Devil-worshipper . . .

'Do you swear on the four Gospels?' Joan asked as the light of dawn began to filter through the window on the ground floor of the house.

The man nodded.

'I know you have sinned,' said Joan.

Flanked by two tall soldiers, the man who had bought a moment's pleasure from the young widow turned pale. Drops of sweat stood out on his forehead.

'What is your name?'

'Gaspar.'

'I know you have sinned, Gaspar,' said Joan.

The man stammered: 'I . . . I . . .'

'Confess!' said Joan, raising his voice.

'I . . .'

'Flog him until he confesses!' shouted Joan, thumping the table with both fists.

One of the soldiers moved his hand to his belt, where a leather whip was hanging. The man fell to his knees in front of the table where Joan and the scribe were sitting.

'No. I beg you. Don't flog me.'

'Confess.'

With the whip still rolled up in his hand, the soldier pushed him in the back.

'Confess!' cried Joan.

'It . . . it isn't my fault. It's this woman. She has bewitched me,' the man said in a sudden rush. 'Her husband no longer sleeps with her.' Joan did not react. 'She seeks me out; she pursues me. We have only done it a few times, but . . . but I will never do it again. I will never see her again. I swear it.'

'Have you fornicated with her?'

'Ye . . . yes.'

'How often?'

'I don't know . . .'

'Four times? Five? Ten?'

'Four. Yes. That's right. Four times.'

'What is the name of this woman?'

The scribe wrote it down.

'What other sins have you committed?'

'No . . . nothing more, I swear.'

'Do not swear oaths in vain,' said Joan with slow emphasis. 'Whip him.'

After ten lashes, the man confessed to fornicating with the woman and with several prostitutes when he went to market at Puigcerdà. He also confessed to having blasphemed, lied and committed an endless number of minor sins. After a further five lashes he remembered the young widow.

'I have your confession,' Joan declared. 'Tomorrow you are to be in the square to hear my *sermo generalis*, when I will tell you what your punishment is to be.'

The man did not even have time to protest before he

was dragged out of the room on his knees by the soldiers.

Marta, Peregrina's sister-in-law, confessed without any need to threaten her further. Joan ordered her to appear in the square the next day, then urged the scribe to move on to the next case.

'Bring in Anton Sinom,' the scribe told the captain, reading from his list.

As soon as he saw the Devil-worshipper enter the room, Joan sat upright in his hard wooden chair. The man's hooked nose, his high forehead, those dark eyes of his . . .

He wanted to hear his voice.

'Do you swear on the four Gospels?'

'I do.'

'What is your name?' asked Joan, before even the man was standing in front of him.

'Anton Sinom.' The small, slightly stooped man answered his question flanked by two soldiers who towered over him. Joan was quick to catch the note of resignation in his voice.

'Has that always been your name?'

Anton Sinom hesitated. Joan waited.

'People here have always known me by that name,' Sinom said finally.

'And elsewhere?'

'Elsewhere I had another name.'

Joan and Anton stared at each other. The little man did not lower his eyes.

'Was it a Christian one?'

Anton shook his head. Joan suppressed a smile. How should he start? By saying that he knew the man had sinned? This converted Jew would not fall for that. No one in the village had discovered his secret; if they had, there would have been more than one accusation against him. Converted Jews were often a target. This Sinom must be clever. Joan regarded him for a few moments while he thought about it: what could this man be hiding? Why did he keep a light on at night in his house?

Joan stood up and went outside; neither the scribe nor the soldiers made a move to follow him. As he shut the door behind him, the curious onlookers who had gathered outside the building froze. Joan ignored them and spoke to the guard captain: 'Are the family of that man inside here?'

The captain pointed to a woman and two children who were staring in their direction. There was something . . .

'What does this man do for a living? What is his house like? What did he do when you told him to appear before the tribunal?'

'He's a baker,' replied the soldier. 'He has his shop on the ground floor of his house. What's that like? It's normal enough, it's clean. But we didn't see him to tell him to appear, we talked to his wife.'

'Wasn't he in the bakery?'

'No.'

'Did you go at first light as I ordered?'

'Yes, Brother Joan.'

'Some nights he wakes me up . . .' His neighbour had said 'he wakes me up'. A baker . . . a baker has to get up before dawn. *Don't you sleep, Sinom? If you have to get up before dawn* . . . Joan looked across again at the convert's family, who were standing slightly apart from the others. He walked round in circles for a moment or two, then plunged back inside the house. The scribe, soldiers and Sinom had not moved from where he had left them.

'Take his clothes off,' he ordered the soldiers.

'I am circumcised. I've already admitted—'

'Take his clothes off!'

The soldiers turned to Sinom, but before they even

557

laid their hands on him, the look the converted Jew gave Joan convinced him he was right.

'Now,' said Joan once Sinom was completely naked, 'what do you have to say to me?'

The convert tried as best he could to maintain his composure. 'I don't know what you mean,' he said.

'I mean', said Joan, lowering his voice and emphasizing each word as he said it, 'that your face and neck are dirty, but from the chest down, your skin is white. I mean that your hands and wrists are dirty, but your forearms are spotless. I mean that your feet and ankles are dirty, but your legs are clean.'

'Dirty where I wear no clothes, clean where I do,' Sinom countered.

'Not even flour, and you a baker? Would you have me believe that the clothes a baker wears protect him completely from flour? Would you have me believe that you work in the same clothes you wear to protect yourself from the winter cold? Where is the flour on your arms? Today is Monday, Sinom. Did you keep God's day holy?'

'Yes.'

Joan thumped the table and rose from his chair. 'But you also purified yourself according to your heretic rites!' he shouted, pointing straight at him.

'No!' groaned Sinom.

'We shall see, Sinom, we shall see. Lock him up and bring me his wife and children.'

'No!' begged Sinom as the soldiers dragged him out towards the cellar. 'They have nothing to do with this.'

'Stop!' Joan ordered. The soldiers halted, and turned their prisoner to face the inquisitor once more. 'What do they have nothing to do with, Sinom? What do they have nothing to do with?'

Trying to save his family, Sinom confessed. When he had finished, Joan ordered his arrest . . . and that of his family. Then he ordered the others brought in.

* * *

Joan went out into the square before first light.

'Does he never sleep?' asked one of the soldiers between yawns.

'No,' another one answered. 'We often hear him pacing up and down his room all night.'

The two soldiers looked at Joan, who was busy preparing everything for his final sermon. His threadbare black habit was so stiff with dirt it seemed unwilling to follow his movements.

'But if he doesn't sleep and doesn't eat . . .' said the first soldier.

'He lives on hatred,' said the captain, who had overheard them talking.

At first light, the villagers began to file into the square. The accused were led to the front by the soldiers: among them was Alfons, the nine-year-old boy.

Joan began the *auto de fe*. The village authorities came to pledge their oath of obedience to the Inquisition, and to swear they would see that the sentences were carried out. Those who had appeared before Joan during the period of grace were given lesser punishments: to make a pilgrimage to Girona cathedral. Alfons was sentenced to help the neighbour he had stolen from for free one day a week for a month.

When the scribe read Gaspar's testimony, he was interrupted by a man shouting: 'Whore!' A man in the crowd threw himself on the woman who had fornicated with Gaspar. The soldiers moved in to protect her. 'So that was the sin you would not tell me?' he went on shouting behind the line of soldiers.

As soon as the wronged husband had fallen silent, Joan read out the sentence: 'Every Sunday for the next three years, wearing the cloak of repentance, you will kneel outside the church from sun-up to sunset. As for you . . .' he began, turning to the woman.

'I claim the right to punish her,' cried the husband.

Joan looked at her. 'Do you have any children?' he almost asked her. What wrong could they have done to deserve having to talk to her from on top of a crate outside a tiny window, their only consolation that of feeling a hand stroke their hair? But the man had a right to . . .

'As for you,' he repeated, 'I hand you over to the lay authorities, who will see to it that the laws of Catalonia are respected, as your husband requests.'

Joan continued to pass sentence and hand out punishments.

'Anton Sinom. You and your family are to be put at the disposition of the inquisitor general.'

'Let's go,' Joan ordered after loading his scant belongings on a mule.

Joan took one last look at the village. He could hear his own words still echoing round the small square; later that day they would arrive at another one, and then another, and still another. And in each of them, thought Joan, the people will stare at me and listen fearfully to my sermon. Then they will accuse each other, and their sins will come out. And I shall have to investigate everything. I shall have to interpret the way they move, their expressions, their silences, their feelings, in order to uncover sin.

'Hurry up, captain. I want to arrive before noon.'

PART FOUR

CHAINED TO DESTINY

46

Arnau remained on his knees in front of his Virgin of the Sea while the priests said the Easter mass. He had strode into Santa Maria with Eleonor on his arm. The church was full to overflowing, but the congregation gave way to allow them to reach the front. He recognized their smiles: this man had asked him for a loan for his new boat; that one had entrusted him with his savings; over there was someone who wanted a dowry for his daughter; and there was another who had not paid him the sum they had agreed on. The man avoided his gaze, but Arnau paused next to him and, to Eleonor's disgust, shook him by the hand. 'Peace be with you,' he said.

The man's eyes lit up. Arnau continued on his way towards the main altar. That was all he had, he told the Virgin: humble people who appreciated him because he helped them. Joan was tracking down sin, and he did not know what had become of Guillem. As for Mar, what could he say?

Eleonor kicked his ankle. When Arnau glanced across at her, she flapped her hand for him to get up. 'Have you ever seen a noble who stays on his knees as long as you do?' she had already chided him on several occasions. Arnau paid no attention, but Eleonor continued flicking her foot at his ankles.

I have this too, Mother. A wife who is more concerned with appearances than anything else, except for wanting me to make her a mother too. Should I? She only wants an heir, a son who can guarantee her future. Eleonor was still kicking his ankles. When Arnau turned to her, she lifted her chin towards the other nobles in Santa Maria. Some were standing; the rest were seated on their pews. Arnau was the only one still down on his knees.

'Sacrilege!'

The cry resounded through the church. The priests fell silent. Arnau got to his feet, and everyone turned to look at the main doorway.

'Sacrilege!' came the cry again.

Several men pushed their way to the altar, still shouting, 'Sacrilege! Heresy! The Devil's work! . . . Jews!' They wanted to talk to the priests, but one of them came to a halt and addressed the congregation: 'The Jews have profaned a sacred host!'

A murmur rose from the ranks of the faithful.

'As if they hadn't done enough by killing Jesus Christ!' the first man cried out again from the altar. 'Now they want to profane his body!'

The murmur grew to an uproar. Arnau turned to face the congregation, but Eleonor's scornful countenance was all he saw.

'Your Jewish friends,' she scoffed.

Arnau knew what his wife meant. Ever since Mar had married, he had found it almost impossible to be at home, and so on most evenings he went to see his old friend Hasdai Crescas, and stayed talking to him until late into the night. Before he could say anything to Eleonor, the nobles and other leading citizens began to discuss what they had heard.

'They want Christ to suffer even after his death,' said one of them.

'By law they are obliged to stay at home with doors and windows shut during Holy Week. How could they have done such a thing?'

'They must have escaped,' another man asserted.

'What about our children?' said a woman. 'What if they have taken a Christian child to crucify him and then eat his heart?'

'And drink his blood,' another voice chimed in.

Arnau could not take his eyes off this group of enraged nobles. How could they . . .? He caught Eleonor's eye again. She was smiling.

'Your friends,' she said sarcastically.

Then the entire congregation started to shout, demanding vengeance. 'To the Jewish quarter!' they cried, driving each other on with more shouts of 'Heresy!' and 'Sacrilege!' Arnau watched them all rushing out of the church, with the nobles bringing up the rear.

'If you don't hurry,' he heard Eleonor hiss, 'you won't get into the Jewry.'

Arnau turned to look at her again, and then glanced up at the Virgin. The noise from the crowd of people was dying away down Carrer de la Mar.

'Why so much hatred, Eleonor? Don't you have everything you want?'

'No, Arnau. You know I don't have what I want, and perhaps that's exactly what you give your Jewish friends.'

'What are you talking about, woman?'

'About you, Arnau, about you. You know you have never fulfilled your conjugal duties.'

For a few brief seconds, Arnau recalled all the occasions he had rejected Eleonor's advances, at first gently, trying not to hurt her feelings, but gradually more roughly and impatiently.

'The King forced me to marry you. He said nothing about satisfying your needs.'

'The King may not have done so,' she replied, 'but the Church does.'

'God cannot force me to lie with you!'

Eleonor withstood his rebuff, staring straight at him, then turned her face towards the main altar. They were alone in Santa Maria . . . apart from the three priests standing there, openly listening to the couple arguing. Arnau also looked at the three priests. When he confronted Eleonor once more, her eyes narrowed, but she said nothing. He turned his back on her and headed for the doorway out of the church.

'Go to your Jewish lover!' he heard his wife shout behind him.

A shudder ran the length of his backbone.

That year, Arnau was once again Consul of the Sea. Dressed in his robes of office, he made his way to the Jewish quarter. The din of the crowd grew still louder as it advanced along Carrer de la Mar, Plaça del Blat, then down Baixada de la Presó to Sant Jaume church. The people were baying for vengeance, and rushed towards the gates of the Jewry, which was defended by a troop of the King's soldiers. Despite the crush, Arnau had little difficulty pushing his way to the front.

'You cannot enter the Jewry, honourable consul,' the captain of the guard told him. 'We're awaiting orders from the King's lieutenant, the Infante Don Juan.'

The orders duly arrived. The next morning, King Pedro's son Don Juan ordered all the Jews to be shut in the main synagogue of Barcelona, without food or water, until those guilty of the profanation of the host came forward.

'Five thousand people,' Arnau growled in his office at the exchange when he heard the news. 'Five thousand people shut up in the synagogue without food or water!

What will happen to the children, the newborn babies? What does the Infante want? What fool could expect any Jew to admit to profaning the host and condemn himself to death?'

Arnau thumped his table and stood up. The bailiff who had brought him the news looked startled.

'Tell the guard,' Arnau ordered him.

The honourable Consul of the Sea made his way hastily through the streets of the city, accompanied by half a dozen armed *missatges*. Still guarded by soldiers, the gates to the Jewry stood wide open. Outside, the angry mob had disappeared, but there were at least a hundred curious onlookers trying to get a glimpse inside, despite being pushed and jostled by the soldiers.

'Who is in charge here?' Arnau asked the captain.

'The magistrate is inside,' the officer told him.

'Tell him I'm here.'

The magistrate soon appeared. 'What do you want, Arnau?' he asked, holding out his hand.

'I want to talk to the Jews.'

'The Infante has given the order—'

'I know,' Arnau interrupted him. 'That's exactly why I need to talk to them. I've got a lot of outstanding business with Jews. I need to talk to them.'

'But the Infante . . .' the magistrate began to protest.

'The Infante lives off the Jewish quarters in Catalonia! The King has ordered that they pay him twelve thousand shillings every year.' The magistrate nodded. 'The Infante would like those responsible for the profanation to be found, but you know very well that he also wants Jewish commerce to continue, because if it doesn't . . . remember, the Jews of Barcelona contribute most of those twelve thousand shillings.'

The magistrate was convinced, and allowed Arnau and his men through. 'They are in the main synagogue,' he said as they passed by.

'I know, I know.'

Even though all the Jews were shut in, the streets of the quarter were thronged with people. As he walked towards the synagogue, Arnau could see a swarm of black-robed monks searching each and every house for the bleeding host.

At the synagogue entrance, Arnau came up against more guards. 'I've come to talk to Hasdai Crescas.'

The captain tried to stand in his way, but the other guard who had accompanied Arnau explained he had permission.

While they were waiting for Hasdai to appear, Arnau looked back at the Jewish quarter. The houses stood wide open and had obviously been ransacked. The friars came and went, carrying out objects and showing them to each other. They shook their heads, then threw them on to the growing pile of Jewish possessions. Who are the profaners? thought Arnau.

'Your worship,' he heard behind him.

Arnau wheeled round and found Hasdai standing there. For a few seconds he stared into the Jew's eyes, full of tears at the violation of his intimate world. Arnau ordered all the soldiers to withdraw. His *missatges* obeyed at once, but the King's soldiers stayed where they were.

'Since when did the Consul of the Sea's affairs interest you?' Arnau asked them. 'Stand back with my men. The consul's concerns are secret.'

The soldiers obeyed reluctantly. Arnau and Hasdai studied each other.

'I'd like to embrace you,' Arnau said when nobody could hear them.

'Better not.'

'How are you?'

'Not good, Arnau. We old people are unimportant, the young can cope, but the children have had nothing to eat or drink for hours. There are several infants; when their mothers have no more milk to give them . . . We've only been here a few hours, but bodies have their needs . . .'

'Can I help?'

'We've tried to negotiate, but the magistrate will not listen. You know there is only one way out: we have to buy our freedom.'

'How much should I—?'

Hasdai's stare prevented him finishing. How much were the lives of five thousand Jews worth?

'I trust you, Arnau. My community is in danger.'

Arnau held out his hand.

'We all trust you,' said Hasdai again, taking it in his.

Arnau went back among the black friars. Could they have found the bleeding host already? The contents of the houses, including pieces of furniture, were being heaped ever higher in the streets. As he left the Jewry, Arnau thanked the magistrate. He would ask for an official audience with him that afternoon: but how much should he offer for a man's life? Or for an entire community? Arnau had bargained with all kinds of goods: fabrics, spices, grain, animals, ships, gold and silver; he knew the price of slaves, but how much was a friend worth?

Arnau left the Jewry. He turned left, took Carrer dels Banys Nous down to Plaça del Blat, but when he was in Carrer dels Carders by the corner with Carrer de Montcada close to his own house, he suddenly halted. What was the point? To clash yet again with Eleonor? He turned on his heel to go back to Carrer de la Mar and his exchange table. From the day he had agreed to Mar's marriage . . . Ever since that day Eleonor had pursued him relentlessly. At first she did it stealthily. Why, she had not even called him her beloved before then! She had never concerned herself about his business, what he ate or even how he felt. When that tactic failed, she tried a frontal attack. 'I'm a woman,' she told him one day. She must have been discouraged by the way Arnau looked at her, because she said nothing more . . . until a few days later: 'We have to consummate our marriage; we're living in sin.'

'Since when were you so interested in my salvation?' Arnau asked.

Despite her husband's gruff rejection, she did not give up. Eventually she decided to talk about it to Father Juli Andreu, one of the priests at Santa Maria. He was interested in the salvation of the faithful, among whom Arnau was one of the most highly regarded. With him, Arnau could not find excuses as he did with Eleonor.

'I can't do it, Father,' he told the priest when he was confronted by him one day in the church.

It was true. Immediately after handing Mar to the knight Felip de Ponts, Arnau had tried to forget her: why not have a family of his own? He was all alone. All the people he loved had gone from his life. He could have children, play with them, devote himself to them and perhaps find what was missing. But he could only do this with Eleonor, and whenever she sidled up to him, or pursued him through the palace chambers, or he heard her false, forced voice, so different from the way she usually spoke to him, all his resolve came to nought.

'What do you mean, my son?' asked the priest.

'The King forced me to marry Eleonor, Father, but he never asked what my feelings were for his ward.'

'The baroness . . .'

'The baroness does not attract me, Father. My body refuses.'

'I could recommend a good doctor?'

Arnau smiled. 'No, Father, no. It's not that. Physically I'm fine; it's simply . . .'

'Well then, you should make an effort to fulfil your matrimonial obligations. Our Lord expects . . .'

Arnau listened to the priest's harangue, imagining the stories Eleonor must have told him. Who did they think they were?

'Listen, Father,' he said, interrupting him, 'I cannot oblige my body to desire a woman if it doesn't.' The priest raised his hand as though to intervene, but Arnau stopped him. 'I swore to be faithful to my wife, and I am; nobody can accuse me of being otherwise. I come often to Santa Maria to pray. I donate large sums of money to the Church. It seems to me that my contributions to building this church should compensate for the shortcomings of my body.'

The priest stopped rubbing his hands. 'My son . . .'

'What do you think, Father?'

The priest searched among his scant theological knowledge for ways of refuting Arnau's arguments. He was defeated, and soon hastened away among the men still working on Santa Maria. Left alone, Arnau went to find the Virgin in her chapel. He knelt before her statue: 'I think only of her, Mother. Why did you allow me to give her to Lord de Ponts?'

He had not seen Mar since her marriage to Felip de Ponts. When her husband died a few months later, he tried to approach the widow, but Mar refused to see him. Perhaps it's for the best, Arnau told himself. The oath he had sworn to the Virgin bound him even more than ever now: he was condemned to be faithful to a woman who did not love him and whom he could not love. And to give up the only person with whom he might have been happy . . .

'Have they found the host yet?' Arnau asked the magistrate as they sat opposite each other in the palace overlooking Plaça del Blat.

'No,' said the magistrate.

'I've been talking to the city councillors,' Arnau told

him, 'and they agree with me. Imprisoning the entire Jewish community could seriously affect Barcelona's commercial interests. The seagoing season has just begun. If you went down to the port, you would see there are several ships ready to depart. They have Jewish goods on board; they will either have to be unloaded or will need to wait for the traders. The problem is that not all the cargoes belong to Jews; part of them are owned by Christians.'

'Why not unload them then?'

'The cost of transporting the Christians' merchandise would go up.'

The magistrate spread his hands in a gesture of frustration. 'Then put all the Jews' merchandise on some ships, and the Christians' goods on others,' he suggested finally.

Arnau shook his head. 'That's impossible. Not all the ships are headed for the same destination. You know the sailing season is short. If the ships cannot leave, all our trade will be held up. They will not be back in time, and so will miss some journeys. That will push the price of everything up again. We will all lose money.' You included, thought Arnau. 'On top of which, it's danger-ous for ships to wait too long in Barcelona: if a storm blows up . . .'

'So what do you suggest?'

That you set them all free. That you order the friars to stop searching their homes. That you give them back their belongings, that . . . thought Arnau. 'Impose a fine on the whole Jewish community,' was what he said.

'The people are demanding the guilty be punished, and the Infante has promised to find them. The profanation of a host—'

'The profanation of a host, whether or not the bleed-ing host appears, will of course be more expensive than any other kind of crime,' Arnau interrupted him. Why bother to argue? The Jews had been judged and condemned. The magistrate wrinkled his brow. 'Why not make the attempt? If we succeed, it will be the Jews and only they who pay. If not, it's going to be a bad year for trade, and all of us will lose.'

Surrounded by workmen, noise and dust, Arnau looked up at the keystone that topped the second of the four vaults above Santa Maria's central nave, the latest completed. On the end of the keystone was an image of the Annunciation, with the Virgin dressed in a red cape edged with gold, kneeling as the angel brought her the news that she was to give birth. Arnau's attention was caught by the bright reds, blues and especially the golden hues of the delicate scene. The magistrate had considered Arnau's arguments and finally yielded.

Twenty-five thousand shillings and fifteen guilty men! That was the answer the magistrate gave Arnau the next day after he had consulted with the Infante Don Juan's court.

'Fifteen culprits? You want to execute fifteen people because of the ravings of four madmen?'

The magistrate thumped the table. 'Those madmen belong to the holy Catholic Church.'

'You know it's an impossible demand,' said Arnau.

The two men stared at each other.

'No culprits,' Arnau insisted.

'That's not possible. The Infante—'

'No culprits! Twenty-five thousand shillings is a fortune.'

Arnau left the magistrate's palace not knowing where to go. What could he say to Hasdai? That fifteen Jews had to die? Yet he could not get the image of those five thousand people packed into the synagogue with no water or food out of his mind . . .

'When will I have my answer?' he asked the magistrate.

'The Infante is out hunting.'

Hunting! Five thousand people were shut up on his orders and he had gone hunting. It could not have been more than three hours by horse from Barcelona to Girona, where the Infante, Duke of Girona and Cervera, had his lands, but Arnau had to wait until late the following afternoon to be summoned again by the magistrate.

'Thirty-five thousand shillings and five culprits.'

Ten Jews for ten thousand shillings. Perhaps that's the price of a man, thought Arnau.

'Forty thousand, and no culprits.'

'No.'

'I'll appeal to the King.'

'You know that the King has enough problems with the war against Castile than to look for more with his son. That was why he named him his lieutenant.'

'Forty-five thousand, but no one guilty.'

'No, Arnau, no—'

'Ask him!' Arnau exploded. 'I beg you,' he added apologetically.

When he was still several yards from the synagogue, Arnau was hit by the stench. The streets of the Jewry looked still more wretched than before: furniture and possessions were strewn everywhere. From inside the houses came the sounds of the friars demolishing walls and floors in their search for the body of Christ. When Arnau saw Hasdai, he had to struggle to keep his composure. Hasdai was accompanied by two rabbis and two leaders of the community. Arnau's eyes were stinging. Could it be from the acid fumes of urine coming from inside the synagogue, or simply because of the news he had to give them?

For a few moments, to a background noise of groans and wails, Arnau watched as the others tried to get fresh air into their lungs: what could it be like inside? All of them cast anxious glances at the streets around them; for a while they seemed to hold their breath.

'They want culprits,' Arnau told him when the five men had recovered. 'We started with fifteen. Now it's down to five, and I hope that—'

'We can't wait, Arnau Estanyol,' one of the rabbis interrupted him. 'One old man has died today; he was sick, and our doctors could do nothing for him, not even moisten his lips. And we are not allowed to bury him. Do you know what that means?' Arnau nodded. 'Tomorrow, the stink of his decomposing body will be added to . . .'

'Inside the synagogue we have no room to move,' Hasdai said. 'No one . . . no one can even get up to relieve themselves. The nursing mothers have no more milk: they have suckled their own babies and tried to feed the other infants. If we have to wait many more days, five culprits will be nothing.'

'Plus forty-five thousand shillings,' Arnau pointed out.

'What do we care about money when we could all die?' the other rabbi added.

'Well?' asked Arnau.

'You have to try, Arnau,' Hasdai begged him.

Ten thousand more shillings speeded up the Infante's reply . . . or perhaps he never even got the message. Arnau was summoned the next morning. Three culprits.

'They are men!' Arnau said accusingly to the magistrate.

'They are Jews, Arnau. Only Jews. Heretics who belong to the Crown. Without the King's favour they would already be dead, and the King has decided that three of them have to pay for the profanation of the host. The people demand it.'

Since when has the King been so concerned about his people? thought Arnau.

'Besides,' the magistrate insisted, 'it will mean that our seafarers' problems are solved.'

The old man's body, the mothers' dried-up breasts, the weeping children, the wailing and the stench: Arnau nodded in agreement. The magistrate leant back in his chair.

'On two conditions,' said Arnau, forcing him to listen closely once more. 'First, the Jews themselves must choose the guilty men.' The magistrate nodded. 'And secondly, the agreement has to be ratified by the bishop, who must promise to calm the faithful.'

'I've already done that, Arnau. Do you think I want to see another massacre of Jews?'

The procession left the Jewry. All the doors and windows were shut and, apart from the piles of furniture, the streets seemed deserted. The silence inside the Jewry was in stark contrast to the hubbub outside, where a crowd had gathered around the bishop, standing there with his gold vestments gleaming in the Mediterranean sunlight, and with the countless priests and black friars lining Carrer de la Boqueria, separated from the people by two lines of the King's soldiers.

When three figures appeared at the gates of the Jewish quarter, a loud shout rent the air. The crowd raised their fists and their insults mingled with the sound of swords being drawn as the soldiers prepared to defend the members of the procession. Shackled hand and foot, the three men were brought in between the two lines of black friars. Then, with the Bishop of Barcelona at its head, the group set off down the street. The presence of the soldiers and the friars was not enough to prevent the mob throwing stones and spitting at the three men being slowly dragged past them.

Arnau was in Santa Maria, praying. It was he who had taken the Infante's final decision to the synagogue, where he had been met by Hasdai, the rabbis and the community leaders.

'Three culprits,' he said, trying to meet their gazes, 'and you can . . . you can choose them yourselves.'

None of them said a word. They merely gazed at the streets of the Jewry and let the cries and laments from inside the synagogue guide their thoughts. Arnau did not have the heart to negotiate any further, but told the magistrate as he left the Jewry: 'Three innocent men . . . because you and I know that this idea of the profanation of Christ's body is false.'

Arnau began to hear the uproar from the crowd as it approached Carrer de la Mar. The hubbub filled Santa Maria; it filtered in through the gaps in the unfinished doors, it climbed the wooden scaffolding surrounding the unfinished structures as rapidly as any workman, and filled the vaults of the new church. Three innocent men! How had they chosen them? Did the rabbis make the choice, or did they come forward voluntarily? Arnau remembered Hasdai's expression as he looked out at the devastated streets of the Jewry. What had been in his eyes? Resignation? Or had it been the look of someone . . . saying goodbye? Arnau trembled; his legs almost gave way, and he had to cling on to the prayer-stool. The procession was drawing near to Santa Maria. The noise was getting louder and louder. Arnau stood up and looked towards the door that gave on to Plaça de Santa Maria. The procession would soon be there. He stayed inside the church, staring out at the square, until the shouts and insults became a reality.

He ran to the church door. Nobody heard his cry. Nobody saw him in tears. Nobody saw him fall to his knees when he caught sight of Hasdai being dragged along in chains with curses, stones and spit raining down on him. As Hasdai went past Santa Maria, he looked straight at the man who was on his knees beating the ground in despair. Arnau did not see him, and continued flailing at the beaten earth until the sad procession had disappeared and the earth was turning red from his bleeding fists. Someone knelt in front of him and gently took his hands in theirs.

'My father wouldn't want you to harm yourself for him,' said Raquel. Arnau glanced up at her.

'They're going . . . they're going to kill him.'

'Yes.'

Arnau searched the face of this girl who had grown into a woman. Many years ago, he had hidden her underneath this very church. Raquel was not crying, and although it was very dangerous, was wearing her Jewish costume and the yellow and red badge.

'We have to be strong,' said the girl he remembered.

'Why, Raquel? Why him?'

'For me. For Jucef. For my children and Jucef's children, and for our grandchildren. For all the Jews of Barcelona. He said he was already old, that he had lived enough.'

With Raquel's help, Arnau got to his feet. They followed the noise of the crowd.

The three men were burnt alive. They were tied to stakes on the top of bonfires of twigs and branches, which were set alight while the Christians were still baying for revenge. As the flames enveloped his body, Hasdai looked up to the heavens. Now it was Raquel's turn to burst into tears: she hugged Arnau and buried her face in his chest.

His arms round Hasdai's daughter, Arnau could not take his eyes off his friend's burning body. At first he thought he saw him bleeding, but the flames quickly took hold. All of a sudden, he could no longer hear the crowd shouting: all he saw was them raising their fists menacingly . . . and then something made him look to his right. Fifty paces or so from the crowd, he saw the bishop and the grand inquisitor standing next to Eleonor. She was talking to them and pointing directly at him. Beside her was another elegantly dressed woman, whom he did not at first recognize. Arnau met the inquisitor's gaze as Eleonor continued pointing at him and shouting.

'That Jewish girl is his lover. Just look at them. Look at the way he is embracing her.'

Arnau had his arms tightly round Raquel, who was sobbing desperately on his chest as the flames rose skywards, accompanied by the cheers of the mob. Turning his eyes away from this horror, Arnau found himself looking at Eleonor. When he saw the mixture of deep-rooted hatred and joyous revenge on her face, he shuddered. It was then that he heard the woman standing next to his wife laugh, the same scornful, unforgettable laugh that had been engraved on his memory since childhood: the laugh of Margarida Puig.

47

This was a revenge that had been a long time coming, and involved many more than Eleonor. A revenge for which the accusation against Arnau and Raquel was only the beginning.

The decisions Arnau Estanyol had made as Baron of Granollers, Sant Vicenç dels Horts and Caldes de Montbui had ruffled the feathers of the other Catalan nobles. They were afraid of the winds of rebellion stirring their own serfs: several of them had been obliged to use more force than they had ever needed before to stifle a revolt that was demanding the abolition of privileges which Arnau – that baron who had been born a serf – had reneged on. Among them were Jaume de Bellera, son of the lord of Navarcles, whom Francesca had suckled as a boy, and someone else, someone whom Arnau had deprived of his house, his fortune, and his way of life: Genís Puig. After losing everything, Genís had been forced to live in the old Navarcles house that belonged to his grandfather, Grau's father. The house was a world away from the palace on Carrer de Montcada where he had spent most of his life. Both these men spent hours lamenting their ill fortune and plotting revenge. Revenge which, if his sister Margarida's letters were true, was about to come to fruition . . .

Arnau asked the sailor giving evidence to wait. He turned to the court usher of the Consulate of the Sea who had burst into the chamber.

'A captain and soldiers sent by the Holy Inquisition wish to see you,' the usher whispered in Arnau's ear.

'What do they want?' asked Arnau. The usher shrugged. 'Tell them to wait until the hearing is over,' Arnau told him, before urging the sailor to continue his testimony.

Another sailor had died during a journey, and the owner of the ship was refusing to pay his heirs more than two months' wages. The widow claimed that the contract had not been in terms of months, and that since her husband had died at sea, she ought to be paid half of the agreed sum.

'Go on,' said Arnau, looking over at the widow and her three children.

'No sailor is ever paid by the month—'

Suddenly the courtroom doors crashed open. A captain and six soldiers of the Inquisition came in wielding their swords. They pushed the usher aside and stood in the middle of the room.

'Arnau Estanyol?' the captain asked, looking directly at him.

'What is the meaning of this?' Arnau protested. 'How dare you interrupt—?'

The captain stepped forward until he was directly in front of Arnau. 'Are you Arnau Estanyol, Consul of the Sea, Baron of Granollers—?'

'You know very well I am, captain,' Arnau interrupted him, 'but—'

'By order of the tribunal of the Holy Inquisition, you are under arrest. Come with me.'

The court *missatges* made to defend the consul, but Arnau motioned to them to be still.

'Be so kind as to stand aside,' Arnau asked the captain.

The soldier hesitated a moment. Arnau calmly motioned with his hand for the intruders to move closer to the door. Still glaring at his prisoner, the captain stepped aside just enough for Arnau to be able to see the dead sailor's relatives.

'I find in favour of the widow and her children,' Arnau ruled imperturbably. 'They are to receive half of the total wage for the journey, and not the two months as the ship owner is claiming. That is the resolution of this court.'

Arnau thumped the table, stood up, and faced the captain.

'Now we can go,' he said.

The news of Arnau Estanyol's arrest spread throughout Barcelona and from there, nobles, merchants and even peasants took it to the rest of Catalonia.

A few days later, in a small village in the north of the principality, an inquisitor who was busy putting the fear of God into a group of inhabitants heard it from an officer of the Inquisition.

Joan stared at him.

'It seems it is true,' the officer insisted.

The inquisitor turned towards the group of people. What had he been saying to them? What was this about Arnau being arrested?

He glanced at the captain, who nodded.

Arnau?

The small crowd began to shift uneasily. Joan wanted to go on, but could not find the words. He turned to the captain again: the man was smiling.

'Aren't you going to continue, Brother Joan?' said the officer. 'These sinners are waiting.'

Joan turned to him. 'Let's go to Barcelona,' he said.

On their way back to the city, Joan passed close by the Baron of Granollers's lands. If he had turned aside a little from his route, he would have seen how the thane of Montbui and other knights who owed allegiance to Arnau were already riding through their lands to threaten the peasants that they would soon see the return of practices Arnau had abolished. 'They say it was the baroness herself who accused Arnau,' someone said.

But Joan did not pass through Arnau's lands. Ever since they had begun their journey, he had not said another word to the captain or anyone else in their small party, not even the scribe. There was no way he could not hear what they were saying, however.

'It seems they've arrested him for heresy,' said one of the soldiers, loud enough for Joan to hear.

'The brother of an inquisitor?' another soldier shouted.

'Nicolau Eimerich will make him confess everything he is trying to hide,' the captain replied.

Joan remembered Nicolau Eimerich well. How often had he congratulated him on his work as inquisitor?

'We have to fight heresy, Brother Joan . . . We have to seek out sin beneath people's virtuous exterior: in their bedrooms, their children, their spouses.'

And Joan had done the same. 'You should not hesitate to use torture to obtain a confession.' He had done the same, tirelessly. What torture could they have used on Arnau for him to confess to heresy?

Joan quickened his pace. His filthy, shabby black habit hung stiffly down his legs.

'It's his fault I am in this situation,' Genís Puig said, pacing up and down the chamber. 'I, who once had—'

'Money, women and power,' the baron interrupted him.

But Genís paid no attention. 'My parents and brother

died as starving peasants. They died from illnesses that thrive only among the poor, and I—'

'A mere knight who has no soldiers to offer the King,' the baron said, wearily finishing the phrase he had heard a thousand times.

Genís Puig came to a halt in front of Jaume, Llorenç de Bellera's son. 'Do you think it's amusing?'

Lord de Bellera did not move from the seat from which he had been watching Genís roving round the chamber in the keep of Navarcles Castle. 'Yes,' he replied after a while. 'Extremely amusing. Your reasons for hating Arnau Estanyol are grotesque compared to mine.' Jaume de Bellera looked up towards the roof of the keep. 'And will you please stop walking up and down?'

'How long will your man be?' Genís asked, still on the move.

Both of them were waiting for confirmation of the news Margarida Puig had hinted at in a previous letter. From Navarcles, Genís Puig had convinced his sister stealthily to win the confidence of the baroness in the long hours Eleonor spent alone in the former Puig family house. It was not difficult: Eleonor was desperate for a confidante who hated her husband as much as she did. It was Margarida who insinuated to Eleonor where the baron had come from that day. It was Margarida who had invented the adultery between Arnau and Raquel. And now that Arnau Estanyol had been arrested for having congress with a Jewess, Jaume de Bellera and Genís Puig were ready to take the next step as planned.

'The Inquisition has arrested Arnau Estanyol,' the captain confirmed as soon as he came into the keep.

'So Margarida was—' Genís exclaimed.

'Be quiet,' Lord de Bellera warned him from his seat. 'Go on.'

'He was arrested three days ago, while presiding over a tribunal at the Consulate of the Sea.'

'What is he accused of?' asked the baron.

'That isn't very clear. Some say heresy, others say it's because he consorts with Jews, still others say it is because he has had relations with a Jewish woman. He has not been brought before the Inquisition yet; he is being held in the dungeons of the bishop's palace. Half the city supports him; the other half is against, but they are all clamouring at his counting house to claim their deposits back. I've seen them. They're all fighting to get their money.'

'Are they being paid?' asked Genís.

'For the moment, yes, but everyone knows that Arnau Estanyol lent a lot of money to people who didn't have a penny, and if he cannot call in those loans . . . That's why everyone is fighting to get there first: they don't think he'll be able to pay up for long.'

Jaume de Bellera and Genís Puig exchanged looks.

'The fall has begun,' said the knight.

'Find the whore who gave me suck!' the baron ordered the captain. 'Shut her in the castle dungeons!'

Genís Puig added his voice to that of Lord de Bellera, urging the official to hurry up.

'That diabolical milk was not meant for me,' he had heard the baron complain time and again, 'it was for that son of hers, Arnau Estanyol. And now he's the one who has money and is the King's favourite, while I have to endure the consequences of the sickness his mother gave me.'

Jaume de Bellera had been forced to petition the bishop that the epilepsy he suffered should not be considered the Devil's work. All the same, the Holy Inquisition would no doubt see Francesca as possessed by the Devil.

'I'd like to see my brother,' Joan abruptly asked Nicolau Eimerich as soon as he entered the bishop's palace.

The grand inquisitor's eyes narrowed. 'Your duty is to make him confess and repent.'

'What is he accused of?'

Nicolau Eimerich stiffened behind the table where he had received Joan. 'You're asking me to tell you what he is accused of? You are an accomplished inquisitor – but you wouldn't be trying to help your brother, would you?'

Joan looked at the floor.

'All I can tell you is that it is very serious. I'll permit you to see him provided you confirm that the reason for your visits is to obtain Arnau's confession.'

Ten lashes! Fifteen, twenty-five . . . How often had he himself given that command in the past few years? 'Until he confesses!' he would instruct the captain accompanying him. And now . . . now he was being asked to obtain his own brother's confession. How was he supposed to do that? Joan's only reply was to spread his hands in a mute appeal.

'It's your duty,' Eimerich reminded him.

'He's my brother. He's all I have . . .'

'You have the Church. You have all of us, your brothers in Christ.' The grand inquisitor fell silent for a while. 'Brother Joan, I was waiting for you to arrive. If you don't accept the terms, I'll have to take charge of him myself.'

Joan could not repress a grimace of distaste when the stench from the dungeons in the bishop's palace hit him. As he was being led down the dark passageway to where Arnau was imprisoned, he could hear water dripping from the walls and rats scuttling out of the way. He felt one run between his legs. He shuddered, as he had done when he heard Nicolau Eimerich's threat: *I'll have to take charge of him myself*. What could Arnau have done? How was he going to tell him that he, his own brother, had promised to . . .?

The gaoler opened the door to the dungeon. A vast, evil-smelling chamber appeared before Joan. Shadowy figures moved in the darkness, and the clink of the chains that bound them grated on Joan's ears. The Dominican friar could feel his stomach reacting against the foul conditions; he tasted bile in his mouth. 'Over there,' said the gaoler, pointing to a dark shape hunched in a corner. He left without waiting for any answer. The sound of the door slamming behind him made Joan start. He stood close to the door searching in the gloom: the only light came in through a small window high up on the outer wall. As soon as the gaoler had left, he heard the sounds of chains once more. What seemed like a dozen shadows shifted in front of him. Did that mean they were relieved because it was not them he and the gaoler had come for, or were they desperate for the same reason? Joan had no idea, unable to interpret the groans and laments that surrounded him. He went up to the shadowy bundle that he thought the gaoler had pointed to, but when he knelt in front of the figure, the scarred, toothless face of an old woman peered up at him.

He fell backwards; the old crone stared at him for a few moments, then hastened to conceal her misery in the darkness once more.

'Arnau?' whispered Joan, still spread-eagled on the floor. Then, when he got no reply, he repeated his brother's name out loud.

'Joan?'

Joan hastened in the direction the voice had come from. He knelt before another shadowy figure, then took his brother's head in his hands and pulled him towards him. 'Holy Mother of God! What . . . what have they done to you? How are you?' Joan felt Arnau's head: the hair was matted, his cheekbones were beginning to stand out from the gaunt cheeks. 'Don't they feed you?'

'Yes,' Arnau replied. 'A crust of bread and water.'

When Joan's fingers came up against the shackles round his brother's ankles, he quickly drew his hands away.

'Could you do something for me?' asked Arnau. Joan said nothing. 'You're one of them. You've always told me the grand inquisitor holds you in great esteem. This is unbearable, Joan. I don't know how many days I've been in here. I was waiting for you . . .'

'I came as soon as I could.'

'Have you spoken to the grand inquisitor?'

'Yes.' Despite the darkness, Joan tried to hide his features. The two of them fell silent.

'And?' asked Arnau eventually.

'What have you done, Arnau?'

Arnau's hand tightened on Joan's arm.

'How could you think that . . .?'

'I need to know, Arnau. If I'm to help you, I need to know what they are accusing you of. You must be aware that they never say what the accusation is. Nicolau refused to tell me.'

'So what did you talk about?'

'Nothing,' Joan said. 'I didn't want to talk about anything with him until I had seen you. I need to know what sort of accusation they are making if I am to convince Nicolau.'

'Go and ask Eleonor.' Arnau remembered how he had seen his wife pointing at him through the flames licking around the body of an innocent man. 'Hasdai is dead,' he said.

'Eleonor?' queried Joan.

'Does that surprise you?'

Joan lost his balance, and leant on Arnau for support.

'What's the matter, Joan?' his brother asked, trying to steady him.

'It's this place . . . and seeing you like this . . . I feel faint.'

'Get out of here then,' Arnau encouraged him. 'You'll be more use to me on the outside than you will be trying to comfort me in here.'

Joan stood up. His legs were weak. 'Yes, I think you're right.'

Joan called the gaoler and left the dungeon. He followed the fat man back up the passageway. He had a few coins on him. 'Take these,' he said. The gaoler put them in his purse without a word. 'Tomorrow there'll be more if you treat my brother properly.'

The only sound was from rats scurrying along the passage.

'Did you hear me?' he insisted. This time the reply was a deep growl that at least silenced the rats.

Joan needed money. As soon as he left the bishop's palace, he headed for Arnau's counting house. When he arrived, he saw a crowd outside the small building on the corner of Canvis Vells and Canvis Nous from where Arnau had conducted his business affairs. Joan drew back.

'That's his brother!' one of the crowd shouted.

Several of them rushed up to him. Joan was about to turn tail, but stopped when he saw that they came to a halt a few steps from him. Of course they would not attack a Dominican. He stood as upright as possible and carried on walking.

'What's happened to your brother, friar?' one of the men asked as he passed by.

Joan confronted a man who was a good head taller than he. 'My name is Brother Joan. I'm an inquisitor with the Holy Office,' he said, raising his voice as he explained his position. 'When you speak to me, call me "my lord inquisitor".' Joan looked up, staring the man straight in the eye. What sins do you have to confess? he enquired silently. The man took a couple of steps backwards. Joan strode on towards the counting house, the crowd giving way before him.

'I am Brother Joan, an inquisitor from the Holy Office!' he shouted outside the closed doors of the building.

Three of Arnau's assistants allowed him in. The room inside was in turmoil: account books were strewn all over the rumpled red cloth covering his brother's accounting table. If Arnau could have seen it . . .

'I need money,' he told them.

The three men looked at him in disbelief.

'So do we,' responded the eldest, a man by the name of Remigi who had taken over from Guillem.

'What's that?'

'We have hardly any money left, Brother Joan.' Remigi opened several money boxes on the table. 'Look, there's nothing in them.'

'Doesn't my brother have money?'

'Not in cash. Why do you think all those people are outside? They want their money. They've been besieging us for days now. Arnau is still a very rich man,' he said, trying to reassure the friar, 'but it's all invested – in loans, commissions, in business deals . . .'

'Can't you demand repayment of the loans?'

'The main debtor is the King, and you know what his majesty's coffers are like.'

'Is there no one who owes Arnau money?'

'Yes, lots of people do, but either they are loans which have not come to term, or ones which have, but . . . you know Arnau lent money to many people who have nothing. They can't pay him back. Even so, when they heard about his situation, many of them came and paid back part of what they owed him, what little they could afford. But that is no more than a gesture. We cannot hope to cover all the deposits that way.'

Joan turned back and pointed to the door. 'So how is it that they can demand their money?'

'In fact, they don't have the right to. They all deposited their funds for Arnau to use on their behalf, but money is slippery, and the Inquisition . . .'

Joan gestured for him to forget that he was also a member of the Holy Office. The gaoler's growl echoed in his ears. 'I need money,' he repeated out loud.

'I've already told you, there isn't any,' Remigi protested.

'But I need some,' Joan insisted. 'Arnau needs it.'

Arnau needs it, and, above all, thought Joan, turning to look at the door again, he needs a breathing space. This scandal can only do him harm. People will think he is ruined, and then no one will want to know him . . . We'll need help.

'Is there nothing we can do to calm those people down? Is there nothing we can sell?'

'We could pass on some commissions. We could put the creditors together in them, instead of Arnau,' said Remigi. 'But to do that, we would need his authority.'

'Is mine enough?'

The official stared at him.

'It has to be done, Remigi.'

'I suppose you're right,' the other man said after a few moments' thought. 'In fact, we would not be losing money. We would simply be switching things around; they could keep some investments; we would still have others. If Arnau were not involved, that would calm them down . . . but you will have to give me your written authority.'

Remigi quickly prepared a document. Joan signed it.

'Gather some money by first thing tomorrow,' he said as he signed. 'It's cash we need,' he insisted when the assistant looked at him hesitantly. 'Sell something off cheaply if necessary, but we must have money.'

As soon as Joan had left the counting house and calmed down the creditors outside once more, Remigi began to redistribute the investments. That same afternoon, the last ship leaving Barcelona carried with it instructions for Arnau's agents all over the Mediterranean. Remigi acted swiftly; by the next day, the satisfied creditors were spreading the news of how Arnau's business affairs were sound.

48

For the first time in almost a week, Arnau drank fresh water and ate something other than a crust of bread. The gaoler forced him to his feet by kicking him, and then sluiced a bucket of water on the floor. Better water than excrement, thought Arnau. For a few seconds, all that could be heard was the water splashing on the stones, and the obese gaoler's laboured breathing. Even the old woman who had given herself up to death and kept her face buried in her filthy rags looked up at Arnau.

'Leave the bucket,' the *bastaix* ordered the gaoler as he was about to leave.

Arnau had seen him mistreat prisoners just because they had dared to meet his gaze. Now the gaoler lunged at him with outstretched arm, but when he saw Arnau defying him, he pulled away just before making contact. He spat and threw the bucket on the ground. Before he shut the door behind him, he kicked at one of the shadows looking on.

After the ground had absorbed the water, Arnau sat down again. He could hear a church bell ringing. That and the feeble rays of sun that managed to penetrate the filthy window, which was at street level outside, were his only links to the world. Arnau raised his eyes to the tiny window and strained to hear more. Santa Maria was bathed in light, but still did not have any bells, and yet the sound of chisels on stone, the hammering on timbers and the workmen's calls on the scaffolding could be heard some distance from the church. Whenever the distant echo of those sounds reached the dungeons, together with the sunlight it transported Arnau's spirit to accompany all those working so devotedly for the Virgin of the Sea. Arnau felt once more the weight of that first block of stone he had carried to Santa Maria. How long ago had that been? How things had changed! He had been little more than a boy, a boy who found in the Virgin the mother he had never known . . .

At least, thought Arnau, he had managed to save Raquel from the terrible fate that seemed to await her. As soon as he had seen Eleonor and Margarida pointing to them, Arnau had made sure Raquel and her family fled the Jewish quarter. Not even he knew where they had gone . . .

'I want you to go and look for Mar,' he told Joan on his next visit.

Still two paces away from his brother, the friar tensed.

'Did you hear me, Joan?' Arnau tried to approach him, but the chains cut into his legs. Joan had not moved. 'Joan, did you hear me?'

'Yes . . . yes . . . I heard you.' Joan went up to his brother and embraced him. 'But . . .' he started to say.

'I have to see her, Joan.' He gripped him by the shoulders, and gently shook him. 'I don't want to die without speaking to her again . . .'

'My God! Don't say that!'

'Yes, Joan. I might well die in here, all alone, with only a dozen helpless unfortunates as witnesses. I don't want to perish without having had the chance to see Mar. It's something—'

'What do you want to say to her? What can be that important?'

'Her forgiveness, Joan, I need her forgiveness.' Joan tried to struggle free from his brother's hands, but Arnau would not let him go. 'You know me. You are a man of God. You know I've never done anyone any harm, apart from that . . . child.'

Joan succeeded in freeing his shoulders . . . and fell on his knees before his brother. 'It wasn't—' he began to say.

'You're the only one I have, Joan,' Arnau interrupted him. He too sank to his knees. 'You have to help me. You've never let me down. You can't do so now. You're all I have, Joan!'

Joan said nothing.

'What about her husband?' was all he could think of to say. 'He might not allow . . .'

'He's dead,' Arnau replied. 'I found that out when he ceased making payments on a cheap loan I had offered him. He died fighting for the King, in the defence of Calatayud.'

'But—' Joan tried to say again.

'Joan, I'm tied to my wife by an oath that prevents me from being with Mar as long as she lives – but I must see her. I have to tell her my feelings, even though we can't be together . . .' Arnau slowly recovered his composure. There was another favour he wanted to ask his brother. 'Would you visit my counting house? I want to know how things are going.'

Joan gave a sigh. That very morning, when he had gone to his brother's money exchange, Remigi had handed him a bag of money.

'It wasn't a good deal,' he told Joan.

Nothing was a good deal. When he left Arnau after promising to do his best to find Mar, Joan handed over money to the gaoler at the door to the dungeon.

'He asked for a bucket.'

How much was a bucket worth to Arnau? Joan gave the gaoler another coin.

'I want that bucket cleaned constantly.' The gaoler stuffed the coins in his purse and set off up the passageway. 'One of the prisoners in there is dead,' added Joan.

The gaoler merely shrugged.

Joan did not even emerge from the bishop's palace. After leaving the dungeons, he went in search of Nicolau Eimerich. He knew all the palace corridors. How often in his younger days had he walked down them, proud of his responsibilities? Now other young men hastened along, neat and tidy priests who openly stared at him in astonishment.

'Has he confessed?'

Joan had promised Arnau he would try to find Mar.

'Has he confessed?' repeated the grand inquisitor.

Joan had spent a sleepless night preparing for this conversation, but nothing he had thought of was any use now.

'If he did, what penalty—?'

'I have already told you it is a very serious matter.'

'My brother is very rich.'

Joan met Nicolau Eimerich's gaze.

'Are you, an inquisitor, trying to buy the Holy Office?'

'Fines are permitted as payment for lesser offences. I am sure that if you offered Arnau a fine . . .'

'As you well know, that depends on how serious the offence is. The accusation against him—'

'Eleonor has no right to accuse him of anything,' Joan interrupted.

The grand inquisitor got up from his seat and confronted Joan, pressing his hands on the table. 'So,' he said, raising his voice, 'both of you know it was the

King's ward who made the accusation. His own wife, the King's ward! How could you imagine she would do such a thing if Arnau had nothing to hide? What man mistrusts his wife? Why not a business rival, or one of his assistants, or even a neighbour? How many people has Arnau sentenced as Consul of the Sea? Why couldn't it have been one of them? Answer me, Brother Joan: why the baroness? What sins is your brother hiding for him to be so sure it was her?'

Joan shrank back in his seat. How often had he used the same tactic? Plucking words from the air in order to . . . But how did Arnau know it had been Eleonor? Could it be that he had really . . .?

'It wasn't Arnau who put the blame on his wife,' Joan lied, 'it was I.'

Nicolau Eimerich raised his hands to the heavens. 'And how do you know it was she, Brother Joan?'

'She hates him . . . No!' he tried to correct himself, but Nicolau was already pouncing on his words.

'Why would she do that?' cried the inquisitor. 'Why would the King's ward hate her husband? Why would a good, God-fearing Christian wife come to hate her husband? What kind of wrong can her husband have done her to awaken such hatred? Women were born to serve men; that is the law on earth and in heaven. Men beat women, but the women do not hate them for it; men keep women shut up, and are not hated for that either. Women work for their husbands, and fornicate with them when the man so wishes. They have to look after them and submit to them – but none of that creates hatred. So what precisely do you know, Brother Joan?'

Joan clenched his teeth. He should not say anything more. He felt defeated.

'You are an inquisitor. I demand you tell me all you know,' shouted Nicolau.

Joan still said nothing.

'You are forbidden to protect sin. Whoever is silent about a sin is more guilty than a person who commits one.'

In his mind's eye, Joan saw an endless number of village squares, with the inhabitants shrinking in the face of his diatribes.

'Brother Joan,' Nicolau spat the words as though they were distasteful, pointing to him across the table, 'I want his confession by tomorrow. And pray that I don't decide to judge you as well. Oh, and Brother Joan!' he added as the friar was about to leave the room. 'Make sure you change your habit. I have already received complaints. And from what I can see . . .' Nicolau waved disdainfully at Joan's habit.

As Joan left the chamber, glancing down at the filthy, threadbare folds of his tunic, he almost bumped into two men waiting in the grand inquisitor's ante-chamber. With them were three armed men who stood guard over two women in chains: an old woman, and a younger one, whose face . . .

'What are you doing still here, Brother Joan?' asked Nicolau Eimerich, coming to the door to receive his visitors.

Joan delayed no longer, but scurried off down the corridor.

Jaume de Bellera and Genís Puig went into Nicolau Eimerich's office. After casting a rapid glance at Francesca and Aledis, the inquisitor left them in the ante-chamber.

'We have heard,' said Lord de Bellera once they had presented themselves and taken seats, 'that you have arrested Arnau Estanyol.'

Genís Puig fiddled nervously with his hands in his lap.

'Yes,' said Nicolau curtly, 'it's public knowledge.'

'What is he accused of?' Genís Puig interjected. The

nobleman at his side glared at him. 'Don't speak; don't say a word until the inquisitor asks you to,' he had warned him many times.

Nicolau turned to Genís. 'Don't you know that is a secret?'

'I beg you to forgive my friend,' Jaume de Bellera quickly said, 'but you will soon see why we are so interested. We have heard that there is an accusation against Arnau Estanyol, and we wish to back it up.'

The grand inquisitor straightened in his seat. A ward of the King, three priests from Santa Maria who had heard Estanyol blaspheme in the church itself, arguing out loud with his wife. Now a nobleman and a knight. Few accusations could have more convincing witnesses. He nodded to the two men to continue.

Jaume de Bellera narrowed his eyes to caution Genís Puig, then began the speech he had so often rehearsed.

'We think that Arnau Estanyol is the incarnation of the Devil.' Nicolau did not move. 'He is the son of a murderer and a witch. His father, Bernat Estanyol, killed a groom in Navarcles Castle and then fled with his son, Arnau, whom my father was keeping locked up because he knew what he was capable of. It was Bernat Estanyol who led the rising in Plaça del Blat during the first bad year we had: do you remember it? He was executed on the same spot—'

'And his son set fire to his body,' Genís Puig could not stop himself exclaiming.

Nicolau gave a start. Jaume de Bellera gave his companion another warning look.

'He set fire to the body?' asked Nicolau.

'Yes, yes, I saw it myself,' lied Genís Puig, recalling what his mother had told him.

'Did you report him to the authorities then?'

'I . . .' Genís faltered. Lord de Bellera tried to intervene, but Nicolau gestured to him not to interrupt. 'I . . . was only a child. I was afraid he might do the same to me.'

Nicolau raised his hand to his chin, to hide a sly smile. Then he motioned for Lord de Bellera to continue.

'His mother, that old woman outside, is a witch. Nowadays she is the mistress of a bawdy house, but she was the one who suckled me, and bewitched me with milk intended for her son.' When he heard this from the nobleman, Nicolau's eyes opened wide. The lord of Navarcles realized: 'Don't worry,' he said quickly, 'as soon as the sickness became apparent, my father brought me to the lord bishop. I am the son of Llorenç and Caterina de Bellera, the lords of Navarcles. You can verify that no one in my family has ever had the Devil's sickness. It can only have been that accursed milk!'

'You say she is a harlot now?'

'Yes, that too you can verify. She calls herself Francesca.'

'And the other woman?'

'She wanted to accompany her.'

'Is she another witch?'

'That is for you to decide.'

Nicolau thought for a few moments. 'Is there anything more?' he asked.

'Yes,' Genís Puig intervened. 'Arnau killed my brother Guiamon when he refused to take part in his diabolic rites. He tried to drown him one night on the beach. My brother died soon afterwards.'

Nicolau stared at the knight once more.

'My sister Margarida can confirm it. She was there. She grew frightened and tried to run away when Arnau began to summon the Devil. She can confirm all this for you.'

'And you did not report Arnau then either?'

'I've only recently learnt about it, when I told my sister what I was thinking of doing. She is still terrified that Arnau might harm her; she has lived with that fear for years.'

'These are very serious accusations.'

'They are nothing more than Arnau Estanyol deserves,' said Lord de Bellera. 'You well know that this man has spent a lifetime undermining authority. On his lands, contrary to his spouse's wishes, he abolished customary practices. Here in Barcelona he lends money to the poor, and as Consul of the Sea he is well known for his habit of giving judgements in favour of the common people.' Nicolau Eimerich listened attentively. 'Throughout his life he has sought to undermine the principles on which our social harmony is based. God created the peasants to work the land under the tutelage of their feudal lords. Even the Church, in order not to lose them, has forbidden its serfs to take the habit—'

'In New Catalonia many of those customary practices no longer exist,' Nicolau intervened.

Genís Puig was glancing anxiously at each of them in turn.

'That is precisely what I am trying to say.' Lord de Bellera chopped the air with his hands. 'In New Catalonia there are no abuses . . . thanks to our Prince, thanks to the Church. We have to populate the lands won from the infidel, and the only way to do that is by attracting new people. That is what our Prince has decided. But Arnau is nothing more than the Prince . . . of Darkness.'

When he saw the grand inquisitor nod imperceptibly at these words, Genís Puig smiled broadly.

'He lends money to the poor,' the nobleman went on, 'money he knows he is never likely to recover. God created the rich – and the poor. It is not right that the poor should have money and marry off their daughters as though they were rich; that is against the will of Our Lord. What are those poor people going to think of you churchmen, or of us nobles? Are we not following the precepts of the Church when we treat the poor as they should be treated? Arnau is a devil, the son of devils. Everything he does is designed to prepare for the coming of the Devil through the rebellion of the common people. I beg you to think on all this.'

Nicolau Eimerich thought about what he had heard. He called in his scribe to note down all the accusations that Lord de Bellera and Genís Puig had made. He sent for Margarida Puig, and ordered that Francesca be imprisoned.

'What about the other woman?' he asked. 'Is she accused of anything?' The two men hesitated. 'In that case, let her be set free.'

Francesca was sent to the huge palace dungeon. She was chained to the wall at the opposite end to Arnau. Aledis was thrown out on to the street.

When he had finished organizing everything, Nicolau Eimerich slumped in his chair. Blaspheming in the temple of Our Lord; having sexual congress with a Jewess; befriending Jews; committing murder; engaging in diabolic practices; going against the precepts of the Church . . . and all of this backed up by priests, nobles, knights . . . and by the King's ward herself. The grand inquisitor leant back in his chair and smiled to himself.

How rich is your brother, Joan? Stupid man! What fine are you talking about, when all that money will fall into the hands of the Inquisition anyway as soon as your brother is condemned to die?

Aledis stumbled as the soldiers pushed her into the street outside the bishop's palace. When she regained her balance, she realized that several passers-by were staring at her. What was it that the soldiers had shouted? Witch? She was almost in the middle of the street by now, and people were still peering at her. She looked down at her filthy clothes. She felt her brittle, unkempt hair. A well-dressed man walked by, openly staring at her. Aledis stamped her foot and leapt towards him, baring her teeth like a dog attacking its prey. The man jumped backwards and then ran off, only slowing down when he realized Aledis was not following him. Now it was Aledis who scrutinized all those around her, forcing them to lower their eyes one by one, although some of them still cast covert glances out of the corner of their eyes to see what she was doing.

What had happened? Men sent by Lord de Bellera had broken into her house and arrested Francesca as she rested on a chair. Nobody had given them any explanation. The soldiers roughly pushed the girls aside when they tried to intervene; they all turned to Aledis to see what she would do, but she was paralysed by fear. A few clients ran out of the house, hose around their ankles.

Aledis confronted the soldier who seemed to be in charge: 'What does this mean? Why are you arresting this woman?'

'On the orders of Lord de Bellera,' the man replied.

Lord de Bellera! Aledis looked towards Francesca, who was being held under the arms by two soldiers. The old woman's body had begun to shake. De Bellera! Ever since Arnau had put an end to the privileges at Montbui Castle and Francesca had told Aledis her secret, the two women had overcome the only remaining barrier between them. How often had she heard the story of Llorenç de Bellera from Francesca's lips? How often had she seen her weep when she remembered those days? And now . . . another de Bellera; and Francesca was being taken to the castle, just as when . . .

Francesca was still trembling, held by the two soldiers.

'Let her go!' she shouted at them. 'Can't you see you're hurting her?' The two soldiers turned to their captain. 'We'll go of our own accord,' said Aledis, also looking in his direction.

The captain shrugged, and the soldiers handed the old woman over to Aledis.

They were taken to Navarcles Castle, where they were shut in the dungeons. They were not mistreated, however. On the contrary, they were given food, water and even bundles of straw to sleep on. It was only now that Aledis understood the reason: Lord de Bellera had wanted Francesca to reach Barcelona in good health. They were taken to the city two days later, in a cart, in complete silence. What for? Why? What did it all mean?

The noise all around her brought Aledis back to reality. She had been so caught up in her own thoughts, she had hardly realized she had walked all the way down Carrer del Bisbe, then Carrer dels Seders, and had finally entered Plaça del Blat. The fine, sunny spring day had brought even more people than usual into the square. Alongside the grain-sellers were dozens of curious onlookers. Aledis was standing under the old gateway to the city: she turned when the smell of freshly baked bread from a barrow on her left reached her nostrils. The baker glanced at her suspiciously, and Aledis remembered how she looked. She did not have a single coin on her. She swallowed hard and walked away, avoiding catching the baker's gaze.

Twenty-five years; it had been twenty-five years since she had last been in these streets, seen these people, and breathed the air of Barcelona. Could the Pia Almoina still exist? They had been given nothing to eat that morning in the castle, and her stomach was reminding her of the fact. She walked back the way she had come, up towards the cathedral and the bishop's palace. Her mouth began to water as she approached the line of beggars queueing for food outside the Pia Almoina. How often in her youth had she passed this very same spot, feeling nothing but pity for these hungry people who openly showed to anyone who passed by their need for public charity?

Aledis joined the queue. She lowered her head so that her hair would cover her face, and shuffled along with the rest of them towards the food. She concealed her face still further when she reached the novice, and stretched out her hands. Why did she have to ask for charity? She had a good house, and had saved enough money to live comfortably for the rest of her days. Men still found her desirable and . . . a crust of hard bean bread, a cup of wine and a bowl of soup. She ate everything, with as much enjoyment as all the poor beggars around her.

When she had finished, she lifted her gaze for the first time. She looked at the throng of beggars, cripples and old people sitting at the tables. They all kept an eye on their neighbours, and clutched their hunk of bread and bowl of soup tightly. What was the reason for her being there? Why had they kept Francesca in the bishop's palace? Aledis got up. Her attention was caught by a young blonde woman dressed in a scarlet robe, walking towards the cathedral. A noblewoman . . . out on her own? But if she were not a noble, dressed like that she could only be a . . . Teresa! Aledis ran over to her.

'We took turns outside the castle to find out what was happening to you,' Teresa explained after they had embraced. 'It wasn't hard convincing the soldiers at the gate to tell us.' The young woman winked one of her beautiful green eyes. 'When you were taken out and the soldiers told us you were headed for Barcelona, we had to find some way of getting here. That's what took us so long. Where's Francesca?'

'She's under arrest in the bishop's palace.'

'For what reason?'

Aledis shrugged. When the two of them had been split up and the soldiers told her to get out of the palace, she had tried to hear what was going on. 'Take the old woman to the dungeons,' was all she had heard. Nobody had answered her questions, though, and they had pushed her out of the way. Her insistence on knowing why Francesca had been arrested led a young friar whose sleeve she was tugging to call the guard. She was thrown out of the palace to shouts of 'Witch!'

'How many of you came?'

'Eulàlia and me.'

A glittering green dress came running towards them.

'Did you bring money?'

'Of course.'

'What about Francesca?' asked Eulàlia when she caught up with the other two.

'She's been arrested,' Aledis told her. Eulàlia wanted to know why, but Aledis silenced her with a gesture. 'I don't know why.'

Aledis studied the two young women – what mightn't they discover? 'I don't know why she's been arrested,' she repeated, 'but we'll find out, won't we, girls?'

They both smiled mischievously at her.

Joan dragged the muddy folds of his habit through all Barcelona. His brother had asked him to find Mar. How could he appear before her? After leaving Arnau, he had tried to make a pact with Eimerich. Instead of that, like one of the hapless villains he was used to judging as inquisitor, he had condemned himself with his own words, and had only served to make his brother seem more guilty. What could Eleonor have accused him of? For a few moments he thought of going to see his sister-in-law, but when he remembered the smile she had given him in Felip de Ponts's house, he knew that would be no use. If she had denounced her own husband, what was she going to say to him?

Joan walked down Carrer de la Mar to Santa Maria. Arnau's church. Joan came to a halt and surveyed it.

Although still covered in wooden scaffolding where masons came and went ceaselessly, the proud outlines of Santa Maria were plain to see. All the external walls and their buttresses had been completed. So had the apse and two of the four vaults in the main nave. The tracery of the third vault, on the end of whose keystone the King had paid for the image of his father King Alfonso on horseback to be sculpted, was already rising in a perfect arch, supported by a complicated network of scaffolding until the keystone could be lowered into place and the arch soar free. All that was left to build were the two remaining vaults, and then Santa Maria's new roof would be complete.

How could one not fall in love with a church like this? Joan recalled Father Albert and the first time Arnau and he had set foot in Santa Maria. He had not even known how to pray! Years later, while he was learning to pray, to read and to write, his brother was hauling blocks of stone to this very spot. Joan remembered the bloody wounds on his brother's back those first days of work as a *bastaix* . . . and yet he had smiled! He watched the master builders busy with the jambs and archivolts on the main doorway, while other experts worked on the statues, the doorways, the tracery that was different around each door, the forged iron grilles and the gargoyles with all their vast array of allegorical figures, the capitals of the columns. But what most caught his attention were the stained-glass windows, those works of art intended to filter the magical light of the Mediterranean so that it could play, hour by hour, almost minute after minute, with the shapes and colours inside the church.

The composition of the impressive rose window above the main doorway was already hinted at: in the centre lay a small rondel, from the edge of which, like whimsical arrows or a carefully sculpted sunstone, grew the stone mullions that divided up the shapes of the main window. Beyond these, the tracery gave way to a row of pointed trefoils, with above them another row of quatrefoil lights that ended in rounded curves. It was in between all this stone tracery, as elsewhere in the narrow lights of the façade, that the pieces of leaded stained glass would eventually be placed; for now, though, the rose window looked like a huge spider's web made of finely carved stone, just waiting for the master glaziers to fill in the gaps.

They still have a lot to do, thought Joan as he watched the hundred or so workmen who carried the hopes and illusions of a whole people on their backs. At that moment, a *bastaix* arrived carrying another huge block. Sweat poured down from his forehead to his calves; all his muscles stood out tautly as they rocked to the rhythm of each step that brought him closer to the church. But he was smiling, just as his brother had all those years ago. Joan could not take his eyes off him. The masons stopped their work up on the scaffolding to watch this fresh load of stones arriving. Another *bastaix* appeared after the first one, then another, and still another, all of them bent double under the weight. The sound of chisels on stone ceased, as the masons paid homage to these humble workers of La Ribera. For a few moments the whole of Santa Maria lay in enchanted silence. Then a mason broke the spell with his shout of encouragement from high on the scaffolding. His cry pierced the air, bounced off the stones and entered the hearts of everyone there.

'Keep going!' Joan whispered, adding his voice to the clamour that had arisen. The *bastaixos* were smiling. As each of them deposited his stone on the ground, the shouts grew louder. Afterwards, they were handed waterskins, which they raised high over their heads for the contents to run off their faces before they drank. Joan saw himself running along the beach to offer the *bastaixos* Bernat's waterskin. Then he raised his eyes to the heavens. He had to go and find her: if that was the penitence the Lord was imposing on him, he would seek out Mar and confess the truth. He went round Santa Maria to Plaça del Born, then Pla de'n Llull and Santa Clara convent, leaving Barcelona by the Sant Daniel gate.

It was not difficult for Aledis to find Lord de Bellera and Genís Puig. Apart from the exchange, where visiting merchants stayed, Barcelona had only five inns. She ordered Teresa and Eulàlia to hide on the way out to Monjuïc hill until she came to fetch them. Aledis was silent as she watched them walk away, fond memories flooding her mind . . .

When she could no longer see the bright gleam of their robes, she began her search. She went first to the Hostal del Bou, close by the bishop's palace and Plaça Nova. When she appeared at the kitchen door to the rear of the inn, the scullion boy rudely shooed her away when she asked for Lord de Bellera. At the Hostal de la Massa in Portaferrissa, also near the bishop's palace, a woman kneading bread told her no two such gentlemen were staying there. So Aledis headed for the Estanyer inn, on Plaça de la Llana. There another young lad brazenly stared her up and down.

'Who wants to know about Lord de Bellera?' he asked.

'My mistress,' replied Aledis. 'She has been following him from Navarcles.'

The lad was tall and thin as a rake. He stared at Aledis's breasts, then reached out his right hand and fondled one.

'What interest does your mistress have in this nobleman?'

Aledis did not move away; she stifled a smile. 'It's not

for me to know.' The lad began to rub her breasts more vigorously. Aledis stepped closer to him, and brushed the top of his thigh. He tensed. 'But,' Aledis said, drawling her words, 'if they are staying here, I may have to spend the night sleeping in the garden while my mistress . . .' By now she was stroking his groin.

'This morning,' the lad stammered, 'two gentlemen came asking for somewhere to stay.'

This time, Aledis smiled openly. For a moment she thought of leaving the boy, but then . . . why not? It had been so long since she had felt a young, clumsy body on top of her, someone driven only by passion . . .

She pushed him into a small hut. The first time, the lad did not even have time to remove his hose, but after that Aledis was able to take advantage of every thrust of this casual object of her desire.

When Aledis stood up to get dressed again, the youth was lying on the ground on his back. He was out of breath, and staring blindly up at the rafters on the roof of the hut.

'If you see me again,' Aledis told him, 'whatever happens, remember you don't know me!'

She had to repeat this twice before she could secure his promise.

'You two will be my daughters,' she told Teresa and Eulàlia as she gave them the dresses she had just bought. 'I have been recently widowed, and we are in Barcelona on our way to Girona, where we are hoping one of my brothers will take us in. We have been left with nothing. Your father was a tradesman . . . a tanner from Tarragona.'

'For someone who has just become a widow and has been left penniless, you look very cheerful,' Eulàlia exclaimed as she took off her green robe and smiled at Teresa.

'It's true,' the other girl agreed. 'You need to avoid looking so pleased with yourself. It's as though you had just met—'

'Don't worry,' Aledis intervened, 'when necessary I'll display all the grief that befits a recent widow.'

'And until it becomes necessary,' Teresa insisted, 'could you not forget the widow and tell us why it is you are looking so happy?'

The two girls laughed out loud at her story. Hidden among the bushes on the slopes of Montjuïc hill, Aledis could not help noticing how perfect and sensual their naked bodies were. Such was youth. For a brief moment, she saw herself here on the same spot, many years earlier . . .

'Ow!' Eulàlia protested. 'This . . . scratches.'

Aledis stopped daydreaming and saw Eulàlia wearing a long, washed-out smock that came down to her ankles. 'The orphaned daughters of a tanner don't wear silk.'

'But does it have to be this?' protested Eulàlia, plucking at the cloth with her fingers.

'It's quite normal,' Aledis insisted. 'Anyway, you have both forgotten something.'

Aledis showed them two strips of clothing that were as faded and shapeless as their smocks. They came to get a closer look.

'What is it?' asked Teresa.

'Decent women cover their breasts properly. These are used to—'

'No, you can't want us to wear—'

The two young women made as though to protest.

'First your breasts,' Aledis said sternly, 'then your smocks, and on top of them the kirtles. And you can thank the Lord that I bought you smocks and not hairshirts, because a little penance would not go amiss.'

The three women had to help each other wrap the strips of cloth round themselves.

'I thought you wanted us to seduce two noblemen,' Eulàlia complained while Aledis was pulling the cloth tight round her abundant breasts. 'I don't see how, dressed like this.'

'You leave that to me,' Aledis told her. 'The kirtles are . . . almost white, as a sign of virginity. Those two rogues will never miss the chance to sleep with virgins. You know nothing about men,' Aledis said as she finished dressing. 'Don't flirt or take liberties. Refuse all the time. Reject their advances as often as necessary.'

'What if we reject them so much they change their minds?'

Aledis raised her eyebrows at Teresa. 'Poor little innocent,' she said, smiling. 'All you two have to do is make sure they drink. The wine will do the rest. As long as you are with them they will have only one thought in mind. Believe me. And remember, Francesca has been arrested by the Church, and not by the city magistrate or the bailiff. Turn your conversation towards religious topics.'

The two girls looked at her in surprise.

'Religious?' they exclaimed as one.

'I realize you don't know much about them,' said Aledis, 'but use your imagination. I think she's accused of something to do with witchcraft . . . when they threw me out of the palace, they shouted about me being a witch.'

A few hours later, the soldiers guarding the Trentaclaus gate allowed in a woman dressed in mourning clothes, with her hair coiled round her head. With her were her two daughters, dressed in near-white kirtles, with demurely plaited locks. They had common rope sandals on their feet, wore no make-up or perfume, and walked with downcast eyes behind their mother, staring at her ankles, as she had instructed them.

49

The dungeon door suddenly clanged open. This was not the usual time; the sun had not yet gone down sufficiently, and daylight was still struggling to find a way in through the bars of the tiny ground-level window, although the scene of misery inside seemed to make this almost impossible as the light was absorbed by all the dust and the foul vapours emanating from the prisoners' bodies. This was not the usual time for the door to open, and all the shadowy figures stirred. Arnau heard the sound of chains, which ceased when the gaoler came in with the new prisoner. That meant he had not come in search of one of them. Another man . . . or rather, another woman, Arnau thought, correcting himself when he saw the outline of the old woman in the doorway. What sin could that poor woman have committed?

The gaoler pushed her inside the dungeon. She fell to the floor.

'Get up, witch!' his voice resonated round the entire dungeon. The old woman did not stir. The gaoler gave the bundle at his feet two hefty kicks. The echoing sound of the two dull thuds seemed to last an eternity. 'I said, get up!'

Arnau noticed how the other shadows tried to merge into the walls of the prison. The same shouts, the same gruff bark, the same voice. He had heard that voice often during the days he had been imprisoned, thundering from the far side of the door after one or other of the prisoners had been unchained. Then too he had noticed how the shadows shrank away from it, consumed with the fear of torture. First came the voice, then the shout, then a few moments later the heart-rending cry of a body in pain.

'Get up, you old whore!'

The gaoler kicked her again, but still she would not move. Eventually, puffing and blowing, he bent down, grasped her by the arm, and dragged her over to where he had been told to chain her up: as far as possible from the moneychanger. The sound of keys and chains told all of them what had happened to her. Before leaving the dungeon, the gaoler came over to where Arnau was.

'Why?' he had asked when he had been ordered to chain the witch up as far away as possible from Arnau.

'This witch is the moneychanger's mother,' the officer of the inquisition told him: he had heard it from one of Lord de Bellera's men.

'Don't think that you can pay the same to have your mother eat properly,' said the gaoler when he was next to Arnau. 'Even if she is your mother, she is still a witch, and witches cost money.'

Nothing had changed: the farmhouse, with the tower to one side, still dominated the low rise. Joan looked up the hill and in his mind saw again the assembled *host*, the nervous men with their drawn swords, the shouts of joy when he, on this very spot, succeeded in convincing Arnau to give up Mar in marriage. He had never got on well with the girl: what was he going to say to her now?

Joan looked up at the heavens and then, stooping and

with downcast eyes, started to climb the gentle slope.

Outside, the farmhouse seemed deserted. The silence was broken only by the rustle of animals moving on the straw in the stables.

'Is anybody there?' shouted Joan.

He was about to call out again when he spotted something moving by a corner of the house. A boy was staring at him, his eyes wide open in astonishment.

'Come here, boy,' Joan ordered him.

The youngster hesitated.

'Come here—'

'What's going on?'

Joan turned to look at the external staircase leading to the upper floor of the farmhouse. At the top was Mar, staring straight at him.

The two of them stood motionless for long silent moments. Joan tried to discern in this woman the image of the girl whose life he had handed to the knight Felip de Ponts, but the air of severity about her seemed far distant from the explosion of feelings that had occurred in this same farmhouse six years earlier. The minutes ticked by, and Joan felt more and more inhibited. Mar meanwhile pierced him with her steady, unflinching gaze.

Finally she asked him: 'What are you here for, friar?'

'I came to talk to you.' Joan had to raise his voice to reach her.

'I'm not interested in anything you might have to say.'

Mar made as though to turn on her heel, but Joan quickly added: 'I promised Arnau I would talk to you.'

Contrary to his expectations, the mention of Arnau's name did not seem to make any impact on her: but she did not go inside either. 'It's not I who wishes to talk to you.' Joan let a few moments go by. 'May I come up?'

Mar turned her back on him and went into the farmhouse. Joan walked to the foot of the staircase. He peered up at the heavens. Was this truly the penance he deserved?

He cleared his throat to show her he was there. Mar was busy at the hearth, stirring a pot that hung from a hook over the fire.

'Speak,' was all she said.

Joan studied her back as she leant over. Her hair cascaded down below her waist, almost as far as a pair of firm buttocks whose outline was very clear beneath her smock. She had turned into an . . . attractive woman.

'Have you got nothing to say?' asked Mar, turning her head towards him briefly.

'Arnau has been put in gaol by the Inquisition,' the Dominican blurted out.

Mar stopped stirring the food in the pot.

Joan said nothing more.

Her voice seemed to waver and dance as delicately as the flames of the fire itself: 'Some of us have been incarcerated for much longer.'

Mar still had her back to him. She straightened up, staring at the beams of the hearth.

'It wasn't Arnau who put you there.'

Mar turned quickly to face him. 'Wasn't he the one who gave me to Lord de Ponts?' she cried. 'Wasn't he the one who agreed to my marriage? Wasn't he the one who decided not to avenge my dishonour? Ponts raped me! He kidnapped me and raped me!'

She had spat out the words. Her whole body was shaking, from her top lip to her hands, which she now raised to her breast. Joan could not bear to see the pain in her eyes.

'It wasn't Arnau,' the friar repeated in a faint voice. 'It was . . . it was I!' He was speaking loudly now. 'Do you understand? It was I. I was the one who convinced him he should marry you off. What future was there for a raped girl? What would have become of you when the whole of Barcelona learnt of your misfortune? Eleonor convinced me, and I was the one who arranged your kidnap. I agreed to your dishonour to get Arnau to allow you to be married to someone else. It was I who was guilty of everything. Arnau would never have done it otherwise.'

They stared at each other. Joan could feel the weight of his habit lightening. Mar stopped shaking as tears welled up in her eyes.

'He loved you,' said Joan. 'He loved you then and he loves you now. He needs you . . .'

Mar lifted her hands to her face. She bent her knees to one side, and her body sank until she was prostrate before the friar.

That was it. He had done it. Now Mar would go to Barcelona. She would tell Arnau and . . . The thoughts raced through Joan's mind as he bent to help Mar up . . .

'Don't touch me!'

Joan jumped away from her.

'Is something wrong, my lady?'

The friar turned towards the door. On the threshold stood a giant of a man. He was carrying a scythe and stared at him menacingly. Joan could see the little boy's head poking out from behind his legs. He was only a couple of feet from the friar, and seemed head and shoulders taller than him.

'Nothing is wrong,' said Joan, but the man came into the room, brushing him aside like a feather. 'I've told you, there's nothing wrong,' Joan insisted. 'Go about your business.'

The little boy ran and hid behind the door-frame. Joan glanced at him and then turned back to the others; he saw that the man with the scythe was kneeling in front of Mar, without touching her.

'Didn't you hear me?' asked Joan. The man did not answer. 'Do as you are told, and get about your business.'

This time the man did turn and look at him. 'I take orders only from my mistress,' he said.

How many big, strong, proud men like him had fallen at Joan's feet? How many had he seen sobbing and begging for forgiveness before he passed sentence? Joan's eyes narrowed. He clenched his fists and took two steps towards the servant. 'How dare you disobey the Inquisition?' he cried.

Before he could even finish, Mar was on her feet. She was shaking again. The man with the scythe also stood up, but more slowly.

'Friar, how dare *you* come into my house and threaten my servant? Inquisitor? Ha! You're no more than a devil disguised as a friar. You were the one who had me raped!' Joan could see the man's fingers gripping the handle of the scythe. 'You've admitted it!'

'I . . .' Joan stammered.

The servant came over to him and pushed the blunt edge of the scythe into his stomach. 'Nobody would find out, mistress. He came on his own.'

Joan looked at Mar. There was no fear in her eyes, or compassion. There was only . . . He turned as quickly as he could to make for the door, but the little boy slammed it shut and confronted him.

Behind his back, the man reached out with the scythe until it was hooked round Joan's neck. This time it was the sharp edge he pressed against his throat. Joan did not move. The boy no longer looked fearful: his expression now mirrored that of the two people near the hearth.

'What . . . what are you going to do, Mar?' As Joan spoke, he could feel the scythe cutting into his neck.

Mar said nothing for a few moments. Joan could hear her breathing.

'Shut him in the tower, Esteve,' she ordered.

Mar had not been in there since the day when the Barcelona *host* first made ready for its attack, then exploded in shouts of joy. Ever since her husband had fallen at Calatayud, she had kept it locked.

50

The widow and her two daughters crossed Plaça de la Llana to the Estanyer inn. This was a tall, two-storey building with the kitchen and the guests' dining room on the ground floor, and all the bedrooms on the first floor. The innkeeper greeted them. The kitchen lad was with him: when she saw him staring open-mouthed at her, Aledis winked at him. 'What are you staring at?' the innkeeper shouted, cuffing him round the head. The lad ran off to the back of the building. Teresa and Eulàlia had noticed the wink, and both smiled.

'You're the ones who deserve a good slap,' Aledis whispered when the innkeeper turned his back for a moment. 'Stand still and stop scratching, will you? The next one who does will get—'

'These clothes are impossible.'

'Be quiet,' Aledis ordered them as the innkeeper turned his attention back to her.

He had a room where the three of them could sleep, although there were only two mattresses.

'Don't worry, my man,' said Aledis. 'My daughters are used to sharing a bed.'

'Did you see how that innkeeper looked at us when you told him we were used to sleeping together?' asked Teresa once they were safely in their room. Two straw pallets and a small chest on which stood an oil lamp was all the furniture in the room.

'He was imagining lying between the two of us,' said Eulàlia with a laugh.

'And that was without him being able to appreciate any of your charms,' said Aledis. 'I told you so.'

'We could work dressed like this. It seems to be successful.'

'It only works once,' Aledis said. 'Or twice at most. Men like the idea of innocence, of virginity. But as soon as they've had it . . . We would have to go from place to place, practising the deception, and we wouldn't be able to ask them to pay.'

'There isn't enough gold in all Catalonia that would make me wear this . . .' Teresa started furiously scratching from her thighs to her breasts.

'Don't scratch!'

'But no one can see us now,' the girl protested.

'The more you scratch, the more it will itch.'

'What about that wink you gave the scullion?'

Aledis stared at them. 'That's none of your business.'

'Did you ask him to pay?'

Aledis remembered the look on the lad's face when he realized he did not even have time to take off his hose, and the clumsy, violent way he had climbed on top of her. It wasn't only men who liked innocence, virginity . . .

She smiled. 'He gave me something.'

They waited in their room until suppertime. Then they went down and sat at a rough table of unpolished wood. Soon afterwards, Jaume de Bellera and Genís Puig made their appearance. From the moment they sat at their table on the far side of the room, they could not take their eyes off the two girls. There was no one else in the dining room. Aledis caught the girls' attention. They both crossed themselves and made a start on the bowls of soup the innkeeper had brought.

'Wine? Only for me,' Aledis told him. 'My daughters don't drink.'

'It's one jug of wine after the other for her . . . since our father died,' Teresa said apologetically to the innkeeper.

'To get over her grief,' Eulàlia explained.

'Listen,' Aledis whispered to them some time later, 'that makes three jugs of wine, and they have had their effect. In a moment I'm going to let my head drop on the table, and I'll start snoring. From then on, you know what you have to do. We need to know why Francesca's been arrested, and what they intend to do with her.'

Soon afterwards, Aledis's head drooped on to the table between her hands. But she was listening intently.

'Why not come over here?' came the sound of a man's voice. Silence. 'She's drunk . . .' the voice insisted.

'We won't harm you,' said a second voice. 'How could we, in a place like this, with the innkeeper as witness?'

Aledis thought of the innkeeper: he wouldn't say a word, providing they let him lay his hands on something . . .

'Don't worry, we are gentlemen . . .'

The two girls eventually gave in. Aledis heard them scraping their chairs back and standing up.

'You're not snoring loudly enough,' Teresa whispered to her.

Aledis allowed herself a smile.

'A castle!'

Aledis could imagine Teresa and those incredible green eyes of hers opening wide as she stared at Lord de Bellera, making sure he got an eyeful of all her charms.

'Did you hear that, Eulàlia? A castle. He's a real

nobleman. We've never talked with a noble before . . .'

'Tell us about all your battles,' Aledis heard Eulàlia encouraging him. 'Have you met King Pedro? Have you talked to him?'

'Who else do you know?' Teresa wanted to know.

The two girls pressed round Lord de Bellera. Aledis was tempted to open her eyes, just enough to see them at work – but there was no point. Her girls knew what they were doing.

The castle, the King, the royal court – had they ever been there? The war . . . squeals of terror when Genís Puig, who had no castle, no King, and had never been to court, tried to capture their attention by playing up all the battles he had fought in. And wine, lots and lots of wine . . .

'What's a nobleman like you doing in the city, in this inn? Are you waiting to see someone important?' Aledis heard Teresa asking.

'We've brought in a witch,' Genís Puig burst out.

The girls had been talking to Lord de Bellera. Teresa saw him cast a disapproving look at his companion. Now was the time.

'A witch!' gushed Teresa, throwing herself on Jaume de Bellera and clasping both his hands in hers. 'In Tarragona we saw one being burnt. She shrieked as the flames leapt up her legs to her body, then her breasts, and . . .'

Teresa looked up at the ceiling as though following the path of the flames. She raised her hands to her own breast, but soon came back to reality, and looked embarrassedly at the nobleman, whose face was already flushed with desire.

Still holding her hands, Jaume de Bellera stood up. 'Come with me.' It sounded more like an order than a request. Teresa let herself be dragged away.

Genís Puig watched them leave. 'What about us?' he

said to Eulàlia, suddenly dropping his hand on to her calf.

Eulàlia made no move to lift it off. 'First I want to hear everything about the witch. It excites me . . .'

The knight slid his hand up her thigh. He began to tell her the story. When she heard the name 'Arnau', Aledis almost gave the game away by raising her head. 'The witch is his mother,' she heard Genís Puig say. Revenge, revenge, revenge . . .

'Now can we go?' Genís Puig pleaded when he had finished his account.

There was a moment's silence as Eulàlia hesitated.

'I'm not sure . . .' said the girl.

Genís Puig stood up, swaying. He slapped Eulàlia's face.

'That's enough nonsense. Come with me!'

'All right, let's go,' she yielded.

Once she realized she was alone in the dining room, Aledis struggled to her feet. She put her hands to the back of her head and rubbed her neck. So they were going to try Arnau and Francesca – the Devil and the witch, according to Genís Puig.

'I'd take my own life before letting Arnau know I'm his mother,' Francesca had told her during one of their few conversations after Arnau's speech on the plains of Montbui. 'He's a well-respected man,' Francesca went on before Aledis could say anything, 'and I'm nothing more than the mistress of a bawdy house. Besides, there are many things I could never explain to him: why I didn't follow his father and him, why I left him to die . . .'

Aledis looked down.

'I've no idea what his father told him about me,' Francesca continued, 'but whatever it was, there's nothing I can do about it now. Time makes one forget even a mother's love. Whenever I think of him, I like to picture him on that platform defying the nobles; I have no wish to see him brought down from on high. Best leave things as they are, Aledis. You're the only person in the world who knows my secret; I'm trusting you not to give it away even after my death. Promise me that, Aledis.'

But what use was her promise now?

When Esteve came back up into the tower, he was no longer carrying the scythe.

'The mistress says you are to put this over your eyes,' he said, throwing Joan a piece of cloth.

'Who do you think you are?' Joan exclaimed, kicking the cloth away.

There was not much room inside the tower: scarcely three steps in any direction. With a single bound, Esteve was beside Joan. He slapped him hard twice, once on either cheek.

'The mistress says you are to cover your eyes.'

'I'm an inquisitor!'

This time, the blow from Esteve sent Joan crashing against the wall. He lay there at Esteve's feet.

'Put the blindfold on.' Esteve lifted him with one hand. 'Put it on,' he repeated when Joan was upright.

'Do you think that by using violence you can intimidate an inquisitor? You cannot imagine—'

Esteve did not let him finish. First he punched him hard in the face, and Joan went hurtling against the wall once again. Then Mar's servant began to kick him – in the groin, the stomach, his chest, his face . . .

Joan curled up in a ball to protect himself from more pain. Esteve picked him up with one hand.

'The mistress says you are to put it on.'

Joan was bleeding from the mouth. His legs gave way under him. When the servant let go, he tried to stay on his feet, but a stab of pain in his knee made him lurch forward and clutch Esteve's body. The giant pushed him away.

'Put it on.'

The cloth was beside him. Joan realized he had wet himself, and that his habit was sticking to his thighs.

He picked up the blindfold and put it on.

Joan heard the servant close the tower door and go down the steps. Silence. On and on. Then he heard several footsteps on the stairs. Joan clambered up, gripping the wall. The door opened. They had brought some pieces of furniture with them: could they be chairs?

'I know you have sinned.' Seated on a footstool as she intoned the Inquisition's charge, Mar's voice reverberated around the room. Next to her, the little boy was watching the friar closely.

Joan said nothing.

'The Inquisition never blindfolds its . . . prisoners,' he complained finally. 'Perhaps if I could see you face to face . . .'

'That's true,' he heard Mar reply. 'You only blindfold their souls, their dignity, their decency, their honour. I know you have sinned,' she said again.

'I won't accept a trick like that.'

Mar signalled to Esteve. The servant went over to Joan and punched him hard in the stomach. Joan bent double, gasping for breath. By the time he had managed to straighten up again there was complete silence in the room. He was panting so hard he could not even hear the others breathing. His legs and chest ached; his face felt raw. Nobody said a word. A knee to the outside of his thigh toppled him to the floor again.

Pain surged through him. He curled up into a ball once more.

Still silence.

A kick to his kidneys sent him arcing in the opposite direction.

'What do you want from me?' Joan screamed between the waves of pain.

Nobody answered. Finally the pain subsided, and it was then that Esteve picked him up again and hauled him in front of Mar.

Joan struggled to stay on his feet. 'What do you . . .?'

'I know you have sinned.'

How far would she go? Would she really beat him to death? Was she capable of killing him? Yes, he had sinned; but what authority did Mar have to judge him? He shuddered so violently he thought he was about to collapse again.

'You've already condemned me,' Joan managed to say. 'Why judge me then?'

Silence. Darkness.

'Tell me! Why do you want to sit in judgement on me?'

'You are right,' he heard her say at length. 'I've already condemned you, but remember it was you who confessed your guilt. On this very spot, it was you who robbed me of my virginity; this was where you had me raped time and again. Hang him and get rid of his body,' Mar told Esteve abruptly.

Mar's footsteps began to descend the staircase. Joan felt Esteve tie his hands behind his back. He could not move: none of his muscles responded. The servant lifted him in order to get him to stand on the stool where Mar had been sitting. Then Joan heard the noise of a rope being thrown up over one of the wooden beams in the ceiling. Esteve missed his aim, and the rope clattered to the floor. Joan wet himself again, and his bowels loosened. The noose was round his neck.

'I have sinned!' shouted Joan with what little strength he had left.

At the foot of the stairs, Mar heard his anguished confession.

At last.

Mar walked back up to the top of the tower, followed by the little boy.

'Now I'll listen to you,' she told Joan.

At first light, Mar was ready to leave for Barcelona. Dressed in her finest robes, and wearing the few jewels she possessed, she allowed Esteve to lift her on to her mule. She urged the animal on.

'Take care of the house,' she told the servant as her mount set off. 'And you, help your father,' she said to the boy.

Esteve pushed Joan behind the mule. 'Keep your word, friar,' he said.

With downcast eyes, Joan stumbled after Mar. What would happen now? That night, when the blindfold had finally been removed, he had found himself face to face with her by the light of the torches hanging on the tower's circular walls.

She had spat in his face.

'You don't deserve any reprieve . . . but Arnau might need you,' she said. 'That's the only thing stopping me killing you with my own bare hands here and now.'

The mule's small, sharp hooves clopped their way along the track. Joan followed their rhythm, his eyes fixed on his feet. He had confessed everything to her: from his conversations with Eleonor to the hatred that had made him such a ferocious inquisitor. It was then that Mar had snatched off the blindfold and spat in his face.

The mule plodded on slowly and docilely towards Barcelona. To his left, Joan could smell the sea, accompanying him on his pilgrimage.

51

The sun was already beating down by the time Aledis left the Estanyer inn and mingled with the people crossing Plaça de la Llana. Barcelona was wide awake. Some women, equipped with buckets, pots and jars, were queueing at the Cadena well, next to the inn, while others were crowding round the butcher's stall on the far side. They were all talking loudly and laughing. Aledis would have liked to be out earlier, but donning her widow's disguise with the doubtful help of two girls who never ceased pestering her with questions about what was going to happen next, what was going to become of Francesca, if she were really going to be burnt as a witch as the noblemen had said, had taken her longer than she had anticipated. At least no one was staring at her as she walked down Carrer de la Bòria towards Plaça del Blat. Aledis felt odd: she had always attracted men's attention and won scornful looks from women, but now, with the heat making her black robes stick to her, she looked all round and did not see anyone so much as giving her a second glance.

The noise from Plaça del Blat told her she could expect

more people, more sun, more heat. She was perspiring heavily, and her breasts chafed against the coarse girdle wrapped tightly round them. Just before she reached Barcelona's main market, Aledis turned right, heading for the shade of Carrer dels Semolers. She walked up the street until she reached Plaça de l'Oli, where customers had come in search of the best olive oil or were buying bread at the stall. She crossed the square until she came to the Sant Joan fountain, where none of the women lined up gave her a second look either.

Turning to her left, Aledis soon arrived at the cathedral and the bishop's palace. The day before they had thrown her out, calling her a witch. Would they recognize her now? The lad at the inn . . . Aledis smiled while she searched for a side entrance: that lad was much more likely to have recognized her than any of the Inquisition's soldiers.

'I'm looking for the gaoler. I have a message for him,' she said in reply to the question from the guard at the door.

The soldier let her past, and showed her the way down to the dungeons.

As she advanced down the stairs, all light and colours were gradually extinguished. At the foot, she found herself in an empty rectangular ante-chamber. It had a beaten earth floor and was lit by torches in the wall. At one end of the room, the gaoler was resting his mounds of flesh on a stool, at the other opened a dark passageway.

The man studied her in silence as she approached.

Aledis took a deep breath. 'I would like to see the old woman brought in yesterday,' she said, clinking her purse.

Without so much as moving or replying, the gaoler spat close to her feet, and waved his hand dismissively. Aledis took a step back.

'No,' was all he said.

Aledis opened the purse. The man's eyes greedily followed the gleam of coins that fell out on her hand. He had strict orders: no one was to enter the dungeons without express authorization by Nicolau Eimerich, and he had no wish to have to face the grand inquisitor. He knew what Eimerich was like when he grew angry . . . and the methods he used on those who disobeyed him. But those coins the woman was offering him . . . and besides, hadn't the officer added that what the inquisitor really wanted to avoid was anyone having contact with the moneychanger? And this woman did not want to see him; she was interested in the witch.

'All right,' he agreed.

Nicolau thumped the table. 'What can that idiot have thought he was doing?'

The young monk who had brought him the news started back. His brother, a wine merchant, had told him what had happened that same evening, while they were having supper in his house, with five children playing merrily in the background.

'It's the best bit of business I've done in years,' his brother had told him. 'Apparently Arnau's brother the friar has given instructions to sell off commissions in order to raise money and, by God, if he carries on this way, he'll succeed: Arnau's assistant is selling everything at half price.' At that, he raised his cup of wine and, still smiling, proposed a toast to Arnau.

When he heard the news, Nicolau fell silent. Then he flushed, and finally exploded. The young monk heard the orders he shouted to his captain: 'Go and fetch Brother Joan here! Tell the guards to find him!'

As the wine merchant's brother hurriedly left the room, Nicolau shook his head. What had that impudent little friar imagined? That he could cheat the Inquisition by emptying his brother's coffers? That fortune was destined for the Holy Office! All of it! Eimerich clenched his fists until his knuckles were white. 'Even if I have to see him on a bonfire!' he growled.

'Francesca.' Aledis knelt beside the old woman, who pulled a face that might have been a smile. 'What have they done to you? How are you?' The old woman did not answer. The groaning and wailing of the other prisoners filled the silence. 'Francesca, they have taken Arnau. That's why they brought us here.'

'I know . . .'

Aledis shook her head, but before she could ask how she knew, Francesca went on: 'He's over there.'

Aledis turned her head to look at the opposite end of the dungeon. She saw a dark figure standing there, studying them.

'Listen to me,' the words rang out, 'you who are visiting the old woman.' Aledis turned again to look in the direction of the figure. 'I want to talk to you. I'm Arnau Estanyol.'

'What's going on, Francesca?'

'Ever since I was thrown in here, he's been asking me why the gaoler says I'm his mother. He says his name is Arnau Estanyol, and that he's been put in prison by the Inquisition. You can imagine what a torture that has been.'

'What have you told him?'

'Nothing.'

'Listen!'

This time Aledis did not turn round. 'The Inquisition wants to prove that Arnau is a witch's son,' she explained to Francesca.

'Listen to me, please.'

Aledis could feel Francesca's hands gripping her forearms. The old woman's grip tightened as Arnau's entreaties echoed around them.

'Aren't you . . .?' Aledis struggled to speak. 'Aren't you going to tell him anything?'

'Nobody must know Arnau is my son. Do you hear me, Aledis? If I've never admitted it before, now that the Inquisition is on his heels I am even less likely to . . . You are the only one who knows it.' The old woman's voice was clearer now.

'Jaume de Bellera . . .'

'Please!' came the voice in the gloom.

Aledis turned towards Arnau. She could not see him through her tears, but forced herself not to wipe them away.

'Only you, Aledis,' Francesca insisted. 'Swear to me you will never tell anyone.'

'But Lord de Bellera—'

'Nobody can prove it. Swear to me, Aledis.'

'They will torture you.'

'More than life already has? More than the silence now is doing, when I have to say nothing in the face of Arnau's pleas? Swear it.' Francesca's eyes gleamed in the darkness.

'I swear.'

Aledis swore her oath, then flung her arms round Francesca. For the first time in many years, she realized how frail she was.

'I . . . I don't want to leave you here,' she said, sobbing. 'What will become of you?'

'Don't worry about me,' the old woman whispered in her ear. 'I'll withstand everything until I've convinced them Arnau is not my son.' She struggled to breathe. 'One de Bellera ruined my life. I won't let his son ruin Arnau's.'

Aledis kissed Francesca and sat for a few moments with her mouth pressed against the old woman's cheek. Then she got to her feet.

'Listen to me!'

Aledis stared at the dark figure.

'Don't go to him,' Francesca begged her from the floor. 'Come here! I beg you!'

'You won't be able to bear it, Aledis. You swore to me.'

Arnau and Aledis stared at each other in the darkness. Two shadowy figures. Aledis's tears glistened as they rolled down her cheeks.

Arnau sank to the ground when he saw the unknown visitor head straight for the dungeon door.

That same morning, a woman riding a mule entered Barcelona by the Sant Daniel gate. Behind her limped a Dominican friar who did not even look up at the soldiers on guard. The two of them walked in silence through the city until they reached the bishop's palace, with the friar still trailing behind the mule.

'Brother Joan?' asked one of the guards at the palace doorway.

The Dominican raised his battered face to the soldier.

'Brother Joan?' he asked again.

Joan nodded.

'The grand inquisitor has given orders for us to take you to him as soon as possible.'

The soldier called for the guard, and several of his colleagues came to take charge of Joan.

The woman did not even dismount from her mule.

52

Sahat burst into the store the old merchant had in Pisa, down in the port on the banks of the Arno. Some workmen and apprentices tried to greet him, but the Moor paid them no heed. 'Where is your master?' he asked everyone he met, striding among the huge bales of merchandise piled up in the vast establishment. Sahat finally found him at the far end of the building, bent over some lengths of silk.

'What's happening, Filippo?'

The old merchant straightened up with difficulty. He turned to Sahat. 'Yesterday a ship bound for Marseilles arrived.'

'I know. Is something wrong?'

Filippo studied Sahat. How old could he be? One thing was for sure: he was no longer young. He was as well-dressed as ever, although he avoided the ostentation that many far less rich than him fell into. What had happened between him and Arnau? Sahat had never wanted to tell him. Filippo remembered the slave arriving from Catalonia, his certificate of emancipation, the money order he brought from Arnau . . .

'Filippo!'

Sahat's cry brought him back to the present. There was no denying, he thought, that the Moor still had the force and energy of a young, hopeful man. He did everything with the same great determination . . .

'Filippo! Please!'

'You're right, you're right. I'm sorry.' The old man hobbled over to him and leant on his arm. 'You're quite right. Help me, and we'll go to my office.'

In the trading circles of Pisa, Filippo Tescio asked few people for help. This public show of confidence by the old man could open more doors than a thousand gold florins. On this occasion, however, Sahat stopped the old man's slow advance.

'Filippo, please.'

The old man tugged at his sleeve. 'News – bad news. Arnau . . .' he said, giving Sahat time to recover his balance. 'Arnau has been arrested by the Inquisition.'

Sahat said nothing.

'The reasons aren't very clear,' Filippo went on. 'His assistants have started selling his commissions, and apparently his situation . . . but that is only a rumour, and probably a spiteful one. Sit down,' said the old man when they reached what he called his office. This was no more than a table on a raised platform from where he supervised the work of three clerks who sat at similar tables noting down all the transactions in huge account books, and from where he could keep an eye on all the activity in the warehouse.

Filippo sighed as he sat down. 'That's not all,' he added. Seated opposite him, Sahat did not react. 'This Easter the people of Barcelona attacked the Jewry. The Jews were said to have profaned a Christian host. They were fined a huge amount, and three of them were executed . . .' Filippo could see Sahat's lower lip start to tremble. 'Hasdai.'

The old man looked away from Sahat for a few seconds, to allow him to recover. When he looked back, he saw the Moor's lips were drawn in a firm line. Sahat took a deep breath and raised his hands to his face to wipe his eyes.

'Here,' said Filippo, handing him a letter. 'It's from Jucef. A ship from Barcelona bound for Alexandria left it with my agent in Naples, and the captain of the ship heading for Marseilles brought it to me. Jucef has taken over from his father. In the letter he tells me everything that has happened, although he does not say much about Arnau.'

Sahat took the letter, but did not open it.

'Hasdai burnt at the stake, and Arnau arrested,' he said, 'and me here!'

'I've booked you a passage to Marseilles,' Filippo told him. 'The ship leaves at dawn tomorrow. From Marseilles it should be easy to reach Barcelona.'

'Thank you,' said Sahat in almost a whisper.

Filippo sat silent.

'I came here in search of my origins,' Sahat began. 'To search for the family I thought I had lost. Do you know what I found?' Filippo didn't reply. 'When I was sold as a boy, my mother and five brothers and sisters were alive. I only ever found one of them . . . and I'm not sure he was my real brother. He was the slave of a workman in the port of Genoa. When he was pointed out to me, I did not recognize him – I couldn't even remember his name. He was limping, the little finger of his right hand was missing, and so were both his ears. At first I thought he must have had a very cruel master if that was how he punished him, but later I learnt that . . .' Sahat paused and looked across at the old man. Filippo still made no comment. 'I bought his freedom and made sure he was given a good sum of money, without telling him I was the one behind all this. The money only lasted him six days: six days during which he was constantly drunk, and managed to spend on gambling and women what to him must have been a fortune. He sold himself as a slave again to his former master in return for a bed and food.' Sahat waved his hand dismissively. 'That's all I found here: a drunken, brawling brother.'

'You also found a few friends,' said Filippo.

'That's true. I'm sorry. I meant . . .'

'I know what you meant.'

The two men sat gazing at the documents on the table. They could hear the noise and bustle of the warehouse all around them.

'Sahat,' Filippo said finally, 'for many years I was Hasdai's agent, and now, as long as God grants me life, I'll do the same for his son. In addition, thanks to Hasdai and you, I also became Arnau's agent. During all that time, I have heard only good things of Arnau, from traders, sailors or sea captains. The news of what he did for his serfs reached even here! What happened between the two of you? If you had fallen out, he would not have rewarded you with your freedom, still less instructed me to give you all that money. What happened for you to abandon him, while he rewarded you in that way?'

'It was a girl . . . an extraordinary girl.'

'Ah!'

'No,' the Moor protested, 'it's not what you think.'

And for the first time in six years, Sahat revealed everything that he had until then kept to himself.

'How dare you!' Nicolau Eimerich's angry shout echoed along the corridors of the bishop's palace. He did not even wait for the guards to leave the room. The inquisitor strode up and down the chamber, waving his arms. 'How dare you put at risk something that by right belongs to the Holy Office?' Nicolau turned abruptly towards Joan, who was standing in the centre of the room. 'How dare you sell off commissions cheaply like that?'

Joan did not reply. He had spent a sleepless night, being mistreated and humiliated. He had just had to walk several miles behind the back end of a mule. His whole body ached. He stank, and his filthy, mud-caked habit scratched at his skin. He had not had a bite to eat since the previous day, and he was thirsty. No. He was not going to reply.

Nicolau came up behind him. 'What are you trying to do, Brother Joan?' he whispered in his ear. 'Could it be you wish to sell off your brother's fortune so that the Inquisition cannot have it?'

He stood close to Joan for a few seconds.

'By God, you stink!' he said, leaping away from him. He waved his arms in the air once more. 'You smell like a peasant.' He paced the room muttering to himself, before he finally sat down again. 'The Inquisition has taken possession of your brother's account books. There will be no more selling.' Joan did not move. 'I've forbidden all visits to the dungeons, so do not try to see him. His trial will start in a few days.'

Still Joan did not react.

'Didn't you hear me, friar? Within a few days I'll sit in judgement on your brother!' Nicolau thumped the table. 'That's enough! Get out of here!'

Joan dragged the hem of his filthy habit across the shiny floor tiles of the grand inquisitor's office.

Joan paused in the doorway to allow his eyes to get accustomed to the bright sunlight. Mar was standing there waiting for him, the mule's halter in her hand. He had brought her here from the farmhouse: how could he possibly tell her that the grand inquisitor had forbidden any visits to Arnau? How was he going to bear that guilt on top of all the rest?

'Are you going out, friar?' he heard behind him.

Joan turned, and found himself confronted by a widow in black. Her face was streaming with tears. They looked at each other.

'Joan?' the woman asked.

Those big brown eyes. That face . . .

'Joan?' she asked again. 'Joan, it's me, Aledis. Don't you remember me?'

'The tanner's daughter—' Joan started to say.

'What's going on, friar?' Mar had walked up to the doorway. Aledis saw Joan turn towards the newcomer, then look back at her, and once again at the woman with the mule.

'A childhood friend,' he said. 'Aledis, this is Mar. Mar, this is Aledis.'

The two women nodded at each other.

'This is no place to stand and talk!' The guard's barked command startled all three of them. 'Clear the doorway, will you?'

'We've come to see Arnau Estanyol,' said Mar, still gripping the mule's halter.

The soldier looked her up and down. A mocking smile appeared on his lips. 'The moneychanger?' he asked.

'Yes,' said Mar.

'The grand inquisitor has forbidden any visits to him.' He went to push Aledis and Joan out of the doorway.

'Why has he done that?' asked Mar, as the other two stepped out into the street.

'You should ask the friar here that,' said the soldier, gesturing towards Joan.

The three of them moved away from the palace.

'I should have killed you yesterday.'

Aledis saw Joan lower his eyes to the ground. He said nothing. Then she studied the woman, standing there erect, leading her mule with confidence. What could have happened the day before? Joan made no attempt to hide his battered face, and his companion wanted to see Arnau. Who could this woman be? Arnau was married to the baroness. It was she who had stood beside him on the platform at Montbui Castle when he had renounced all his privileges . . .

'Arnau's trial is to start in a few days' time . . .'

Mar and Aledis came to an abrupt halt. Joan walked on a few paces, until he realized the women were no longer with him. When he turned back towards them, he saw they were looking intently at each other, as though asking: Who are you?

'I doubt whether the friar ever had a childhood – and still less knew anything about girls,' said Mar.

Aledis met her gaze. Mar stood there proudly: her bright young eyes seemed to want to pierce her through. Even the mule appeared to be listening to her every word, its ears pricked.

'You are nothing if not blunt,' Aledis told her.

'That's what life has taught me.'

'Thirty years ago, if my parents had given their consent, I would have been married to Arnau.'

'And six years ago, if I'd been treated like a human being rather than an animal' – Mar glanced at Joan – 'I would still be at Arnau's side.'

The two women fell silent as they again measured each other with their gaze.

'But I haven't seen Arnau in thirty years,' Aledis finally admitted. I'm not trying to compete with you, she was trying to tell her, in a language only two women could understand.

Mar shifted her weight from one leg to the other and relaxed her grip on the mule's halter. She rolled her eyes, and stopped challenging Aledis.

'I live outside Barcelona: do you have anywhere to put me up?' she asked after a few moments.

'I live outside the city as well. I am being put up . . .'

with my daughters, in the Estanyer inn. But we could arrange something,' she added quickly when she saw Mar hesitate. 'What about him?' Aledis lifted her chin at Joan.

The two women surveyed him, standing there with bruised face and his filthy, torn habit hanging down from his stooped shoulders.

'He has a lot to explain,' said Mar, 'and we might need him. He can sleep with the mule.'

Joan waited for the two women to set off again, then followed a few steps behind.

Why are you here? she will ask me. What were you doing in the bishop's palace? Aledis cast a sideways glance at her new companion; she was walking on serenely, pulling at the mule, and not stepping aside for anyone they came across on the way. What could have happened between Mar and Joan? The friar seemed completely crushed . . . how on earth could a Dominican allow a woman to send him to sleep with a mule? They crossed Plaça del Blat. Aledis had admitted she knew Arnau, but had not told them she had seen him in the dungeons, begging for her to come close. *What about Francesca? What should I tell them about her? That she's my mother? No. Joan knew who she was, and knows she wasn't called Francesca. My dead husband's mother? What will they say when she is brought in during Arnau's trial? I ought to have an answer. And when they find out she is a whore? How could my mother-in-law be a whore? Better to pretend I know nothing: but then what was I doing in the bishop's palace?*

'Oh,' Aledis replied when Mar asked her the question, 'it was some business related to my deceased husband. Since we were passing through Barcelona . . .'

Eulàlia and Teresa glanced at her, but carried on eating from their bowls. The two women had reached the inn and persuaded the innkeeper to place a third straw pallet in the room where Aledis and her daughters were staying. When she told him he had to sleep in the stable with the mule, Joan made no demur.

'Whatever you may hear,' Aledis whispered to the girls, 'don't say a thing. Try to avoid answering any questions, and remember: we don't know anyone called Francesca.'

The five of them sat down to eat.

'Well, friar,' Mar began, 'why has the inquisitor forbidden all visits to Arnau?'

Joan had not touched his food. 'I needed money for the gaoler,' he said wearily, 'and since Arnau's business had no cash, I ordered the sale of some of his commissions. Eimerich thought I was trying to spend Arnau's fortune so that the Inquisition could not get hold of it . . .'

At that moment, Lord de Bellera and Genís Puig came in. They both beamed when they saw the girls.

'Joan,' Aledis said quickly, 'yesterday those two noblemen were bothering my daughters, and I have the impression that their intentions . . . Could you help me make sure they don't trouble my daughters again?'

Joan turned towards the two men while they stood there ogling Teresa and Eulàlia, obviously remembering the previous night. When they caught sight of Joan's black habit, their smiles vanished. The friar looked at them steadily, and the two nobles sat down quietly at their table, then stared down at the food the innkeeper had brought them.

'On what charges are they trying Arnau?' Aledis asked Joan when he turned his attention back to them.

Sahat watched as the final preparations were made for the ship bound for Marseilles to leave. It was a solid, single-masted galley, with a rudder at the stern and two leeboards, and with room for 120 oarsmen.

'It's a very rapid and safe ship,' Filippo told him.

'They've had several run-ins with pirates and have always managed to escape. You'll be in Marseilles in three or four days.' Sahat nodded. 'From there you'll have no problem finding a cargo vessel bound for Barcelona.'

As he pointed to the galley with his stick, Filippo clung to Sahat with his other hand. Officials, traders and workmen alike greeted him as they went past, and then did the same with Sahat, the Moor he was leaning on for support.

'The weather is fine,' Filippo added, this time pointing his cane up at the sky. 'You won't have any problems.'

The galley captain came to the side of the ship and waved at Filippo.

'I have the feeling I may not see you again,' said the old man. Sahat turned to look at him, but Filippo clung to him even more tightly. 'I'm growing old, Sahat.'

The two men embraced at the foot of the ship.

'Take care of my affairs,' Sahat said, stepping back.

'I will, and when I am no longer able to,' Filippo said in a shaky voice, 'my sons will carry on for me. Then, wherever you may be, it will be for you to give them a helping hand.'

'I will,' Sahat promised in turn.

Filippo drew Sahat to him again and kissed him full on the lips. The crowd waiting for this last passenger to come aboard murmured at this show of affection from Filippo Tescio.

'God speed,' the old man said.

Sahat ordered the two slaves carrying his possessions to go on ahead, then went on board himself. By the time he emerged at the galley's side, Filippo had vanished.

The sea was calm. There was no wind, but the galley sped along thanks to the efforts of its 120 oarsmen.

'I didn't have the courage', wrote Jucef in his letter after he had explained what had happened following the theft of the host, 'to escape from the Jewry to be with my father in his final moments. I hope he understands, wherever he may be now.'

Standing in the prow of the galley, Sahat raised his eyes to the horizon. 'You and your kind had the courage to live in a Christian city,' he said to himself. He had read and reread the letter many times: 'Raquel did not want to escape, but we convinced her she must.'

Sahat jumped to the end of the letter:

Yesterday, the Inquisition arrested Arnau. Today, thanks to a Jew who works in the bishop's household, I discovered that it was Arnau's wife, Eleonor, who accused him of being a friend of Jews. Since the Inquisition needs two witnesses to bring a charge, Eleonor has called several priests from Santa Maria de la Mar to testify that they overheard an argument between her and her husband; apparently what Arnau said then is considered sacrilegious and supports Eleonor's accusation.

It was a very complicated affair, Jucef added. On the one hand, Arnau was a very rich man, and the Inquisition was interested in his fortune; on the other, he was in the hands of a man like Nicolau Eimerich. Sahat had a strong memory of the arrogant inquisitor, who had occupied the post six years before the Moor had left Catalonia, and whom he had seen at some religious ceremonies to which he had been obliged to accompany Arnau.

Ever since you left, Eimerich has been gathering more and more power. He has not even been afraid to publicly challenge the monarch. For years, the King has not paid revenues to the Pope, and as a result Urban IV has offered Sardinia to the lord of Arborea, the leader of the rebellion against the Catalans. And after the long war with Castile, there is unrest again among the Corsican nobles. Eimerich, who depends directly on the Pope, has taken advantage of all this to openly oppose the King. He insists the Inquisition should have the right to try Jews and other non-Christians, God forbid! But the King, who is responsible for all the Jewries in Catalonia, is strongly opposed to this. Eimerich is still trying to convince the Pope, who has no great wish to defend our monarch's interests.

But in addition to attempting to attack the Jewries, against the King's interests, Eimerich has also dared denounce the works of the Catalan theologian Ramon Llull as heresy. For more than half a century now, Llull's doctrines have been treated with respect by the Catalan Church. Seeing this attack as a personal insult, the King has appointed jurists and philosophers to defend his work.

In view of all this, I am afraid that Eimerich will try to turn the trial against Arnau, a Catalan baron and Consul of the Sea, into a new confrontation with the King in order to cement still further his position, while at the same time securing a considerable fortune for the Inquisition. I understand that Eimerich has already written to Urban IV to inform him that he will keep what the King is owed by Arnau to pay the revenues Pedro owes him; so that at one and the same time the inquisitor can wreak his revenge on the King through a Catalan nobleman, and also strengthen his position with the Pope.

I also think that Arnau's personal situation is delicate, if not desperate. His brother Joan is known to be a cruel inquisitor; his wife is the one who has made the accusation against him; my father is dead and the rest of us, given the charge of befriending Jews and for his own good, dare not show our support for him. You are the only one he has left.

That was how Jucef ended his letter: *You are the only one he has left.* Sahat put the letter into the small chest in which he kept all the correspondence he had had with Hasdai over the past six years. *You are the only one he has left.* Standing at the prow of the galley, with the box in his hands, Sahat gazed out at the horizon. *Row, men . . . I am the only one he has left.*

* * *

At a signal from Aledis, Eulàlia and Teresa retired to bed. Joan had already left them some time earlier; Mar had not responded to his farewell.

'Why do you treat him like that?' Aledis asked once the two of them were alone in the dining room. The only sound was the crackling of the almost spent logs on the fire. Mar said nothing. 'After all, he is Arnau's brother.'

'That friar deserves no better.'

As she spoke, Mar did not even raise her eyes from the table, where she was trying to remove a splinter of wood. She is a beautiful woman, thought Aledis. Her long, wavy hair hung down over her shoulders. Her features were well-defined: plump lips, prominent cheekbones, a strong chin and a straight nose. On their way from the palace to the inn, Aledis had been surprised at how white and perfect her teeth looked, and could not help noticing how firm and shapely her body was. Yet her hands were those of someone who had worked hard in the fields: they were rough and calloused.

Mar left the splinter and looked up at Aledis. The two women stared at each other in silence.

'It's a long story,' Mar admitted.

'If you want to tell it, I have the time,' said Aledis.

Mar's mouth twitched, and she let several more seconds go by. Why not, after all? It had been years since she had talked to a woman; years that she had lived wrapped up in herself, doing nothing but work inhospitable land, hoping that the ears of wheat and the sun would understand her misfortune and take pity on her. Why not? Aledis seemed like a good woman.

'My parents died in the plague outbreak, when I was no more than a child . . .'

Mar told her everything. Aledis trembled when Mar spoke of the love she had felt on the plain outside Montbui Castle. 'I understand,' she almost blurted out, 'I also . . .' Arnau, Arnau, Arnau; his name came up after every few words. Aledis remembered the sea breeze playing on her young body, betraying her innocence, stirring her desire. Then Mar told her about how she was kidnapped and forced to marry her husband; her confession reduced her to tears.

'Thank you,' said Mar when she could speak again.

Aledis took her hand.

'Do you have any children?' she asked.

'I had one,' said Mar, squeezing her hand. 'He died four years ago, as an infant, when there was another outbreak of plague among children. His father never knew him; he didn't even know I was pregnant. He died at Calatayud defending a King who instead of leading his troops preferred to board ship in Valencia and set sail for Roussillon to safeguard his family from the plague.' As she spoke, Mar smiled disdainfully.

'What has all this got to do with Joan?' asked Aledis.

'He knew I loved Arnau . . . and that Arnau loved me too.'

When she had heard everything, Aledis slapped the table. Night had crept up on them, and the noise resounded through the empty inn. 'Do you intend to denounce him?'

'Arnau has always protected the friar. He is his brother, and he loves him,' Mar replied. Aledis recalled the two young lads who slept in Pere and Mariona's kitchen; Arnau carrying blocks of stone, Joan studying. 'I don't want to harm Arnau and yet now . . . now I can't even see him, and I don't even know if he is aware that I am here and still love him . . . They are going to try him. Perhaps, perhaps they will condemn him to . . .' Mar burst into tears once more.

'Don't be afraid I'm going to break the promise I made you, but I have to talk to him,' Aledis said to Francesca as she was leaving the dungeon. Francesca tried to make out her features in the gloom. 'Trust me,' Aledis added.

Arnau had stood up as soon as Aledis came back into the dungeon, but he had not called out to her. He simply listened in silence to the two women whispering together. Where was Joan? He had not been for two days now, and Arnau had many things to ask him. He wanted him to find out who this old woman was. What was she doing there? Why had the gaoler said she was his mother? What was happening with his trial? And his business affairs? And Mar? What had happened to Mar? Something was wrong. Ever since the last time Joan had visited him, the gaoler had started treating him just like the rest again: all he got to eat was a crust of bread with stale water, and the bucket had disappeared.

Arnau saw the stranger move apart from the old woman. He started to slump down against the wall, but . . . but she was heading his way.

He could see in the darkness that she was coming towards him, and struggled to his feet. She stopped a few paces away, outside the range of the feeble light that dimly lit this end of the dungeon.

Arnau half closed his eyes to get a better glimpse of her.

'They've forbidden all visits to you,' he heard the unknown woman say.

'Who are you?' he asked. 'How do you know?'

'We don't have time, Arn . . . Arnau.' She had called him Arnau! What if the gaoler came . . .

'Who are you?'

Why not tell him? Why not embrace him, offer him some comfort? She wouldn't be able to bear it. Francesca's words echoed through her mind. Aledis looked back at her, and then again at Arnau. The sea breeze, the beach, her youth, the long journey to Figueres . . .

'Who are you?' she heard once more.

'That doesn't matter. All I want to tell you is that Mar is in Barcelona, waiting for you. She loves you. She still loves you.'

Aledis could see Arnau slump back against the wall. She waited a few moments. There were noises in the passage. The gaoler had only given her a few minutes. More noise. The key in the lock. Arnau heard it too and turned towards the door.

'Would you like me to give her a message?'

The door creaked open. The light from the torches in the passageway cast a stronger light on Aledis.

'Tell her that I too . . .' The gaoler came into the dungeon. 'I love her. Even though I cannot . . .'

Aledis turned on her heel and walked towards the door.

'What were you doing talking to the moneychanger?' the fat gaoler wanted to know as he locked the door behind her.

'He called me over as I was leaving.'

'It's forbidden to talk to him.'

'I didn't know that. I didn't know he was the moneychanger either. I didn't say anything. I didn't even go over to him.'

'The inquisitor has forbidden . . .'

Aledis took out her purse and jingled the coins.

'I don't want to see you here again,' said the gaoler, taking the money. 'If you come, you won't leave.'

All this time, inside the dungeon, Arnau was desperately trying to understand what the strange woman had said to him: *She loves you. She still loves you.* But the memory of Mar was obscured by the light that the torches had cast on a pair of huge brown eyes. He recognized them. Where had he seen them before?

Aledis had told Mar she would give him the message.

'Don't worry,' she insisted. 'Arnau will know you're here, waiting for him.'

'Tell him I love him,' Mar shouted after Aledis as she began to cross Plaça de la Llana.

From the doorway, Mar saw the widow turn back and smile at her. Once Aledis was out of sight, Mar left the inn. She had thought about it on the journey from Mataró; again, when they had not been allowed to see Arnau; and that night over and over again. She left Plaça de la Llana and went part of the way down Carrer de la Bòria. She passed in front of the Bernat Marcús chapel and turned right. She came to a halt at the start of Carrer de Montcada and stood for a few minutes looking at the noble palaces lining the street.

'My lady!' exclaimed Pere, Eleonor's aged servant, as he opened one of the big gates to Arnau's palace. 'What a joy to see you again. It's been such a long time . . .' Pere fell silent, and nervously motioned her to step into the cobbled yard. 'What brings you here?'

'I've come to see Dona Eleonor.'

Pere nodded and disappeared.

Mar was overwhelmed by her memories. Everything looked the same: the cool, clean yard with its gleaming cobblestones; the stables opposite; and to the right the impressive staircase leading up to the principal rooms. This was where Pere had headed.

He came back down the stairs looking disturbed. 'My lady will not see you.'

Mar looked up at the first floor of the palace. A shadow flitted behind one of the windows. When had she been in this situation before? When . . .? She looked up again at the windows.

'Once before,' she muttered up towards the windows, while Pere looked on, unable to offer any words of comfort, 'I have lived through this scene. Arnau won that battle, Eleonor. I'm warning you: he has paid his debt in full.'

53

As the soldiers escorted him along the endless high corridors of the bishop's palace, the noise of their swords and leather straps echoed all around them. The group marched along, the captain at its head, two soldiers in front of Arnau, and another two behind. When they had reached the top of the passage up from the dungeons, Arnau had halted to let his eyes adjust to the light streaming into the palace, until a sharp blow in the middle of his back forced him to keep pace with the soldiers.

Arnau passed by friars, priests and scribes, all of them squeezing against the walls to let him and his guard through. Nobody had wanted to answer his question: 'Where are you taking me?' The gaoler had come into the dungeon and silently undone his chains. A Dominican in black crossed himself as he went by; another raised a crucifix. The soldiers marched on impassively, their mere presence enough to clear a path. For days now, Arnau had heard nothing from Joan or the brown-eyed woman: where had he seen those eyes before? He asked the old crone in the dungeon but got no reply. 'Who was that woman?' he had shouted four times at least. Some of the shadows chained to the walls had groaned; others did not stir. Nor did the old woman, and yet, when the gaoler pushed him out of the dungeon, Arnau thought he saw her shifting nervously.

Arnau bumped into the back of one of the soldiers in front of him. They had come to a halt outside an imposing double door. The soldier pushed him back, while the captain banged on the wooden panel. The doors opened and the escort marched into a huge chamber. The walls were hung with rich tapestries. The soldiers accompanied Arnau to the centre of the room, then returned to stand guard at the door.

Sitting behind an elaborately carved table, seven men were staring at him. Nicolau Eimerich, the grand inquisitor, sat in the middle, together with Berenguer d'Eril, the Bishop of Barcelona. Both of them were wearing fine robes embroidered in gold. To the inquisitor's left sat the Holy Office clerk; Arnau had seen him on occasion, but had never had any dealings with the man. On either side sat two black Dominican friars, whom Arnau did not know.

Arnau looked steadily at the members of the tribunal until one of the friars turned away in disgust. Arnau raised a hand to his face: it was covered in a greasy beard that had grown during his days in the dungeon. His torn clothes had lost all their original colour. He was barefoot, and his feet, hands and nails were caked with black dirt. He stank. He himself found his smell unbearable.

Eimerich smiled when he saw Arnau reacting to his own sorry state.

'First they will get him to swear on the four Gospels,' Joan explained to Aledis as they sat round a table at the inn. 'The trial could last days, or even months,' he had already told them, when they had urged him to go to the bishop's palace, 'it's better to wait at the inn.'

'Will there be someone to defend him?' asked Mar.

Joan shook his head wearily. 'He will be appointed a lawyer . . . but that person is not allowed to defend him.'

'Why not?' the two women asked together.

'It is forbidden for lawyers and notaries to aid heretics,' Joan recited, 'to advise or support them or to believe their word and defend them.' Mar and Aledis looked nonplussed at Joan. 'That's what the bull by Pope Innocent the Third says.'

'What do they do then?' asked Mar.

'The lawyer's task is to obtain the heretic's voluntary confession; if he were to defend a heretic, he would be defending heresy.'

'I have nothing to confess,' Arnau told the young priest who had been appointed as his lawyer.

'He's an expert in civil and canon law,' said Nicolau Eimerich, 'and also a passionate believer,' he added with a smile.

The priest spread his arms wide in a helpless gesture, in the same way as he had done in the dungeon, when he had encouraged Arnau to confess his heresy. 'You ought to do so,' he had said, 'and put your faith in the tribunal's mercy.' Now he repeated the same gesture – how often had he done that in the past as a lawyer for heretics? – and then, at a sign from Eimerich, withdrew from the chamber.

'After that,' Joan continued at Aledis's prompting, 'they will ask him to name his enemies.'

'Why is that?'

'If he were to name any of the witnesses accusing him, the tribunal could consider their testimony unsound.'

'But Arnau doesn't know who denounced him,' Mar said.

'No, not at the moment. He might find out in due course . . . if Eimerich concedes him that right. In fact, he is entitled to know,' said Joan, noticing how the two women reacted. 'That is what Pope Boniface the Eighth decreed, but the Pope is a long way away, and each inquisitor conducts his own trials as he sees fit.'

'I think my wife hates me,' Arnau replied in answer to Eimerich's question.

'Why should Dona Eleonor hate you?' the inquisitor insisted.

'Because we have no children.'

'Have you tried? Have you lain with her?'

Arnau had sworn on the four Gospels.

'No.'

The clerk's quill copied all the words on to the pile of parchments in front of him. Nicolau Eimerich turned to the bishop.

'Can you name any other enemy?' asked Berenguer d'Eril.

'The nobles on my lands, in particular the thane of Montbui.' The clerk went on writing. 'I have also judged many people as Consul of the Sea, but I consider I have always been just in my decisions.'

'Do you have any enemies among members of the Church?'

Why were they asking him that? He had always got on well with the Church.

'Apart from some of those here—'

'The members of this tribunal are impartial,' said Eimerich, interrupting him.

'I trust they are.' Arnau looked directly at the inquisitor.

'Anyone else?'

'As you well know, I have been a moneychanger for many years, and perhaps—'

'It's not for you' – Eimerich interrupted him again – 'to speculate on who might or might not be your enemies, or for what reason. If you have enemies, you are to name them; if not, say nothing. Do you have enemies?'

'I do not think so.'

'What then?' Aledis wanted to know.

'Then the inquisition proper begins.' Joan thought back to all the village squares, the chambers in rich houses, the sleepless nights . . . but a heavy blow on the table in front of him brought him back to reality.

'What do you mean, friar?' Mar shouted at him.

Joan sighed and looked her in the eye. 'The word "inquisition" means a search. The inquisitor has to search out heresy and sin. Even when there have been accusations, the trial is not based on them or restricted to them. If the person on trial refuses to confess, they will search for the hidden truth.'

'How will they do that?' asked Mar.

Before he replied, Joan closed his eyes. 'If you're asking about torture, yes, that is one of the ways.'

'What will they do to him?'

'They might decide torture is not necessary.'

'What will they do to him?' insisted Mar.

'Why do you want to know?' said Aledis, taking her by the hand. 'It will only torment you . . . still further.'

'The law forbids death or the loss of any limb under torture,' Joan explained, 'and suspected heretics may only be tortured once.'

Joan could see how the two women, their faces streaming tears, sought some comfort in that. Yet he knew that Eimerich had found a way to make a mockery of this legal requirement. '*Non ad modum iterationis sed continuationis*,' he used to say, with a strange gleam in his eye: not repeatedly but continuously, he translated for the novices who did not yet have a good grasp of Latin.

'What happens if they torture him and he still doesn't confess?' asked Mar, after taking a deep breath.

'His attitude will be taken into account at the moment of handing down a sentence,' Joan said, without further explanation.

'Will it be Eimerich who sentences him?' asked Aledis.

'Yes, unless the sentence is life imprisonment or burning at the stake; in that case, he will need the bishop's approval. And yet,' the friar went on, anticipating the women's next question, 'if the inquisition considers that it is a complex matter, it has been known for them to consult the *boni viri*, between thirty and eighty people, not members of the Church, so that they can give their opinion as to the guilt of the accused, and the appropriate sentence. That means the trial drags on for months and months.'

'During which time Arnau would remain in gaol,' said Aledis.

Joan nodded. The three of them sat in silence. The women were trying to take in everything they had heard; Joan was remembering another of Eimerich's maxims: 'The gaol is to be forbidding, placed underground so that no light, and especially no sun or moonlight, may enter. It has to be harsh and tough, in order to shorten the prisoner's life to the point that he faces death.'

Filthy, in rags, Arnau stood in the centre of the chamber while the inquisitor and the bishop put their heads together and started whispering. The clerk took advantage of the interruption to tidy his papers. The four Dominicans continued to stare at the prisoner.

'How are you going to conduct the interrogation?' Berenguer d'Eril asked.

'We'll start as usual and as we progress, we'll inform him what the charges are.'

'You're going to tell him?'

'Yes. I think he is the sort of person who will react more to dialectic pressure than to a physical threat, although if necessary . . .'

Arnau tried to withstand the looks from the black friars. One, two, three, four . . . He shifted his weight on to his other foot and glanced again at the inquisitor and the bishop. They were still whispering to each other. The Dominicans on the other hand were observing him closely. The chamber was absolutely quiet apart from the unintelligible muttering.

'He's growing nervous,' said the bishop, glancing up at Arnau before turning back to the inquisitor.

'He is someone who is used to giving commands and being obeyed,' said Eimerich. 'He needs to understand what the situation is; he has to accept the tribunal and its authority, and submit to it. Only then will he respond to interrogation. Humiliation is the first step.'

Bishop and inquisitor continued their conversation. Throughout the whole time, the Dominicans did not take their eyes off Arnau. Arnau tried to think of other things: of Mar, or Joan, but whenever he did so, he could feel one of the Dominicans' eyes clawing at him as if he had guessed what he was thinking. He shifted his weight time and again, felt his unruly beard and unkempt hair. In their gleaming gold robes, Berenguer d'Eril and Nicolau Eimerich sat comfortably behind the tribunal bench, glancing at him and continuing their discussion at their own leisure.

After a long pause, Nicolau Eimerich addressed him in a loud voice: 'Arnau Estanyol, I know you have sinned.'

The trial proper had begun.

Arnau took a deep breath. 'I do not know what you mean. I consider I have always been a good Christian. I have tried—'

'You yourself have admitted to this tribunal that you

have not lain with your wife. Is that the attitude of a good Christian?'

'I cannot have carnal relations. I do not know if you are aware that I was married before, and could . . . could not have children then either.'

'Are you telling the tribunal you have a physical problem?' said the bishop.

'Yes.'

Eimerich studied Arnau for a few moments. He leant forward on his elbows and then hid his mouth behind his hands. He turned to the clerk and whispered an order to him.

'"Declaration by Juli Andreu, priest at Santa Maria de la Mar,"' the clerk read out from one of his pieces of parchment. '"I, Juli Andreu, priest at Santa Maria de la Mar, questioned by the grand inquisitor of Catalonia, do declare that in approximately the month of March in the year of Our Lord 1364, I held a conversation with Arnau Estanyol, baron of Catalonia, at the request of his wife Dona Eleonor, baroness, ward of King Pedro. She had expressed to me her concern at her husband's neglect of his conjugal duties. I declare that Arnau Estanyol confided to me that he was not attracted to his wife, and that his body refused to allow him to enjoy relations with her. He said that it was not a physical problem, but that he could not force his body to desire a woman for whom he felt no attraction. He further said that he knew he was in a state of sin"' – Nicolau Eimerich's eyes narrowed – '"and that for this reason he prayed as often as he could in Santa Maria and made substantial donations towards the construction of the church."'

The chamber fell silent again. Nicolau stared fixedly at Arnau.

'Do you still affirm that you have a physical problem?' the inquisitor asked finally.

Arnau remembered his conversation with the priest,

but could not remember exactly what . . . 'I cannot recall what I said to him.'

'Do you admit that you had this conversation with Father Juli Andreu?'

'Yes.'

Arnau could hear the clerk's quill scratching across the parchment.

'Yet you are calling into question the declaration by a man of God. What possible interest could the priest have in lying about you?'

'He might be mistaken. I do not remember exactly what was said.'

'Are you saying that a priest who was not certain what he heard would make a declaration like the one Father Juli Andreu has made?'

'All I am saying is that he might be mistaken.'

'Father Andreu is not an enemy of yours, is he?' intervened the bishop.

'I have never considered him one.'

Nicolau spoke to the clerk again.

' "Declaration by Pere Salvete, canon at Santa Maria de la Mar. I, Pere Salvete, canon at Santa Maria de la Mar, questioned by the grand inquisitor of Catalonia, declare that at Easter in the year of Our Lord 1367, while I was saying holy mass, the service was interrupted by a number of citizens of Barcelona who alerted us to the theft of a host by heretics. The mass was suspended, and the faithful left the church, with the exception of Arnau Estanyol, Consul of the Sea."' *Go to your Jewish lover!* Eleonor's words rang out in his head once more. Arnau shuddered, exactly as he had when he first heard them. He looked up. Nicolau was staring at him . . . and smiling. Had he seen his reaction? The clerk was still reading the declaration: ' ". . . and the consul answered that God could not oblige him to lie with her . . ."'

Nicolau silenced the scribe. The smile vanished. 'So is the canon lying too?'

Go to your Jewish lover! Why had he not let the clerk finish? What was Nicolau up to? *Your Jewish lover, your Jewish lover* . . . The flames licking at Hasdai's body, the silence, the enraged mob baying for justice, shouting words that were never properly spoken, Eleonor pointing at him, the bishop standing next to her, staring . . . and Raquel clinging to him.

'Is the canon lying as well?'

'I have not accused anyone of lying,' said Arnau. He needed time to think.

'Do you deny God's commandments? Do you object to the duties demanded of you as a Christian husband?'

'No . . . no . . .' stammered Arnau.

'Well then?'

'Well then what?'

'Do you deny God's commandments?' Nicolau repeated, his voice rising.

His words reverberated from the stone walls of the vast chamber. Arnau's legs felt heavy after all those days in the dungeon.

'The tribunal could take your silence for a confession,' said the bishop.

'No, I don't deny them.' His legs began to ache. 'Why does the Holy Office take such an interest in my relations with Dona Eleonor? Is it a sin to—?'

'Be careful, Estanyol,' the inquisitor cut in. 'It is for the tribunal to ask the questions, not you.'

'Ask them, then.'

Nicolau could see Arnau moving unsteadily, shifting his weight from foot to foot.

'He's beginning to feel pain,' he whispered in Berenguer d'Eril's ear.

'Leave him to think about it,' replied the bishop.

They began to whisper together again. Arnau could

sense the four Dominicans' eyes fixed on him once more. His legs ached dreadfully, but he had to resist. He could not bow down before Nicolau Eimerich. What would happen if he collapsed to the floor? He needed . . . a stone! A stone on his back, a long road on which to carry a stone for his Virgin. *Where are you now? Can these people really be your representatives? I was little more than a boy, and yet* . . . Of course he could resist now. He had walked across all Barcelona with a stone that weighed more than he did, sweating, bleeding, with everyone's shouts of encouragement ringing in his ears. Was there none of that strength left? Was a fanatic friar going to defeat him? Him? The boy *bastaix* admired by all the other boys in the city? Step by step, fighting his way along the path to Santa Maria, and then returning home to rest until the next day. His home . . . those brown eyes, those big brown eyes. Then all at once, with a shudder that almost knocked him off his feet, he realized that the person who had spoken to him in the dungeon was Aledis.

When they saw Arnau suddenly straighten, Nicolau Eimerich and Berenguer d'Eril exchanged looks. For the first time, one of the Dominicans' stares wavered, and he looked towards the centre of the table.

'He's not going to fall,' the bishop whispered nervously.

'Where do you satisfy your needs?' Nicolau asked loudly.

That explained why she had known his name. Her voice . . . Yes, that was the voice he had heard so often on the slopes of Montjuïc hill.

'Arnau Estanyol!' The inquisitor's cry brought him back to the tribunal. 'I asked how you satisfy your needs.'

'I do not understand your question.'

'You are a man. You have had no physical contact with your wife for years. It's a very simple question: where do you satisfy your needs as a man?'

'For the same number of years, I have had no contact with any woman.'

He had answered without thinking. *The gaoler had said she was his mother.*

'That's a lie!' Arnau gave a start. 'This tribunal has seen you embracing a heretic. Is that not contact with a woman?'

'Not the kind of contact you were referring to.'

'What can drive a man and a woman to embrace in public' – Nicolau waved his hands – 'if not lasciviousness?'

'Grief.'

'What grief?' the bishop wanted to know.

'What grief?' Nicolau insisted when Arnau did not reply. Arnau still said nothing. The flames from the funeral pyre lit the chamber. 'Grief because a heretic who had profaned the sacred host had been executed?' the inquisitor insisted, pointing a bejewelled finger at him. 'Is that the grief you feel as a true Christian? Because the weight of justice fell on a monster, a profaner, a wretch, a thief—?'

'He did nothing!' Arnau shouted.

All the members of the tribunal, including the clerk, stirred in their seats.

'Those three men confessed their guilt. Why do you defend heretics? The Jews—'

'Jews! Jews!' Arnau faced them defiantly. 'What does the world have against them?'

'Do you not know?' asked the inquisitor, anger in his voice. 'They crucified Jesus Christ!'

'Haven't they paid enough for that?' Arnau stared at the men ranged in front of him. They were all sitting up attentively.

'Are you saying they should be pardoned?' asked Berenguer d'Eril.

'Isn't that what Our Lord teaches us?'

'Their only salvation is through conversion! There can

be no pardon for those who do not repent,' shouted Nicolau.

'You're talking about something that happened more than thirteen hundred years ago. What do the Jews born in our time have to repent for? They are not to blame for what might have happened all those years ago.'

'Anyone who accepts the Jewish doctrine is making himself responsible for what his forebears did; he is taking on their guilt.'

'They only adopt ideas, beliefs, just like . . .'. At this, Nicolau and Berenguer gave a start. Why not? Was it not true? Didn't that poor man who had died under a hail of insults and given his life for his community deserve the truth? 'Just like us,' Arnau said in a loud, firm voice.

'You dare equate the Catholic faith with heresy?' roared the bishop.

'It is not for me to compare anything: I leave that to you, the men of God. All I said was—'

'We are well aware of what you said!' Nicolau Eimerich interrupted. 'You compared the one, true Christian faith with the heretical doctrines of the Jews.'

Arnau faced the tribunal. The clerk was still writing on his papers. Even the soldiers, standing stiffly to attention by the doors behind him, appeared to be listening to the scrape of his quill on the parchment. Nicolau smiled. The scratching pierced Arnau to the backbone and a shudder ran through his entire body. The inquisitor saw it, and smiled even more broadly. Yes, he seemed to be saying, that is what you said.

'They are just like us,' Arnau repeated.

Nicolau silenced him with a wave of his hand.

The clerk continued writing for a few more moments. Everything you said is recorded there, the inquisitor's look told Arnau. When the clerk raised his quill, Nicolau gave a satisfied smile. 'The session is suspended until tomorrow,' he cried, getting up from his seat.

*　*　*

Mar was tired of listening to Joan.

'Where are you going?' Aledis asked her. Mar merely looked at her. 'There again? You've been every day, and you haven't succeeded—'

'I've succeeded in letting her know I'm here, and that I won't forget what she did to me.' Joan hid his face. 'I succeeded in catching sight of her through the window, and in letting her know that Arnau is mine. I saw it in her eyes, and I intend to remind her of it every day of her life. I intend to succeed by making her think every moment of the day that I was the one who won.'

Aledis watched her leave the inn. Mar took the same route as she had done every day since her arrival in Barcelona, and ended up outside the gates of the palace in Carrer de Montcada. She pounded with the doorknocker as hard as she could. Eleonor might refuse to see her, but she wanted her to know she was there.

As on every other day, the ancient servant peered at her through the peephole. 'My lady,' he said, 'you know that Dona Eleonor—'

'Open the door. I just want to see her, even if it is only through the window she hides behind.'

'But she does not want that.'

'Does she know who I am?'

Mar saw Pere turn towards the palace windows. 'Yes.'

Mar banged again with the knocker.

'My lady, do not insist, or Dona Eleonor will call the soldiers,' the old man advised her.

'Open up, Pere.'

'She won't see you, my lady.'

Mar felt a hand on her shoulder, pulling her away from the door. 'Perhaps she will see me,' she heard, before she saw someone stepping in front of her.

'Guillem!' cried Mar, flinging herself on him.

'Do you remember me, Pere?' asked the Moor, with Mar clinging to him.

'How could I not remember?'

'Well then, tell your mistress I want to see her.'

When the old man shut the peephole, Guillem took Mar by the waist and lifted her into the air. Laughing, Mar let him whirl her round. Then Guillem put her down, took a step back, and lifted her arms so that he could get a good look at her.

'My little girl,' he said, his voice choking with emotion. 'How often I've dreamt of holding you in my arms again! But now you weigh a lot more. You've become a real—'

Mar broke free, and ran to embrace him. 'Why did you abandon me?' she asked, tears in her eyes.

'I was no more than a slave, child. What could a mere slave do?'

'You were like a father to me.'

'Am I not that any more?'

'You always will be.'

Mar hugged Guillem tight. You always will be, thought the Moor. How many years had he wasted so far from here? He turned back to the door.

'Dona Eleonor will not see you either,' he heard from inside.

'Tell her she will be hearing from me.'

The soldiers took him back down to the dungeons. As the gaoler chained him up again, Arnau could not take his eyes off the dark bundle at the far end of the gloomy cell. He was still standing observing it when the gaoler left.

'What do you have to do with Aledis?' he shouted at the old woman as soon as the gaoler's footsteps had faded in the distance.

Arnau thought he could make out a slight movement in the shadowy figure, but after that, nothing.

'What do you have to do with Aledis?' he repeated. 'What was she doing here? Why does she visit you?'

The silence that was his only reply made him think again of that pair of huge brown eyes.

'What do Aledis and Mar have to do with each other?' he begged the shadow.

No reply. Arnau tried at least to hear the old woman's breathing, but the countless groans and snores from the other prisoners prevented him making out any sound from Francesca. Arnau looked desperately along the walls of the dungeon: nobody paid him any heed.

As soon as he saw Mar enter accompanied by a splendidly dressed Moor, the innkeeper stopped stirring the big cooking-pot hanging over the fire. He became even more troubled when he saw two slaves follow them in carrying Guillem's possessions. Why didn't he go to the corn exchange where all the merchants stay? he thought as he went to receive them.

'This is truly an honour,' the innkeeper said, bowing to the ground before them.

Guillem waited for him to finish his exaggerated display. 'Do you have rooms?'

'Yes. The slaves can sleep in the—'

'Rooms for three,' Guillem cut in. 'One room for me, and another for the two of them.'

The innkeeper glanced at the two youngsters with big dark eyes and curly locks waiting silently behind their master. 'Yes,' he said. 'If that is what you require. Follow me.'

'They will see to everything. Bring us some water.'

Guillem went with Mar to one of the tables. Only the two of them were left in the dining room. 'Did you say the trial began today?'

'Yes, although I couldn't say for sure. I'm not sure about anything. I haven't even been able to see him.'

Guillem heard the emotion choking Mar. He stretched out his hand to comfort her, but in the end withdrew it without touching her. She was no longer a little girl, and he . . . well, he was only a Moor. Nobody ought to think . . . It was enough to have whirled her round in the air outside Eleonor's palace. Mar's hand reached out and took his.

'I'm still the same. I always will be, for you.'

Guillem smiled. 'What about your husband?'

'He died.' Mar's face did not show the least sign of distress.

Guillem changed the subject: 'Have you done anything for Arnau?'

Mar half closed her eyes and twisted her lips. 'What do you mean? There's nothing we—'

'What about Joan? Joan is an inquisitor. Have you heard anything from him? Hasn't he interceded on Arnau's behalf?'

'That friar?' Mar laughed scornfully and said nothing: what was the point in telling him? Arnau's situation was bad enough, and that was what had brought Guillem to Barcelona. 'No. He hasn't done anything. Besides, he can't go against the grand inquisitor. He is at the inn with us—'

'With us?'

'Yes. I've met a widow called Aledis. She's staying here with her two daughters. She was a friend of Arnau's when they were young. Apparently she happened to be in Barcelona when he was arrested. I sleep in their room. She's a good woman. You'll meet them all when we eat.'

Guillem squeezed her hand.

'Tell me about you,' said Mar.

As the sun climbed in the sky, Mar and Guillem told each other all that had happened to them in the six years since they had last met. Mar was careful not to mention Joan.

667

The first to appear back at the inn were Teresa and Eulàlia. They were hot, but looked happy, although the smiles disappeared from their pretty faces as soon as they saw Mar and remembered that Francesca was still in jail.

They had walked all over the city, delighted at the new identity that being dressed as orphans – and virgins – had lent them. They had never before enjoyed such freedom, because according to the law they always had to wear bright silks and colours to show everyone that they were prostitutes. 'Shall we go in?' suggested Teresa, surreptitiously pointing to the doorway of Sant Jaume. She said it in a whisper, as though afraid that the very idea might arouse the ire of the whole of Barcelona. But nothing happened. The faithful inside the church paid them no attention, nor did the priest whom they avoided looking at, pressing closer to each other as he went by.

Chattering and laughing, they went down Carrer de la Boqueria towards the sea. If they had gone in the opposite direction, up Carrer del Bisbe to Plaça Nova, they would have run into Aledis. She was standing outside the bishop's palace, trying to recognize Arnau or Francesca in the shadows behind the stained-glass windows. She did not even know which window concealed the chamber where Arnau was being tried! Had Francesca been called to testify yet? Joan did not know anything about her. Aledis peered at window after window. She must have done, but what use was it knowing that if she could not do anything for her? Arnau was strong, and Francesca . . . they did not know what she was like.

'What are you doing standing there?' Aledis turned and saw one of the soldiers of the Inquisition next to her. She had not seen him arrive. 'What are you looking at so closely?'

Aledis ducked down and fled without a word. You

don't know Francesca, she thought as she ran away. None of your tortures will be able to make her give away the secret she has kept hidden all her life.

Before Aledis arrived back at the inn, Joan had appeared. He was wearing a clean habit borrowed from the Sant Pere de les Puelles monastery. When he saw Guillem sitting with Mar and Aledis's two daughters, he came to a halt in the centre of the dining room.

Guillem studied him. Was that a smile, or a grimace of distaste?

Joan himself would not have been able to say. What if Mar had told him about the kidnap?

The way the friar had treated him when he was with Arnau flashed through Guillem's mind, but this was no time to relive old quarrels, so he stood up to greet the newcomer. They all needed to be united to help Arnau.

'How are you, Joan?' he asked, taking him by the shoulders. 'What happened to your face?' he added, when he saw all the bruises.

Joan looked over at Mar, but her face held the same harsh, emotionless expression he had seen on it ever since he had gone in search of her. But no, Guillem could not be so cynical . . .

'An unfortunate encounter,' said Joan. 'It happens to friars as well.'

'I suppose you will have already excommunicated them,' joked Guillem as he led the friar over to the table. 'Isn't that what the *Constitutions of Peace and Truce* establish?' Joan and Mar exchanged glances. 'Isn't that what it says: "Anyone who disturbs the peace against unarmed priests . . ." You weren't armed, were you, Joan?'

Guillem did not have the chance to notice how strained the relationship was between Mar and the friar, because at that moment Aledis came in. Guillem greeted her briefly: it was Joan he wanted to talk to.

'You're an inquisitor,' he said. 'What do you make of Arnau's situation?'

'I think Nicolau wants to find him guilty, but he cannot have much against him. I think it may end with him having to wear the cloak of repentance and paying a hefty fine – that's what most interests Eimerich. I know Arnau: he has never harmed anyone. Even if Eleonor has denounced him, they won't be able to find—'

'What if Eleonor's accusation were backed up by several priests?'

Joan looked startled. Would priests stoop to that kind of thing? 'What do you mean?'

'That doesn't matter,' said Guillem, remembering Jucef's letter. 'Tell me though: what would happen if priests backed her up?'

Aledis did not hear Joan's reply. Should she tell them what she knew? Could that Moor possibly help? He was rich, and he looked . . . Eulàlia and Teresa were watching her. They had stayed silent as she had instructed them, but it seemed they were anxious to say something now. She had no need to ask them, she could see what they wanted. That meant . . . Oh, what did it matter? Somebody had to do something, and that Moor . . .

'There is quite a lot more,' she said, interrupting Joan's conjectures as to what might happen.

The two men and Mar all turned their attention to her.

'I have no intention of telling you how I found out, and I have no wish to talk about this again once I have said what I have to say. Do you agree?'

'What do you mean?' asked Joan.

'It's perfectly clear, friar,' snapped Mar.

Guillem looked at her with surprise: why was she speaking to Joan like that? He turned to the friar, but he was staring at the floor.

'Go on, Aledis. We agree,' said Guillem.

'Do you remember the two noblemen who are staying at the inn?'

When he heard the name Genís Puig, Guillem gasped. Aledis paused, then told him: 'He has a sister called Margarida.'

Guillem raised his hands to his face. 'Are they still here?' he asked.

Aledis nodded, and continued telling them what her girls had discovered; the favours Eulàlia had granted Genís Puig had not been in vain. Once he had exhausted his drunken passion on her, he had been more than happy to tell her of all the charges Arnau was facing.

'They say Arnau burnt his father's body,' said Aledis, 'but I can't believe . . .'

Joan was about to retch. All the others turned towards him. The friar had his hand over his mouth, as though he were choking. The darkness, Bernat's body hanging from the makeshift scaffold, the flames . . .

'What do you have to say now, Joan?' he heard Guillem asking him.

'They will put him to death,' he managed to say before he ran out of the inn, still covering his mouth with his hand.

Joan's verdict floated in the air around them. None of them dared look at each other.

'What has happened between you and Joan?' Guillem whispered to Mar after a while, when the friar had still not reappeared.

He was no more than a slave. What could a mere slave do? Guillem's words rattled round Mar's brain. If she told him . . . They needed to be united! Arnau needed them all to fight for him – including Joan.

'Nothing,' she said. 'You know we never got on very well.' She avoided looking at him.

'Will you tell me some day?' insisted Guillem.

Mar looked down at the table.

54

The members of the tribunal were already assembled: the four Dominicans and the clerk sitting behind the desk, the soldiers on guard at the door, and Arnau, as filthy as he had been the previous day, standing at the centre of the chamber. All eyes were on him.

A short while later Nicolau Eimerich and Berenguer d'Eril came in. Everything about them spoke of luxury and arrogance. The soldiers snapped alert, and the others stood until the two men had taken their seats.

'The session is open,' declared Nicolau. 'May I remind you,' he added, addressing Arnau, 'that you are still under oath.'

'That man', the bishop had warned him on their way into the tribunal, 'will give away more because of the oath he has taken than from any fear of being tortured.'

'Please read the prisoner's last declaration,' said Nicolau to the clerk.

' "They only adopt ideas and beliefs just like us." ' Arnau was struck by his own words. All night he had been unable to get the images of Mar and Aledis out of his mind, and had gone over what he had said time and again. Nicolau had not allowed him to explain what he meant, but then again, what could he say? What could he tell those hunters of heretics about his relations with Raquel and her family? The clerk was still reading out his declaration. He must not allow the questions to focus on Raquel: she and her family had suffered more than enough with the death of Hasdai. The last thing they needed was to have the Inquisition on their heels again . . .

'So you think that the Christian faith is no more than a few ideas and beliefs, which men are free to accept or not as they see fit?' Berenguer d'Eril asked him. 'How dare a mere mortal judge God's designs?'

Why shouldn't he? Arnau looked steadily at Nicolau. Aren't you two mere mortals as well? he thought. They would burn him. They would burn him just as they had burnt Hasdai and so many others. He shuddered.

'I expressed myself badly,' he said finally.

'How would you care to express yourself then?' asked Nicolau.

'I'm not sure. I do not have your learning. All I can say is that I believe in God, that I am a good Christian, and that I have always followed his commandments.'

'Do you think that burning the body of your father is following God's commandments?' shouted the inquisitor, rising to his feet and thumping the table with both hands.

Hurrying along in the shadows, Raquel ran to her brother's house as agreed.

'Sahat,' was all she said when she stood on the threshold.

Guillem got up from the table he was sharing with Jucef. 'I'm sorry, Raquel.'

Her only reply was a twist of the mouth. Guillem was a few steps away from her, but when she raised her arms in a helpless gesture, he strode over and embraced her. Guillem pressed her to him and tried to comfort her, but words failed him. Let the tears flow, Raquel, he thought, let them put out the fire still burning in your eyes.

After a few moments, Raquel pulled away from Guillem and dried her tears. 'You've come for Arnau, haven't you?' she asked once she had regained her composure. 'You must help him,' she added when Guillem nodded. 'We can't do much without making things even more difficult for him.'

'I was just telling your brother that I need a letter of introduction to the royal court.'

Raquel looked enquiringly at her brother, who was still seated at the table.

'We'll get one,' said Jucef. 'The Infante Don Juan, his retinue, the other members of the court and prominent men from all over the kingdom are meeting in Barcelona to discuss Sardinia. It's an excellent opportunity.'

'What are you planning, Sahat?' asked Raquel.

'I don't know yet,' he said, turning to Jucef. 'You wrote to me that the King is at loggerheads with the grand inquisitor.' Jucef nodded. 'What about his son?'

'He's even angrier with him,' said Jucef. 'The Infante is a patron of art and culture. He loves music and poetry. He invited many writers and philosophers to his court in Girona. None of them can accept the way Eimerich has attacked Ramon Llull. Catalan thinkers have little regard for the Inquisition: early this century fourteen works by the doctor Arnau de Vilanova were condemned as heretical; more recently the work of Nicolás de Calabria was declared heresy by Eimerich himself, and now they are attacking someone as important as Ramon Llull. It's as though they despise anything Catalan. Nowadays, only a few people dare write, out of fear of the interpretation Eimerich might put on their words; Nicolás de Calabria ended up at the stake. In addition, if anyone could put a stop to the grand inquisitor's plan to extend his jurisdiction to the Catalan Jewries, that person is the Infante. Don't forget, he lives on the taxes we pay him. He will listen to you,' said Jucef, 'but make no mistake, he will not want to confront the Inquisition openly.'

Guillem took silent note of all this.

Burning the body?

Nicolau Eimerich was still standing, hands pressed on the table, staring at Arnau. He was purple with rage. 'Your father was a devil who roused the people to rebellion,' he growled. 'That is why he was executed, and why you burnt him.'

Nicolau ended by pointing an accusing finger at Arnau.

How did he know? There was only one person who knew what he had done . . . The clerk's quill scratched its way across the page. It was impossible. Not Joan . . . Arnau could feel his legs buckling beneath him.

'Do you deny having burnt your father's body?' asked Berenguer d'Eril.

Joan could not have told anyone!

'Do you deny it?' Nicolau insisted, raising his voice.

The faces of the tribunal in front of him became a blur. Arnau thought he was going to be sick.

'We were hungry!' he shouted. 'Do you know what it feels like to be hungry?' He saw his father's purple face with its tongue lolling out, superimposed on those of the people watching him now. Joan? Why hadn't he been to see him again? 'We were hungry!' he shouted. Arnau could hear his father's words: *If I were you, I wouldn't give in* . . . 'Have you ever been hungry?'

Arnau tried to throw himself on Nicolau, who was still standing there arrogantly challenging him, but before he could reach the table, he was grabbed by the soldiers and dragged back to the centre of the chamber.

'Did you burn your father as a devil?' Nicolau shouted again.

'My father was not a devil!' Arnau replied, shouting and struggling to free himself from the soldiers.

'But you did burn your father's body.'

Why did you do it, Joan? You are my brother, and Bernat . . . Bernat always loved you like a son. Arnau lowered his head and went limp in the soldiers' hands. *Why?*

'Did your mother tell you to do it?'

Arnau could barely lift his head.

'Your mother is a witch who transmits the Devil's sickness,' said the bishop.

What were they talking about?

'Your father killed a boy in order to set you free. Do you confess it?' howled Nicolau.

'What—?' Arnau started to say.

'You,' Nicolau interrupted him, 'you also killed a Christian boy. What were you planning to do with him?'

'Did your parents tell you to kill him?'

'Did you want his heart?' said Nicolau.

'How many other boys have you killed?'

'What are your relations with heretics?'

The inquisitor and the bishop assailed him with questions. Your father, your mother, boys, murders, hearts, heretics, Jews . . . Joan! Arnau's head fell on to his chest again. His whole body was quivering.

Nicolau rounded on him. 'Do you confess?'

Arnau did not move. His interrogators were silent as he hung in the arms of the soldiers. Eventually, Nicolau signalled to them to take him out of the chamber. Arnau was aware of them dragging him away.

'Wait!' came the order from the inquisitor just as they were opening the doors. The guards turned back to him. 'Arnau Estanyol!' he shouted. And again: 'Arnau Estanyol!'

Arnau slowly raised his head and peered at Nicolau.

'You can take him out,' said the inquisitor once he had met Arnau's gaze. 'Take this down,' Arnau heard him instructing the clerk as he was bundled out of the room. 'The prisoner did not deny any of the accusations made by this tribunal, and has avoided confessing by pretending to have fainted, the falseness of which has been discovered when, no longer under oath in the tribunal, the prisoner responded to calls for him to answer his name.'

The sound of the scratching quill followed Arnau all the way to the dungeons.

Despite the innkeeper's protests, Guillem gave instructions to his slaves to organize his move to the corn exchange, which was close to the Estanyer inn. He left Mar behind, but he could not risk being recognized by Genís Puig. The slaves only shook their heads when the innkeeper tried desperately to get them and their rich master to stay on. 'What use to me are nobles who won't pay?' he growled as he counted out the money the slaves had given him.

Guillem went straight from the Jewry to his new lodgings. None of the merchants staying in Barcelona knew of his former connections with Arnau.

'I have a business in Pisa,' he told a Sicilian trader who sat down to eat at the same table and showed an interest in him.

'What brings you to Barcelona?' he asked.

He almost said: a friend who is in trouble, then thought better of it. The Sicilian was a short, bald man with rough-hewn features. He said his name was Jacopo Lercardo. Guillem had discussed the situation in Barcelona thoroughly with Jucef, but it was always a good idea to get another opinion.

'Years ago I had good contacts in Catalonia, so I

thought I would take advantage of a trip to Valencia to see how things are here now.'

'There's not much to see,' said the Sicilian, continuing to eat.

Guillem waited for him to go on, but the other man seemed more interested in his stew. It was obvious he would not say anything more unless he thought he was talking to someone who knew as much about business as he did.

'I've noticed the situation has changed a lot since I was last here. There don't seem to be many peasants in the markets: their stalls are empty. I can remember when, years ago, the inspector had to struggle to keep order among all the traders and peasants selling produce.'

'The inspector has no work to do these days,' said the Sicilian with a smile. 'The peasants don't produce, and don't bring anything to sell. Epidemics have decimated the countryside, the land is poor, and even the land-owners no longer plant crops. Many peasant farmers have been heading to where you came from: Valencia.'

'I've visited some people I knew before,' Guillem commented. The Sicilian looked up from his food. 'They no longer want to risk their money in commerce: they prefer to buy the city's debt. They live on the interest. They've told me that nine years ago, Barcelona's debt was around a hundred and sixty-nine thousand pounds; nowadays it must be nearer two hundred thousand, and it's still increasing. The city can no longer pay the interest on the different loans it has given as guarantee for the debt; it is facing ruin.'

Guillem reflected on the endless debate among Christians about whether it was permitted to earn money through interest. With the collapse of trade and the consequent lack of money from commerce, the city authorities had once again sought to get round the prohibition by creating these new types of loan, which entailed the rich lending them money in return for a guarantee of a yearly payment – which obviously included interest. Repayment of the property levy implied handing over a third more than the original sum. The advantage of these loans was that there was much less risk than that involved in commercial ventures . . . as long as Barcelona could pay.

'But until that moment of ruin arrives,' said the Sicilian, 'there is a great opportunity to make money in Catalonia—'

'By selling,' Guillem intervened.

'In the main, yes,' said the Sicilian. Guillem could tell he trusted him more now. 'But you can also buy, provided you do so in the proper currency. The parity between the gold florin and silver croat is a complete fiction; it has nothing to do with the rate that you can get in foreign exchanges. Silver is pouring out of Catalonia, yet the King is determined to defend the value of his gold florin against the market; his attitude is going to cost him dear.'

'Why do you think he persists in it then?' Guillem asked. 'King Pedro has always behaved very sensibly . . .'

'It's purely out of political interest,' said Jacopo. 'The florin is a royal currency: it is minted in Montpellier under his direct control. But the croat is minted in cities like Barcelona and Valencia under licence. The King is determined to support the value of his own currency even if it's a mistake – but for us, his obstinacy is very fortunate. He has put parity between gold and silver at thirteen times more than its real value in other markets!'

'What about the royal coffers?' That was what most interested Guillem.

'Thirteen times over-valued!' laughed the Sicilian trader. 'The King is still fighting Castile, although it seems the war may soon be over. King Pedro the Cruel is having problems with his barons, who are deserting him in favour of the House of Trastámara. Pedro the Ceremonious can only count on support from the cities and, apparently, the Jews. The war with Castile has ruined him. Four years ago, the Monzón parliament provided him with two hundred and sixty thousand pounds for his war chest in return for fresh concessions for nobles and cities. The King is spending the money on the war, but he is giving up privileges that might affect him in the future. And now there's a rebellion in Corsica . . . If you are owed money by the King, you can forget it.'

Guillem's attention wandered from what the Sicilian was saying. He merely nodded and smiled when it seemed appropriate. So the King was ruined, and Arnau was one of his biggest creditors. When Guillem had left Barcelona, Arnau had lent the royal house more than ten thousand pounds: how much could it be now? The King had probably not even been able to pay off the interest on the cheap loans. *They will put him to death.* Joan's words came back into Guillem's mind. 'Nicolau will use Arnau to help strengthen his position,' Jucef had told him. 'The King does not pay any revenues to the Pope, and Eimerich has promised him part of Arnau's fortune.' Would the King want to owe money to a Pope who had just backed a revolt in Corsica by denying the rights of the Crown of Aragon? But how could he get the King to stand up to the Inquisition?

'Your proposal interests us.'

The Infante's voice was lost in the vastness of the Tinell chamber in Barcelona's royal palace. He was only sixteen, but he had just presided, in the name of his father, over the parliament which dealt with the revolt in Sardinia. Guillem glanced surreptitiously at the King's heir, seated on the throne flanked by his two counsellors, Joan Fernández d'Heredia and Francesc de Perellós, both of whom were standing. It was said that the Infante was weak, and yet, two years earlier, he had found the strength to try, pass sentence and execute the man who had been his tutor since birth: Bernat de Cabrera. And after ordering his beheading in Zaragoza market square, he had been obliged to send the viscount's head to his father, King Pedro.

The same evening as he had spoken to the Sicilian trader, Guillem had met with Francesc de Perellós. The counsellor had listened closely to what he had to say, and then asked him to wait behind a small door. When after many minutes he was told to come in, Guillem found himself in the most imposing chamber he had ever seen: it was an airy room more than thirty paces wide, with six long arches that almost reached the floor. The walls were bare apart from the torches that lit the chamber. The Infante and his counsellors were waiting for him at the far end.

When he was still several steps away from the throne, Guillem knelt down on one knee.

'Yet remember,' said the Infante, 'we cannot oppose the Inquisition.'

Guillem waited until Francesc de Perellós nodded for him to speak.

'You would not have to, my liege.'

'So be it,' the Infante ruled, then stood up and left the chamber, accompanied by Joan Fernández d'Heredia.

'You may rise,' Francesc de Perellós told Guillem. 'When can you arrange this?'

'Tomorrow, if possible. If not, the day after.'

'I will inform the magistrate.'

Guillem left the royal palace as night was falling. He stared up at the clear Mediterranean sky and took a deep breath. There was still a lot to do.

That same afternoon, when he was still talking to Jacopo the Sicilian, he had received a message from

Jucef: 'The counsellor Francesc de Perelló will see you today in the royal palace, when the parliament has finished.' He knew how to interest the Infante. It was easy: he would cancel the substantial debts that the Catalan Crown owed Arnau, thus making sure they did not end up in the hands of the Pope. But how could he set Arnau free and yet avoid the Duke of Girona having to confront the Inquisition?

Before he headed for the royal palace, Guillem went for a walk. His steps led him in the direction of Arnau's counting house. It was boarded up: Nicolau Eimerich must have all his account books in order to avoid any further sales. All Arnau's assistants had gone. Guillem looked towards Santa Maria, still surrounded in scaffolding. How was it possible that someone who had given everything for a church like that . . .? He walked on to the Consulate of the Sea, and then the beach.

'How is your master?' he heard behind him.

Guillem turned, and saw a *bastaix* carrying an enormous sack on his shoulders. Years earlier, Arnau had lent him money, which he had returned coin by coin. Guillem shrugged and twisted his mouth. Almost immediately, he was surrounded by a line of *bastaixos* who were unloading a ship. 'What's happened to Arnau?' he heard. 'How can they accuse him of heresy?' That man had borrowed money from Arnau as well . . . for his daughter's dowry? How many of them had turned to Arnau for help? 'If you see him,' said another *bastaix*, 'tell him we've lit a candle for him beneath the statue in Santa Maria. We make sure it never goes out.' Guillem tried to explain he knew nothing, but they all launched into attacks on the Inquisition before continuing on their way.

Emboldened by their passion, Guillem strode off determinedly to the royal palace.

Now, with the silhouette of Santa Maria picked out

against the night sky, Guillem found himself once more outside Arnau's counting house. He needed the bill of payment that the Jew Abraham Levi had once signed, which he himself had hidden behind a stone in the wall. The door to the counting house was shut, but there was a window on the ground floor which had never closed properly. Guillem strained his ears: there was no one around. Arnau had never known the document existed. Guillem and Hasdai had decided to conceal the profits they received from a sale of slaves as if it were a deposit made by a Jew passing through Barcelona: that was Abraham Levi. Arnau would never have accepted money made from slavery. The window grated in the night-time silence. Guillem froze. After all, he was a Moor, an infidel entering the house of a prisoner of the Inquisition in the middle of the night. If he were caught, the fact that he had been baptized a Christian would be of little help. But the night-time sounds around him made him realize that the universe did not depend on him: the lapping of the waves, the creaking of the scaffolding at Santa Maria, babies crying, men shouting at their wives . . .

He opened the window wider and slipped inside. Abraham Levi's fictitious deposit had allowed Arnau to put the money to good use and earn healthy profits, but each time he did so, he made sure that a quarter of the earnings were noted down in Levi's name. Guillem waited until his eyes grew used to the darkness, and the moonlight could guide him. Before Abraham Levi left Barcelona, Hasdai had gone with him to a scribe for him to sign a receipt for the money he had deposited with Arnau. The money was Arnau's, but on his books it still showed as belonging to the Jew, and it had accumulated year after year.

Guillem knelt by the wall. It was the second stone from the right. He began to pull at it.

He had never confessed to Arnau about that first

operation he had done behind his back, but in his name. The stone would not budge. 'Don't worry,' he remembered Hasdai telling Arnau once when he had mentioned the Jew, 'I have instructions for the deposit to remain as it is. Don't worry about it.' When Arnau turned to look at them, Hasdai had stared at Guillem, who limited himself to shrugging and sighing.

The stone began to move. No. Arnau would never have used money that came from the sale of slaves. The stone came away, and behind it Guillem soon found the document, carefully wrapped in a cloth. He did not bother reading it because he remembered exactly what it said. He pushed the stone back, and returned to the window. He could hear nothing unusual outside, so he slipped out again, and left Arnau's counting house.

55

The soldiers had to come into the dungeon to get him. Two of them lifted him under the arms and dragged him out, while Arnau struggled to stand. His ankles banged against the stairs up to the palace; he did not have the strength to make his own way. He did not even notice the monks and priests peering at him as he was led to face Nicolau again. Arnau had not been able to sleep for a moment: how could Joan have denounced him?

When he had been thrown back into the dungeon the previous evening, Arnau had wept and wailed and flung himself at the wall. Why Joan? And if Joan had denounced him, what role was Aledis playing in all this? And the old woman in the dungeon with him? Aledis had reason to hate him: he had abandoned her and then refused to receive her. Could she be in league with Joan? Had they really gone to fetch Mar? If that were so, why hadn't she visited him? Was it so hard to bribe a simple gaoler?

Francesca listened to him weeping and crying out. When she heard her son in such pain, her body shrank still further. She would have loved to look at him and respond, to console him even if she had to lie. 'You won't be able to stand it,' she had warned Aledis. But what about her? Would she be able to bear this situation for much longer? Arnau went on howling his anguish to the world, and Francesca pressed herself closer to the dank walls of the prison.

The doors to the chamber opened and Arnau was pushed in. The members of the tribunal were all assembled. The soldiers dragged him to the centre of the room and let him go: Arnau fell to his knees with his legs splayed out beneath him. He heard Nicolau's voice breaking the silence, but could not understand a word of what he was saying. Why should he care what this friar could do to him, when his own brother had already passed sentence on him? He had no one. He had nothing.

'Make no mistake,' the bailiff had told him when he tried to buy him off with a small fortune, 'you don't have any money any more.' Money! Money had been the reason why the King had married him to Eleonor; money was behind his wife's accusations; it was money that had led to his imprisonment. Could it have been money that led Joan to . . .?

'Bring in the mother!'

The barked command stirred a response in Arnau's befuddled brain.

Mar and Aledis, with Joan a few paces away, were waiting outside the bishop's palace in Plaça Nova. 'The Infante will see my master this evening,' was all that one of Guillem's slaves had told them the day before. This morning, at first light, the same slave had appeared and told them his master wanted them to go to the Plaça Nova.

So the three of them waited, wondering why Guillem had called them there like that.

* * *

Arnau heard the doors opening behind him. Then he heard the soldiers come back in and approach the centre of the chamber close by him. After that, they marched back to stand guard at the doors.

He could sense her presence. He saw her bare, cracked feet, filthy and bleeding. Nicolau and the bishop smiled when they saw Arnau apparently fascinated by his mother's feet. He turned to look at her properly. Although he was on his knees and she was standing, she was so shrunken that she was only a hand taller than he. The time she had spent in the dungeons had left its mark: her sparse grey hair was matted and stiff; her profile as she stared at the tribunal bench was a mass of slack skin. The eye in the side of her face he could see was sunk so deep into what looked like purple, mottled flesh that Arnau could scarcely make it out.

'Francesca Esteve,' said Nicolau, 'do you swear on the four Gospels?'

The old woman's strong, firm voice took everyone by surprise. 'I swear,' she said, 'but you are wrong; my name is not Francesca Esteve.'

'What is it then?' asked Nicolau.

'My name is Francesca, but not Esteve. It's Ribes. Francesca Ribes,' she said, raising her voice.

'Do we have to remind you that you are under oath?' the bishop said.

'No. On my oath, I am telling the truth. My name is Francesca Ribes.'

'Are you not the daughter of Pere and Francesca Esteve?' Nicolau insisted.

'I never knew who my parents were.'

'Did you contract marriage with Bernat Estanyol in the lands of the lord of Navarcles?'

Arnau stiffened. Bernat Estanyol?

'No. I have never been in such a place and have never been married.'

'And did you not bear a son by the name of Arnau Estanyol?'

'No. I know of no such Arnau Estanyol.'

Arnau turned to her again.

Nicolau Eimerich and Berenguer d'Eril whispered together. Then the inquisitor addressed the clerk.

'Listen,' he told Francesca.

' "Declaration by Jaume de Bellera, lord of Navarcles",' the clerk began to read.

When he heard the name de Bellera, Arnau's eyes narrowed. His father had told him about that family. He listened closely to the supposed story of his life, the story cut short by his father's death. The way his mother had been called to the castle to suckle Llorenç de Bellera's new son. A witch? He heard Jaume de Bellera's version of how his mother had run away when soon afterwards he had begun to suffer from the Devil's sickness.

' "Arnau Estanyol's father, Bernat," ' went on the clerk, ' "succeeded in eluding the guard after he had killed an innocent youth, and then abandoned his lands and fled to Barcelona with his son. Once in the city, they were taken in by the family of Grau Puig, the merchant. The witness understands that the witch became a common whore. Arnau Estanyol is the son of a witch and a murderer." '

'What do you have to say to that?' Nicolau asked Francesca.

'That you've got the wrong whore,' the old woman said coldly.

'You!' shouted the bishop, pointing an accusing finger at her. 'How dare you challenge the Inquisition's evidence?'

'I'm not here for being a whore,' Francesca said, 'and that's not what I'm being tried for. Saint Augustine wrote that only God can judge fallen women.'

The bishop went bright red with rage: 'How dare you quote Saint Augustine? How . . .?'

Berenguer d'Eril went on ranting and raving, but Arnau was no longer listening. Saint Augustine wrote that God would judge fallen women. Saint Augustine said . . . Years ago, in an inn at Figueres, he had heard those words from a common whore – hadn't she been called Francesca? Saint Augustine wrote . . . could it be?

Arnau turned to look at Francesca: he had seen her only twice in his life, but both were crucial moments. Everyone in the tribunal saw how he reacted to her.

'Look at your son!' shouted Eimerich. 'Do you deny you are his mother?'

Arnau and Francesca heard his accusation reverberate from the chamber walls. Arnau was on his knees, staring at her; she was looking ahead of her, straight at the grand inquisitor.

'Look at him!' Nicolau raged, pointing at Arnau.

Faced with all the hatred of that accusatory finger, Francesca's entire body quivered. Only Arnau noticed how the skin of her neck pulled back almost imperceptibly. She did not take her eyes off the inquisitor.

'You will confess,' Nicolau assured her, rolling his tongue round the word. 'I can assure you, you will confess.'

'*Via fora!*'

The cry disturbed the peace and quiet of Plaça Nova. A boy ran across the square, shouting the call to arms: '*Via fora! Via fora!*' Aledis and Mar looked at each other, and then at Joan.

'The bells aren't ringing,' he replied with a shrug.

Yet the cry of '*Via fora!*' had echoed round the city. Curious citizens came out into Plaça del Blat, expecting to see the Sant Jordi banner next to the stone in the centre. Instead of that, they found two *bastaixos* armed with crossbows, who led them to Santa Maria.

In the square outside the church, the Virgin of the Sea had been hoisted on her dais on to the shoulders of more *bastaixos*, who were waiting for the people of the city to gather round. Beside her, the guild aldermen had hoisted their banner and were receiving the steady stream of people coming down Carrer de la Mar. One of them had the key to the Sacred Urn round his neck. The crowd round the Virgin grew and grew. To one side, outside Arnau's counting house, Guillem was watching and listening closely.

'The Inquisition has seized a citizen of Barcelona, the Consul of the Sea,' one of the guild aldermen explained.

'But the Inquisition—' someone said.

'The Inquisition is not part of our city,' one of the aldermen interrupted him. 'It is not subject to the King either. It does not take orders from the Council of a Hundred, or the city magistrate, or the bailiff. None of them chooses its members – that is done by the Pope, who is a foreigner and is only interested in our money. How can they accuse someone of heresy who has devoted his life to the Virgin of the Sea?'

'They only want our consul's money!' shouted someone in the crowd.

'They're lying so they can get their hands on our money!'

'They hate the Catalan people,' another alderman said.

The news spread like wildfire among all those gathered in the square. Angry shouts could soon be heard along Carrer de la Mar.

Guillem saw the aldermen explaining what was going on to the leaders of the other guilds. Who wasn't fearful about what might happen to their money? Although of course the Inquisition was to be feared as well. It was an absurd accusation . . .

'We have to defend our privileges,' shouted one of those who had been talking to the *bastaixos*.

The crowd grew agitated. Soon swords, crossbows and fists were being waved in the air to more cries of '*Via fora!*'

The noise grew louder and louder. Guillem saw some city councillors arrive. He immediately went over to the group talking together round the statue.

'What about the King's soldiers?' he heard one of the newcomers ask.

The alderman repeated the exact words that Guillem had suggested to him: 'Let's go to Plaça del Blat and see what the magistrate does.'

Guillem left them. For a brief moment, he stared at the small stone image the *bastaixos* were carrying. Help him! he said in silent prayer.

The group set off. 'To Plaça del Blat!' was the cry.

Guillem joined the stream of people flocking back up Carrer de la Mar to the square where the magistrate's palace stood. Few among them knew that the aim of the *host* was to determine what attitude the magistrate would adopt, so that while the Virgin on her dais was placed in the centre of the square where usually the banner of Sant Jordi and the other guild banners would hang, he had no difficulty in getting close to the palace itself.

In the centre of the square, the councillors and guild aldermen gathered round the Virgin and the pennant. All had their eyes fixed on the palace. When the rest of the crowd realized what was happening, they all fell silent and turned towards the palace as well. Guillem could feel the tension rising. Had the Infante kept his side of the bargain? The King's soldiers were lined up, swords drawn, between the crowd and the palace. The magistrate appeared at one of the windows, squinted down at the people gathered below him, and disappeared again. A few moments later, a captain appeared in the square. Hundreds of pairs of eyes, Guillem's included, turned to him.

'The King cannot intervene in the affairs of the city of Barcelona,' the captain shouted. 'It is for the city to decide whether to call the *host* or not.'

With that, he ordered the line of soldiers to withdraw.

The crowd watched as the soldiers filed out of the square and disappeared beneath the old city gate. Before they had all left the square, a huge cry of '*Via fora!*' rent the air. Guillem trembled.

Just as Nicolau de Eimerich was about to order that Francesca be taken back to the dungeons to be tortured, the sound of bells interrupted him. First came Sant Jaume, the call for the *host* to gather, and then one by one all the other church bells in the city began to chime. Most of the priests in Barcelona's churches were faithful followers of Ramon Llull's doctrines, and so were not opposed to the lesson the city intended to teach the Inquisition.

'The *host*?' the grand inquisitor asked enquiringly of Berenguer d'Eril.

The bishop shrugged.

The Virgin of the Sea still stood in the centre of Plaça del Blat, waiting for the banners of all the guilds to join that of the *bastaixos*. Already, though, many people were heading for the bishop's palace.

Aledis, Mar and Joan could hear them approaching. Then all of a sudden, cries of '*Via fora*' began to fill Plaça Nova.

Nicolau Eimerich and Berenguer d'Eril went over to one of the leaded windows. When they opened it, they saw more than a hundred people down below, shouting and waving their weapons in the air. The shouts grew louder when they spied the two provosts.

'What's going on?' Nicolau asked the guard, starting back from the window.

'Barcelona has come to set its Consul of the Sea free,' a boy shouted when Joan asked the same question.

Aledis and Mar closed their eyes and set their mouths in a firm line. They felt for each other's hand, and stared up with tear-filled eyes at the window that had remained half-open.

'Go and fetch the magistrate!' Nicolau ordered the captain of the guard.

With no one paying any attention to him, Arnau got up from his knees and took Francesca by the arm.

'What made you tremble?' he asked her.

Francesca just managed to stop a teardrop falling down her cheek, but she could not prevent her mouth twisting in pain. 'Forget me,' she said, her voice choking with emotion.

The uproar outside the windows made all further conversation or thought almost impossible. The *host* had assembled, and was heading for Plaça Nova. It passed beneath the old city gate, and on past the magistrate's palace. He watched it go by from one of his windows. Then the men marched along Carrer dels Seders up to Carrer de la Boqueria and the church of Sant Jaume, whose bells were still ringing out, and then up Carrer del Bisbe to the bishop's palace.

Still clutching each other by the hand, Mar and Aledis rushed to the end of the street. Everyone was pressed up against the walls to leave room for the *host* to go by: in the vanguard was the banner of the *bastaixos*, then the Virgin under her canopy, and behind her in a riot of colour came the banners of all the other guilds of the city.

The magistrate refused to see the Inquisition's envoy.

'The King cannot interfere in the *host* of Barcelona's affairs,' the King's officer told him.

'But they will attack the bishop's palace,' said the other man, still panting.

The royal officer shrugged. Do you use that sword to torture with? he was on the point of asking him. The Inquisition envoy saw his look, and the two men glared at each other.

'I'd like to see you measure it against a Castilian blade or a Moorish scimitar,' the soldier said, spitting between the other man's feet.

Meanwhile, the Virgin's statue had reached the bishop's palace, swaying on the shoulders of the *bastaixos*, who had been forced almost to run up the street to keep pace with the enraged people of Barcelona.

Somebody threw a stone at the leaded windows.

This one missed, but not the next one, or many of the others that followed.

Nicolau Eimerich and Berenguer d'Eril retreated from the windows. Arnau was still waiting for an answer from Francesca. Neither of them moved.

Several people started banging on the palace doors. A youth with a crossbow slung over his back climbed up the wall, cheered on by the crowd below. Others followed suit.

'That's enough!' shouted one of the city councillors, trying to push the people away from the door. 'Enough!' he said again. 'Nobody is to attack without the city's approval.'

The men stopped hammering on the door.

'Nobody can attack the building without an order from the councillors and the guild aldermen,' the official repeated.

The people nearest the door fell silent, and word ran through the square. The Virgin was steadied, and there was silence throughout all the *host*. Everyone in the square was staring up at the six men who had scaled the palace walls; the first of them was already level with the smashed window of the tribunal chamber.

'Come down from there!' came the cry.

The five city councillors and the *bastaixos*' alderman, who was wearing the key to the Sacred Urn round his neck, all shouted at the locked palace door: 'Open in the name of the Barcelona *host*!'

'Open up!' The Inquisition's envoy banged on the doors of the Jewry, which had been shut as the *host* approached. 'Open up for the Inquisition!'

He had tried to reach the bishop's palace, but all the streets leading to it were thronged with people. There was only one way to get there: by crossing the Jewish quarter, which ran alongside the palace. If he could do that, he might be able to send his master the message: the magistrate was not going to intervene.

Nicolau and Berenguer were still in the tribunal chamber when they heard the news: the King's soldiers would not come to their defence, and the Barcelona *host* was threatening to assault the palace if they did not let them in.

'What do they want?'

The guard looked towards Arnau. 'They want the Consul of the Sea set free.'

Nicolau went up to Arnau until their faces were almost touching. 'How dare they!' he spat. Then he turned on his heel and sat down again behind the tribunal bench. Bishop Berenguer went with him. 'Let them in,' ordered Nicolau.

To set the Consul of the Sea free . . . Arnau straightened up as much as his enfeebled condition would allow. Ever since her son had asked her his question, Francesca had been staring blindly in front of her. *Consul of the Sea.* I'm that person, Arnau's steady gaze told Nicolau.

The five city councillors and the *bastaixos*' alderman

burst into the tribunal. Behind them, trying to go un-noticed, came Guillem, who had asked the *bastaixos* for permission to enter with them. He remained at the door while the other six, weapons drawn, faced Nicolau. One of the councillors stepped forward.

'What—?' Nicolau started to say.

'The Barcelona *host*', cut in the councillor, raising his voice above the inquisitor's, 'orders you to hand over Arnau Estanyol, Consul of the Sea.'

'You presume to give orders to the Inquisition?' asked Nicolau.

The councillor did not flinch. 'For a second time,' he warned, 'the *host* orders you to hand over the Consul of the Sea of Barcelona.'

Nicolau blustered, and turned to the bishop for support.

'They'll attack the palace,' Berenguer said.

'They would not dare,' Nicolau whispered. 'He's a heretic!' he shouted.

'Should you not try him before you decide that?' one of the councillors said.

Nicolau's eyes narrowed. 'He is a heretic,' he insisted.

'For the third and last time, hand over the Consul of the Sea to us.'

'What do you mean, "for the last time"?' asked Berenguer d'Eril.

'Look outside if you really wish to know.'

'Arrest them!' shouted the grand inquisitor, waving his arms at the soldiers guarding the door.

Guillem took a few steps away from them. None of the councillors moved. Some of the soldiers put their hands to their swords, but the captain in charge signalled them to do nothing.

'Arrest them!' shrieked Nicolau.

'They've come to negotiate,' argued the captain.

'How dare you—?' Nicolau yelled, rising to his feet.

The captain interrupted him: 'Tell me how you expect me to defend this palace, and then I will arrest them; the King is not going to come to our aid.' The captain gestured towards the square outside, from where the sounds of the crowd were growing louder every minute. He turned to the bishop for help.

'You can take your Consul of the Sea,' said the bishop, 'he's free to go.'

Nicolau's face flushed. 'What are you saying . . .?' he cried, grasping the bishop by the arm.

Berenguer d'Eril shook himself free.

'You don't have the authority to hand over Arnau Estanyol,' the councillor told the bishop. 'Nicolau Eimerich,' he went on, 'the Barcelona *host* has given you three chances: now hand over the Consul of the Sea to us or face the consequences.'

As he was saying this, a stone flew into the chamber and smashed against the front of the long table where the members of the tribunal were placed: even the Dominican friars jumped in their seats. The shouts from Plaça Nova were even louder and more insistent. Another stone came flying in; the clerk gathered up his papers and sought refuge at the far end of the chamber. The black friars who were closest to the window tried to do the same, but the inquisitor gestured for them to remain where they were.

'Are you mad?' whispered the bishop.

Nicolau gazed at everyone in the tribunal one by one, until finally he looked at Arnau. He was smiling. 'Heretic!' he bellowed.

'That is enough,' said the councillor, turning on his heel.

'Take him with you!' pleaded the bishop.

'We only came here to negotiate,' said the councillor, halting as he raised his voice above the noise from out-side. 'If the Inquisition does not accept the city's demands and free the prisoner, the *host* will do so. That is the law.'

Nicolau stood facing them all. He was shaking with rage: his bloodshot eyes bulged. Two more stones crashed into the chamber.

'They will attack the palace,' said the bishop, not caring whether he was heard or not. 'What do you care? You have his declaration and his possessions. Declare him a heretic anyway; he will be an outlaw for ever.'

By now, the councillors and the *bastaixos*' alderman had reached the doors of the chamber. The soldiers, all of whom looked terrified, stepped to one side. Guillem was more interested in the conversation between the bishop and the grand inquisitor. All this time, Arnau remained standing in the centre of the room with Francesca, defying Nicolau, who could not now look at him.

'Take him with you!' the inquisitor finally yielded.

As soon as Arnau appeared with the councillors in the palace doorway the roars of jubilation spread from the square to the crowded streets nearby. Francesca limped behind them: nobody had noticed when Arnau took her by the arm and led her out of the chamber. As they left the building, though, he had to let go of her, and she stayed in the background. Inside the tribunal chamber, Nicolau stood behind the bench watching them leave, oblivious to the hail of stones coming in through the window. One of them hit him full on his left arm, but the inquisitor did not even move. All the other members of the tribunal had sought refuge on the far side of the room, as far away as possible from the *host's* anger.

Arnau had come to a halt behind the soldiers, although the councillors were urging him to go on out into the square.

'Guillem . . .'

The Moor came over to him, put his arms round his shoulders, and kissed him on the mouth. 'Go with them, Arnau,' he told him. 'Mar is waiting for you – and your brother, outside. I still have things to do here. I'll come and see you later.'

In spite of the councillors' efforts to protect him, the crowd rushed towards Arnau as soon as he was out in the square. They embraced him, patted him on the back, congratulated him. Row upon row of beaming faces confronted him. None of them wanted to move away to allow the councillors through; all the faces seemed to be calling to him.

The commotion was so great that the group of five councillors and the *bastaixos'* alderman were jostled from one side to another. The uproar and the endless sea of faces shook Arnau to the core. His legs began to weaken. He raised his eyes above the crowd, but all he could see was a forest of crossbows, swords and fists waving to the shouts of the *host*, over and over again . . . He leant back on the councillors for support, but just as he was about to collapse, he saw a tiny stone figure appear among the weapons, bobbing along with them.

Guillem was back, and his Virgin was smiling at him. Arnau closed his eyes and allowed himself to be carried shoulder-high by the councillors.

However hard they tried to push their way through the crowd, neither Mar and Aledis nor Joan could get anywhere near Arnau. They caught sight of him being carried along as the Virgin of the Sea and the banners began to make their way back to Plaça del Blat. Two others who saw him from amid the crowd were Jaume de Bellera and Genís Puig. Until that moment, they had added their swords to the thousands of other weapons raised at the bishop's palace. They had even been forced to join in the shouting against the inquisitor, even though deep inside they both urged Nicolau to resist and for the King to change his attitude and come to the defence of the Holy Office. How was it possible that the King they had so often risked their lives for . . .

When he saw Arnau, Genís Puig began to whirl his sword in the air and howl like a man possessed. The lord of Navarcles recognized that cry – he had heard it many times when the knight galloped to the attack, flailing his weapon round his head. Genís's blade clattered against the crossbows and swords of all those around him. As people started to move away from him, he made straight for the small group carrying the Consul of the Sea, which by now was about to leave Plaça Nova and head down Carrer del Bisbe. How did he imagine he could take on the entire Barcelona *host*? They would kill him, and then . . .

Jaume de Bellera threw himself on his friend and forced him to lower his sword. The men next to them looked on in a puzzled fashion, but the crush of the crowd swept them on towards Carrer del Bisbe. As soon as Genís stopped shouting and waving his sword in the air, the gap around them closed up.

Lord de Bellera took him to one side, away from anyone who might have seen him launch his charge. 'Have you gone mad?' he asked.

'They've set him free . . . Free!' answered Genís, staring all the while at the banners that by now were advancing down Carrer del Bisbe. Jaume de Bellera forced Genís to look at him.

'What are you trying to do?'

Genís Puig stared after the banners again and tried to break out of his companion's grasp. 'To have revenge!' he shouted.

'This isn't the way,' Lord de Bellera warned him. 'This

isn't the way.' He shook Genís Puig until he was forced to respond. 'We'll find a better one.'

Genís stared at him; his lips were trembling. 'Do you swear it?'

'On my honour.'

As the *host* moved out of Plaça Nova, silence returned to the tribunal chamber. The shouts of victory of the last citizens disappeared down Carrer del Bisbe and the grand inquisitor's laboured breathing became evident. Nobody in the room had moved. The soldiers were still standing to attention, keeping as still as possible. Nicolau's gaze settled on everyone in turn: he had little need to say anything. 'Traitor!' he spat at Berenguer d'Eril. 'Cowards!' he shouted at the others. When he looked over towards the soldiers, he discovered Guillem standing among them.

'What is that infidel doing in here?' he cried. 'Do they have to mock us in this way?'

The captain of the guard did not know what to say. He had been concentrating so intently on the inquisitor that he had not seen Guillem come in with the councillors. Guillem was on the point of telling him that he was in fact baptized a Christian, but thought better of it: despite the grand inquisitor's efforts, the Holy Office did not have any jurisdiction over Jews and Moors. Nicolau could not threaten or arrest him.

'My name is Sahat de Pisa,' Guillem said out loud, 'and I should like to speak to you.'

'I have nothing to say to an infidel. Throw him out—'

'I think you will be interested in what I have to say.'

'I don't care what you think.' Nicolau gestured to the captain, who drew his sword.

'Perhaps you will be interested to learn that Arnau Estanyol is *abatut*,' said Guillem, backing away from the soldier's sword. 'You will not be able to use a single penny of his fortune.'

Nicolau gave a deep sigh and stared up at the chamber roof. Although the captain received no fresh order, he put down his weapon and stopped threatening Guillem.

'What do you mean, infidel?' the inquisitor asked.

'You have Arnau Estanyol's books; look at them closely.'

'Do you think we haven't?'

'Did you know that the King's debts have been pardoned?'

It was Guillem himself who had signed the receipt and given it to Francesc de Perellós. As the Moor had discovered, Arnau had never withdrawn Guillem's authority over his affairs.

Nicolau did not move a muscle. Everyone in the tribunal had the same thought: that was why the magistrate had refused to intervene.

Several seconds went by, with Guillem and Nicolau staring at each other. Guillem knew precisely what was going through the grand inquisitor's mind. *What are you going to tell the Pope? How are you going to pay the money you promised him? You've already dispatched the letter; he is bound to receive it. What will you say to him? And you need his support against a king whom you have always defied.*

'And what has all this got to do with you?' Nicolau eventually asked.

'I could explain . . . in private,' said Guillem, when Nicolau gestured impatiently at him.

'Barcelona has risen against the Inquisition, and now an infidel dares demand a private audience with me!' Nicolau complained in a loud voice. 'Who do you think you are?'

What will you say to your Pope? Guillem's eyes questioned him. Do you really want the whole of Barcelona to hear about your machinations?

'Search him,' the inquisitor commanded the captain. 'Make sure he is not carrying any weapons, and take him to the ante-chamber to my office. Wait for me there.'

Flanked by the captain and two soldiers, Guillem stood and waited in the ante-chamber. He had never dared tell Arnau where his fortune had come from: the slave trade. Now that the King's debts had been pardoned, if the Inquisition seized Arnau's possessions, it also took on his debts. Only he, Guillem, knew that the entries in favour of Abraham Levi were false; if he did not show anyone the receipt that the Jewish merchant had signed all those years ago, Arnau's wealth did not exist.

56

As soon as she emerged from the bishop's palace, Francesca moved away from the doors and stood pressed up against the wall. From there she could see how the crowd launched itself at Arnau, and watched as the councillors struggled unsuccessfully to keep them away. *Look at your son!* Nicolau's words in her memory drowned out the shouts of the *host*. *Didn't you want me to look at him, inquisitor? Well, there he is, and he's won.* When she saw Arnau falter and stumble, she stiffened, but then he disappeared in a waving sea of heads, weapons and banners, with the small statue of the Virgin bobbing up and down in the midst of them.

Little by little, still shouting and waving their weapons in the air, the *host* made its way down Carrer del Bisbe. Francesca did not move. Her legs were giving way beneath her, and she needed to hold herself up against the wall. It was as the square gradually emptied that she saw her: Aledis had refused to follow Mar and Joan, suspecting that the old woman had been left behind. There she was! Aledis was overcome with emotion when she saw her clinging to the only support she could find: she looked so old, frail and helpless . . .

Aledis ran towards her at the very moment the Inquisition guards finally dared poke their noses outside the bishop's palace as the shouts of the crowd died away in the distance. Francesca was standing only a few steps away.

'Witch!' the first soldier spat at her.

Aledis came to an abrupt halt a few steps from them. 'Let her be,' she shouted. Several more soldiers had come running out of the palace. 'Leave her alone or I'll call the *host*,' she threatened them, pointing towards the last backs disappearing down Carrer del Bisbe.

Some of the soldiers followed her gaze, but another one drew his sword. 'The inquisitor will be pleased with the death of a witch,' he said.

Francesca did not even look at them. She was staring intently at the woman who had run towards her. How many years had they spent together? How much suffering had they seen?

'Leave her, you dogs!' shouted Aledis, stepping back and pointing towards the *host* once more. She wanted to run and fetch them, but the soldier had already lifted his sword high over Francesca's head. The blade seemed bigger than she did. 'Leave her!' she shrieked.

Francesca saw Aledis cover her face in her hands and sink to her knees. She had taken her in all that time ago in Figueres and ever since . . . Was she going to die without one last embrace?

The soldier had drawn back his arm to strike when Francesca's cold eyes stopped him in his tracks.

'Swords can't kill witches,' she warned him in an even voice. The blade wavered in his hand. What was she saying? 'Only fire can purify a witch at death.' Could it be true? The soldier turned to his companions for support, but they were already backing away. 'If you kill me with your sword, I'll pursue you for the rest of your life – all of you!' None of them could have imagined that the threat they had just heard could have come from such a shrivelled old body. Aledis looked up. 'I'll pursue you,' hissed Francesca, 'I'll pursue your wives, your children and your children's children, and their wives too! A curse on all of you!' For the first time since she had left the palace, Francesca felt strong enough to move away from the wall. By now, the other soldiers had retreated back into the palace, leaving the one with his raised sword on his own. 'I curse you,' Francesca said, pointing her finger at him. 'If you kill me, your corpse will never find rest. I'll turn into a thousand worms and devour you. I'll make your eyes mine for all eternity.'

As Francesca continued with her curses, Aledis got up from her knees and went over to her. She put an arm round her shoulder and started to lead her away.

'Your children will be lepers . . .' The two women passed beneath the sword blade. 'Your wife will become the Devil's whore . . .'

They did not look round. For some time, the soldier stood with his arm still raised. He lowered it slowly, and watched the two women crossing the square.

'Let's get out of here, my child,' Francesca said as soon as they were in Carrer del Bisbe, which by now was completely empty.

Aledis was trembling. 'I have to pass by the inn.'

'No. No. Let's just go. Now. This very minute.'

'What about Teresa and Eulàlia?'

'We'll send word to them,' said Francesca, clinging to the girl from Figueres.

They came to Plaça Sant Jaume, then skirted the Jewry heading for the Boqueria gate, the nearest way out of Barcelona. They walked silently, arm in arm.

'What about Arnau?' asked Aledis.

Francesca did not reply.

* * *

The first part of his plan had worked. By now, Arnau should be with the *bastaixos* in the small boat Guillem had hired. The agreement with the Infante had been very precise: 'The only commitment his highness makes is not to oppose the Barcelona *host*,' Francesc de Perellós had told him. 'Under no circumstance will he challenge the Inquisition, try to oblige it to do anything, or question its resolutions. If your plan is successful and Estanyol is set free, the Infante will not defend him if the Inquisition arrests him again or condemns him. Is all that clear?' Guillem agreed, and handed him the bill of payment for the loans made to the King. Now Guillem had to tackle the second part of his scheme: convincing Nicolau that Arnau was ruined and that there was little to be gained from pursuing or sentencing him. They could all have fled to Pisa and left Arnau's possessions to the Inquisition; but the fact was, the Inquisition already controlled his wealth, and if sentence was pronounced on Arnau, even *in absentia*, there would be a warrant for his arrest. This was why Guillem wanted to try to deceive Eimerich; there was nothing to lose, and a lot to gain: Arnau would have peace of mind, and the Inquisition would not pursue him for the rest of his life.

Nicolau kept Guillem waiting several hours. When he finally appeared, he was accompanied by a small Jewish man dressed in a black coat and wearing the obligatory yellow badge. The Jew scurried after the inquisitor, carrying several account books under his arm. He avoided looking at Guillem when Nicolau gestured to both of them to step inside his chamber.

Nicolau did not ask them to sit down, but himself took a seat behind his big table.

'If what you say is true,' he said, addressing Guillem, 'Estanyol is *abatut*, ruined.'

'You know it's true,' Guillem replied. 'The King does not owe Arnau Estanyol a penny.'

'In that case, I could call the city's finance inspector,' said the inquisitor. 'How ironic if the same city that freed him from the Holy Office were to execute him for being *abatut.*'

That will never happen, Guillem was tempted to reply. I can easily secure Arnau's freedom, simply by showing Abraham Levi's receipt . . . But no: Nicolau had not agreed to receive him just to denounce Arnau to the finance inspector. What he wanted was his money, the money he had promised the Pope, the money that this Jew (who must be a friend of Jucef's) had told him was available.

Guillem said nothing.

'I could do so,' insisted Nicolau.

Guillem spread his palms. The inquisitor looked at him more closely.

'Who are you?' he asked at length.

'My name is—'

'I know, I know,' Eimerich said, with a chopping, impatient gesture, 'your name is Sahat de Pisa. What I should like to know is what someone from Pisa is doing in Barcelona defending a heretic.'

'Arnau Estanyol has a lot of friends, even in Pisa.'

'Infidels and heretics!' cried Nicolau.

Guillem spread his palms once more. How long would it be before the inquisitor succumbed to the idea of money? Nicolau seemed to have understood. He said nothing for a few moments.

'What do those friends of Arnau Estanyol have to offer the Inquisition?' he finally asked.

'In those books' – Guillem nodded towards the tiny Jew, who had not taken his eyes off Nicolau's table – 'there are entries in favour of one of Arnau Estanyol's creditors. They amount to a fortune.'

For the first time, the inquisitor addressed the Jew. 'Is this true?'

'Yes,' replied the Jew. 'From the outset, there are entries in the name of Abraham Levi—'

'Another heretic!' Nicolau exploded.

The three men fell silent.

'Go on,' ordered the inquisitor.

'Those entries have added up over the years. By now, they must amount to more than fifteen thousand pounds.'

A glint appeared in the inquisitor's narrowed eyes. Neither Guillem nor the little Jew failed to notice it.

'Well?' asked the inquisitor.

'Arnau Estanyol's friends could see to it that Levi renounced his right to the money.'

Nicolau sat back in his chair. 'Your friend is a free man,' he said. 'Nobody gives money away. Why would anyone, however great a friend, give away fifteen thousand pounds?'

'Arnau Estanyol has only been set free by the *host*.'

Guillem stressed the word 'only'; Arnau could still be seen to be subject to the Holy Inquisition. The crucial moment had arrived. He had been weighing it up during the long hours he was kept waiting in the ante-chamber, while he was staring at the weapons of the Inquisition guards. He had to be careful not to underestimate Nicolau's intelligence. The Inquisition had no authority over a Moor . . . unless Nicolau could prove there had been a direct attack on the institution. Guillem could never offer an inquisitor a deal directly. It had to be Eimerich who made the suggestion first. An infidel could not be seen to be trying to buy off the Holy Office.

Nicolau looked at him challengingly. You're not going to catch me out, thought Guillem.

'Perhaps you are right,' said Guillem. 'It's true, there is no logical reason why, with Arnau a free man, anyone should want to offer such a large amount of money.' The inquisitor's eyes narrowed to slits. 'I don't really understand why they asked me to come here. I was told you would understand, but I share your invaluable opinion. I'm sorry to have wasted your time.'

Guillem waited for Nicolau to make up his mind. When the inquisitor sat up in his seat and opened his eyes wide, he knew he had won.

'Leave us,' Nicolau instructed the Jew. As soon as the little man had shut the door, Nicolau went on, although he still did not offer Guillem a seat. 'It may be true that your friend is free, but the case against him has not been completed. Even if he is a free man, I can still sentence him as a relapsed heretic. The Inquisition cannot dictate death sentences,' he continued, as though talking to himself; 'that must come from the secular power, the King. Your friends ought to know that the King's will may change. Perhaps some day . . .'

'I am sure that both you and his majesty will do what you have to,' replied Guillem.

'The King has a very clear idea of what is for the best: that is, fighting against the infidel and taking Christianity to the farthest corners of the kingdom. But as for the Church: sometimes it is difficult to know what is best for a people with no frontiers. Your friend Arnau Estanyol has confessed his guilt, and that confession must lead to punishment.' Nicolau paused, and stared again at Guillem. You have to be the one, the other man insisted with his look. 'And yet,' said the inquisitor when he saw that Guillem was not going to say anything, 'the Church and the Inquisition have to show themselves merciful, if by that attitude they can secure benefits for the common good. Would your friends – the people who have sent you – accept a lesser sentence?'

I'm not going to bargain with you, Eimerich, thought Guillem. Only Allah, praised be his name, knows what you might obtain if you arrested me, only Allah knows if there are eyes spying on us from behind these walls, or ears listening to us. It has to be you who proposes the solution.

'Nobody would call into question whatever the Inquisition decides,' he answered.

Nicolau stirred in his chair. 'You asked for a private audience on the pretext of having something to offer me. You've said that some friends of Arnau Estanyol could arrange it so that his main creditor renounces a debt of fifteen thousand pounds. What is it you want, infidel?'

'I know what I don't want,' was all Guillem replied.

'All right,' said Nicolau, rising from his seat. 'A minimum punishment: he is to wear the cloak of repentance in the cathedral every Sunday for a year, and in return your friends will ensure that the credit is cancelled.'

'In Santa Maria,' Guillem said, somewhat to his own surprise. The words seemed to have come spontaneously from deep inside him. Where else but Santa Maria could Arnau fulfil his punishment?

57

Mar tried to keep up with the men carrying Arnau on their shoulders, but could not force her way through the crowd. She remembered Aledis's last words: 'Take care of him,' she had shouted above the uproar of the *host*. She was smiling.

Mar rushed off, pushing against the human tide that threatened to sweep her away.

'Take good care of him,' Aledis repeated, with Mar still looking at her and trying to get out of the way of the rush of people. 'I wanted to, but that was many years ago . . .'

All of a sudden she was gone.

Mar almost fell to the ground and was trampled. 'The *host* is no place for women,' grumbled a man who pushed her out of his way. Mar managed to turn round. She looked for the banners that were already entering Plaça Sant Jaume at the far end of Carrer del Bisbe. For the first time that morning, Mar dried her tears, and from her throat came a roar so loud it silenced all those around her. She did not even think about Joan. She shouted, pushed, kicked at the men in front of her, forcing them to make room for her.

The *host* gathered in Plaça del Blat. Mar found herself quite close to the Virgin, which was still dancing on the *bastaixos'* shoulders over the stone in the centre of the square. But there was no sign of Arnau ... Mar thought she could see some men arguing with the city councillors. Perhaps ... yes, he was in the midst of them. She was only a few steps away, but the square was very crowded. She clawed at the arm of a man who would not let her through. The man drew a dagger and for a brief moment ... but in the end he burst out laughing and gave way. Arnau should have been directly behind him, but when Mar managed to get past, the only people she found were the councillors and the *bastaixos'* alderman.

'Where is Arnau?' she asked. She was panting and perspiring freely.

The imposing *bastaix*, wearing the key to the Sacred Urn round his neck, looked down at her. It was a secret. The Inquisition ...

'I'm Mar Estanyol,' she said, stumbling over the words. 'I'm the orphaned daughter of Ramon the *bastaix*. You must have known him.'

No, he had not known him, but he had heard of him and his daughter, and of the fact that Arnau had adopted her.

'Run down to the beach,' was all he said.

Mar crossed the square and flew down Carrer de la Mar, which had emptied of people. She caught up with them outside the consulate: six *bastaixos* were carrying Arnau shoulder high. He was still stunned from all that had happened.

Mar wanted to throw herself on them, but one of the *bastaixos* stood in her way. The man from Pisa had given them clear instructions: nobody should know where they were taking Arnau.

'Let go of me!' shouted Mar, her feet flailing in the air.

The *bastaix* had lifted her by the waist, trying not to hurt her. She weighed less than half of any of the stones or bundles he had to carry every day.

'Arnau! Arnau!'

How often had he dreamt he was hearing that voice? When he opened his eyes he saw he was being carried by a group of men whose faces he could not even make out. They were taking him somewhere in a hurry, without speaking. What was going on? Where was he? Arnau! Yes, it was the same plea he had once seen in the eyes of a young girl he had betrayed, in the farmhouse of Felip de Ponts.

Arnau! The beach. His memories mingled with the sound of the waves and the salty breeze. What was he doing on the beach?

'Arnau!'

The voice came from afar.

The *bastaixos* entered the water, heading for the small boat that would take Arnau to the larger vessel Guillem had hired, which was waiting further offshore. The salt water splashed Arnau.

'*Arnau*.'

'Wait,' he muttered, trying to raise himself. That voice . . . who . . .?

'A woman,' said one of the *bastaixos*. 'She won't cause any problem. We ought to . . .'

Arnau was standing by the side of the boat, still supported under the arms by the *bastaixos*. He looked back at the beach. *Mar is waiting for you*. Guillem's words silenced everything going on around him. Guillem, Nicolau, the Inquisition, the dungeons: it all came flooding back to him.

'My God!' he cried. 'Bring her here, I beg you.'

One of the *bastaixos* rushed over to where she was still being held.

Arnau saw her running towards him.

The *bastaixos*, who were also looking at her, turned their attention to Arnau when he struggled free of their grasp: it seemed as though the gentlest of the waves might knock him over at any time.

Mar came to a halt beside Arnau, who was standing there with his arms by his sides. She saw a tear roll down his cheek. She stepped forward and kissed it away.

Neither of them said a word. Mar herself helped the *bastaixos* lift him into the boat.

There was no point in him going openly against the King.

Ever since Guillem had left, Nicolau had been pacing up and down his chamber. If Arnau had no money, there was no point sentencing him either. The Pope would never release him from the promise he had made. The man from Pisa had him trapped. If he wanted to keep his word to the Pope . . .

His attention was distracted by hammering at the door, but after glancing at it, he carried on walking up and down.

Yes. A lesser punishment would safeguard his reputation as an inquisitor. It would also avoid any confrontation with the King, as well as providing him with enough money to . . .

More hammering on the door. Nicolau looked over at it again.

He would have loved to have sent that Estanyol to the stake. What about his mother? What had become of her? She must have taken advantage of the confusion . . .

The hammering echoed through the room. Nicolau flung the door open. 'What . . .?'

Jaume de Bellera was standing there, his fist raised to pound once more.

'What do you want?' asked the grand inquisitor,

glancing across at the captain who should have been guarding the ante-chamber, and who was pinioned against the wall by Genís Puig's sword. 'How dare you threaten a soldier of the Holy Inquisition?' he roared.

Genís lowered his sword and stared at his companion.

'We've been waiting a long time,' said the lord of Navarcles.

'I have no wish to see anyone,' Nicolau said to the captain, who had struggled free from Genís. 'I've already told you that.'

The inquisitor made to close the door, but Jaume de Bellera prevented him doing so.

'I am a Catalan baron,' he said slowly and carefully, 'and I demand respect for my rank.'

Genís bellowed his agreement, and lifted his sword again to prevent the captain coming to Nicolau's aid.

Nicolau looked into Lord de Bellera's face. He could call for help; the rest of the guards could be there in a moment, but those desperate eyes . . . who knew what two men used to imposing their authority could do? He sighed. This was far from being the happiest day of his life.

'Very well, baron,' he said, 'what do you want?'

'You promised you would sentence Arnau Estanyol, but you have let him escape.'

'I do not recall having promised anything, and as for letting him go, it was your King, the man whose noble line you support, who refused to come to the aid of the Church. Go and demand an explanation from him.'

Jaume de Bellera muttered some unintelligible words and waved his hands in the air. 'You could still condemn him,' he said.

'He has escaped,' Nicolau admitted.

'We'll bring him to you!' shouted Genís Puig, who was still threatening the captain, but was listening closely to what they were saying.

716

Nicolau turned to look at him. Why did he have to explain anything to them?

'We provided you with more than enough proof of his sin,' said Jaume de Bellera. 'The Inquisition cannot—'

'What proof?' barked Eimerich. These two dolts were offering him a way to save his honour. If he could question their proof . . . 'What proof?' he repeated. 'The accusation by someone possessed by the Devil like you, baron?' Jaume de Bellera tried to say something, but Nicolau silenced him with a scything movement of his hand. 'I've looked for the documents you said the bishop drew up when you were born.' The two men glared at each other. 'But I couldn't find them.'

Genís Puig let his sword hand drop to his side.

'They must be somewhere in his archives,' Jaume de Bellera spluttered.

'And you, sir?' Nicolau shouted, turning to Genís. 'What do you have against Arnau Estanyol?' The inquisitor could tell that he was trying to hide the truth: that was what he was good at. 'Did you know that to lie to the inquisition is a crime?' Genís looked to Jaume de Bellera for support, but the nobleman's gaze was staring up at some point on the chamber ceiling. Genís was on his own. 'What do you have to say?' Genís shifted uncomfortably, not knowing where to look. 'What did the moneychanger do to you?' Nicolau insisted. 'Did he ruin you, perhaps?'

Genís reacted. It was only for a split second, a second in which he glanced at the inquisitor out of the corner of his eye. That must be it! What could a moneychanger do to a nobleman if not ruin him financially?

'Not me,' Genís replied naively.

'Not you? Who then? Your father?'

Genís looked down at the floor.

'So you tried to use the Holy Office by lying! You made a false accusation for your own personal revenge!'

Hearing the inquisitor scream at his companion brought Jaume de Bellera back to reality.

'But he burnt his father,' Genís insisted almost inaudibly.

Nicolau waved his hand angrily. What should he do now? If he arrested and tried them that would only mean keeping alive something that was much better dead and buried as soon as possible.

'You are to appear before the clerk to the Inquisition and withdraw your charges. If you do not do so . . . Do you understand?' he shouted when neither of them appeared to react. They nodded. 'The Inquisition cannot judge a man on the basis of false accusations. Get out of here,' he concluded, signalling to the guard captain.

'You swore on your honour you would have revenge,' Genís Puig said to Jaume de Bellera as they turned to leave.

Nicolau heard the recrimination. He also heard the response.

'No lord of Navarcles has ever broken his oath,' Jaume de Bellera retorted.

The grand inquisitor's eyes narrowed. That was enough. He had allowed a prisoner to go free. He had just ordered two witnesses to withdraw their charges. He was making a bargain with . . . a man from Pisa? What if Jaume de Bellera carried out his revenge before Nicolau had a chance to get his hands on the fortune Arnau had left? Would the man from Pisa keep his side of the bargain? All this had to be kept quiet once and for all.

'Well, on this occasion,' he bellowed at the men's retreating backs, 'the lord of Navarcles is not going to keep his word.'

The two men turned back to him.

'What are you saying?' said Jaume de Bellera.

'That the Holy Office cannot allow two . . .' He dismissed them with a gesture. '. . . two laymen to question a sentence that it has passed. That is divine justice. There is to be no other revenge! Do you understand that, de Bellera?' The nobleman hesitated. 'If you carry out your threat, I will try you for being possessed by the Devil. Do you understand now?'

'But I've sworn an oath—'

'In the name of the Holy Inquisition, I relieve you of your promise.' Jaume de Bellera nodded. 'And you,' added Nicolau, turning to Genís Puig, 'you are to take great care not to wreak vengeance in a matter already resolved by the Inquisition. Is that clear?'

Genís Puig nodded.

The catboat, a small lateen-rigged craft about thirty feet long, had pulled into a tiny cove on the Garraf coast, hidden from passing ships and only approachable by sea.

A rough wooden hut built by fishermen from the flotsam the Mediterranean had deposited on the shore of the cove was the only thing that broke the monotony of grey stones and pebbles that vied with the sun to reflect the light and warmth it brought them.

Together with a weighty bag of coins, the helmsman had received strict instructions from Guillem. 'You are to leave him there with food and water and a man you can trust. Then you can go about your business, but stick to nearby ports and return to Barcelona at least every two days to receive further instructions from me. There will be more money for you when all this is over,' he had promised in order to secure the man's loyalty. In fact, there was no real need for this: Arnau was known and loved by all seagoing folk, who saw him as an honest consul. The man accepted the money anyway. However, he had not taken Mar into account. She refused to share the responsibility of looking after Arnau with anyone else.

'I'll take care of him,' she said, once they had disembarked in the cove and she had installed Arnau in the
shade of the hut.

'But the man from Pisa—' the helmsman tried to
argue.

'Tell him that Mar is with Arnau, and if that doesn't
satisfy him, come back with your man.'

She spoke with an authority he had rarely heard in a
woman. He stared her up and down and again tried to
object.

'Be on your way,' was all she said.

When his boat had disappeared behind the rocks at
the cove entrance, Mar took a deep breath and peered up
at the sky. How often had she denied herself a fantasy
like this? How often, with the memory of Arnau fresh in
her mind, had she tried to convince herself her destiny
lay elsewhere? And now . . . Mar glanced towards the
hut. Arnau was still asleep. During the crossing, Mar had
been able to check he did not have a fever and was not
wounded. She had sat down next to him, crossed her legs
and lifted his head on to her lap.

Arnau had opened his eyes on several occasions,
stared up at her, then closed them again, a smile on his
lips. She took one of his hands in hers and, whenever
Arnau gazed at her, squeezed it until he fell back into a
contented sleep. This had happened time and again, as
though he were trying to prove to himself that she was
real. And now . . . Mar went back to the hut and sat at
Arnau's feet.

He spent two days going round Barcelona, remembering
the places that had been part of his life for so long. Little
seemed to have changed during the six years Guillem
had been in Pisa. Despite the crisis, the city teemed with
activity. Barcelona was still open to the sea, defended
only by the *tasques* where Arnau had scuttled the whaling

ship when Pedro the Cruel had threatened the coast with his fleet. The western wall Pedro III had ordered built was still under construction, as were the royal shipyards. Until they were finished, all the ships came aground for repairs or to be rebuilt in the old yards at the foot of the beach opposite the Regomir tower. Guillem breathed in the sharp smell of tar that the caulkers used, mixed with oakum, to make the ships' hulls watertight. He watched the carpenters at work, the oarmakers, blacksmiths and ropemakers. In times gone by, he had accompanied Arnau to make sure that they did not mix new hemp with old when they twisted cables or ropes for rigging. They would walk up and down, supervised by solemn-looking carpenters. Then, after checking the ropes, Arnau would invariably head for the caulkers. He would send away everyone else, so that just he and Guillem could talk in private with these men.

'Their work is essential: they are forbidden by law to be paid by how much they do,' Arnau had explained the first time. That was why the consul wanted to talk to them, to ensure that none of the caulkers had been forced by necessity to do his work hurriedly, and so put the fleet at risk.

Now, Guillem watched a caulker on his knees carefully checking the seal he had just finished on a ship's hull. Seeing him made Guillem close his eyes. He tightened his mouth and shook his head. He and Arnau had fought alongside each other so often, and now his friend was hiding in a distant cove, waiting for the inquisitor to sentence him to a lesser punishment. Christians! At least he had Mar with him . . . his little child. Guillem had not been surprised when the captain of the catboat had appeared at the corn exchange and explained what had happened with Mar and Arnau. His little child!

'Good luck to you, my pretty one,' he had murmured.

'What did you say?'

'Nothing, nothing. You did the right thing. Put to sea again, and come back in a couple of days.'

The first day, he had no news from Eimerich. On the second, he went back into Barcelona. He could not just sit there waiting; he left his servants in the exchange, with orders to find him if anyone appeared asking for him.

The merchants' districts were exactly the same. He could walk through the city with his eyes closed, letting himself be guided by the distinctive smells from each of them. The cathedral, like Santa Maria or the Pi church, was still under construction, although work on the shrine to the Virgin of the Sea was much further advanced. Santa Clara and Santa Anna were also covered in scaffolding. Guillem paused in front of each church and watched the carpenters and masons hard at work. What about the sea wall? And the secure harbour? How strange Christians were.

On the third day, one of his servants rushed panting up to him. 'Someone at the corn exchange is asking for you.'

Have you given way then, Nicolau? Guillem wondered as he hurried back.

Nicolau Eimerich signed the Inquisition's sentence with Guillem standing on the far side of the table. He added his seal, and handed it over without a word.

Guillem picked it off the table and began to read it.

'Read the end, that's all you need bother with,' the grand inquisitor urged him.

He had forced the clerk to work all night, and had no intention of spending all day waiting for this infidel to read the document through.

Guillem peered at him over the top of the parchment

and carried on reading the inquisitor's arguments. So Jaume de Bellera and Genís Puig had withdrawn their charges: how had Nicolau managed to achieve that? Margarida Puig's testimony had been thrown into doubt because the tribunal had discovered that her family had been ruined in dealings with Arnau. As for Eleonor . . . she had refused to accept the surrender and submission every wife ought to show her lord and master!

In addition, Eleonor claimed that the accused had publicly embraced a Jewish woman with whom he was suspected of having carnal relations. As witnesses, she cited Nicolau himself and Bishop Berenguer d'Eril. Guillem looked up again at Nicolau: the inquisitor held his gaze. 'It is not true,' Nicolau had written, 'that the accused embraced a Jewish woman on the occasion Dona Eleonor was referring to.' Neither he nor Berenguer d'Eril, who had also signed the document – at this point, Guillem did turn to the last sheet to confirm the bishop's signature and seal – could support this charge. 'The smoke, flames, the noise, the crowd's passion' – Nicolau had written – 'could have led a woman who was by nature weak to have thought this was what she had seen. And since the accusation made by Dona Eleonor regarding Arnau's relationship with this Jewish woman was obviously false, little credibility could be afforded to the rest of her testimony.'

Guillem smiled.

This meant that the only actions that could be held against Arnau were those described by the priests of Santa Maria de la Mar. The blasphemy had been admitted by the prisoner, but he had repented of it in front of the whole tribunal, and this was the ultimate goal of every trial held by the Inquisition. For this reason, Arnau Estanyol was sentenced to pay a penalty consisting of the seizure of all his goods, and to do penance every Sunday for a year outside Santa Maria de la Mar, wearing the cloak of repentance that all those found guilty by the Inquisition were obliged to wear.

Guillem finished reading all the grandiloquent legal formulas, then checked that the document was properly signed and sealed by the grand inquisitor and the bishop. He had done it!

He rolled up the parchment, then searched in his clothes for the bill of payment signed by Abraham Levi. He handed it to Nicolau and watched in silence as he read it. The document signified Arnau's ruin, but guaranteed his freedom and his life. In any case, Guillem would never have been able to explain to Arnau where the money had come from, or why he had hidden the piece of paper for so many years.

58

Arnau slept the rest of that day. At nightfall, Mar lit a fire with twigs and the wood the fishermen had collected in the hut. The sea was calm. Mar looked up at the stars coming out in the night sky. Then she peered out at the cliffs surrounding the cove: the moonlight was playing here and there on the edges of the rocks, creating fantastic shapes.

She breathed in the silence and savoured the calm. The world did not exist. Barcelona did not exist. Nor did the Inquisition, or Eleonor or Joan. There was only her . . . and Arnau.

Around midnight she heard sounds from inside the hut. She got up to see what it was, and saw Arnau emerging into the moonlight. They stood in silence a few steps from each other.

Mar was standing between Arnau and the bonfire. The glow from the fire picked out her silhouette but hid her features. Am I in heaven already? thought Arnau. As his eyes grew used to the darkness, he was able to distinguish the details he had so often pursued in dreams: first of all, her bright eyes – how many nights had he shed tears over them? Then her nose, her cheek-bones, her chin . . . and her mouth, and those lips . . . The figure opened its arms to him and the light from the flames streamed round her, caressing a body clothed in ethereal robes that the light and dark complemented. She was calling him.

Arnau answered her call. What was happening? Where was he? Could it really be Mar? When he took her hands, saw her smiling at him, and then kissing him on the lips, he had his reply.

Mar clung to him as tightly as she could, and the world returned to normal. 'Hold me,' he heard her ask. Arnau put his arm round her shoulder and held her to him. He heard her start to cry. He could feel her sobbing against him, and gently stroked her hair. How many years had gone by before they could enjoy a moment like this? How many mistakes had he made?

Arnau raised Mar's head from his shoulder and forced her to look up into his eyes. 'I'm sorry,' he began to say. 'I'm sorry I forced you to—'

'Don't say anything,' she interrupted him. 'The past doesn't exist. There is nothing to be sorry for. Today is when we start to live. Look,' she said, pulling away from him and taking his hand, 'look at the sea. The sea has no past. It is just there. It will never ask us to explain. The stars, the moon, they are there to light our way, to shine for us. What do they care what might have happened in the past? They are accompanying us, and are happy with that: can you see them shine? The stars are twinkling in the sky: would they do that if the past mattered? Wouldn't there be a huge storm if God wanted to punish us? We are alone, you and I, with no past, no memories, no guilt, nothing that can stand in the way of . . . our love.'

Arnau stood looking up at the sky, then lowered his gaze to the sea and the gentle waves lapping at the shore without even breaking. He looked at the wall of rock protecting them and swayed in the silent darkness.

He turned back to Mar, still holding her hand. There was something he had to tell her, something painful that he had sworn before the Virgin after the death of his first wife, something he could not renounce. Staring her in the eyes, he told her everything in a whisper.

When he had finished, Mar sighed.

'All I know is that I have no intention of ever leaving you again, Arnau. I want to be with you, to be close to you . . . in whatever way you choose.'

On the morning of the fifth day, a small boat arrived. The only person to disembark was Guillem. The three of them met on the seashore. Mar stood aside to let the two men fling their arms round each other.

'God!' sobbed Arnau.

'Which God?' asked Guillem, almost too moved to speak. He pushed Arnau away and smiled a broad smile.

'The God of everyone,' replied Arnau, as happy as he was.

'Come here, my child,' said Guillem, releasing one arm.

Mar came up to the two men and put her arms round their waists.

'I'm not your child any more,' she told him with a mischievous smile.

'You always will be,' said Guillem.

'Yes, that you will always be,' Arnau confirmed.

And so arm in arm they walked over and sat down by the remains of the previous evening's fire.

'You are a free man, Arnau,' said Guillem when he had settled on the sand. 'Here is the Inquisition's ruling.'

'Tell me what it says,' Arnau asked him, refusing to take the document. 'I've never read anything that came from you.'

'It says they are seizing your goods . . .' Guillem glanced at Arnau, but saw no reaction. 'And that you are sentenced to a year's penance wearing the cloak of repentance every Sunday for a year outside the doors of Santa Maria de la Mar. Beyond that, the Inquisition declares you are free.'

Arnau saw himself wearing the long penitent's cloak with two white crosses painted on it, standing outside the doors of Santa Maria.

'I should have known you could do it when I saw you in the tribunal, but I was in no state—'

'Arnau,' said Guillem, interrupting him, 'did you hear what I said? The Inquisition has seized all your possessions.'

For a while, Arnau said nothing.

'I was a dead man, Guillem,' he replied at length. 'Eimerich wanted my blood. Besides, I would have given everything I have . . . everything I used to have,' he corrected himself, taking Mar's hand, 'for these past few days.' Guillem looked at Mar and saw her beaming smile and glistening eyes. His child. He smiled too. 'I have been thinking . . .'

'Traitor!' said Mar, pouting her lips in mock reproach.

Arnau patted her hand. 'As far as I can remember, it must cost a lot of money for the King not to oppose the Barcelona *host.*'

Guillem nodded.

'Thank you,' said Arnau.

The two men stared at each other.

'Well,' said Arnau, deciding to break the spell. 'What about you? What has happened to you in all this time?'

The sun was high in the sky by the time the three of them headed out to the catboat, which the helmsman brought in close to shore at their signal. Arnau and Guillem climbed on board.

'Just one minute,' Mar begged them.

The girl turned towards the cove and looked at the hut for one last time. What would the future hold for her? Arnau and his penance, Eleonor . . .

Mar looked down.

'Don't worry about her,' Arnau said when she was on board the boat. 'She won't have any money, and won't bother us. The palace in Carrer de Montcada is part of my wealth, so now it belongs to the Inquisition. All that's left for her is Montbui. She will have to move there.'

'The castle,' murmured Mar. 'Will the Inquisition take that too?'

'No. The castle and its lands were given to us by the King on our marriage. The Inquisition has no authority to seize them.'

'I feel sorry for the peasants,' said Mar, remembering the day when Arnau abolished all the ancient privileges.

Neither of them mentioned Mataró and Felip de Ponts's farmhouse.

'We'll get by somehow—' Arnau started to say.

'What are you talking about?' Guillem cut in. 'You will have all the money you need. If you wish, you could buy the Carrer de Montcada palace all over again.'

'But that's your money,' Arnau protested.

'It's our money. Look,' said Guillem, addressing them both. 'Apart from you two, I have no one. What am I meant to do with the money I have thanks to your generosity? Of course it's yours.'

'No, no,' Arnau insisted.

'You are my family. My child . . . and the man who gave me freedom and riches. Does this mean you do not want me as part of your family?'

Mar stretched out her arm to him.

Arnau stuttered: 'No . . . that wasn't what I meant at all . . . Of course . . .'

'Well, if you accept me, you accept my money,' said Guillem. 'Or would you rather the Inquisition took it?'

His question forced a smile from Arnau.

'Besides, I have great plans,' said Guillem.

Mar sat looking back at the cove. A tear trickled down her cheek. She did not try to wipe it away as it ran down and into the corner of her mouth. They were on their way back to Barcelona. Back to an unjust punishment, to the Inquisition, to Joan, the brother who had betrayed Arnau . . . and a wife he hated but from whom he could never be free.

59

Guillem had rented a house in La Ribera district. It was not luxurious, but was spacious enough for the three of them; with a room for Joan as well, Guillem thought when he gave his instructions. When he disembarked from the catboat in the port of Barcelona, Arnau was received with great affection by the workmen on the beach. Some merchants supervising the loading of their goods or coming and going from the warehouses only nodded as he passed by.

'I'm not a rich man any more,' Arnau said to Guillem as he returned the greetings.

'News spreads quickly,' Guillem replied.

Arnau had said that the first thing he wanted to do when he returned was to visit Santa Maria to thank the Virgin for his freedom. The confused image he had of the tiny statue dancing in the air above the heads of the crowd while he was being carried by the city councillors had become much clearer. But his plan was interrupted when they passed by the corner of Canvis Vells and Canvis Nous: the door and windows of his house – his counting house – had been thrown wide open. A group of curious onlookers had gathered outside. They stepped aside when they saw Arnau arrive, but he did not go in. The three of them recognized some of the pieces of furniture and other effects that the soldiers of the Inquisition were carrying out and piling on a cart by the front door: the long table, which hung over the back of the cart and had been tied on with ropes, the red cloth, the metal shears to test fake coins, the abacus, the money chests . . .

Arnau's attention was caught by a figure dressed in black noting down all the goods seized. The Dominican paused in his work and stared defiantly at him. The onlookers fell silent as Arnau realized where he had seen those eyes before: they belonged to one of the friars who had studied him during the tribunal sessions, behind the bench next to the bishop.

'Vultures,' Arnau muttered.

These were his possessions, his past, his moments of joy and of defeat. He had never thought he would ever witness the way they were stripping him . . . He had never attached any importance to material things, and yet it was a whole life they were carting away.

Mar could feel Arnau's palm grow sweaty.

Someone in the small crowd started to jeer at the friar. At once, the soldiers left the furniture and drew their weapons. Three other armed men appeared from inside the house.

'They won't allow the common people to humiliate them again,' warned Guillem, dragging Mar and Arnau away.

The soldiers charged the group of spectators, who scattered in all directions. Arnau let himself be led away by Guillem, although he constantly looked back at the cart.

They forgot about Santa Maria, where the soldiers were still chasing some of the onlookers. Instead, they skirted round the church until they came to Plaça del Born and their new home.

The news of Arnau's return spread quickly through the city. The first people to arrive at his new house were *missatges* from the Consulate of the Sea. The official did not dare look Arnau in the face. When he addressed him, he used the title 'your worship', but he was there to give him the letter in which the Council of a Hundred stripped him of his position. Arnau held out his hand to the official, who finally raised his eyes.

'It's been an honour to work with you,' the official said.

'The honour was all mine,' replied Arnau. 'They don't want anyone poor,' he told Guillem and Mar when the official and his soldiers had left the house.

'We need to talk about that,' said Guillem.

But Arnau shook his head. Not yet, he pleaded.

Many other people came to visit Arnau in his new home. Some of them, like the alderman of the *bastaixos'* guild, he received personally; others of more humble station were happy simply to offer their best wishes to the servant who attended them.

On the second day, Joan appeared. Ever since he had heard that Arnau was in Barcelona, Joan had been wondering what Mar could have told him. When the uncertainty became unbearable, he decided to face his fears and go to see his brother.

When Joan entered the dining room, Arnau and Guillem stood up to greet him. Mar remained seated at the table.

But you did burn your father's body! Nicolau Eimerich's accusation rang through Arnau's mind as soon as he saw Joan. Until then, he had been trying to push the thought away.

Still standing in the doorway, Joan stammered out a

few words. Then he walked over towards Arnau, head lowered.

Arnau's eyes narrowed. So he had come to ask forgiveness. How could a brother . . .?

'How could you do it?' he said when Joan was by his side.

Joan's gaze shifted from the floor to Mar. Had she not punished him enough? Did he have to confess everything to Arnau as well? She seemed surprised at his presence.

'Why did you come here?' asked Arnau coldly.

Joan searched desperately for an excuse.

'We have to pay the expenses at the inn,' he heard himself say.

Arnau's hand chopped the air, and then he turned on his heel.

Guillem called one of his servants and gave him a bag of money.

'Go with the friar and pay the hostel bill,' he commanded.

Joan turned to the Moor for support, but Guillem did not so much as blink. The friar walked back to the door and vanished through it.

'What happened between you?' asked Mar as soon as Joan had gone.

Arnau said nothing. Ought they to know? How could he explain that he had burnt his father's body, and that his own brother had denounced him to the Inquisition? He was the only one who knew.

'Let's forget the past,' he said at length, 'at least as much as we can.'

Mar sat in silence for a while, and then nodded.

Joan followed Guillem's slave out of the house. The young lad had to stop and wait for the friar several times on the way, because he kept stopping and peering blindly around him. They had taken the way to the corn exchange, which the boy knew well, but when they came to Carrer de Montcada, the slave could not get Joan to follow him any further. The friar would not budge from the gateway to Arnau's palace.

'You go and pay,' Joan told the boy, to be free of him. 'I have another debt to settle,' he muttered to himself.

Pere, the aged servant, led him into Eleonor's chamber. As Joan walked along he started mumbling something, at first in a low whisper as he crossed the threshold, then louder as he climbed the stone staircase with Pere, who looked round at him in astonishment, and then in a roar as he entered the room where Eleonor was waiting for him:

'I know you have sinned!'

On her feet at the far end of the room, the baroness surveyed him haughtily. 'What nonsense are you talking, friar?' she said.

'I know you have sinned,' repeated Joan.

Eleonor burst out laughing and turned her back on him.

Joan stared at her richly embroidered robe. Mar had suffered. He had suffered. Arnau . . . Arnau must have suffered even more than they had.

Eleonor was still laughing, her face turned from him. 'Who do you think you are, friar?'

'I am an inquisitor of the Holy Office,' Joan replied. 'And in your case, I do not need any confession.'

When she heard this harsh rejoinder, Eleonor turned to face him. She saw he had an oil lamp in his hand.

'What . . .?'

Joan did not give her time to finish. He threw the lamp at her. The oil soaked the heavy material of her robe and caught fire.

Eleonor screamed.

By the time Pere could come to her aid, she was a

flaming torch. He called the rest of the servants, and pulled down a tapestry to smother the flames. Joan pushed him aside, but other slaves were already rushing in, wild-eyed.

Someone shouted for water.

Joan looked at Eleonor, who was on her knees enveloped in flames.

'Forgive me, Lord,' he muttered.

He seized another lamp and went up to Eleonor. The hem of his habit also caught fire.

'Repent!' he shouted, before he too was engulfed in flames.

He emptied the second lamp on Eleonor and fell to the floor beside her.

The rug they were on started to burn fiercely. Then the flames began to lick at the furniture in the room.

By the time the slaves appeared with water, all they could do was throw it in from the doorway. Then, overcome by the dense smoke, they covered their faces and ran.

60

15 August 1384
Feast of the Assumption
Church of Santa Maria de la Mar

Seventeen years had gone by.

In the square outside Santa Maria, Arnau raised his eyes to the sky. The pealing of the bells filled the whole city of Barcelona. The sound made the hairs on his forearms stand on end, and he shuddered as the four church bells chimed. He had stood and watched as the four of them were raised to the bell-tower: Assumpta, the largest, weighing almost a ton; Conventual, more than half a ton; Andrea, half that weight; and Vedada, the smallest; all hauled to the very top of the tower.

Today Santa Maria, his church, was being inaugurated and the bells seemed to give off a different sound to the one he had heard since they had been installed . . . or was it he who was hearing them differently? He looked up at the octagonal towers flanking the west front: they were tall, slender and light, built in three levels, each one narrower than the one below. They had tall arched windows open to the winds, with balustrades round the outside, and were topped by flat roofs. While they were being built, Arnau had been assured they would be simple, natural, with no spires or capitals – as natural as the sea, whose patron saint they were there to protect – and yet at the same time imposing and full of fantasy, as the sea also was.

People dressed in their finest were congregating at Santa Maria. Some went straight into the church; others, like Arnau, stayed outside to admire its beauty and listen to its bells' music. Arnau drew Mar to him. He was holding her on his right-hand side; to his left, tall, sharing his father's joy, stood a youth of thirteen, with a birthmark by his right eye.

Surrounded by his family, and with the bells still ringing, Arnau went into Santa Maria de la Mar. The others entering the church stopped to allow him through. This was Arnau Estanyol's church. As a *bastaix*, he had carried its first stones on his back. As a moneychanger and Consul of the Sea, he had offered it important donations. More recently, as a maritime insurance agent, he had donated more funds. Santa Maria had suffered its fair share of catastrophes: on 28 February 1373, an earthquake which devastated Barcelona brought its bell-tower crashing to the ground. Arnau was the first to contribute to its rebuilding.

'I need money,' he had said to Guillem on that occasion.

'It is yours,' replied the Moor, well aware of the disaster and of the fact that a member of the Commission of Works for Santa Maria had visited him that same morning.

The fact was, fortune had smiled on them once more. On Guillem's advice, Arnau had dedicated himself to maritime insurance. Unlike Genoa, Venice or Pisa, Catalonia had no such provision, which made it a paradise for the first people to venture into this area of commerce. However, it was only the wise few like Arnau and Guillem who managed to survive. The Catalan financial system was on the verge of collapse, and threatened to take with it all those who had hoped to make quick profits either by insuring a cargo for more than its worth, which was often the last they heard of it, or by offering insurance on ships and goods even after it was known they had been seized by pirates, in the hope that the news was false. But Arnau and Guillem chose their ships and the risk involved carefully, and soon had the same vast network of agents working for them in their new business as they had used in times gone by.

On 26 December 1379, Arnau could no longer ask Guillem if he might use some of their money for Santa Maria. The Moor had died suddenly a year earlier. Arnau had found him sitting in his chair out in the garden, as usual facing Mecca, to where, in what was an open secret, he always prayed. Arnau informed the members of the Moorish community, and they took Guillem's body away under cover of night.

That night in December 1379, Santa Maria was ravaged by a terrible fire. It reduced the sacristy, choir, organs, altars, and everything else in the interior not made of stone, to a pile of ashes. The stonework too suffered the effects of the fire, and the keystone depicting King Alfonso the Kind, father of Pedro the Ceremonious (who had paid for this part of the work), was completely destroyed.

The King flew into a rage at the destruction of this homage to his august forebear, and demanded the effigy be recreated. The La Ribera district had more than enough to worry about to pay much heed to the monarch's demands. All their money and effort went into a new sacristy, choir, organs, and altars; the equestrian figure of King Alfonso was cleverly reconstructed in plaster, stuck on to the stone, and painted red and gold.

On 3 November 1383, the final keystone above the central nave, the one closest to the main door, was put in place. On the end was sculpted the coat of arms of the Commission of Works, in honour of all the anonymous citizens who had contributed to the construction of the church.

Arnau glanced up at the keystone. Mar and Bernat did the same and then, wreathed in smiles, the three of them made their way to the high altar.

From the moment the heavy keystone had been lifted on to its scaffold, waiting for the columns of the arches to reach up to it, Arnau had repeated the same thing over and over: 'That is our emblem,' he told his son.

'Father,' Bernat retorted, 'that's the people of Barcelona's emblem. Important people like you have their coats of arms engraved on the arches, the columns, in the chapels and in—' Arnau raised his hand to try to stem the flow of his son's words, but the boy rushed on: 'You don't even have your stall in the choir!'

'This is the church of the people, my boy. Many men have given their lives for it, yet their names are nowhere to be found.'

In his mind's eye, Arnau saw himself as a youngster carrying blocks of stone from the royal quarry down to Santa Maria.

'Your father has engraved many of these stones with his blood,' Mar said. 'There can be no greater homage than that.'

Bernat turned to look at his father, eyes wide open.

'I and many others, my son,' said Arnau, 'many, many others.'

August in the Mediterranean; August in Barcelona. The sun was shining with a splendour hard to equal anywhere else on earth. Before it filtered in through the stained glass of Santa Maria and played on colour and stone inside, the sea reflected the light back to the sun, lending its rays an unmatched beauty. Inside the church, the shafts of light mingled with the quivering flames of thousands of candles lit on the high altar and the side chapels. The smell of incense filled the air, and organ music swelled in the perfect acoustics of the central nave.

Arnau, Mar and Bernat walked up to the high altar. Beneath the magnificent apse, surrounded by eight graceful columns and in front of a reredos, stood the small figure of the Virgin of the Sea. Behind the altar, which was covered in fine French lace that King Pedro had lent for the occasion (not without sending word beforehand from Vilafranca del Penedès that the cloths should be returned immediately after the celebration), Bishop Pere de Planella was preparing to say mass to consecrate the church.

Santa Maria was so full that the three of them could not get close to the altar. Some of those in the congregation recognized Arnau and stood back to let him through, but he thanked them and stood where he was among the crowd: they were his people, his family. The only ones missing were Guillem . . . and Joan. Arnau preferred to remember his brother as the young boy with whom he had discovered the world rather than as the bitter monk who had sacrificed himself in flames.

Bishop Pere de Planella began the mass.

Arnau was troubled. Guillem, Joan, Maria, his father . . . and that old woman. Why, whenever he thought of those no longer with him, did he always end up remembering her? He had asked Guillem to search for her and Aledis.

'They have vanished,' the Moor reported.

'They said she was my mother,' Arnau remembered, and told Guillem so. 'Search harder.'

'I haven't been able to find them,' Guillem told him again, some time later.

'But . . .'

'Forget them,' Guillem had advised him, in a tone that brooked no argument.

Pere de Planella was still saying mass.

Arnau was sixty-three years old. He felt tired, and leant on his son.

Bernat squeezed his father's arm affectionately. Arnau bent his mouth to his son's ear and pointed towards the high altar.

'Can you see her smile, my son?' he asked.

THE END

AUTHOR'S NOTE

In writing this novel I have closely followed the *Crónica* written by King Pedro III, adapting it where necessary to the requirements of a work of fiction.

The choice of Navarcles as the site of the castle and estates of the lord of Navarcles is entirely fictional, but the baronies of Granollers, Sant Vicenç dels Horts and Caldes de Montbui which King Pedro offers Arnau as the dowry for his ward Eleonor (another fictional creation) did exist. These baronies were ceded in 1380 by the Infante Martín, son of Pedro the Ceremonious, to Guillem Ramon de Montcada, of the Sicilian branch of the Montcada family, as reward for his good offices in support of the marriage between Queen Maria and one of Martín's sons, who subsequently reigned known as 'the Humane'. Guillem de Montcada held these estates for a much shorter time than the protagonist of my novel: no sooner had he been granted them than he sold them to the Count of Urgell and used the money to equip a fleet and dedicate himself to piracy.

According to the *Usatges* of Catalonia, a feudal lord did have the right to lie with the bride of any of his serfs on her wedding night. The existence of privileges in old Catalonia, compared to the new Catalan territories, led the serfs to rebel repeatedly against their lords, until the 1486 Judgement of Guadalupe abolished these privileges, although it did stipulate at the same time that the lords stripped of their rights in this way should be paid generous compensation.

The royal judgement against Joan's mother, which obliged her to live enclosed in a room on bread and water until her death, was pronounced in 1330 by Alfonso III against a woman by the name of Eulàlia, consort of one Juan Dosca.

The author in no way shares the opinions about women or peasants expressed throughout this novel: nearly all of them have been faithfully copied from the book written by the monk Francesc Eiximenis, in approximately 1381, entitled *Lo crestià*.

As occurs with the marriage between Mar and Felip de Ponts, in medieval Catalonia rapists could marry their victim, even if the abduction had been a violent one, thanks to the *usatge: Si quis virginem*. This was not true in the rest of Spain, which was governed by the legal tradition of the Visigoths in the *Fuero Juzgo*, which prohibited it.

The violator's duty was to provide the woman with a dowry so that she could find a husband, or to marry her himself. If she was already married, she was treated as an adulteress.

No one is sure whether the episode in which King Jaime of Mallorca tries to abduct his brother-in-law Pedro III, which fails because a friar who is close to Pedro hears details of the plot during confession (helped in the novel by Joan), actually happened or not. It may well have been invented by Pedro III as an excuse for the legal action taken by him against the King of Mallorca which ended with his requisitioning Jaime's kingdoms. What does appear to be true is King Jaime's demand to have a wooden bridge built to link his galleys, anchored in the port of Barcelona, with Framenors convent. Perhaps this served to arouse King Pedro's imagination to invent the plot mentioned in his chronicles.

The attempt to invade Barcelona by Pedro the Cruel of Castile is described in minute detail in Pedro III's *Crónica*. The build-up of land along the Barcelona coast meant that its earlier harbours could no longer be used, with the result that the city was defenceless against natural phenomena and enemy attacks. It was not until 1340 that, during the reign of Alfonso the Magnanimous, a new, more adequate port was built.

The sea battle took place as Pedro III describes it, and the Castilian fleet was prevented from gaining access to the city because a ship – a whaling ship, according to Capmany – was grounded on the offshore *tasques* (sandbanks) to halt their advance. It was during this battle that the first references are made to the use of artillery – a bricola mounted on the prow of the King's galley – in naval warfare. It was not long before ships, which until then had been used chiefly as a means of troop transport, were equipped with heavy cannons, changing the whole concept of naval battles. In his *Crónica*, Pedro III delights in the way that the Catalan *host*, ranged on the shore or on the numerous small craft which set out to defend the capital, mocked and insulted Pedro the Cruel's army. He considers it, together with the effective use of the bricola, one of the main reasons why the King of Castile was forced to reconsider his plans to invade Barcelona.

In the revolt of Plaça del Blat during the first so-called 'bad year', when the citizens of Barcelona were demanding grain, the leaders were given summary justice and hanged. For plot reasons, I have placed these executions in Plaça del Blat. It is also true that the authorities thought that a simple oath could help put a stop to the hunger.

Another person who was executed, in the year 1360, was the moneychanger F. Castelló. As stipulated by law, he was beheaded outside his counting house close to what nowadays is Pla del Palau.

In 1367, after being accused of profaning a host and having been locked in the synagogue without food or water, three Jews were executed on the orders of Infante Don Juan, King Pedro's deputy.

Jews were strictly forbidden to leave their houses during the Christian Holy Week. They were also ordered to keep the doors and windows of their homes closed so that they could not see or interfere with the numerous processions. Even so, Easter saw an increase in the fears of the Christian fanatics, and accusations of the celebration of heretical rites also grew at a time of year which the Jews came to have just reason to fear.

Two main accusations were made against the Jews during Easter: the ritual murder of Christians, and especially children, in order to crucify and torture them, drink their blood or eat their hearts; and the profanation of the host. Both of these were commonly seen as designed to recreate the pain and suffering of the Catholics' Christ.

The first known accusation of the crucifixion of a Christian child comes from the Holy Roman Empire in Würzburg, Germany, in 1147. As was so often the case with accusations against the Jews, popular feeling led to similar charges spreading quickly throughout Europe. Only a year later, in 1148, the English Jews in the city of Norwich were accused of crucifying a Christian boy. From then on, accusations of ritual murder, usually during Easter and often involving crucifixion, became widespread: Gloucester, 1168; Fulda, 1235; Lincoln, 1255, Munich, 1286 . . . hatred of the Jews and popular credulity was so strong that in the fifteenth century an Italian Franciscan friar, Bernardino da Feltre, predicted that a Christian child was to be crucified: an event that actually happened in Trent, where a little boy called Simon was found dead on a cross. The Catholic Church beatified Simon, but the friar went on 'prophesying' further crucifixions, in Reggio, Bassano and Mantua. Simon was a martyr of fanaticism rather than faith, but it was not until the mid-twentieth century that the Catholic Church finally annulled his beatification.

One occasion when the Barcelona *host* was summoned – although this took place in the year 1369, later than I have situated it in the book – was against the village of Creixell, when the local lord prevented the free passage and grazing of cattle headed for Barcelona, where by law the animals had to arrive alive. The seizure of animals was one of the main reasons why the *host* was called upon to defend the city's privileges against other towns and feudal lords.

Santa Maria de la Mar is without doubt one of the most beautiful churches to be found anywhere. It may lack the monumentality of others built at the same time or later, but its interior is filled with the spirit with which Berenguer de Montagut sought to infuse it: the people's church, built by the people of Barcelona for Barcelona, is like an airy Catalan farmhouse. It is austere, protected and protecting, and the light of the Mediterranean sets it apart from any other church in the world.

According to the experts, the great virtue of Santa Maria is that it was built over an uninterrupted period of fifty-five years. This means it benefits from a unified architectural style, with few elements added on, making it the leading example of Catalan Gothic. As was usual at that time, and in order not to interrupt the religious services, Santa Maria was built on and around the former construction. In the 1920s, the architect Bassegoda

Amigó placed the original church on the corner of Carrer de l'Espaseria. He calculated that the new church had been built in front of the old one, further to the north, with what nowadays is Carrer de Santa Maria between them. However, when a new presbytery and crypt were being built in 1966, the discovery of a Roman necropolis underneath Santa Maria led to a modification of Bassegoda's original idea. His grandson, also an architect and expert on Santa Maria, asserts that the successive versions of Santa Maria were always built on the same spot, one on top of the other. The Roman cemetery is said to have been where the body of Saint Eulàlia, patron saint of Barcelona, was buried. As described in the novel, her remains were transferred by King Pedro from Santa Maria to the cathedral.

The statue of the Virgin of the Sea which figures in the novel is the one now on the high altar, and was previously part of the tympanum of the main doorway in Passeig del Born.

Nothing is known of the bells of Santa Maria until 1714, when King Felipe V of Castile defeated the Catalans. The King imposed a special tax on church bells in Catalonia in reprisal for the way they were constantly rung to call Catalan patriots to *sometent*: that is, to take up arms to defend their land. It was not only the Castilians who were enraged by bells calling citizens to defend a city. Pedro the Ceremonious himself, after he had put down an uprising in Valencia, ordered that the leaders of the uprising be killed by forcing them to swallow molten metal from the Union bell that had rung to call the people of Valencia to battle.

Santa Maria occupied such a special place in Barcelona that King Pedro did choose to urge the citizens to aid him in his campaign against Sardinia from the square in front of it, rather than the Plaça del Blat outside the magistrate's palace.

The humble *bastaixos*, the port workers who offered to carry blocks of stone to Santa Maria without payment, are the clearest example of the popular fervour which helped build the church. The parish accorded them many privileges, and even today their devotion to the cult of Mary can be seen in the bronze figures on the main doorway and reliefs in the presbytery or marble capitals, on all of which are portrayed figures of port workmen.

The Jew Hasdai Crescas existed. There was also a Bernat Estanyol, who was a captain of the Company of Almogavars. I deliberately chose the first of these two; the second is a simple coincidence. But it was my decision to make Crescas a moneylender and the details of his life are my invention. In 1391, seven years after the official inauguration of Santa Maria (and more than a century before the Catholic monarchs ordered the expulsion of the Jews from their kingdoms) the Barcelona Jewry was burnt down by the people. Its inhabitants were put to death, while those who managed to avoid that, for example by seeking refuge in a convent, were forced to convert to Christianity. The Barcelona Jewry was totally destroyed, and churches were built inside it, until King Juan, worried at the economic consequences for the royal coffers of the disappearance of the Jews, attempted to coax them back to the city. He promised them tax exemptions until their community reached two hundred members, and annulled specific impositions such as having to give up their beds and other furniture whenever the royal court was visiting the city, or having to feed the lions and other wild animals kept by the sovereign. The Jews did not return, however, so that in 1397 the King conceded Barcelona the right not to have a Jewry.

The grand inquisitor Nicolau Eimerich took refuge with the Pope in Avignon, but on the death of King

Pedro returned to Catalonia and continued his attacks on the works of Ramon Llull. In 1393, King Juan banished him from Catalonia, and the inquisitor again sought refuge with the Pope. However, that same year Eimerich returned to La Seu d'Urgell, so that King Juan had to urge the bishop to expel him at once. Nicolau fled to Avignon a second time, but on the death of King Juan was granted permission by King Martín the Humane to spend the last years of his life in his native Girona, where he died aged eighty. The references to Eimerich's assertions that torturing several times was merely a continuation of the first torture, and on the conditions that prisoners should be held in, are true.

Unlike Castile where the Inquisition was only created in 1487, in Catalonia inquisition tribunals had existed since 1249. These were completely separate from and independent of the traditional ecclesiastical jurisdiction as exercised by the episcopal tribunals. This early establishment of the Inquisition in Catalonia is explained by its original objective: to fight against heresy, which at that time was identified with the Cathars in the south of France and the Waldensians who followed Peter Waldo in Lyons. Both these doctrines, considered heretical by the Catholic Church, found supporters among the inhabitants of old Catalonia because of geographical proximity. Many Catalan nobles in the Pyrenees became part of these movements, including Viscount Arnau and his wife Ermessenda; Ramon, lord of Cadí; and Guillem de Niort, magistrate for Count Nuño Sanç in the Cerdagne and Coflent.

This explains why the Inquisition began its sad journey through the Iberian peninsula in Catalonia. In 1286, however, the Cathar movement was finally extinguished, and by the fourteenth century the Catalan Inquisition was being instructed by Pope Clement V to direct its efforts against the banned order of the Knights

Templar, as was happening in the neighbouring kingdom of France. Yet in Catalonia the Knights were not regarded with such antipathy as they were by the French King (although this was principally for economic reasons). At a provincial synod called by the Archbishop of Tarragona, the bishops unanimously adopted a resolution declaring the Knights Templar free of all blame, and finding no reason to accuse them of heresy.

After the Templars, the Catalan Inquisition turned its attention to the Beghards, who had also won support in Catalonia. Several death sentences were passed, which, as was customary, were carried out by the secular authorities after the accused was handed over to them. By 1348, with the attacks on Jewries throughout Europe following the outbreak of the Black Death and widespread accusations against the Jews, the Catalan Inquisition began to persecute those whom it regarded as befriending or sympathizing with the Jews.

My thanks go to my wife Carmen, without whom this novel would not have been possible; to Pau Pérez, who has lived it with as much passion as I have; to the Escola d'Escriptura of the Ateneo of Barcelona for their wonderful work in teaching and spreading Catalan literature; and also to my agent, Sandra Bruna, and my editor, Ana Liarás.

Barcelona, November 2005